THE BEST OF KIPLING

Three Complete Books
Three Short Stories
Barrack-Room Ballads

89

THE BEST OF KIPLING

NELSON DOUBLEDAY, INC.   *Garden City, New York*

kím

1

Chapter 1

"Oh ye who tread the Narrow Way
By Tophet-flare to Judgment Day,
Be gentle when the heathen pray
To Buddha at Kamakura!"

HE SAT, in defiance of municipal orders, astride the gun Zam-Zammah on her brick platform opposite the old Ajaib-Gher—the Wonder House, as the natives call the Lahore Museum. Who hold Zam-Zammah, that "fire-breathing dragon," hold the Punjab, for the great green-bronze piece is always first of the conqueror's loot.

There was some justification for Kim,—he had kicked Lala Dinanath's boy off the trunnions,—since the English held the Punjab and Kim was English. Though he was burned black as any native; though he spoke the vernacular by preference, and his mother-tongue in a clipped uncertain sing-song; though he consorted on terms of perfect equality with the small boys of the bazar; Kim was white—a poor white of the very poorest. The half-caste woman who looked after him (she smoked opium, and pretended to keep a second-hand furniture shop by the square where the cheap cabs wait) told the missionaries that she was Kim's mother's sister; but his mother had been nursemaid in a colonel's family and had married Kimball O'Hara, a young colour-sergeant of the Mavericks, an Irish regiment. He afterwards took a post on the Sind, Punjab, and Delhi railway, and his regiment went home without him. The wife died of cholera in Ferozepore, and O'Hara fell to drink and loafing up and down the line with the keen-eyed three-year-old baby. Societies and chaplains, anxious for the child, tried to catch him, but O'Hara drifted away, till he came across the woman who took opium and learned the taste from her, and died as poor whites die in India. His estate at death consisted of three papers—one he called his "ne varietur" because those words were written below his signature thereon, and another his "clearance-certificate." The third was Kim's birth-certificate. Those things, he was used to say, in his glorious opium-hours, would yet make little Kimball a man. On no account was Kim to part with them, for they belonged to a

great piece of magic—such magic as men practised over yonder behind
the Museum, in the big blue and white Jadoo-Gher—the Magic House,
as we name the Masonic Lodge. It would, he said, all come right some
day, and Kim's horn would be exalted between pillars—monstrous pillars
—of beauty and strength. The Colonel himself, riding on a horse, at the
head of the finest regiment in the world, would attend to Kim,—little
Kim that should have been better off than his father. Nine hundred
first-class devils, whose god was a Red Bull on a green field, would attend
to Kim, if they had not forgotten O'Hara—poor O'Hara that was gang-
foreman on the Ferozepore line. Then he would weep bitterly in the
broken rush chair on the veranda. So it came about after his death that
the woman sewed parchment, paper, and birth-certificate into a leather
amulet-case which she strung round Kim's neck.

"And some day," she said, confusedly remembering O'Hara's prophecies,
"there will come for you a great Red Bull on a green field, and the
Colonel riding on his tall horse, yes, and"—dropping into English—"nine
hundred devils."

"Ah," said Kim, "I shall remember. A Red Bull and a Colonel on a
horse will come, but first, my father said, will come the two men making
ready the ground for these matters. That is how, my father said, they always did; and it is always so when men work magic."

If the woman had sent Kim up to the local Jadoo-Gher with those
papers, he would, of course, have been taken over by the Provincial Lodge
and sent to the Masonic Orphanage in the Hills; but what she had heard
of magic she distrusted. Kim, too, held views of his own. As he reached
the years of indiscretion, he learned to avoid missionaries and white men
of serious aspect who asked who he was, and what he did. For Kim did
nothing with an immense success. True, he knew the wonderful walled
city of Lahore from the Delhi Gate to the outer Fort Ditch; was hand in
glove with men who led lives stranger than anything Haroun al Raschid
dreamed of; and he lived in a life wild as that of the Arabian Nights,
but missionaries and secretaries of charitable societies could not see the
beauty of it. His nickname through the wards was "Little Friend of all
the World"; and very often, being lithe and inconspicuous, he executed
commissions by night on the crowded housetops for sleek and shiny young
men of fashion. It was intrigue, of course,—he knew that much, as he
had known all evil since he could speak,—but what he loved was the
game for its own sake—the stealthy prowl through the dark gullies and
lanes, the crawl up a water-pipe, the sights and sounds of the women's
world on the flat roofs, and the headlong flight from housetop to housetop
under cover of the hot dark. Then there were holy men, ash-smeared
faquirs by their brick shrines under the trees at the riverside, with whom

he was quite familiar—greeting them as they returned from begging-tours, and, when no one was by, eating from the same dish. The woman who looked after him insisted with tears that he should wear European clothes—trousers, a shirt, and a battered hat. Kim found it easier to slip into Hindu or Mohammedan garb when engaged on certain businesses. One of the young men of fashion—he who was found dead at the bottom of a well on the night of the earthquake—had once given him a complete suit of Hindu kit, the costume of a low-caste street boy, and Kim stored it in a secret place under some baulks in Nila Ram's timber-yard, beyond the Punjab High Court, where the fragrant deodar logs lie seasoning after they have driven down the Ravee. When there was business or frolic afoot, Kim would use his properties, returning at dawn to the veranda, all tired out from shouting at the heels of a marriage procession, or yelling at a Hindu festival. Sometimes there was food in the house, more often there was not, and then Kim went out again to eat with his native friends.

As he drummed his heels against Zam-Zammah he turned now and again from his king-of-the-castle game with little Chota Lal, and Abdullah the sweetmeat-seller's son, to make a rude remark to the native policeman on guard over rows of shoes at the Museum door. The big Punjabi grinned tolerantly: he knew Kim of old. So did the water-carrier, sluicing water on the dry road from his goat-skin bag. So did Jawahir Singh, the Museum carpenter, bent over new packing-cases. So did everybody in sight except the peasants from the country, hurrying up to the Wonder House to view the things that men made in their own Province and elsewhere. The Museum was given up to Indian arts and manufactures, and anybody who sought wisdom could ask the curator to explain.

"Off! Off! Let me up!" cried Abdullah, climbing up Zam-Zammah's wheel.

"Thy father was a pastry-cook, Thy mother stole the ghi," sang Kim. "All Mussalmans fell off Zam-Zammah long ago!"

"Let me up!" shrilled little Chota Lal in his gilt-embroidered cap. His father was worth perhaps half a million sterling, but India is the only democratic land in the world.

"The Hindus fell off Zam-Zammah too. The Mussalmans pushed them off. Thy father was a pastry-cook—"

He stopped; for there shuffled round the corner, from the roaring Motee Bazar, such a man as Kim, who thought he knew all castes, had never seen. He was nearly six feet high, dressed in fold upon fold of dingy stuff like horse-blanketing, and not one fold of it could Kim refer to any known trade or profession. At his belt hung a long open-work iron pen-case and a wooden rosary such as holy men wear. On his head was a gigantic sort of tam-o'-shanter. His face was yellow and wrinkled, like that of Fook Shing, the Chinese bootmaker in the bazar. His eyes turned up at the corners and looked like little slits of onyx.

"Who is that?" said Kim to his companions.

"Perhaps it is a man," said Abdullah, finger in mouth, staring.

"Without doubt," returned Kim; "but he is no man of India that I have ever seen."

"A priest, perhaps," said Chota Lal, spying the rosary. "See! He goes into the Wonder House!"

"Nay, nay," said the policeman, shaking his head. "I do not understand your talk." The constable spoke Punjabi. "Oh, Friend of all the World, what does he say?"

"Send him hither," said Kim, dropping from Zam-Zammah, flourishing his bare heels. "He is a foreigner, and thou art a buffalo."

The man turned helplessly and drifted towards the boys. He was old, and his woollen gaberdine still reeked of the stinking artemisia of the mountain passes.

"O Children, what is that big house?" he said in very fair Urdu.

"The Ajaib-Gher, the Wonder House!" Kim gave him no title—such as Lala or Mian. He could not divine the man's creed.

"Ah! The Wonder House! Can any enter?"

"It is written above the door—all can enter."

"Without payment?"

"I go in and out. I am no banker," laughed Kim.

"Alas! I am an old man. I did not know." Then, fingering his rosary, he half turned to the Museum.

"What is your caste? Where is your house? Have you come far?" Kim asked.

"I came by Kulu—from beyond the Kailas—but what know you? From the Hills where"—he sighed—"the air and water are fresh and cool."

"Aha! Khitai" (Chinaman), said Abdullah proudly. Fook Shing had once chased him out of his shop for spitting at the joss above the boots.

"Pahari?" (a hillman), said little Chota Lal.

"Aye, child—a hillman from Hills thou'lt never see. Didst hear of Bhotiyal (Tibet)? I am no Khitai, but a Bhotiya (Tibetan), since you must know—a lama—or, say a guru in your tongue."

"A guru from Tibet," said Kim. "I have not seen such a man. They be Hindus in Tibet, then?"

"We be followers of the Middle Way, living in peace in our lamasseries, and I go to see the Four Holy Places before I die. Now do you, who are children, know as much as I do who am old." He smiled benignantly on the boys.

"Hast thou eaten?"

He fumbled in his bosom and drew forth a worn wooden begging-bowl. The boys nodded. All priests of their acquaintance begged.

"I do not wish to eat yet." He turned his head like an old tortoise in the sunlight. "Is it true that there are many images in the Wonder House of Lahore?" He repeated the last words as one making sure of an address.

"That is true," said Abdullah. "It is full of heathen buts. Thou also art an idolater."

"Never mind him," said Kim. "That is the Government's house and there is no idolatry in it, but only a Sahib with a white beard. Come with me and I will show."

"Strange priests eat boys," whispered Chota Lal.

"And he is a stranger and a but-parast" (idolater), said Abdullah, the Mohammedan.

Kim laughed. "He is new. Run to your mothers' laps, and be safe. Come!"

Kim clicked round the self-registering turnstile; the old man followed and halted amazed. In the entrance-hall stood the larger figures of the Greco-Buddhist sculptures done, savants know how long since, by forgotten workmen whose hands were feeling, and not unskilfully, for the mysteriously transmitted Grecian touch. There were hundreds of pieces, friezes of figures in relief, fragments of statues and slabs crowded with figures that had encrusted the brick walls of the Buddhist stupas and viharas of the North Country and now, dug up and labelled, made the pride of the Museum. In open-mouthed wonder the lama turned to this and that, and finally checked in rapt attention before a large alto-relief representing a coronation or apotheosis of the Lord Buddha. The Master was represented seated on a lotus the petals of which were so deeply undercut as to show almost detached. Round Him was an adoring hierarchy of kings, elders, and old-time Buddhas. Below were lotus-covered waters with fishes and water-birds. Two butterfly-winged dewas held a wreath over His head; above them another pair supported an umbrella surmounted by the jewelled headdress of the Bodhisat.

"The Lord! The Lord! It is Sakya Muni himself," the lama half sobbed; and under his breath began the wonderful Buddhist invocation:—

"To Him the Way—the Law—Apart—
Whom Maya held beneath her heart
Ananda's Lord—the Bodhisat."

"And He is here! The Most Excellent Law is here also! My pilgrimage is well begun. And what work! What work!"

"Yonder is the Sahib," said Kim, and dodged sideways among the cases of the arts and manufacture wing. A white-bearded Englishman was looking at the lama, who gravely turned and saluted him and after some fumbling drew forth a note-book and a scrap of paper.

"Yes, that is my name," smiling at the clumsy, childish print.

"One of us who had made pilgrimage to the Holy Places—he is now Abbot of the Lung-Cho Monastery—gave it me," stammered the lama. "He spoke of these." His lean hand moved tremulously round.

"Welcome, then, O lama from Tibet. Here be the images, and I am here"—he glanced at the lama's face—"to gather knowledge. Come to my office awhile." The old man was trembling with excitement.

The office was but a little wooden cubicle partitioned off from the sculpture-lined gallery. Kim laid himself down, his ear against a crack in the heat-split cedar door, and, following his instinct, stretched out to listen and watch.

Most of the talk was altogether above his head. The lama, haltingly at first, spoke to the curator of his own lamassery, the Suchzen, opposite the Painted Rocks, four months' march away. The curator brought out a huge book of photos and showed him that very place, perched on its crag, overlooking the gigantic valley of many-hued strata.

"Ay, ay!" The lama mounted a pair of horn-rimmed spectacles of Chinese work. "Here is the little door through which we bring wood before winter. And thou—the English know of these things? He who is now Abbot of Lung-Cho told me, but I did not believe. The Lord—the Excellent One—He has honour here too? And His life is known?"

"It is all carven upon the stones. Come and see, if thou art rested."

Out shuffled the lama to the main hall, and, the curator beside him, went through the collection with the reverence of a devotee and the appreciative instinct of a craftsman.

Incident by incident in the beautiful story he identified on the blurred stone, puzzled here and there by the unfamiliar Greek convention, but delighted as a child at each new trove. Where the sequence failed, as in the Annunciation, the curator supplied it from his mound of books—French and German, with photographs and reproductions.

Here was the devout Asita, the pendant of Simeon in the Christian story, holding the Holy Child on his knee while mother and father listened; and here were incidents in the legend of the cousin Devadatta. Here was the wicked woman who accused the Master of impurity, all confounded; here was the teaching in the Deer-park; the miracle that stunned the fire-worshippers; here was the Bodhisat in royal state as a prince; the miraculous birth; the death at Kusinagara, where the weak disciple fainted; while there were almost countless repetitions of the meditation under the Bodhi tree; and the adoration of the alms-bowl was everywhere. In a few minutes the curator saw that his guest was no mere bead-telling mendicant, but a scholar of parts. And they went at it all over again, the lama taking snuff, wiping his spectacles, and talking at railway speed in a bewildering mixture of Urdu and Tibetan. He had heard of the travels of the Chinese pilgrims, Fo-Hian and Hwen-Thiang, and was anxious to know if there was any translation of their record. He drew in his breath as he turned helplessly over the pages of Beal and Stanislas Julien. "'Tis all here. A treasure locked." Then he composed himself reverently to listen to fragments, hastily rendered into Urdu. For the first time he heard of the labours of European scholars, who by the help of these and a hundred other documents have identified the Holy Places of Buddhism. Then he was shown a mighty map, spotted and traced with yellow. The brown finger followed the curator's pencil from point to point. Here was Kapilavastu, here the Middle Kingdom, and here Mahabodi, the Mecca of Buddhism; and here was Kusinagara, sad place of the Holy One's death. The old man bowed his head over the sheets in silence for a while, and the curator lit another pipe. Kim had fallen asleep. When he waked, the talk, still in spate, was more within his comprehension.

"And thus it was, O Fountain of Wisdom, that I decided to go to the Holy Places which His foot had trod—to the Birthplace, even to Kapila; then to Maha Bodhi, which is Buddh Gaya—to the Monastery—to the Deer-park—to the place of His death."

The lama lowered his voice. "And I come here alone. For five—seven—eighteen—forty years it was in my mind that the Old Law was not well followed; being overlaid, as thou knowest, with devildom, charms, and idolatry. Even as the child outside said but now. Ay, even as the child said, with but-parasti."

"So it comes with all faiths."

"Thinkest thou? The books of my lamassery I read, and they were dried pith; and the later ritual with which we of the Reformed Law have cumbered ourselves—that, too, had no worth to these old eyes. Even the followers of the Excellent One are at feud on feud with one another. It is all illusion. Ay, maya, illusion. But I have another desire"—the seamed yellow face drew within three inches of the curator, and the long fore-finger nail tapped on the table. "Your scholars, by these books, have followed the Blessed Feet in all their wanderings; but there are things which they have not sought out. I know nothing,—nothing do I know,—but I go to free myself from the Wheel of Things by a broad and open road." He smiled with most simple triumph. "As a pilgrim to the Holy Places I acquire merit. But there is more. Listen to a true thing. When our gracious Lord, being as yet a youth, sought a mate, men said, in His father's court, that He was too tender for marriage. Thou knowest?"

The curator nodded, wondering what would come next.

"So they made the triple trial of strength against all comers. And at the test of the Bow, our Lord first breaking that which they gave Him, called for such a bow as none might bend. Thou knowest?"

"It is written. I have read."

"And, overshooting all other marks, the arrow passed far and far beyond sight. At the last it fell; and, where it touched earth, there broke out a stream which presently became a River, whose nature, by our Lord's beneficence, and that merit He acquired ere He freed himself, is that whoso bathes in it washes away all taint and speckle of sin."

"So it is written," said the curator sadly.

The lama drew a long breath. "Where is that River? Fountain of Wisdom, where fell the arrow?"

"Alas, my brother, I do not know," said the curator.

"Nay, if it please thee to forget—the one thing only that thou hast not told me. Surely thou must know? See, I am an old man! I ask with my head between thy feet, O Fountain of Wisdom. We know He drew the bow! We know the arrow fell! We know the stream gushed! Where, then is the River? My dream told me to find it. So I came. I am here. But where is the River?"

"If I knew, think you I would not cry it aloud?"

"By it one attains freedom from the Wheel of Things," the lama went on, unheeding. "The River of the Arrow! Think again! Some little stream, may be—dried in the heats? But the Holy One would never so cheat an old man."

"I do not know. I do not know."

The lama brought his thousand-wrinkled face once more a handsbreadth from the Englishman's. "I see thou dost not know. Not being of the Law, the matter is hid from thee."

"Ay—hidden—hidden."

"We are both bound, thou and I, my brother. But I"—he rose with a sweep of the soft thick drapery—"I go to cut myself free. Come also!"

"I am bound," said the curator. "But whither goest thou?"

"First to Kashi (Benares): where else? There I shall meet one of the pure faith in a Jain temple of that city. He also is a Seeker in secret, and from him haply I may learn. May be he will go with me to Buddh Gaya. Thence north and west to Kapilavastu, and there will I seek for the River. Nay, I will seek everywhere as I go—for the place is not known where the arrow fell."

"And how wilt thou go? It is a far cry to Delhi, and farther to Benares."

"By road and the trains. From Pathankot, having left the Hills, I came hither in a te-rain. It goes swiftly. At first I was amazed to see those tall poles by the side of the road snatching up and snatching up their threads,"—he illustrated the stoop and whirl of a telegraph-pole flashing past the train. "But later I was cramped and desired to walk, as I am used."

"And thou art sure of thy road?" said the curator.

"Oh, for that one but asks a question and pays money, and the appointed persons despatch all to the appointed place. That much I knew in my lamassery from sure report," said the lama proudly.

"And when dost thou go?" The curator smiled at the mixture of old-world piety and modern progress that is the note of India today.

"As soon as may be. I follow the places of His life till I come to the River of the Arrow. There is, moreover, a written paper of the hours of the trains that go south."

"And for food?" Lamas, as a rule, have good store of money somewhere about them, but the curator wished to make sure.

"For the journey, I take up the Master's begging-bowl. Yes. Even as He went so go I, forsaking the ease of my monastery. There was with me when I left the Hills a chela (disciple) who begged for me as the Rule demands, but halting in Kulu awhile a fever took him and he died. I have now no chela, but I will take the alms-bowl and thus enable the charitable to acquire merit." He nodded his head valiantly.

Learned doctors of a lamassery do not beg, but the lama was an enthusiast in this quest.

"Be it so," said the curator, smiling. "Suffer me now to acquire merit. We be craftsmen together, thou and I. Here is a new book of white English paper: here be sharpened pencils two and three—thick and thin, all good for a scribe. Now lend me thy spectacles."

The curator looked through them. They were heavily scratched, but the power was almost exactly that of his own pair, which he slid into the lama's hand, saying: "Try these."

"A feather! A very feather upon the face!" The old man turned his head delightedly and wrinkled up his nose. "How scarcely do I feel them! How clearly do I see!"

"They be bilaur—crystal and will never scratch. May they help thee to thy River, for they are thine."

"I will take them and the pencils and the white note-book," said the lama, "as a sign of friendship between priest and priest—and now"—he fumbled at his belt, detached the open ironwork pencase, and laid it on the curator's table. "That is for a memory between thee and me—my pencase. It is something old—even as I am."

It was a piece of ancient design, Chinese, of an iron that is not smelted these days; and the collector's heart in the curator's bosom had gone out to it from the first. For no persuasion would the lama resume his gift.

"When I return, having found the River, I will bring thee a written picture of the Padma Samthora—such as I used to make on silk at the lamassery. Yes—and of the Wheel of Life," he chuckled, "for we be craftsmen together, thou and I."

The curator would have detained him: they are few in the world who still have the secret of the conventional brush-pen Buddhist pictures which are, as it were, half written and half drawn. But the lama strode out, head high in air, and pausing an instant before the great statue of a Bodhisat in meditation, brushed through the turnstile.

Kim followed like a shadow. What he had overheard excited him wildly. This man was entirely new to all his experience, and he meant to investigate further: precisely as he would have investigated a new building or a strange festival in Lahore city. The lama was his trove, and he purposed to take possession. Kim's mother had been Irish too.

The old man halted by Zam-Zammah and looked round till his eye fell on Kim. The inspiration of his pilgrimage had left him for a while, and he felt old, forlorn, and very empty.

"Do not sit under that gun," said the policeman loftily.

"Huh! Owl!" was Kim's retort on the lama's behalf. "Sit under that gun if it please thee. When didst thou steal the milk-woman's slippers, Dunnoo?"

That was an utterly unfounded charge sprung on the spur of the moment, but it silenced Dunnoo, who knew that Kim's clear yell could call up legions of bad bazar boys if need arose.

"And whom didst thou worship within?" said Kim affably, squatting in the shade beside the lama.

"I worshipped none, child. I bowed before the Excellent Law."

Kim accepted this new god without emotion. He knew already a few score.

"And what dost thou do?"

"I beg. I remember now it is long since I have eaten or drunk. What is the custom of charity in this town? In silence, as we do of Tibet, or speaking aloud?"

"Those who beg in silence starve in silence," said Kim, quoting a native proverb. The lama tried to rise, but sank back again, sighing for his disciple, dead in faraway Kulu. Kim watched—head to one side, considering and interested.

"Give me the bowl. I know the people of this city—all who are charitable. Give, and I will bring it back filled."

Simply as a child the old man handed him the bowl.

"Rest thou. I know the people."

He trotted off to the open shop of a kunjri, a low-caste vegetable-seller, which lay opposite the belt-tramway line down the Motee Bazar. She knew Kim of old.

"Oho, hast thou turned yogi with thy begging-bowl?" she cried.

"Nay," said Kim proudly. "There is a new priest in the city—a man such as I have never seen."

"Old priest—young tiger," said the woman angrily. "I am tired of new priests! They settle on our wares like flies. Is the father of my son a well of charity to give to all who ask?"

"No," said Kim. "Thy man is rather yagi (bad-tempered) than yogi (a holy man). But this priest is new. The Sahib in the Wonder House has talked to him like a brother. O my mother, fill me this bowl. He waits."

"That bowl indeed! That cow-bellied basket! Thou hast as much grace as the holy bull of Shiv. He has taken the best of a basket of onions already, this morn; and forsooth, I must fill thy bowl. He comes here again."

The huge, mouse-coloured Brahminee bull of the ward was shouldering his way through the many-coloured crowd, a stolen plantain hanging out of his mouth. He headed straight for the shop, well knowing his privileges as a sacred beast, lowered his head, and puffed heavily along the line of baskets ere making his choice. Up flew Kim's hard little heel and caught him on his moist blue nose. He snorted indignantly, and walked away across the tram rails, his hump quivering with rage.

"See! I have saved more than the bowl will cost thrice over. Now, mother, a little rice and some dried fish atop—yes, and some vegetable curry."

A growl came out of the back of the shop, where a man lay.

"He drove away the bull," said the woman in an undertone. "It is good to give to the poor." She took the bowl and returned it full of hot rice.

"But my yogi is not a cow," said Kim gravely, making a hole with his fingers in the top of the mound. "A little curry is good, and a fried cake, and a morsel of conserve would please him, I think."

"It is a hole as big as thy head," said the woman fretfully. But she filled it, none the less, with good, steaming vegetable curry, clapped a dried cake atop, and a morsel of clarified butter on the cake, dabbed a lump of sour tamarind conserve at the side; and Kim looked at the load lovingly.

"That is good. When I am in the bazar the bull shall not come to this house. He is a bold beggarman."

"And thou?" laughed the woman. "But speak well of bulls. Hast thou not told me that some day a Red Bull will come out of a field to help thee? Now hold all straight and ask for the holy man's blessing upon me. Perhaps, too, he knows a cure for my daughter's sore eyes. Ask him that also, O thou Little Friend of all the World."

But Kim had danced off ere the end of the sentence, dodging pariah dogs and hungry acquaintances.

"Thus do we beg who know the way of it," said he proudly to the lama, who opened his eyes at the contents of the bowl. "Eat now and— I will eat with thee. Ohe bhistie!" he called to the water-carrier, sluicing the crotons by the Museum. "Give water here. We men are thirsty."

"We men!" said the bhistie, laughing. "Is one skinful enough for such a pair? Drink then, in the name of the Compassionate."

He loosed a thin stream into Kim's hands, who drank native fashion; but the lama must needs pull out a cup from his inexhaustible upper draperies and drink ceremonially.

"Pardesi" (a foreigner), Kim explained, as the old man delivered in an unknown tongue what was evidently a blessing.

They ate together in great content, clearing the beggar's bowl. Then the lama took snuff from a portentous wooden snuff-gourd, fingered his rosary awhile, and so dropped into the easy sleep of age, as the shadow of Zam-Zammah grew long.

Kim loafed over to the nearest tobacco-seller, a rather lively young Mohammedan woman, and begged a rank cigar of the brand that they sell to students of the Punjab University who copy English customs. Then he smoked and thought, knees to chin, under the belly of the gun, and the outcome of his thoughts was a sudden and stealthy departure in the direction of Nila Ram's timber-yard.

The lama did not wake till the evening life of the city had begun with lamp-lighting and the return of white-robed clerks and subordinates from the Government offices. He stared dizzily in all directions, but none looked at him save a Hindu urchin in a dirty turban and Isabella-coloured clothes. Suddenly he bowed his head on his knees and wailed.

"What is this?" said the boy, standing before him. "Hast thou been robbed?"

"It is my new chela (my disciple) that is gone away from me, and I know not where he is."

"And what like of man was thy disciple?"

"It was a boy who came to me in place of him who died, on account of the merit which I had gained when I bowed before the Law within there." He pointed towards the Museum. "He came upon me to show me a road which I had lost. He led me into the Wonder House, and by his talk emboldened to speak to the Keeper of the Images, so that I was cheered and made strong. And when I was faint with hunger he begged for me, as would a chela for his teacher. Suddenly was he sent. Suddenly has he gone away. It was in my mind to have taught him the Law upon the road to Benares."

Kim stood amazed at this, because he had overheard the talk in the Museum, and knew that the old man was speaking the truth, which is a thing a native on the road seldom presents to a stranger.

"But I see now that he was but sent for a purpose. By this I know that I shall find a certain River for which I seek."

"The River of the Arrow?" said Kim, with a superior smile.

"Is this yet another Sending?" cried the lama. "To none have I spoken of my search, save to the Priest of the Images. Who art thou?"

"Thy chela," said Kim simply, sitting on his heels. "I have never seen any one like to thee in all this my life. I go with thee to Benares. And, too, I think that so old a man as thou, speaking the truth to chance-met people at dusk, is in great need of a disciple."

"But the River—the River of the Arrow?"

"Oh, that I heard when thou was speaking to the Englishman. I lay against the door."

The lama sighed. "I thought thou hadst been a guide permitted. Such things fall sometimes—but I am not worthy. Thou dost not, then, know of the River?"

"Not I." Kim laughed uneasily. "I go to look for—for a bull—a Red Bull on a green field who shall help me." Boylike, if an acquaintance had a scheme, Kim was quite ready with one of his own; and, boylike, he had really thought for as much as twenty minutes at a time of his father's prophecy.

"To what, child?" said the lama.

"God knows, but so my father told me. I heard thy talk in the Wonder House of all those new strange places in the Hills, and if one so old and so little—so used to truth-telling—may go out for the small matter of a river, it seemed to me that I too must go a-travelling. If it is our fate to find those things we shall find them—thou, thy River; and I, my Bull, and the strong pillars and some other matters that I forget."

"It is not pillars but a Wheel from which I would be free," said the lama.

"That is all one. Perhaps they will make me a king," said Kim, serenely prepared for anything.

"I will teach thee other and better desires upon the road," the lama replied in the voice of authority. "Let us go to Benares."

"Not by night. Thieves are abroad. Wait till the day."

"But there is no place to sleep." The old man was used to the order of his monastery, and though he slept on the ground, as the Rule decrees, preferred a decency in these things.

"We shall get good lodging at the Kashmir Serai," said Kim, laughing at his perplexity. "I have a friend there. Come!"

The hot and crowded bazars blazed with light as they made their way through the press of all the races in Upper India, and the lama mooned through it like a man in a dream. It was his first experience of a large manufacturing city, and the crowded tram-car with its continually squealing brakes frightened him. Half pushed, half towed, he arrived at the high gate of the Kashmir Serai: that huge open square over against the railway station, surrounded with arched cloisters where the camel and horse caravans put up on their return from Central Asia. Here were all manner of Northern folk, tending tethered ponies and kneeling camels; loading and unloading bales and bundles; drawing water for the evening meal at the creaking well-windlasses; piling grass before the shrieking, wild-eyed stallions; cuffing the surly caravan dogs; paying off camel-drivers, taking on new grooms; swearing, shouting, arguing, and chaffering in the packed square. The cloisters, reached by three or four masonry steps, made a haven of refuge around this turbulent sea. Most of them were rented to traders, as we rent the arches of a viaduct; the space between pillar and pillar being bricked or boarded off into rooms, which were guarded by heavy wooden doors and cumbrous native padlocks. Locked doors showed that the owner was away, and a few rude—sometimes very rude—chalk or paint scratches told where he had gone. Thus: "Lutuf Ullah is gone to Kurdistan." Below, in coarse verse: "O Allah, who sufferest lice to live on the coat of a Kabuli, why has thou allowed this louse Lutuf to live so long?"

Kim, fending the lama between excited men and excited beasts, sidled along the cloisters to the far end, nearest the railway station, where Mahbub Ali, the horse-trader, lived when he came in from that mysterious land beyond the Passes of the North.

Kim had had many dealings with Mahbub in his little life,—especially between his tenth and his thirteenth year,—and the big burly Afghan, his beard dyed scarlet with lime (for he was elderly and did not wish his gray hairs to show), knew the boy's value as a gossip. Sometimes he would tell Kim to watch a man who had nothing whatever to do with horses: to follow him for one whole day and report every soul with whom he talked. Kim would deliver himself of his tale at evening, and Mahbub would listen without a word or gesture. It was intrigue of some kind, Kim knew; but its worth lay in saying nothing whatever to any one except Mahbub, who gave him beautiful meals all hot from the cookshop at the head of the serai, and once as much as eight annas in money.

"He is here," said Kim, hitting a bad-tempered camel on the nose. "Ohe, Mahbub Ali!" He halted at a dark arch and slipped behind the bewildered lama.

The horse-trader, his deep, embroidered Bokhariot belt unloosed, was lying on a pair of silk carpet saddle-bags, pulling lazily at an immense silver hookah. He turned his head very slightly at the cry; and seeing only the tall silent figure, chuckled in his deep chest.

"Allah! A lama! A Red Lama! It is far from Lahore to the Passes. What dost thou do here?"

The lama held out the begging-bowl mechanically.

"God's curse on all unbelievers!" said Mahbub. "I do not give to a lousy Tibetan; but ask my Baltis over yonder behind the camels. They may value your blessings. Oh, horse-boys, here is a countryman of yours. See if he be hungry."

A shaven, crouching Balti, who had come down with the horses, and who was nominally some sort of degraded Buddhist, fawned upon the priest, and in thick gutturals besought the Holy One to sit at the horse-boys' fire.

"Go!" said Kim, pushing him lightly, and the lama strode away, leaving Kim at the edge of the cloister.

"Go!" said Mahbub Ali, returning to his hookah. "Little Hindu, run away. God's curse on all unbelievers! Beg from those of my tail who are of thy faith."

"Maharaj," whined Kim, using the Hindu form of address, and thoroughly enjoying the situation; "my father is dead—my mother is dead—my stomach is empty."

"Beg from my men among the horses, I say. There must be some Hindus in my tail."

"Oh, Mahbub Ali, but am I a Hindu?" said Kim in English.

The trader gave no sign of astonishment, but looked under shaggy eyebrows.

"Little Friend of all the World," said he, "what is this?"

"Nothing. I am now that holy man's disciple; and we go a pilgrimage together—to Benares, he says. He is quite mad, and I am tired of Lahore city. I wish new air and water."

"But for whom dost thou work? Why come to me?" The voice was harsh with suspicion.

"To whom else should I come? I have no money. It is not good to go about without money. Thou wilt sell many horses to the officers. They are very fine horses, these new ones: I have seen them. Give me a rupee, Mahbub Ali, and when I come to my wealth I will give thee a bond and pay."

"Um," said Mahbub Ali, thinking swiftly. "Thou hast never before lied to me. Call that lama—stand back in the dark."

"Oh, our tales will agree," said Kim laughing.

"We go to Benares," said the lama, as soon as he understood the drift of Mahbub Ali's questions. "The boy and I. I go to seek for a certain River."

"Maybe—but the boy?"

"He is my disciple. He was sent, I think, to guide me to that River. Sitting under a gun was I when he came suddenly. Such things have befallen the fortunate to whom guidance was allowed. But I remember now, he said he was of this world—a Hindu."

"And his name?"

"That I did not ask. Is he not my disciple?"

"His country—his face—his village? Mussalman—Sikh—Hindu—Jain—low caste or high?"

"Why should I ask? There is neither high nor low in the Middle Way. If he is my chela—does—will—can any one take him from me? for, look you, without him I shall not find my River." He wagged his head solemnly.

"None shall take him from thee. Go, sit among my Baltis," said Mahbub Ali, and the lama drifted off, soothed by the promise.

"Is he not quite mad?" said Kim, coming forward to the light again. "Why should I lie to thee, Hajji?"

Mahbub puffed his hookah in silence. Then he began, almost whispering: "Umballa is on the road to Benares—if indeed ye two go there."

"Tck! Tck! I tell thee he does not know how to lie—as we two know."

"And if thou wilt carry a message for me as far as Umballa, I will give thee money. It concerns a horse—a white stallion which I have sold to an officer upon the last time I returned from the Passes. But then—stand nearer and hold up hands as begging—the pedigree of the white stallion was not fully established, and that officer, who is now at Umballa, bade me make it clear." (Mahbub here described the horse and the appearance of the officer.) "So the message to that officer will be: 'The pedigree of the white stallion is fully established.' By this will he know that thou comest from me. He will then say 'What proof has thou?' and thou wilt answer: 'Mahbub Ali has given me the proof.' "

"And all for the sake of a white stallion," said Kim, with a giggle, his eyes aflame.

"That pedigree I will give thee now—in my own fashion—and some hard words as well." A shadow passed behind Kim, and a feeding camel. Mahbub Ali raised his voice.

"Allah! Art thou the only beggar in the city? Thy mother is dead. Thy father is dead. So is it with all of them. Well, well—" he turned as feeling on the floor beside him and tossed a flap of soft, greasy Mussalman bread to the boy. "Go and lie among my horse-boys for to-night—thou and the lama. To-morrow I may give thee service."

Kim slunk away, his teeth in the bread, and, as he expected, he found a small wad of folded tissue-paper wrapped in oil-skin, with three silver rupees—enormous largesse. He smiled and thrust money and paper into his leather amulet-case. The lama, sumptuously fed by Mahbub's Baltis, was already asleep in a corner of one of the stalls. Kim lay down beside him and laughed. He knew he had rendered a service to Mahbub Ali, and not for one little minute did he believe the tale of the stallion's pedigree.

But Kim did not suspect that Mahbub Ali, known as one of the best horse-dealers in the Punjab, a wealthy and enterprising trader, whose caravans penetrated far and far into the Back of Beyond, was registered in one of the locked books of the Indian Survey Department as C.25.1B. Twice or thrice yearly C.25 would send in a little story, badly told but most interesting, and generally—it was checked by the statements of R.17 and M.4—quite true. It concerned all manner of out-of-the-way mountain principalities, explorers of nationalities other than English, and the gun-trade—was, in brief, a small portion of that vast mass of "information received" on which the Indian Government acts. But, recently, five confederated Kings, who had no business to confederate, had been informed by a kindly Northern Power that there was a leakage of news from their territories into British India. So those Kings' prime ministers were seriously annoyed and took steps, after the Oriental fashion. They suspected, among many others, the bullying red-bearded horse-dealer whose caravans ploughed through their fastnesses belly deep in snow. At least, his caravan that season had been ambushed and shot at twice on the way down, when Mahbub's men accounted for three strange ruffians who might, or might not, have been hired for the job. Therefore Mahbub had avoided halting at the insalubrious city of Peshawur, and had come through without stop to Lahore, where, knowing his country-people, he anticipated curious developments.

And there was that on Mahbub Ali which he did not wish to keep an hour longer than was necessary—a wad of closely folded tissue-paper, wrapped in oil-skin—an impersonal, unaddressed statement, with five microscopic pin-holes in one corner, that most scandalously betrayed the five confederated Kings, the sympathetic Northern Power, a Hindu banker in Peshawur, a firm of gun-makers in Belgium, and an important, semi-independent Mohammedan ruler to the south. This last was R.17's work, which Mahbub had picked up beyond the Dora Pass and was carrying in for R.17, who, owing to circumstances over which he had no control, could not leave his post of observation. Dynamite was milky and innocuous beside that report of C.25; and even an Oriental, with an Oriental's views of the value of time, could see that the sooner it was in the proper hands the better. Mahbub had no particular desire to die by violence, because two or three family blood-feuds across the border hung unfinished on his hands, and when these scores were cleared he intended to settle down as a more or less virtuous citizen. He had never passed the serai gate since his arrival two days ago, but had been ostentatious in sending telegrams to Bombay, where he banked some of his money; to Delhi, where a sub-partner of his own clan was selling horses to the agent of a Rajputana state; and to Umballa, where an Englishman was excitedly demanding the pedigree of a white stallion. The public letter-writer, who knew English, composed excellent telegrams, such as:—"Creighton, Laurel Bank, Umballa.—Horse is Arabian as already advised. Sorrowful delayed-pedigree which am translating." And later to the same address: "Much sorrowful delay. Will forward pedigree." To this sub-partner at Delhi he wired: "Lutuf Ullah.—Have wired two thousand rupees your credit Luchman Narain's bank." This was entirely in the way of trade, but every one of those telegrams was discussed and re-discussed, by parties who conceived themselves to be interested, before they went over to the railway station in charge of a foolish Balti, who allowed all sorts of people to read them on the road.

When, in Mahbub's own picturesque language, he had muddied the wells of inquiry with the stick of precaution, Kim had dropped on him, sent from heaven; and, being as prompt as he was unscrupulous, Mahbub Ali, used to taking all sorts of gusty chances, pressed him into service on the spot.

A wandering lama with a low-caste boy-servant might attract a moment's interest as they wandered about India, the land of pilgrims; but no one would suspect them or, what was more to the point, rob.

He called for a new light-ball to his hookah, and considered the case. If the worst came to the worst, and the boy came to harm, the paper would incriminate nobody. And he would go up to Umballa leisurely and—at a certain risk of exciting fresh suspicion—repeat his tale by word of mouth to the people concerned.

But R.17's report was the kernel of the whole affair, and it would be distinctly inconvenient if that failed to come to hand. However, God was great, and Mahbub Ali felt he had done all he could for the time being. Kim was the one soul in the world who had never told him a lie. That would have been a fatal blot on Kim's character if Mahbub had not known that to others, for his own ends or Mahbub's business, Kim could lie like an Oriental.

Then Mahbub Ali rolled across the serai to the Gate of the Harpies who paint their eyes and trap the stranger, and was at some pains to call on the one girl who, he had reason to believe, was a particular friend of a smooth-faced Kashmiri pundit who had waylaid his simple Balti in the matter of the telegrams. It was an utterly foolish thing to do; because they fell to drinking perfumed brandy against the Law of the Prophet, and Mahbub grew wonderfully drunk, and the gates of his mouth were loosened, and he pursued the Flower of Delight with the feet of intoxication till he fell flat among the cushions, where the Flower of Delight, aided by a smooth-faced Kashmiri pundit, searched him from head to foot most thoroughly.

About the same hour Kim heard soft feet in Mahbub's deserted stall. The horse-trader, curiously enough, had left his door unlocked, and his men were busy celebrating their return to India with a whole sheep of Mahbub's bounty. A sleek young gentleman from Delhi, armed with a bunch of keys which the Flower had unshackled from the senseless one's belt, went through every single box, bundle, mat, and saddle-bag in Mahbub's possession even more systematically than the Flower and the pundit were searching the owner.

"And I think," said the Flower scornfully an hour later, one rounded elbow on the snoring carcase, "that he is no more than a pig of an Afghan horse-dealer, with no thought except women and horses. Moreover, he may have sent it away by now—if ever there were such a thing."

"Nay—in a matter touching Five Kings it would be next his black heart," said the pundit. "Was there nothing?"

The Delhi man laughed and resettled his turban as he entered. "I searched between the soles of his slippers as the Flower searched his clothes. This is not the man but another. I leave little unseen."

"They did not say he was the very man," said the pundit thoughtfully. "They said, 'Look if he be the man, since our councils are troubled.'"

"That North country is full of horse-dealers as an old coat of lice. There is Sikandar Khan, Nur Ali Beg, and Farrukh Shah—all heads of Kafilas—who deal there," said the Flower.

"They have not yet come in," said the pundit. "Thou must ensnare them later."

"Phew!" said the Flower with deep disgust, rolling Mahbub's head from her lap. "I earn my money. Farrukh Shah is a bear, Ali Beg a swashbuckler, and old Sikandar Khan—yaie! Go! I sleep now. This swine will not stir till dawn."

When Mahbub woke, the Flower talked to him severely on the sin of drunkenness. Asiatics do not wink when they have out-manoeuvred an enemy, but as Mahbub Ali cleared his throat, tightened his belt, and staggered forth under the early morning stars, he came very near to it.

"What a colt's trick," said he to himself. "As if every girl in Peshawur did not use it! But 'twas prettily done. Now God He knows how many more there be upon the road who have orders to test me—perhaps with the knife. So it stands that the boy must go to Umballa—and by rail—for the writing is something urgent. I abide here, following the Flower and drinking wine as an Afghan coper should."

He halted at the stall next but one to his own. His men lay there heavy with sleep. There was no sign of Kim or the lama.

"Up!" He stirred a sleeper. "Whither went those who lay here last even —the lama and the boy? Is aught missing?"

"Nay," grunted the man; "the old madman rose at second cock-crow saying he would go to Benares, and the young one led him away."

"The curse of Allah on all unbelievers," said Mahbub heartily, and climbed into his own stall, growling in his beard.

But it was Kim who had wakened the lama—Kim with one eye laid against a knot-hole in the planking, who had seen the Delhi man's search through the boxes. This was no common thief that turned over letters, bills, and saddles—no mere burglar who ran a little knife sideways into the soles of Mahbub's slippers, or picked the seams of the saddle-bags so deftly. At first Kim had been minded to give the alarm—the long-drawn "cho-or —choor!" (thief! thief!) that sets the serai ablaze of nights; but he looked more carefully, and, hand on amulet, drew his own conclusions.

"It must be the pedigree of that made-up horse-lie," said he, "the thing that I carry to Umballa. Better that we go now. Those who search bags with knives may presently search bellies with knives. Surely there is a woman behind this. Hai! Hai!" in a whisper to the light-sleeping old man. "Come. It is time—time to go to Benares."

The lama rose obediently, and they passed out of the serai like shadows.

Chapter 2

"For whoso will, from Pride released,
Contemning neither creed nor priest,
May hear the Soul of all the East
About him at Kamakura."

THEY entered the fort-like railway station, black in the end of night; the electrics sizzling over the goods yard where they handle the heavy Northern grain-traffic.

"This is the work of devils!" said the lama, recoiling from the hollow echoing darkness, the glimmer of rails between the masonry platforms, and the maze of girders above. He stood in a gigantic stone hall paved, it seemed, with the sheeted dead—third-class passengers who had taken their tickets overnight and were sleeping in the waiting-rooms. All hours of the twenty-four are alike to Orientals, and their passenger traffic is regulated accordingly.

"This is where the fire-carriages come. One stands behind that hole"— Kim pointed to the ticket-office—"who will give thee a paper to take thee to Umballa."

"But we go to Benares," he replied petulantly.

"All one. Benares then. Quick: she comes!"

"Take thou the purse."

The lama, not so well used to trains as he had pretended, started as the 3.25 a. m. south bound roared in. The sleepers sprang to life, and the station filled with clamour and shoutings, cries of water and sweetmeat vendors, shouts of native policemen, and shrill yells of women gathering up their baskets, their families, and their husbands.

"It is the train—only the te-rain. It will come here. Wait!" Amazed at the lama's immense simplicity (he handed him a small bag full of rupees), Kim asked and paid for a ticket to Umballa. A sleepy clerk grunted and flung out a ticket to the next station, just six miles distant.

"Nay," said Kim, scanning it with a grin. "This may serve for farmers, but I live in the city of Lahore. It was cleverly done, babu. Now give the ticket to Umballa."

The babu scowled and dealt the proper ticket.

"Now another to Amritzar," said Kim, who had no notion of spending Mahbub Ali's money on anything so crude as a paid ride to Umballa. "The price is so much. The small money in return is just so much. I know the ways of the te-rain. . . . Never did yogi need chela as thou dost," he went on merrily to the bewildered lama. "They would have flung thee out at Mian Mir but for me. This way! Come." He returned the money, keeping only one anna in each rupee of the price of the Umballa ticket as his commission—the immemorial commission of Asia.

The lama jibbed at the open door of a crowded third-class carriage. "Were it not better to walk?" said he weakly.

A burly Sikh artisan thrust forth his bearded head. "Is he afraid? Do not be afraid. I remember the time when I was afraid of the te-rain. Enter! This thing is the work of the Government."

"I do not fear," said the lama. "Have ye room within for two?"

"There is no room even for a mouse," shrilled the wife of a well-to-do cultivator—a Hindu Jat from the rich Jullundur district. "Our night trains are not as well looked after as the day ones, where the sexes are very strictly kept to separate carriages."

"Oh, mother of my son, we can make space," said the blue-turbaned husband. "Pick up the child. It is a holy man, seest thou?"

"And my lap full of seventy times seven bundles! Why not bid him sit on my knee, Shameless? But men are ever thus!" She looked round for approval. An Amritzar courtesan near the window sniffed behind her head drapery.

"Enter! Enter!" cried a fat Hindu money-lender, his folded account-book in a cloth under his arm. With an oily smirk: "It is well to be kind to the poor."

"Ay, at seven per cent a month with a mortgage on the unborn calf," said a young Dogra soldier going south on leave; and they all laughed.

"Will it travel to Benares?" said the lama.

"Assuredly. Else why should we come? Enter, or we are left," cried Kim.

"See!" shrilled the Amritzar girl. "He has never entered a train. Oh see!"

"Nay, help," said the cultivator, putting out a large brown hand and hauling him in. "Thus is it done, father."

"But—but—I sit on the floor. It is against the Rule to sit on a bench," said the lama. "Moreover, it cramps me."

"I say," began the money-lender, pursing his lips, "that there is not one rule of right living which these te-rains do not cause us to break. We sit, for example, side by side with all castes and peoples."

"Yea, and with most outrageously shameless ones," said the wife, scowling at the Amritzar girl making eyes at the young sepoy.

"I said we might have gone by cart along the road," said the husband, "and thus have saved some money."

"Yes—and spent twice over what we saved on food by the way. That was talked out ten thousand times."

"Ay, by ten thousand tongues," grunted he.

"The Gods help us poor women if we may not speak. Oho! He is of that sort which may not look at or reply to a woman." For the lama, constrained by his Rule, took not the faintest notice of her. "And his disciple is like him?"

"Nay, mother," said Kim most promptly. "Not when the woman is well-looking and above all charitable to the hungry."

"A beggar's answer," said the Sikh, laughing. "Thou hast brought it on thyself, sister!" Kim's hands were crooked in supplication.

"And whither goest thou?" said the woman, handing him the half of a cake from a greasy package.

"Even to Benares."

"Jugglers belike?" the young soldier suggested. "Have ye any tricks to pass the time? Why does not that yellow man answer?"

"Because," said Kim stoutly, "he is holy, and thinks upon matters hidden from thee."

"That may be well. We of the Loodhiana Sikhs," he rolled it out sonorously, "do not trouble our heads with doctrine. We fight."

"My sister's brother's son is naik (corporal) in that regiment," said the Sikh craftsman quietly. "There are also some Dogra companies there." The soldier glared, for a Dogra is of other caste than a Sikh, and the banker tittered.

"They are all one to me," said the Amritzar girl.

"That we believe," snorted the cultivator's wife malignantly.

"Nay, but all who serve the Sirkar with weapons in their hands are, as it were, one brotherhood. There is one brotherhood of the caste, but beyond that again"—she looked round timidly—"the bond of the Pulton—the Regiment—eh?"

"My brother is in a Jat regiment," said the cultivator. "Dogras be good men."

"Thy Sikhs at least were of that opinion," said the soldier, with a scowl at the placid old man in the corner. "Thy Sikhs thought so when our two companies came to help them at the Pirzai Kotal in the face of eight Afreedee standards on the ridge not three months gone."

He told the story of a border action in which the Dogra companies of the Loodhiana Sikhs had acquitted themselves well. The Amritzar girl smiled; for she knew the tale was to win her approval.

"Alas!" said the cultivator's wife at the end. "So their villages were burnt and their little children made homeless?"

"They had marked our dead. They paid a great payment after we of the Sikhs had schooled them. So it was. Is this Amritzar?"

"Ay, and here they cut our tickets," said the banker, fumbling at his belt.

The lamps were paling in the dawn when the half-caste guard came round. Ticket-collecting is a slow business in the East, where people secrete their tickets in all sorts of curious places. Kim produced his and was told to get out.

"But I go to Umballa," he protested. "I go with this holy man."

"Thou canst go to Jehannum for aught I care. This ticket is only to Amritzar. Out!"

Kim burst into a flood of tears, protesting that the lama was his father and his mother, that he was the prop of the lama's declining years, and that the lama would die without his care. All the carriage bade the guard be merciful,—the banker was specially eloquent here,—but the guard hauled Kim on to the platform. The lama blinked, he could not overtake the situation and Kim lifted up his voice and wept outside the carriage window.

"I am very poor. My father is dead—my mother is dead. Oh, charitable ones, if I am left here, who shall tend that old man?"

"What—what is this?" the lama repeated. "He must go to Benares. He must come with me. He is my chela. If there is money to be paid—"

"Oh, be silent," whispered Kim; "are we Rajahs to throw away good silver when the world is so charitable?"

The Amritzar girl stepped out with her bundles, and it was on her that Kim kept his watchful eye. Ladies of that persuasion, he knew, were generous.

"A ticket—a little tikkut to Umballa—O Breaker of Hearts!" She laughed. "Hast thou no charity?"

"Does the holy man come from the North?"

"From far and far in the North he comes," cried Kim. "From among the Hills."

"There is snow among the pine trees in the North—in the hills there is snow. My mother was from Kulu. Get thee a ticket. Ask him for a blessing."

"Ten thousand blessings," shrilled Kim. "O Holy One, a woman has given us in charity so that I can come with thee—a woman with a golden heart. I run for the tikkut."

The girl looked up at the lama, who had mechanically followed Kim to the platform. He bowed his head that he might not see her, and muttered in Tibetan as she passed on with the crowd.

"Light come—light go," said the cultivator's wife viciously.

"She has acquired merit," returned the lama. "Beyond doubt it was a nun."

"There be ten thousand such nuns in Amritzar alone. Return, old man, or the train may depart without thee," cried the banker.

"Not only was it sufficient for the ticket, but for a little food also," said Kim, leaping to his place. "Now eat, Holy One. Look. Day comes!"

Golden, rose, saffron, and pink, the morning mists smoked away across the flat green levels. All the rich Punjab lay out in the splendour of the keen sun. The lama flinched a little as the telegraph-posts swung by.

"Great is the speed of the train," said the banker, with a patronising grin. "We have gone farther since Lahore than thou couldst walk in two days: at even, we shall enter Umballa."

"And that is still far from Benares," said the lama wearily, mumbling over the cakes that Kim offered. They all unloosed their bundles and made their morning meal. Then the banker, the cultivator, and the soldier prepared their pipes and wrapped the compartment in choking, acrid smoke, spitting and coughing and enjoying themselves. The Sikh and the cultivator's wife chewed pan; the lama took snuff and told his beads, while Kim, cross-legged, smiled over the comfort of a full stomach.

"What rivers have ye by Benares?" said the lama of a sudden to the carriage at large.

"We have Gunga," returned the banker, when the little titter had subsided.

"What others?"

"What other than Gunga?"

"Nay, but in my mind was the thought of a certain River of healing."

"That is Gunga. Who bathes in her is made clean and goes to the Gods. Thrice have I made pilgrimage to Gunga." He looked round proudly.

"There was need," said the young sepoy drily, and the travellers' laugh turned against the banker.

"Clean—to return again to the Gods," the lama muttered. "And to go forth on the round of lives anew—still tied to the Wheel." He shook his head testily. "But maybe there is a mistake. Who, then, made Gunga in the beginning?"

"The Gods. Of what known faith art thou?" the banker said, appalled.

"I follow the Law—the Most Excellent Law. So it was the Gods that made Gunga. What like of Gods were they?"

The carriage looked at him in amazement. It was inconceivable that any one should be ignorant of Gunga.

"What—what is thy God?" said the money-lender at last.

"Hear!" said the lama, shifting the rosary to his hand. "Hear: for I speak of Him now! O people of Hind, listen!"

He began in Urdu the tale of the Lord Buddha, but, borne by his own thoughts, slid into Tibetan and long-droned texts from a Chinese book of the Buddha's life. The gentle, tolerant folk looked on reverently. All India is full of holy men stammering gospels in strange tongues; shaken and consumed in the fires of their own zeal; dreamers, babblers, and visionaries: as it has been from the beginning and will continue to the end.

"Um!" said the soldier of the Loodhiana Sikhs. "There was a Mohammedan regiment lay next to us at the Pirzai Kotal, and a priest of theirs,— he was, as I remember, a naik,—when the fit was on him, spake prophecies. But the mad all are in God's keeping. His officers overlooked much in that man."

The lama fell back on Urdu, remembering that he was in a strange land. "Hear the tale of the Arrow which our Lord loosed from the bow," he said.

This was much more to their taste, and they listened curiously while he told it. "Now, O people of Hind, I go to seek that River. Know ye aught that may guide me, for we be all men and women in evil case."

"There is Gunga—and Gunga alone—who washes away sin," ran the murmur round the carriage.

"Though past question we have good Gods Jullundurway," said the cultivator's wife, looking out of window. "See how they have blessed the crops."

"To search every river in the Punjab is no small matter," said her husband. "For me, a stream that leaves good silt on my land suffices, and I thank Bhumia, the God of the Homestead." He shrugged one knotted, bronzed shoulder.

"Think you our Lord come so far north?" said the lama, turning to Kim.

"It may be," Kim replied soothingly, as he spat red pan-juice on the floor.

"The last of the Great Ones," said the Sikh with authority, "was Sikander Julkarn (Alexander the Great). He paved the streets of Jullundur and built a great tank near Umballa. That pavement holds to this day; and the tank is there also. I never heard of thy God."

"Let thy hair grow long and talk Punjabi," said the young soldier jestingly to Kim, quoting a Northern proverb. "That is all that makes a Sikh." But he did not say this very loud.

The lama sighed and shrank into himself, a dingy, shapeless mass. In the pauses of their talk they could hear the low droning—"Om mane pudme hum! Om mane pudme hum!"—and the thick click of the wooden rosary beads.

"It irks me," he said at last. "The speed and the clatter irk me. Moreover, my chela, I think that may be we have overpassed that River."

"Peace, peace," said Kim. "Was not the River near Benares? We are yet far from the place."

"But—if our Lord came north, it may be any one of these little ones that we have run across."

"I do not know."

"But thou wast sent to me—wast thou sent to me?—for the merit I had acquired over yonder at Suchzen. From beside the cannon didst thou come—bearing two faces—and two garbs."

"Peace. One must not speak of these things here," whispered Kim. "There was but one of me. Think again and thou wilt remember. A boy—a Hindu boy—by the great green cannon."

"But was there not also an Englishman with a white beard—holy—among images—who himself made more sure my assurance of the River of the Arrow?"

"He—we—went to the Ajaib-Gher in Lahore to pray before the Gods there," Kim explained to the openly listening company. "And the Sahib of the Wonder House talked to him—yes, this is truth—as a brother. He is a very holy man, from far beyond the Hills. Rest thou. In time we come to Umballa."

"But my River—the River of my healing?"

"And then, if it please thee, we will go hunting for that River on foot. So that we miss nothing—not even a little rivulet in a field-side."

"But thou hast a Search of thine own?" The lama—very pleased that he remembered so well—sat bolt upright.

"Ay," said Kim, humouring him. The boy was entirely happy to be out chewing pan and seeing new people in the great good-tempered world. "It was a Bull—a Red Bull that shall come and help thee—and carry thee—whither? I have forgotten. A Red Bull on a green field, was it not?"

"Nay, it will carry me nowhere," said Kim. "It is but a tale I told thee."

"What is this?" the cultivator's wife leaned forward, her bracelets clinking on her arm. "Do ye both dream dreams? A Red Bull on a green field, that shall carry thee to the Heavens—or what? Was it a vision? Did one make a prophecy? We have a Red Bull in our village behind Jullundur city, and he grazes by choice in the very greenest of our fields!"

"Give a woman an old wife's tale and a weaver-bird a leaf and a thread, they will weave wonderful things," said the Sikh. "All holy men dream dreams, and by following holy men their disciples attain that power."

"A Red Bull on a green field, was it?" the lama repeated. "In a former life it may be thou hast acquired merit, and the Bull will come to reward thee."

"Nay—nay—it was but a tale one told to me—for a jest belike. But I will seek the Bull about Umballa, and thou canst look for thy River and rest from the clatter of the train."

"It may be that the Bull knows—that he is sent to guide us both," said the lama, hopefully as a child. Then to the company, indicating Kim: "This one was sent to me but yesterday. He is not, I think, of this world."

"Beggars a plenty have I met, and holy men to boot, but never such a yogi nor such a disciple," said the woman.

Her husband touched his forehead lightly with one finger and smiled. But the next time the lama would eat they took care to give him their best.

And at last—tired, sleepy, and dusty—they reached Umballa City Station.

"We abide here upon a law-suit," said the cultivator's wife to Kim. "We lodge with my man's cousin's younger brother. There is room also in the courtyard for thy yogi and for thee. Will—will he give me a blessing?"

"O holy man! A woman with a heart of gold gives us lodging for the night. It is a kindly land, this land of the South. See how we have been helped since the dawn!"

The lama bowed his head in benediction.

"To fill my cousin's younger brother's house with wastrels—" the husband began, as he shouldered his heavy bamboo staff.

"Thy cousin's younger brother owes my father's cousin something yet on his daughter's marriage-feast," said the woman crisply. "Let him put their food to that account. The yogi will beg, I doubt not."

"Ay, I beg for him," said Kim, anxious only to get the lama under shelter for the night, that he might seek Mahbub Ali's Englishman and deliver himself of the white stallion's pedigree.

"Now," said he, when the lama had come to an anchor in the inner courtyard of a decent Hindu house behind the cantonments, "I go away for a while—to—to buy us victual in the bazar. Do not stray abroad till I return."

"Thou wilt return? Thou wilt surely return?" The old man caught at his wrist. "And thou wilt return in this very same shape? Is it too late to look to-night for the River?"

"Too late and too dark. Be comforted. Think how far thou art on the road—an hundred kos from Lahore already."

"Yea—and farther from my monastery. Alas! It is a great and terrible world."

Kim stole out and away, as unremarkable a figure as ever carried his own and a few score thousand other folk's fate slung round his neck. Mahbub Ali's directions left him little doubt of the house in which his Englishman lived; and a groom, bringing a dog-cart home from the Club, made him quite sure. It remained only to identify his man, and Kim slipped through the garden hedge and hid in a clump of plumed grass close to the veranda. The house blazed with lights, and servants moved about tables dressed with flowers, glass, and silver. Presently forth came an Englishman, dressed in black and white, humming a tune. It was too dark to see his face, so Kim, beggar-wise, tried an old experiment.

"Protector of the Poor!"

The man backed towards the voice.

"Mahbub Ali says—"

"Hah! What says Mahbub Ali?" He made no attempt to look for the speaker, and that showed Kim that he knew.

"The pedigree of the white stallion is fully established."

"What proof is there?" The Englishman switched at the rose hedge in the side of the drive.

"Mahbub Ali has given me this proof." Kim flipped the wad of folded paper into the air, and it fell on the path beside the man, who put his foot on it as a gardener came round the corner. When the servant passed he picked it up, dropped a rupee,—Kim could hear the clink,—and strode into the house, never turning round. Swiftly Kim took up the money; but, for all his training, he was Irish enough by birth to reckon silver the least part of any game. What he desired was the visible effect of action; so, instead of slinking away, he lay close in the grass and wormed nearer to the house.

He saw—Indian bungalows are open through and through—the Englishman return to a small dressing-room, in a corner of the veranda, and that was half-office, littered with papers and despatch-boxes, and sit down to study Mahbub Ali's message. His face, by the full ray of the kerosene lamp, changed and darkened, and Kim, used as every beggar must be to watching countenances, took good note.

"Will! Will, dear!" called a woman's voice. "You ought to be in the drawing-room. They'll be here in a minute."

The man still read intently.

"Will!" said the voice, five minutes later. "He's come. I can hear the troopers in the drive."

The man dashed out bareheaded as a big landau with four native troopers behind it halted at the veranda, and a tall, black-haired man, erect as an arrow, swung out, preceded by a young officer who laughed pleasantly.

Flat on his belly lay Kim, almost touching the high wheels. His man and the black stranger exchanged two sentences.

"Certainly, sir," said the young officer promptly. "Everything waits while a horse is concerned."

"We shan't be more than twenty minutes," said Kim's man. "You can do the honours—keep 'em amused, and all that."

"Tell one of the troopers to wait," said the tall man, and they both passed into the dressing-room together as the landau rolled away. Kim saw their heads bent over Mahbub Ali's message, and heard the voices—one low and deferential, the other sharp and decisive.

"It isn't a question of weeks. It is a question of days—hours almost," said the elder. "I'd been expecting it for some time, but this"—he tapped Mahbub Ali's paper—"clenches it. Grogan's dining here to-night, isn't he?"

"Yes, sir, and Macklin too."

"Very good. I'll speak to them myself. That matter will be referred to the Council, of course, but this is a case where one is justified in assuming that we take action at once. Warn the Pindi and Peshawur brigades. It will disorganize all the summer reliefs, but we can't help that. This comes of not smashing them thoroughly the first time. Eight thousand should be enough."

"What about artillery, sir?"

"I must consult Macklin."

"Then it means war?"

"No. Punishment. When a man is bound by the action of his predecessor—"

"But C.25 may have lied."

"He bears out the other's information. Practically, they showed their hand six months back. But Devenish would have it there was a chance of peace. Of course they used it to make themselves stronger. Send off those telegrams at once,—the new code, not the old,—mine and Wharton's. I don't think we need keep the ladies waiting any longer. We can settle the rest over the cigars. I thought it was coming. It's punishment—not war."

As the trooper cantered off Kim crawled round to the back of the house, where, going on his Lahore experiences, he judged there would be food—and information. The kitchen was crowded with excited scullions, one of whom kicked him.

"Aie," said Kim, feigning tears. "I came only to wash dishes in return for a bellyful."

"All Umballa is on the same errand. Get hence. They go in now with the soup. Think you that we who serve Creighton Sahib need strange scullions to help us through a big dinner?"

"It is a very big dinner," said Kim, looking at the plates.

"Small wonder. The guest of honor is none other than the Jang-i-Lat Sahib" (the Commander-in-Chief).

"Ho!" said Kim, with the correct guttural note of wonder. He had learned what he wanted, and when the scullion turned he was gone.

"And all that trouble," said he to himself, thinking as usual in Hindustanee, "for a horse's pedigree! Mahbub Ali should have come to me to learn a little lying. Every time before that I have borne a message it concerned a woman. Now it is men. Better. The tall man said that they will loose a great army to punish some one—somewhere—the news goes to Pindi and Peshawur. There are also guns. Would I had crept nearer. It is big news!"

He returned to find the cultivator's cousin's younger brother discussing the family law-suit in all its bearings with the cultivator and his wife and a few friends, while the lama dozed. After the evening meal some one passed him a water-pipe; and Kim felt very much of a man as he pulled at the smooth cocoanut-shell, his legs spread abroad in the moonlight, his tongue clicking in remarks from time to time. His hosts were most polite; for the cultivator's wife had told them of his vision of the Red Bull, and of his probable descent from another world. Moreover, the lama was a great and venerable curiosity. The family priest, an old, tolerant Sarsut Brahmin, dropped in later, and naturally started a theological argument to impress the family. By creed, of course, they were all on their priest's side, but the lama was the guest and the novelty. His gentle kindliness, and his impressive Chinese quotations, that sounded like spells, delighted them hugely; and in this sympathetic, simple air he expanded like the Bodhisat's own lotus, speaking of his life in the great Hills of Suchzen, before, as he said, "I rose up to seek enlightenment."

Then it came out that in those worldly days he had been a master-hand at casting horoscopes and nativities; and the family priest led him on to describe his methods; each giving the planets names that the other could not understand, and pointing upwards as the big stars sailed across the dark. The children of the house tugged unrebuked at his rosary; and he clean forgot the Rule which forbids looking at women as he talked of enduring snows, landslips, blocked passes, the remote cliffs where men find sapphires and turquoise, and that wonderful upland road that leads at last into Great China itself.

"How thinkest thou of this one?" said the cultivator aside to the priest.

"A holy man—a holy man indeed. His Gods are not the Gods, but his feet are upon the Way," was the answer. "And his methods of nativities, though that is beyond thee, are wise and sure."

"Tell me," said Kim lazily, "whether I find my Red Bull on a green field, as was promised me."

"What knowledge hast thou of thy birth-hour?" the priest asked, swelling with importance.

"Between first and second cock-crow of the first night in May."

"Of what year?"

"I do not know; but upon the hour that I cried first fell the great earthquake in Srinagur which is in Kashmir." This Kim had from the woman who took care of him, and she again from Kimball O'Hara. The earthquake had been felt in India, and for long stood a leading date in the Punjab.

"Ai!" said a woman excitedly. This seemed to make Kim's supernatural origin more certain. "Was not such an one's daughter born then—"

"And her mother bore her husband four sons in four years—all likely boys," cried the cultivator's wife, sitting outside the circle in the shadow.

"None reared in the knowledge," said the family priest, "forget how the planets stood in their Houses upon that night." He began to draw in the dust of the courtyard. "At least thou hast good claim to a half of the House of the Bull. How runs thy prophecy?"

"Upon a day," said Kim, delighted at the sensation he was creating, "I shall be made great by means of a Red Bull on a green field, but first there will enter two men making all things ready."

"Yes: thus ever at the opening of a vision. A thick darkness that clears slowly; anon one enters with a broom making ready the place. Then begins the Sight. Two men—thou sayest? Ay, ay. The Sun, leaving the House of the Bull, enters that of the Twins. Hence the two men of the prophecy. Let us now consider. Fetch me a twig, little one."

He knitted his brows, scratched, smoothed out, and scratched again in the dust mysterious signs—to the wonder of all save the lama, who, with fine instinct, forbore to interfere.

At the end of half an hour he tossed the twig from him with a grunt.

"Hm. Thus say the stars. Within three days come the two men to make all things ready. After them follows the Bull; but the sign over against him is the sign of War and armed men."

"There was indeed a man of the Loodhiana Sikhs in the carriage from Lahore," said the cultivator's wife hopefully.

"Tck! Armed men—many hundreds. What concern hast thou with war?" said the priest to Kim. "Thine is red and an angry sign of War to be loosed very soon."

"None—none," said the lama earnestly. "We seek only peace and our River."

Kim smiled, remembering what he had overheard in the dressing-room. Decidedly he was a favourite of the stars.

The priest brushed his foot over the rude horoscope. "More than this I cannot see. In three days comes the Bull to thee, boy."

"And my River, my River," pleaded the lama. "I had hoped his Bull would lead us both to the River."

"Alas, for that wondrous River, my brother," the priest replied. "Such things are not common."

Next morning, though they were pressed to stay, the lama insisted on departure. They gave Kim a large bundle of good food and nearly three annas in copper money for the needs of the road, and with many blessings watched the two go southward in the dawn.

"Pity it is that these and such as these could not be freed from the Wheel of Things," said the lama.

"Nay, then would only evil people be left on the earth, and who would give us meat and shelter?" quoth Kim, stepping merrily under his burden.

"Yonder is a small stream. Let us look," said the lama, and he led from the white road across the fields; walking into a very hornets'-nest of pariah dogs.

Chapter 3

"Yea, voice of every Soul that clung
To Life that strove from rung to rung
When Devadatta's rule was young,
The warm wind brings Kamakura."

BEHIND them an angry farmer brandished a bamboo pole. He was a market-gardener, Arain by caste, growing vegetables and flowers for Umballa city, and well Kim knew the breed.

"Such an one," said the lama, disregarding the dogs, "is impolite to strangers, intemperate of speech and uncharitable. Be warned by his demeanour, my disciple."

"Ho, shameless beggars!" shouted the farmer. "Begone! Get hence!"

"We go," the lama returned, with quiet dignity. "We go from these unblessed fields."

"Ah," said Kim, sucking in his breath. "If the next crop fails, thou canst only blame thy own tongue."

The man shuffled uneasily in his slippers. "The land is full of beggars," he began, half apologetically.

"And by what sign didst thou know that we would beg from thee, O Mali?" said Kim tartly, using the name that a market-gardener least likes. "All we sought was to look at that river beyond the field there."

"River, forsooth!" the man snorted. "What city do ye hail from not to know a canal-cut? It runs as straight as an arrow, and I pay for the water as though it were molten silver. There is a branch of a river beyond. But if ye need water I can give that—and milk."

"Nay, we will go to the river," said the lama, striding out.

"Milk and a meal," the man stammered, as he looked at the strange tall figure. "I—I would not draw evil upon myself—or my crops; but beggars are so many in these hard days."

"Take notice," the lama turned to Kim. "He was led to speak harshly by the Red Mist of anger. That clearing from his eyes, he becomes courteous and of an affable heart. May his fields be blessed. Beware not to judge men too hastily, O farmer."

"I have met holy ones who would have cursed thee from hearthstone to byre," said Kim to the abashed man. "Is he not wise and holy? I am his disciple."

He cocked his nose in the air loftily and stepped across the narrow field-borders with great dignity.

"There is no pride," said the lama, after a pause, "there is no pride among such as follow the Middle Way."

"But thou hast said he was low caste and discourteous."

"Low caste I did not say, for how can that be which is not? Afterwards he amended his discourtesy, and I forgot the offense. Moreover, he is as we are, bound upon the Wheel of Things; but he does not tread the way of deliverance." He halted at a little runlet among the fields, and considered the hoof-pitted bank.

"Now, how wilt thou know thy River?" said Kim, squatting in the shade of some tall sugar-cane.

"When I find it, an enlightenment will surely be given. This, I feel, is not the place. O littlest among the waters, if only thou couldst tell me where runs my River! But be thou blessed to make the fields bear!"

"Look! Look!" Kim sprang to his side and dragged him back. A yellow and brown streak glided from the purple rustling stems to the bank, stretched its neck to the water, drank, and lay still—a big cobra with fixed, lidless eyes.

"I have no stick—I have no stick," said Kim. "I will get me one and break his back."

"Why? He is upon the Wheel as we are—a life ascending or descending—very far from deliverance. Great evil must the soul have done that is cast into this shape."

"I hate all snakes," said Kim. No native training can quench the white man's horror of the Serpent.

"Let him live out his life." The coiled thing hissed and half opened its hood. "May thy release come soon, brother," the lama continued placidly. "Hast thou knowledge, by chance, of my River?"

"Never have I seen such a man as thou art," Kim whispered, overwhelmed. "Do the very snakes understand thy talk?"

"Who knows?" He passed within a foot of the cobra's poised head. It flattened itself among the dusty coils.

"Come thou!" he called over his shoulder.

"Not I," said Kim. "I go round."

"Come. He does no hurt."

Kim hesitated for a moment. The lama backed his order by some droned Chinese quotation which Kim took for a charm. He obeyed and bounded across the rivulet, and the snake, indeed, made no sign.

"Never have I seen such a man." Kim wiped the sweat from his forehead. "And now, whither go we?"

"That is for thee to say. I am old, and a stranger—far from my own place. But that the rel-carriage fills my head with noises of devil-drums I would go in it to Benares now. . . . Yet by so going we may miss the River. Let us find another river."

Where the hard-worked soil gives three and even four crops a year—through patches of sugar-cane, tobacco, long white radishes, and nol-kol, all that day they strolled on, turning aside to every glimpse of water; rousing village dogs and sleeping villages at noonday; the lama replying to the vollied questions with an unswerving simplicity. They sought a River—a River of miraculous healing. Had any one knowledge of such a stream? Sometimes men laughed, but more often heard the story out to the end and offered them a place in the shade, a drink of milk, and a meal. The women were always kind, and the little children as children are the world over, alternately shy and venturesome. Evening found them at rest under the village tree of a mud-walled, mud-roofed hamlet, talking to the headman as the cattle came in from the grazing-grounds and the women prepared the day's last meal. They had passed beyond the belt of market-gardens round hungry Umballa, and were among the mile-wide green of the staple crops.

He was a white-bearded and affable elder, used to entertaining strangers. He dragged out a string bedstead for the lama, set warm cooked food before him, prepared him a pipe, and, the evening ceremonies being finished in the village temple, sent for the village priest.

Kim told the older children tales of the size and beauty of Lahore, of railway travel, and such-like city things, while the men talked, slowly as their cattle chew the cud.

"I cannot fathom it," said the headman at last to the priest. "How readest thou this talk?" The lama, his tale told, was silently telling his beads.

"He is a Seeker," the priest answered. "The land is full of such. Remember him who came only last month—the faquir with the tortoise?"

"Ay, but that man had right and reason, for Krishna Himself appeared in a vision promising him Paradise without the burning-pyre if he journeyed to Prayag. This man seeks no god who is within my knowledge."

"Peace, he is old: he comes from far off, and he is mad," the smooth-shaven priest replied. "Hear me." He turned to the lama. "Three kos (six miles) to the westward runs the great road to Calcutta."

"But I would go to Benares—to Benares."

"And to Benares also. It crosses all streams on this side of Hind. Now my word to thee, Holy One, is rest here till to-morrow. Then take the road" (it was the Grand Trunk Road he meant) "and test each stream that it overpasses; for, as I understand, the virtue of thy River lies neither in one pool nor place, but throughout its length. Then, if thy gods will, be assured that thou wilt come upon thy freedom."

"That is well said." The lama was much impressed by the plan. "We will begin to-morrow, and a blessing on thee for showing old feet such a near road." A deep, sing-song Chinese half-chant closed the sentence. Even the priest was impressed, and the headman feared an evil spell: but none could look at the lama's simple, eager face and doubt him long.

"Seest thou my chela?" he said, diving into his snuff-gourd with an important sniff. It was his duty to repay courtesy with courtesy.

"I see—and hear." The headman rolled his eye where Kim was chatting to a girl in blue as she laid crackling thorns on a fire.

"He also has a Search of his own. No river but a Bull. Yea, a Red Bull on a green field will some day raise him to honour. He is, I think, not altogether of this world. He was sent of a sudden to aid me in this search, and his name is Friend of all the World."

The priest smiled. "Ho there, Friend of all the World," he cried across the sharp-smelling smoke, "What art thou?"

"This Holy One's disciple," said Kim.

"He says thou art a but" (a spirit).

"Can buts eat?" said Kim, with a twinkle. "For I am hungry."

"It is no jest," cried the lama. "A certain astrologer of that city whose name I have forgotten—"

"That is no more than the city of Umballa where we slept last night," Kim whispered to the priest.

"Ay, Umballa was it? He cast a horoscope and declared that my chela should find his desire within two days. But what said he of the meaning of the stars, Friend of all the World?"

Kim cleared his throat and looked around at the village gray-beards. "The meaning of my Star is War," he replied pompously.

Somebody laughed at the little tattered figure strutting on the brickwork plinth under the great tree. Where a native would have lain down, Kim's white blood set him upon his feet.

"Ay, War," he answered.

"That is a sure prophecy," rumbled a deep voice. "For there is always war along the Border—as I know."

It was an old, withered man, who had served the Government in the days of the Mutiny as a native officer in a newly raised cavalry regiment. The Government had given him a good holding in the village, and though the demands of his sons, now gray-bearded officers on their own account, had impoverished him, he was still a person of consequence. English officials—Deputy Commissioners even—turned aside from the main road to visit him, and on those occasions he dressed himself in the uniform of ancient days, and stood up like a ramrod.

"But this shall be a great war—a war of eight thousand," Kim's voice shrilled across the quick-gathering crowd, astonishing himself.

"Redcoats or our own regiments?" the old man snapped, as though he were asking an equal. His tone made men respect Kim.

"Redcoats," said Kim at a venture. "Redcoats and guns."

"But—but the astrologer said no word of this," cried the lama, snuffing prodigiously in his excitement.

"But I know. The word has come to me, who am this Holy One's disciple. There will rise a war—a war of eight thousand redcoats. From Pindi and Peshawur they will be drawn. This is sure."

"The boy has heard bazar-talk," said the priest.

"But he was always by my side," said the lama. "How should he know? I did not know."

"He will make a clever juggler when the old man is dead," muttered the priest to the headman. "What new trick is this?"

"A sign. Give me a sign," thundered the old soldier suddenly. "If there were war my sons would have told me."

"When all is ready, thy sons, doubt not, will be told. But it is a long road from thy sons to the man in whose hands these things lie." Kim warmed to the game, for it reminded him of experiences in the letter-carrying line, when, for the sake of a few pice, he pretended to know more than he knew. But now he was playing for larger things—the sheer excitement and the sense of power. He drew a new breath and went on.

"Old man, give me a sign. Do underlings order the goings of eight thousand redcoats—with guns?"

"No." Still the old man answered as though Kim were an equal.

"Dost thou know who He is then that gives the order?"

"I have seen Him."

"To know again?"

"I have known Him since he was a lieutenant in the topkhana" (the Artillery).

"A tall man. A tall man with black hair, walking thus?" Kim took a few paces in a stiff, wooden style.

"Ay. But that any one may have seen." The crowd were breathless-still through all this talk.

"That is true," said Kim. "But I will say more. Look now. First the great man walks thus. Then He thinks thus. (Kim drew a forefinger over his forehead and downwards till it came to rest by the angle of the jaw.)

Anon He twitches his fingers thus. Anon He thrusts his hat under his left armpit." Kim illustrated the motion and stood like a stork.

The old man groaned, inarticulate with amazement; and the crowd shivered.

"So—so—so. But what does He when He is about to give an order?"

"He rubs the skin at the back of his neck—thus. Then falls one finger on the table and he makes a small sniffing noise through his nose. Then He speaks, saying: 'Loose such and such a regiment. Call out such guns.'"

The old man rose stiffly and saluted.

"'For'"—Kim translated into the vernacular the clinching sentences he had heard in the dressing-room at Umballa—"'For,' says He, 'we should have done this long ago. It is not war—it is a chastisement. Snff!'"

"Enough. I believe. I have seen Him thus in the smoke of battles. Seen and heard. It is He!"

"I saw no smoke"—Kim's voice shifted to the rapt sing-song of the way-side fortune-teller. "I saw this in darkness. First came a man to make things clear. Then came horsemen. Then came He, standing in a ring of light. The rest followed as I have said. Old man, have I spoken truth?"

"It is He. Past all doubt it is He."

The crowd drew a long, quavering breath, staring alternately at the old man, still at attention, and ragged Kim against the purple twilight.

"Said I not—said I not he was from the other world?" cried the lama proudly. "He is the Friend of all the World. He is the Friend of the Stars!"

"At least it does not concern us," a man cried. "O thou young soothsayer, if the gift abides with thee at all seasons, I have a red-spotted cow. She may be sister to thy Bull for aught I know—"

"Or I care," said Kim. "My Stars do not concern themselves with thy cattle."

"Nay, but she is very sick," a woman struck in. "My man is a buffalo, or he would have chosen his words better. Tell me if she recover?"

Had Kim been at all an ordinary boy, he would have carried on the play; but one does not know Lahore city, and least of all the faquirs by the Taksali Gate, for thirteen years without also knowing human nature.

The priest looked at him sideways, something bitterly—a dry and blight-ing smile.

"Is there no priest then in the village? I thought I had seen a great one even now," cried Kim.

"Ay—but—" the woman began.

"But thou and thy husband hoped to get the cow cured for a handful of thanks." The shot told: they were notoriously the closest-fisted couple in the village. "It is not well to cheat the temples. Give a young calf to thy own priest, and, unless thy gods are angry past recall, she will give milk within a month."

"A master-beggar art thou," purred the priest approvingly. "Not the cunning of forty years could have done better. Surely thou hast made the old man rich?"

"A little flour, a little butter and a mouthful of cardamoms," Kim retorted, flushed with the praise, but still cautious—"does one grow rich on that? And, as thou canst see, he is mad. But it serves me while I learn the road at least."

He knew what the faquirs of the Taksali Gate were like when they talked among themselves, and copied the very inflection of their lewd disciples.

"Is his Search, then, truth or a cloak to other ends? It may be treasure."

"He is mad—many times mad. There is nothing else."

Here the old soldier hobbled up and asked if Kim would accept his hospitality for the night. The priest recommended him to do so, but insisted that the honour of entertaining the lama belonged to the temple— at which the lama smiled guilelessly. Kim glanced from one face to the other, and drew his own conclusions.

"Where is the money?" he whispered, beckoning the old man off into the darkness.

"In my bosom. Where else?"

"Give it me. Quietly and swiftly give it me."

"But why? Here is no ticket to buy."

"Am I thy chela, or am I not? Do I not safeguard thy old feet about the ways? Give me the money and at dawn I will return it." He slipped his hand above the lama's girdle and brought away the purse.

"Be it so—be it so." The old man nodded his head. "This is a great and terrible world. I never knew there were so many men alive in it."

Next morning the priest was in a very bad temper, but the lama was quite happy; and Kim had enjoyed a most interesting evening with the old man, who brought out his cavalry sabre and, balancing it on his dry knees, told tales of the Mutiny and young captains thirty years in their graves, till Kim dropped off to sleep.

"Certainly the air of this country is good," said the lama. "I sleep lightly, as do all old men; but last night I slept unwaking till broad day. Even now I am heavy."

"Drink a draught of hot milk," said Kim, who had carried not a few such remedies to opium-smokers of his acquaintance. "It is time to take the road again."

"The long road that overpasses all the rivers of Hind," said the lama gaily. "Let us go. But how thinkest thou, chela, to recompense these people, and especially the priest, for their great kindness? Truly they are but-parast, but in other lives, may be, they will receive enlightenment. A rupee to the temple? The thing within is no more than stone and red paint, but the heart of man we must acknowledge when and where it is good."

"Holy One, hast thou ever taken the road alone?" Kim looked up sharply, like the Indian crows so busy about the fields.

"Surely, child: from Kulu to Pathankot—from Kulu, where my first chela died. When men were kind to us we made offerings, and all men were well-disposed throughout all the Hills."

"It is otherwise in Hind," said Kim drily. "Their gods are many-armed and malignant. Let them alone."

"I would set thee on thy road for a little, Friend of all the World—thou and thy yellow man." The old soldier ambled up the village street, all shadowy in the dawn, on a gaunt, scissor-hocked pony. "Last night broke up the fountains of remembrance in my so-dried heart, and it was as a blessing to me. Truly there is war abroad in the air. I smell it. See! I have brought my sword."

He sat long-legged on the little beast, with his big sword at his side,— hand dropped on the pommel,—staring fiercely over the flat lands towards the north. "Tell me again how He showed in thy vision. Come up and sit behind me. The beast will carry two."

"I am this Holy One's disciple," said Kim, as they cleared the village-gate. The villagers seemed almost sorry to be rid of them, but the priest's farewell was cold and distant. He had wasted some opium on a man who carried no money.

"That is well spoken. I am not much used to holy men, but respect is always good. There is no respect in these days—not even when a Commissioner Sahib comes to see me. But why should one whose Star leads him to war follow a holy man?"

"But he is a holy man," said Kim earnestly. "In truth, and in talk and in act, holy. He is not like the others. I have never seen such an one. We be not fortune-tellers, or jugglers, or beggars."

"Thou art not, that I can see; but I do not know that other. He marches well, though."

The first freshness of the day carried the lama forward with long, easy, camel-like strides. He was deep in meditation, mechanically clicking his rosary.

They followed the rutted and worn country road that wound across the flat between the great dark-green mango-groves, the line of the snow-capped Himalayas faint to the eastward. All India was at work in

the fields, to the creaking of well-wheels, the shouting of ploughmen behind their cattle, and the clamour of the crows. Even the pony felt the
good influence and almost broke into a trot as Kim laid a hand on the
stirrup-leather.

"It repents me that I did not give a rupee to the shrine," said the lama
on the last bead of his eighty-one.

The old soldier growled in his beard, so that the lama for the first time
was aware of him.

"Seekest thou the River also?" said he, turning.

"The day is new," was the reply. "What need of a river save to water
at before sundown? I come to show thee a short lane to the Big Road."

"That is a courtesy to be remembered, O man of good will; but why
the sword?"

The old soldier looked as abashed as a child interrupted in his game
of make-believe.

"'The sword," he said, fumbling it. "Oh, that was a fancy of mine—an
old man's fancy. Truly the police orders are that no man must bear weapons throughout Hind, but"—he cheered up and slapped the hilt—"all the
constabeels hereabout know me."

"It is not a good fancy," said the lama. "What profit to kill men?"

"Very little—as I know; but if evil men were not now and then slain
it would not be a good world for weaponless dreamers. I do not speak
without knowledge who have seen the land from Delhi south awash with
blood."

"What madness was that, then?"

"The Gods, who sent it for a plague, alone know. A madness ate into
all the Army, and they turned against their officers. That was the first evil,
but not past remedy if they had then held their hands. But they chose
to kill the Sahibs' wives and children. Then came the Sahibs from over
the sea and called them to most strict account."

"Some such rumour, I believe, reached me once long ago. They called
it the Black Year, as I remember."

"What manner of life hast thou led, not to know The Year? A rumour
indeed! All earth knew, and trembled."

"Our earth never shook but once—upon the day that the Excellent One
received Enlightenment."

"Umph! I saw Delhi shake at least; and Delhi is the navel of the world."

"So they turned against women and children? That was a bad deed,
for which the punishment cannot be avoided."

"Many strove to do so, but with very small profit. I was then in a
regiment of cavalry. It broke. Of six hundred and eighty sabres stood fast
to their salt—how many think you? Three. Of whom I was one."

"The greater merit."

"Merit! We did not consider it merit in those days. My people, my friends, my brothers fell from me. They said: 'The time of the English is accomplished. Let each strike out a little holding for himself.' But I had talked with the men of Sobraon, of Chillianwallah, of Moodkee and Ferozeshah. I said: 'Abide a little and the wind turns. There is no blessing in this work.' In those days I rode seventy miles with an English mem-sahib and her babe on my saddle-bow. (Wow! That was a horse fit for a man!) I placed them in safety, and back came I to my officer—the one that was not killed of our five. 'Give me work,' said I, 'for I am an outcast among my own kin, and my cousin's blood is wet on my sabre.' 'Be content,' said he. 'There is great work forward. When this madness is over there is a recompense.' "

"Ay, there is a recompense when the madness is over, surely?" the lama muttered half to himself.

"They did not hang medals in those days on all who by accident had heard a gun fired. No! In nineteen pitched battles was I; in six-and-forty skirmishes of horse; and in small affairs without number. Nine wounds I bear; a medal and four clasps and the medal of an Order, for my captains who are now generals, remembered me when the Kaiser-i-Hind had accomplished fifty years of her reign, and all the land rejoiced. They said: 'Give him the order of Berittish India.' I carry it upon my neck now. I have also my jaghir (holding) from the hands of the State—a free gift to me and mine. The men of the old days—they are now Commissioners —come riding to me through the crops,—high upon horses so that all the village sees,—and we talk out the old skirmishes, one dead man's name leading to another."

"And after?" said the lama.

"Oh, afterwards they go away, but not before my village has seen."

"And at the last what wilt thou do?"

"At the last I shall die."

"And after?"

"Let the Gods order it. I have never pestered Them with prayers: I do not think they will pester me. Look you, I have noticed in my long life that those who eternally break in upon Those Above with complaints and reports and bellowings and weepings are presently sent for in haste, as our colonel used to send for slack-jawed down-country men who talked too much. No, I have never wearied the Gods. They will remember this, and give me a quiet place where I can drive my lance in the shade, and wait to welcome my sons: I have no less than three—ressaldar-majors all—in the regiments."

"And they likewise, bound upon the Wheel, go forth from life to life—

from despair to despair," said the lama below his breath, "hot, uneasy, snatching."

"Ay," the old soldier chuckled. "Three ressaldar-majors in three regiments. Gamblers a little, but so am I. They must be well mounted; and one cannot take the horses as in the old days one took women. Well, well, my holding can pay for all. How thinkest thou? It is a well-watered strip, but my men cheat me. I do not know how to ask save at the lance's point. Ugh! I grow angry and I curse them, and they feign penitence, but behind my back I know they call me a toothless old ape."

"Hast thou never desired any other thing?"

"Yes—yes—a thousand times! A straight back and a close-clinging knee once more; a quick wrist and a keen eye; and the marrow that makes a man. Oh, the old days—the good days of my strength!"

"That strength is weakness."

"It has turned so; but fifty years since I could have proved it otherwise," the old soldier retorted, driving his stirrup-edge into the pony's lean flank.

"But I know a River of great healing."

"I have drunk Gunga-water to the edge of dropsy. All she gave me was a flux, and no sort of strength."

"It is not Gunga. The River that I know washes from all taint of sin. Ascending the far bank one is assured of Freedom. I do not know thy life, but thy face is the face of the honourable and courteous. Thou hast clung to thy Way, rendering fidelity when it was hard to give, in that Black Year of which I now remember other tales. Enter now upon the Middle Way, which is the path to Freedom. Hear the Most Excellent Law, and do not follow dreams."

"Speak then, old man," the soldier smiled, half saluting. "We be all babblers at our age."

The lama squatted under the shade of a mango, whose shadow played checkerwise over his face; the soldier sat stiffly on the pony; and Kim, making sure that there were no snakes, lay down in the crotch of the twisted roots.

There was a drowsy buzz of small life in hot sunshine, a cooing of doves, and a sleepy drone of well-wheels across the fields. Slowly and impressively the lama began. At the end of ten minutes the old soldier slid from his pony, to hear better as he said, and sat with the reins round his wrist. The lama's voice faltered—the periods lengthened. Kim was busy watching a gray squirrel. When the little scolding bunch of fur, close pressed to the branch, disappeared, preacher and audience were fast asleep, the old officer's strong-cut head pillowed on his arm, the lama's thrown back against the tree bole, where it showed like yellow ivory. A naked child toddled up, stared, and, moved by some quick impulse of reverence made a solemn little obeisance before the lama—only the child was so short and fat that it toppled over sideways, and Kim laughed at the sprawling, chubby legs. The child, scared and indignant, yelled aloud.

"Hai! Hai!" said the soldier leaping to his feet. "What is it? What orders? . . . It is . . . a child! I dreamed it was an alarm. Little one—little one—do not cry. Have I slept? That was discourteous indeed!"

"I fear! I am afraid!" roared the child.

"What is it to fear? Two old men and a boy? How wilt thou ever make a soldier, Princeling?"

The lama had waked too, but, taking no direct notice of the child, clicked his rosary.

"What is that?" said the child, stopping a yell midway. "I have never seen such things. Give them me."

"Aha," said the lama, smiling, and trailing a loop of it on the grass:

> "This is a handful of cardamoms,
> This is a lump of ghi:
> This is millet and chillies and rice,
> A supper for thee and me!"

The child shrieked with joy, and snatched at the dark, glancing beads.

"Oho!" said the old soldier. "Whence had thou that song, despiser of this world?"

"I learned it in Pathankot—sitting on a door-step," said the lama shyly. "It is good to be kind to babes."

"As I remember, before the sleep came on us, thou hadst told me that marriage and bearing were darkeners of the true light, stumbling-blocks upon the way. Do children drop from heaven in thy country? Is it the Way to sing them songs?"

"No man is all perfect," said the lama gravely, recoiling the rosary. "Run now to thy mother, little one."

"Hear him!" said the soldier to Kim. "He is ashamed for that he has made a child happy. There was a very good householder lost in thee, my brother. Hai, child!" He threw it a pice. "Sweetmeats are always sweet." And as the little figure capered away into the sunshine: "They grow up and become men. Holy One, I grieve that I slept in the midst of thy preaching. Forgive me."

"We be two old men," said the lama. "The fault is mine. I listened to thy talk of the world and its madness, and one fault led to the next."

"Hear him! What harm do thy Gods suffer from play with a babe? And that song was very well sung. Let us go on and I will sing thee the song of Nikal Seyn before Delhi—the old song."

And they fared out from the gloom of the mango tope, the old man's high, shrill voice ringing across the field, as wail by long-drawn wail he unfolded the story of Nikal Seyn (Nicholson)—the song that men sing in the Punjab to this day. Kim was delighted, and the lama listened with deep interest.

"Ahi! Nikal Seyn is dead—he died before Delhi! Lances of North take vengeance for Nikal Seyn." He quavered it out to the end, marking the trills with the flat of his sword on the pony's rump.

"And now we come to the Big Road," said he, after receiving the compliments of Kim; for the lama was markedly silent. "It is long since I have ridden this way, but thy boy's talk stirred me. See, Holy One—the Great Road which is the backbone of all Hind. For the most part it is shaded, as here, with four lines of trees; the middle road—all hard—takes the quick traffic. In the days before rail-carriages the Sahibs travelled up and down here in hundreds. Now there are only country-carts and such like. Left and right is the rougher road for the heavy carts—grain and cotton and timber, bhoosa, lime and hides. A man goes in safety here—for at every few kos is a police-station. The police are thieves and extortioners (I myself would patrol it with cavalry—young recruits under a strong captain), but at least they do not suffer any rivals. All castes and kinds of men move here. Look! Brahmins and chumars, bankers and tinkers, barbers and bunnias, pilgrims and potters—all the world going and coming. It is to me as a river from which I am withdrawn like a log after a flood."

And truly the Grand Trunk Road is a wonderful spectacle. It runs straight, bearing without crowding India's traffic for fifteen hundred miles —such a river of life as nowhere else exists in the world. They looked at the green-arched, shade-flecked length of it, the white breadth speckled with slow-pacing folk; and the two-roomed police-station opposite.

"Who bears arms against the law?" a constable called out laughingly, as he caught sight of the soldier's sword. "Are not the police enough to destroy evil-doers?"

"It was because of the police I bought it," was the answer. "Does all go well in Hind?"

"Ressaldar Sahib, all goes well."

"I am like an old tortoise, look you, who puts his head out from the bank and draws it in again. Ay, this is the road of Hindustan. All men come by this way. . . ."

"Son of a swine, is the soft part of the road meant for thee to scratch thy back upon? Father of all the daughters of shame and husband of ten thousand virtueless ones, thy mother was devoted to a devil, being led thereto by her mother; thy aunts have never had a nose for seven generations! Thy sister—What owl's folly told thee to draw thy carts across the road? A broken wheel? Then take a broken head and put the two together at leisure!"

The voice and a venomous whip-cracking came out of a pillar of dust fifty yards away, where a cart had broken down. A thin, high Kattiwar mare, with eyes and nostrils aflame, rocketed out of the jam, snorting and wincing as her rider bent her across the road in chase of a shouting man. He was tall and gray-bearded, sitting the almost mad beast as a piece of her, and scientifically lashing his victim between plunges.

The old man's face lit with pride. "My child!" said he briefly, and strove to rein the pony's neck to a fitting arch.

"Am I to be beaten before the police?" cried the carter. "Justice! I will have Justice—"

"Am I to be blocked by a shouting ape who upsets ten thousand sacks under a young horse's nose? That is the way to ruin a mare."

"He speaks truth. He speaks truth. But she follows her man close," said the old man. The carter ran under the wheels of his cart and thence threatened all sorts of vengeance.

"They are strong men, thy sons," said the policeman serenely, picking his teeth.

The horseman delivered one last vicious cut with his whip and came on at a canter.

"My father!" He reined back ten yards and dismounted.

The old man was off his pony in an instant, and they embraced as do father and son in the East.

Chapter 4

Good Luck, she is never a lady,
But the cursedest quean alive.
Tricksy, wincing, and jady—
Kittle to lead or drive.
Greet her—she's hailing a stranger!
Meet her—she's busking to leave!
Let her alone for a shrew to the bone
And the hussy comes plucking your sleeve!
  Largesse! Largesse, O Fortune!
  Give or hold at your will
  If I've no care for Fortune,
  Fortune must follow me still!

"The Wishing Caps."

THEN, lowering their voices, they spoke together. Kim came to rest under a tree, but the lama tugged impatiently at his elbow.

"Let us go on. The River is not here."

"Hai mai? Have we not walked enough for a little? Our River will not run away. Patience, and he will give us a dole."

"That," said the old soldier suddenly, "is the Friend of the Stars. He brought me the news yesterday. Having seen the very man Himself, in a vision, giving orders for the war."

"Hm!" said his son, all deep in his broad chest. "He came by a bazar-rumour and made profit of it."

His father laughed. "At least he did not ride to me begging for a new charger and the gods know how many rupees. Are thy brothers' regiments also under orders?"

"I do not know. I took leave and came swiftly to thee in case—"

"In case they ran before thee to beg. O gamblers and spendthrifts all! But thou hast never yet ridden in a charge. A good horse is needed there, truly. A good follower and a good pony also for the marching. Let us see—let us see." He thrummed on the pommel.

"This is no place to cast thy accounts in, my father. Let us go to thy house."

"At least pay the boy then: I have no pice with me, and he brought auspicious news. Ho! Friend of all the World, a war is toward as thou hast said."

"Nay, as I know, the war," returned Kim composedly.

"Eh?" said the lama, fingering his beads, all eager for the road.

"My master does not trouble the Stars for hire. We brought the news— bear witness we brought the news, and now we go." Kim half-crooked his hand at his side.

The son tossed a silver coin through the sunlight, grumbling something about beggars and jugglers. It was a four-anna piece, and would feed them well for some days. The lama, seeing the flash of the metal, droned a blessing.

"Go thy way, Friend of all the World," piped the old soldier, wheeling his scrawny mount. "For once in all my days I have met a true prophet— who was not in the Army."

Father and son swung round together: the old man sitting as erect as the younger.

A Punjabi constable in yellow linen trousers slouched across the road. He had seen the money pass.

"Halt!" he cried in impressive English. "Know ye not that there is a takkus of two annas a head, which is four annas, on those who enter the road from this side-road. It is the order of the Sirkar, and the money is spent for the planting of trees and the beautification of the ways."

"And the bellies of the police," said Kim, skipping out of arm's reach. "Consider for a while, man with a mud head. Think you we came from the nearest pond like the frog, thy father-in-law. Hast thou ever heard the name of thy brother?"

"And who was he? Leave the boy alone," cried the senior constable, immensely delighted, as he squatted down to smoke his pipe in the veranda.

"He took a label from a bottle of belaitee-pani (soda-water), and, affix- ing it to a bridge, collected taxes for a month from those who passed, saying that it was the Sirkar's order. Then came an Englishman and broke his head. Ah, brother, I am a town-crow, not a village-crow!"

The policeman drew back abashed, and Kim hooted at him all down the road.

"Was there ever such a disciple as I?" he cried merrily to the lama. "All earth would have picked thy bones within ten mile of Lahore city if I had not guarded thee."

"I consider in my own mind whether thou art a spirit, sometimes, or sometimes an evil imp," said the lama, smiling slowly.

"I am thy chela." Kim dropped into step at his side—that indescribable gait of the long-distance tramp all the world over.

"Now let us walk," muttered the lama, and to the click of his rosary they walked in silence mile upon mile. The lama, as usual, was deep in meditation, but Kim's bright eyes were open wide. This broad, smiling river of life, he considered, was a vast improvement on the cramped and crowded Lahore streets. There were new people and new sights at every stride—castes he knew and castes that were altogether out of his experience.

They met a troop of long-haired, strong-scented Sansis with baskets of lizards and other unclean food on their backs, their lean dogs sniffing at their heels. These people kept their own side of the road, moving at a quick, furtive jog-trot, and all other castes gave them ample room; for the Sansi is deep pollution. Behind them, walking wide and stiffly across the strong shadows, the memory of his leg-irons still on him, strode one newly released from the jail; his full stomach and shiny skin to prove that the Government fed its prisoners better than most honest men could feed themselves. Kim knew that walk well, and made broad jest of it as they passed. Then an Akali, a wild-eyed, wild-haired Sikh devotee in the blue-checked clothes of his faith, with polished-steel quoits glistening on the cone of his tall blue turban, stalked past, returning from a visit to one of the independent Sikh States, where he had been singing the ancient glories of the Khalsa to college-trained princelings in top-boots and white-cord breeches. Kim was careful not to irritate that man; for the Akali's temper is short and his arm quick. Here and there they met or were overtaken by the gaily dressed crowds of whole villages turning out to some local fair; the women, with their babes on their hips, walking behind the men, the older boys prancing on sticks of sugar-cane, dragging rude brass models of locomotives such as they sell for a half-penny, or flashing the sun into the eyes of their betters from cheap toy mirrors. One could see at a glance what each had bought; and if there were any doubt it needed only to watch the wives comparing, brown arm against brown arm, the newly purchased dull glass bracelets that come from the North-West. These merry-makers stepped slowly, calling one to the other and stopping to haggle with sweetmeat-sellers, or to make a prayer before one of the wayside shrines—sometimes Hindu, sometimes Mussalman—which the low caste of both creeds share with beautiful impartiality. A solid line of blue, rising and falling like the back of a caterpillar in haste, would swing up through the quivering dust and trot past to a chorus of quick cackling. That was a gang of changars—the women who have taken all the embankments of all the Northern railways under their charge—a flat-footed, big-bosomed, strong-limbed, blue-petticoated clan of earth-carriers, hurrying north on news of a job, and wasting no time by the road. They belong to the caste whose men do not count, and they walked with squared elbows, swing-

ing hips, and heads on high, as suits women who carry heavy weights.
A little later a marriage procession would strike into the Grand Trunk
with music and shoutings, and a smell of marigold and jasmine stronger
even than the reek of the dust. One could see the bride's litter, a blur of
red and tinsel, staggering through the haze, while the bridegroom's be-
wreathed pony turned aside to snatch a mouthful from a passing fodder-
cart. Then Kim would join the Kentish-fire of good wishes and bad jokes,
wishing the couple a hundred sons and no daughters, as the saying is.
Still more interesting and more to be shouted over it was when a strolling
juggler with some half-trained monkeys, or a panting, feeble bear, or a
woman who tied goats' horns to her feet, and with these danced on a
slack-rope, set the horses to shying and the women to shrill, long-drawn
quavers of amazement.

The lama never raised his eyes. He did not note the money-lender on
his goose-rumped pony, hastening along to collect the cruel interest; or
the long-shouting, deep-voiced little mob—still in military formation—of
native soldiers on leave, rejoicing to be rid of their breeches and puttees,
and saying the most outrageous things to the most respectable women in
sight. Even the seller of Ganges-water he did not see, and Kim expected
that he would at least buy a bottle of that precious stuff. He looked
steadily at the ground, and strode as steadily hour after hour, his soul
busied elsewhere. But Kim was in the seventh heaven of joy. The Grand
Trunk at this point was built on an embankment to guard against winter
floods from the foothills, so that one walked, as it were, a little above the
country, along a stately corridor, seeing all India spread out to left and
right. It was beautiful to behold the many-yoked grain and cotton wag-
gons crawling over the country-roads: one could hear their axles, complaining a mile away, coming nearer, till with shouts and yells and bad
words they climbed up the steep incline and plunged on to the hard main
road, carter reviling carter. It was equally beautiful to watch the people,
little clumps of red and blue and pink and white and saffron, turning
aside to go to their own villages, dispersing and growing small by twos
and threes across the level plain. Kim felt these things, though he could
not give tongue to his feelings, and so contented himself with buying
peeled sugar-cane and spitting the pith generously about his path. From
time to time the lama took snuff, and at last Kim could endure the silence
no longer.

"This is a good land—the land of the South!" said he. "The air is good;
the water is good. Eh?"

"And they are all bound upon the Wheel," said the lama. "Bound from
life after life. To none of these has the Way been shown." He shook
himself back to this world.

"And now we have walked a weary way," said Kim. "Surely we shall soon come to a parao (a resting-place). Shall we stay there? Look, the sun is sloping."

"Who will receive us this evening?"

"That is all one. This country is full of good folk. Besides,"—he sunk his voice beneath a whisper,—"we have money."

The crowd thickened as they neared the resting-place which marked the end of their day's journey. A line of stalls selling very simple food and tobacco, a stack of firewood, a police-station, a well, a horse-trough, a few trees, and, under them, some trampled ground dotted with the black ashes of old fires, are all that mark a parao on the Grand Trunk; if you except the beggars and the crows—both hungry.

By this time the sun was driving broad golden spokes through the lower branches of the mango trees; the parakeets and doves were coming home in their hundreds; the chattering, gray-backed Seven Sisters, talking over the day's adventures, walked back and forth in twos and threes almost under the feet of the travellers; and shufflings and scufflings in the branches showed that the bats were ready to go out on the night-picket. Swiftly the light gathered itself together, painted for an instant the faces and the cart-wheels and the bullocks' horns as red as blood. Then the night fell, changing the touch of the air, drawing a low, even haze, like a gossamer veil of blue, across the face of the country, and bringing out, keen and distinct, the smell of wood-smoke and cattle and the good scent of wheaten cakes cooked on ashes. The evening patrol hurried out of the police-station with important coughings and reiterated orders; and a live charcoal-ball in the cup of a wayside carter's hookah glowed red while Kim's eye mechanically watched the last flicker of the sun on the brass tweezers.

The life of the parao was very like that of the Kashmir Serai on a small scale. Kim dived into the happy Asiatic disorder which, if you only allow time, will bring you everything that a simple man needs.

His wants were few, because, since the lama had no caste scruples, cooked food from the nearest stall would serve; but, for luxury's sake, Kim bought a handful of dung-cakes to build a fire. All about, coming and going round the little flames, men cried for oil, or grain, or sweetmeats, or tobacco, jostling one another while they waited their turn at the well; and under the men's voices you heard from halted, shuttered carts the high squeals and giggles of women whose faces should not be seen in public.

Nowadays, well-educated natives are of opinion that when their women-folk travel—and they visit a good deal—it is better to take them quickly by rail in a properly screened compartment; and that custom is spreading.

But there are always those of the old rock who hold by the use of their forefathers; and, above all, there are always the old women,—more conservative than the men,—who toward the end of their days go a pilgrimage. They, being withered and undesirable, do not, under certain circumstances, object to unveiling. After their long seclusion, during which they have always been in business touch with a thousand outside interests, they love the bustle and stir of the open road, the gatherings at the shrines, and the infinite possibilities of gossip with like-minded dowagers. Very often it suits a long-suffering family that a strong-tongued, iron-willed old lady should disport herself about India in this fashion; for certainly pilgrimage is grateful to the Gods. So all about India, in the most remote places, as in the most public, you find some knot of grizzled servitors in nominal charge of an old lady who is more or less curtained and hid away in a bullock-cart. Such men are staid and discreet, and when a European or a high-caste native is near will net their charge with most elaborate precautions; but in the ordinary haphazard chances of pilgrimage the precautions are not taken. The old lady is, after all, intensely human, and lives to look upon life.

Kim marked down a gaily ornamented ruth or family bullock-cart, with a broidered canopy of two domes, like a double-humped camel, which had just been drawn into the parao. Eight men made its retinue, and two of the eight were armed with rusty sabres—sure signs that they followed a person of distinction, for the common folk do not bear arms. An increasing cackle of complaints, orders, and jests, and what to a European would have been bad language, came from behind the curtains. Here was evidently a woman used to command.

Kim looked over the retinue critically. Half of them were thin-legged, gray-bearded Ooryas from down country. The other half were duffle-clad, felt-hatted hillmen of the North: and that mixture told its own tale, even if he had not overheard the incessant sparring between the two divisions. The old lady was going south on a visit—probably to a rich relative, most probably to a son-in-law, who had sent up an escort as a mark of respect. The hillmen would be of her own people—Kulu or Kangra folk. It was quite clear that she was not taking her daughter down to be wedded, or the curtains would have been laced home and the guard would have allowed no one near the car. A merry and a high-spirited dame, thought Kim, balancing the dung-cake in one hand, the cooked food in the other, and piloting the lama with a nudging shoulder. Something might be made out of the meeting. The lama would give him no help, but, as a conscientious chela, Kim was delighted to beg for two.

He built his fire as close to the cart as he dared, waiting for one of the escort to order him away. The lama dropped wearily to the ground, much as a heavy fruit-eating bat cowers, and returned to his rosary.

"Stand farther off, beggar!" The order was shouted in broken Hindustanee by one of the hillmen.

"Huh! It is only a pahari" (a hillman), said Kim over his shoulder. "Since when have the hill-asses owned all Hindustan?"

The retort was a swift and brilliant sketch of Kim's pedigree for three generations.

"Ah!" Kim's voice was sweeter than ever, as he broke the dung-cake into fit pieces. "In my country we call that the beginning of love-talk."

A harsh, thin cackle behind the curtains put the hillman on his mettle for a second shot.

"Not so bad—not so bad," said Kim with calm. "But have a care, my brother, lest we—we, I say—be minded to give a curse or so in return. And our curses have the knack of biting home."

The Ooryas laughed; the hillman sprang forward threateningly; the lama suddenly raised his head, bringing his huge tam-o'-shanter cap into the full light of Kim's new-started fire.

"What is it?" said he.

The man halted as though struck to stone. "I—I—am saved from a great sin," he stammered.

"The foreigner has found him a priest at last," whispered one of the Ooryas.

"Hai! Why is that beggar-brat not well beaten?" the old woman cried.

The hillman drew back to the cart and whispered something to the curtain. There was dead silence, then a muttering.

"This goes well," thought Kim, pretending neither to see nor hear.

"When—when—he has eaten,"—the hillman fawned on Kim—"it—it is requested that the Holy One will do the honour to talk to one who would speak to him."

"After he has eaten he will sleep," Kim returned loftily. He could not quite see what new turn the game had taken, but stood resolute to profit by it. "Now, I will get him his food." The last sentence, spoken loudly, ended with a sigh as of faintness.

"I—I myself and the others of my people will look to that—if it is permitted."

"It is permitted," said Kim, more loftily than ever. "Holy One, these people will bring us food."

"The land is good. All the country of the South is good—a great and terrible world," mumbled the lama drowsily.

"Let him sleep," said Kim, "but look to it that we are well fed when he wakes. He is a very holy man."

Again one of the Ooryas said something contemptuously.

"He is not a faquir. He is not a down-country beggar," Kim went on severely, addressing the stars. "He is the most holy of holy men. He is above all castes. I am his chela."

"Come here!" said the flat thin voice behind the curtain; and Kim came, conscious that eyes he could not see were staring at him. One skinny brown finger heavy with rings lay on the edge of the cart, and the talk went this way:

"Who is that one?"

"An exceedingly holy one. He comes from far off. He comes from Tibet."

"Where in Tibet?"

"From behind the snows—from a very far place. He knows the stars; he makes horoscopes; he reads nativities. But he does not do this for money. He does it for kindness and great charity. I am his disciple. I am called also the Friend of the Stars."

"Thou art no hillman."

"Ask him. He will tell thee I was sent to him from the stars to show him an end to his pilgrimage."

"Humph! Consider, brat, that I am an old woman and not altogether a fool. Lamas I know, and to these I give reverence, but thou art no more a lawful chela than this my finger is the pole of this waggon. Thou art a casteless Hindu—a bold and unblushing beggar, attached, belike, to the Holy One for the sake of gain."

"Do we not all work for gain?" Kim changed his tone promptly to match that altered voice. "I have heard"—this was a bow drawn at a venture—"I have heard—"

"What hast thou heard?" she snapped, rapping with the finger.

"Nothing that I well remember, but some talk in the bazars, which is doubtless a lie, that even Rajahs—small hill Rajahs—"

"But none the less of good Rajput blood."

"Assuredly of good blood. That these even sell the more comely of their womenfolk for gain. Down South they sell them—to zemindars and such-all of Oudh."

If there be one thing in the world that the small hill Rajahs deny it is just this charge; but it happens to be one thing that the bazars believe, when they discuss the mysterious slave-traffics of India. The old lady explained to Kim, in a tense, indignant whisper, precisely what manner and fashion of malignant liar he was. Had Kim hinted this when she was a girl, he would have been pommelled to death that same evening by an elephant. This was perfectly true.

"Ahai! I am only a beggar's brat, as the Eye of Beauty has said," he wailed in extravagant terror.

"Eye of Beauty, forsooth! Who am I that thou shouldst fling beggar-endearments at me?" And yet she laughed at the long-forgotten word. "Forty years ago that might have been said, and not without truth. Ay, thirty years ago. But it is the fault of this gadding up and down Hind that a king's widow must jostle all the scum of the land, and be made a mock by beggars."

"Great Queen," said Kim promptly, for he heard her shaking with indignation, "I am even what the Great Queen says I am; but none the less is my master holy. He has not yet heard the Great Queen's order that—"

"Order? I order a Holy One—a Teacher of the Law—to come and speak to a woman? Never!"

"Pity my stupidity. I thought it was given as an order—"

"It was not. It was a petition. Does this make all clear?"

A silver coin clicked on the edge of the cart. Kim took it and salaamed profoundly. The old lady recognized that, as the eyes and the ears of the lama, he was to be propitiated.

"I am but the Holy One's disciple. When he has eaten perhaps he will come."

"Oh, villain and shameless rogue!" The jewelled forefinger shook itself at him reprovingly; but he could hear the old lady's chuckle.

"Nay, what is it?" he said, dropping into his most caressing and confidential tone—the one, he well knew, that few could resist. "Is—is there any need of a son in thy family? Speak freely, for we priests—" That last was a direct plagiarism from a faquir by the Taksali Gate.

"We priests! Thou art not yet old enough to—" She checked the joke with another laugh. "Believe me, now and again, we women, O priest, think of other matters than sons. Moreover, my daughter has borne her man-child."

"Two arrows in the quiver are better than one; and three are better still." Kim quoted the proverb with a meditative cough, looking discreetly earthward.

"True—oh, true. But perhaps that will come. Certainly those down-country Brahmins are utterly useless. I sent gifts and monies and gifts again to them and they prophesied."

"Ah," drawled Kim, with infinite contempt, "they prophesied!" A professional could have done no better.

"And it was not till I remembered my own Gods that my prayers were heard. I chose an auspicious hour, and—perhaps thy Holy One has heard of the Abbot of the Lung-Cho Lamassery. It was to him I put the matter, and behold in the due time all came about as I desired. The Brahmin in the house of the father of my daughter's son has since said that it was through his prayers—which is a little error that I will explain to him

when we reach our journey's end. And so afterwards I go to Buddh Gaya,
to make shraddha for the father of my children."

"Thither go we."

"Doubly auspicious," chirruped the old lady. "A second son at least!"

"O Friend of all the World!" The lama had waked, and, simply as a child
bewildered in a strange bed, called for Kim.

"I come! I come, Holy One!" He dashed to the fire, where he found
the lama already surrounded by dishes of food, the hillmen visibly adoring
him and the Southerners looking sourly.

"Go back! Withdraw!" Kim cried. "Do we eat publicly like dogs?" They
finished the meal in silence, each turned a little from the other, and Kim
topped it with a native-made cigarette.

"Have I not said an hundred times that the South is a good land? Here
is a virtuous and high-born widow of a Hill Rajah on pilgrimage, she says,
to Buddh Gaya. She it is sends us those dishes; and when thou art well
rested she would speak to thee."

"Is this also thy work?" The lama dipped deep into his snuffgourd.

"Who else watched over thee since our wonderful journey began?"
Kim's eyes danced in his head as he blew the rank smoke through his
nostrils and stretched him on the dusty ground. "Have I failed to oversee
thy comforts, Holy One?"

"A blessing on thee." The lama inclined his solemn head. "I have known
many men in my so long life, and disciples not a few. But to none among
men, if so be thou art woman-born, has my heart gone out as it has to
thee—thoughtful, wise, and courteous, but something of a small imp."

"And I have never seen such a priest as thou." Kim considered the
benevolent yellow face wrinkle by wrinkle. "It is less than three days since
we took road together, and it is as though it were a hundred years."

"Perhaps in a former life it was permitted that I should have rendered
thee some service. May be"—he smiled—"I freed thee from a trap; or, having caught thee on a hook in the days when I was not enlightened, cast
thee back into the river."

"May be," said Kim quietly. He had heard this sort of speculation again
and again, from the mouths of many whom the English would not consider imaginative. "Now, as regards that woman in the bullock-cart, I think
she needs a second son for her daughter."

"That is no part of the Way," sighed the lama. "But at least she is from
the Hills. Ah, the Hills, and the snow of the Hills!"

He rose and stalked to the cart. Kim would have given his ears to come
too, but the lama did not invite him; and the few words he caught were
in an unknown tongue, for they spoke some common speech of the mountains. The woman seemed to ask questions which the lama turned over in

his mind before answering. Now and again he heard the sing-song cadence of a Chinese quotation. It was a strange picture that Kim watched between drooped eyelids. The lama very straight and erect, the deep folds of his yellow clothing slashed with black in the light of the parao fires precisely as a knotted tree-trunk is slashed with the shadow of the long sun, addressed a tinsel and lacquered ruth which burned like a many-coloured jewel in the same uncertain light. The patterns on the gold-worked curtains ran up and down, melting and re-forming as the folds shook and quivered to the night wind; and when the talk grew more earnest the jewelled forefinger snapped out little sparks of light between the embroideries. Behind the cart was a wall of uncertain darkness speckled with little flames and alive with half-caught forms and faces and shadows. The voices of early evening had settled down to one soothing hum whose deepest note was the steady chumping of the bullocks above their chopped straw, and whose highest was the tinkle of a Bengali dancing-girl's sitar. Most men had eaten and pulled deep at their gurgling, grunting hookahs, which in full blast sound like bull-frogs.

At last the lama returned. A hillman walked behind him with a wadded cotton-quilt and spread it carefully by the fire.

"She deserves ten thousand grandchildren," thought Kim. "None the less, but for me, these gifts would not have come."

"A virtuous woman—and a wise one." The lama slackened off, joint by joint, like a slow camel. "The world is full of charity to those who follow the Way." He flung a fair half of the quilt over Kim.

"And what said she?" Kim rolled up in his share of it.

"She asked me many questions and propounded many problems—the most of which were idle tales which she had heard from devil-serving priests who pretend to follow the Way. Some I answered, and some I said were foolish. Many wear the Robe, but few keep the Way."

"True. That is true." Kim used the thoughtful, conciliatory tone of those who wish to draw confidences.

"But by her lights she is most right-minded. She desires greatly that we should go with her to Buddh Gaya; her road being ours, as I understand, for many days' journey to the southward."

"And?"

"Patience a little. To this I said that my Search came before all things. She had heard many foolish legends, but this great truth of my River she had never heard. Such are the priests of the lower hills! She knew the Abbot of Lung-Cho, but she did not know of my River—nor the tale of the Arrow."

"And?"

"I spoke therefore of the Search, and of the Way, and of matters that were profitable; she desiring only that I should accompany her and make prayer for a second son."

"Aha! 'We women' do not think of anything save children," said Kim sleepily.

"Now, since our roads run together for a while, I do not see that we in any way depart from our Search if so be we accompany her—at least as far as—I have forgotten the name of the city."

"Ohe!" said Kim, turning and speaking in a sharp whisper to one of the Ooryas a few yards away. "Where is your master's house?"

"A little behind Saharunpore, among the fruit gardens." He named the village.

"That was the place," said the lama. "So far, at least, we can go with her."

"Flies go to carrion," said the Oorya, in an abstracted voice.

"For the sick cow a crow; for the sick man a Brahmin." Kim breathed the proverb impersonally to the shadow-tops of the trees overhead.

The Oorya grunted and held his peace.

"So then we go with her, Holy One?"

"Is there any reason against? I can still step aside and try all the rivers that the road overpasses. She desires that I should come. She very greatly desires it."

Kim stifled a laugh in the quilt. When once that imperious old lady had recovered from her natural awe of a lama he thought it probable that she would be worth listening to.

He was nearly asleep when the lama suddenly quoted a proverb: "The husbands of the talkative have a great reward hereafter." Then Kim heard him snuff thrice, and dozed off, still laughing.

The diamond-bright dawn woke men and crows and bullocks together. Kim sat up and yawned, shook himself, and thrilled with delight. This was seeing the world in real truth; this was life as he would have it—bustling and shouting, the buckling of belts, and beating of bullocks and creaking of wheels, lighting of fires and cooking of food, and new sights at every turn of the approving eye. The morning mist swept off in a whorl of silver, the parrots shot away to some distant river in shrieking green hosts: all the well-wheels within earshot went to work. India was awake, and Kim was in the middle of it, more awake and more excited than any one, chewing on a twig that he would presently use as a toothbrush; for he borrowed right- and left-handedly from all the customs of the country he knew and loved. There was no need to worry about food—no need to spend a cowrie at the crowded stalls. He was the disciple of a holy man annexed by a strong-willed old lady. All things would be prepared for them, and when they were respectfully invited so to do they would sit and eat. For the rest,—Kim giggled here as he cleaned his teeth,—his hostess would rather heighten the enjoyment of the road. He inspected her bullocks critically, as they came up grunting and blowing under the yokes. If they went too fast—it was not likely—there would be a pleasant seat for himself along the pole; the lama would sit beside the driver. The escort, of course, would walk. The old lady, equally of course, would talk a great deal, and by what he had heard that conversation would not lack salt. She was already ordering, haranguing, rebuking, and, it must be said, cursing her servants for delays.

"Get her her pipe. In the name of the Gods, get her her pipe and stop her ill-omened mouth," cried an Oorya, tying up his shapeless bundles of bedding. "She and the parrots are alike. They screech in the dawn."

"The lead-bullocks! Hai! Look to the lead-bullocks!" They were backing and wheeling as a grain-cart's axle caught them by the horns. "Son of an owl, where dost thou go?" This to the grinning carter.

"Ai! Yai! Yai! That within there is the Queen of Delhi going to pray for a son," the man called back over his high load. "Room for the Queen of Delhi and her prime minister the gray monkey climbing up his own sword!" Another cart loaded with bark for a down-country tannery followed close behind, and its driver added a few compliments as the ruth-bullocks backed and backed again.

From behind the shaking curtains came one volley of invective. It did not last long, but in kind and quality, in blistering, biting appropriateness, it was beyond anything that even Kim had heard. He could see the carter's bare chest collapse with amazement, as the man salaamed reverently to the voice, leaped from the pole, and helped the escort haul their volcano on to the main road. Here the voice told him truthfully what sort of wife he had wedded, and what she was doing in his absence.

"Oh, shabash!" murmured Kim, unable to contain himself, as the man slunk away.

"Well done, indeed? It is a shame and a scandal that a poor woman may not go to make prayer to her gods except she be jostled and insulted by all the refuse of Hindustan—that she must eat gali (abuse) as men eat ghi. But I have yet a wag left to my tongue—a word or two well spoken that serves the occasion. And still am I without my tobacco! Who is the one-eyed and luckless son of shame that has not yet prepared my pipe?"

It was hastily thrust in by a hillman, and a trickle of thick smoke from each corner of the curtains showed that peace was restored.

If Kim had walked proudly the day before, disciple of a holy man, to-day he paced with tenfold pride in the train of a semi-royal procession, with a recognised place under the patronage of an old lady of charming manners and infinite resource. The escort, their heads tied up native fashion, fell in on either side the cart, shuffling enormous clouds of dust.

The lama and Kim walked a little to one side; Kim chewing his stick of sugar-cane, and making way for no one under the status of a priest. They could hear the old lady's tongue clack as steadily as a rice-husker. She bade the escort tell her what was going on on the road; and so soon as they were clear of the parao she flung back the curtains and peered out, her veil a third across her face. Her men did not eye her directly when she addressed them, and thus the proprieties were more or less observed.

A dark, sallowish District Superintendent of Police, faultlessly uniformed, an Englishman, trotted by on a tired horse, and, seeing from her retinue what manner of person she was, chaffed her.

"O mother," he cried, "do they do this in the zenanas? Suppose an Englishman came by and saw that thou hadst no nose?"

"What?" she shrilled back. "Thy own mother has no nose? Why say so, then, on the open road?"

It was a fair counter. The Englishman threw up his hand with the gesture of a man hit at sword-play. She laughed and nodded.

"Is this a face to tempt virtue aside?" She withdrew all her veil and stared at him.

It was by no means lovely, but as the man gathered up his reins he called it a Moon of Paradise, a Disturber of Integrity, and a few other fantastic epithets which doubled her up with mirth.

"That is a nut-cut" (rogue), she said. "All police-constables are nut-cuts; but the police-wallahs are the worst. Hai, my son, thou hast never learned all that since thou camest from Belait (Europe). Who suckled thee?"

"A pahareen—a hillwoman of Dalhousie, my mother. Keep thy beauty under a shade—O Dispenser of Delights," and he was gone.

"These be the sort"—she took a fine judicial tone, and stuffed her mouth with pan. "These be the sort to oversee justice. They know the land and the customs of the land. The others, all new from Europe, suckled by white women and learning our tongues from books, are worse than the pestilence. They do harm to Kings." Then she told a long, long tale to the world at large, of an ignorant young policeman who had disturbed some small Hill Rajah, a ninth cousin of her own, in the matter of a trivial land-case, winding up with a quotation from a work by no means devotional.

Then her mood changed, and she bade one of the escort ask whether the lama would walk alongside and discuss matters of religion. So Kim dropped back into the dust and returned to his sugar-cane. For an hour or more the lama's tam-o'-shanter showed like a moon through the haze;

and, from all he heard, Kim gathered that the old woman wept. One of
the Ooryas half apologised for his rudeness overnight, saying that he had
never known his mistress of so bland a temper, and he ascribed it to the
presence of the strange priest. Personally, he believed in Brahmins, though,
like all natives, he was acutely aware of their cunning and their greed.
Still, when Brahmins but irritated with begging demands the mother of
his master's wife, and when she sent them away so angry that they cursed
the whole retinue (which was the real reason of the second off-side bullock
going lame, and of the pole breaking the night before), he was prepared to accept any priest of any other denomination in or out of India.
To this Kim assented with wise nods, and bade the Oorya observe that
the lama took no money, and that the cost of his and Kim's food would
be repaid a hundred times in the good luck that would attend the caravan henceforward. He also told stories of Lahore city, and sang a song
or two which made the escort laugh. As a town-mouse well acquainted
with the latest songs by the most fashionable composers,—they are women
for the most part,—Kim had a distinct advantage over men from a little
fruit-village behind Saharunpore, but he let that advantage be inferred.

At noon they turned aside to eat, and the meal was good, plentiful, and
well served on plates of clean leaves, in decency, out of drift of the dust.
They gave the scraps to certain beggars, that all requirements might be
fulfilled, and sat down to a long, luxurious smoke. The old lady had
retreated behind her curtains, but mixed most freely in the talk, her servants arguing with and contradicting her as servants do through out the
East. She compared the cool and the pines of the Kangra and Kulu hills
with the dust and the mangoes of the South; she told a tale of some old
local Gods at the edge of her husband's territory; she roundly abused the
tobacco which she was then smoking, reviled all Brahmins, and speculated
without reserve on the coming of many grandsons.

Chapter 5

Here come I to my own again—
Fed, forgiven, and known again—
Claimed by bone of my bone again,
    And sib to flesh of my flesh!
The fatted calf is dressed for me,
But the husks have greater zest for me . . .
I think my pigs will be best for me,
So I'm off to the styes afresh.

"The Prodigal Son."

ONCE more the lazy, string-tied, shuffling procession got under way, and she slept till they reached the next halting-stage. It was a very short march, and time lacked an hour to sundown, so Kim cast about for means of amusement.

"But why not sit and rest?" said one of the escort. "Only the devils and the English walk to and fro without reason."

"Never make friends with the Devil, a monkey, or a boy. No man knows what they will do next," said his fellow.

Kim turned a scornful back—he did not want to hear the old story how the Devil played with the boys and repented of it—and walked idly across country.

The lama strode after him. All that day, whenever they passed a stream, he had turned aside to look at it, but in no case had he received any warning that he had found his River. Insensibly too the comfort of speaking to some one in a reasonable tongue, and of being properly considered and respected as her spiritual adviser by a well-born woman, had weaned his thoughts a little from the Search. And further, he was prepared to spend serene years in his quest; having nothing of the white man's impatience, but a great faith.

"Where goest thou?" he called after Kim.

"No whither—it was a small march, and all this"—Kim waved his hands abroad—"is new to me."

"She is beyond question a wise and discerning woman. But it is hard to meditate when—"

"All women are thus." Kim spoke as might have Solomon.

"Before the lamassery was a broad platform," the lama muttered, looping up the well-worn rosary, "of stone. On that I have left the marks of my feet—pacing to and fro with these."

He clicked the beads, and began the "Om mane pudme hum" of his devotion; grateful for the cool, the quiet, and the absence of dust.

One thing after another drew Kim's idle eye across the plain. There was no purpose in his wanderings, except that the build of the huts near by seemed new, and he wished to investigate.

They came out on a broad tract of grazing-ground, brown and purple in the afternoon light, with a heavy clump of mangoes in the centre. It struck Kim as curious that no shrine stood in so eligible a spot: the boy was observing as any priest for these things. Far across the plain walked side by side four men, made small by the distance. He looked intently under his curved palms and caught the sheen of brass.

"Soldiers. White soldiers!" said he. "Let us see."

"It is always soldiers when thou and I go out alone together. But I have never seen the white soldiers."

"They do no harm except when they are drunk. Keep behind this tree."

They stepped behind the thick trunks in the cool dark of the mango-tope. Two little figures halted; the other two came forward uncertainly. They were the advance-party of a regiment on the march, sent out, as usual, to mark the camp. They bore five-foot sticks with fluttering flags, and called to each other as they spread over the flat earth.

At last they entered the mango-grove, walking heavily.

"It's here or hereabouts—officers' tents under the trees, I take it, an' the rest of us can stay outside. Have they marked out for the baggage-waggons behind?"

They cried again to their comrades in the distance, and the rough answer came back faint and mellowed.

"Shove the flag in here, then," said one.

"What do they prepare?" said the lama, wonder-struck. "This is a great and terrible world. What is the device on the flag?"

A soldier thrust a stave within a few feet of them, grunted discontentedly, pulled it up again, conferred with his companion, who looked up and down the shaded cave of greenery, and returned it.

Kim stared with all his eyes, his breath coming short and sharp between his teeth. The soldiers stamped off into the sunshine.

"O Holy One," he gasped, "my horoscope! The drawing in the dust by the priest at Umballa! Remember what he said. First come two—ferashes—to make all things ready—in a dark place, as it is always at the beginning of a vision."

"But this is not vision," said the lama. "It is the world's illusion, and no more."

"And after them comes the Bull—the Red Bull on the green field. Look! It is he!"

He pointed to the flag that was snap-snapping in the evening breeze not ten feet away. It was no more than an ordinary camp marking-flag; but the regiment, always punctilious in matters of millinery, had charged it with the regimental device, the Red Bull, which is the crest of the Mavericks—the great Red Bull on the background of Irish green.

"I see, and now I remember," said the lama. "Certainly it is thy Bull. Certainly, also, the two men came to make all ready."

"They are soldiers—white soldiers. What said the priest? 'The sign over against the Bull is the sign of War and armed men.' Holy One, this thing touches my Search."

"True. It is true." The lama stared fixedly at the device that flamed like a ruby in the dusk. "The priest at Umballa said that thine was the sign of War."

"What is to do now?"

"Wait. Let us wait."

"Even now the darkness clears," said Kim. It was only natural that the descending sun should at last strike through the tree-trunks, across the grove, filling it with mealy gold light for a few minutes; but to Kim it was crown of the Umballa Brahmin's prophecy.

"Hark!" said the lama. "One beats a drum—far off!"

At first the sound, carrying diluted through the still air, resembled the beating of an artery in the head. Soon a sharpness was added.

"Ah! The music," Kim explained. He knew the sound of a regimental band, but it amazed the lama.

At the far end of the plain a heavy, dusty column crawled in sight. Then the wind brought the tune:—

> *"We crave your condescension*
> *To tell you what we know*
> *Of marching in the Mulligan Guards*
> *To Sligo Port below."*

Here broke in the shrill-tongued fifes:—

"We shouldered arms,
We marched—we marched away
From Phoenix Park
We marched to Dublin Bay.
The drums and the fifes,
Oh, sweetly they did play,
As we marched—marched—marched—with the Mulligan Guards!"*

It was the band of the Mavericks playing the regiment to camp; for the men were route-marching with their baggage. The rippling column swung into the level—carts behind it—divided left and right, ran about like an ant-hill, and . . .

"But this is sorcery!" said the lama.

The plain dotted itself with tents that seemed to rise, all spread, from the carts. Another rush of men invaded the grove, pitched a huge tent in silence, ran up yet eight or nine more by the side of it, unearthed cooking-pots, pans, and bundles, which were taken possession of by a crowd of native servants; and behold the mango-tope turned into an orderly town as they watched!

"Let us go," said the lama, sinking back afraid, as the fires twinkled and white officers with jingling swords stalked into the mess-tent.

"Stand back in the shadow. No one can see beyond the light of a fire," said Kim, his eyes still on the flag. He had never before watched the routine of a seasoned regiment pitching camp in thirty minutes.

"Look! look! look!" clucked the lama. "Yonder comes a priest."

It was Bennett, the Church of England chaplain of the regiment, limping in dusty black. One of his flock had made some rude remarks about the chaplain's mettle; and to abash him Bennett had marched step by step with the men that day. The black dress, gold cross on the watch-chain, the hairless face, and the soft, black wide-awake hat would have marked him as a holy man anywhere in all India. He dropped into a camp-chair by the door of the mess-tent and slid off his boots. Three or four officers gathered round him, laughing and joking over his exploit.

"The talk of white men is wholly lacking in dignity," said the lama, who judged only by tone. "But I have considered the countenance of that priest, and I think he is learned. Is it likely that he will understand our talk? I would talk to him of my Search."

"Never speak to a white man till he is fed," said Kim, quoting a well-known proverb. "They will eat now, and—and I do not think they are good to beg from. Let us go back to the resting-place. After we have eaten we will come again. It certainly was a Red Bull—my Red Bull."

They were both noticeably absent-minded when the old lady's retinue set their meal before them; so none broke their reserve, for it is not lucky to annoy guests.

"Now," said Kim, picking his teeth, "we will return to that place; but thou, O Holy One, must wait a little way off, because thy feet are heavier than mine and I am anxious to see more of that Red Bull."

"But how canst thou understand the talk? Walk slowly. The road is dark," the lama replied uneasily.

Kim put the question aside. "I marked a place near to the trees," said he, "where thou canst sit till I call. Nay," as the lama made some sort of protest, "remember this is my Search—the Search for my Red Bull. The sign in the Stars was not for thee. I know a little of the customs of white soldiers, and I always desire to see some new things."

"What dost thou not know of this world?" The lama squatted obediently in a little hollow of the ground not a hundred yards from the hump of the mango trees dark against the star-powdered sky.

"Stay till I call." Kim flitted into the dusk. He knew that in all probability there would be sentries round the camp, and smiled to himself as he heard the thick boots of one. A boy who can dodge over the roofs of Lahore city on a moonlight night, using every little patch and corner of darkness to discomfit his pursuer, is not likely to be checked by a line of well-trained soldiers. He paid them the compliment of crawling between a couple, and, running and halting, crouching and dropping flat, worked his way towards the lighted mess-tent where, close pressed behind the mango tree, he waited till some chance word should give him a returnable lead.

The one thing in his mind now was further information as to the Red Bull. For aught he knew, and Kim's limitations were as curious and sudden as his expansions, the men, the nine hundred thorough devils of his father's prophecy, might pray to the beast after dark, as Hindus pray to the Holy Cow. That at least would be entirely right and logical, and the Padre with the gold cross would be therefore the man to consult in the matter. On the other hand, remembering sober-faced padres whom he had avoided in Lahore city, the priest might be an inquisitive nuisance who would bid him learn. But had it not been proven at Umballa that his sign in the high heavens portended war and armed men? Was he not the Friend of the Stars as well as of all the world, crammed to the teeth with dreadful secrets? Lastly,—and firstly as the undercurrent of all his quick thoughts,—this adventure, though he did not know the English word, was a stupendous lark—a delightful continuation of his old flights across the housetops, as well as the fulfilment of sublime prophecy. He lay belly-flat and wriggled towards the mess-tent door, a hand on the amulet round his neck. It was as he suspected. The Sahibs prayed to their

God; for in the centre of the mess-table—its sole ornament when they were on the line of march—stood a golden bull fashioned from old-time loot of the Summer Palace at Pekin—a red-gold bull with lowered head, ramping upon a field of Irish green. To him the Sahibs held out their glasses and cried aloud confusedly.

Now the Reverend Arthur Bennett always left mess after that toast, and being rather tired by his march his movements were more abrupt than usual. Kim, with slightly raised head, was still staring at his totem on the table, when the chaplain stepped on his right shoulder-blade. Kim flinched under the leather, and, rolling sideways, brought down the chaplain, who, ever a man of action, caught him by the throat and nearly choked the life out of him. Kim then kicked him desperately in the stomach. Mr. Bennett gasped and doubled up but without relaxing his grip, rolled over again, and silently hauled Kim to his own tent. The Mavericks were incurable practical jokers; and it occurred to the Englishman that silence was best till he had made complete inquiry.

"Why, it's a boy!" he said, as he drew his prize under the light of the tent-pole lantern, then shaking him severely cried: "What were you doing? You're a thief. Choor? Mallum?" His Hindustanee was very limited, and the ruffled and disgusted Kim intended to keep to the character laid down for him. As he recovered his breath he was inventing a beautifully plausible tale of his relations to some mess-scullion, and at the same time keeping a keen eye on and a little under the chaplain's left armpit. The chance came; he ducked for the doorway, but a long arm shot out and clutched at his neck, snapping the amulet string and closing on the amulet.

"Give it me. O give it me. Is it lost? Give me the papers."

The words were in English—the tinny, saw-cut English of the native-bred, and the chaplain jumped.

"A scapular," said he, opening his hand. "No, some sort of heathen charm. Why—why, do you speak English? Little boys who steal are beaten. You know that?"

"I do not—I did not steal." Kim danced in agony like a terrier at a lifted stick. "O give it me. It is my charm. Do not thieve it from me."

The chaplain took no heed, but, going to the tent door, called aloud. A fattish, clean-shaven man appeared.

"I want your advice, Father Victor," said Bennett. "I found this boy in the dark outside the mess-tent. Ordinarily, I should have chastised him and let him go, because I believe him to be a thief. But it seems he talks English, and he attaches some sort of value to a charm round his neck. I thought perhaps you might help me."

Between himself and the Roman Catholic chaplain of the Irish contingent lay, as Bennett believed, an unbridgeable gulf, but it was noticeable that whenever the Church of England dealt with a human problem she was likely to call in the Church of Rome. Bennett's official abhorrence of the Scarlet Woman and all her ways was only equalled by his private respect for Father Victor.

"A thief talking English is it? Let's look at his charm. No, it's not a scapular, Bennett." He held out his hand.

"But have we any right to open it? A sound whipping—"

"I did not thieve," protested Kim. "You have hit me kicks all over my body. Now give me my charm and I will go away."

"Not quite so fast; we'll look first," said Father Victor, leisurely rolling out poor Kimball O'Hara's "ne varietur" parchment, his clearance-certificate, and Kim's baptismal-certificate. On this last O'Hara—with some confused idea that he was doing wonders for his son—had scrawled scores of times: "Look after the boy. Please look after the boy,"—signing his name and regimental number in full.

"Powers of Darkness below!" said Father Victor, passing all over to Mr. Bennett. "Do you know what these things are?"

"Yes," said Kim. "They are mine, and I want to go away."

"I do not quite understand," said Mr. Bennett. "He probably brought them on purpose. It may be a begging trick of some kind."

"I never saw a beggar less anxious to stay with his company, then. There's the makings of a gay mystery here. Ye believe in Providence, Bennett?"

"I hope so."

"Well, I believe in miracles, so it comes to the same thing. Powers of Darkness! Kimball O'Hara! And his son! But then he's a native, and I saw Kimball married myself to Annie Shott. How long have you had these things, boy?"

"Ever since I was a little baby." Father Victor stepped forward quickly and opened the front of Kim's upper garment. "You see, Bennett, he's not very black. What's your name?"

"Kim."

"Or Kimball?"

"Perhaps. Will you let me go away?"

"What else?"

"They call me Kim Rishti ke. That is Kim of the Rishti."

"What is that—'Rishti'?"

"Eye-rishti—that was the regiment—my father's."

"Irish, oh I see."

"Yess. That was how my father told me. My father, he has lived."

"Has lived where?"

"Has lived. Of course he is dead—gone-out."

"Oh. That's your abrupt way of putting it, is it?"

Bennett interrupted. "It is possible I have done the boy an injustice. He is certainly white, though evidently neglected. I am sure I must have bruised him. I do not think spirits—"

"Get him a glass of sherry, then, and let him squat on the cot. Now, Kim," continued Father Victor, "no one is going to hurt you. Drink that down and tell us about yourself. The truth, if you've no objection."

Kim coughed a little as he put down the empty glass, and considered. This seemed a time for caution and fancy. Small boys who prowl about camps are generally turned out after a whipping. But he had received no stripes; the amulet was evidently working in his favour, and it looked as though the Umballa horoscope and the few words that he could remember of his father's maunderings fitted in most miraculously. Else why did the fat padre seem so impressed, and why the glass of hot yellow wine from the lean one?

"My father, he is dead in Lahore city since I was very little. The woman, she kept kabarri-shop near where the hire-carriages are." Kim began with a plunge, not quite sure how far the truth would serve him.

"Your mother?"

"No"—with a gesture of disgust. "She went out when I was born. My father, he got these papers from the Jadoo-Gher—what do you call that?" (Bennett nodded) "because he was in—good-standing. What do you call that?" (again Bennett nodded). "My father told me that. He said too, and also the Brahmin who made the drawing in the dust at Umballa two days ago, he said, that I shall find a Red Bull on a green field and that the Bull shall help me."

"A phenomenal little liar," muttered Bennett.

"Powers of Darkness below, what a country!" murmured Father Victor. "Go on, Kim."

"I did not thieve. Besides, I am just now disciple of a very holy man. He is sitting outside. We saw two men come with flags, making the place ready. That is always so in a dream, or on account of a—a—prophecy. So I knew it was come true. I saw the Red Bull on the green field, and my father he said: 'Nine hundred pukka devils and the Colonel riding on a horse will look after you when you find the Red Bull!' I did not know what to do when I saw the Bull, but I went away and I came again when it was dark. I wanted to see the Bull again, and I saw the Bull again with the—the Sahibs praying to it. I think the Bull shall help me. The holy man said so too. He is sitting outside. Will you hurt him, if I call him a shout now? He is very holy. He can witness to all the things I say, and he knows I am not a thief."

" 'Officers praying to a bull!' What in the world do you make of that?" said Bennett. " 'Disciple of a holy man!' Is the boy mad?"

"It's O'Hara's boy, sure enough. O'Hara's boy leagued with all the Powers of Darkness. It's very much what his father would have done—if he was drunk. We'd better invite the holy man. He may know something."

"He does not know anything," said Kim. "I will show you him if you come. He is my master. Then afterwards we can go."

"Powers of Darkness!" was all that Father Victor could say, as Bennett marched off, with a firm hand on Kim's shoulder.

They found the lama where he had dropped.

"The search is at an end for me," shouted Kim in the vernacular. "I have found the Bull, but God knows what comes next. They will not hurt you. Come to the fat priest's tent with this thin man and see the end. It is all new, and they cannot talk Hindi. They are only uncurried donkeys."

"Then it is not well to make a jest of their ignorance," the lama returned. "I am glad if thou art rejoiced, chela."

Dignified and unsuspicious, he strode into the little tent, saluted the Churches as a Churchman, and sat down by the open charcoal brazier. The yellow lining of the tent reflected in the lamplight made his face red-gold.

Bennett looked at him with the triple-ringed uninterest of the creed that lumps nine-tenths of the world under the title of "heathen."

"And what was the end of the search? What gift has the Red Bull brought?" The lama addressed himself to Kim.

"He says, 'What are you going to do?'" Bennett was staring uneasily at Father Victor, and Kim, for his own ends, took upon himself the office of interpreter.

"I do not see what concern this faquir has with the boy, who is probably his dupe or his confederate," Bennett began. "We cannot allow an English boy— Assuming that he is the son of a Mason, the sooner he goes to the Masonic Orphanage the better."

"Ah! That's your opinion as Secretary to the Regimental Lodge," said Father Victor; "but we might as well tell the old man what we are going to do. He doesn't look like a villain."

"My experience is that one can never fathom the Oriental mind. Now, Kimball, I wish you to tell this man what I say—word for word."

Kim gathered the import of the next few sentences and began thus:

"Holy One, the thin fool who looks like a camel says that I am the son of a Sahib."

"But how?"

"Oh, it is true. I knew it since my birth, but he could only find it out by rending the amulet from my neck and reading all the papers. He thinks that once a Sahib is always a Sahib, and between the two of them they purpose to keep me in this regiment or to send me to a madrissah (a school). It has happened before. I have always avoided it. The fat fool is of one mind and the camel-like one of another. But that is no odds. I may spend one night here and perhaps the next. It has happened before. Then I will run away and return to thee."

"But tell them that thou art my chela. Tell them how thou didst come to me when I was faint and bewildered. Tell them of our Search, and they will surely let thee go now."

"I have already told them. They laugh, and they talk of the Police."

"What are you saying?" asked Mr. Bennett.

"Oah. He only says that if you do not let me go it will stop him in his business—his ur-gent private affairs." This last was a reminiscence of some talk with a Eurasian clerk in the Canal Department, but it only drew a smile, which nettled him. "And if you did know what his business was you would not be in such a beastly hurry to interfere."

"What is it then?" said Father Victor, not without feeling, as he watched the lama's face.

"There is a River in this country which he wishes to find so verree much. It was put out by an Arrow which—" Kim tapped his foot impatiently as he translated in his own mind from the vernacular to his clumsy English. "Oah, it was made by our Lord God Buddha, you know, and if you wash there you are washed away from all your sins and made as white as cotton-wool." (Kim had heard mission-talk in his time.) "I am his disciple, and we must find that River. It is so verree valuable to us."

"Say that again," said Bennett. Kim obeyed, with amplifications.

"But this is gross blasphemy!" cried the Church of England.

"Tck! Tck!" said Father Victor sympathetically. "I'd give a good deal to be able to talk the vernacular. A river that washes away sin! And how long have you two been looking for it?"

"Oh, many days. Now we wish to go away and look for it again. It is not here, you see."

"I see," said Father Victor gravely. "But he can't go on in that old man's company. It would be different, Kim, if you were not a soldier's son. Tell him that the regiment will take care of you and make you as good a man as your—as good a man as can be. Tell him that if he believes in miracles he must believe that—"

"There is no need to play on his credulity," Bennett interrupted.

"I'm doing no such thing. He must believe that the boy's coming here —to his own regiment—in search of his Red Bull is in the nature of a miracle. Consider the chances against it, Bennett. This one boy in all India, and our regiment of all others on the line o' march for him to meet with! It's predestined on the face of it. Yes, tell him it's Kismet. Kismet, mallum?" (Fate! Do you understand?)

He turned towards the lama, to whom he might as well have talked of Mesopotamia.

"They say,"—the old man's eye lighted at Kim's speech,—"they say that the meaning of my horoscope is now accomplished, and that being led back—though as thou knowest I went out of curiosity—to these people and their Red Bull I must needs go to a madrissah and be turned into a Sahib. Now I make pretence of agreement, for at the worst it will be but a few meals eaten away from thee. Then I will slip away and follow down the road to Saharunpore. Therefore, Holy One, keep with that Kulu woman—on no account stray far from her cart till I come again. Past question, my sign is of War and of armed men. See how they have given me wine to drink and set me upon a bed of honour! My father must have been some great person. So if they raise me to honour among them, good. If not, good again. However it goes, I will run back to thee when I am tired. But stay with the Rajputni, or I shall miss thy feet. . . . Oah yess," said the boy, "I have told him everything you tell me to say."

"And I cannot see any need why he should wait," said Bennett, feeling in his trouser-pocket. "We can investigate the details later—and I will give him a ru—"

"Give him time. May be he's fond of the lad," said Father Victor, half-arresting the clergyman's motion.

The lama dragged forth his rosary and pulled his huge hat-brim over his eyes.

"What can he want now?"

"He says"—Kim put up one hand. "He says: Be quiett. He wants to speak to me by himself. You see you do not know one little word of what he says, and I think if you talk he will perhaps give you very bad curses. When he takes those beads like that, you see he always wants to be quiett."

The two Englishmen sat overwhelmed, but there was a look in Bennett's eye that promised ill for Kim when he should be relaxed to the religious arm.

"A Sahib and the son of a Sahib—" The lama's voice was harsh with pain. "But no white man knows the land and the customs of the land as thou knowest. How comes it this is true?"

"What matter, Holy One: but remember it is only for a night or two. Remember, I can change swiftly. It will be as it was when I first spoke to thee under Zam-Zammah the great gun—"

"As a boy in the dress of white men—when I first went to the Wonder House. And a second time thou wast a Hindu. What shall the third incarnation be?" He chuckled drearily. "Ah, chela, thou hast done a wrong to an old man because my heart went out to thee."

"And mine to thee. But how could I know that the Red Bull would bring me to this business?"

The lama covered his face afresh, and nervously rattled the rosary. Kim squatted beside him and laid hold upon a fold of his clothing.

"Now it is understood that the boy is a Sahib?" he went on in a muffled tone. "Such a Sahib as was he who kept the images in the Wonder House." The lama's experience of white men was limited. He seemed to be repeating a lesson. "So then it is not seemly that he should do other than as the Sahibs do. He must go back to his own people."

"For a day and a night and a day," Kim pleaded.

"No, ye don't!" Father Victor saw Kim edging towards the door, and interposed a strong leg.

"I do not understand the customs of white men. The Priest of the Images in the Wonder House in Lahore was more courteous than the thin one here. This boy will be taken from me. They will make a Sahib of my disciple? Woe to me, how shall I find my River? Have they no disciples? Ask."

"He says he is very sorry that he cannot find the River now any more. He says, Why have you no disciples, and stop bothering him? He wants to be washed of his sins."

Neither Bennett nor Father Victor found any answer ready.

Said Kim in English, distressed for the lama's agony: "I think if you will let me go now we will walk away quietly and not steal. We will look for that River like before I was caught. I wish I did not come here to find the Red Bull and all that sort of thing. I do not want it."

"It's the very best day's work you ever did for yourself, young man," said Bennett.

"Good heavens, I don't know how to console him," said Father Victor, watching the lama intently. "He can't take the boy away with him, and yet he's a good man—I'm sure he's a good man. Bennett, if you give him that rupee he'll curse you root and branch!"

They listened to each other's breathing—three—five full minutes. Then the lama raised his head, and looked forth across them into space and emptiness.

"And I am a follower of the Way," he said bitterly. "The sin is mine and the punishment is mine. I made believe to myself—for now I see it was but make-belief—that thou wast sent to me to aid in the Search. So my heart went out to thee for thy charity and thy courtesy and the wisdom of the little years. But those who follow the Way must permit not the fire of any desire or attachment, for that is all illusion. As says . . ." He quoted an old, old Chinese text, backed it with another, and reinforced these with a third. "I stepped aside from the Way, my chela. It was no fault of thine. I delighted in the sight of life, the new people upon the roads, and in thy joy at seeing these things. I was pleased with thee who should have considered my Search and my Search alone. Now I am sorrowful because thou art taken away and my River is far from me. It is the Law which I have broken!"

"Powers of Darkness below!" said Father Victor, who, wise in the confessional, heard the pain in every sentence.

"I see now that the sign of the Red Bull was a sign for me as well as for thee. All Desire is red—and evil. I will do penance and find my River alone."

"At least go back to the Kulu woman," said Kim, "otherwise thou wilt be lost upon the roads. She will feed thee till I run back to thee."

The lama waved a hand to show that the matter was finally settled in his mind.

"Now,"—his tone altered as he turned to Kim,—"what will they do with thee? At least I may, acquiring merit, wipe out past ill."

"Make me a Sahib—so they think. The day after to-morrow I return. Do not grieve."

"Of what sort? Such an one as this or that man?" He pointed to Father Victor. "Such an one as those I saw this evening—men wearing swords and stamping heavily?"

"May be."

"That is not well. These men follow desire and come to emptiness. Thou must not be of their sort."

"The Umballa priest said that my Star was War," Kim interjected. "I will ask these fools—but there is truly no need. I will run away this night, for all I wanted to see the new things."

Kim put two or three questions in English to Father Victor, translating the replies to the lama.

Then: "He says, 'You take him from me and you cannot say what you will make him.' He says, 'Tell me before I go, for it is not a small thing to make a child.'"

"You will be sent to a school. Later on, we shall see. Kimball, I suppose you'd like to be a soldier?"

"Gorah-log (white-folk). No-ah! No-ah!" Kim shook his head violently. There was nothing in his composition to which drill and routine appealed. "I will not be a soldier."

"You will be what you're told to be," said Bennett; "and you should be grateful that we're going to help you."

Kim smiled compassionately. If these men lay under the delusion that he would do anything that he did not fancy, so much the better.

Another long silence followed. Bennett fidgeted with impatience, and suggested calling a sentry to evict the faquir.

"Do they give or sell learning among the Sahibs? Ask them," said the lama, and Kim interpreted.

"They say that money is paid to the teacher—but that money the regiment will give. . . . What need? It is only for a night."

"And—the more money is paid the better learning is given?" The lama disregarded Kim's plans for an early flight. "It is no wrong to pay for learning; to help the ignorant to wisdom is always a merit." The rosary clicked furiously as an abacus. Then he faced his oppressors.

"Ask them for how much money do they give a wise and suitable teaching? and in what city is that teaching given?"

"Well," said Father Victor in English, when Kim had translated, "that depends. The regiment would pay for you all the time you are at the Military Orphanage; or you might go on the Punjab Masonic Orphanage's list (not that he or you 'ud understand what that means); but the best schooling a boy can get in India is, of course, at St. Xavier's in Partibus at Lucknow." This took some time to interpret, for Bennett wished to cut it short.

"He wants to know how much?" said Kim placidly.

"Two or three hundred rupees a year." Father Victor was long past any sense of amazement. Bennett, impatient, did not understand.

"He says: 'Write that name and the money upon a paper and give it him.' And he says you must write your name below, because he is going to write a letter in some days to you. He says you are a good man. He says the other man is a fool. He is going away."

The lama rose suddenly. "I follow my Search," he cried, and was gone.

"He'll run slap into the sentries," cried Father Victor, jumping up as the lama stalked out; "but I can't leave the boy." Kim made swift motion to follow, but checked himself. There was no sound of challenge outside. The lama had disappeared.

Kim settled himself composedly on the chaplain's cot. At least the lama had promised that he would stay with the Rajput woman from Kulu, and the rest was of the smallest importance. It pleased him that the two padres were so evidently excited. They talked long in undertones, Father Victor urging some scheme on Mr. Bennett, who seemed incredulous. All this was very new and fascinating, but Kim felt sleepy. They called men into

the tent—one of them certainly was the Colonel, as his father had prophesied—and they asked him an infinity of questions, chiefly about the
woman who looked after him, all of which Kim answered truthfully. They
did not seem to think the woman a good guardian.

After all, this was the newest of his experiences. Sooner or later, if
he chose, he could escape into great, gray, formless India, beyond tents
and padres and colonels. Meantime, if the Sahibs were to be impressed,
he would do his best to impress them. He too was a white man.

After much talk that he could not comprehend, they handed him over
to a sergeant, who had strict instructions not to let him escape. The regiment would go on to Umballa, and Kim would be sent up, partly at the
expense of the Lodge and in part by subscription, to a place called Sanawar.

"It's miraculous past all whooping, Colonel," said Father Victor, when
he had talked without a break for ten minutes. "His Buddhist friend
has levanted after taking my name and address. I can't quite make out
whether he'll pay for the boy's education or whether he is preparing some
sort of witchcraft on his own account." Then to Kim: "You'll live to be
grateful to your friend the Red Bull yet. We'll make a man of you at
Sanawar—even at the price o' making you a Protestant."

"Certainly—most certainly," said Bennett.

"But you will not go to Sanawar," said Kim.

"But we will go to Sanawar, little man. That's the order of the
Commander-in-Chief, who's a trifle more important than O'Hara's son."

"You will not go to Sanawar. You will go to thee war."

There was a shout of laughter from the full tent.

"When you know your own regiment a trifle better you won't confuse
the line of march with line of battle, Kim. We hope to go to 'thee war'
sometime."

"Oah, I know all thatt." Kim drew his bow again at a venture. If they
were not going to the war, at least they did not know what he knew of
the talk in the veranda at Umballa.

"I know you are not at thee war now; but I tell you that as soon as
you get to Umballa you will be sent to the war—the new war. It is a
war of eight thousand men, besides the guns."

"That's explicit. D'you add prophecy to your other gifts? Take him
along, Sergeant. Take up a suit for him from the Drums, an' take care
he doesn't slip through your fingers. Who says the age of miracles is
gone by? I think I'll go to bed. My poor mind's weakening."

At the far end of the camp, silent as a wild animal, an hour later sat
Kim, newly washed all over, in a horrible stuff suit that rasped his arms
and legs.

"A most amazin' young bird," said the Sergeant. "He turns up in charge of a yellow-headed buck-Brahmin priest, with his father's Lodge certificates round his neck, talkin' God knows what all of a red bull. The buck-Brahmin evaporates without explanations, an' the bhoy sets cross-legged on the chaplain's bed prophesyin' bloody war to the men at large. Injia's a wild land for a God-fearin' man. I'll just tie his leg to the tent-pole in case he'll go through the roof. What did ye say about the war?"

"Eight thousand men, besides guns," said Kim. "Very soon you will see."

"You're a consolin' little imp. Lie down between the Drums an' go to bye-bye. Those two boys beside ye will watch your slumbers."

Chapter 6

Now I remember comrades—
Old playmates on new seas—
Whenas we traded orpiment
Among the savages.
Ten thousand leagues to southward,
And thirty years removed—
They knew not noble Valdez,
But me they knew and loved.

"Song of Diego Valdez."

Very early in the morning the white tents came down and disappeared as the Mavericks took a side road to Umballa. It did not skirt the resting-place, and Kim, trudging beside a baggage-cart under fire of comments from soldiers' wives, was not so confident as overnight. He discovered that he was closely watched—Father Victor on the one side, and Mr. Bennett on the other.

In the forenoon the column checked. A camel-orderly handed the Colonel a letter. He read it, and spoke to a major. Half a mile in the rear, Kim heard a hoarse and joyful clamour rolling down on him through the thick dust. Then some one beat him on the back, crying: "Tell us how ye knew, ye little limb of Satan? Father dear, see if ye can make him tell."

A pony ranged alongside, and he was hauled on to the priest's saddle-bow.

"Now, my son, your prophecy of last night has come true. Our orders are to entrain at Umballa for the front to-morrow."

"What is thatt?" said Kim, for "front" and "entrain" were newish words to him.

"We are going to 'thee war,' as you called it."

"Of course you are going to thee war. I said last night."

"Ye did; but, Powers o' Darkness, how did ye know?"

Kim's eyes sparkled. He shut his lips, nodded his head, and looked unspeakable things. The chaplain moved on through the dust, and privates, sergeants, and subalterns called one another's attention to the boy. The Colonel, at the head of the column, stared at him curiously. "It was probably some bazar rumour," he said; "but even then—" He referred to the paper in his hand. "Hang it all, the thing was only decided within the last forty-eight hours."

"Are there many more like you in India?" said Father Victor, "or are you by way o' being a lusus naturae?"

"Now I have told you," said the boy, "will you let me go back to my old man? If he has not stayed with that woman from Kulu, I am afraid he will die."

"By what I saw of him he's as well able to take care of himself as you. No. Ye've brought us luck, an' we're goin' to make a man of you. I'll take ye back to your baggage-cart and ye'll come to me this evening."

For the rest of the day Kim found himself an object of distinguished consideration among a few hundred white men. The story of his appearance in camp, the discovery of his parentage, and his prophecy, had lost nothing in the telling. A big, shapeless white woman of a pile of bedding asked him mysteriously whether he thought her husband would come back from the war. Kim reflected gravely, and said that he would, and the woman gave him food. In many respects, this big procession that played music at intervals—this crowd that talked and laughed so easily—resembled a festival in Lahore city. So far, there was no sign of hard work, and he resolved to lend the spectacle his patronage. At evening there came out to meet them bands of music, and played the Mavericks into camp near Umballa railway station. That was an interesting night. Men of other regiments came to visit the Mavericks. The Mavericks went visiting on their own account. Their pickets hurried forth to bring them back, met pickets of strange regiments on the same duty; and, after a while, the bugles blew madly for more pickets with officers to control the tumult. The Mavericks had a reputation for liveliness to live up to. But they fell in on the platform next morning in perfect shape and condition; and Kim, left behind with the sick, women, and boys, found himself shouting farewells excitedly as the trains drew away. Life as a Sahib was amusing so far; but he touched it with a cautious hand. Then they marched him back in charge of a drummer-boy to empty, lime-washed barracks, whose floors were covered with rubbish and string and paper, and whose ceilings gave back his lonely footfall. Native fashion, he curled himself up on a stripped cot and went to sleep. An angry man stumped down the veranda, woke him up, and said he was a schoolmaster. This was enough for Kim, and he retired into his shell. He could just puzzle out the various English Police notices in Lahore city, because they affected his comfort; and among the many guests of the woman who looked after him had been a queer

German who painted scenery for the Parsee travelling theatre. He told Kim that he had been "on the barricades in Forty-eight," and therefore—at least that was how it struck Kim—he would teach the boy to write in return for food. Kim had been kicked as far as single letters, but did not think well of them.

"I do not know anything. Go away!" said Kim, scenting evil. Hereupon the man caught him by the ear, dragged him to a room in a far-off wing where a dozen drummer-boys were sitting on forms, and told him to be still if he could do nothing else. This he managed very successfully. The man explained something or other with white lines on a black board for at least half an hour, and Kim continued his interrupted nap. He much disapproved of the present aspect of affairs, for this was the very school and discipline he had spent two-thirds of his young life in avoiding. Suddenly a beautiful idea occurred to him, and he wondered that he had not thought of it before.

The man dismissed them, and first to spring through the veranda into the open sunshine was Kim.

"'Ere you! 'Alt! Stop!" said a high voice at his heels. "I've got to look after you. My orders are not to let you out of my sight. Where are you goin'?"

It was the drummer-boy who had been hanging round him all the fore-noon—a fat and freckled person of about fourteen, and Kim loathed him from the soles of his boots to his cap-ribbons.

"To the bazar—to get sweets—for you," said Kim, after thought.

"Well, the bazar's out o' bounds. If we go there we'll get a dressing-down. You come back."

"How near can we go?" Kim did not know what bounds meant, but he wished to be polite—for the present.

"'Ow near? 'Ow far, you mean? We can go as far as that tree down the road."

"Then I will go there."

"All right. I ain't goin'. It's too 'ot. I can watch you from 'ere. It's no good runnin' away. If you did, they'd spot you by your clothes. That's regimental stuff you're wearin'. There ain't a picket in Umballa wouldn't 'ead you back quicker than you started out."

This did not impress Kim as much as the knowledge that his raiment would tire him out if he tried to run. He slouched to the tree at the corner of a bare road leading towards the bazar, and eyed the natives passing. Most of them were barrack-servants of the lowest caste. Kim hailed a sweeper, who promptly retorted with a piece of unnecessary insolence, in the natural belief that the European boy could not follow. The low, quick answer undeceived him. Kim put his fettered soul into it, thankful for the late chance to abuse somebody in the tongue he knew best. "And now, go to the nearest letter-writer in the bazar and tell him to come here. I would write a letter."

"But—but what manner of white man's son art thou, to need a bazar letter-writer? Is there not a schoolmaster in the barracks?"

"Ay; and Hell is full of the same sort. Do my order, you—you Od! Thy mother was married under a basket! Servant of Lal Beg" (Kim knew the god of the sweepers), "run on my business or we will talk again."

The sweeper shuffled off in haste. "There is a white boy by the barracks waiting under a tree who is not a white boy," he stammered to the first bazar letter-writer he came across. "He needs thee."

"Will he pay?" said that spruce scribe, gathering up his desk and pens and sealing-wax all in order.

"I do not know. He is not like other boys. Go and see. It is well worth."

Kim danced with impatience when the slim young Kayeth hove in sight. As soon as his voice could carry he cursed him volubly.

"First I will take my pay," the letter-writer said. "Bad words have made the price higher. But who art thou, dressed in that fashion, to speak in this fashion?"

"Aha! That is in the letter which thou shalt write. Never was such a tale. But I am in no haste. Another writer will serve me. Umballa city is as full of them as is Lahore."

"Four annas," said the writer, sitting down and spreading his cloth in the shade of a deserted barrack-wing.

Mechanically Kim squatted beside him,—squatted as only the natives can,—in spite of the abominable clinging trousers.

The writer regarded him sideways.

"That is the price to ask of Sahibs," said Kim. "Now fix me a true one."

"An anna and a half. How do I know, having written the letter, that thou wilt not run away?"

"I must not go beyond this tree, and there is also the stamp to be considered."

"I get no commission on the price of the stamp. Once more, what manner of white boy art thou?"

"That shall be said in the letter, which is to Mahbub Ali, the horse-dealer in the Kashmir Serai, at Lahore. He is my friend."

"Wonder on wonder!" murmured the letter-writer, dipping a reed in the inkstand. "To be written in Hindi?"

"Assuredly. To Mahbub Ali then. Begin! 'I have come down with the old man as far as Umballa in the train. At Umballa I carried the news of the bay mare's pedigree.'" After what he had seen in the garden, he was not going to write of white stallions.

"Slower a little. What has a bay mare to do. . . . Is it Mahbub Ali the great dealer?"

"Who else? I have been in his service. Take more ink. Again. 'As the order was, so I did it. We then went on foot towards Benares, but on the third day we found a certain regiment.' Is that down?"

"Ay, 'pulton,'" murmured the writer, all ears.

"'I went into their camp and was caught, and by means of the charm about my neck, which thou knowest, it was established that I was the son of some man in the regiment: according to the prophecy of the Red Bull, which thou knowest was common talk of our bazar.'" Kim waited for this shaft to sink into the letter-writer's heart, cleared his throat, and continued: "'A priest clothed me and gave me a new name. . . . One priest, however, was a fool. The clothes are very heavy, but I am a Sahib and my heart is heavy too. They send me to a school and beat me. I do not like the air and water here. Come then and help me, Mahbub Ali, or send me some money, for I have not sufficient to pay the writer who writes this.'"

"'Who writes this.' It is my own fault that I was tricked. Thou art as clever as Husain Bux that forged the Treasury stamps at Nucklao. But what a tale! What a tale! Is it true by any chance?"

"It does not profit to tell lies to Mahbub Ali. It is better to help his friends by lending them a stamp. When the money comes I will repay."

The writer grunted doubtfully, but took a stamp out of his desk, sealed the letter, handed it over to Kim, and departed. Mahbub Ali's was a name of power in Umballa.

"That is the way to win a good account with the Gods," Kim shouted after him.

"Pay me twice over when the money comes," the man cried over his shoulder.

"What was you bukkin' to that nigger about?" said the drummer-boy when Kim returned to the veranda. "I was watchin' you."

"I was only talkin' to him."

"You talk the same as a nigger, don't you?"

"No-ah! No-ah! I onlee speak a little. What shall we do now?"

"The bugles 'ill go for dinner in arf a minute. My Gawd! I wish I'd gone up to the front with the regiment. It's awful doin' nothin' but school down 'ere. Don't you 'ate it?"

"Oah yess!"

"I'd run away if I knew where to go to, but, as the men say, in this bloomin' Injia you're only a prisoner at large. You can't desert without bein' took back at once. I'm fair sick of it."

"You have been in Be—England?"

"W'y, I only come out last troopin' season with my mother. I should think I 'ave been in England. What a ignorant little beggar you are. You was brought up in the gutter, wasn't you?"

"Oah yess. Tell me something about England. My father he came from there."

Though he would not say so, Kim of course disbelieved every word the drummer-boy spoke about the Liverpool suburb which was his England. It passed the heavy time till dinner—a most unappetising meal served to the boys and a few invalids in a corner of a barrack-room. But that he had written to Mahbub Ali, Kim would have been almost depressed. The indifference of native crowds he was used to; but this strong loneliness among white men preyed on him. He was grateful when, in the course of the afternoon, a big soldier took him over to Father Victor, who lived in another wing across another dusty parade-ground. The priest was reading an English letter written in purple ink. He looked at Kim more curiously than ever.

"An' how do you like it, my son, as far as you've gone? Not much, eh? It must be hard—very hard on a wild animal. Listen now. I've an amazin' epistle from your friend."

"Where is he? Is he well? Oah! If he knows to write me letters, it is all right."

"You're fond of him then?"

"Of course I am fond of him. He was fond of me."

"It seems so by the look of this. He can't write English, can he?"

"Oah no. Not that I know, but of course he found a letter-writer who can write English verree well, and so he wrote. I do hope you understand."

"That accounts for it. D'you know anything about his money affairs?" Kim's face showed that he did not.

"How can I tell?"

"That's what I'm askin'. Now listen if you can make head or tail o' this. We'll skip the first part. . . . It's written from Jagadhir Road. . . . 'Sitting on wayside in grave meditation, trusting to be favoured with your Honour's applause of present step, which recommend your Honour to execute for Almighty God's sake. Education is greatest blessing if of best sorts. Otherwise no earthly use.' Faith, the old man's hit the bull's-eye that time! 'If your Honour condescending giving my boy best educations Xavier' (I suppose that's St. Xavier in Partibus) 'in terms of our conversation dated in your tent 15th instant' (a business-like touch there!) 'then Almighty God blessing your Honour's succeedings to third an' fourth generation and'—now listen!—'confide in your Honour's humble servant for adequate remuneration per hoondie per annum three hundred rupees a year to one expensive education St. Xavier, Lucknow, and allow small time to forward same per hoondie sent to any part of India as your Honour shall address yourself. This servant of your Honour has presently no place to lay crown of his head, but going to Benares by train on account of persecution of old woman talking so much and unanxious residing Saharunpore in any domestic capacity.' Now what in the world does that mean?"

"She has asked him to be puro—her clergyman—at Saharunpore, I think. He would not do that on account of his River. She did talk."

"It's clear to you, is it? It beats me altogether. 'So going to Benares, where will find address and forward rupees for boy who is apple of eye, and for Almighty God's sake execute this education, and your petitioner as in duty bound shall ever awfully pray. Written by Sobrao Satai, Failed Entrance Allahabad University, for Venerable Teshoo Lama the priest of Suchzen looking for a River, address care of Tirthankers' Temple, Benares. P.M.—Please note boy is apple of eye, and rupees shall be sent per hoondie three hundred per annum. For God Almighty's sake.' Now, is that ravin' lunacy or a business proposition? I ask you, because I'm fairly at my wits' end."

"He says he will give me three hundred rupees a year, so he will give me them."

"Oh, that's the way you look at it, is it?"

"Of course. If he says so!"

The priest whistled; then he addressed Kim as an equal.

"I don't believe it; but we'll see. You were goin' off to-day to the Military Orphanage at Sanawar, where the regiment would keep you till you were old enough to enlist. Ye'd be brought up to the Church of England. Bennett arranged for that. On the other hand, if ye go to St. Xavier's ye'll get a better education an'—an' can have the religion. D'ye see my dilemma?"

Kim saw nothing save a vision of the lama going south in a train with none to beg for him.

"Like most people, I'm going to temporise. If your friend sends the money from Benares—Powers of Darkness below, where's a street-beggar to raise three hundred rupees?—ye'll go down to Lucknow and I'll pay your fare, because I can't touch the subscription money if I intend, as I do, to make ye a Catholic. If he doesn't, ye'll go to the Military Orphanage at the regiment's expense. I'll allow him three days' grace, though I don't believe it at all. Even then, if he fails in his payments later on . . . but it's beyond me. We can only walk one step at a time in this world, praise God! An' they sent Bennett to the front an' left me behind. Bennett can't expect anything."

"Oah yess," said Kim vaguely.

The priest leaned forward. "I'd give a month's pay to find what's goin' on inside that little round head of yours."

"There is nothing," said Kim, and scratched it. He was wondering whether Mahbub Ali would send him as much as a whole rupee. Then he could pay the letter-writer and write letters to the lama at Benares. Perhaps Mahbub Ali would visit him next time he came south with horses. Surely he must know that Kim's delivery of the letter to the officer at Umballa had caused the great war which the men and boys had discussed so loudly over the barrack dinner-tables. But if Mahbub Ali did not know this, it would be very unsafe to tell him so. Mahbub Ali was hard upon boys who knew, or thought they knew, too much.

"Well, till I get further news"—Father Victor's voice interrupted the reverie—"ye can run along and play with the other boys. They'll teach ye something—but I don't think ye'll like it."

The day dragged to its weary end. When he wished to sleep he was instructed how to fold up his clothes and set out his boots; the other boys deriding. Bugles waked him in the dawn; the schoolmaster caught him after breakfast, thrust a page of meaningless characters under his nose, gave them senseless names, and whacked him without reason. Kim meditated poisoning him with opium borrowed from a barrack-sweeper, but reflected that, as they all ate at one table in public (this was peculiarly revolting to Kim, who preferred to turn his back on the world at his meals), the stroke might be dangerous. Then he attempted running off to the village where the priest had tried to drug the lama—the village where the old soldier lived. But far-seeing sentries at every exit headed back the little scarlet figure. Trousers and jacket crippled body and mind alike, so he abandoned the project and fell back, Oriental fashion, on time and chance. Three days of torment passed in the big, echoing white rooms. He walked out of afternoons under escort of the drummer-boy, and all he heard from his companion were the few useless words which seemed to make two-thirds of the white man's abuse. Kim knew and despised them all long ago. The boy resented his silence and lack of interest by beating him, as was only natural. He did not care for any of the bazars which were in bounds. He styled all natives "niggers"; yet servants and sweepers called him abominable names to his face, and, misled by their deferential attitude, he never understood. This somewhat consoled Kim for the beatings.

On the morning of the fourth day a judgment overtook that drummer. They had gone out together towards Umballa race-course. He returned alone, weeping, with news that young O'Hara, to whom he had been doing nothing in particular, had hailed a scarlet-bearded nigger on horseback; that the nigger had then and there laid into him with a peculiarly adhesive quirt, picked up young O'Hara, and borne him off at full gallop.

These tidings came to Father Victor, and he drew down his long upper lip. He was already sufficiently startled by a letter from the Temple of the Tirthankers at Benares, enclosing a native banker's note of hand for three hundred rupees, and an amazing prayer to "Almighty God." The lama would have been more annoyed than the priest had he known how the bazar letter-writer had translated his phrase "to acquire merit."

"Powers of Darkness below!" Father Victor fumbled with the note. "An' now he's off with another of his peep-o'-day friends. I don't know whether it will be a greater relief to me to get him back or to have him lost. He's beyond my comprehension. How the Divil—yes, He's the man I mean—can a street-beggar raise money to educate white boys?"

Three miles off, on Umballa race-course, Mahbub Ali, reining a gray Cabuli stallion with Kim in front of him, was saying:

"But, Little Friend of all the World, there is my honour and reputation to be considered. All the officer-sahibs in all the regiments, and all Umballa, know Mahbub Ali. Men saw me pick thee up and chastise that boy. We are seen now from far across this plain. How can I take thee away, or account for thy disappearing if I set thee down and let thee run off into the crops? They would put me in jail. Be patient. Once a Sahib, always a Sahib. When thou art a man—who knows—thou wilt be grateful to Mahbub Ali."

"Take me beyond their sentries where I can change this red. Give me money and I will go to Benares and be with my lama again. I do not want to be a Sahib, and remember I did deliver that message."

The stallion bounded wildly. Mahbub Ali had incautiously driven home the sharp-edged stirrup. (He was not the new sort of fluent horse-dealer who wears English boots and spurs.) Kim drew his own conclusions from that betrayal.

"That was a small matter. It lay on the straight road to Benares. I and the Sahib have by this time forgotten it. I send so many letters and messages to men who ask questions about horses, I cannot well remember one from the other. Was it some matter of a bay mare that Peters Sahib wished the pedigree of?"

Kim saw the trap at once. If he had said "bay mare" Mahbub would have know by his very readiness to fall in with the amendment that the boy suspected something. Kim replied therefore:

"Bay mare? No. I do not forget my messages thus. It was a white stallion."

"Ay, so it was. A white Arab stallion. But thou didst write bay mare to me."

"Who cares to tell truth to a letter-writer?" Kim answered, feeling Mahbub's palm on his heart.

"Hi! Mahbub, you old villain, pull up!" cried a voice, and an English-man raced alongside on a little polo-pony. "I've been chasing you half over the country. That Cabuli of yours can go. For sale, I suppose?"

"I have some young stuff coming on made by Heaven for the delicate and difficult polo-game. He has no equal. He—"

"Plays polo and waits at table. Yes. We know all that. What the deuce have you got there?"

"A boy," said Mahbub gravely. "He was being beaten by another boy. His father was once a white soldier in the big war. The boy was a child in Lahore city. He played with my horses when he was a babe. Now I think they will make him a soldier. He has been newly caught by his father's regiment that went up to the war last week. But I do not think he wants to be a soldier. I take him for a ride. Tell me where thy barracks are and I will set thee there."

"Let me go. I can find the barracks alone."

"And if thou runnest away who will say it is not my fault?"

"He'll run back to his dinner. Where has he to run to?" the English-man asked.

"He was born in the land. He has friends. He goes where he chooses. He is a chabuk sawai (a sharp chap). It needs only to change his clothing, and in a twinkling he would be a low-caste Hindi boy."

"The deuce he would!" The Englishman looked critically at the boy as Mahbub headed towards the barracks. Kim ground his teeth. Mahbub was mocking him, as faithless Afghans will; for he went on:

"They will send him to a school and put heavy boots on his feet and swaddle him in these clothes. Then he will forget all he knows. Now which of the barracks is thine?"

Kim pointed—he could not speak—to Father Victor's wing, all staring white near by.

"Perhaps he will make a good soldier," said Mahbub reflectively. "He will make a good orderly at least. I sent him to deliver a message once from Lahore. A message concerning the pedigree of a white stallion."

Here was deadly insult on deadlier injury—and the Sahib to whom he had so craftily given that war-making letter heard it all. Kim beheld Mahbub Ali frying in flame for his treachery, but for himself he saw one long gray vista of barracks, schools, and barracks again. He gazed implor-ingly at the clear-cut face in which there was no glimmer of recognition; but even at this extremity it never occurred to him to throw himself on the white man's mercy or to denounce the Afghan. And Mahbub stared deliberately at the Englishman, who stared as deliberately at Kim, quiver-ing and tongue-tied.

"My horse is well trained," said the dealer. "Others would have kicked, Sahib."

"Ah," said the Englishman at last, rubbing his pony's damp withers with his whip-butt. "Who makes the boy a soldier?"

"He says the regiment that found him, and especially the padre-sahib of that regiment."

"There is the padre!" Kim choked as bare-headed Father Victor sailed down upon them from the veranda.

"Powers o' Darkness below, O'Hara! How many more mixed friends do you keep in Asia?" he cried, as Kim slid down and stood helplessly before him.

"Good morning, Padre," the Colonel said cheerily. "I know you by reputation well enough. Meant to have come over and called before this. I'm Creighton."

"Of the Ethnological Survey?" said Father Victor. The Colonel nodded. "Faith I'm glad to meet ye then; an' I owe you some thanks for bringing back the boy."

"No thanks to me, Padre. Besides, the boy wasn't going away. You don't know old Mahbub Ali"—the horse-dealer sat impassive in the sunlight. "You will when you have been in the station a month. He sells us all our crocks. That boy is rather a curiosity. Can you tell me anything about him?"

"Can I tell you?" puffed Father Victor. "You'll be the one man that could help me in my quandaries. Tell you! Powers o' Darkness, I'm bursting to tell some one who knows something o' the native!"

A groom came round the corner. Colonel Creighton raised his voice, speaking in Urdu. "Very good, Mahbub Ali, but what is the use of telling me all those stories about the pony. Not one pie more than three hundred and fifty rupees will I give."

"The Sahib is a little hot and angry after riding," the horse-dealer returned, with the leer of a privileged jester. "Presently, he will see my horse's points more clearly. I will wait till he has finished his talk with the padre. I will wait under that tree."

"Confound you!" The Colonel laughed. "That comes of looking at one of Mahbub's horses. He's a regular old leech, Padre. Wait then, if thou hast so much time to spare, Mahbub. Now I'm at your service, Padre. Where is the boy? Oh, he's gone off to collogue with Mahbub. Queer sort of boy. Might I ask you to send my mare round under cover?"

He dropped into a chair which commanded a clear view of Kim and Mahbub Ali in conference beneath the tree. The padre went indoors for cheroots.

Creighton heard Kim say bitterly: "Trust a Brahmin before a snake, and a snake before a harlot, and a harlot before an Afghan, Mahbub Ali."

"That is all one," the great red beard wagged solemnly. "Children should not see a carpet on the loom till the pattern is made plain. Believe me, Friend of all the World, I do thee great service. They will not make a soldier of thee."

"You crafty old sinner," thought Creighton. "But you're not far wrong. That boy mustn't be wasted if he is as advertised."

"Excuse me half a minute," cried the padre from within, "but I'm gettin' the documents of the case."

"If through me the favour of this bold and wise Colonel Sahib comes to thee, and thou art raised to honour, what thanks wilt thou give Mahbub Ali when thou art a man?"

"Nay, nay; I begged thee to let me take the road again, where I should have been safe; and thou hast sold me back to the English. What will they give thee for blood-money?"

"A cheerful young demon!" The Colonel bit his cigar, and turned politely to Father Victor.

"What are the letters that the fat priest is waving before the Colonel? Stand behind the stallion as though looking at my bridle!" said Mahbub Ali.

"A letter from my lama which he wrote from Jagadhir Road, saying that he will pay three hundred rupees by the year for my schooling."

"Oho! Is old Red Hat of that sort? At which school?"

"God knows. I think in Nucklao."

"Yes. There is a big school there for the sons of Sahibs—and half-Sahibs. I have seen it when I sell horses there. So the lama also loved the Friend of all the World?"

"Ay; and he did not tell lies, or return me to captivity."

"Small wonder the padre does not know how to unravel the thread. How fast he talks to the Colonel Sahib." Mahbub Ali chuckled. "By Allah!"—the keen eyes swept the veranda for an instant—"thy lama has sent what to me looks like a note of hand. I have had some small dealing in hoondies. The Colonel Sahib is looking at it."

"What good is all this to me?" said Kim wearily. "Thou wilt go away, and they will return me to those empty rooms where there is no good place to sleep and where the boys beat me."

"I do not think that. Have patience, child. All Pathans are not faithless —except in horseflesh."

Five—ten—fifteen minutes passed, Father Victor talking energetically or asking questions which the Colonel answered.

"Now I've told you everything that I know about the boy from beginnin' to end; and it's a blessed relief to me. Did ye ever hear the like?"

"At any rate, the old man has sent the money. Gobind Sahia's notes of hand are good from here to China," said the Colonel. "The more one knows about natives the less can one say what they will or won't do."

"That's consolin'—from the head of the Ethnological Survey. It's this mixture of Red Bulls and Rivers of Healing (poor heathen, God help him!) an' notes of hand and Masonic certificates. Are you a Mason, by any chance?"

"By Jove, I am, now I come to think of it. That's an additional reason," said the Colonel absently.

"I'm glad ye see a reason in it. But as I said, it's the mixture o' things that's beyond me. An' his prophesyin' to our Colonel sitting on my bed with his little shimmy torn open showing his white skin; an' the prophecy comin' true! They'll cure all that nonsense at St. Xavier's, eh?"

"Sprinkle him with holy water," the Colonel laughed.

"On my word, I fancy I ought to sometimes. But I'm hoping he'll be brought up as a good Catholic. All that troubles me is what'll happen if the old beggar-man—"

"Lama, lama, my dear sir; and some of them are gentlemen in their own country."

"The lama, then, fails to pay next year. He's a fine business head to plan on the spur of the moment, but he's bound to die some day. An' takin' a heathen's money to give a child a Christian education—"

"But he said explicitly what he wanted. As soon as he knew the boy was white he seems to have made his arrangements accordingly. I'd give a month's pay to hear how he explained it all at the Tirthankers' Temple at Benares. Look here, Padre, I don't pretend to know much about natives, but if he says he'll pay, he'll pay—dead or alive. I mean his heirs will assume the debt. My advice to you is, send the boy down to Lucknow. If your Anglican chaplain thinks you've stolen a march on him—"

"Bad luck to Bennett! He was sent to the front instead o' me. Doughty certified me medically unfit. I'll excommunicate Doughty if he comes back alive! Surely Bennett ought to be content with—"

"Glory, leaving you the religion. Quite so! As a matter of fact I don't think Bennett will mind. Put the blame on me. I—er—strongly recommend sending the boy to St. Xavier's. He can go down on pass as a soldier's orphan, so the railway fare will be saved. You can buy him an outfit from the regimental subscription. The Lodge will be saved the expense of his education, and that will put the Lodge in a good temper. It's perfectly easy. I've got to go down to Lucknow next week. I'll look after the boy on the way—give him in charge of my servants, and so on."

"You're a good man."

"Not in the least. Don't make that mistake. The lama has sent us money for a definite end. We can't very well return it. We shall have to do as he says. Well, that's settled, isn't it? Shall we say that, Tuesday next, you'll hand him over to me at the night train south? That's only three days. He can't do much harm in three days."

"It's a weight off my mind, but—this thing here?"—he waved the note of hand—"I don't know Gobind Sahai: or his bank, which may be a hole in a wall."

"You've never been a subaltern in debt. I'll cash it if you like, and send you the vouchers in proper order."

"But with all your own work too! It's askin'—"

"It's not the least trouble indeed. You see, as an ethnologist, the thing's very interesting to me. I'd like to make a note of it for some Government work that I'm doing. The transformation of a regimental badge like your Red Bull into a sort of fetish that the boy follows is very interesting."

"But I can't thank you enough."

"There's one thing you can do. All we Ethnological men are as jealous as jackdaws of one another's discoveries. They're of no interest to any one but ourselves, of course, but you know what book-collectors are like. Well, don't say a word, directly or indirectly, about the Asiatic side of the boy's character—his adventures and his prophecy, and so on. I'll worm them out of the boy later on and—you see?"

"I do. Ye'll make a wonderful account of it. Never a word will I say to any one till I see it in print."

"Thank you. That goes straight to an ethnologist's heart. Well, I must be getting back to my breakfast. Good heavens! Old Mahbub here still?" He raised his voice, and the horse-dealer came out from under the shadow of the tree. "Well, what is it?"

"As regards that young horse," said Mahbub, "I say that when a colt is born to be a polo-pony, closely following the ball without teaching—when such a colt knows the game by divination—then I say it is a great wrong to break that colt to a heavy cart, Sahib!"

"So do I say also, Mahbub. The colt will be entered for polo only. (These fellows think of nothing in the world but horses, Padre.) I'll see you to-morrow, Mahbub, if you've anything likely for sale."

The dealer saluted, horseman fashion, with a sweep of the off hand. "Be patient a little, Friend of all the World," he whispered to the agonised Kim. "Thy fortune is made. In a little while thou goest to Nucklao, and—here is something to pay the letter-writer. I shall see thee again, I think, many times," and he cantered off down the road.

"Listen to me," said the Colonel from the veranda, speaking in the vernacular. "In three days thou wilt go with me to Lucknow, seeing and hearing new things all the while. Therefore sit still for three days and do not run away. Thou wilt go to school at Lucknow."

"Shall I meet my Holy One there?" Kim whimpered.

"At least Lucknow is nearer to Benares than Umballa. It may be thou wilt go under my protection. Mahbub Ali knows this, and he will be angry if thou returnest to the road now. Remember—much has been told to me which I do not forget."

"I will wait," said Kim, "but the boys will beat me."

Then the bugles blew for dinner.

Chapter 7

Unto whose use the pregnant suns are poised
With idiot moons and stars retracting stars?
Creep thou betweene—thy coming's all unnoised.
Heaven hath her high, as earth her baser, wars.
Heir to these tumults, this affright, that fray
(By Adam's, fathers, own, sin bound alway);
Peer up, draw out thy horoscope and say
Which planet mends thy threadbare fate or mars!

Sir John Christie.

In the afternoon the red-faced schoolmaster told Kim that he had been "struck off the strength," which conveyed no meaning to him till he was ordered to go away and play. Then he ran to the bazar, and found the young letter-writer to whom he owed a stamp.

"Now I pay," said Kim royally, "and now I need another letter to be written."

"Mahbub Ali is in Umballa," said the writer jauntily. He was, by virtue of his office, a bureau of general misinformation.

"This is not to Mahbub, but to a priest. Take thy pen and write quickly. 'To Teshoo Lama, the holy one from Bhotiyal seeking for a River, who is now in the Temple of the Tirthankers at Benares.' Take more ink! 'In three days I am to go down to Nucklao to the school at Nucklao. The name of the school is Xavier. I do not know where that school is, but it is at Nucklao.'"

"But I know Nucklao," the writer interrupted. "I know the school."

"Tell him where it is, and I give half an anna."

The reed pen scratched busily. "He cannot mistake." The man lifted his head. "Who watches us across the street?"

Kim looked up hurriedly and saw Colonel Creighton in tennis-flannels.

"Oh, that is some Sahib who knows the fat priest in the barracks. He is beckoning me."

"What dost thou?" said the Colonel, when Kim trotted up.

"I—I am not running away. I send a letter to my Holy One at Benares."

"I had not thought of that. Hast thou said that I take thee to Lucknow?"

"Nay, I have not. Read the letter, if there be a doubt."

"Then why hast thou left out my name in writing to that Holy One?" The Colonel smiled a queer smile. Kim took his courage in both hands.

"It was said once to me that it is inexpedient to write the names of strangers concerned in any matter, because by the naming of names many good plans are brought to confusion."

"Thou has been well taught," the Colonel replied, and Kim flushed. "I have left my cheroot-case in the padre's veranda. Bring it to my house this even."

"Where is the house?" said Kim. His quick wit told him that he was being tested in some fashion or another, and he stood on guard.

"Ask any one in the big bazar." The Colonel walked on.

"He has forgotten his cheroot-case," said Kim, returning. "I must bring it to him this evening. That is all my letter except, thrice over, 'Come to me! Come to me! Come to me!' Now I will pay for a stamp and put it in the post." He rose to go, and as an afterthought asked, "Who is that angry-faced Sahib who lost the cheroot-case?"

"Oh, he is only Creighton Sahib—a very foolish Sahib, who is a Colonel Sahib without a regiment."

"What is his business?"

"God knows. He is always buying horses which he cannot ride, and asking riddles about the works of God—such as plants and stones and the customs of people. The dealers call him the father of fools, because he is so easily cheated about a horse. Mahbub Ali says he is madder than all other Sahibs."

"Oh!" said Kim, and departed. His training had given him some small knowledge of character, and he argued that fools are not given information which leads to calling out eight thousand men, besides guns. The Commander-in-Chief of all India does not talk, as Kim had heard him talk, to fools. Nor would Mahbub Ali's tone have changed, as it did every time he mentioned the Colonel's name, if the Colonel had been a fool. Consequently—and this set Kim to skipping—there was a mystery some-where, and Mahbub Ali probably spied for the Colonel much as Kim had spied for Mahbub. And, like the horse-dealer, the Colonel evidently respected people who did not show themselves to be too clever.

He rejoiced that he had not betrayed his knowledge of the Colonel's house; and when, on his return to barracks, he discovered that no cheroot-case had been left behind, he beamed with delight. Here was a man after his own heart—a tortuous and indirect person playing a hidden game. Well, if he could be a fool, so could Kim.

He showed nothing of his mind when Father Victor, for three long mornings, discoursed to him of an entirely new set of gods and godlings—notably of a goddess called Mary, who, he gathered, was one with Bibi Miriam of Mahbub Ali's theology. He betrayed no emotion when, after the lecture, Father Victor dragged him from shop to shop buying articles of outfit, nor when envious drummer-boys kicked him because he was going to a superior school did he complain, but awaited the play of circumstances with an interested soul. Father Victor, good man, took him to the station, put him into an empty second-class next to Colonel Creighton's first, and bade him farewell with genuine feeling.

"They'll make a man o' you, O'Hara, at St. Xavier's—a white man, an', I hope, a good man. They know all about your comin', an' the Colonel will see that ye're not lost or mislaid anywhere on the road. I've given you a notion of religious matters,—at least I hope so,—and you'll remember, when they ask you your religion, that you're a Cath'lic. Better say Roman Cath'lic, tho' I'm not fond of the word."

Kim lit a rank cigarette—he had been careful to buy a stock in the bazar—and lay down to think. This solitary passage was very different from that joyful down-journey in the third-class with the lama. "Sahibs get little pleasure of travel," he reflected. "Hai mai! I go from one place to another as it might be a kickball. It is my Kismet. No man can escape his Kismet. But I am to pray to Bibi Miriam and I am a Sahib"—he looked at his boots ruefully. "No; I am Kim. This is the great world, and I am only Kim. Who is Kim?" He considered his own identity, a thing he had never done before, till his head swam. He was one insignificant person in all this roaring whirl of India, going southward to he knew not what fate.

Presently the Colonel sent for him, and talked for a long time. So far as Kim could gather, he was to be diligent and enter the Survey of India as a chain-man. If he were very good, and passed the proper examinations, he would be earning thirty rupees a month at seventeen years old, and Colonel Creighton would see that he found a suitable employment.

Kim pretended at first to understand perhaps one word in three of this talk. Then the Colonel, seeing his mistake, turned to fluent and picturesque Urdu and Kim was contented. No man could be a fool who knew the language so intimately, who moved so gently and silently, and whose eyes were so different from the dull fat eyes of other Sahibs.

"Yes, and thou must learn how to make pictures of roads and mountains and rivers—to carry these pictures in thy eye till a suitable time comes to set them upon paper. Perhaps some day, when thou art a chain-man, I may say to thee when we are working together: 'Go across those hills and see what lies beyond.' Then one will say: 'There are bad people living in those hills who will slay the chain-man if he be seen to look like a Sahib.' What then?"

Kim thought. Would it be safe to return the Colonel's lead?

"I would tell what the other man had said."

"But if I answered: 'I will give thee a hundred rupees for knowledge of what is behind those hills—for a picture of a river and a little news of what the people say in the villages there'?"

"How can I tell? I am only a boy. Wait till I am a man." Then, seeing the Colonel's brow clouded, he went on: "But I think I should in a few days earn the hundred rupees."

"By what road?"

Kim shook his head resolutely. "If I said how I would earn them, another man might hear and forestall me. It is no good to sell knowledge for nothing."

"Tell now." The Colonel held up a rupee. Kim's hand half reached towards it, and dropped.

"Nay, Sahib; nay. I know the price that will be paid for the answer, but I do not know why the question is asked."

"Take it for a gift, then," said Creighton, tossing it over. "There is a good spirit in thee. Do not let it be blunted at St. Xavier's. There are many boys there who despise the black men."

"Their mothers were bazar-women," said Kim. He knew well there is no hatred like that of the half-caste for his brother-in-law.

"True; but thou art a Sahib and the son of a Sahib. Therefore, do not at any time be led to contemn the black men. I have known boys newly entered into the service of the Government who feigned not to understand the talk or the customs of black men. Their pay was cut for ignorance. There is no sin so great as ignorance. Remember this."

Several times in the course of the long twenty-four hours' run south did the Colonel send for Kim, always developing this latter text.

"We be all on one lead-rope, then," said Kim at last, "the Colonel, Mahbub Ali, and I—when I become a chain-man. He will use me as Mahbub Ali employed me, I think. That is good, if it allows me to return to the road again. This clothing grows no easier by wear."

When they came to the crowded Lucknow station there was no sign of the lama. He swallowed his disappointment, while the Colonel bundled him into a ticca-garri with his neat belongings and despatched him alone to St. Xavier's.

"I do not say farewell, because we shall meet again," he cried. "Again, and many times, if thou art one of good spirit. But thou art not yet tried."

"Not when I brought thee"—Kim actually dared to use the tum of equals—"a white stallion's pedigree that night?"

"Much is gained by forgetting, little brother," said the Colonel, with a look that pierced through Kim's shoulder-blades as he scuttled into the carriage.

It took him nearly five minutes to recover. Then he sniffed the new air appreciatively. "A rich city," he said. "Richer than Lahore. How good the bazars must be! Coachman, drive me a little through the bazars here."

"My order is to take thee to the school." The driver used the "thou," which is rudeness when applied to a white man. In the clearest and most fluent vernacular Kim pointed out his error, climbed on to the box-seat, and, perfect understanding established, drove for a couple of hours up and down, estimating, comparing, and enjoying. There is no city—except Bombay, the queen of all—more beautiful in her garish style than Lucknow, whether you see her from the bridge over the river, or from the top of the Imambara looking down on the gilt umbrellas of the Chutter Munzil, and the trees in which the town is bedded. Kings have adorned her with fantastic buildings, endowed her with charities, crammed her with pensioners, and drenched her with blood. She is the centre of all idleness, intrigue, and luxury, and shares with Delhi the claim to talk the only pure Urdu.

"A fair city—a beautiful city." The driver, as a Lucknow man, was pleased with the compliment, and told Kim many astounding things where an English guide would have talked of the Mutiny.

"Now we will go to the school," said Kim at last. The great old school of St. Xavier's in Partibus, block on block of low white buildings, stands in vast grounds over against the Gumti River, at some distance from the city.

"What like of folk are they within?" said Kim.

"Young Sahibs—all devils; but to speak truth, and I drive many of them to and fro from the railway station, I have never seen one that had in him the making of a more perfect devil than thou—this young Sahib whom I am now driving."

Naturally, for he was never trained to consider them in any way improper, Kim had passed the time of day with one or two frivolous ladies at upper windows in a certain street, and naturally, in the exchange of compliments, had acquitted himself well. He was about to acknowledge the driver's last insolence, when his eye—it was growing dusk—caught a figure sitting by one of the white plaster gate-pillars in the long sweep of wall.

"Stop!" he cried. "Stay here! I do not go to the school at once."

"But what is to pay me for this coming and recoming?" said the driver petulantly. "Is the boy mad? Last time it was a dancing-girl. This time it is a priest."

Kim was in the road headlong, patting the dusty feet beneath the dirty yellow robe.

"I have waited here a day and a half," the lama's level voice began. "Nay, I had a disciple with me. He that was my friend at the Temple of the Tirthankers gave me a guide for this journey. I came from Benares in the train, when thy letter was given me. Yes, I am well fed. I need nothing."

"But why didst thou not stay with the Kulu woman, O Holy One? In what way didst thou get to Benares? My heart has been heavy since we parted."

"The woman wearied me by constant flux of talk and requiring charms for children. I separated myself from that company, permitting her to acquire merit by gifts. She is at least a woman of open hands, and I made a promise to return to her house if need arose. Then, perceiving myself alone in this great and terrible world, I bethought me of the te-rain to Benares, where I knew one abode in the Tirthankers' Temple who was a Seeker, even as I."

"Ah! Thy River," said Kim. "I had forgotten the River."

"So soon, my chela? I have never forgotten it; but when I had left thee it seemed better that I should go to the temple and take counsel, for, look you, India is very large, and it may be that wise men before us, some two or three, have left a record of the place of our River. There is debate in the Temple of the Tirthankers on this matter; some saying one thing, and some another. They are courteous folk."

"So be it; but what dost thou do now?"

"I acquire merit in that I help thee, my chela, to wisdom. The priest of that body of men who serve the Red Bull wrote me that all should be as I desired for thee. I sent the money to suffice for one year, and then I came, as thou seest me, to watch for thee going up into the Gates of Learning. A day and a half have I waited—not because I was led by any affection towards thee—that is not part of the Way—but, as they said at the Tirthankers' Temple, because, money having been paid for learning, it was right that I should oversee the end of the matter. They resolved my doubts most clearly. I had a fear that, perhaps, I came because I wished to see thee—misguided by the red mist of affection. It is not so. . . . Moreover, I am troubled by a dream."

"But surely, Holy One, thou hast not forgotten the Road and all that befell on it. Surely it was a little to see me that thou didst come?"

"The horses are cold, and it is past their feeding-time," whined the driver.

"Go to Jehannum and abide there with thy reputationless aunt!" Kim snarled over his shoulder. "I am all alone in this land; I know not where

I go nor what shall befall me. My heart was in that letter I sent thee. Except for Mahbub Ali, and he is a Pathan, I have no friend save thee, Holy One. Do not altogether go away."

"I have considered that also," the lama replied, in a shaking voice. "It is manifest that from time to time I shall acquire merit—if before that I have not found my River—by assuring myself that thy feet are set on wisdom. What they will teach thee I do not know, but the priest wrote me that no son of a Sahib in all India will be better taught than thou. So from time to time, therefore, I will come again. May be thou will be such a Sahib as he who gave me these spectacles"—the lama wiped them elaborately—"in the Wonder House at Lahore. That is my hope, for he was a Fountain of Wisdom—wiser than many abbots. . . . Again, may be thou wilt forget me and our meetings."

"If I eat thy bread," cried Kim passionately, "how shall I ever forget thee?"

"No—no." He put the boy aside. "I must go back to Benares. From time to time, now that I know the customs of letter-writers in this land, I will send thee a letter, and from time to time I will come and see thee."

"But whither shall I send my letters?" wailed Kim, clutching at the robe, all forgetful that he was a Sahib.

"To the Temple of the Tirthankers at Benares. That is the place I have chosen till I find my River. Do not weep; for, look you, all Desire is illusion and a new binding upon the Wheel. Go up to the Gates of Learning. Let me see thee go. . . . Dost thou love me? Then go, or my heart cracks. . . . I will come again. Surely I will come again."

The lama watched the ticca-garri rumble into the compound, and strode off, snuffing between each long stride.

"The Gates of Learning" shut with a clang.

The country born and bred boy has his own manners and customs, which do not resemble those of any other land; and his teachers approach him by roads which an English master would not understand. Therefore, you would scarcely be interested in Kim's experiences as a St. Xavier's boy among two or three hundred precocious youths, most of whom had never seen the sea. He suffered the usual penalties for breaking out of bounds when there was cholera in the city. This was before he had learned to write fair English, and so was obliged to find a bazar letter-writer. He was, of course, indicted for smoking and for the use of abuse more full-flavoured than even St. Xavier's had ever heard. He learned to wash himself with the Levitical scrupulosity of the native-born, who in his heart considers the Englishman rather dirty. He played the usual tricks on the patient coolies pulling the punkahs in the sleeping-rooms where the boys thrashed through the hot nights telling tales till the dawn; and quietly he measured himself against his self-reliant mates.

They were sons of subordinate officials in the Railway, Telegraph, and Canal services; of warrant-officers sometimes retired and sometimes acting as commanders-in-chief to a feudatory Rajah's army; of captains of the Indian Marine, Government pensioners, planters, Presidency shopkeepers, and missionaries. A few were cadets of the old Eurasian houses that have taken strong root in Dhurrumtollah—Pereiras, De Souzas, and D'Silvas. Their parents could well have educated them in England, but they loved the school that had served their own youth, and generation followed sallow-hued generation at St. Xavier's. Their homes ranged from Howrah of the railway people to abandoned cantonments like Monghyr and Chunar; lost tea-gardens Shillong-way; villages where their fathers were large land-holders in Oudh or the Deccan; Mission-stations a week from the nearest railway line; seaports a thousand miles south, facing the brazen Indian surf; and cinchona-plantations south of all. The mere story of their adventures, which to them were no adventures, on their road to and from school would have crisped a Western boy's hair. They were used to jogging off alone through a hundred miles of jungle, where there was always the delightful chance of being delayed by tigers; but they would no more have bathed in the English Channel in an English August than their brothers across the world would have lain still while a leopard snuffed at their palanquin. There were boys of fifteen who had spent a day and a half on an islet in the middle of a flooded river, taking charge, as by right, of a camp of frantic pilgrims returning from a shrine; there were seniors who had requisitioned a chance-met Rajah's elephant, in the name of St. Francis Xavier, when the rains once blotted out the cart-track that led to their father's estate, and had all but lost the huge beast in a quicksand. There was a boy who, he said, and none doubted, had helped his father to beat off with rifles from the veranda a rush of Akas in the days when those head-hunters were bold against lonely plantations.

And every tale was told in the even, passionless voice of the native-born, mixed with quaint reflections, borrowed unconsciously from native foster-mothers, and turns of speech that showed they had been that instant translated from the vernacular. Kim watched, listened, and approved. This was not insipid, single-word talk of drummer-boys. It dealt with a life he knew and in part understood. The atmosphere suited him, and he throve by inches. They gave him a white drill suit as the weather warmed, and he rejoiced in the new-found bodily comforts as he rejoiced to use his sharpened mind over the tasks they set him. His quickness would have delighted an English master; but at St. Xavier's they know the first rush of minds developed by sun and surroundings, as well as they know the half-collapse that sets in at twenty-two or twenty-three.

None the less he remembered to hold himself lowly. When tales were told of hot nights, Kim did not sweep the board with his reminiscences; for St. Xavier's looks down on boys who "go native altogether." One must never forget that one is a Sahib, and that some day, when examinations are passed, one will command natives. Kim made a note of this, for he began to understand where examinations led.

Then came the holidays from August to October—the long holidays imposed by the heat and the rains. Kim was informed that he would go north to some station in the hills behind Umballa, where Father Victor would arrange for him.

"A barrack-school?" said Kim, who had asked many questions and thought more.

"Yes, I suppose so," said the master. "It will not do you any harm to keep you out of mischief. You can go up with young De Castro as far as Delhi."

Kim considered it in every possible light. He had been diligent, even as the Colonel advised. A boy's holiday was his own property,—of so much the talk of his companions had advised him,—and a barrack-school would be torment after St. Xavier's. Moreover—this was magic worth anything else—he could write. In three months he had discovered how men can speak to each other without a third party, at the cost of half an anna and a little knowledge. No word had come from the lama, but there remained the Road. Kim yearned for the caress of soft mud squishing up between the toes, as his mouth watered for mutton stewed with butter and cabbages, for rice speckled with strong-scented cardamoms, for the saffron-tinted rice, garlic and onions, and the forbidden greasy sweetmeats of the bazars. They would feed him raw beef on a platter at the barrack-school, and he must smoke by stealth. But again, he was a Sahib and was at St. Xavier's, and that pig Mahbub Ali . . . No, he would not test Mahbub's hospitality—and yet . . . He thought it out alone in the dormitory, and came to the conclusion he had been unjust to Mahbub.

The school was empty; nearly all the masters had gone away; Colonel Creighton's railway-pass lay in his hand, and Kim puffed himself that he had not spent Colonel Creighton's or Mahbub's money in riotous living. He was still lord of two rupees seven annas. His new bullock-trunk, marked "K. O'H.," and bedding-roll lay in the empty sleeping-room. "Sahibs are always tied to their baggage," said Kim, nodding at them. "You will stay here." He went out into the warm rain, smiling sinfully, and sought a certain house whose outside he had noted down some time before. . . .

"Arre! Dost thou know what manner of women we be in this quarter? O shame!"

"Was I born yesterday?" Kim squatted native fashion on the cushions of that upper room. "A little dye-stuff and three yards of cloth to help out a jest. Is it much to ask?"

"Who is she? Thou art full young, as Sahibs go, for this devilry."

"Oh, she? She is the daughter of a certain schoolmaster of a regiment in the cantonments. He has beaten me twice because I went over their wall in these clothes. Now I would go as a gardener's boy. Old men are very jealous."

"That is true. Hold thy face still while I dab on the juice."

"Not too black, Naikan. I would not appear to her as a hubshi" (nigger).

"Oh, love makes nought of these things. And how old is she?"

"Twelve years, I think," said the shameless Kim. "Spread it also on the breast. It may be her father will tear my clothes off me and if I am pie-bald—" he laughed.

The girl worked busily, dabbing a twist of cloth into a little saucer of brown dye that holds longer than any walnut juice.

"Now send out and get me a cloth for the turban. Woe is me, my head is all unshaved! And he will surely knock off my turban."

"I am not a barber, but I will make shift. Thou wast born to be a breaker of hearts! All this disguise for one evening? Remember, the stuff does not wash away." She shook with laughter till her bracelets and anklets jingled. "But who is to pay me for this? Huneefa herself could not have given thee better stuff."

"Trust in the Gods, my sister," said Kim gravely screwing his face round as the stain dried. "Besides, hast thou ever helped to paint a Sahib thus before?"

"Never indeed. But a jest is not money."

"It is worth much more."

"Child, thou art beyond all dispute the most shameless son of Shaitan that I have ever known to take up a poor girl's time with this play, and then to say: 'Is not the jest enough?' Thou wilt go very far in this world." She gave the dancing-girls' salutation in mockery.

"All one. Make haste and rough-cut my head." Kim shifted from foot to foot, his eyes ablaze with mirth as he thought of the fat days before him. He gave the girl four annas, and ran down the stairs in the likeness of a low-caste Hindu boy—perfect in every detail. A cookshop was his next point of call, where he feasted in extravagance and greasy luxury.

On Lucknow station platform he watched young De Castro, all covered with prickly-heat, get into a second-class compartment. Kim patronised a third, and was the life and soul of it. He explained to the company that he was assistant to a juggler who had left him behind sick with fever, and that he would pick up his master at Umballa. As the occupants of the carriage changed, he varied this tale, or adorned it with all the shoots of a budding fancy, the more rampant for being held off native speech so long. In all India that night was no human being so joyful as Kim. At Umballa he got out and headed eastward, plashing over the sodden fields to the village where the old soldier lived.

About this time Colonel Creighton at Simla was advised from Lucknow by wire that young O'Hara had disappeared. Mahbub Ali was in town selling horses, and to him the Colonel confided the affair one morning cantering around Annandale race-course.

"Oh, that is nothing," said the horse-dealer. "Men are like horses. At certain times they need salt, and if that salt is not in the mangers they will lick it up from the earth. He has gone back to the Road again for a while. The madrissah wearied him. I knew it would. Another time, I will take him up on the Road myself. Do not be troubled, Creighton Sahib. It is as though a polo-pony, breaking loose, ran out to learn the game alone."

"Then he is not dead, think you?"

"Fever might kill him. I do not fear for the boy otherwise. A monkey does not fall among trees."

Next morning, on the same course, Mahbub's stallion ranged alongside the Colonel.

"It is as I had thought," said the horse-dealer. "He has come through Umballa at least, and there he has written a letter to me, having learned in the bazar that I was here."

"Read," said the Colonel, with a sigh of relief. It was absurd that a man of his position should take an interest in a little country-bred vagabond; but the Colonel remembered the conversation in the train, and often in the past few months had caught himself thinking of the queer, silent, self-possessed boy. His evasion, of course, was the height of insolence, but it argued some resource and nerve.

Mahbub's eyes twinkled as he reined out into the centre of the cramped little plain, where none could come near unseen.

" 'The Friend of the Stars, who is the Friend of all the World—' "

"What is this?"

"A name we give him in Lahore city. 'The Friend of all the World takes leave to go to his own places. He will come back upon the appointed day. Let the box and the bedding-roll be sent for; and if there has been a fault, let the Hand of Friendship turn aside the Whip of Calamity.' There is yet a little more, but—"

"No matter, read."

" 'Certain things are not known to those who eat with forks. It is better to eat with both hands for a while. Speak soft words to those who do not understand this that the return may be propitious.' Now the manner in which that was cast is of course the work of the letter-writer, but see how wisely the boy has devised the matter of it so that no hint is given except to those who know!"

"Is this the Hand of Friendship to avert the Whip of Calamity?" laughed the Colonel.

"See how wise is the boy. He would go back to the Road again, as I said. Not knowing yet thy trade—"

"I am not quite sure of that," the Colonel muttered.

"He turns to me to make a peace between you. Is he not wise? He says he will return. He is but perfecting his knowledge. Think, Sahib! He has been three months at the school. And he is not mouthed to that bit. For my part, I rejoice: the pony learns the game."

"Ay, but another time he must not go alone."

"Why? He went alone before he came under the Colonel Sahib's protection. When he comes to the Great Game he must go alone—alone, and at peril of his head. Then, if he spits, or sneezes, or sits down other than as the people do whom he watches, he may be slain. Why hinder him now? Remember how the Persians say: The jackal that lives in the wilds of Mazanderan can only be caught by the hounds of Mazanderan."

"True. It is true, Mahbub Ali. And if he comes to no harm, I do not desire anything better. But it is great insolence on his part."

"He does not tell me, even, whither he goes," said Mahbub. "He is no fool. When his time is accomplished he will come to me. It is time the healer of pearls took him in hand. He ripens too quickly—as Sahibs reckon."

This prophecy was fulfilled to the letter a month later. Mahbub had gone down to Umballa to bring up a fresh consignment of horses, and Kim met him on the Kalka road at dusk riding alone, begged an alms of him, was sworn at, and replied in English. There was nobody within earshot to hear Mahbub's gasp of amazement.

"Oho! And where hast thou been?"

"Up and down—down and up."

"Come under a tree, out of the wet, and tell."

"I stayed for a while with an old man near Umballa; anon with a household of my acquaintance in Umballa. With one of these I went as far as Delhi to the southward. That is a wondrous city. Then I drove a bullock for a teli (an oilman) coming north; but I heard of a great feast forward in Puttiala, and thither went I in the company of a firework-maker. It was a great feast" (Kim rubbed his stomach). "I saw Rajahs, and elephants with gold and silver trappings; and they lit all the fireworks at once, whereby eleven men were killed, my firework-maker among them, and I was blown across a tent but took no harm. Then I came back to the rel with a Sikh horseman, to whom I was groom for my bread; and so here."

"Shabash!" said Mahbub Ali.

"But what does the Colonel Sahib say? I do not wish to be beaten."

"The Hand of Friendship has averted the Whip of Calamity; but another time, when thou takest the Road it will be with me. This is too early."

"Late enough for me. I have learned to read and to write English a little at the madrissah. I shall soon be altogether a Sahib."

"Hear him!" laughed Mahbub, looking at the little drenched figure dancing in the wet. "Salaam—Sahib," and he saluted ironically. "Well, art tired of the Road, or wilt thou come on to Umballa with me and work back with the horses?"

"I come with thee, Mahbub Ali."

Chapter 8

"Something I owe to the soil that grew—
More to the life that fed—
But most to Allah Who gave me two
Separate sides to my head.

I would go without shirts or shoes,
Friends, tobacco or bread
Sooner than for an instant lose
Either side of my head."

"THEN in God's Name take blue for red," said Mahbub, alluding to the Hindu colour of Kim's disreputable turban.

Kim countered with the old proverb, "I will change my faith and my bedding, but thou must pay for it."

The dealer laughed till he nearly fell from his horse. At a shop on the outskirts of the city the change was made, and Kim stood up, externally at least, a Mohammedan.

Mahbub hired a room over against the railway station, sent for a cooked meal of the finest with almond-curd sweetmeats (balushai we call it) and fine-chopped Lucknow tobacco.

"This is better than some other meat that I ate with the Sikh," said Kim, grinning as he squatted, "and assuredly they give no such victuals at my madrissah."

"I have a desire to hear of that same madrissah." Mahbub stuffed himself with great boluses of spiced mutton fried in fat with cabbage and golden-brown onions. "But tell me first, altogether and truthfully, the manner of thy escape. For, O Friend of all the World,"—he loosed his cracking belt,—"I do not think it is often that a Sahib and the son of a Sahib runs away from there."

"How should they? They do not know the land. It was nothing," said Kim, and began his tale. When he came to the disguisement and the interview with the girl in the bazar, Mahbub Ali's gravity went from him. He laughed aloud and beat his hand on his thigh.

"Shabash! Shabash! Oh, well done, little one! What will the healer of turquoises say to this? Now, slowly, let us hear what befell afterwards— step by step, omitting nothing."

Step by step then, Kim told his adventures between coughs as the full- flavoured tobacco caught his lungs.

"I said," growled Mahbub Ali to himself, "I said it was the pony break- ing out to play polo. The fruit is ripe already—except that he must learn his distances and his pacings, and his rods and his compasses. Listen now. I have turned aside the Colonel's whip from thy skin, and that is no small service."

"True." Kim puffed serenely. "That is all true."

"But it is not to be thought that this running out and in is any way good."

"It was my holiday, Hajji. I was a slave for many weeks. Why should I not run away when the school was shut? Look, too, how I, living upon my friends or working for my bread, as I did with the Sikh, have saved the Colonel Sahib a great expense."

Mahbub's lips twitched under his well-pruned Mohammedan mous- tache.

"What are a few rupees"—the Pathan threw out his open hand care- lessly—"to the Colonel Sahib? He spends them for a purpose, not in any way for love of thee."

"That," said Kim slowly, "I knew a very long time ago."

"Who told?"

"The Colonel Sahib himself. Not in those many words, but plainly enough for one who is not altogether a mud head. Yea, he told me in the te-rain when we went down to Lucknow."

"Be it so. Then I will tell thee more, Friend of all the World, though in the telling I lend thee my head."

"It was forfeit to me," said Kim, with deep relish, "in Umballa, when thou didst pick me up on the horse after the drummer-boy beat me."

"Speak a little plainer. All the world may tell lies save thou and I. For equally is thy life forfeit to me if I chose to raise my finger here."

"And this is known to me also," said Kim, readjusting the live charcoal- ball on the weed. "It is a very sure tie between us. Indeed thy hold is surer even than mine; for who would miss a boy beaten to death, or, it may be, thrown into a well by the roadside? Many people here and in Simla and across the passes behind the Hills would, on the other hand, say: 'What has come to Mahbub Ali,' if he were found dead among his horses. Surely too the Colonel Sahib would make inquiries. But again,"—Kim's face puck- ered with cunning,—"he would not make overlong inquiry, lest people

should ask: 'What has this Colonel Sahib to do with that horse-dealer?'
But I—if I lived—"

"As thou wouldst surely die—"

"It may be; but I say, if I lived, I, and I alone, would know that one
had come by night, as a common thief perhaps, to Mahbub Ali's bulkhead
in the serai, and there had slain him, either before or after that thief had
made a full search into his saddle-bags and between the soles of his slippers. Is that news to tell to the Colonel, or would he say to me—(I have
not forgotten when he sent me back for a cigar-case that he had not left
behind him)—'What is Mahbub Ali to me?' "

Up went a gout of heavy smoke. There was a long pause; then Mahbub
Ali spoke in admiration: "And with these things on thy mind, dost thou
lie down and rise again among all the Sahibs' little sons at the madrissah
and meekly take instruction from thy teachers?"

"It is an order," said Kim blandly. "Who am I to dispute an order?"

"A most finished son of Eblis," said Mahbub Ali. "But what is this
tale of the thief and the search?"

"That which I saw," said Kim, "the night that my lama and I lay next
thy place in the Kashmir Serai. The door was left unlocked, which I
think is not thy custom, Mahbub. He came in as one assured that thou
wouldst not soon return. My eye was against a knot-hole in the plank.
He searched as it were for something—not a rug, not stirrups, nor a bridle,
nor brass pots—something little and most carefully hid. Else why did
he prick with an iron between the soles of thy slippers?"

"Ha!" Mahbub Ali smiled gently. "And seeing these things, what tale
didst thou fashion to thyself, Well of the Truth?"

"None. I put my hand upon my amulet, which lies always next to my
skin, and, remembering the pedigree of a white stallion that I had bitten
out of a piece of Mussalmani bread, I went away to Umballa perceiving
that a heavy trust was laid upon me. At that hour, had I chosen, thy head
was forfeit. It needed only to say to that man, 'I have here a paper concerning a horse which I cannot read.' And then?" Kim peered at Mahbub
under his eyebrows.

"Then thou wouldst have drunk water twice—perhaps thrice, afterwards. I do not think more than thrice," said Mahbub simply.

"It is true. I thought of that a little, but most I thought that I loved
thee, Mahbub. Therefore I went to Umballa, as thou knowest, but (and
this thou dost not know) I lay hid in the garden-grass to see what Colonel Creighton Sahib might do upon reading the white stallion's pedigree."

"And what did he?" for Kim had bitten off the conversation.

"Dost thou give news for love, or dost thou sell it?" Kim asked.

"I sell and—I buy." Mahbub took a four-anna piece out of his belt and held it up.

"Eight!" said Kim, mechanically following the huckster instinct of the East.

Mahbub laughed, and put away the coin. "It is too easy to deal in that market, Friend of all the World. Tell me for love. Our lives lie in each other's hand."

"Very good. I saw the Jang-i-Lat Sahib (the Commander-in-Chief) come to a big dinner. I saw him in Creighton Sahib's office. I saw the two read the white stallion's pedigree. I heard the very orders given for the opening of a great war."

"Hah!" Mahbub nodded with deepset eyes afire. "The game is well played. That war is done now, and the evil, we hope, nipped before the flower—thanks to me—and thee. What didst thou later?"

"I made the news as it were a hook to catch me victual and honour among the villagers in a village whose priest drugged my lama. But I bore away the old man's purse, and the Brahmin found nothing. So next morning he was angry. Ho! Ho! And I also used the news when I fell into the hands of that white regiment with their Bull!"

"That was foolishness." Mahbub scowled. "News is not meant to be thrown about like dung-cakes, but used sparingly—like bhang."

"So I think now, and, moreover it did me no sort of good. But that was very long ago,"—he made as to brush it all away with a thin brown hand,—"and since then, and especially in the nights under the punkah at the madrissah, I have thought very greatly."

"Is it permitted to ask whither the Heaven-born's thought might have led?" said Mahbub, with an elaborate sarcasm, smoothing his scarlet beard.

"It is permitted," said Kim, and threw back the very tone. "They say at Nucklao that no Sahib must tell a black man that he has made a fault."

Mahbub's hand shot into his bosom, for to call a Pathan a "black man" (kala admi) is a blood-insult. Then he remembered and laughed. "Speak, Sahib: thy black man hears."

"But," said Kim, "I am not a Sahib, and I say I made a fault when I cursed thee, Mahbub Ali, on the day at Umballa I thought I was betrayed by a Pathan. I was senseless; for I was but newly caught, and I wished to kill that low-caste drummer-boy. I say now, Hajji, that it was well done; and I see my road all clear before me to a good service. I will stay in the madrissah till I am ripe."

"Well said. Especially are distances and numbers and the manner of using compasses to be learned in that game. One waits in the Hills above to show thee."

"I will learn their teaching upon a condition—that my time is given to me without question when the madrissah is shut. Ask that for me of the Colonel."

"But why not ask the Colonel in the Sahib's tongue?"

"The Colonel is the servant of the Government. He is sent hither and yon at a word, and must consider his own advancement. (See how much I have already learned at Nucklao!) Moreover, the Colonel I know since three months only. I have known one Mahbub Ali for six years. So! To the madrissah I will go. At the madrissah I will learn. In the madrissah I will be a Sahib. But when the madrissah is shut, then must I be free and go among my people. Otherwise I die!"

"And who are thy People, Friend of all the World?"

"This great and beautiful land," said Kim, waving his paw round the little clay-walled room where the oil-lamp in its niche burned heavily through the tobacco-smoke. "And, further, I would see my lama again. And further, I need money."

"That is the need of every one," said Mahbub ruefully. "I will give thee eight annas, for much money is not picked out of horses' hooves, and it must suffice for many days. As to all the rest, I am well pleased, and no further talk is needed. Make haste to learn, and in three years, or it may be less, thou wilt be an aid—even to me."

"Have I been such a hindrance till now?" said Kim, with a boy's giggle.

"Do not give answers," Mahbub grunted. "Thou art my new horse-boy. Go and bed among my men. They are near the north end of the station, with the horses."

"They will beat me to the south end of the station if I come without authority."

Mahbub felt in his belt, wetted his thumb on a cake of Chinese ink, and dabbed the impression on a piece of soft native paper. From Balkh to Bombay men know that rough-ridged print with the old scar running diagonally across it.

"That is enough to show my headman. I come in the morning."

"By which road?" said Kim.

"By the road from the City. There is but one, and then we return to Creighton Sahib. I have saved thee a beating."

"Allah! What is a beating when the very head is loose on the shoulders?"

Kim slid out quietly into the night, walked half round the house, keeping close to the walls, and headed away from the station for a mile or so. Then, fetching a wide compass, he worked back at leisure, for he needed time to invent a story if any of Mahbub's retainers asked questions.

They were camped on a piece of waste ground beside the railway, and, being natives, had not, of course, unloaded the two trucks in which Mahbub's animals stood among a consignment of country-breds bought by the Bombay tram-company. The headman, a broken-down, consumptive-looking Mohammedan, promptly challenged Kim, but was pacified at sight of Mahbub's sign-manual.

"The Hajji has of his favour given me service," said Kim testily. "If this be doubted, wait till he comes in the morning. Meantime, a place by the fire."

Followed the usual aimless babble that every low-caste native must raise on every occasion. It died down, and Kim lay out behind the little knot of Mahbub's followers, almost under the wheels of a horse-truck, a borrowed blanket for covering. Now a bed among brickbats and ballast-refuse on a damp night, between overcrowded horses and unwashen Baltis, would not appeal to many white boys; but Kim was utterly happy. Change of scene, service, and surroundings were the breath of his little nostrils, and thinking of the neat white cots of St. Xavier's all arow under the punkah gave him joy as keen as the repetition of the multiplication-table in English.

"I am very old," he thought sleepily. "Every month I become a year more old. I was very young, and a fool to boot, when I took Mahbub's message to Umballa. Even when I was with that white regiment I was very young and small and had no wisdom. But now I learn every day, and in three years the Colonel will take me out of the madrissah and let me go upon the Road with Mahbub hunting for horses' pedigrees, or maybe I shall go by myself; or maybe I shall find the lama and go with him. Yes; that is best. To walk again as a chela with my lama when he comes back to Benares." The thoughts came more slowly and disconnectedly. He was plunging into a beautiful dreamland when his ears caught a whisper, thin and sharp, above the monotonous babble round the fire. It came from behind the iron-skinned horse-truck.

"He is not here then?"

"Where should he be but roystering in the City. Who looks for a rat in a frog-pond? Come away. He is not our man."

"He must not go back beyond the Passes a second time. It is the order."

"Hire some woman to drug him. It is a few rupees only, and there is no evidence."

"Except the woman. It must be more certain; and remember the price upon his head."

"Ay, but the police have a long arm, and we are far from the Border. If it were in Peshawur now!"

"Yes—in Peshawur," the second voice sneered. "Peshawur, full of his blood-kin—full of bolt-holes and women behind whose clothes he will hide. Yes, Peshawur or Jehannum would suit us equally well."

"Then what is the plan?"

"O fool, have I not told it a hundred times. Wait till he comes to lie down, and then one sure shot. The trucks are between us and pursuit. We have but to run back over the lines and go our way. They will not see whence the shot came. Wait here at least till the dawn. What manner of faquir art thou to shiver at a little watching?"

"Oho!" thought Kim, behind close-shut eyes. "Once again it is Mahbub. Indeed a white stallion's pedigree is not a good thing to peddle to Sahibs! Or maybe Mahbub has been selling other news. Now what is to do, Kim? I know not where Mahbub houses, and if he comes here before dawn they will shoot him. That would be no profit for thee, Kim. And this is not a matter for the police. That would be no profit for Mahbub; and," he giggled almost aloud, "I do not remember any lesson at Nucklao which will help me. Allah! Here is Kim and yonder are they. First then, Kim must wake and go away, so that they shall not suspect. A bad dream wakes a man—thus—"

He threw the blanket off his face, and raised himself suddenly with the terrible, bubbling, meaningless yell of the Asiatic roused by nightmare.

"Urr-urr-urr-urr! Ya-la-la-la-la! Narain! The churel! The churel!"

A churel is the peculiarly malignant ghost of a woman who has died in child-bed. She haunts lonely roads, her feet are turned backwards on the ankles, and she leads men to torment.

Louder rose Kim's quavering howl, till at last he leaped to his feet and staggered off sleepily, while the camp cursed him for waking them. Some twenty yards farther up the line he lay down again, as he recomposed himself. After a few minutes he rolled towards the road and stole away into the thick darkness.

He paddled along swiftly till he came to a culvert, and dropped behind it, his chin on a level with the coping-stone. Here he could command all the night-traffic, himself unseen.

Two or three carts passed, jingling out to the suburbs; a coughing policeman and a hurrying foot-passenger or two who sang to keep off evil spirits. Then rapped the shod feet of a horse.

"Ah! This is more like Mahbub," thought Kim, as the beast shied at the little head above the culvert.

"Ohe, Mahbub Ali," he whispered, "have a care!"

The horse was reined back almost on its haunches, and forced towards the culvert.

"Never again," said Mahbub, "will I take a shod horse for nightwork. They pick up all the bones and nails in the city." He stooped to lift its forefoot, and that brought his head within a foot of Kim's. "Down—keep down," he muttered. "The night is full of eyes."

"Two men wait thy coming behind the horse-trucks. They will shoot thee at thy lying down, because there is a price on thy head. I heard, sleeping near the horses."

"Didst thou see them? . . . Hold still, Sire of Devils!" This furiously to the horse.

"No."

"Was one dressed belike as a faquir?"

"One said to the other, 'What manner of a faquir art thou, to shiver at a little watching?' "

"Good. Go back to the camp and lie down. I do not die to-night."

Mahbub wheeled his horse and vanished. Kim tore back down the ditch till he reached a point opposite his second resting-place, slipped across the road like a weasel, and recoiled himself in the blanket.

"At least Mahbub knows," he thought contentedly. "And certainly he spoke as one expecting it. I do not think those two men will profit by to-night's watch."

An hour passed, and, with the best will in the world to keep awake all night, he slept deeply. Now and again a night train roared along the metals within twenty feet of him; but he had all the Oriental's indifference to mere noise, and it did not even weave a dream through his slumber.

Mahbub was anything but asleep. It annoyed him vehemently that people outside his tribe and unaffected by his casual amours should pursue him for the life. His first and natural impulse was to cross the line lower down, work up again, and, catching his well-wishers from behind, summarily slay them. Here, he reflected with sorrow, another branch of the Government, totally unconnected with Colonel Creighton, might demand explanations which would be hard to supply; and he knew that south the Border a perfectly ridiculous fuss is made about a corpse or so. He had not been troubled in this way since he sent Kim to Umballa with the message, and hoped that suspicion had been finally diverted.

Then a most brilliant notion struck him.

"The English do eternally tell the truth," he said, "therefore we of this country are eternally made foolish. By Allah, I will tell the truth to an Englishman! Of what use is the Government police if a poor Kabuli be robbed of his horses in their very trucks. This is as bad as Peshawur! I should lay a complaint at the station. Better still, some young Sahib on the Railway! They are zealous, and if they catch thieves it is remembered to their honour."

He tied up his horse outside the station, and strode on to the platform.

"Hullo, Mahbub Ali!" said a young Assistant District Traffic Superintendent who was waiting to go down the line—a tall, tow-haired, horsey youth in dingy white linen. "What are you doing here? Selling weeds —eh?"

"No; I am not troubled for my horses. I come to look for Lutuf Ullah. I have a truck-load up the line. Could any one take them out without the Railway's knowledge?"

"Shouldn't think so, Mahbub. You can claim against us if they do."

"I have seen two men crouching under the wheels of one of the trucks nearly all the night. Faquirs do not steal horses, so I gave them no more thought. I would find Lutuf Ullah, my partner."

"The deuce you did? And you didn't bother your head about it? 'Pon my word, it's just almost as well that I met you. What were they like, eh?"

"They were only faquirs. They will no more than take a little grain perhaps from one of the trucks. There are many up the line. The State will never miss the dole. I came here seeking for my partner, Lutuf Ullah—"

"Never mind your partner. Where are your horse-trucks?"

"A little to this side of the farthest place where they make lamps for the trains."

"The signal-box. Yes."

"And upon the rail nearest to the road upon the right-hand side—looking up the line thus. But as regards Lutuf Ullah—a tall man with a broken nose, and a Persian greyhound—Aie!"

The boy had hurried off to wake up a young and enthusiastic policeman; for, as he said, the Railway had suffered much from depredations in the goods-yard. Mahbub Ali chuckled in his dyed beard.

"They will walk in their boots, making a noise, and then they will wonder why there are no faquirs. They are very clever boys—Barton Sahib and Young Sahib."

He waited idly for a few minutes, expecting to see them hurry up the line girt for action. A light engine slid through the station, and he caught a glimpse of young Barton in the cab.

"I did that child an injustice. He is not altogether a fool," said Mahbub Ali. "To take a fire-carriage for a thief is a new game!"

When Mahbub Ali came to his camp in the dawn, no one thought it worth while to tell him any news of the night. No one, at least, but one small horse-boy, newly advanced to the great man's service, whom Mahbub called to his tiny tent to assist in some packing.

"It is all known to me," whispered Kim, bending above saddle-bags. "Two Sahibs came up on a te-rain. I was running to and fro in the dark on this side of the trucks as the te-rain moved up and down slowly. They fell upon two men sitting under this truck—Hajji, what shall I do with this lump of tobacco? Wrap it in paper and put it under the salt-bag? Yes—and struck them down. But one man struck at a Sahib with a faquir's buck's horn" (Kim meant the conjoined black-buck horns, which are a faquir's sole temporal weapon)—"the blood came. So the other Sahib, first smiting his own man senseless, smote the stabber with a short gun which had rolled from the first man's hand. They all raged as though mad together."

Mahbub smiled with heavenly resignation. "No! That is not so much dewanee (madness, or a case for the civil court—the word can be punned upon both ways) as nizamut (a criminal case). A gun sayest thou? Ten good years in jail."

"Then they both lay still, but I think they were nearly dead when they were put on the te-rain. Their heads moved thus. And there is much blood on the line. Come and see?"

"I have seen blood before. Jail is the sure place—and assuredly they will give false names, and assuredly no man will find them for a long time. They were unfriends of mine. Thy Fate and mine seem on one string. What a tale for the healer of pearls! Now swiftly with the saddle-bags and the cooking-platter. We will take out the horses and away to Simla."

Swiftly,—as Orientals understand speed,—with long explanations, with abuse and windy talk, carelessly, amid a hundred checks for little things forgotten, the untidy camp broke up and led the half-dozen stiff and fretful horses along the Kalka road in the fresh of the rain-swept dawn. Kim, regarded as Mahbub Ali's favourite by all who wished to stand well with the Pathan, was not called upon to work. They strolled on by the easiest of stages, halting every few hours at a wayside shelter. Very many Sahibs travel along the Kalka road; and, as Mahbub Ali says, every young Sahib must needs esteem himself a judge of a horse, and, though he be over head in debt to the money-lender, must make as if to buy. That was the reason that Sahib after Sahib, rolling along in stage-carriage, would stop and open talk. Some would even descend from their vehicles and feel the horses' legs; asking inane questions, or, through sheer ig-norance of the vernacular, grossly insulting the imperturbable trader.

"When first I dealt with Sahibs, and that was when Colonel Soady Sahib was Governor of Fort Abazai and flooded the Commissioner's camping-ground for spite," Mahbub confided to Kim as the boy filled his pipe under a tree, "I did not know how greatly they were fools, and this made me wroth. As thus—" and he told Kim a tale of an expression, misused in all innocence, that doubled Kim up with mirth. "Now I see, however,"—he exhaled smoke slowly,—"that it is with them as with all men—in certain matters they are wise, and in others most foolish. Very foolish it is to use the wrong word to a stranger; for though the heart may be clean of offence, how is the stranger to know that? He is more like to search truth with a dagger."

"True. True talk," said Kim solemnly. "Fools speak of a cat when a woman is brought to bed, for instance. I have heard them."

"Therefore, in one situate as thou art, it particularly behoves thee to remember this with both kinds of faces. Among Sahibs, never forgetting thou art a Sahib; among the folk of Hind, always remembering thou art—" he paused, with a puzzled smile.

"What am I? Mussalman, Hindu, Jain, or Buddhist? That is a hard nut."

"Thou art beyond question an unbeliever, and therefore thou wilt be damned. So says my Law—or I think it does. But thou art also my Little Friend of all the World, and I love thee. So says my heart. This matter of creeds is like horseflesh. The wise man knows horses are good—that there is a profit to be made from all; and for myself—but that I am a good Sunni and hate the men of Tirah—I could believe the same of all the Faiths. Now manifestly a Kattiawar mare taken from the sands of her birthplace and removed to the west of Bengal founders—nor is even a Balkh stallion (and there are no better horses than those of Balkh, were they not so heavy in the shoulder) of any account in the great Northern deserts beside the snow-camels I have seen. Therefore I say in my heart the Faiths are like the horses. Each has merit in its own country."

"But my lama said altogether a different thing."

"Oh, he is an old dreamer of dreams from Bhotiyal. My heart is a little angry, Friend of all the World, that thou shouldst see such worth in a man so little known."

"It is true, Hajji; but that worth do I see; and to him my heart is drawn."

"And his to thine, I hear. Hearts are like horses. They come and they go against bit or spur. Shout Gul Sher Khan yonder to drive in that bay stallion's pickets more firmly. We do not want a horse-fight at every resting-stage, and the dun and the black will be locked in a little. . . . Now hear me. Is it necessary to the comfort of thy heart to see that lama?"

"It is one part of my bond," said Kim. "If I do not see him, and if he is taken from me, I will go out of that madrissah in Nucklao and, and— once gone, who is to find me again?"

"It is true. Never was colt held on a lighter heel-rope than thou." Mahbub nodded his head.

"Do not be afraid." Kim spoke as though he could have evanished on the moment. "My lama has said that he will come to see me at the madrissah—"

"A beggar and his bowl in the presence of those young Sa—"

"Not all!" Kim cut in with a snort. "Their eyes are blued and their nails are blackened with low-caste blood, many of them. Sons of metheeranees—brothers-in-law to the bhungi" (sweeper).

We need not follow the rest of the pedigree; but Kim made his little point clearly and without heat, chewing a piece of sugar-cane the while.

"Friend of all the World," said Mahbub, pushing over the pipe for the boy to clean, "I have met many men, women, and boys, and not a few Sahibs. I have never in all my days met such an imp as thou art."

"And why? When I always tell thee the truth."

"Perhaps the very reason, for this is a world of danger to honest men."

Mahbub Ali hauled himself off the ground, girt in his belt, and went over to the horses.

"Or sell it?"

There was that in the tone that made Mahbub halt and turn. "What new devilry?"

"Eight annas, and I will tell," said Kim, grinning. "It touches thy peace."

"O Shaitan!" Mahbub gave the money.

"Rememberest thou the little business of the thieves in the dark, down yonder at Umballa?"

"Seeing they sought my life, I have not altogether forgotten. Why?"

"Rememberest thou the Kashmir Serai?"

"I will twist thy ears in a moment—Sahib."

"No need—Pathan. Only, the second faquir, whom the Sahibs beat senseless, was the man who came to search thy bulkhead at Lahore. I saw his face as they helped him on the engine. The very same man."

"Why didst thou not tell before?"

"Oh, he will go to jail, and be safe for some years. There is no need to tell more than is necessary at any one time. Besides, I did not then need money for sweetmeats."

"Allah Karim!" said Mahbub Ali. "Wilt thou some day sell my head for a few sweetmeats if the fit takes thee?"

Kim will remember till he dies that long, lazy journey from Umballa, through Kalka and the Pinjore Gardens near by, up to Simla. A sudden spate in the Gugger River swept down one horse (the most valuable, be sure), and nearly drowned Kim among the dancing boulders. Farther up the road the horses were stampeded by a Government elephant, and being in high condition of grass food, it cost a day and a half to get them together again. Then they met Sikandar Khan coming down with a few unsaleable screws,—remnants of his string,—and Mahbub, who has more of horse-coping in his little finger nail than Sikandar Khan in all his tents, must needs buy two of the worst, and that meant eight hours, laborious diplomacy and untold tobacco. But it was all pure delight—the wandering road, climbing, dipping, and sweeping about the growing spurs; the flush of the morning laid along the distant snows; the branched cacti, tier upon tier on the stony hillsides; the voices of a thousand water-channels; the chatter of the monkeys; the solemn deodars, climbing one after another with down-drooped branches; the vista of the Plains rolled out far beneath them; the incessant twanging of the tonga-horns and the wild rush of the led horses when a tonga swung round a curve; the halts for prayers (Mahbub was very religious in dry-washings and bellowings when time did not press); the evening conferences by the halting-places, when camels and bullocks chewed solemnly together and the stolid drivers told the news of the Road—all these things lifted Kim's heart to song within him.

"But, when the singing and dancing is done," said Mahbub Ali, "comes the Colonel Sahib's, and that is not so sweet."

"A fair land—a most beautiful land is this of Hind—and the land of the Five Rivers is fairer than all," Kim half chanted. "Into it I will go again if Mahbub Ali or the Colonel lift hand or foot against me. Once gone, who shall find me? Look, Hajji, is yonder the city of Simla? Allah, what a city!"

"My father's brother, and he was an old man when Mackerson Sahib's well was new at Peshawur, could recall when there were but two houses in it."

He led the horses below the main-road into the lower Simla bazar—the crowded rabbit-warren that climbs up from the valley to the town-hall at an angle of forty-five. A man who knows his way there can defy all the police of India's summer capital; so cunningly does veranda communicate with veranda, alley-way with alley-way, and bolt-hole with bolt-hole. Here live those who minister to the wants of the glad city—jhampanis who pull the pretty ladies' rickshaws by night and gamble till the dawn; grocers, oil-sellers, curio-vendors, firewood dealers, priests, pickpockets, and native employees of the Government: here are discussed by courtesans the things which are supposed to be profoundest secrets of the India Council; and here gather all the sub-sub-agents of half the native States. Here, too, Mahbub Ali rented a room, much more securely locked than his bulkhead at Lahore, in the house of a Mohammedan cattle-dealer. It was a place of miracles, too, for there went in at twilight a Mohammedan horse-boy, and there came out an hour later a Eurasian lad—the Lucknow girl's dye was of the best—in badly fitting shop-clothes.

"I have spoken with Creighton Sahib," quoth Mahbub Ali, "and a second time has the Hand of Friendship averted the Whip of Calamity. He says that thou hast altogether wasted sixty days upon the Road, and it is too late, therefore, to send thee to any hill-school."

"I have said that my holidays are my own. I do not go to school twice over. That is one part of my bond."

"The Colonel Sahib is not yet aware of the contract. Thou art to lodge in Lurgan Sahib's house till it is time to go again to Nucklao."

"I had sooner lodge with thee, Mahbub."

"Thou dost not know the honour. Lurgan Sahib himself asked for thee. Thou wilt go up the hill and along the road atop, and there thou must forget for a while that thou hast ever seen or spoken to me, Mahbub Ali, who sells horses to Creighton Sahib, whom thou dost not know. Remember this order."

Kim nodded. "Good," said he, "and who is Lurgan Sahib? Nay"—he caught Mahbub's sword-keen glance—"indeed I have never heard his name. Is he by chance"—he lowered his voice—"one of us?"

"What talk is this of us, Sahib?" Mahbub Ali returned, in the tone he used towards Europeans. "I am a Pathan; thou art a Sahib and the son of a Sahib. Lurgan Sahib has a shop among the European shops. All Simla knows it. Ask there . . . and, Friend of all the World, he is one to be obeyed to the last wink of his eyelashes. Men say he does magic, but that should not touch thee. Go up the hill and ask. Here begins the Great Game."

Chapter 9

S'doaks was son of Yelth the wise—
  Chief of the Raven clan.
Itswoot the Bear had him in care
  To make him a medicine-man.

He was quick and quicker to learn—
  Bold and bolder to dare:
He danced the dread Kloo-Kwallie Dance
  To tickle Itswoot the Bear!

                                                    "Oregon Legend."

KIM flung himself whole-heartedly upon the next turn of the Wheel. He would be a Sahib again for a while. In that idea, so soon as he had reached the broad road under Simla town-hall, he cast about for one to impress. A Hindu child, some ten years old, squatted under a lamp-post.

"Where is Mr. Lurgan's house?" demanded Kim.

"I do not understand English," was the answer, and Kim shifted his speech accordingly.

"I will show."

Together they set off through the mysterious dusk, full of the noises of a city below the hillside, and the breath of a cool wind in deodar-crowned Jakko, shouldering the stars. The house-lights, scattered on every level, made, as it were, a double firmament. Some were fixed, others belonged to the rickshaws of the careless, open-spoken English folk, going out to dinner.

"It is here," said Kim's guide, and halted in a veranda flush with the main road. No door stayed them, but a curtain of beaded reeds that split up the lamp-light beyond.

"He is come," said the boy, in a voice little louder than a sigh, and vanished. Kim felt sure that the boy had been posted to guide him from the first, but putting a bold face on it, parted the curtain. A black-bearded man, with a green shade over his eyes, sat at a table, and, one by one, with short, white hands, picked up globules of light from a tray before

him, threaded them on a glancing silken string, and hummed to himself
the while. Kim was conscious that beyond the circle of light the room
was full of things that smelt like all the temples of all the East. A whiff
of musk, a puff of sandalwood, and a breath of sickly jessamine-oil caught
his opened nostrils.

"I am here," said Kim at last, speaking in the vernacular: the smells
made him forget that he was to be a Sahib.

"Seventy-nine, eighty, eighty-one," the man counted to himself, stringing pearl after pearl so quickly that Kim could scarcely follow his fingers.
He slid off the green shade and looked fixedly at Kim for a full half-
minute. The pupils of the eye dilated and closed to pin-pricks, as if at
will. There was a faquir by the Taksali Gate who had just this gift and
made money by it, especially when cursing silly women. Kim stared with
interest. His disreputable friend could further twitch his ears, almost like
a goat, and Kim was disappointed that this new man could not imitate
him.

"Do not be afraid," said Mr. Lurgan suddenly.

"Why should I fear?"

"Thou wilt sleep here to-night, and stay with me till it is time to go
again to Nucklao. It is an order."

"It is an order," Kim repeated. "But where shall I sleep?"

"Here, in this room." Lurgan Sahib waved his hand towards the darkness behind him.

"So be it," said Kim composedly. "Now?"

He nodded and held the lamp above his head. As the light swept
them, there leaped out from the walls a collection of Tibetan devil-dance
masks, hanging above the fiend-embroidered draperies of those ghastly
functions—horned masks, scowling masks, and masks of idiotic terror. In
a corner, a Japanese warrior, mailed and plumed, menaced him with
a halberd, and a score of lances and khandas and kuttars gave back the
unsteady gleam. But what interested Kim more than all these things—he
had seen devil-dance masks at the Lahore Museum—was a glimpse of the
soft-eyed Hindu child who had left him in the doorway, sitting cross-
legged under the table of pearls with a little smile on his scarlet lips.

"I think that Lurgan Sahib wishes to make me afraid. And I am sure
that the devil's brat below the table wishes to see me afraid. This place,"
he said aloud, "is like a Wonder House. Where is my bed?"

Lurgan Sahib pointed to a native quilt in a corner by the loathsome
masks, picked up the lamp, and left the room black.

"Was that Lurgan Sahib?" Kim asked as he cuddled down. No answer.
He could hear the Hindu boy breathing, however and, guided by the

sound, crawled across the floor, and cuffed into the darkness, crying: "Give answer, devil! Is this the way to lie to a Sahib?"

From the darkness he fancied he could hear the echo of a chuckle. It could not be his soft-fleshed companion, because he was weeping. So Kim lifted up his voice and called aloud: "Lurgan Sahib! O Lurgan Sahib! Is it an order that thy servant does not speak to me?"

"It is an order." The voice came from behind him and he started.

"Very good. But remember," he muttered, as he resought the quilt, "I will beat thee in the morning. I do not love Hindus."

That was no cheerful night; the room being overfull of voices and music. Kim was waked twice by some one calling his name. The second time he set out in search, and ended by bruising his nose against a box that certainly spoke with a human tongue, but in no sort of human accent. It seemed to end in a tin trumpet and to be joined by wires to a smaller box on the floor—so far, at least, as he could judge by touch. And the voice, very hard and whirring, came out of the trumpet. Kim rubbed his nose and grew furious, thinking, as usual, in Hindi.

"This with a beggar from the bazar might be good but—I am a Sahib and the son of a Sahib and, which is twice as much more beside, a student of Nucklao. Yess" (here he turned to English), "a boy of St. Xavier's. Damn Mr. Lurgan's eyes!—It is some sort of machinery like a sewing-machine. Oh, it is a great cheek of him—we are not frightened that way at Lucknow—No!" Then in Hindi: "But what does he gain? He is only a trader—I am in his shop. But Creighton Sahib is a Colonel—and I think Creighton Sahib gave orders that it should be done. How I will beat the Hindu in the morning! What is this?"

The trumpet-box was pouring out a string of the most elaborate abuse that even Kim had ever heard, in a high uninterested voice, that for a moment lifted the short hairs of his neck. When the vile thing drew breath, Kim was reassured by the soft, sewing-machine-like whirr.

"Chup!" (be still) he cried, and again he heard a chuckle that decided him. "Chup—or I break your head."

The box took no heed. Kim wrenched at the tin trumpet and something lifted with a click. He had evidently raised a lid. If there were a devil inside, now was its time for—he sniffed—thus did the sewing-machines of the bazar smell. He would clean that shaitan. He slipped off his jacket, and plunged it into the box's mouth. Something long and round bent under the pressure, there was a whirr and the voice stopped—as voices must if you ram a thrice-doubled coat on to the wax cylinder and into the works of an expensive phonograph. Kim finished his slumbers with a serene mind.

In the morning he was aware of Lurgan Sahib looking down on him.
"Oah!" said Kim, firmly resolved to cling to his Sahibdom. "There was
a box in the night that gave me bad talk. So I stopped it. Was it your
box?"

The man held out his hand.

"Shake hands, O'Hara," he said. "Yes, it was my box. I keep such things
because my friends the Rajahs like them. That one is broken, but it was
cheap at the price. Yes, my friends the Kings are very fond of toys—and
so am I sometimes."

Kim looked him over out of the corners of his eyes. He was a Sahib in
that he wore Sahib's clothes; the accent of his Urdu, the intonation of his
English, showed that he was anything but a Sahib. He seemed to understand what moved in Kim's mind ere the boy opened his mouth, and he
took no pains to explain himself as did Father Victor or the Lucknow
masters. Sweetest of all—he treated Kim as an equal on the Asiatic side.

"I am sorry you cannot beat my boy this morning. He says he will kill
you with a knife or poison. He is jealous, so I have put him in the corner
and I shall not speak to him to-day. He has just tried to kill me. You must
help me with the breakfast. He is almost too jealous to trust, just now."

Now a genuine imported Sahib from England would have made a
great to do over this tale. Lurgan Sahib stated it as simply as Mahbub
Ali was used to record his little affairs in the North.

The back veranda of the shop was built out over the sheer hillside, and
they looked down into their neighbors' chimney-pots, as is the custom of
Simla. But even more than the purely Persian meal cooked by Lurgan Sahib
with his own hands, the shop fascinated Kim. The Lahore Museum was
larger, but here were more wonders—ghost-daggers and prayer-wheels
from Tibet; turquoise and raw amber necklaces; green jade bangles;
curiously packed incense-sticks in jars crusted over with raw garnets;
the devil-masks of overnight and a wall of peacock-blue draperies; gilt
figures of Buddha, and little portable lacquer altars; Russian samovars
with turquoises on the lid; egg-shell china sets in quaint octagonal cane
boxes; yellow ivory crucifixes—from Japan of all places in the world, so
Lurgan Sahib said; carpets in dusty bales, smelling atrociously, pushed
back behind torn and rotten screens of geometrical work; Persian water-
jugs for the hands after meals; dull copper incense-burners neither Chinese
nor Persian, with friezes of fantastic devils running round them; tarnished silver belts that knotted like raw hide; hairpins of jade, ivory, and
plasma; arms of all sorts and kinds, and a thousand other oddments were
cased, or piled, or merely thrown into the room, leaving a clear space only
round the rickety deal table, where Lurgan Sahib worked.

"Those things are nothing," said his host, following Kim's glance. "I buy them because they are pretty, and sometimes I sell—if I like the buyer's look. My work is on the table—some of it."

It blazed in the morning light—all red and blue and green flashes, picked out with the vicious blue-white spurt of a diamond here and there. Kim opened his eyes.

"Oh, they are quite well, those stones. It will not hurt them to take the sun. Besides, they are cheap. But with sick stones it is very different." He piled Kim's plate anew. "There is no one but me can doctor a sick pearl and re-blue turquoises. I grant you opals—any fool can cure an opal—but for a sick pearl there is only me. Suppose I were to die! Then there would be no one. . . . Oh no! You cannot do anything with jewels. It will be quite enough if you understand a little about the turquoise—some day."

He moved to the end of the veranda to refill the heavy, porous clay water-jug from the filter.

"Do you want drink?"

Kim nodded. Lurgan Sahib, fifteen feet off, laid one hand on the jar. Next instant, it stood at Kim's elbow, full to within half an inch of the brim—the white cloth only showing, by a small wrinkle, where it had slid into place.

"Wah!" said Kim in most utter amazement. "That is magic." Lurgan Sahib's smile showed that the compliment had gone home.

"Throw it back."

"It will break."

"I say, throw it back."

Kim pitched it at random. It fell short and crashed into fifty pieces, while the water dripped through the rough veranda boarding.

"I said it would break."

"All one. Look at it. Look at the largest piece."

That lay with a sparkle of water in its curve, as it were a star on the floor. Kim looked intently; Lurgan Sahib laid one hand gently on the nape of the neck, stroked it twice or thrice, and whispered: "Look! It shall come to life again, piece by piece. First the big piece shall join itself to two others on the right and left—on the right and the left. Look!"

To save his life, Kim could not have turned his head. The light touch held him as in a vise, and his blood tingled pleasantly through him. There was one large piece of the jar where there had been three, and above them the shadowy outline of the entire vessel. He could see the veranda through it, but it was thickening and darkening with each beat of his pulse. Yet the jar—how slowly the thoughts came!—the jar had been smashed before his eyes. Another wave of prickling fire raced down his neck, as Lurgan Sahib moved his hand.

"Look! It is coming into shape," said Lurgan Sahib.

So far Kim had been thinking in Hindi, but a tremor came on him, and with an effort like that of a swimmer before sharks, who hurls himself half out of the water, his mind leaped up from a darkness that was swallowing it and took refuge in—the multiplication-table in English!

"Look! It is coming into shape," whispered Lurgan Sahib.

The jar had been smashed—yess, smashed—not the native word, he would not think of that—but smashed—into fifty pieces, and twice three was six, and thrice three was nine, and four times three was twelve. He clung desperately to the repetition. The shadow-outline of the jar cleared like a mist after rubbing eyes. There were the broken shards; there was the spilt water drying in the sun, and through the cracks of the veranda showed, all ribbed, the white house-wall below—and thrice twelve was thirty-six!

"Look! Is it coming into shape?" asked Lurgan Sahib.

"But it is smashed—smashed," he gasped—Lurgan Sahib had been muttering softly for the last half-minute. Kim wrenched his head aside. "Look! Dekho! It is there as it was there."

"It is there as it was there," said Lurgan, watching Kim closely while the boy rubbed his neck. "But you are the first of a many who have ever seen it so." He wiped his broad forehead.

"Was that more magic?" Kim asked suspiciously. The tingle had gone from his veins; he felt unusually wide awake.

"No, that was not magic. It was only to see if there was—a flaw in a jewel. Sometimes very fine jewels will fly all to pieces if a man holds them in his hand, and knows the proper way. That is why one must be careful before one sets them. Tell me, did you see the shape of the pot?"

"For a little time. It began to grow like a flower from the ground."

"And then what did you do? I mean, how did you think?"

"Oah! I knew it was broken, and so, I think, that was what I thought—and it was broken."

"Hm! Has any one ever done that same sort of magic to you before?"

"If it was," said Kim, "do you think I should let it again? I should run away."

"And now you are not afraid—eh?"

"Not now."

Lurgan Sahib looked at him more closely than ever. "I shall ask Mahbub Ali—not now, but some day later," he muttered. "I am pleased with you—yes; and I am pleased with you—no. You are the first that ever saved himself. I wish I knew what it was that . . . But you are right. You should not tell that—not even to me."

He turned into the dusky gloom of the shop, and sat down at the table, rubbing his hands softly. A small, husky sob came from behind a pile of carpets. It was the Hindu child obediently facing towards the wall: his thin shoulders worked with grief.

"Ah! He is jealous, so jealous. I wonder if he will try to poison me again in my breakfast, and make me cook it twice."

"Kubbee—kubbee nahin," came the broken answer.

"And whether he will kill this other boy?"

"Kubbee—kubbee nahin" (never—never. No!).

"What do you think he will do?" He turned suddenly on Kim.

"Oah! I do not know. Let him go, perhaps. Why did he want to poison you?"

"Because he is so fond of me. Suppose you were fond of some one, and you saw some one come, and the man you were fond of was more pleased with him than he was with you, what would you do?"

Kim thought. Lurgan repeated the sentence slowly in the vernacular.

"I should not poison that man," said Kim reflectively, "but I should beat that boy—if that boy was fond of my man. But first I would ask that boy if it were true."

"Ah! He thinks every one must be fond of me."

"Then I think he is a fool."

"Hearest thou?" said Lurgan Sahib to the shaking shoulders. "The Sahib's son thinks thou art a little fool. Come out, and next time thy heart is troubled, do not try white arsenic quite so openly. Surely the Devil Dasim was lord of our table-cloth that day! It might have made me ill, child, and then a stranger would have guarded the jewels. Come!"

The child, heavy-eyed with much weeping, crept out from behind the bale and flung himself passionately at Lurgan Sahib's feet, with an extravagance of remorse that impressed even Kim.

"I will look into the ink-pools—I will faithfully guard the jewels! Oh, my father and my mother, send him away!" He indicated Kim with a backward jerk of his bare heel.

"Not yet—not yet. In a little while he will go away again. But now he is at school—at a new madrissah—and thou shalt be his teacher. Play the Play of the Jewels against him. I will keep tally."

The child dried his tears at once, and dashed to the back of the shop, whence he returned with a copper tray.

"Give me!" he said to Lurgan Sahib. "Let them come from thy hand, for he may say that I knew them before."

"Gently—gently," the man replied, and from a drawer under the table dealt a half handful of clattering trifles into the tray.

"Now," said the child, waving an old newspaper. "Look on them as long as thou wilt, stranger. Count and, if need be, handle. One look is enough for me." He turned his back proudly.

"But what is the game?"

"When thou hast counted and handled and art sure that thou canst remember them all, I cover them with this paper, and thou must tell over the tally to Lurgan Sahib. I will write mine."

"Oah!" The instinct of competition waked in his breast. He bent over the tray. There were but fifteen stones on it. "That is easy," he said after a minute. The child slipped the paper over the winking jewels and scribbled in a native account-book.

"There are under that paper five blue stones—one big, one smaller, and three small," said Kim, all in haste. "There are four green stones, and one with a hole in it; there is one yellow stone that I can see through, and one like a pipe-stem. There are two red stones, and—and—I made the count fifteen, but two I have forgotten. No! Give me time. One was of ivory, little and brownish; and—and—give me time . . ."

"One—two"—Lurgan Sahib counted him out up to ten. Kim shook his head.

"Hear my count!" the child burst in, trilling with laughter. "First, are two flawed sapphires—one of two ruttees and one of four as I should judge. The four-ruttee sapphire is chipped at the edge. There is one Turkestan turquoise, plain with black veins, and there are two inscribed— one with a Name of God in gilt, and the other being cracked across, for it came out of an old ring, I cannot read. We have now all five blue stones. Four flawed emeralds there are, but one is drilled in two places, and one is a little carven—"

"Their weights?" said Lurgan Sahib impassively.

"Three—five—five—and four ruttees as I judge it. There is one piece of old greenish pipe amber, and a cut topaz from Europe. There is one ruby of Burma, of two ruttees, without a flaw, and there is a balas-ruby, flawed, of two ruttees. There is a carved ivory from China representing a rat sucking an egg; and there is last—ah ha!—a ball of crystal as big as a bean set in a gold leaf."

He clapped his hands at the close.

"He is thy master," said Lurgan Sahib, smiling.

"Huh! He knew the names of the stones," said Kim, flushing. "Try again! With common things such as he and I both know."

They heaped the tray again with odds and ends gathered from the shop, and even the kitchen, and every time the child won, till Kim marvelled.

"Bind my eyes—let me feel once with my fingers, and even then I will leave thee open-eyed behind," he challenged.

Kim stamped with vexation when the lad made his boast good.

"If it were men—or horses," he said, "I could do better. This playing with tweezers and knives and scissors is too little."

"Learn first—teach later," said Lurgan Sahib. "Is he thy master?"

"Truly. But how is it done?"

"By doing it many times over till it is done perfectly—for it is worth doing."

The Hindu boy, in highest feather, actually patted Kim on the back.

"Do not despair," he said. "I myself will teach thee."

"And I will see that thou art well taught," said Lurgan Sahib, still speaking in the vernacular, "for except my boy here—it was foolish of him to buy so much white arsenic when, if he had asked, I could have given it —except my boy here I have not in a long time met with one better worth teaching. And there are ten days more ere thou canst return to Lucknow where they teach nothing—at the long price. We shall, I think, be friends."

They were a most mad ten days, but Kim enjoyed himself too much to reflect on their craziness. In the morning they played the Jewel Game—sometimes with veritable stones, sometimes with piles of swords and daggers, sometimes with photographs of natives. Through the afternoons he and the Hindu boy would mount guard in the shop, sitting dumb behind a carpet-bale or a screen and watching Mr. Lurgan's many and very curious visitors. There were small Rajahs, escorts coughing in the veranda, who came to buy curiosities—such as phonographs and mechanical toys. There were ladies in search of necklaces, and men, it seemed to Kim—but his mind may have been vitiated by early training—in search of the ladies; natives from independent and feudatory courts whose ostensible business was the repair of broken necklaces—rivers of light poured out upon the table—but whose true end seemed to be to raise money for angry Maharanees or young Rajahs. There were Babus to whom Lurgan Sahib talked with austerity and authority, but at the end of each interview he gave them money in coined silver and currency notes. There were occasional gatherings of long-coated theatrical natives who discussed metaphysics in English and Bengali, to Mr. Lurgan's great edification. He was always interested in religions. At the end of the day, Kim and the Hindu boy—whose name varied at Lurgan's pleasure—were expected to give a detailed account of all that they had seen and heard—their view of each man's character, as shown in his face, talk, and manner, and their notions of his real errand. After dinner, Lurgan Sahib's fancy turned more to what might be called dressing-up, in which game he took a most informing interest. He could paint faces to a marvel; with a brush-dab here and a line there changing them past recognition. The shop was full of all manner of dresses and turbans, and Kim was apparelled variously as a young Mohammedan of good family, an oilman, and once—which was a joyous evening—as the son of an Oudh landholder in the fullest of full dress. Lurgan Sahib had a hawk's eye to detect the least flaw in the make-up;

and lying on a worn teak-wood couch, would explain by the half-hour together how such and such a caste talked, or walked, or coughed, or spat, or sneezed, and, since "hows" matter little in this world, the "why" of everything. The Hindu child played this game clumsily. That little mind, keen as an icicle where tally of jewels was concerned, could not temper itself to enter another's soul; but a demon in Kim woke up and sang with joy as he put on the changing dresses, and changed speech and gesture therewith.

Carried away by enthusiasm, he volunteered to show Lurgan Sahib one evening how the disciples of a certain caste of faquir, old Lahore acquaintances, begged doles by the roadside; and what sort of language he would use to an Englishman, to a Punjabi farmer going to a fair, and to a woman without a veil. Lurgan Sahib laughed immensely, and begged Kim to stay as he was, immobile for half an hour—cross-legged, ash-smeared, and wild-eyed, in the back room. At the end of that time entered a hulking, obese Babu whose stockinged legs shook with fat, and Kim opened on him with a shower of wayside chaff. Lurgan Sahib—this annoyed Kim—watched the Babu and not the play.

"I think," said the Babu heavily, lighting a cigarette, "I am of opeenion that it is most extraordinary and effeecient performance. Except that you had told me I should have opined that—that—that you were pulling my legs. How soon can he become approximately effeecient chain-man? Because then I shall indent for him."

"That is what he must learn at Lucknow."

"Then order him to be jolly dam-quick. Good-night, Lurgan." The Babu swung out with the gait of a bogged cow.

When they were telling over the day's list of visitors, Lurgan Sahib asked Kim who he thought the man might be.

"God knows!" said Kim cheerily. The tone might almost have deceived Mahbub Ali, but it failed entirely with the healer of sick pearls.

"That is true. God, He knows; but I wish to know what you think."

Kim glanced sideways at his companion, whose eye had a way of compelling truth.

"I—I think he will want me when I come from the school, but"—confidentially, as Lurgan Sahib nodded approval—"I do not understand how he can wear many dresses and talk many tongues."

"Thou wilt understand many things later. He is a writer of tales for a certain Colonel. His honour is great only in Simla, and it is noticeable that he has no name, but only a number and a letter—that is a custom among us."

"And is there a price upon his head too—as upon Mah—all the others?"

"Not yet; but if a boy rose up who is now sitting here and went—look, the door is open!—as far as a certain house with a red-painted veranda, behind that which was the old theatre in the Lower Bazar, and whispered through the shutters: 'Hurree Chunder Mookerjee bore the bad news of last month,' that boy might take away a belt full of rupees."

"How many?" said Kim promptly.

"Five hundred—a thousand—as many as he might ask for."

"Good. And how long might such a boy live after the news was told?" He smiled merrily at Lurgan Sahib's very beard.

"Ah! That is to be well thought of. Perhaps if he were very clever, he might live out the day—but not the night. By no means the night."

"Then what is the Babu's pay if so much is put upon his head?"

"Eighty—perhaps a hundred—perhaps a hundred and fifty rupees; but the pay is the least part of the work. From time to time, God causes men to be born—and thou art one of them—who have a lust to go abroad at the risk of their lives and discover news—to-day it may be of far-off things, to-morrow of some hidden mountain, and the next of some near-by men who have done a foolishness against the State. These souls are very few; and of these few, not more than ten are of the best. Among these ten I count the Babu, and that is curious. How great therefore and desirable must be a business that brazens the heart of a Bengali!"

"True. But the days go slowly for me. I am yet a boy, and it is only within two months I learned to write Angrezi. Even now I cannot read it well. And there are yet years and years and long years before I can be even a chain-man."

"Have patience, Friend of all the World"—Kim started at the title. "Would I had a few of the years that so irk thee. I have proved thee in several small ways. This will not be forgotten when I make my report to the Colonel Sahib." Then, changing suddenly into English with a deep laugh:—

"By Jove! O'Hara, I think there is a great deal in you; but you must not become proud and you must not talk. You must go back to Lucknow and be a good little boy and mind your book, as the English say, and perhaps, next holidays if you care, you can come back to me!" Kim's face fell. "Oh, I mean if you like. I know where you want to go."

Four days later a seat was booked for Kim and his small trunk at the rear of a Kalka tonga. His companion was the whale-like Babu, who, with a fringed shawl wrapped round his head, and his fat openwork-stockinged left leg tucked under him, shivered and grunted in the morning chill.

"How comes it that this man is one of us?" thought Kim, considering the jelly-back as they jolted down the road; and the reflection threw him into most pleasant day-dreams. Lurgan Sahib had given him five rupees— a splendid sum—as well as the assurance of his protection if he worked.

Unlike Mahbub, Lurgan Sahib had spoken most explicitly of the reward
that would follow obedience, and Kim was content. If only, like the Babu,
he could enjoy the dignity of a letter and a number—and a price upon his
head! Some day he would be all that and more. Some day he might be almost as great as Mahbub Ali! The housetops of his search should be half
India; he would follow Kings and ministers, as in the old days he had
followed vakils and lawyers' touts across Lahore city for Mahbub Ali's
sake. Meantime, there was the present, and not at all unpleasant, fact of
St. Xavier's immediately before him. There would be new boys to condescend to, and there would be tales of holiday adventures to hear. Young
Martin, son of the tea-planter at Manipur, had boasted that he would go
to war, with a rifle, against the head-hunters. That might be, but it was
certain young Martin had not been blown half across the forecourt of a
Patiala palace by an explosion of fireworks; nor had he. . . . Kim fell to
telling himself the story of his own adventures through the last three
months. He could paralyze St. Xavier's—even the biggest boys who shaved
—with the recital, were that permitted. But it was, of course, out of the
question. There would be a price upon his head in good time, as Lurgan
Sahib had assured him; and if he talked foolishly now, not only would
that price never be set, but Colonel Creighton would cast him off—and he
would be left to the wrath of Lurgan Sahib and Mahbub Ali—for the
short space of life that would remain to him.

"So I should lose Delhi for the sake of a fish," was his proverbial phi-
losophy. It behoved him to forget his holidays (there would always remain
the fun of inventing imaginary adventures) and, as Lurgan Sahib had
said, to work.

Of all the boys hurrying back to St. Xavier's, from Sukkur in the sands
to Galle beneath the palms, none was so filled with virtue as Kimball
O'Hara, jiggeting down to Umballa behind Hurree Chunder Mookerjee,
whose name on the books of one section of the Ethnological Survey was
R.17.

And if additional spur were needed, the Babu supplied it. After a huge
meal at Kalka, he spoke uninterruptedly. Was Kim going to school? Then
he, an M.A. of Calcutta University, would explain the advantages of
education. There were marks to be gained by due attention to Latin and
Wordsworth's "Excursion" (all this was Greek to Kim). French, too, was
vital, and the best was to be picked up in Chandernagore, a few miles
from Calcutta. Also a man might go far, as he himself had done, by strict
attention to plays called "Lear" and "Julius Caesar," both much in demand
by examiners. "Lear" was not so full of historical allusions as "Julius Caesar"; the book cost four annas, but could be bought second-hand in Bow
Bazar for two. Still more important than Wordsworth, or the eminent

authors, Burke and Hare, was the art and science of mensuration. A boy who had passed his examination in these branches—for which, by the way, there were no cram-books—could, by merely marching over a country with a compass and a level and a straight eye, carry away a picture of that country which might be sold for large sums in coined silver. But as it was occasionally inexpedient to carry about measuring-chains, a boy would do well to know the precise length of his own foot-pace, so that when he was deprived of what Hurree Chunder called "adventitious aids" he might still tread his distances. To keep count of thousands of paces, Hurree Chunder's experience had shown him nothing more valuable than a rosary of eighty-one or a hundred and eight beads, for "it was divisible and sub-divisible into many multiples and sub-multiples." Through the volleying drifts of English, Kim caught the general trend of the talk, and it interested him very much. Here was a new craft that a man could tuck away in his head; and by the look of the large wide world unfolding itself before him, it seemed that the more a man knew the better for him.

Said the Babu when he had talked for an hour and a half, "I hope some day to enjoy your offeecial acquaintance. Ad interim, if I may be pardoned that expression, I shall give you this betel-box which is highly valuable article and cost me two rupees only four years ago." It was a cheap, heart-shaped brass thing with three compartments for carrying the eternal betel-nut, lime and pan-leaf; but it was filled with little tabloid-bottles. "That is reward of merit for your performance in character of that holy man. You see, you are so young you think you will last for ever and not take care of your body. It is great nuisance to go sick in the middle of business. I am fond of drugs myself, and they are handy to cure poor people too. These are good departmental drugs—quinine and so on. I give it you for souvenir. Now good-bye. I have urgent private business here by the roadside."

He slipped out noiselessly as a cat, on the Umballa road, hailed a passing ekka and jingled away, while Kim, tongue-tied, twiddled the brass betel-box in his hands.

The record of a boy's education interests few save his parents, and, as you know, Kim was an orphan. It is written in the books of St. Xavier in Partibus that a report of Kim's progress was forwarded at the end of each term to Colonel Creighton and to Father Victor, from whose hands duly came the money for his schooling. It is further recorded in the same books that he showed a great aptitude for mathematical studies as well as map-making, and carried away a prize ("The Life of Lord Lawrence," tree-calf, two vols., nine rupees, eight annas) for proficiency therein; and the same term played in St. Xavier's eleven against the Allyghur Mohamme-dan College, his age being fourteen years and ten months. He was also re-vaccinated (from which we may assume that there had been another epidemic of small-pox at Lucknow) about the same time. Pencil notes on the edge of an old muster-roll record that he was punished several times for "conversing with improper persons," and it seems that he was once sentenced to heavy pains for "absenting himself for a day in the company of a street beggar." That was when he got over the gate and pleaded with the lama through a whole day down the banks of the Goomtee to accompany him on the Road next holidays—for one month—for a little week; and the lama set his face as a flint against it, averring that the time had not yet come. Kim's business, said the old man as they ate cakes together, was to get all the wisdom of the Sahibs and then he would see. The hand of friendship must in some way have averted the whip of calamity, for six weeks later Kim seems to have passed an examination in elementary surveying "with great credit," his age being fifteen years and eight months. From this date the record is silent. His name does not appear in the year's batch of those who entered for the subordinate Survey of India, but against it stand the words "removed on appointment."

Several times in those three years, cast up at the Temple of the Tirthankers in Benares the lama, a little thinner and a shade yellower, if that were possible, but gentle and untainted as ever. Sometimes it was from the South that he came—from south of Tuticorin, whence the wonderful fire-boats go to Ceylon where are priests who know Pali; sometimes it was from the wet green West and the thousand cotton-factory chimneys that ring Bombay; and once from the North, where he had doubled back eight hundred miles to talk a day with the Keeper of the Images in the Wonder House. He would stride to his cell in the cool, cut marble—the priests of the temple were good to the old man—wash off the dust of travel, make prayer, and depart for Lucknow, well accustomed now to the ways of the rail, in a third-class carriage. Returning, it was noticeable, as his friend the Seeker pointed out to the head-priest, that he ceased for a while to mourn the loss of his River, or to draw wondrous pictures of the Wheel of Life, but preferred to talk of the beauty and wisdom of a certain mysterious chela whom no man of the temple had ever seen. Yes, he had followed the traces of the Blessed Feet throughout all India. (The curator has still in his possession a most marvellous account of his wanderings and meditations.) There remained nothing more in life but to find the River of the Arrow. Yet it was shown to him in dreams that it was a matter not to be undertaken with any hope of success unless that seeker had with him the one chela appointed to bring the event to a happy issue, and versed in great wisdom—such wisdom as white-haired Keepers of Images possess. For example (here came out the snuff-gourd, and the kindly Jain priests made haste to be silent):—

"Long and long ago, when Devadatta was King of Benares—let all listen to the 'Jataka'!—an elephant was captured for a time by the king's hunters and, ere he broke free, beringed with a grievous leg-iron. This he strove to remove with hate and frenzy in his heart, and hurrying up and down the forests, besought his brother-elephants to wrench it asunder. One by one, with their strong trunks, they tried and failed. At the last they gave it as their opinion that the ring was not to be broken by any bestial power. And in a thicket, new-born, wet with the moisture of birth, lay a day-old calf of the herd whose mother had died. The fettered elephant, forgetting his own agony, said: 'If I do not help this suckling it will perish under our feet.' So he stood above the young thing, making his legs but tresses against the uneasily moving herd; and he begged milk of a virtuous cow, and the calf throve, and the ringed elephant was the calf's guide and defence. Now the days of an elephant—let all listen to the 'Jataka'!—are thirty-five years to his full strength, and through thirty-five Rains the ringed elephant befriended the younger, and all the while the fetter ate into the flesh.

"Then one day the young elephant saw the half-buried iron, and turning to the elder said: 'What is this?' 'It is even my sorrow,' said he who had befriended him. Then that other put out his trunk and in the twinkling of an eyelash abolished the ring, saying: 'The appointed time has come.' So the virtuous elephant who had waited temperately and done kind acts was relieved, at the appointed time, by the very calf whom he had turned aside to cherish—let all listen to the 'Jataka'!—for the Elephant was Ananda, and the Calf that broke the ring was none other than The Lord Himself. . . ."

Then he would shake his head benignly, and over the ever-clicking rosary point out how free that elephant calf was from the sin of pride. He was as humble as a chela who, seeing his master sitting in the dust outside the Gates of Learning, over-leapt the gates (though they were locked) and took his master to his heart in the presence of the proud-stomached city. Rich would be the reward of such a master and such a chela when the time came for them to seek freedom together!

So did the lama speak, coming and going across India as softly as a bat. A sharp-tongued old woman in a house among the fruit-trees behind Saharunpore honoured him as the woman honoured the prophet, but his chamber was by no means upon the wall. In an apartment of the fore-court overlooked by cooing doves he would sit, while she laid aside her useless veil and chattered of spirits and friends of Kulu, of grandchildren unborn, and of the free-tongued brat who had talked to her in the resting-place. Once, too, he strayed alone from the Grand Trunk Road below Umballa to the very village whose priest had tried to drug him, but the kind heaven that guards lamas sent him at twilight through the crops, absorbed and unsuspicious, to the ressaldar's door. Here was like to have been a grave misunderstanding, for the old soldier asked him why the Friend of the Stars had gone that way only six days before.

"That may not be," said the lama. "He has gone back to his own people."

"He sat in that corner telling a hundred merry tales five nights ago," his host insisted. "True, he vanished somewhat suddenly in the dawn after foolish talk with my grand-daughter. He grows apace, but he is the same Friend of the Stars as brought me true word of the war. Have ye parted?"

"Yes—and No," the lama replied. "We—we have not altogether parted, but the time is not ripe that we should take the Road together. He acquires wisdom in another place. We must wait."

"All one—but if it were not the boy how did he come to speak so continually of thee?"

"And what said he?" asked the lama eagerly.

"Sweet words—an hundred thousand—that thou art his father and mother and such all. Pity that he does not take the Queen's service. He is fearless."

This news amazed the lama, who did not then know how religiously Kim kept to the contract made with Mahbub Ali, and perforce ratified by Colonel Creighton. . . .

"There is no holding the young pony from the game," said the horse-dealer when the Colonel pointed out that vagabonding over India in holiday time was absurd. "If permission be refused to go and come as he chooses, he will make light of the refusal. Then who is to catch him? Colonel Sahib, only once in a thousand years is a horse born so well fitted for the game as this our colt. And we need men."

Chapter 10

Your tiercel's too long at hack, Sire. He's no eyass
But a passage-hawk that footed ere we caught him,
Dangerously free o' the air. Faith! were he mine
(As mine's the glove he binds to for his tirings)
I'd fly him with a make-hawk. He's in yarak
Plumed to the very point—so manned so weathered . . .
Give him the firmament God made him for,
And what shall take the air of him?—Old Play.

LURGAN SAHIB did not use as direct speech, but his advice tallied with Mahbub's; and the upshot was good for Kim. He knew better now than to leave Lucknow city in native garb and if Mahbub were anywhere within reach of a letter, it was to Mahbub's camp he headed, and made his change under the Pathan's wary eye. Could the little Survey paint-box that he used for map-tinting in term-time have found a tongue to tell of holiday doings, he might have been expelled. Once Mahbub and he went together as far as the beautiful city of Bombay, with three truck-loads of tram-horses, and Mahbub nearly melted when Kim proposed a sail in a dhow across the Indian Ocean to buy Gulf Arabs, which he understood from a hanger-on of the dealer Abdul Rahman, fetched better prices than mere Cabulis.

He dipped his hand into the dish with that great trader when Mahbub and a few co-religionists were invited to a big Haj dinner. They came back by way of Karachi by sea, when Kim took his first experience of sea-sickness sitting on the fore-hatch of a coasting-steamer, well persuaded he had been poisoned. The Babu's famous drug-box proved useless, though Kim had restocked it at Bombay. Mahbub had business at Quetta, and there Kim, as Mahbub admitted, earned his keep, and perhaps a little over, by spending four curious days as scullion in the house of a fat Commissariat sergeant, from whose office-box, in an auspicious moment, he removed a little vellum ledger which he copied out—it seemed to deal entirely with cattle and camel sales—by moonlight, lying behind an outhouse, all through one hot night. Then he returned the ledger to its place, and, at

Mahbub's word, left that service unpaid, rejoining him six miles down the road, the clean copy in his bosom.

"That soldier is a small fish," Mahbub Ali explained, "but in time we shall catch the larger one. He only sells oxen at two prices—one for himself and one for the Government—which I do not think is a sin."

"Why could not I take away the little book and be done with it?"

"Then he would have been frightened, and he would have told his master. Then he should miss, perhaps, a great number of new rifles which seek their way up from Quetta to the North. The Game is so large that one sees but a little at a time."

"Oho!" said Kim, and held his tongue. That was in the monsoon holidays, after he had taken the prize for mathematics. The Christmas holidays he spent—deducting ten days for private amusements—with Lurgan Sahib, where he sat for the most part in front of a roaring wood-fire —Jakko road was four feet deep in snow that year—and—the small Hindu had gone away to be married—helped Lurgan to thread pearls. He made Kim learn whole chapters of the Koran by heart, till he could deliver them with the very roll and cadence of a mullah. Moreover, he told Kim the names and properties of many native drugs, as well as the runes proper to recite when you administer them. And in the evenings he wrote charms on parchment—elaborate pentagrams crowned with the names of devils— Murra, and Awan the Companion of Kings—all fantastically written in the corners. More to the point, he advised Kim as to the care of his own body, the cure of fever-fits, and simple remedies of the Road. A week before it was time to go down, Colonel Creighton Sahib—this was unfair— sent Kim a written examination-paper that concerned itself solely with rods and chains and links and angles.

Next holidays he was out with Mahbub, and here, by the way, he nearly died of thirst, plodding through the sand on a camel to the mysterious city of Bikaneer, where the wells are four hundred feet deep, and lined throughout with camel-bone. It was not an amusing trip from Kim's point of view, because—in defiance of the contract—the Colonel ordered him to make a map of that wild, walled city; and since Mohammedan horseboys and pipe-tenders are not expected to drag Survey-chains round the capital of an independent native state, Kim was forced to pace all his distances by means of a bead rosary. He used the compass for bearings as occasion served—after dark chiefly, when the camels had been fed— and by the help of his little Survey paint-box of six colour-cakes and three brushes, he achieved something not remotely unlike the city of Jeysalmir. Mahbub laughed a great deal, and advised him to make up a written report as well; and in the back of the big account-book that lay under the flap of Mahbub's pet saddle Kim fell to work.

"It must hold everything that thou hast seen or touched or considered. Write as though the Jung-i-Lat Sahib himself had come by stealth with a vast army outsetting to war."

"How great an army?"

"Oh, half a lakh of men."

"Folly! Remember how few and bad were the wells in the sand. Not a thousand thirsty men could come near by here."

"Then write that down—also all the old breaches in the walls—and whence the firewood is cut—and what is the temper and disposition of the King. I stay here till all my horses are sold. I will hire a room by the gateway, and thou shalt be my accountant. There is a good lock to the door."

The report in its unmistakable St. Xavier's running script, and the brown, yellow, and lake-daubed map, was on hand a few years ago (a careless clerk filed it with the rough notes of E.23's second Seistan survey), but by now the pencil characters must be almost illegible. Kim translated it, sweating under the light of an oil-lamp, to Mahbub, the second day of their return-journey. The Pathan rose and stooped over his dappled saddle-bags.

"I knew it would be worthy a dress of honour, and so I made one ready," he said smiling. "Were I Amir of Afghanistan (and some day we may see him), I would fill thy mouth with gold." He laid the garments formally at Kim's feet. There was a gold-embroidered Peshawur turban-cap, rising to a cone, and a big turban-cloth ending in a broad fringe of gold. There was a Delhi embroidered waistcoat to slip over a milky-white shirt, fastening to the right, ample and flowing; green pyjamas with twisted silk waist-string; and that nothing might be lacking, russia-leather slippers, smelling divinely, with arrogantly curled tips.

"Upon a Wednesday, and in the morning, to put on new clothes is auspicious," said Mahbub solemnly. "But we must not forget the wicked folk in the world. So!"

He capped all the splendour, that was taking Kim's delighted breath away, with a mother-of-pearl, nickel-plated, self-extracting .450 revolver.

"I had thought of a smaller bore, but reflected that this takes Government bullets. A man can always come by those—especially across the Border. Stand up and let me look." He clapped Kim on the shoulder. "May you never be tired, Pathan! Oh, the hearts to be broken! Oh, the eyes under the eyelashes, looking sideways!"

Kim turned about, pointed his toes, stretched, and felt mechanically for the moustache that was just beginning. Then he stooped towards Mahbub's feet to make proper acknowledgment with fluttering, quick-patting hands; his heart too full for words. Mahbub forestalled and embraced him.

"My son," said he, "what need of words between us? But is not the little gun a delight? All six cartridges come out at one twist. It is borne in the bosom next the skin, which, as it were, keeps it oiled. Never put it elsewhere, and please God, thou shalt some day kill a man with it."

"Hai mai!" said Kim ruefully. "If a Sahib kills a man he is hung in the jail."

"True: but one pace beyond the Border, men are wiser. Put it away; but fill it first. Of what use is a gun unfed?"

"When I go back to the madrissah I must return it. They do not allow little guns. Thou wilt keep it for me?"

"Son, I am wearied of that madrissah, where they take the best years of a man to teach him what he can only learn upon the Road. The folly of the Sahibs has neither top nor bottom. No matter. Maybe thy written report shall save thee further bondage; and God He knows we need men more and more in the Game."

They marched, jaw-bound against blowing sand, across the salt desert to Jodhpore, where Mahbub and his handsome nephew Habib-Ullah did much trading; and then sorrowfully, in European clothes, which he was fast outgrowing, Kim went second-class to St. Xavier's. Three weeks later, Colonel Creighton, pricing Tibetan ghost-daggers at Lurgan's shop, faced Mahbub Ali openly mutinous. Lurgan Sahib operated as support in reserve.

"The pony is made—finished—mouthed and paced, Sahib! From now on, day by day, he will lose his manners if he is kept at tricks. Drop the rein on his back and let go," said the horse-dealer. "We need him."

"But he is so young, Mahbub—not more than sixteen—is he?"

"When I was fifteen, I had shot my man and begot my man, Sahib."

"You impenitent old heathen." Creighton turned to Lurgan. The black beard nodded assent to the wisdom of the Afghan's dyed scarlet.

"I should have used him long ago," said Lurgan. "The younger the better. That is why I always have my really valuable jewels watched by a child. You sent him to me to try. I tried him in every way: he is the only boy I could not make to see things."

"In the crystal—in the ink-pool?" demanded Mahbub.

"No. Under my hand, as I told you. That has never happened before. It means that he is strong enough—but you think it skittles, Colonel Creighton—to make any one do anything he wants. And that is three years ago. I have taught him a good deal since, Colonel Creighton. I think you waste him now."

"Hmm! Maybe you're right. But, as you know, there is no Survey work for him at present."

"Let him out—let him go," Mahbub interrupted. "Who expects any colt to carry heavy weight at first? Let him run with the caravans like our white camel-colts—for luck. I would take him myself, but—"

"There is a little business where he would be most useful—in the South," said Lurgan, with peculiar suavity, dropping his heavy nude eyelids.

"E.23 has that in hand," said Creighton quickly. "He must not go down there. Besides, he knows no Turki."

"Only tell him the shape and the smell of the letters we want and he will bring them back," Lurgan insisted.

"No. That is a man's job," said Creighton.

It was a wry-necked matter of unauthorised and incendiary correspondence between a person who claimed to be the ultimate authority in all matters of the Mohammedan religion throughout the world, and a younger member of a royal house who had been brought to book for kidnapping women within British territory. The Moslem Archbishop had been emphatic and overarrogant; the young prince was merely sulky at the curtailment of his privileges, but there was no need he should continue a correspondence which might some day compromise him. One letter indeed had been procured, but the finder was later found dead by the roadside in the habit of an Arab trader, as E.23, taking up the work, duly reported.

These facts, and a few others not to be published, made both Mahbub and Creighton shake their heads.

"Let him go out with his Red Lama," said the horse-dealer with visible effort. "He is fond of the old man. He can learn his paces by the rosary at least."

"I have had some dealings with the old man—by letter," said Colonel Creighton, smiling to himself. "Whither goes he?"

"Up and down the land, as he has these three years. He seeks a River of Healing. God's curse upon all—" Mahbub checked himself. "He beds down at the Temple of the Tirthankers or at Buddh Gaya when he is in from the Road. Then he goes to see the boy at the madrissah as we know, for the boy was punished for it twice or thrice. He is quite mad, but a peaceful man. I have met him. The Babu also has had dealings with him. We have watched him for three years. Red Lamas are not so common in Hind that one loses track."

"Babus are very curious," said Lurgan meditatively. "Do you know what Hurree Babu really wants? He wants to be made a member of the Royal Society by taking ethnological notes. I tell you, I tell him about the lama everything that Mahbub and the boy have told me. Hurree Babu goes down to Benares—at his own expense, I think."

"I don't," said Creighton briefly. He had paid Hurree's travelling expenses, out of a most lively curiosity to learn what the lama might be.

"And he applies to the lama for information on lamaism, and devil dances, and spells and charms, several times in these few years. Holy Virgin! I could have told him all that yee-ars ago. I think Hurree Babu is getting too old for the Road. He likes better to collect manners and customs information. Yes, he wants to be an F. R. S."

"Hurree thinks well of the boy, doesn't he?"

"Oh, very indeed—we have had some pleasant evenings at my little place—but I think it would be waste to throw him away with Hurree on the Ethnological side."

"Not for a first experience. How does that strike you, Mahbub? Let the boy run with the lama for six months. After that we can see. He will get experience."

"He has it already, Sahib—as a fish controls the water he swims in; but for every reason it will be well to loose him from the school."

"Very good, then," said Creighton, half to himself. "He can go with the lama, and if Hurree Babu cares to keep an eye on them so much the better. He won't lead the boy into any danger as Mahbub would. Curious —his wish to be an F. R. S. Very human, too. He is best on the Ethnological side—Hurree."

No money and no preferment would have drawn Creighton from his work on the Indian Survey, but deep in his heart also lay an ambition to write "F. R. S." after his name. Honours of a sort he knew could be obtained by ingenuity and the help of friends, but, to the best of his belief, nothing save work—papers representing a life of it—took a man into the Society which he had bombarded for years with monographs on strange Asiatic cults and unknown customs. Nine men out of ten would flee from a Royal Society soiree in extremity of boredom; but Creighton was the tenth, and at times his soul yearned for the crowded rooms in easy London where silver-haired, bald-headed gentlemen who know nothing of the Army move among spectroscopic experiments, the lesser plants of the frozen tundras, electric flight-measuring machines, and apparatus for slicing into fractional millimetres the left eye of the female mosquito. By all right and reason, it was the Royal Geographical that should have appealed to him, but men are as chancy as children in their choice of playthings. So Creighton smiled, and thought the better of Hurree Babu, moved by like desires.

He dropped the ghost-dagger and looked up at Mahbub.

"How soon can we get the colt from the stable?" said the horse-dealer, reading his eyes.

"Hmm. If I withdraw him by order now—what will he do, think you? I have never before assisted at the teaching of such an one."

"He will come to me," said Mahbub promptly. "Lurgan Sahib and I will prepare him for the Road."

"So be it, then. For six months he shall run at his choice: but who will be his sponsor?"

Lurgan slightly inclined his head. "He will not tell anything, if that is what you are afraid of, Colonel Creighton."

"It's only a boy, after all."

"Ye-es; but first, he has nothing to tell; and secondly, he knows what would happen. Also, he is very fond of Mahbub, and of me a little."

"Will he draw pay?" demanded the practical horse-dealer.

"Food and water allowance only. Twenty rupees a month."

One advantage of the Secret Service is that it has no worrying audit. The service is ludicrously starved, of course, but the funds are administered by a few men who do not call for vouchers or present itemised accounts. Mahbub's eyes lighted with almost a Sikh's love of money. Even Lurgan's impassive face changed. He considered the years to come when Kim would have been entered and made to the Great Game that never ceases day and night, throughout India. He foresaw honour and credit in the mouths of a chosen few, coming to him from his pupil. Lurgan Sahib had made E.23 what E.23 was, out of a bewildered, impertinent, lying, little North-West Province man.

But the joy of these masters was pale and smoky beside the joy of Kim when St. Xavier's Head called him aside, with word that Colonel Creighton had sent for him.

"I understand, O'Hara, that he has found you a place as an assistant chain-man in the Canal Department: that comes of taking up mathematics. It is great luck for you, for you are only seventeen; but of course you understand that you do not become pukka (permanent) till you have passed the autumn examination. So you must not think you are going out into the world to enjoy yourself, or that your fortune is made. There is a great deal of hard work before you. Only, if you succeed in becoming pukka, you can rise, you know, to four hundred and fifty a month." Whereat the Principal gave him much good advice as to his conduct, and his manners, and his morals; and others, his elders, who had not been wafted into billets, talked, as only Anglo-Indian lads can, of favouritism and corruption. Indeed, young Cazalet, whose father was a pensioner at Chunar, hinted very broadly that Colonel Creighton's interest in Kim was directly paternal; and Kim, instead of retaliating, did not even use language. He was thinking of the immense fun to come, of Mahbub's letter of the day before, all neatly written in English, making appointment for that afternoon in a house the very name of which would have crisped the Principal's hair with horror. . . . .

Said Kim to Mahbub in Lucknow railway station that evening, above the luggage-scales—"I feared lest, at the last, the roof would fall upon me and cheat me. Is it indeed all finished, O my father?"

Mahbub snapped his fingers to show the utterness of that end, and his eyes blazed like red coals.

"Then where is the pistol that I may wear it?"

"Softly! A half-year, to run without heel-ropes. I begged that much from Colonel Creighton Sahib. At twenty rupees a month. Old Red Hat knows that thou art coming."

"I will pay thee dustoorie (commission) on my pay for three months," said Kim gravely. "Yea, two rupees a month. But first we must get rid of these." He plucked his thin linen trousers and dragged at his collar. "I have brought with me all that I need on the Road. My trunk has gone up to Lurgan Sahib's."

"Who sends his salaams to thee—Sahib."

"Lurgan Sahib is a very clever man. But what dost thou do?"

"I go North again, upon the Great Game. What else? Is thy mind still set on following old Red Hat?"

"Do not forget he made me what I am—though he did not know it. Year by year, he sent the money that taught me."

"I would have done as much—had it struck my thick head," Mahbub growled. "Come away. The lamps are lit now, and none will mark thee in the bazar. We go to Huneefa's house."

On the way thither, Mahbub gave him much the same sort of advice as his mother gave to Lemuel, and curiously enough, Mahbub was exact to point out how Huneefa and her likes destroyed kings.

"And I remember," he quoted maliciously, "one who said, 'Trust a snake before a harlot and a harlot before a Pathan, Mahbub Ali.' Now, excepting as to Pathans, of whom I am one, all that is true. Most true is it in the Great Game, for it is by means of woman that all plans come to ruin and we lie out in dawning with our throats cut. So it happened to such a one,"—he gave the reddest particulars.

"Then why—?" Kim paused before a filthy staircase that climbed to the warm darkness of an upper chamber in the ward that is behind Azim Ullah's tobacco-shop. Those who know it call it The Bird-cage—it is so full of whisperings and whistlings and chirrupings.

The room, with its dirty cushions and half-smoked hookahs, smelt abominably of stale tobacco. In one corner lay a huge and shapeless woman clad in greenish gauzes, and decked, brow, nose, ear, neck, wrist, arm, waist, and ankle, with heavy native jewellery. When she turned it was like the clashing of copper pots. A lean cat in the balcony outside the window mewed hungrily. Kim checked, bewildered, at the door-curtain.

"Is that the new stuff, Mahbub?" said Huneefa lazily, scarce troubling to remove the mouthpiece from her lips. "O Buktanoos!"—like most of her kind, she swore by the Djinns—"O Buktanoos! He is very good to look upon."

"That is part of the selling of the horse," Mahbub explained to Kim, who laughed.

"I have heard that talk since my Sixth Day," he replied, squatting by the light. "Whither does it lead?"

"To protection. To-night we change thy colour. This sleeping under roofs has blanched thee like an almond. But Huneefa has the secret of a colour that catches. No painting of a day or two. Also, we fortify thee against the chances of the Road. That is my gift to thee, my son. Take out all metals on thee and lay them here. Make ready, Huneefa."

Kim dragged forth his compass, Survey paint-box, and the new-filled medicine-box. They had all accompanied his travels, and boy-like he valued them immensely.

The woman rose slowly and moved with her hands a little spread before her. Then Kim saw that she was blind. "No, no," she muttered, "the Pathan speaks truth—my colour does not go in a week or a month, and those whom I protect are under strong guard."

"When one is far off and alone, it would not be well to grow blotched and leprous of a sudden," said Mahbub. "When thou wast with me I could oversee the matter. Besides, a Pathan is a fair-skin. Strip to the waist now and look how thou are whitened." Huneefa felt her way back from an inner room. "It is no matter, she cannot see." He took a pewter bowl from her ringed hand.

The dye-stuff showed blue and gummy. Kim experimented on the back of his wrist, with a dab of cotton wool; but Huneefa heard him.

"No, no," she cried, "the thing is not done thus, but with the proper ceremonies. The colouring is the least part. I give thee the full protection of the Road."

"Jadoo?" (magic), said Kim, with a half start. He did not like the white, sightless eyes. Mahbub's hand on his neck bowed him to the floor, nose within an inch of the boards.

"Be still. No harm comes to thee, my son. I am thy sacrifice!"

He could not see what the woman was about, but heard the clish-clash of her jewellery for many minutes. A match lit up the darkness; he caught the well-known purr and fizzle of grains of incense. Then the room filled with smoke—heavy, aromatic, and stupefying. Through growing drowse he heard the names of devils—of Zulbazan, Son of Eblis, who lives in bazars and paraos, making all the sudden lewd wickedness of wayside halts; of Dulhan, invisible about mosques, the dweller among the slippers of the Faithful, who hinders folk from their prayers; and Musboot, Lord of lies and panic. Huneefa, now whispering in his ear, now talking as from an immense distance, touched him with horrible soft fingers, but Mahbub's grip never shifted from his neck till, relaxing with a sigh, the boy lost his senses.

"Allah! How he fought! We should never have done it but for the drugs. That was his white blood, I take it," said Mahbub testily. "Go on with the dawut (invocation). Give him full Protection."

"O Hearer! Thou that hearest with ears, be present. Listen, O Hearer!" Huneefa moaned, her dead eyes turned to the west. The dark room filled with moanings and snortings.

From the outer balcony, a ponderous figure raised a round bullet head and coughed nervously.

"Do not interrupt this ventriloquial necromanciss, my friend," it said in English. "I opine that it is very disturbing to you, but no enlightened observer is jolly well upset."

". . . I will lay a plot for their ruin! O Prophet, bear with the unbelievers. Let them alone awhile!" Huneefa's face, turned to the northward, worked horribly, and it was as though voices from the ceiling answered her.

Hurree Babu returned to his note-book, balanced on the windowsill, but his hand shook. Huneefa, in some sort of drugged ecstasy, wrenched herself to and fro as she sat cross-legged by Kim's still head, and called upon devil after devil, in the ancient order of the ritual, binding them to avoid the boy's every action.

"With Him are the keys of the Secret Things! None knoweth them beside Himself. He knoweth that which is in the dry land and in the sea!" Again broke out the unearthly whistling responses.

"I—I apprehend it is not at all malignant in its operation?" said the Babu, watching the throat-muscles quiver and jerk as Huneefa spoke with tongues. "It—it is not likely that she has killed the boy? If so, I decline to be witness at the trial. . . . What was the last hypothetical devil mentioned?"

"Babuji," said Mahbub in the vernacular. "I have no regard for the devils of Hind, but the Sons of Eblis are far otherwise, and whether they be jumalee (well-affected) or jullalee (terrible) they love not Kafirs."

"Then you think I had better go?" said Hurree Babu, half rising. "They are, of course, dematerialised phenomena. Spencer says—"

Huneefa's crisis passed, as these things must, in a paroxysm of howling, with a touch of froth at the lips. She lay spent and motionless beside Kim, and the crazy voices ceased.

"Wah! That work is done. May the boy be better for it; and Huneefa is surely a mistress of dawut. Help haul her aside, Babu. Do not be afraid."

"How am I to fear the absolutely non-existent?" said Hurree Babu, talking English to reassure himself. It is an awful thing still to dread the magic that you contemptuously investigate—to collect folk-lore for the Royal Society with a lively belief in all Powers of Darkness.

Mahbub chuckled. He had been out with Hurree on the Road ere now. "Let us finish the colouring," said he. "The boy is well protected if—if the Lords of the Air have ears to hear. I am a sufi (free-thinker), but when one can get blind-sides of a woman, a stallion, or a devil, why go round to invite a kick? Set him upon the way, Babu, and see that old Red Hat does not lead him beyond our reach. I must get back to my horses."

"All raight," said Hurree Babu. "He is at present a curious spectacle."

About third cock-crow, Kim woke after a sleep of thousands of years. Huneefa, in her corner, snored heavily, but Mahbub was gone.

"I hope you were not frightened," said an oily voice at his elbow. "I superintended entire operation, which was most interesting from ethnological point of view. It was high-class dawut."

"Huh!" said Kim, recognising Hurree Babu, who smiled ingratiatingly.

"And also I had honour to bring down from Lurgan your present costume. I am not in the habit offeecially of carrying such gauds to subordinates, but"—he giggled—"your case is noted as exceptional on the books. I hope Mr. Lurgan will note my action."

Kim yawned and stretched himself. It was good to turn and twist within loose clothes once again.

"What is this?" He looked curiously at the heavy duffle-stuff loaded with the scents of the far North.

"Oho! That is inconspicuous dress of chela attached to service of lamaistic lama. Com-plete in every particular," said Hurree Babu, rolling into the balcony to clean his teeth at a goglet. "I am of opeenion it is not your old gentleman's precise religion, but rather sub-variant of same. I have contributed rejected notes to 'Asiatic Quarterly Review' on these subjects. Now it is curious that the old gentleman himself is totally devoid of religiosity. He is not a dam particular."

"Do you know him?"

Hurree Babu held up his hand to show he was engaged in the prescribed rites that accompany tooth-cleaning and such things among decently bred Bengalis. Then he recited in English an Arya-Somaj prayer of a theistical nature, and stuffed his mouth with pan and betel.

"Oah yes. I have met him several times at Benares, and also at Buddh Gaya, to interrogate him on religious points and devil-worship. He is pure agnostic—same as me."

Huneefa stirred in her sleep, and Hurree Babu jumped nervously to the copper incense-burner, all black and discoloured in morning-light, rubbed a finger in the accumulated lampblack, and drew it diagonally across his face.

"Who has died in thy house?" asked Kim in the vernacular.

"None. But she may have the Evil Eye—that sorceress," the Babu replied.

"What dost thou do now, then?"

"I will set thee on thy way to Benares, if thou goest thither, and tell thee what must be known by Us."

"I go. At what hour runs the te-rain?" He rose to his feet, looked round the desolate chamber and at the yellow-wax face of Huneefa as the low sun stole across the floor. "Is there money to be paid that witch?"

"No. She has charmed thee against all devils and all dangers—in the name of her devils. It was Mahbub's desire." In English: "He is highly obsolete, I think, to indulge in such supersteetion. Why, it is all ventriloquy. Belly-speak—eh?"

Kim snapped his fingers mechanically to avert whatever evil—Mahbub, he knew, meditated none—might have crept in through Huneefa's ministrations; and Hurree giggled once more. But as he crossed the room he was careful not to step in Huneefa's blotched, squat shadow on the boards. Witches—when their time is on them—can lay hold of the heels of a man's soul if he does that.

"Now you must well listen," said the Babu when they were in the fresh air. "Part of these ceremonies which we witnessed they include supply of effeecient amulet to those of our Department. If you feel in your neck you will find one small silver amulet, verree cheap. That is ours. Do you understand?"

"Oah yes, hawa-dilli" (a heart-lifter), said Kim, feeling at his neck.

"Huneefa she makes them for two rupees twelve annas with—oh, all sorts of exorcisms. They are quite common, except they are partially black enamel, and there is a paper inside each one full of names of local saints and such things. Thatt is Huneefa's look-out, you see? Huneefa makes them onlee for us, but in case she does not, when we get them we put in, before issue, one small piece of turquoise. Mr. Lurgan, he gives them. There is no other source of supply; but it was me invented all this. It is strictly unoffeecial of course, but convenient for subordinates. Colonel

Creighton he does not know. He is European. The turquoise is wrapped in the paper. . . . Yes, that is road to railway station. . . . Now suppose you go with the lama, or with me, I hope, some day, or with Mahbub. Suppose we get into a dam-tight place. I am a fearful man—most fearful— but I tell you I have been in dam-tight places more than hairs on my head. You say: 'I am Son of the Charm.' Verree good."

"I do not understand quite. We must not be heard talking English here."

"That is all raight. I am only Babu showing off my English to you. All we Babus talk English to show off," said Hurree, flinging his shoulder-cloth jauntily. "As I was about to say, 'Son of the Charm' means that you may be member of the Sat Bhai—the Seven Brothers, which is Hindi and Tantric. It is popularly supposed to be extinct society, but I have written notes to show it is still extant. You see it is all my invention. Verree good. Sat Bhai has many members, and perhaps before they jolly-well-cut-your-throat they may give you just a chance for life. That is useful, anyhow. And, moreover, these fooolish natives—if they are not too excited—they always stop to think before they kill a man who says he belongs to any specific organisation. You see? You say then when you are in right place, 'I am Son of the Charm,' and you get—perhaps—ah—your second wind. That is only in extreme instances, or to open negotiations with a stranger. Can you quite see? Verree good. But suppose now, I, or any one of the Department, come to you dressed quite different. You would not know me at all unless I choose, I bet you. Some day I will prove it. I come as Ladakhi trader—oh anything—and I say to you: 'You want to buy precious stones?' You say: 'Do I look like a man who buys precious stones?' Then I say: 'Even verree poor man can buy a turquoise or tarkeean.' "

"That is kichree—vegetable curry," said Kim.

"Of course it is. You say: 'Let me see the tarkeean.' Then I say: 'It was cooked by a woman, and perhaps it is bad for your caste.' Then you say: 'There is no caste when men go to—look for tarkeean.' You stop a little between those words, 'to look.' That is thee whole secret. The little stop before the words."

Kim repeated the test-sentence.

"That is all right. Then I will show you my turquoise if there is time, and then you know who I am, and then we exchange views and documents and those-all things. And so it is with any other man of us. We talk sometimes about turquoises and sometimes about tarkeean, but always with that little stop in the words. It is verree easy. First, 'Son of the Charm,' if you are in a tight place. Perhaps that may help you—perhaps not. Then what I have told you about the tarkeean, if you want to transact offeecial business with a strange man. Of course, at present, you have no offeecial business. You are ah ha!—supernumerary on probation. Quite unique specimen. If you were Asiatic of birth you might be employed right off; but this half-year of leave is to make you de-Englishised, you see? The lama, he expects you, because I have demi-offeecially informed him you have passed all your examinations, and you will soon obtain Government appointment. Oh ho! You are on acting-allowance you see: so if you are called upon to help Sons of the Charm mind you jolly well try. Now I shall say good-bye, my dear fellow, and I hope you—ah—will come out top-side all raight."

Hurree Babu stepped back a pace or two into the crowd at the entrance of Lucknow station and—was gone. Kim drew a deep breath and hugged himself all over. The nickel-plated revolver he could feel in the bosom of his sad-coloured robe, the amulet was on his neck; begging-gourd, rosary, and ghost-dagger (Mr. Lurgan had forgotten nothing) were all to hand, with medicine, paint-box, and compass, and in a worn old pursebelt embroidered with porcupine quill-patterns lay a month's pay. Kings could be no richer. He bought sweetmeats in a leafcup from a Hindu trader, and ate them with glad rapture till a policeman ordered him off the steps.

Chapter 11

Give the man who is not made
 To his trade
Swords to fling and catch again,
Coins to ring and snatch again,
Men to harm and cure again,
Snakes to charm and lure again—
He'll be hurt by his own blade,
By his serpents disobeyed,
By his clumsiness bewrayed,
By the people mocked to scorn.
 So 'tis not with juggler born.
Pinch of dust or withered flower,
 Chance-flung fruit or borrowed staff,
Serve his need and shore his power,
 Bind the spell, or loose the laugh!
 "But a man who, etc.," Op. 15.

FOLLOWED a sudden natural reaction.

"Now am I alone—all alone," he thought. "In all India is no one so alone as I! If I die to-day, who shall bring the news—and to whom? If I live and God is good, there will be a price upon my head, for I am a Son of the Charm—I, Kim."

A very few white people, but many Asiatics, can throw themselves into a mazement as it were by repeating their own names over and over again to themselves, letting the mind go free upon speculation as to what is called personal identity. When one grows older, the power, usually, departs, but while it lasts it may descend upon a man at any moment.

"Who is Kim—Kim—Kim?"

He squatted in a corner of the clanging waiting-room, rapt from all other thoughts; hands folded in lap, and pupils contracted to pinpoints. In a minute—in another half second—he felt he would arrive at the solution of the tremendous puzzle; but here, as always happens, his mind dropped away from those heights with the rush of a wounded bird, and passing his hand before his eyes, he shook his head.

A long-haired Hindu bairagi (holy man), who had just bought a ticket, halted before him at that moment and stared intently.

"I also have lost it," he said sadly. "It is one of the Gates to the Way, but for me it has been shut many years."

"What is the talk?" said Kim, abashed.

"Thou wast wondering there in thy spirit what manner of thing thy soul might be. The seizure came of a sudden. I know. Who should know but I? Whither goest thou?"

"Toward Kashi" (Benares).

"There are no Gods there. I have proved them. I go to Prayag (Allahabad) for the fifth time—seeking the road to Enlightenment. Of what faith art thou?"

"I too am a Seeker," said Kim, using one of the lama's pet words. "Though"—he forgot his Northern dress for the moment—"though Allah alone knoweth what I seek."

The old fellow slipped the bairagi's crutch under his armpit and sat down on a patch of ruddy leopard's skin as Kim rose at the call for the Benares train.

"Go in hope, little brother," he said. "It is a long road to the feet of the One; but thither do we all travel."

Kim did not feel so lonely after this, and ere he had sat out twenty miles in the crowded compartment, was cheering his neighbours with a string of most wonderful yarns about his own and his master's magical gifts.

Benares struck him as a peculiarly filthy city, though it was pleasant to find how his cloth was respected. At least one-third of the population prays eternally to some group or other of the many million deities, and so revere every sort of holy man. Kim was guided to the Temple of the Tirthankers, about a mile outside the city, near Sarnath, by a chance-met Punjabi farmer—a Kamboh from Jullundur-way who had appealed in vain to every God of his homestead to cure his small son, and was trying Benares as a last resort.

"Thou art from the North?" he asked, shouldering through the press of the narrow, stinking streets much like his own pet bull at home.

"Ay, I know the Punjab. My mother was a Pahareen, but my father came from Amritzar—by Jandiala," said Kim, oiling his ready tongue for the needs of the Road.

"Jandiala—Jullundur? Oho! Then we be neighbours in some sort, as it were." He nodded tenderly to the wailing child in his arms. "Whom dost thou serve?"

"A most holy man at the Temple of the Tirthankers."

"They are all most holy and—most greedy," said the Jat with bitterness. "I have walked the pillars and trodden the temples till my feet are flayed, and the child is no whit better. And the mother being sick too. . . . Hush, then, little one. . . . We changed his name when the fever came. We put him into girl's clothes. There was nothing we did not do, except—I said to his mother when she bundled me off to Benares—she should have come with me—I said Sakhi Sarwar Sultan would serve us best. We know His generosity, but these down-country Gods are strangers."

The child turned on the cushion of the huge corded arms and looked at Kim through heavy eyelids.

"And was it all worthless?" Kim asked, with easy interest.

"All worthless—all worthless," said the child, lips cracking with fever.

"The Gods have given him a good mind, at least," said the father proudly. "To think he should have listened so cleverly. Yonder is thy temple. Now I am a poor man,—many priests have dealt with me,—but my son is my son, and if a gift to thy master can cure him—I am at my very wits' end."

Kim considered for a while, tingling with pride. Three years ago he would have made prompt profit on the situation and gone his way without a thought; but now, the very respect the Jat paid him proved that he was a man. Moreover, he had tasted fever once or twice already, and knew enough to recognise starvation when he saw it.

"Call him forth and I will give him a bond on my best yoke, so that the child is cured."

Kim halted at the carved outer door of the temple. A white-clad Oswal banker from Ajmir, his sins of usury new wiped out, asked him what he did.

"I am chela to Teshoo Lama, an Holy One from Bhotiyal—within there. He bade me come. I wait. Tell him."

"Do not forget the child," cried the importunate Jat over his shoulder, and then bellowed in Punjabi: "O Holy One—O disciple of the Holy One—O Gods above all the Worlds—behold affliction sitting at the gate!" That cry is so common in Benares that the passers never turned their heads.

The Oswal, at peace with mankind, carried the message into the darkness behind him, and the easy, uncounted Eastern minutes slid by; for the lama was asleep in his cell, and no priest would wake him. When the click of his rosary again broke the hush of the inner court where the calm images of the Arhats stand, a novice whispered, "Thy chela is here," and the old man strode forth, forgetting the end of that prayer.

Hardly had the tall figure shown in the doorway than the Jat ran before him, and, lifting up the child, cried: "Look upon this, Holy One; and if the Gods will, he lives—he lives!"

He fumbled in his waist-belt and drew out a small silver coin.

"What is now?" The lama's eyes turned to Kim. It was noticeable he spoke far clearer Urdu than long ago, under Zam-Zammah; but the father would allow no private talk.

"It is no more than a fever," said Kim. "The child is not well fed."

"He sickens at everything, and his mother is not here."

"If it be permitted, I may cure, Holy One."

"What! Have they made thee a healer? Wait here," said the lama, and he sat down by the Jat upon the lowest step of the temple, while Kim, looking out of the corner of his eyes, slowly opened the little betel-box. He had dreamed dreams at school of returning to the lama as a Sahib—of chaffing the old man before he revealed himself—boy's dreams all. There was more drama in this abstracted, brow-puckered search through the tabloid-bottles, with a pause here and there for thought and a muttered invocation between whiles. Quinine he had in tablets, and dark brown meat-lozenges—beef most probably, but that was not his business. The little thing would not eat, but it sucked at a lozenge greedily, and said it liked the salt taste.

"Take then these six." Kim handed them to the man. "Praise the Gods, and boil three in milk; other three in water. After he has drunk the milk give him this (it was the half of a quinine pill), and wrap him warm. Give him the water of the other three, and the other half of this white pill when he wakes. Meantime, here is another brown medicine that he may suck at on the way home."

"Gods, what wisdom!" said the Kamboh, snatching.

It was as much as Kim could remember of his own treatment in a bout of autumn malaria—if you except the patter that he added to impress the lama.

"Now go! Come again in the morning."

"But the price—the price," said the Jat, and threw back his sturdy shoulders. "My son is my son. Now that he will be whole again, how shall I go back to his mother and say I took help by the wayside and did not even give a bowl of curds in return?"

"They are alike, these Jats," said Kim softly. "The Jat stood on his dung-hill and the King's elephants went by. 'O driver,' said he, 'what will you sell those little donkeys for?'"

The Jat burst into a roar of laughter, stifled with apologies to the lama. "It is the saying of my own country—the very talk of it. So are we Jats all. I will come to-morrow with the child; and the blessing of the Gods of the Homesteads—who are good little Gods—be on you both. . . . Now, son, we grow strong again. Do not spit it out, little Princeling! King of my Heart, do not spit it out, and we shall be strong men, wrestlers and club-wielders, by morning."

He moved away, crooning and mumbling. The lama turned to Kim, and all the loving old soul of him looked out through his narrow eyes.

"To heal the sick is to acquire merit; but first one gets knowledge. That was wisely done, O Friend of all the World."

"I was made wise by thee, Holy One," said Kim, forgetting the little play just ended; forgetting St. Xavier's; forgetting his white blood; forgetting even the Great Game as he stooped, Mohammedan fashion, to touch his master's feet in the dust of the Jain temple. "My teaching I owe to thee. I have eaten thy bread three years. My time is finished. I am loosed from the schools. I come to thee."

"Herein is my reward. Enter! Enter! And is all well?" They passed to the inner court, where the afternoon sun sloped golden across. "Stand that I may see. So!" He peered critically. "It is no longer a child, but a man, ripened in wisdom, walking as a physician. I did well—I did well when I gave thee up to the armed men on that black night. Dost thou remember our first day under Zam-Zammah?"

"Ay," said Kim. "Dost thou remember when I leapt off the carriage the first day I went to—"

"The Gates of Learning? Truly. And the day that we ate the cakes together at the back of the river by Nucklao. Aha! Many times hast thou begged for me, but that day I begged for thee."

"Good reason," quoth Kim. "I was then a scholar in the Gates of Learning, and attired as a Sahib. Do not forget, Holy One," he went on playfully, "I am still a Sahib—by thy favour."

"True. And a Sahib in most high esteem. Come to my cell, chela."

"How is that known to thee?"

The lama smiled. "First by means of letters from the kindly priest whom we met in the camp of armed men; but he is now gone to his own country, and I sent the money to his brother." Colonel Creighton, who had succeeded to the trusteeship when Father Victor went to England with the Mavericks, was hardly the chaplain's brother. "But I do not well understand Sahibs' letters. They must be interpreted to me. I chose a surer way. Many times when I returned from my Search to this temple, which has always been a nest to me, there came one seeking Enlightenment—a man from Leh—that had been, he said, a Hindu, but wearied of all those Gods." The lama pointed to the Arhats.

"A fat man?" said Kim, a twinkle in his eye.

"Very fat; but I perceived in a little his mind was wholly given up to useless things—such as devils and charms and the form and fashion of our tea-drinkings in the monasteries, and by what road we initiated the novices. A man abounding in questions; but he was a friend of thine, chela. He told me that thou wast on the road to much honour as a scribe. And I see thou are a physician."

"Yes, that am I—a scribe, when I am a Sahib, but it is set aside when I come as thy disciple. I have accomplished the years appointed for a Sahib."

"As it were a novice?" said the lama, nodding his head. "Art thou freed from the schools? I would not have thee unripe."

"I am all free. In due time I take service under the Government as a scribe—"

"Not as a warrior. That is well."

"But first I come to wander—with thee. Therefore I am here. Who begs for thee, these days?" he went on quickly. The ice was thin.

"Very often I beg myself; but, as thou knowest, I am seldom here, except when I come to look again at my disciple. From one end to another of Hind have I travelled afoot and in the te-rain. A great and a wonderful land! But here, when I put in, is as though I were in my own Bhotiyal."

He looked round the little clean cell complacently. A low cushion gave him a seat, on which he had disposed himself in the cross-legged attitude of the Bodhisat emerging from meditation; a black teak-wood table, not twenty inches high, set with copper tea-cups, was before him. In one corner stood a tiny altar, also of heavily carved teak, bearing a copper-gilt image of the seated Buddha and fronted by a lamp, an incense-holder, and a pair of copper flower-pots.

"The Keeper of the Images in the Wonder House acquired merit by giving me these a year since," he said, following Kim's eye. "When one is far from one's own land such things carry remembrance; and we must reverence the Lord for that He showed the Way. See!" he pointed to a curiously-built mound of coloured rice crowned with a fantastic metal ornament. "When I was abbot in my own place—before I came to better knowledge—I made that offering daily. It is the Sacrifice of the Universe to the Lord. Thus do we of Bhotiyal offer all the world daily to the Excellent Law. And I do it even now, though I know that the Excellent One is beyond all pinchings and pattings." He snuffed from his gourd.

"It is well done, Holy One," Kim murmured, sinking at ease on the cushions, very happy and rather tired.

"And also," the old man chuckled, "I write pictures of the Wheel of Life. Three days to a picture. I was busied on it—or it may be I shut my eyes a little—when they brought word of thee. It is good to have thee here: I will show thee my art—not for pride's sake, but because thou must learn. The Sahibs have not all this world's wisdom."

He drew from under the table a sheet of strangely scented yellow Chinese paper, the brushes, and slab of India ink. In cleanest, severest outline he had traced the Great Wheel with its six spokes, whose centre is the conjoined Hog, Snake, and Dove (Ignorance, Anger, and Lust), and whose compartments are all the heavens and hells, and all the chances of human life. Men say that the Bodhisat Himself first drew it with grains of rice upon dust, to teach His disciples the cause of things. Many ages have crystallised it into a most wonderful convention crowded with hundreds of little figures whose every line carries a meaning. Few can translate the picture-parable; there are not twenty in all the world who can draw it surely without a copy: of those who can both draw and expound are but three.

"I have a little learned to draw," said Kim. "But this is a marvel beyond marvels."

"I have written it for many years," said the lama. "Time was when I could write it all between one lamp-lighting and the next. I will teach thee the art—after due preparation; and I will show thee the meaning of the Wheel."

"We take the Road, then?"

"The Road and our Search. I was but waiting for thee. It was made plain to me in a hundred dreams—notably one that came upon the night of the day that the Gates of Learning first shut—that without thee I should never find my River. Again and again, as thou knowest, I put this from me, fearing an illusion. Therefore I would not take thee with me that day at Lucknow, when we ate the cakes. I would not take thee till the time was ripe and auspicious. From the Hills to the Sea, from the Sea to the Hills have I gone, but it was vain. Then I remembered the 'Jataka.' "

He told Kim the story of the elephant with the leg-iron, as he had told it so often to the Jain priests.

"Further testimony is not needed," he ended serenely. "Thou wast sent for an aid. That aid removed, my Search came to nought. Therefore we will go out again together, and our Search is sure."

"Whither go we?"

"What matters, Friend of all the World? The Search, I say, is sure. If need be, the River will break from the ground before us. I acquired merit when I sent thee to the Gates of Learning, and gave thee the jewel that is Wisdom. Thou didst return, I saw even now, a follower of Sakyamuni, the Physician, whose altars are many in Bhotiyal. It is sufficient. We are together, and all things are as they were—Friend of all the World—Friend of the Stars—my chela!"

Then they talked of matters secular; but it was noticeable that the lama never demanded any details of life at St. Xavier's, nor showed the faintest curiosity as to the manners and customs of Sahibs. His mind moved all in the past, and he revived every step of their wonderful first journey together, rubbing his hands and chuckling, till it pleased him to curl himself up into the sudden sleep of old age.

Kim watched the last dusty sunshine fade out of the court, and played with his ghost-dagger and rosary. The clamour of Benares, oldest of all earth's cities awake before the Gods, day and night, beat round the walls as the sea's roar round a breakwater. Now and again, a Jain priest crossed the court, with some small offering to the images, and swept the path about him lest by chance he should take the life of a living thing. A lamp twinkled, and there followed the sound of a prayer. Kim watched the stars as they rose one after another in the still, sticky dark, till he fell asleep at the foot of the altar. That night he dreamed in Hindustanee, with never an English word. . . .

"Holy One, there is the child to whom we gave the medicine," he said, about three o'clock in the morning, when the lama, also waking from dreams, would have fared forth on pilgrimage. "The Jat will be here at the light."

"I am well answered. In my haste I would have done a wrong." He sat down on the cushions and returned to his rosary. "Surely old folk are as children," he said pathetically. "They desire a matter—behold, it must be done at once, or they fret and weep! Many times when I was upon the Road I have been ready to stamp with my feet at the hindrance of an oxcart in the way, or a mere cloud of dust. It was not so when I was a man—a long time ago. None the less it is wrongful—"

"But thou art indeed old, Holy One."

"The thing was done. A Cause was put out into the world, and, old or young, sick or sound, knowing or unknowing, who can rein in the effect of that Cause? Does the Wheel hang still if a child spin it—or a drunkard? Chela, this is a great and a terrible world."

"I think it good," Kim yawned. "What is there to eat? I have not eaten since yesterday even."

"I had forgotten thy need. Yonder is good Bhotiyal tea and cold rice."

"We cannot walk far on such stuff." Kim felt all the European's lust for flesh-meat, which is not accessible in a Jain temple. Yet, instead of going out at once with the begging-bowl, he stayed his stomach on slabs of cold rice till the full dawn. It brought the farmer, voluble, stuttering with gratitude.

"In the night the fever broke and the sweat came," he cried. "Feel here —his skin is fresh and new! He esteemed the salt lozenges, and took milk with greed." He drew the cloth from the child's face, and it smiled sleepily at Kim. A little knot of Jain priests, silent but all-observant, gathered by the temple door. They knew, and Kim knew that they knew, how the old lama had met his disciple. Being courteous folk, they had not obtruded themselves overnight by presence, word, or gesture. Wherefore Kim repaid them as the sun rose.

"Thank the Gods of the Jains, brother," he said, not knowing how those Gods were named. "The fever is indeed broken."

"Look! See!" The lama beamed in the background upon his hosts of three years. "Was there ever such a chela? He follows our Lord the Healer."

Now the Jains officially recognise all the Gods of the Hindu creed, as well as the Lingam and the Snake. They wear the Brahminical thread; they adhere to every claim of Hindu caste-law. But, because they knew and loved the lama, because he was an old man, because he sought the Way, because he was their guest, and because he collogued long of nights with the head-priest—as free-thinking a metaphysician as ever split one hair into seventy—they murmured assent.

"Remember,"—Kim bent over the child,—"this trouble may come again."

"Not if thou hast the proper spell," said the father.

"But in a little while we go away."

"True," said the lama to all the Jains. "We go now together upon the Search whereof I have often spoken. I waited till my chela was ripe. Behold him! We go North. Never again shall I look upon this place of my rest, O people of good will."

"But I am not a beggar." The cultivator rose to his feet, clutching the child.

"Be still. Do not trouble the Holy One," a priest cried.

"Go," Kim whispered. "Meet us again under the big railway bridge, and for the sake of all the Gods of our Punjab, bring food—curry, pulse, cakes fried in fat, and sweetmeats. Specially sweetmeats. Be swift!"

The pallor of hunger suited Kim very well as he stood, tall and slim, in his sad-coloured, sweeping robes, one hand on his rosary and the other in the attitude of benediction, faithfully copied from the lama. An English observer might have said that he looked rather like the young saint of a stained-glass window, whereas he was but a growing lad faint with emptiness.

Long and formal were the farewells, thrice ended and thrice renewed. The Seeker—he who had invited the lama to that haven from far-away Tibet, a silver-faced, hairless ascetic—took no part in it, but meditated, as always, alone among the images. The others were very human; pressing small comforts upon the old man,—a betel-box, a fine new iron pencase, a food-bag, and such like,—warning him against the dangers of the world without, and prophesying a happy end to the Search. Meantime Kim, lonelier than ever, squatted on the steps, and swore to himself in the language of St. Xavier's.

"But it is my own fault," he concluded. "With Mahbub, I ate Mahbub's bread, or Lurgan Sahib's. At St. Xavier's, three meals a day. Here I must jolly well look out for myself. Besides, I am not in good training. How I could eat a plate of beef now! . . . Is it finished, Holy One?"

The lama, both hands raised, intoned a final blessing in ornate Chinese. "I must lean on thy shoulder," said he, as the temple-gates closed. "We grow stiff, I think."

The weight of a six-foot man is not light to steady through miles of crowded streets, and Kim, loaded down with bundles and packages for the way, was glad to reach the shadow of the railway bridge.

"Here we eat," he said resolutely, as the Kamboh, blue-robed and smiling, hove in sight, a basket in one hand and the child on the other.

"Fall to, Holy Ones!" he cried from fifty yards. (They were by the shoal under the first bridge-span, out of sight of hungry priests.) "Rice and good curry, cakes all warm and well scented with hing (asafoetida), curds and sugar. King of my fields," this to the small son, "let us show these holy men that we Jats of Jullundur can pay a service. . . . I had heard the Jains would eat nothing that they had not cooked, but truly" —he looked away politely over the broad river—"where there is no eye there is no caste."

"And we," said Kim, turning his back and heaping a leaf-platter for the lama, "are beyond all castes."

They gorged themselves on the good food in silence. Nor till he had licked the last of the sticky sweet-stuff from his little finger did Kim note that the Kamboh too was girt for travel.

"If our roads lie together," he said roughly, "I go with thee. One does not often find a worker of miracles, and the child is still weak. But I am not altogether a reed." He picked up his lathi—a five-foot male-bamboo ringed with bands of polished iron—and flourished it in the air. "The Jats are called quarrelsome, but that is not true. Except when we are crossed, we are like our own buffaloes."

"So be it," said Kim. "A good stick is a good reason."

The lama gazed placidly up-stream, where in long, smudged perspective the ceaseless columns of smoke go up from the burning-ghats by the river. Now and again, despite all municipal regulations, the fragment of a half-burned body bobbed by on the full current.

"But for thee," said the Kamboh to Kim, drawing his child into his hairy breast, "I might to-day have gone thither—with this one. The priests tell us that Benares is holy—which none doubt—and desirable to die in. But I do not know their Gods, and they ask for money; and when one has done one worship a shaved-head vows it is of none effect except one do another. Wash here! Wash there! Pour, drink, lave, and scatter flowers—but always pay the priests. No, the Punjab for me, and the soil of the Jullundur-doab for the best soil in it."

"I have said many times—in the temple I think—that if need be, the River will open at our feet. We will therefore go North," said the lama, rising. "I remember a pleasant place, set about with fruit-trees, where one can walk in meditation—and the air is cooler there. It comes from the Hills and the snow of the Hills."

"What is the name?" said Kim.

"How should I know? Didst thou not—no, that was after the Army rose out of the earth and took thee away. I abode there in meditation in a room against the dovecot—except when she talked eternally."

"Oho! the woman from Kulu. That is by Saharunpore," Kim laughed.

"How does the spirit move thy master? Does he go afoot, for the sake of past sins?" the Jat demanded cautiously. "It is a far cry to Delhi."

"No," said Kim. "I will beg a tikkut for the te-rain." One does not own to the possession of money in India.

"Then in the name of the Gods, let us take the fire-carriage. My son is best in his mother's arms. The Government has brought on us many taxes, but it gives us one good thing—the te-rain that joins friends and unites the anxious. A wonderful matter is the te-rain."

They all piled into it a couple of hours later, and slept through the heat of the day. The Kamboh plied Kim with ten thousand questions as to the lama's walk and work in life, and received some curious answers. Kim was content to be where he was, to look out upon the flat North-Western landscape, and to talk to the changing mob of fellow-passengers. Even to-day, tickets and ticket-clipping are dark oppression to Indian rustics. They do not understand why, when they have paid for a magic piece of paper, strangers should punch great pieces out of the charm. So long and furious are the debates between travellers and Eurasian ticket-collectors. Kim assisted at two or three with grave advice, meant to darken council and to show off his wisdom before the lama and the admiring Kamboh. But at Somna Road the Fates sent him a matter to think upon. There tumbled into the compartment, as the train was moving off, a mean, lean little person—a Mahratta, so far as Kim could judge by the cock of the tight turban. His face was cut, his muslin upper-garment was badly torn, and one leg was bandaged. He told them that a country-cart had upset and nearly slain him: he was going to Delhi, where his son lived. Kim watched him closely. If, as he asserted, he had been rolled over and over on the earth, there should have been signs of gravel-rash on the skin. But all his injuries seemed clean cuts, and a mere fall from a cart could not cast a man into such extremity of terror. As, with shaking fingers, he knotted up the torn cloth about his neck he laid bare an amulet of the kind called a keeper-up of the heart. Now, amulets are common enough, but they are not generally strung on square-plaited copper wire, and still fewer amulets bear black enamel on silver. There were none except the Kamboh and the lama in the compartment, which, luckily, was of an old type with solid ends. Kim made as to scratch in his bosom, and thereby lifted his own amulet. The Mahratta's face changed altogether at the sight, and he disposed the amulet fairly on his breast.

"Yes," he went on to the Kamboh, "I was in haste, and the cart, driven by a bastard, bound its wheel in a water-cut, and besides the harm done to me there was lost a full dish of tarkeean. I was not a Son of the Charm (a lucky man) that day."

"That was a great loss," said Kamboh, withdrawing interest. His experience of Benares had made him suspicious.

"Who cooked it?" said Kim.

"A woman." The Mahratta raised his eyes.

"But all women can cook tarkeean," said the Kamboh. "It is a good curry, as I know."

"Oh, yes, it is a good curry," said the Mahratta.

"And cheap," said Kim. "But what about caste?"

"Oh, there is no caste where men go to—look for tarkeean," the Mahratta replied, in the prescribed cadence. "Of whose service art thou?"

"Of the service of this Holy One." Kim pointed to the happy, drowsy lama, who woke with a jerk at the well-loved word.

"Ah, he was sent from Heaven to aid me. He is called the Friend of all the World. He is also called the Friend of the Stars. He walks as a physician—his time being ripe. Great is his wisdom."

"And a Son of the Charm," said Kim under his breath, as the Kamboh made haste to prepare a pipe lest the Mahratta should beg.

"And who is that?" the Mahratta asked, glancing sideways nervously.

"One whose child I—we have cured, who lies under great debt to us.—Sit by the window, man from Jullundur. Here is a sick one."

"Humph! I have no desire to mix with chance-met wastrels. My ears are not long. I am not a woman wishing to overhear secrets." The Jat slid himself heavily into a far corner.

"Art thou anything of a healer? I am ten leagues deep in calamity," cried the Mahratta, picking up the cue.

"The man is cut and bruised all over. I go about to cure him," Kim retorted. "None interfered between thy babe and me."

"I am rebuked," said the Kamboh meekly. "I am thy debtor for the life of my son. Thou art a miracle-worker—I know it."

"Show me the cuts." Kim bent over the Mahratta's neck, his heart nearly choking him; for this was the Great Game with a vengeance. "Now, tell thy tale swiftly, brother, while I say a charm."

"I come from the South, where my work lay. One of us they slew by the roadside. Hast thou heard?" Kim shook his head. He, of course, knew nothing of E.23's predecessor, slain down South in the habit of an Arab trader. "Having found a certain letter which I was sent to seek, I came away. I escaped from the city and ran to Mhow. So sure was I that none knew, I did not change my face. At Mhow a woman brought charge against me of theft of jewellery in that city which I had left. Then I saw the cry was out against me. I ran from Mhow by night, bribing the police, who had been bribed to hand me over without question to my enemies in the South. Then I lay in old Chitor city a week, a penitent in a temple, but I could not get rid of the letter which was my charge. I buried it under the Queen's Stone, at Chitor, in the place known to us all."

Kim did not know, but not for worlds would he have broken the thread.

"At Chitor, look you, I was all in Kings' country; for Kotah to the east is beyond the Queen's law, and east again lie Jeypur and Gwalior. Neither love spies, and there is no justice. I was hunted like a wet jackal; but I broke through at Bandakui, where I heard there was a charge against me of murder in the city I had left—of the murder of a boy. They have both the corpse and the witnesses waiting."

"But cannot the Government protect?"

"We of the Game are beyond protection. If we die, we die. Our names are blotted from the book. That is all. At Bandakui, where lives one of us, I thought to slip the scent by changing my face, and so made me a Mahratta. Then I came to Agra, and would have turned back to Chitor to recover the letter. So sure I was I had slipped them. Therefore I did not send a tar (telegram) to any one saying where the letter lay. I wished the credit of it all."

Kim nodded. He understood that feeling well.

"But at Agra, walking in the streets, a man cried a debt against me, and approaching with many witnesses, would hale me to the courts then and there. Oh, they are clever in the South! He recognised me as his agent for cotton. May he burn in Hell for it!"

"And wast thou?"

"O fool! I was the man they sought for the matter of the letter! I ran into the Fleshers' Ward and came out by the House of the Jew, who feared a riot and pushed me forth. I came afoot to Somna Road—I had only money for my tikkut to Delhi—and there, while I lay in a ditch with a fever, one sprang out of the bushes and beat me and cut me and searched me from head to foot. Within earshot of the te-rain it was!"

"Why did he not slay thee out of hand?"

"They are not so foolish. If I am taken in Delhi at the instance of lawyers, upon a proven charge of murder, my body is handed over to the State that desires it. I go back guarded, and then—I die slowly for an example to the rest of us. The South is not my country. I run in circles —like a goat with one eye. I have not eaten for two days. I am marked"— he touched the filthy bandage on his leg—"so that they will know me at Delhi."

"Thou are safe in the te-rain, at least."

"Live a year at the Great Game and tell me that again! The wires will be out against me at Delhi, describing every tear and rag upon me. Twenty—a hundred, if need be—will have seen me slay that boy. And thou art useless!"

Kim knew enough of native methods of attack not to doubt that the case would be deadly complete—even to the corpse. The Mahratta twitched his fingers with pain from time to time. The Kamboh in his corner glared sullenly; the lama was busy over his beads; and Kim, fumbling doctor-fashion at the man's neck, thought out his plan between invocations.

"Hast thou a charm to change my shape? Else I am dead. Five—ten minutes alone, if I had not been so pressed, and I might—"

"Is he cured yet, miracle-worker?" said the Kamboh jealously. "Thou hast chanted long enough."

"Nay. There is no cure for his hurts, as I see, except he sit for three days in the habit of a bairagi." This is a common penance, often imposed on a fat trader by his spiritual teacher.

"One priest always goes about to make another priest," was the retort. Like most grossly superstitious folk, the Kamboh could not keep his tongue from deriding his Church.

"Will thy son be a priest, then? It is time he took more of my quinine."

"We Jats are all buffaloes," said the Kamboh, softening anew.

Kim rubbed a finger-tip of bitterness on the child's trusting little lips. "I have asked for nothing," he said sternly to the father, "except food. Dost thou grudge me that? I go to heal another man. Have I thy leave— Prince?"

Up flew the man's huge paws in supplication. "Nay—nay. Do not mock me thus."

"It pleases me to cure this sick one. Thou shalt acquire merit by aiding. What colour ash is there in thy pipe-bowl? White. That is auspicious. Was there raw turmeric among thy foodstuffs?"

"I—I—"

"Open thy bundle!"

It was the usual collection of small oddments: bits of cloth, quack medicines, cheap fairings, a clothful of atta,—grayish, rough-ground native flour,—twists of down-country tobacco, tawdry pipe-stems, and a packet of curry-stuff, all wrapped in a quilt. Kim turned it over with the air of a wise warlock, muttering a Mohammedan invocation.

"This is wisdom I learned from the Sahibs," he whispered to the lama; and here, when one thinks of his training at Lurgan's, he spoke no more than the truth. "There is a great evil in this man's fortune, as shown by the stars, which—which troubles him. Shall I take it away?"

"Friend of the Stars, thou hast done well in all things. Let it be at thy pleasure. Is it another healing?"

"Quick! Be quick!" gasped the Mahratta. "The train may stop."

"A healing against the shadow of death," said Kim, mixing the Kamboh's flour with the mingled charcoal and tobacco ash in the red-earth bowl of the pipe. E.23, without a word, slipped off his turban and shook down his long black hair.

"That is my food—priest," the Jat growled.

"A buffalo in the temple! Hast thou dared to look even thus far?" said Kim. "I must do mysteries before fools; but have a care for thy eyes. Is there a film before them already? I save the babe, and for return thou —oh, shameless!" The man flinched at the direct gaze, for Kim was wholly in earnest. "Shall I curse thee, or shall I—" He picked up the outer cloth of the bundle and threw it over the bowed head. "Dare so much as to think a wish to see, and—and—even I cannot save thee. Sit! Be dumb!"

"I am blind—dumb. Forbear to curse! Co—come, child; we will play a game of hiding. Do not, for my sake, look from under the cloth."

"I see hope," said E.23. "What is thy scheme?"

"This comes next," said Kim, plucking the thin body-shirt. E.23 hesitated, with all a North-West man's dislike of baring his body.

"What is caste to a cut throat?" said Kim, rending it to the waist. "We must make thee a yellow Saddhu all over. Strip—strip swiftly, and shake thy hair over thy eyes while I scatter the ash. Now, a caste-mark on thy forehead." He drew from his bosom the little Survey paint-box and a cake of crimson lake.

"Art thou only a beginner?" said E.23, labouring literally for the dear life, as he slid out of his body-wrappings and stood clear in the loin-cloth while Kim splashed in a noble caste-mark on the ash-smeared brow.

"But two days entered to the Game, brother," Kim replied. "Smear more ash on the bosom."

"Hast thou met—a physician of sick pearls?" He switched out his long, tight-rolled turban-cloth and, with swiftest hands, rolled it over and under about his loins into the intricate devices of a Saddhu's cincture.

"Hah! Dost thou know his touch, then? He was my teacher for a while. We must bar thy legs. Ash cures wounds. Smear it again."

"I was his pride once, but thou art almost better. The Gods are kind to us! Give me that."

It was a tin box of opium pills among the rubbish of the Jat's bundle. E.23 gulped down a half handful. "They are good against hunger, fear, and chill. And they make the eyes red too," he explained. "Now I shall have heart to play the Game. We lack only a Saddhu's tongs. What of the old clothes?"

Kim rolled them small, and stuffed them into the slack folds of his tunic. With a yellow-ochre paint cake he smeared the legs and breast, great streaks against the background of flour, ash, and turmeric.

"The blood on them is enough to hang thee, brother."

"May be; but no need to throw them out of the window. . . . It is finished." His voice thrilled with a boy's pure delight in the Game. "Turn and look, O Jat."

"The Gods protect us," said the hooded Kamboh, emerging like a buffalo from the reeds. "But—whither went the Mahratta? What hast thou done?"

Kim had been trained by Lurgan Sahib; and E.23, by virtue of his business, was no bad actor. In place of the tremulous, shrinking trader there lolled against the corner an all but naked, ash-smeared, ochre-barred, dusty-haired Saddhu, his swollen eyes—opium takes quick effect on an empty stomach—luminous with insolence and bestial lust, his legs crossed under him, Kim's brown rosary round his neck, and a scant yard of worn, flowered chintz on his shoulders. The child buried his face in his amazed father's arms.

"Look up, Princeling! We travel with warlocks, but they will not hurt thee. Oh, do not cry. . . . What is the sense of curing a child one day and killing him with fright the next?"

"The child will be fortunate all his life. He has seen a great healing. When I was a child I made clay men and horses."

"I have made them too. Sir Banas, he comes in the night and makes them all alive at the back of our kitchen-midden," piped the child.

"And so thou art not frightened at anything. Eh, Prince?"

"I was frightened because my father was frightened. I felt his arms shake."

"Oh, chicken-man," said Kim, and even the abashed Jat laughed. "I have done a healing on this poor trader. He must forsake his gains and his account-books, and sit by the wayside three nights to overcome the malignity of his enemies. The Stars are against him."

"The fewer money-lenders the better, say I; but, Saddhu or no Saddhu, he should pay for my stuff on his shoulders."

"So? But that is thy child on thy shoulder—given over to the burning-ghat not two days ago. There remains one thing more. I did this charm in thy presence because need was great. I changed his shape and his soul. None the less, if, by any chance, O man from Jullundur, thou rememberest what thou hast seen, either among the elders sitting under the village tree, or in thy own house, or in company of thy priest when he blesses thy cattle, a murrain will come among the buffaloes, and a fire in thy thatch, and rats in the corn-bin, and the curse of our Gods upon thy fields that they may be barren before thy feet and after thy plough-share." This was part of an old curse picked up from a faquir by the Taksali Gate in the days of Kim's innocence. It lost nothing by repetition.

"Cease, Holy One! In mercy, cease!" cried the Jat. "Do not curse the household. I saw nothing! I heard nothing! I am thy cow!" and he made to grab at Kim's bare foot beating rhythmically on the carriage floor.

"But since thou hast been permitted to aid me in the matter of a pinch of flour and a little opium and such trifles as I have honoured by using in my art, so will the Gods return a blessing," and he gave it at length, to the man's immense relief. It was one that he had learned from Lurgan Sahib.

The lama stared through his spectacles as he had not stared at the business of disguisement.

"Friend of the Stars," he said at last, "thou hast acquired great wisdom. Beware that it do not give birth to pride. No man having the Law before his eyes speaks hastily of any matter which he has seen or encountered."

"No—no—no indeed," cried the farmer, fearful lest the master should be minded to improve on the pupil. E.23, with relaxed mouth, gave himself up to the opium that is meat, tobacco, and medicine to the spent Asiatic.

So, in a silence of awe and great miscomprehension, they slid into Delhi about lamp-lighting time.

Chapter 12

"Who hath desired the Sea—the sight of salt-water unbounded?
The heave and the halt and the hurl and the crash of the comber
*   wind-hounded?*
The sleek-barrelled swell before storm—gray, foamless, enormous,
*   and growing?*
Stark calm on the lap of the Line—or the crazy-eyed hurricane
*   blowing?*
His Sea in no showing the same—his Sea and the same 'neath all
*   showing—*
*   His Sea that his being fulfils?*
So and no otherwise—so and no otherwise Hill-men desire their
*   Hills!"*

"I HAVE found my heart again," said E.23, under cover of the platform's tumult. "Hunger and fear make men dazed, or I might have thought of this escape before. I was right. They come to hunt for me. Thou hast saved my head."

A group of yellow-trousered Punjab policemen, headed by a hot and perspiring young Englishman, parted the crowd about the carriages. Behind them, inconspicuous as a cat, ambled a small fat person who looked like a lawyer's tout.

"See the young Sahib reading from a paper. My description is in his hand," said E.23. "They go carriage by carriage, like fisher-folk netting a pool."

When the procession reached their compartment, E.23 was counting his beads with a steady jerk of the wrist; while Kim jeered at him for being so drugged as to have lost the ringed fire-tongs which are the Sadhu's distinguishing mark. The lama, deep in meditation, stared straight before him; and the farmer, glancing furtively, gathered up his belongings.

"Nothing here but a parcel of holy-bolies," said the Englishman aloud, and passed on amid a ripple of uneasiness; for native police mean extortion to the native all India over.

"The trouble now," whispered E.23, "lies in sending a wire as to the place where I hid that letter I was sent to find. I cannot go to the tar-office in this guise."

"Is it not enough I have saved thy neck?"

"Not if the work be left unfinished. Did never the healer of sick pearls tell thee so? Comes another Sahib! Ah!"

This was a tallish, sallowish District Superintendent of Police,—belt, helmet, polished spurs and all,—strutting and twirling his dark moustache.

"What fools are these Police Sahibs!" said Kim genially. E.23 glanced up under his eyelids. "It is well said," he muttered in a changed voice. "I go to drink water. Keep my place."

He blundered out almost into the Englishman's arms, and was bad-worded in clumsy Urdu.

"Tum-mut? You drunk? You mustn't bang about as though Delhi station belonged to you, my friend."

E.23, not moving a muscle of his countenance, answered with a stream of the filthiest abuse, at which Kim naturally rejoiced. It reminded him of the drummer-boys and the barrack-sweepers at Umballa in the terrible time of his first schooling.

"My good fool," the Englishman drawled. "Nicklejao! Go back to your carriage."

Step by step, withdrawing deferentially, and dropping his voice, the yellow Saddhu clomb back to the carriage, cursing the D. S. P. to re-motest posterity by—here Kim almost jumped—by the curse of the Queen's Stone, by the writing under the Queen's Stone, and by an assortment of Gods with wholly new names.

"I don't know what you're saying,"—the Englishman flushed angrily, —"But it's some piece of blasted impertinence. Come out of that!"

E.23, affecting to misunderstand, gravely produced his ticket, which the Englishman wrenched angrily from his hand.

"Oh zoolum! What oppression!" growled the Jat from his corner. "All for the sake of a jest too." He had been grinning at the freedom of the Saddhu's tongue. "Thy charms do not work well to-day, Holy One!"

The Saddhu followed the policeman, fawning and supplicating. The ruck of passengers, busy with their babies and their bundles, had not noticed the affair. Kim slipped out behind him; for it flashed through his head that he had heard this angry, stupid Sahib discoursing loud personalities to an old lady near Umballa three years ago.

"It is well," the Saddhu whispered, jammed in the calling, shouting, bewildered press—a Persian greyhound between his feet and a cadgeful of yelling hawks under charge of a Rajput falconer in the small of his back. "He has gone now to send word of the letter which I hid. They told me he was in Peshawur. I might have known that he is like the crocodile—always at the other ford. He has saved me from present calamity, but I owe my life to thee."

"Is he also one of Us?" Kim ducked under a Mewar camel-driver's greasy armpit and cannoned off a covey of jabbering Sikh matrons.

"Not less than the greatest. We are both fortunate! I will make report to him of what thou hast done. I am safe under his protection."

He bored through the edge of the crowd besieging the carriages, and squatted by the bench near the telegraph-office.

"Return, or they take thy place! Have no fear for the work, brother—or my life. Thou hast given my breathing-space, and Strickland Sahib has pulled me to land. We may work together at the Game yet. Farewell!"

Kim hurried to his carriage: elated, bewildered, but a little nettled in that he had no key to the secrets about him.

"I am only a beginner at the Game, that is sure. I could not have leaped into safety as did the Saddhu. He knew it was darkest under the lamp. I could not have thought to tell news under pretence of cursing . . . and how clever was the Sahib! No matter, I saved the life of one. . . . Where is the Kamboh gone, Holy One?" he whispered, as he took his seat in the now crowded compartment.

"A fear gripped him," the lama replied, with a touch of tender malice. "He saw thee change the Mahratta to a Saddhu in the twinkling of an eye, as a protection against evil. That shook him. Then he saw the Saddhu fall sheer into the hands of the polis—all the effect of thy art. Then he gathered up his son and fled; for he said that thou didst change a quiet trader into an impudent bandier of words with the Sahibs, and he feared a like fate. Where is the Saddhu?"

"With the polis," said Kim. . . . "Yet I saved the Kamboh's child."

The lama snuffed blandly.

"Ah, chela, see how thou art overtaken! Thou didst cure the Kamboh's child solely to acquire merit. But thou didst put a spell on the Mahratta with prideful workings—I watched thee—and with side-long glances to bewilder an old old man and a foolish farmer: whence calamity and suspicion."

Kim controlled himself with an effort beyond his years. Not more than any other youngster did he like to eat dirt or to be misjudged, but he saw himself in a cleft stick. The train rolled out of Delhi into the night.

"It is true," he murmured. "Where I have offended thee I have done wrong."

"It is more, chela. Thou hast loosed an Act upon the world, and as a stone thrown into a pool so spread the consequences thou canst not tell how far."

This ignorance was well both for Kim's vanity and for the lama's peace of mind, when we think that there was then being handed in at Simla a code-wire reporting the arrival of E.23 at Delhi, and, more important, the whereabouts of a letter he had been commissioned to—abstract. Incidentally, an overzealous policeman had arrested, on charge of murder done in a far southern State, a horribly indignant Ajmir cotton-broker, who was explaining himself to a Mr. Strickland on Delhi platform, while E.23 was paddling through by-ways into the locked heart of Delhi city. In two hours several telegrams had reached the angry minister of a southern State reporting that all trace of a somewhat bruised Mahratta had been lost; and by the time the leisurely train halted at Saharunpore the last ripple of the stone Kim had helped to heave was lapping against the steps of a mosque in far-away Roum—where it disturbed a pious man at prayers.

The lama made his in ample form near the dewy bougainvillea-trellis near the platform, cheered by the clear sunshine and the presence of his disciple. "We will put these things behind us," he said, indicating the brazen engine and the gleaming track. "The jolting of the te-rain—though a wonderful thing—has turned my bones to water. We will use clean air henceforward."

"Let us go to the Kulu woman's house," said Kim, and stepped forth cheerily under the bundles. Early morning Saharunporeway is clean and well scented. He thought of the other mornings at St. Xavier's, and it topped his already thrice-heaped contentment.

"Where is this new haste born from? Wise men do not run about like chickens in the sun. We have come hundreds upon hundreds of kos already, and, till now, I have scarcely been alone with thee an instant. How canst thou receive instruction all jostled of crowds? How can I, whelmed by a flux of talk, meditate upon the Way?"

"Her tongue grows no shorter with the years, then?" The disciple smiled.

"Nor her desire for charms. I remember once when I spoke of the Wheel of Life"—the lama fumbled in his bosom for his latest copy—"she was only curious about the devils that besiege children. She shall acquire merit by entertaining us—in a little while—at an after-occasion—softly, softly. Now we will wander loose-foot, waiting upon the Chain of Things. The Search is sure."

So they travelled very easily across and among the broad bloomful fruit-gardens—by way of Aminabad, Sahaigunge, Akrola of the Ford, and little Phulesa—the line of the Sewaliks always to the north, and behind them again the snows. After long, sweet sleep under the dry stars came the lordly, leisurely passage through a waking village—begging-bowl held forth in silence, but eyes roving in defiance of the Law from sky's edge to sky's edge. Then would Kim return soft-footed through the soft dust to his master under the shadow of a mango tree or the thinner shade of a white Doon siris, to eat and drink at ease. At mid-day, after talk and a little wayfaring, they slept; meeting the world refreshed when the air was cooler. Night found them adventuring into new territory—some chosen village spied three hours before across the fat land, and much discussed upon the road.

There they told their tale,—a new one each evening so far as Kim was concerned,—and there were they made welcome, either by priest or headman, after the custom of the kindly East.

When the shadows shortened and the lama leaned more heavily upon Kim, there was always the Wheel of Life to draw forth, to hold flat under wiped stones, and with a long straw to expound cycle by cycle. Here sat the Gods on high—and they were dreams of dreams. Here was our Heaven and the world of the demi-Gods—horsemen fighting among the Hills. Here were the agonies done upon the beasts, souls ascending or descending the ladder and therefore not to be interfered with. Here were the Hells, hot and cold, and the abodes of tormented ghosts. Let the chela study the troubles that come from overeating—bloated stomach and burning bowels. Obediently then, with bowed head and brown finger alert to follow the pointer, did the chela study; but when they came to the Human World, busy and profitless, that is just above the Hells, his mind was distracted; for by the roadside trundled the very Wheel itself, eating, drinking, trading, marrying, and quarrelling—all warmly alive. Often the lama made the living pictures the matter of his text, bidding Kim—too ready—note how the flesh takes a thousand thousand shapes, desirable or detestable as men reckon, but in truth of no account either way; and how the stupid spirit, bond-slave to the Hog, the Dove, and the Serpent— lusting after betel-nut, a new yoke of oxen, women, or the favour of kings—is bound to follow the body through all the Heavens and all the Hells, and strictly round again. Sometimes a woman or a poor man, watching the ritual—it was nothing less—when the great yellow chart was unfolded, would throw a few flowers or a handful of cowries upon its edge. It sufficed these humble ones that they had met a Holy One who might be moved to remember them in his prayers.

"Cure them if they are sick," said the lama, when Kim's sporting instincts woke. "Cure them if they have fever, but by no means work charms. Remember what befell the Mahratta."

"Then all Doing is evil?" Kim replied lying out under a big tree at the fork of the Doon road, watching the little ants run over his hand.

"To abstain from action is well—except to acquire merit."

"At the Gates of Learning we were taught that to abstain from action was unbefitting a Sahib. And I am a Sahib."

"Friend of all the World,"—the lama looked directly at Kim,—"I am an old man—pleased with shows as are children. To those who follow the Way there is neither black nor white, Hind nor Bhotiyal. We be all souls seeking escape. No matter what thy wisdom learned among Sahibs, when we come to my River thou wilt be freed from all illusion—at my side. Hai! my bones ache for that River, as they ached in the te-rain; but my spirit sits above my bones, waiting. The Search is sure!"

"I am answered. Is it permitted to ask a question?"

The lama inclined his stately head.

"I ate thy bread for three years—as thou knowest. Holy One, whence came—?"

"There is much wealth, as men count it, in Bhotiyal," the lama returned with composure. "In my own place I have the illusion of honour. I ask for that I need. I am not concerned with the account. That is for my monastery. Ai! The black high seats in the monastery, and the novices all in order!"

And he told stories, tracing with a finger in the dust, of the immense and sumptuous ritual of avalanche-guarded cathedrals; of processions and devil-dances; of the changing of monks and nuns into swine; of holy cities fifteen thousand feet in the air; of intrigue between monastery and monastery; of voices among the Hills, and of that mysterious mirage that dances on dry snow. He spoke even of Lhassa and of the Dalai Lama, whom he had seen and adored.

Each long, perfect day rose behind Kim for a barrier to cut him off from his race and his mother-tongue. He slipped back to thinking and dreaming in the vernacular, and mechanically followed the lama's ceremonial observances at eating, drinking, and the like. The old man's mind turned more and more to his monastery as his eyes turned to the steadfast snows. His River troubled him nothing. Now and again, indeed, he would gaze long and long at a tuft or a twig, expecting, he said, the earth to cleave and deliver its blessing; but he was content to be with his disciple, at ease in the temperate wind that comes down from the Doon. This was not Ceylon, nor Buddh Gaya, nor Bombay, nor some grass-tangled ruins that he seemed to have stumbled upon two years ago. He spoke of those places as a scholar removed from vanity, as a Seeker walking in humility, as an old man, wise and temperate, illumining knowledge with brilliant insight. Bit by bit, disconnectedly, each tale called up by some wayside thing, he spoke of all his wanderings up and down Hind; till Kim, who had loved him without reason, now loved him for fifty good reasons. So they enjoyed themselves in high felicity, abstaining, as the Rule demands, from evil words, covetous desires; not overeating, not lying on high beds, nor wearing rich clothes. Their stomachs told them the time, and the people brought them their food, as the saying is. They were lords of the villages of Aminabad, Sahaigunge, Akrola of the Ford, and little Phulesa, where Kim gave the soulless woman a blessing.

But news travels fast in India, and too soon shuffled across the cropland, bearing a basket of fruits with a box of Cabul grapes and gilt oranges, a white-whiskered servitor—a lean, dry Oorya—begging them to bring the honour of their presence to his mistress, distressed in her mind that the lama had neglected her so long.

"Now do I remember"—the lama spoke as though it were a wholly new proposition. "She is virtuous, but an inordinate talker."

Kim was sitting on the edge of a cow's manger, telling stories to a village smith's children.

"She will only ask for another son for her daughter. I have not forgotten her," he said. "Let her acquire merit. Send word that we will come."

They covered eleven miles through the fields in two days, and were overwhelmed with attentions at the end; for the old lady held a fine tradition of hospitality, to which she forced her son-in-law, who was under the thumb of his women-folk and brought peace by borrowing of the money-lender. Age had not weakened her tongue or her memory, and from a discreetly barred upper window, in the hearing of not less than a dozen servants, she paid Kim compliments that would have flung European audiences into unclean dismay.

"But thou art still the shameless beggar-brat of the parao," she shrilled. "I have not forgotten thee. Wash ye and eat. The father of my daughter's son is gone away awhile. So we poor women are dumb and useless."

For proof, she harangued the entire household unsparingly till food and drink were brought; and in the evening—the smoke-scented evening, copper-dun and turquoise across the fields—it pleased her to order her palanquin to be set down in the untidy forecourt by smoky torchlight; and there, behind not too closely drawn curtains, she gossiped.

"Had the Holy One come alone, I should have received him otherwise; but with this rogue, who can be too careful?"

"Maharanee," said Kim, choosing as always the amplest title, "is it my fault that none other than a Sahib—a polis-sahib—called the Maharanee whose face he—"

"Chitt! That was on the pilgrimage. When we travel—thou knowest the proverb."

"Called the Maharanee a Breaker of Hearts and a Dispenser of Delights?"

"To remember that! It was true. So he did. That was in the time of the bloom of my beauty." She chuckled like a contented parrot above the sugar lump. "Now tell me of thy goings and comings—as much as may be without shame. How many maids, and whose wives, hang upon thy eyelashes? Ye hail from Benares? I would have gone there again this year, but my daughter—we have only two sons. Phaii! Such is the effect of these low plains. Now in Kulu men are elephants. But I would ask thy Holy One—stand aside, rogue—a charm against most lamentable windy colics that in mango-time overtake my daughter's eldest. Two years back he gave me a powerful spell."

"Oh, Holy One!" said Kim, bubbling with mirth at the lama's rueful face.

"It is true. I gave her one against wind."

"Teeth—teeth—teeth," snapped the old woman.

"Cure them when they are sick," Kim quoted relishingly, "but by no means work charms. Remember what befell the Mahratta."

"That was two Rains ago; she wearied me with her continual importunity." The lama groaned as the Unjust Judge had groaned before him. "Thus it comes—take note, my chela—that even those who would follow the Way are thrust aside by idle women. Three days through, when the child was sick, she talked to me."

"Arre! and to whom else should I talk? The boy's mother knew nothing, and the father—in the nights of the cold weather it was—'Pray to the Gods,' said he, forsooth, and turning over, snored!"

"I gave her the charm. What is an old man to do?"

" 'To abstain from action is well—except when we acquire merit.' "

"Ah, chela, if thou desertest me, I am all alone."

"He found his milk-teeth easily at any rate," said the old lady. "But all priests are alike."

Kim coughed severely. Being young, he did not approve of her flippancy. "To importune the wise out of season is to invite calamity."

"There is a talking mynah"—the thrust came back with the well-remembered snap of the jewelled fore-finger—"over the stables which has picked up the very tone of the family-priest. Maybe I forget honour to my guests, but if ye had seen him double his fists into his belly, which was like a half-grown gourd, and cry: 'Here is the pain!' ye would forgive. I am half minded to take the hakim's medicine. He sells it cheap, and certainly it makes him fat as Shiv's own bull. He does not deny remedies, but I doubted for the child because of the inauspicious colour of the bottles."

The lama, under cover of the monologue, had faded out into the darkness towards the room prepared.

"Thou hast angered him, belike," said Kim.

"Not he. He is wearied, and I forgot, being a grandmother. (None but a grandmother should ever oversee a child. Mothers are only fit for bearing.) To-morrow, when he sees how my daughter's son is grown, he will write the charm. Then, too, he can judge of the new hakim's drugs."

"Who is the hakim, Maharanee?"

"A wanderer, as thou art, but a most sober Bengali from Dacca—a master of medicine. He relieved me of an oppression after meat by means of a small pill that wrought like a devil unchained. He travels about now, vending preparations of great value. He has even papers, printed in Angrezi, telling what things he has done for weak-backed men and slack women. He has been here four days; but hearing ye were coming (hakims and priests are snake and tiger the world over) he has, as I take it, gone to cover."

While she drew breath after this volley, the ancient servant, sitting unrebuked on the edge of the torch-light, muttered: "This house is a cattle-pound, as it were, for all charlatans and—priests. Let the boy stop eating mangoes . . . but who can argue with a grandmother?" He raised his voice respectfully: "Sahiba, the hakim sleeps after his meat. He is in the quarters behind the dovecot."

Kim bristled like an expectant terrier. To outface and down-talk a Calcutta-taught Bengali, a voluble Dacca drug-vendor, would be a good game. It was not seemly that the lama, and incidentally himself, should be thrown aside for such an one. He knew those curious bastard English advertisements at the backs of native newspapers. St. Xavier's boys sometimes brought them in by stealth to snigger over among their mates; for the language of the grateful patient recounting his symptoms is most simple and revealing. The Oorya, not unanxious to play off one parasite against the other, slunk away towards the dovecot.

"Yes," said Kim, with measured scorn. "Their stock-in-trade is a little coloured water and a very great shamelessness. Their prey are broken-down kings and overfed Bengalis. Their profit is in children—who are not born."

The old lady chuckled. "Do not be envious. Charms are better, eh? I never gainsaid it. See that thy Holy One writes me a good amulet by the morning."

"None but the ignorant deny"—a thick, heavy voice boomed through the darkness, as a figure came to rest squatting—"None but the ignorant deny the value of charms. None but the ignorant deny the value of medicines."

"A rat found a piece of turmeric. Said he: 'I will open a grocer's shop,'" Kim retorted.

Battle was fairly joined now, and they heard the old lady stiffen to attention.

"The priest's son knows the names of his nurse and three Gods. Says he: 'Hear me, or I will curse you by the three million Great Ones.'" Decidedly this invisible had an arrow or two in his quiver. He went on: "I am but a teacher of the alphabet. I have learned all the wisdom of the Sahibs."

"The Sahibs never grow old. They dance and they play like children when they are grandfathers. A strong-backed breed," piped the voice inside the palanquin.

"I have, too, our drugs which loosen humours of the head in hot and angry men. Sina well compounded when the moon stands in the proper House; yellow earths I have—arplan from China that makes a man to renew his youth and astonish his household; saffron from Kashmir, and the best salep of Cabul. Many people have died before—"

"That I surely believe," said Kim.

"They knew the value of my drugs. I do not give my sick the mere ink in which a charm is written, but hot and rending drugs which descend and wrestle with the evil."

"Very mightily they do so," sighed the old lady.

The voice launched into an immense tale of misfortune and bankruptcy, studded with plentiful petitions to the Government. "But for my fate, which overrules all, I had been now in Government employ. I bear a degree from the great school at Calcutta—whither, maybe, the son of this house shall go."

"He shall indeed. If our neighbour's brat can in a few years be made an F. A." (First Arts—she used the English word, of which she had heard so often), "how much more shall children clever as some that I know bear away prizes at rich Calcutta."

"Never," said the voice, "have I seen such a child! Born in an auspicious hour, and—but for that colic which, alas! turning into black cholers, may carry him off like a pigeon—destined to many years, he is enviable."

"Hai mai!" said the old lady. "To praise children is inauspicious, or I could listen to this talk. But the back of the house is unguarded, and even in this soft air men think themselves to be men and women we know. . . . The child's father is away too, and I must be chowkedar (watchman) in my old age. Up! Up! Take up the palanquin. Let the hakim and the young priest settle between them whether charms or medi-

cine most avail. Ho! worthless people, fetch tobacco for the guests, and
—round the homestead go I!"

The palanquin reeled off, followed by straggling torches and a horde
of dogs. Twenty villages knew the Sahiba—her failings, her tongue, and
her large charity. Twenty villages cheated her after immemorial custom,
but no man would have stolen or robbed within her jurisdiction for any
gift under Heaven. None the less, she made great parade of her formal
inspections, the riot of which could be heard half-way to Mussoorie.

Kim relaxed, as one augur must when he meets another. The hakim,
still squatting, slid over his hookah with a friendly foot, and Kim pulled
at the good weed. The hangers-on expected grave professional debate,
and perhaps a little free doctoring.

"To discuss medicine before the ignorant is of one piece with teaching
the peacock to sing," said the hakim.

"True courtesy," Kim echoed, "is very often inattention."

These, be it understood, were company-manners, designed to impress.

"Hi! I have an ulcer on my leg," cried a scullion. "Look at it!"

"Get hence! Remove!" said the hakim. "Is it the habit of the place to
pester honoured guests? Ye crowd in like buffaloes."

"If the Sahiba knew—" Kim began.

"Ai! Ai! Come away. They are meat for our mistress. When her young
Shaitan's colics are cured perhaps we poor people may be suffered to—"

"The mistress fed thy wife when thou wast in jail for breaking the
money-lender's head. Who speaks against her?" The old servitor curled
his white moustaches savagely in the young moonlight. "I am responsible
for the honour of this house. Go!" and he drove the underlings before
him.

Said the hakim, hardly more than shaping the words with his lips:
"How do you do, Mr. O'Hara? I am jolly glad to see you again."

Kim's hand clenched about the pipe-stem. Anywhere on the open road,
perhaps, he would not have been astonished; but here, in this quiet back-
water of life, he was not prepared for Hurree Babu. It annoyed him, too,
that he had been hoodwinked.

"Ah ha! I told you at Lucknow—resurgam—I shall rise again and you
shall not know me. How much did you bet—eh?"

He chewed leisurely upon a few cardamom seeds, but he breathed
uneasily.

"But why come here, Babuji?"

"Ah! Thatt is the question, as Shakespeare hath said. I come to con-
gratulate you on your extraordinary effeecient performance at Delhi. Oah!
I tell you we are all proud of you. It was verree neat and handy. Our
mutual friend, he is old friend of mine. He has been in some dam-tight

places. Now he will be in some more. He told me; I tell Mr. Lurgan; and he is pleased you graduate so nicely. All the Department is pleased."

For the first time in his life, Kim thrilled to the clean pride (it can be a deadly pitfall, none the less) of Departmental praise—ensnaring praise from an equal of work appreciated by fellow-workers. Earth has nothing on the same plane to compare with it. But, cried the Oriental in him, Babus do not travel far to retail compliments.

"Tell thy tale, Babu," he said authoritatively.

"Oah, it is nothing. Onlee I was at Simla when the wire came in about what our mutual friend said he had hidden, and old Creighton—" He looked to see how Kim would take this piece of audacity.

"The Colonel Sahib," the boy from St. Xavier's corrected.

"Of course. He found me at a loose string, and I had to go down to Chitor to find that beastly letter. I do not like the South—too much railway travel; but I drew good travelling allowance. Ha! Ha! I meet our mutual at Delhi on the way back. He lies quiett just now, and says Saddhu-disguise suits him to the ground. Well, there I hear what you have done so well, so quickly, upon the instantaneous spur of the moment. I tell our mutual friend you take the bally bun, by Jove! It was splendid. I come to tell you so."

"Umm!"

The frogs were busy in the ditches, and the moon slid to her setting. Some happy servant had gone out to commune with the night and to beat upon a drum. Kim's next sentence was in the vernacular.

"How didst thou follow us?"

"Oah. Thatt was nothing. I know from our mutual friend you go to Saharunpore. So I come on. Red Lamas are not inconspicuous persons. I buy myself my drug-box, and I am very good doctor really. I go to Akrola by the Ford, and hear all about you, and I talk here and talk there. All the common people know what you do. I know when the hospitable old lady sent the dooli. They have great recollections of the old lama's visits here. I know old ladies cannot keep their hands from medicines. So I am a doctor, and—you hear my talk? I think it is verree good. My word, Mister O'Hara, they know about you and the lama for fifty miles—the common people. So I come. Do you mind?"

"Babuji," said Kim, looking up at the broad, grinning face "I am a Sahib."

"My dear Mister O'Hara—"

"And I hope to play the Great Game."

"You are subordinate to me departmentally at present."

"Then why talk like an ape up in a tree? Men do not come after one from Simla and change their dress, for the sake of a few sweet words.

I am not a child. Talk Hindi and let us get to the yolk of the egg. Thou
art here—speaking not one word of truth in ten. Why art thou here? Give
a straight answer."

"That is so verree disconcerting of the European, Mister O'Hara. You
should know a heap better at your time of life."

"But I want to know," said Kim, laughing. "If it is the Game, I may
help. How can I do anything if you bukh (babble) all round the shop."

Hurree Babu reached for the pipe, and sucked it till it guggled again.

"Now I will speak vernacular. You sit tight, Mister O'Hara. . . . . .
It concerns the pedigree of a white stallion."

"Still? That was finished long ago."

"When every one is dead the Great Game is finished. Not before. Listen
to me till the end. There were Five Kings who prepared a sudden war
three years ago, when thou wast given the stallion's pedigree by Mahbub
Ali. Upon them, because of that news, and ere they were ready, fell our
Army."

"Ay—eight thousand men with guns. I remember that night."

"But the war was not pushed. That is the Government custom. The
troops were recalled because the Government believed the Five Kings
were cowed; and it is not cheap to feed men among the high Passes. Hilas
and Bunar—Rajahs with guns—undertook for a price to guard the Passes
against all coming from the North. They protested both fear and friendship." He broke off with a giggle into English: "Of course, I tell you this
unoffeecially to elucidate political situation, Mister O'Hara. Offeecially,
I am debarred from criticising any action of superior. Now I go on.—
This pleased the Government, anxious to avoid expense, and a bond was
made for so many rupees a month that Hilas and Bunar should guard
the Passes as soon as the State's troops were withdrawn. At that time—
it was after we two met—I, who had been selling tea in Leh, became
a clerk of accounts in the Army. When the troops were withdrawn, I
was left behind to pay the coolies who made new roads in the Hills.
This road-making was part of the bond between Bunar, Hilas, and the
Government."

"So; and then?"

"I tell you, it was jolly beastly cold up there too, after summer," said
Hurree Babu confidentially. "I was afraid these Bunar men would cut
my throat every night for thee pay-chest. My native sepoy-guard, they
laughed at me! By Jove! I was such a fearful man! Nevar mind thatt. I
go on colloquially. . . . I send word many times that these two Kings
were sold to the North; and Mahbub Ali, who was yet farther north,
amply confirmed it. Nothing was done. Only my feet were frozen, and
a toe dropped off. I sent word that the roads for which I was paying

money to the diggers were being made for the feet of strangers and enemies."

"For?"

"For the Russians. The thing was an open jest among the coolies. Then I was called down to tell what I knew by speech of tongue. Mahbub came South too. See the end! Over the Passes this year after snow-melting" —he shivered afresh—"come two strangers under cover of shooting wild goats. They bear guns, but they bear also chains and levels and compasses."

"Oho! The thing gets clearer."

"They are well received by Hilas and Bunar. They make great promises; they speak as the mouthpiece of a Kaisar, with gifts. Up the valleys, down the valleys go they, saying, 'Here is a place to build a breastwork; here can ye pitch a fort. Here can ye hold the road against an army'—the very roads for which I paid out the rupees monthly. The Government knows, but does nothing. The three other Kings, who were not paid for guarding the Passes, tell them by runner of the bad faith of Bunar and Hilas. When all the evil is done, look you—when these two strangers with the levels and the compasses make the Five Kings to believe that a great army will sweep the Passes to-morrow or the next day—Hill-people are all fools—comes the order to me, Hurree Babu, 'Go North and see what those strangers do.' I say to Creighton Sahib, 'This is not a lawsuit, that we go about to collect evidence.'" Hurree returned to his English with a jerk: "'By Jove,' I said, 'why the dooce do you not issue demi-offeecial orders to some brave man to poison them, for an example? It is, if you permit the observation, most reprehensible laxity on your part.' And Colonel Creighton, he laughed at me! It is all your beastly English pride. You think no one dare conspire! That is all tommy-rott."

Kim smoked slowly, revolving the business, so far as he understood it, in his quick mind.

"Then thou goest forth to follow the strangers?"

"No; to meet them. They arc coming in to Simla to send down their horns and heads to be dressed at Calcutta. They are exclusively sporting gentlemen, and they are allowed special faceelities by the Government. Of course, we always do that. It is our British pride."

"Then what is to fear from them?"

"By Jove, they are not black people. I can do all sorts of things with black people, of course. They are Russians, and highly unscrupulous people. I—I do not want to consort with them without a witness."

"Will they kill thee?"

"Oah, thatt is nothing. I am good enough Herbert Spencerian, I trust, to meet little thing like death, which is all in my fate, you know. But— but they may beat me."

"Why?"

Hurree Babu snapped his fingers with irritation. "Of course I shall affeeliate myself to their camp in supernumerary capacity as perhaps interpreter, or person mentally impotent and hungree, or some such thing. And then I must pick up what I can, I suppose. That is as easy for me as playing Mister Doctor to the old lady. Onlee—onlee—you see, Mister O'Hara, I am unfortunately Asiatic, which is serious detriment in some respects. And all-so I am Bengali—a fearful man."

"God made the Hare and the Bengali. What shame?" said Kim, quoting the proverb.

"It was process of Evolution, I think, from Primal Necessity, but the fact remains in all its cui bono. I am, oh, awfully fearful!—I remember once they wanted to cut off my head on the road to Lhassa. (No, I have never reached to Lhassa.) I sat down and cried, Mister O'Hara, anticipating Chinese tortures. I do not suppose these two gentlemen will torture me, but I like to provide for possible contingency with European assistance in emergency." He coughed and spat out his cardamoms. "It is purely unoffeecial indent, to which you can say, 'No, Babu.' If you have no pressing engagement with your old man—perhaps you might divert him; perhaps I can seduce his fancies—I should like you to keep in Departmental touch with me till I find those sporting coves. I have great opeenion of you since I met my friend at Delhi. And also I will embody your name in my offeecial report when matter is finally adjudicated. It will be a great feather in your cap. That is why I come really."

"Humph! The end of the tale, I think, is true; but what of the fore-part?"

"About the Five Kings? Oah! there is ever so much truth in it. A lots more than you would suppose," said Hurree earnestly. "You come—eh? I go from here straight into the Doon. It is verree verdant and painted meads. I shall go to Mussoorie—to good old Mussoorie Pahar, as the gentlemen and ladies say. Then by Rampur into Chini. That is the only way they can come. I do not like waiting in the cold, but we must wait for them. I want to walk with them to Simla. You see, one Russian is a Frenchman, and I know my French pretty well. I have friends in Chandernagore."

"He would certainly rejoice to see the Hills again," said Kim meditatively. "All his speech these ten days past has been of little else. If we go together—"

"Oah! We can be quite strangers on the road, if your lama prefers. I shall just be four or five miles ahead. There is no hurry for Hurree—that is an Europe pun, ha! ha!—and you come after. There is plenty of time; they will plot and survey and map of course. I shall go to-morrow, and you the next day, if you choose. Eh? You go think on it till morning.

By Jove, it is near morning now." He yawned ponderously, and with never a civil word lumbered off to his sleeping-place. But Kim slept little, and his thoughts ran in Hindustanee:

"Well is the Game called great! I was four days a scullion at Quetta, waiting on the wife of the man whose book I stole. And that was part of the Great Game! From the South—God knows how far—came up the Mahratta, playing the Great Game in fear of his life. Now I shall go far and far into the North playing the Great Game. Truly, it runs like a shuttle throughout all Hind. And my share and my joy"—he smiled to the darkness—"I owe to the lama here. Also to Mahbub Ali—also to Creighton Sahib, but chiefly to the Holy One. He is right—a great and a wonderful world—and I am Kim—Kim—Kim—alone—one person—in the middle of it all. But I will see these strangers with their levels and chains . . ."

"What was the upshot of last night's babble?" said the lama, after his orisons.

"There came a strolling seller of drugs—a hanger-on of the Sahiba's. Him I abolished by arguments and prayers, proving that our charms are worthier than his coloured waters."

"Alas! my charms. Is the virtuous woman still bent upon a new one?"

"Very strictly."

"Then it must be written, or she will deafen me with her clamour." He fumbled at his pencase.

"In the Plains," said Kim, "are always too many people. In the Hills, as I understand, there are fewer."

"Oh! the Hills, and the snow upon the Hills." The lama tore off a tiny square of paper fit to go in an amulet. "But what dost thou know of the Hills?"

"They are very close." Kim thrust open the door and looked at the long, peaceful line of the Himalayas flushed in morning-gold. "Except in the dress of a Sahib, I have never set foot among them."

The lama snuffed the wind wistfully.

"If we go north,"—Kim put the question to the walking sunrise,—"would not much mid-day heat be avoided by walking among the lower hills at least? . . . Is the charm made, Holy One?"

"I have written the names of seven silly devils—not one of whom is worth a grain of dust in the eye. Thus do foolish women drag us from the Way!"

Hurree Babu came out from behind the dovecot, washing his teeth with ostentatious ritual. Full-fleshed, heavy-haunched, bull-necked, and deep-voiced, he did not look like a "fearful man." Kim signed almost imperceptibly that matters were in good train, and when the morning

toilet was over Hurree Babu, in flowery speech, came to do honour to
the lama. They ate, of course, apart, and afterwards the old lady, more
or less veiled behind a window, returned to the vital business of green-
mango colics in the young. The lama's knowledge of medicine was of
course sympathetic only. He believed that the dung of a black horse,
mixed with sulphur, and carried in a snake-skin, was a sound remedy for
cholera; but the symbolism interested him far more than the science.
Hurree Babu deferred to these views with enchanting politeness, so that
the lama called him a courteous physician. Hurree Babu replied that he
was no more than an inexpert dabbler in the mysteries; but at least—
thanked the Gods therefor—he knew when he sat in the presence of
a master. He himself had been taught by the Sahibs, who do not consider expense, in the lordly halls of Calcutta; but, as he was ever first
to acknowledge, there lay a wisdom behind earthly wisdom—the high and
lonely lore of meditation. Kim looked on with envy. The Hurree Babu
of his knowledge—oily, effusive, and nervous—was gone; gone too was
the brazen drug-vendor of overnight. There remained—polished, polite,
attentive—a sober, learned son of experience and adversity, gathering wisdom from the lama's lips. The old lady confided to Kim that these rare
levels were beyond her. She liked charms with plenty of ink that one
could wash off in water, swallow, and be done with. Else what was
the use of the Gods? She liked men and women, and she spoke of them
—of kinglets she had known in the past; of her own youth and beauty;
of the depredations of leopards and the eccentricities of love Asiatic; of
the incidence of taxation, rack-renting, funeral ceremonies, her son-in-
law (this by allusion, easy to be followed), the care of the young, and
the age's lack of decency. And Kim, as interested in the life of this world
as she soon to leave it, squatted with his feet under the hem of his robe,
drinking all in, while the lama demolished one after another every theory
of body-curing put forward by Hurree Babu.

At noon the Babu strapped up his brass-bound drug-box, took his
patent-leather shoes of ceremony in one hand, a gay blue and white umbrella in the other, and set off northwards to the Doon, where, he said,
he was in demand among the lesser kings of those parts.

"We will go in the cool of the evening, chela," said the lama. "That
doctor, learned in physic and courtesy, affirms that the people among
these lower hills are devout, generous, and much in need of a teacher.
In a very short time—so says the hakim—we come to cool air and the
smell of pines."

"Ye go to the Hills. And by Kulu road? Ah, thrice happy!" shrilled the
old lady. "But that I am a little pressed with the care of the homestead
I would take palanquin . . . but that would be shameless, and my reputa-

tion would be cracked. Ho! Ho! I know the road—every march of the road I know. Ye will find charity throughout—it is not denied to the well-looking. I will give orders for provision. A servant to set you forth upon your journey? No. . . . Then I will at least cook ye good food."

"What a woman is the Sahiba!" said the white-bearded Oorya, when a tumult rose by the kitchen quarters. "She has never forgotten a friend: she has never forgotten an enemy in all her years. And her cookery—wah!" He rubbed his slim stomach.

There were cakes, there were sweetmeats, there was cold fowl stewed to rags with rice and prunes—enough to burden Kim like a mule.

"I am old and useless," she said. "None now love me—and none respect —but there are few to compare with me when I call on the Gods and squat to my cooking-pots. Come again, O people of good will! Holy One and disciple, come again! The room is always prepared; the welcome is always ready. . . . See the women do not follow thy chela too openly. I know the women of Kulu. Take heed, chela, lest he run away when he smells his Hills again. . . . Hai! Do not tilt the rice-bag upside down. . . . Bless the household, Holy One, and forgive thy servant her stupidities."

She wiped her red old eyes on a corner of her veil, and clucked throatily.

"Women talk," said the lama at last, "but that is a woman's infirmity. I gave her a charm. She is upon the Wheel and wholly given over to the shows of this life, but none the less, chela, she is virtuous, kindly, hospitable—of a whole and zealous heart. Who shall say she does not acquire merit?"

"Not I, Holy One," said Kim, reslinging the bountiful provision on his shoulders. "In my mind—behind my eyes—I have tried to picture such an one altogether freed from the Wheel—desiring nothing, causing nothing—a nun, as it were."

"And, O imp?" The lama almost laughed aloud.

"I cannot make the picture."

"Nor I. But there are many, many millions of lives before her. She will get wisdom a little, it may be, in each one."

"And will she forget how to make stews with saffron upon that road?"

"Thy mind is set on things unworthy. But she has skill. I am refreshed all over. When we reach the lower hills I shall be yet stronger. The hakim spoke truly to me this morn when he said a breath from the snows blows away twenty years from the life of a man. We will go up into the Hills—the high Hills—up to the sound of snow-water and the sound of the trees—for a little while. The hakim said that at any time we may return to the Plains, for we do no more than skirt the pleasant places.

The hakim is full of learning; but he is in no way proud. I spoke to him—when thou wast talking to the Sahiba—of a certain dizziness that lays hold upon the back of my neck in the night, and he said it rose from excessive heat—to be cured by cool air. Upon consideration, I marvelled that I had not thought of such a simple remedy."

"Didst thou tell him of thy Search?" said Kim, a little jealously. He preferred to sway the lama by his own speech—not through the wiles of Hurree Babu.

"Assuredly. I told him of my dream, and of the manner by which I had acquired merit by causing thee to be taught wisdom."

"Thou didst not say I was a Sahib?"

"What need? I have told thee many times we be but two souls seeking escape. He said—and he is just herein—that the River of Healing will break forth even as I dreamed—at my feet if need be. Having found the Way, seest thou, that shall free me from the Wheel, need I trouble to find a way about the mere fields of earth—which are illusion? That were senseless. I have my dreams, night upon night repeated; I have the 'Jataka'; and I have thee, Friend of all the World. It was written in thy horoscope that a Red Bull on a green field—I have not forgotten—should bring thee to honour. Who but I saw that prophecy accomplished? Indeed, I was the instrument. Thou shalt find me my River, being in return the instrument. The Search is sure!"

He set his ivory-yellow face, serene and untroubled, towards the beckoning Hills; his shadow shouldering far before him in the dust.

Chapter 13

"Who hath desired the Sea—the immense and contemptuous surges?
The shudder, the stumble, the swerve ere the star-stabbing bow-
* sprit emerges—*
The orderly clouds of the Trades and the ridged roaring sapphire
* thereunder—*
Unheralded cliff-lurking flaws and the head-sails' low-volleying
* thunder?*
His Sea is no wonder the same—his Sea and the same in each won-
* der—*
*   His Sea that his being fulfils?*
So and no otherwise—so and no otherwise Hill-men desire their
* Hills!"*

"WHO goes to the Hills goes to his mother."

They had crossed the Sewaliks and the half-tropical Doon, left Mussoorie behind them, and headed north along the narrow hill-roads. Day after day they struck deeper into the huddled mountains, and day after day Kim watched the lama return to a man's strength. Among the terraces of the Doon he had leaned on the boy's shoulder, ready to profit by wayside halts. Under the great ramp to Mussoorie he drew himself together as an old hunter faces a well-remembered bank, and where he should have sunk exhausted swung his long draperies about him, drew a deep double-lungful of the diamond air, and walked as only a hillman can. Kim, plains-bred and plains-fed, sweated and panted astonished. "This is my country," said the lama. "Besides Suchzen, this is flatter than a rice-field"; and with steady, driving strokes from the loins he strode upwards. But it was on the steep downhill marches, three thousand feet in three hours, that he went utterly away from Kim, whose back ached with holding back, and whose big toe was nigh cut off by his grass sandal-string. Through the speckled shadow of the great deodar-forests; through oak feathered and plumed with ferns; birch, ilex, rhododendron, and pine, out on to the bare hillsides' slippery sunburnt grass, and back into the woodlands' coolth again, till oak gave way to bamboo and palm of the valley, the lama swung untiring.

Glancing back in the twilight at the huge ridges behind him and the faint, thin line of the road whereby they had come, he would lay out, with a hillman's generous breadth of vision, fresh marches for the morrow; or, halting in the neck of some uplifted pass that gave on Spiti and Kulu, would stretch out his hands yearningly towards the high snows of the horizon. In the dawns they flared windy-red above stark blue, as Kedarnath and Badrinath—kings of that wilderness—took the first sunlight. All day long they lay like molten silver under the sun, and at evening put on their jewels again. At first they breathed temperately upon the travellers, winds good to meet when one crawled over some gigantic hogback; but in a few days, at a height of nine or ten thousand feet, those breezes bit; and Kim kindly allowed a village of hillmen to acquire merit by giving him a rough blanket-coat. The lama was mildly surprised that any one should object to the knife-edged breezes which had cut the years off his shoulders.

"These are but the lower hills, chela. There is no cold till we come to the true Hills."

"Air and water are good, and the people are devout enough, but the food is very bad," Kim growled; "and we walk as though we were mad—or English. It freezes at night, too."

"A little, maybe; but only enough to make old bones rejoice in the sun. We must not always delight in the soft beds and rich food."

"We might at the least keep to the road."

Kim had all a plains-man's affection for the well-trodden track, not six feet wide, that snaked among the mountains; but the lama, being Tibetan, could not refrain from short cuts over spurs and the rims of gravel-strewn slopes. As he explained to his limping disciple, a man bred among mountains can prophesy the course of a mountain-road, and though low-lying clouds might be a hindrance to a short-cutting stranger, they made no earthly difference to a thoughtful man. Thus, after long hours of what would be reckoned very fair mountaineering in civilised countries, they would pant over a saddle-back, sidle past a few landslips, and drop through forest at an angle of forty-five on to the road again. Along their track lay the villages of the hillfolk—mud and earth huts, the timbers now and then rudely curved with an axe—clinging like swallows' nests against the steeps, huddled on tiny flats half-way down a three-thousand-foot glissade; jammed into a corner between cliffs that funnelled and focused every wandering blast; or, for the sake of summer pasture, cowering down on a neck that in winter would be ten feet deep in snow. And the people—the sallow, greasy, duffle-clad people, with short bare legs and faces almost Esquimaux—would flock out and adore. The Plains—kindly and gentle—had treated the lama as a holy man among holy men. But the Hills worshipped him as one in the confidence of all the devils. Theirs was an almost obliterated Buddhism, overlaid with a nature-worship fantastic as their own landscapes, elaborate as the terracing of their tiny fields; but they recognised the big hat, the clicking rosary, and the rare Chinese texts for great authority; and they respected the man under the hat.

"We saw thee come down over the black Breasts of Eua," said a Betah who gave them cheese, sour milk, and stone-hard bread one evening. "We do not use that often—except when calving cows stray in summer. There is a sudden wind among those stones that casts men down on the stillest day. But what should such folk care for the Devil of Eua!"

Then did Kim, aching in every fibre, dizzy with looking down, footsore with cramping desperate toes into inadequate crannies, take joy in the day's march—such joy as a boy of St. Xavier's who had won the quarter-mile on the flat might take in the praises of his friends. The Hills sweated the ghi and sugar suet off his bones; the dry air, taken sobbingly at the head of cruel passes, firmed and built out his upper ribs; and tilted levels put new hard muscles into calf and thigh.

They meditated often on the Wheel of Life—the more so since, as the lama said, they were freed from its visible temptations. Except the gray eagle and an occasional far-seen bear grubbing and rooting on the hillside, the vision of a furious painted leopard met at dawn in a still valley devouring a goat, and now and again a bright-coloured bird, they were alone with the winds and the grass singing under the wind. The women of the smoky huts over whose roofs the two walked as they descended the mountains, were unlovely and unclean, wives of many husbands, and afflicted with goitre. The men were woodcutters when they were not farmers—meek, and of an incredible simplicity. But that suitable discourse might not fail, Fate sent them, overtaking and overtaken upon the road, the courteous Dacca physician, who paid for his food in ointments good for goitre and counsels that restore peace between men and women. He seemed to know these Hills as well as he knew the hill dialects, and gave the lama the lie of the land towards Ladakh and Tibet. He said they could return to the Plains at any moment. Meantime, for such as loved mountains, yonder road might amuse. This was not all revealed in a breath, but at evening encounters on the stone threshing-floors, when, patients disposed of, the doctor would smoke and the lama snuff, while Kim watched the wee cows grazing on the housetops, or threw his soul after his eye across the deep blue gulfs between range and range. And there were talks apart in the dark woods, when the doctor would seek herbs, and Kim, as budding physician, must accompany him.

"You see, Mister O'Hara, I do not know what the deuce-an'-all I shall do when I find our sporting friends; but if you will kindly keep within sight of my umbrella, which is fine fixed point for cadastral survey, I feel much better."

Kim looked out across the jungle of peaks. "This is not my country, hakim. Easier, I think, to find one louse in a bearskin."

"Oah, thatt is my strong points. There is no hurry for Hurree. They were at Leh not so long ago. They said they had come down from the Kara Korum with their heads and horns and all. I am onlee afraid they will have sent back all their letters and compromising things from Leh into Russian territoree. Of course they will walk away as far to the East as possible—just to show that they were never among the Western States. You do not know the Hills?" He scratched with a twig on the earth. "Look! They should have come in by Srinagar or Abbottabad. Thatt is their short road—down the river by Bunji and Astor. But they have made mischief in the West. So"—he drew a furrow from left to right—"they march and they march away East to Leh (ah! it is cold there), and down the Indus to Han-le (I know that road), and then down, you see, to Bushahar and Chini valley. That is ascertained by process of elimination, and also by asking questions from people that I cure so well. Our friends have been a long time playing about and producing impressions. So they are well known from far off. You will see me catch them somewhere in Chini valley. Please keep your eye on the umbrella."

It nodded like a wind-blown harebell down the valleys and round the mountain sides, and in due time the lama and Kim, who steered by compass, would overhaul it, vending ointments and powders at eventide. "We came by such and such a way!" The lama would throw a careless finger backward at the ridges, and the umbrella would expend itself in compliments.

They crossed a snowy pass in cold moonlight, when the lama, mildly chaffing Kim, went through up to his knees, like a Bactrian camel—the snow-bred, shag-haired sort that come into the Kashmir Serai. They dipped across beds of light snow and snow-powdered shale, where they took refuge from a gale in a camp of Tibetans hurrying down tiny sheep, each laden with a bag of borax. They came out upon grassy shoulders still snow-speckled, and through forest, to grass anew. For all their marchings, Kedarnath and Badrinath were not impressed; and it was only after days of travel that Kim, uplifted upon some insignificant ten-thousand-foot hummock, could see that a shoulder-knot or horn of the two great lords had—ever so slightly—changed outline.

At last they entered a world within a world—a valley of leagues where the high Hills were fashioned of the mere rubble and refuse from off the knees of the mountains. Here one day's march carried them no farther, it seemed, than a dreamer's clogged pace bears him in a nightmare. They skirted a shoulder painfully for hours, and, behold, it was but an outlying boss in an outlying buttress of the main pile! A rounded meadow revealed itself, when they had reached it, for a vast tableland running far into the valley. Three days later, it was a dim fold in the earth to southward.

"Surely the Gods live here," said Kim, beaten down by the silence and the appalling sweep and dispersal of the cloud-shadows after rain. "This is no place for men!"

"Long and long ago," said the lama, as to himsélf, "it was asked of the Lord whether the world were everlasting. To this the Excellent One returned no answer. . . . When I was in Ceylon, a wise Seeker confirmed that from the gospel which is written in Pali. Certainly, since we know the way to Freedom, the question were unprofitable, but—look, and know illusion, chela! These are the true Hills! They are like my hills by Suchzen. Never were such hills!"

Above them, still enormously above them, earth towered away towards the snow-line, where from east to west across hundreds of miles, ruled as with a ruler, the last of the bold birches stopped. Above that, in scarps and blocks upheaved, the rocks strove to fight their heads above the white smother. Above these again, changeless since the world's beginning, but changing to every mood of sun and cloud, lay out the eternal snow. They could see blots and blurs on its face where storm and wandering wulliewa got up to dance. Below them, as they stood, the forest slid away in a sheet of blue-green for mile upon mile; below the forest was a village in its sprinkle of terraced fields and steep grazing-grounds; below the village they knew, though a thunderstorm worried and growled there for the moment, a pitch of twelve or fifteen hundred feet gave to the moist valley where the streams gather that are the mothers of young Sutluj.

As usual, the lama had led Kim by cow-track and by-road, far from the main route along which Hurree Babu, that "fearful man," had bucketed three days before through a storm to which nine Englishmen out of ten would have given full right of way. Hurree was no game-shot,—the snick of a trigger made him change colour,—but, as he himself would have said, he was "fairly effeecient stalker," and he had raked the huge valley with a pair of cheap binoculars to some purpose. Moreover, the white of worn canvas tents against green carries far. Hurree Babu had seen all he wanted to see when he sat on the threshing-floor of Ziglaur, twenty miles away as the eagle flies, and forty by road—that is to say, two small dots which one day were just below the snow-line, and the next had moved downward perhaps six inches on the hillside. Once cleaned out and set to the work, his fat bare legs could cover a surprising amount of ground, and this was the reason why, while Kim and the lama lay in a leaky hut at Ziglaur till the storm should be overpassed, an oily, wet, but always smiling Bengali, talking the best of English with the vilest of phrases, was ingratiating himself with two sodden and rather rheumatic foreigners. He had arrived, revolving many wild schemes, on the heels of a thunderstorm which had split a pine over against their camp, and so convinced a dozen or two forcibly impressed baggage-coolies the day was inauspicious for farther travel that with one accord they had thrown down their loads and jibbed. They were subjects of a Hill-Rajah who farmed out their services, as is the custom, for his private gain; and, to add to their personal distresses, the strange Sahibs had already threatened them with rifles. The most of them knew rifles and Sahibs of old; they were trackers and shikarris of the Northern valleys, keen after bear and wild goat; but they had never been thus treated in their lives. So the forest took them to her bosom, and, for all oaths and clamour, refused to restore. There was no need to feign madness or—the Babu had thought of another means of securing a welcome. He wrung out his wet clothes, slipped on his patent-leather shoes, opened the blue-and-white umbrella, and with mincing gait and a heart beating against his tonsils appeared as "agent for His Royal Highness, the Rajah of Rampur, gentlemen. What can I do for you, please?"

The gentlemen were delighted. One was visibly French, the other Russian, but they spoke English not much inferior to the Babu's. They begged his kind offices. Their native servants had gone sick at Leh. They had hurried on because they were anxious to bring the spoils of the chase to Simla ere the skins grew moth-eaten. They bore a general letter of introduction (the Babu salaamed to it orientally) to all Government officials. No, they had not met any other shooting-parties en route. They did for themselves. They had plenty of supplies. They only wished to push on as soon as might be. At this he waylaid a cowering hillman among the trees, and after three minutes' talk and a little silver (one cannot be economical upon State service, though Hurree's heart bled at the waste) the eleven coolies and the three hangers-on reappeared. At least the Babu would be a witness to oppression.

"My royal master, he will be much annoyed, but these people are onlee common people and grossly ignorant. If your honours will kindly over-look unfortunate affair, I shall be much pleased. In a little while rain will stop and we can then proceed. You have been shooting, eh? That is fine performance!"

He skipped nimbly from one kilta to the next, making pretence to adjust each conical basket. The Englishman is not, as a rule, familiar with the Asiatic, but he would not strike across the wrist a kindly Babu who had accidentally upset a kilta with a red oil-skin top. On the other hand, he

would not press drink upon a Babu were he never so friendly, nor would
he invite him to meat. The strangers did all these things, and asked many
questions,—about women mostly,—to which Hurree returned gay and un-
studied answers. They gave him a glass of whitish fluid like to gin, and
then more; and in a little time his gravity departed from him. He became
thickly treasonous, and spoke in terms of sweeping indecency of a Government which had forced upon him a white man's education and neglected
to supply him with a white man's salary. He babbled tales of oppression
and wrong till the tears ran down his cheeks for the miseries of his land.
Then he staggered off, singing love-songs of Lower Bengal, and collapsed
upon a wet tree-trunk. Never was so unfortunate a product of English rule
in India more unhappily thrust upon aliens.

"They are all just of that pattern," said one sportsman to the other in
French. "When we get into India proper thou wilt see. I should like to
visit his Rajah. One might speak the good word there. It is possible that
he has heard of us and wishes to signify his goodwill."

"We have not time. We must get into Simla as soon as may be," his
companion replied. "For my own part, I wish our reports had been sent
back from Hilas, or even Leh."

"The English post is better and safer. Remember we are given all
facilities—and name of God!—they give them to us too! Is it unbelievable
stupidity?"

"It is pride—pride that deserves and will receive punishment."

"Yes! To fight a fellow-Continental in our game is something. There is
a risk attached, but these people—bah! It is too easy."

"Pride—all pride, my friend."

"Now what the deuce is good of Chandernagore being so close to Calcutta and all," said Hurree, snoring open-mouthed on the sodden moss,
"if I cannot understand their French. They talk so par-tic-ularly fast!
It would have been much better to cut their beastly throats."

When he presented himself again he was racked with a headache—
penitent, and volubly afraid that in his drunkenness he might have been
indiscreet. He loved the British Government—it was the source of all
prosperity and honour, and his master at Rampur held the very same
opinion. Upon this the men began to deride him and to quote past
words, till step by step, with deprecating smirks, oily grins, and leers of
infinite cunning, the poor Babu was beaten out of his defences and
forced to speak—truth! When Lurgan was told the tale later, he mourned
aloud that he could not have been in the place of the stubborn, inattentive
coolies, who with grass mats over their heads and the raindrops puddling
in their foot-prints, waited on the weather. All the Sahibs of their acquaintance—rough-clad men joyously returning year after year to their

chosen gullies—had servants and cooks and orderlies, very often hillmen. These Sahibs travelled without any retinue. Therefore they were poor Sahibs, and ignorant; for no Sahib in his senses would follow a Bengali's advice. But the Bengali, appearing from somewhere, had given them money, and would make shift with their dialect. Used to comprehensive ill-treatment from their own colour, they suspected a trap somewhere, and stood by to run if occasion offered.

Then through the new-washed air, steaming with delicious earth-smells, the Babu led the way down the slopes—walking ahead of the coolies in pride; walking behind the foreigners in humility. His thoughts were many and various. The least of them would have interested his companions beyond words. But he was an agreeable guide, ever keen to point out the beauties of his royal master's domain. He peopled the hills with anything they had a mind to slay—thar, ibex, or markhor, and bear by Elisha's allowance. He discoursed of botany and ethnology with unimpeachable inaccuracy, and his store of local legends—he had been a trusted agent of the State for fifteen years, remember—was inexhaustible.

"Decidedly this fellow is an original," said the taller of the two foreigners. "He is like the nightmare of a Viennese courier."

"He represents in petto India in transition—the monstrous hybridism of East and West," the Russian replied. "It is we who can deal with Orientals."

"He has lost his own country and has not acquired any other. But he has a most complete hatred of his conquerors. Listen. He confides to me last night," etc.

Under the striped umbrella Hurree Babu was straining ear and brain to follow the quick-poured French, and keeping both eyes on a kilta full of maps and documents—an extra large one with a double red oilskin cover. He did not wish to steal anything. He only desired to know what to steal, and, incidentally, how to get away when he had stolen it. He thanked all the Gods of Hindustan, and Herbert Spencer, that there remained some valuables to steal.

On the second day the road rose steeply to a grass spur above the forest; and it was here, about sunset, that they came across an aged lama —but they called him a bonze—sitting cross-legged above a mysterious chart held down by stones, which he was explaining to a young man, evidently a neophyte, of singular, though unwashen, beauty. The striped umbrella had been sighted half a march away, and Kim had suggested a halt till it came up to them.

"Ha!" said Hurree Babu, resourceful as Puss-in-Boots. "That is eminent local holy man. Probably subject of my royal master."

"What is he doing? It is very curious."

"He is expounding holy picture—all hand-worked."

The two men stood bare-headed in the wash of the afternoon sunlight low across the gold-coloured grass. The sullen coolies, glad of the check, halted and slid down their loads.

"Look!" said the Frenchman. "It is like a picture for the birth of a religion—the first teacher and the first disciple. Is he a Buddhist?"

"Of some debased kind," the other answered. "There are no true Buddhists among the Hills. But look at the folds of the drapery. Look at his eyes—how insolent! Why does this make one feel that we are so young a people?" The speaker struck passionately at a tall weed. "We have nowhere left our mark yet. Nowhere! That, do you understand, is what disquiets me." He scowled at the placid face, and the monumental calm of the pose.

"Have patience. We shall make your mark together—we and you young people. Meantime, draw his picture."

The Babu advanced loftily; his back out of all keeping with his deferential speech, or his wink towards Kim.

"Holy One, these be Sahibs. My medicines cured one of a flux, and I go into Simla to oversee his recovery. They wish to see thy picture—"

"To heal the sick is always good. This is the Wheel of Life," said the lama, "the same I showed thee in the hut at Ziglaur when the rain fell."

"And to hear thee expound it."

The lama's eyes lighted at the prospect of new listeners. "To expound the Most Excellent Way is good. Have they any knowledge of Hindi, such as had the Keeper of Images?"

"A little, maybe."

Hereat, simply as a child engrossed with a new game, the lama threw back his head and began the full-throated invocation of the Doctor of Divinity ere he opens the full doctrine. The strangers leaned on their alpen-stocks and listened. Kim, squatting humbly, watched the red sunlight on their faces, and the blend and parting of their long shadows. They wore un-English leggings and curious girt-in belts that reminded him hazily of the pictures in a book at St. Xavier's library: "The Adventures of a Young Naturalist in Mexico" was its name. Yes, they looked very like the wonderful M. Sumichrast of that tale, and very unlike the "highly unscrupulous folk" of Hurree Babu's imagining. The coolies, earth-coloured and mute, crouched reverently some twenty or thirty yards away, and the Babu, the slack of his thin gear snapping like a marking-flag in the chill breeze, stood by with an air of happy proprietorship.

"These are the men," Hurree whispered, as the ritual went on and the two whites followed the grass blade sweeping from Hell to Heaven and back again. "All their books are in the large kilta with the reddish top,—

books and reports and maps,—and I have seen a King's letter that either
Hilas or Bunar has written. They guard it most carefully. They have
sent nothing back from Hilas or Leh. That is sure."

"Who is with them?"

"Only the beggar-coolies. They have no servants. They are so close
they cook their own food."

"But what am I to do?"

"Wait and see. Only if any chance comes to me thou wilt know where
to seek for the papers."

"This were better in Mahbub Ali's hands than a Bengali's," said Kim
scornfully.

"There are more ways of getting to a sweetheart than butting down a
wall."

"See here the Hell appointed for avarice and greed. Flanked upon the
one side by Desire and on the other by Weariness." The lama warmed to
his work, and one of the strangers sketched him in the quick-fading light.

"That is enough," the man said at last brusquely. "I cannot understand
him, but I want that picture. He is a better artist than I. Ask him if he
will sell it."

"He says 'No sar,'" the Babu replied. The lama, of course, would no
more have parted with his chart to a casual wayfarer than an archbishop
would pawn the holy vessels of a cathedral. All Tibet is full of cheap reproductions of the Wheel; but the lama was an artist, as well as a wealthy
abbot in his own place.

"Perhaps in three days, or four, or ten, if I perceive that the Sahib is a
Seeker and of good understanding, I may myself draw him another. But
this was used for the initiation of a novice. Tell him so, hakim."

"He wishes it now—for money."

The lama shook his head slowly and began to fold up the Wheel. The
Russian, on his side, saw no more than an unclean old man haggling
over a dirty piece of paper. He drew out a handful of rupees, and snatched
half-jestingly at the chart, which tore in the lama's grip. A low murmur of
horror went up from the coolies—some of whom were Spiti men and, by
their lights, good Buddhists. The lama rose at the insult; his hand went
to the heavy iron pencase that is the priest's weapon, and the Babu danced
in agony.

"Now you see—you see why I wanted witnesses. They are highly unscrupulous people. Oh Sar! Sar! You must not hit holy man!"

"Chela! He has defiled the Written Word!"

It was too late. Before Kim could ward him off, the Russian struck the
old man full on the face. Next instant he was rolling over and over down
the hill with Kim at his throat. The blow had waked every unknown Irish

devil in the boy's blood, and the sudden fall of his enemy did the rest. The lama dropped to his knees, half-stunned; the coolies under their loads fled up the hill as fast as plainsmen run across the level. They had seen sacrilege unspeakable, and it behoved them to get away before the Gods and devils of the hills took vengeance. The Frenchman ran towards the lama, fumbling at his revolver with some notion of making him a hostage for his companion. A shower of cutting stones—hillmen are very straight shots—drove him away, and a coolie from Ao-chung snatched the lama into the stampede. All came about as swiftly as the sudden mountain-darkness.

"They have taken the baggage and all the guns," yelled the Frenchman, firing blindly into the twilight.

"All right, Sar! All right! Don't shoot. I go to rescue," and Hurree, pounding down the slope, cast himself bodily upon the delighted and astonished Kim, who was banging his breathless foe's head against a boulder.

"Go back to the coolies," whispered the Babu in his ear. "They have the baggage. The papers are in the kilta with the red top, but look through all. Take their papers, and specially the murasla (King's letter). Go! The other man comes!"

Kim tore up hill. A revolver-bullet rang on a rock by his side, and he cowered partridge-wise.

"If you shoot," shouted Hurree, "they will descend and annihilate us. I have rescued the gentleman, Sar. This is par-tic-ularly dangerous."

"By Jove!" Kim was thinking hard in English. "This is dam-tight place, but I think it is self-defence." He felt in his bosom for Mahbub's gift, and uncertainly—save for a few practice shots in the Bikaner desert, he had never used the little gun—pulled trigger.

"What did I say, Sar!" The Babu seemed to be in tears. "Come down here and assist to resuscitate. We are all up a tree, I tell you."

The shots ceased. There was a sound of stumbling feet, and Kim hurried upward through the gloom, swearing like a cat—or a country-bred.

"Did they wound thee, chela?" called the lama above him.

"No. And thou?" He dived into a clump of stunted firs.

"Unhurt. Come away. We go with these folk to Shamlegh-under-the-Snow."

"But not before we have done justice," a voice cried. "I have got the Sahibs' guns—all four. Let us go down."

"He struck the Holy One—we saw it! Our cattle will be barren—our wives will cease to bear! The snows will slide upon us as we go home. . . . Atop of all other oppression too!"

The little fir-clump filled with clamouring coolies—panic-stricken, and in their terror capable of anything. The man from Ao-chung clicked the breech-bolt of his gun impatiently, and made as to go down hill.

"Wait a little, Holy One; they cannot go far: wait till I return."

"It is this person who has suffered wrong," said the lama, his hand over his brow.

"For that very reason," was the reply.

"If this person overlooks it, your hands are clean. Moreover, ye acquire merit by obedience."

"Wait, and we will all go to Shamlegh together," the man insisted.

For a moment, for just so long as it needs to stuff a cartridge into a breech-loader, the lama hesitated. Then he rose to his feet, and laid a finger on the man's shoulder.

"Hast thou heard? I say there shall be no killing—I who was Abbot of Suchzen. Is it any lust of thine to be re-born as a rat, or a snake under the eaves—a worm in the belly of the most mean beast? Is it thy wish to—"

The man from Ao-chung fell to his knees, for the voice boomed like a Tibetan devil-gong.

"Ai! ai!" cried the Spiti men. "Do not curse us—do not curse him. It was but his zeal, Holy One! . . . Put down the rifle, fool!"

"Anger on anger! Evil on evil! There will be no killing. Let the priest-beaters go in bondage to their own acts. Just and sure is the Wheel, swerving not a hair! They will be born many times—in torment." His head drooped, and he leaned heavily on Kim's shoulder.

"I have come near to great evil, chela," he whispered in that dead hush under the pines. "I was tempted to loose the bullet; and truly, in Tibet there would have been a heavy and a slow death for them. . . . He struck me across the face . . . upon the flesh . . ." He slid to the ground, breathing heavily, and Kim could hear the over-driven heart bump and check.

"Have they hurt him to the death?" said the Ao-chung man, while the others stood mute.

Kim knelt over the body in deadly fear. "Nay," he cried passionately, "this is only a weakness." Then he remembered that he was a white man, with a white man's camp-fittings at his service. "Open the kiltas! The Sahibs may have a medicine."

"Oho! Then I know it," said the Ao-chung man with a laugh. "Not for five years was I Yankling Sahib's shikarri without knowing that medicine. I too have tasted it. Behold!"

He drew from his breast a bottle of cheap whisky—such as is sold to explorers at Leh—and cleverly forced a little between the lama's teeth.

"So I did when Yankling Sahib twisted his foot beyond Astor. Aha! I have already looked into their baskets—but we will make fair division at Shamlegh. Give him a little more. It is good medicine. Feel! His heart goes better now. Lay his head down and rub a little on the chest. If he had waited quietly while I accounted for the Sahibs this would never have come. But perhaps the Sahibs may chase us here. Then it would not be wrong to shoot them with their own guns, heh?"

"One is paid, I think, already," said Kim between his teeth. "I kicked him in the groin as we went down hill. Would I had killed him!"

"It is well to be brave when one does not live in Rampur," said one whose hut lay within a few miles of the Rajah's rickety palace. "If we get a bad name among the Sahibs, none will employ us as Shikarris any more."

"Oh, but these are not Angrezi Sahibs—not merry-minded men like Fostum Sahib or Yankling Sahib. They are foreigners—they cannot speak Angrezi as do Sahibs."

Here the lama coughed and sat up, groping for the rosary.

"There shall be no killing," he murmured. "Just is the Wheel! Evil on evil—"

"Nay, Holy One. We are all here." The Ao-chung man timidly patted his feet. "Except by thy order, no one shall be slain. Rest awhile. We will make a little camp here, and later, as the moon rises, we go to Shamlegh-under-the-Snow."

"After a blow," said a Spiti man sententiously, "it is best to sleep."

"There is, as it were, a dizziness at the back of my neck, and a pinching in it. Let me lay my head on thy lap, chela. I am an old man, but not free from passion. . . . We must think of the Cause of Things."

"Give him a blanket. We dare not light a fire lest the Sahibs see."

"Better get away to Shamlegh. None will follow us to Shamlegh."

This was the nervous Rampur man.

"I have been Fostum Sahib's shikarri, and I am Yankling Sahib's shikarri. I should have been with Yankling Sahib now but for this cursed beegar (the corvee). Let two men watch below with the guns lest the Sahibs do more foolishness. I shall not leave this Holy One."

They sat down a little apart from the lama, and, after listening awhile, passed round a water-pipe whose receiver was an old Day and Martin blacking-bottle. The glow of the red charcoal as it went from hand to hand lit up the narrow, blinking eyes, the high Chinese cheek-bones, and the bull-throats that melted away into the dark duffle folds round the shoulders. They looked like kobolds from some magic mine—gnomes of the hills in conclave. And while they talked, the voices of the snow-waters round them diminished one by one as the night-frost choked and clogged the runnels.

"How he stood up against us!" said a Spiti man admiring. "I remember an old ibex, out Ladakh-way, that Dupont Sahib missed on a shoulder-shot, seven seasons back, standing up just like him. Dupont Sahib was a good shikarri."

"Not as good as Yankling Sahib." The Ao-chung man took a pull at the whisky-bottle and passed it over. "Now hear me—unless any other man thinks he knows more."

The challenge was not taken up.

"We go to Shamlegh when the moon rises. There we will fairly divide the baggage between us. I am content with this new little rifle and all its cartridges."

"Are the bears only bad on thy holding?" said a mate, sucking at the pipe.

"No; but musk-pods are worth six rupees apiece now, and thy women can have the canvas of the tents and some of the cooking-gear. We will do all that at Shamlegh before dawn. Then we all go our ways, remembering that we have never seen or taken service with these Sahibs, who may, indeed, say that we have stolen their baggage."

"That is well for thee, but what will our Rajah say?"

"Who is to tell him? Those Sahibs, who cannot speak our talk, or the Babu, who for his own ends gave us money? Will he lead an army against us? What evidence will remain? That we do not need we shall throw on Shamlegh midden, where no man has yet set foot."

"Who is at Shamlegh this summer?" The place was only a grazing centre of three or four huts.

"The Woman of Shamlegh. She has no love for Sahibs, as we know. The others can be pleased with little presents; and here is enough for us all." He patted the fat sides of the nearest basket.

"But—but—"

"I have said they are not true Sahibs. All their skins and heads were bought in the bazar at Leh. I know the marks. I showed them to ye last march."

"True. They were all bought skins and heads. Some had even the moth in them."

That was a shrewd argument, and the Ao-chung man knew his fellows.

"If the worst comes to the worst, I shall tell Yankling Sahib, who is a man of a merry mind, and he will laugh. We are not doing any wrong to any Sahibs whom we know. They are priest-beaters. They frightened us. We fled! Who knows where we dropped the baggage? Do ye think Yankling Sahib will permit down-country police to wander all over the hills, disturbing his game? It is a far cry from Simla to Chini, and farther from Shamlegh to Shamlegh midden."

"So be it, but I carry the big kilta. The basket with the red top that the Sahibs pack themselves every morning."

"Thus it is proved," said the Shamlegh man adroitly, "that they are Sahibs of no account. Who ever heard of Fostum Sahib, or Yankling Sahib, or even the little Peel Sahib that sits up of nights to shoot serow—I say, who ever heard of these Sahibs coming into the hills without a down-country cook, and a bearer, and—and all manner of well-paid, high-handed and oppressive folk in their tail? How can they make trouble? What of the kilta?"

"Nothing, but that it is full of the Written Word—books and papers in which they wrote, and strange instruments, as of worship."

"Shamlegh midden will take them all."

"True! But how if we insult the Sahibs' Gods thereby? I do not like to handle the Written Word in that fashion. And their brass idols are beyond my comprehension. It is no plunder for simple hill-folk."

"The old man still sleeps. Hst! We will ask his chela." The Ao-chung man refreshed himself, and swelled with pride of leadership.

"We have here," he whispered, "a kilta whose nature we do not know."

"But I do," said Kim cautiously. The lama drew breath in natural, easy sleep, and Kim had been thinking of Hurree's last words. As a player of the Great Game, he was disposed just then to reverence the Babu. "It is a kilta with a red top full of very wonderful things, not to be handled by fools."

"I said it; I said it," cried the bearer of that burden. "Thinkest thou it will betray us?"

"Not if it be given to me. I will draw out its magic. Otherwise it will do great harm."

"A priest always takes his share." Whisky was demoralising the Ao-chung man.

"It is no matter to me," Kim answered, with the craft of his mother-country. "Share it among you, and see what comes!"

"Not I. I was only jesting. Give the order. There is more than enough for us all. We go our way from Shamlegh in the dawn."

They arranged and re-arranged their artless little plans for another hour, while Kim shivered with cold and pride. The humour of the situation tickled the Irish and the Oriental in his soul. Here were the emissaries of the dread Power of the North, very possibly as great in their own land as Mahbub or Colonel Creighton, suddenly smitten helpless. One of them, he privately knew, would be lame for a time. They had made promises to Kings. To-night they lay out somewhere below him, chartless, food-less, tentless, gunless—except for Hurree Babu, guideless. And this collapse of their Great Game (Kim wondered to whom they would report it), this panicky bolt into the night, had come about through no craft of Hurree's or contrivance of Kim's, but simply, beautifully, inevitably as the capture of Mahbub's faquir-friends by the zealous young policeman at Umballa.

"They are there—with nothing; and, by Jove, it is cold! I am here with all their things. Oh, they will be angry! I am sorry for Hurree Babu."

Kim might have saved his pity, for though at that moment the Bengali suffered acutely in the flesh, his soul was puffed and lofty. A mile down the hill, on the edge of the pine-forest, two half-frozen men—one powerfully sick at intervals—were varying mutual recriminations with the most poignant abuse of the Babu, who seemed distraught with terror. They demanded a plan of action. He explained that they were very lucky to be alive; that their coolies, if not then stalking them, had passed beyond recall; that the Rajah, his master, was ninety miles away, and, so far from lending them money and a retinue for the Simla journey, would surely cast them into prison if he heard that they had hit a priest. He enlarged on this sin and its consequences till they bade him change the subject. Their one hope, said he, was unostentatious flight from village to village till they received civilisation; and, for the hundredth time dissolved in tears, he demanded of the high stars why the Sahibs "had beaten holy man."

Ten steps would have taken Hurree into the creaking gloom utterly beyond their reach—to the shelter and food of the nearest village, where glib-tongued doctors were scarce. But he preferred to endure cold, belly-pinch, bad words, and occasional blows in the company of his honoured employers. Crouched against a tree-trunk, he sniffed dolefully.

"And have you thought," said the uninjured man hotly, "what sort of spectacle we shall present wandering through these hills among these aborigines?"

Hurree Babu had thought of little else for some hours, but the remark was not to his address.

"We cannot wander! I can hardly walk," groaned Kim's victim.

"Perhaps the holy man will be merciful in loving-kindness, Sar, otherwise—"

"I promise myself a peculiar pleasure in emptying my revolver into that young bonze when next we meet," was the unchristian answer.

"Revolvers! Vengeance! Bonzes!" Hurree crouched lower. The war was breaking out afresh. "Have you no consideration for our loss? The baggage! The baggage!" He could hear the speaker literally dancing on the grass. "Everything we bore! Everything we have secured! Our gains! Eight months' work! Do you know what that means? 'Decidedly it is we who can deal with Orientals!' Oh, you have done well."

They fell to it in several tongues, and Hurree smiled. Kim was with the kiltas, and in the kiltas lay eight months of good diplomacy. There was no means of communicating with the boy, but he could be trusted. For the rest, he could so stage-manage the journey through the hills that Hilas, Bunar, and four hundred miles of hill-roads should tell the tale for a generation. Men who cannot control their own coolies are little respected in the Hills, and the hillman has a very keen sense of humour.

"If I had done it myself," thought Hurree, "it would not have been better; and, by Jove, now I think of it, of course I arranged it myself. How quick I have been! Just when I ran down hill I thought it! Thee outrage was accidental, but onlee me could have worked it—ah—for all it was dam well worth. Consider the moral effect upon these ignorant peoples! No treaties—no papers—no written documents at all—and me to interpret for them. How I shall laugh with the Colonel! I wish I had their papers also: but you cannot occupy two places in space simultaneously. Thatt is axiomatic."

Chapter 14

My brother kneels (so saith Kabir)
To stone and brass in heathen-wise,
But in my brother's voice I hear
My own unanswered agonies.
His God is as his Fates assign—
His prayer is all the world's—and mine.
                                    Kabir.

AT MOONRISE the cautious coolies got under way. The lama, refreshed by his sleep and the spirit, needed no more than Kim's shoulder to bear him along—a silent, swift-striding man. They held the shale-sprinkled grass for an hour, swept round the shoulder of an immortal cliff, and climbed into a new country entirely blocked off from all sight of Chini valley. A huge pasture-ground ran up fan-shaped to the living snow. At its base was perhaps half an acre of flat land, on which stood a few soil and timber huts. Behind them—for, hill-fashion, they were perched on the edge of all things—the ground fell sheer two thousand feet to Shamlegh midden, where never yet man has set foot.

The men made no motion to divide the plunder till they had seen the lama bedded down in the best room of the place, with Kim shampooing his feet, Mohammedan fashion.

"We will send food," said the Ao-chung man, "and the red-topped kilta. By dawn there will be none to give evidence, one way or the other. If anything is not needed in the kilta—see here!"

He pointed through the window—opening into space that was filled with moonlight reflected from the snow—and threw out an empty whisky-bottle.

"No need to listen for the fall. This is the world's end," he said, and swung off. The lama looked forth, a hand on either sill, with eyes that shone like yellow opals. From the enormous pit before him white peaks lifted themselves yearning to the moonlight. The rest was as the darkness of interstellar space.

"These," he said slowly, "are indeed my Hills. Thus should a man abide, perched above the world, separated from delights, considering vast matters."

"Yes; if he has a chela to prepare tea for him, and to fold a blanket for his head, and to chase out calving cows."

A smoky lamp burned in a niche, but the full moonlight beat it down; and by the mixed light, stooping above the food-bag and cups, Kim moved like a tall ghost.

"Ai! But now I have let the blood cool my head still beats and drums, and there is a cord round the back of my neck."

"No wonder. It was a strong blow. May he who dealt it—"

"But for my own passions there would have been no evil."

"What evil? Thou hast saved the Sahibs from death they deserved a hundred times."

"The lesson is not well learnt, chela." The lama came to rest on a folded blanket, as Kim went forward with his evening routine. "The blow was but a shadow upon a shadow. Evil in itself—my legs weary apace these latter days!—it met evil in me—anger, rage, and a lust to return evil. These wrought in my blood, woke tumult in my stomach, and dazzled my ears." Here he drank scalding block-tea ceremonially, taking the hot cup from Kim's hand. "Had I been passionless, the evil blow would have done only bodily evil—a scar, or a bruise—which is illusion. But my mind was not abstracted, for rushed in straightway a lust to let the Spiti men kill. In fighting that lust, my soul was torn and wrenched beyond a thousand blows. Not till I had repeated the Blessings (he meant the Buddhist Beatitudes) did I achieve calm. But the evil planted in me by that moment's carelessness works out to its end. Just is the Wheel, swerving not a hair! Learn the lesson, chela."

"It is too high for me," Kim muttered. "I am still all shaken. I am glad I hurt the man."

"I felt that sleeping upon thy knees, in the wood below. It disquieted me in my dreams—the evil in thy soul working through to mine. Yet on the other hand"—he loosed his rosary—"I have acquired merit by saving two lives—the lives of those that wronged me. Now I must see into the Cause of Things. The boat of my soul staggers."

"Sleep, and be strong. That is wisest."

"I meditate: there is a need greater than thou knowest."

Till the dawn, hour after hour, as the moonlight paled on the high peaks, and that which had been belted blackness on the sides of the far hills showed as tender green forest, the lama stared fixedly at the wall. From time to time he groaned. Outside the barred door, where discomfited kine came to ask for their old stable, Shamlegh and the coolies gave itself up to plunder and riotous living. The Ao-chung man was their leader, and once they had opened the Sahibs' tinned foods and found that they were very good they dared not turn back. Shamlegh kitchen-midden took the dunnage.

When Kim, after a night of bad dreams, stole forth to brush his teeth in the morning chill, a fair-coloured woman with turquoise-studded head-gear drew him aside.

"The others have gone. They left thee this kilta as the promise was. I do not love Sahibs, but thou wilt make us a charm in return for it. We do not wish little Shamlegh to get a bad name on account of the—accident. I am the Woman of Shamlegh." She looked him over with bold, bright eyes, unlike the usual furtive glance of hillwomen.

"Assuredly. But it must be done in secret."

She raised the heavy kilta like a toy and slung it into her own hut.

"Out and bar the door! Let none come near till it is finished."

"But afterwards—we may talk?"

Kim tilted the kilta on the floor—a cascade of Survey-instruments, books, diaries, letters, maps, and queerly scented native correspondence. At the very bottom was an embroidered bag covering a sealed, gilded, and illuminated document such as one King sends to another. Kim caught his breath with delight, and reviewed the situation from a Sahib's point of view.

"The books I do not want. Besides, they are logarithms—Survey, I suppose." He laid them aside. "The letters I do not understand, but Colonel Creighton will. They must all be kept. The maps—they draw better maps than me—of course. All the native letters—oho!—and particularly the murasla." He sniffed the embroidered bag. "That must be from Hilas or Bunar, and Hurree Babu spoke truth. By Jove! It is a fine haul. I wish Hurree could know. . . . The rest must go out of the window." He fingered a superb prismatic compass and the shiny top of a theodolite. But after all, a Sahib cannot very well steal, and the things might be inconvenient evidence later. He sorted out every scrap of manuscript, every map, and the native letters. They made one softish slab. The three locked ferril-backed books, with five worn pocketbooks, he put aside.

"The letters and the murasla I must carry inside my coat and under my belt, and the hand-written books I must put into the food-bag. It will be very heavy. No. I do not think there is anything more. If there is, the coolies have thrown it down the khud, so thatt is all right. Now you go too." He repacked the kilta with all he meant to lose, and hove it up on to the window-sill. A thousand feet below lay a long, lazy, round-shouldered bank of mist, as yet untouched by the morning sun. A thousand feet below that was an hundred-year-old pine-forest. He could see the green tops looking like a bed of moss when a wind-eddy thinned the cloud.

"No! I don't think any one will go after you!"

The wheeling basket vomited its contents as it dropped. The theodolite hit a jutting cliff-ledge and exploded like a shell; the books, inkstand, paint-boxes, compasses, and rulers showed for a few seconds like a swarm of bees. Then they vanished; and, though Kim, hanging half out of window, strained his young ears, never a sound came up from the gulf.

"Five hundred—a thousand rupees could not buy them," he thought sorrowfully. "It was verree wasteful, but I have all their other stuff—everything they did—I hope. Now how the deuce am I to tell Hurree Babu, and whatt the deuce am I to do? And my old man is sick. I must tie up the letters in oil-cloth. That is something to do first—else they will get all sweated. . . . And I am all alone!" He bound them into a neat packet, swedging down the stiff, sticky oil-cloth at the corners, for his roving life had made him as methodical as an old hunter in matters of the road. Then with double care he packed away the books at the bottom of the food-bag.

The woman rapped at the door.

"But thou hast made no charm," she said, looking about.

"There is no need." Kim had completely overlooked the necessity for a little patter-talk. The woman laughed at his confusion irreverently.

"None—for thee. Thou canst cast a spell by the mere winking of an eye. But think of us poor people when thou art gone! They were all too drunk last night to hear a woman. Thou art not drunk?"

"I am a priest." Kim had recovered himself, and, the woman being aught but unlovely, thought best to stand on his office.

"I warned them that the Sahibs will be angry and will make an inquisition and a report to the Rajah. There is also the Babu with them. Clerks have long tongues."

"Is that all thy trouble?" The plan rose fully formed in Kim's mind, and he smiled ravishingly.

"Not all," quoth the woman, putting out a hard brown hand all covered with turquoises set in silver.

"I can finish that in a breath," he went on quickly. "The Babu is the very hakim (thou hast heard of him?) who was wandering among the hills by Ziglaur. I know him."

"He will tell for the sake of a reward. Sahibs cannot distinguish one hillman from another, but Babus have eyes for men—and women."

"Carry a word to him from me."

"There is nothing I would not do for thee."

He accepted the compliment calmly, as men must in lands where women make the love, tore a leaf from a note-book, and with a patent indelible pencil wrote in gross Shikast—the script that bad little boys use when they write dirt on walls: "I have everything that they have written:

their pictures of the country, and many letters. Especially the murasla. Tell me what to do. I am at Shamlegh-under-the-Snow. The old man is sick."

"Take this to him. It will altogether shut his mouth. He cannot have gone far."

"Indeed no. They are still in the forest across the spur. Our children went to watch them when the light came, and have cried the news as they moved."

Kim looked his astonishment; but from the edge of the sheep-pasture floated a shrill, kite-like trill. A child tending cattle had picked it up from a brother or sister on the far side of the slope that commanded Chini valley.

"My husbands are also out there gathering wood." She drew a handful of walnuts from her bosom, split one neatly, and began to eat. Kim affected blank ignorance.

"Dost thou not know the meaning of the walnut—priest?" she said coyly, and handed him the half-shells.

"Well thought of." He slipped the piece of paper between them quickly. "Hast thou a little wax to close them on this letter?"

The woman sighed aloud, and Kim relented.

"There is no payment till service has been rendered. Carry this to the Babu, and say it was sent by the Son of the Charm."

"Ai! Truly! Truly! By a magician—who is like a Sahib."

"Nay, Son of the Charm: and ask if there be any answer."

"But if he offer a rudeness? I—I am afraid."

Kim laughed. "He is, I have no doubt, very tired and very hungry. The Hills make cold bedfellows. Hai, my"—it was on the tip of his tongue to say Mother, but he turned it to Sister—"thou art a wise and witty woman. By this time all the villages know what has befallen the Sahibs—eh?"

"True. News was at Ziglaur by midnight, and by to-morrow should be at Kotgarh. The villages are both afraid and angry."

"No need. Tell the villages to feed the Sahibs and pass them on, in peace. We must get them quietly away from our valleys. To steal is one thing—to kill another. The Babu will understand, and there will be no after-complaints. Be swift. I must tend my master when he wakes."

"So be it. After service—thou hast said?—comes the reward. I am the Woman of Shamlegh, and I hold from the Rajah. I am no common bearer of babes. Shamlegh is thine: hoof and horn and hide, milk and butter. Take or leave."

She turned resolutely uphill, her silver necklaces clicking on her broad breast, to meet the morning sun fifteen hundred feet above them. This

time Kim thought in the vernacular as he waxed down the oil-skin edges
of the packets.

"How can a man follow the Way or the Great Game when he is
eternally pestered by women? There was that girl at Akrola by the Ford;
and there was the scullion's wife behind the dovecot—not counting the
others—and now comes this one! When I was a child it was well enough,
but now I am a man and they will not regard me as a man. Walnuts indeed! Ho! ho! It is almonds in the Plains!"

He went out to levy on the village—not with a begging-bowl, which
might do for down country, but in the manner of a prince. Shamlegh's
summer population is only three families—four women and eight or nine
men. They were all full of tinned meats and mixed drinks, from ammo-
niated quinine to white vodka, for they had taken their full share in the
overnight loot. The neat Continental tents had been cut up and shared
long ago, and there were patent aluminum saucepans abroad.

But they considered the lama's presence a perfect safeguard against all
consequences, and impenitently brought Kim of their best—even to a drink
of chang—the barley-beer that comes from Ladakh-way. Then they thawed
out in the sun, and sat with their legs hanging over infinite abysses, chattering, laughing, and smoking. They judged India and its Government
solely from their experience of wandering Sahibs who had employed them
or their friends as shikarris. Kim heard tales of shots missed upon ibex,
serow, or markhor, by Sahibs twenty years in their graves—every detail
lighted from behind like twigs on treetops seen against lightning. They
told him of their little diseases, and, more important, the diseases of their
tiny, sure-footed cattle; of trips as far as Kotgarh, where the strange
missionaries live, and beyond even to marvellous Simla, where the streets
are paved with silver, and any one, look you, can get service with the Sahibs, who ride about in two-wheeled carts and spend money with a spade.
Presently, grave and aloof, walking very heavily, the lama joined himself to the chatter under the eaves, and they gave him great room. The
thin air refreshed him, and he sat on the edge of precipices with the
best of them, and when talk languished, flung pebbles into the void.
Thirty miles away, as the eagle flies, lay the next range, seamed and chan-
nelled and pitted with little patches of brush—forests, each a day's dark
march. Behind the village, Shamlegh hill itself cut off all view to southward. It was like sitting in a swallow's nest under the eaves of the roof of
the world.

From time to time the lama stretched out his hand, and with a little,
low-voiced prompting would point out the road to Spiti and north across
the Parungla.

"Beyond, where the hills lie thickest, lies De-ch'en" (he meant Han-le), "the great Monastery. s'Tag-stan-ras-ch'en built it, and of him there runs this tale." Whereupon he told it: a fantastic piled narrative of bewitchment and miracles that set Shamlegh agasping. Turning west a little, he speered for the green hills of Kulu, and sought Kailung under the glaciers. "For thither came I in the old, old days. From Leh I came, over the Baralachi."

"Yes, yes; we know it," said the far-faring people of Shamlegh.

"And I slept two nights with the priests of Kailung. These are the hills of my delight! Shadows blessed above all other shadows! There my eyes opened on this world; there my eyes were opened to this world; there I found Enlightenment; and there I girt my loins for my Search. Out of the Hills I came—the high Hills and the strong winds. Oh, just is the Wheel!" He blessed them in detail—the great glaciers, the naked rocks, the piled moraines and tumbled shale; dry up-land, hidden salt-lake, age-old timber and fruitful water-shot valley one after the other, as a dying man blesses his folk, and Kim marvelled at his passion.

"Yes—yes. There is no place like our Hills," said the people of Shamlegh. And they fell to wondering how a man could live in the hot terrible Plains where the cattle run as big as elephants, unfit to plough on a hillside; where village touches village, they had heard, for a hundred miles; where folk went about stealing in gangs, and what the robbers spared the police carried utterly away.

So the still forenoon wore through, and at the end of it Kim's messenger dropped from the steep pasture as unbreathed as when she had set out.

"I sent a word to the hakim," Kim explained, while she made reverence.

"He joined himself to the idolaters? Nay, I remember he did a healing upon one of them. He has acquired merit, though the healed employed his strength for evil. Just is the Wheel! What of the hakim?"

"I feared that thou hadst been bruised and—and I knew he was wise." Kim took the waxed walnut-shell and read in English on the back of his note: "Your favour received. Cannot get away from present company at present, but shall take them into Simla. After which, hope to rejoin you. Inexpedient to follow angry gentlemen. Return by same road you came, and will overtake. Highly gratified about correspondence due to my forethought." "He says, Holy One, that he will escape from the idolaters, and will return to us. Shall we wait awhile at Shamlegh, then?"

The lama looked long and lovingly upon the Hills and shook his head.

"That may not be, chela. From my bones outward I do desire it, but it is forbidden. I have seen the Cause of Things."

"Why? When the Hills give thee back thy strength day by day? Remember we were weak and fainting down below there in the Doon."

"I became strong to do evil and to forget. A brawler and a swashbuckler upon the hillsides was I." Kim bit back a smile. "Just and perfect is the Wheel, swerving not a hair. When I was a man—a long time ago—I did pilgrimage to Guru Ch'wan among the poplars" (he pointed Bhotan-wards), "where they keep the Sacred Horse."

"Quiet, be quiet!" said Shamlegh, all arow. "He speaks of Jam-lin-nin-k'or, The Horse That Can Go Round The World In a Day."

"I speak to my chela only," said the lama, in gentle reproof, and they scattered like frost on south eaves of a morning. "I did not seek truth in those days, but the talk of doctrine. All illusion! I drank the beer and ate the bread of Guru Ch'wan. Next day one said: 'We go out to fight Sangor Gutok down the valley to discover (mark again how Lust is tied to Anger!) which abbot shall bear rule in the valley, and take the profit of the prayers they print at Sangor Gutok.' I went, and we fought a day."

"But how, Holy One?"

"With our long pencases as I could have shown. . . . I say, we fought under the poplars, both abbots and all the monks, and one laid open my forehead to the bone. See!" He tilted back his cap and showed a puckered silvery scar. "Just and perfect is the Wheel! Yesterday the scar itched, and after fifty years I recalled how it was dealt and the face of him who dealt it; dwelling a little in illusion. Followed that which thou didst see—strife and stupidity. Just is the Wheel! The idolater's blow fell upon the scar. Then I was shaken in my soul: my soul was darkened, and the boat of my soul rocked upon the waters of illusion. Not till I came to Shamlegh could I meditate upon the Cause of Things, or trace the running grass-roots of Evil. I strove all the long night."

"But, Holy One, thou art innocent of all evil. May I be thy sacrifice!"

Kim was genuinely distressed at the old man's sorrow, and Mahbub Ali's phrase slipped out unawares.

"In the dawn," he went on more gravely, ready rosary clicking between the slow sentences, "came enlightenment. It is here. . . . I am an old man . . . hill-bred, hill-fed, never to sit down among my Hills. Three years I travelled through Hind, but—can earth be stronger than Mother Earth? My stupid body yearned to the Hills and the snow of the Hills, from below there. I said, and it is true, my Search is sure. So, at the Kulu woman's house I turned hillward, over-persuaded by myself. There is no blame to the hakim. He—following Desire—foretold that the Hills would make me strong. They strengthened me to do evil, to forget my Search. I delighted in life and the lust of life. I desired strong slopes to climb. I cast about to find them. I measured the strength of my body, which is evil, against the high Hills. I made a mock of thee when thy breath came short under Jamnotri. I jested when thou wouldst not face the snow of the Pass."

"But what harm? I was afraid. It was just. I am not a hillman; and I loved thee for thy new strength."

"More than once I remember," he rested his cheek dolefully on his hand, "I sought thy praise and the hakim's for the mere strength of my legs. Thus evil followed evil till the cup was full. Just is the Wheel! All Hind for three years did me all honour. From the Fountain of Wisdom in the Wonder House to"—he smiled—"a little child playing by a big gun—the world prepared my road. And why?"

"Because we loved thee. It is only the fever of the blow. I myself am still sick and shaken."

"No! It was because I was upon the Way—tuned as are sinen (cymbals) to the purpose of the Law. I departed from that ordinance. The tune was broken: followed the punishment. In my own Hills, on the edge of my own country, in the very place of my evil desire, comes the buffet—here!" (He touched his brow.) "As a novice is beaten when he misplaces the cups, so am I beaten, who was Abbot of Suchzen. No word, look you, but a blow, chela."

"But the Sahibs did not know thee, Holy One?"

"We were well matched. Ignorance and Lust met Ignorance and Lust upon the road, and they begat Anger. The blow was a sign to me, who am no better than a strayed yak, that my place is not here. Who can read the Cause of an act is half-way to Freedom! 'Back to the path,' says the Blow. 'The Hills are not for thee. Thou canst not choose Freedom and go in bondage to the delight of life.'"

"If we had never met that thrice-cursed Russian!"

"Our Lord Himself cannot make the Wheel swing backward. And for my merit that I had acquired I gain yet another sign." He put his hand in his bosom, and drew forth the Wheel of Life. "Look! I considered this after I had meditated. There remains untorn by the idolater no more than the breadth of my fingernail."

"I see."

"So much, then, is the span of my life in this body. I have served the Wheel all my days. Now the Wheel serves me. But for the merit I have acquired in guiding thee upon the Way, there would have been added to me yet another life ere I had found my River. Is it plain, chela?"

Kim stared at the brutally disfigured chart. From left to right diagonally the rent ran—from the Eleventh House where Desire gives birth to the Child (as it is drawn by Tibetans)—across the human and animal worlds, to the Fifth House—the empty House of the Senses. The logic was unanswerable.

"Before our Lord won enlightenment," the lama folded all away with
reverence, "He was tempted. I too have been tempted, but it is finished.
The Arrow fell in the Plains—not in the Hills. Therefore, what make we
here?"

"Shall we at least wait for the hakim?"

"I know how long I live in this body. What can a hakim do?"

"But thou art all sick and shaken. Thou canst not walk."

"How can I be sick if I see Freedom?" He rose unsteadily to his feet.

"Then I must get food from the village. Oh, the weary Road!" Kim felt
that he too needed rest.

"That is lawful. Let us eat and go. The Arrow fell in Plains . . . but I
yielded to Desire. Make ready, chela."

Kim turned to the woman with the turquoise head-gear who had been
idly pitching pebbles over the cliff. She smiled very kindly.

"I found him like a strayed buffalo in a corn-field—the Babu; snorting
and sneezing with cold. He was so hungry that he forgot his dignity and
gave me sweet words. The Sahibs have nothing." She flung out an empty
palm. "One is very sick about the stomach. Thy work?"

Kim nodded, with a bright eye.

"I spoke to the Bengali first—and to the people of a nearby village after.
The Sahibs will be given food as they need it—nor will the people ask
money. The plunder is already distributed. That makes lying speeches to
the Sahibs. Why does he not leave them?"

"Out of the greatness of his heart."

" 'Was never a Bengali yet had one bigger than a dried walnut. But it is
no matter. . . . Now as to walnuts. After service comes reward. I have
said the village is thine."

"It is my loss," Kim began. "Even now I had planned desirable things
in my heart which"—there is no need to go through the compliments
proper to these occasions. He sighed deeply . . . "But my master, led by a
vision—"

"Huh! What can old eyes see except a full begging-bowl?"

"—turns from this village to the Plains again."

"Bid him stay."

Kim shook his head. "I know my Holy One, and his rage if he be
crossed," he replied impressively. "His curses shake the Hills."

"Pity they did not save him from a broken head! I heard that thou wast
the tiger-hearted one who smote the Sahib. Let him dream a little longer.
Stay!"

"Hillwoman," said Kim, with austerity that could not harden the out-
lines of his young oval face, "these matters are too high for thee."

"The Gods be good to us! Since when have men and women been other than men and women?"

"A priest is a priest. He says he will go upon this hour. I am his chela, and I go with him. We need food for the Road. He is an honoured guest in all the villages, but"—he broke into a pure boyish grin—"the food here is good. Give me some."

"What if I do not give it thee? I am the woman of this village."

"Then I curse thee—a little—not greatly, but enough to remember." He could not help smiling.

"Thou hast cursed me already by the down-dropped eyelash and the uplifted chin. Curses? What should I care for mere words?" She clenched her hands upon her bosom. . . . "But I would not have thee to go in anger, thinking hardly of me—a gatherer of cow-dung and grass at Shamlegh, but still a woman of substance."

"I think nothing," said Kim, "but that I am grieved to go, for I am very tired, and that we need food. Here is the bag."

The woman snatched it angrily. "I was foolish," said she. "Who is thy woman in the Plains? Fair or black? I was fair once. Laughest thou? Once, long ago, if thou canst believe, a Sahib looked on me with favour. Once, long ago, I wore European clothes at the Mission-house yonder." She pointed towards Kotgarh. "Once, long ago, I was Ker-lis-ti-an and spoke English—as the Sahibs speak it. Yes. My Sahib said he would return and wed me—yes, wed me. He went away—I had nursed him when he was sick—but he never returned. Then I saw that the Gods of the Kerlistians lied, and I went back to my own people. . . . I have never set eyes on a Sahib since. (Do not laugh at me. The fit is past, little priestling.) Thy face and thy walk and thy fashion of speech put me in mind of my Sahib, though thou art only a wandering mendicant to whom I give a dole. Curse me? Thou canst neither curse nor bless!" She set her hands on her hips and laughed bitterly. "Thy Gods are lies; thy works are lies; thy words are lies. There are no Gods under all the heavens. I know it. . . . But for a while I thought it was my Sahib come back, and he was my God. Yes, once I made music on a pianno in the Mission-house at Kotgarh. Now I give alms to priests who are heatthen." She wound up with the English word, and tied the mouth of the brimming bag.

"I wait for thee, chela," said the lama, leaning against the door-post.

The woman swept the tall figure with her eyes. "He walk? He cannot cover half a mile. Whither would old bones go?"

At this Kim, already perplexed by the lama's collapse, and foreseeing the weight of the bag, fairly lost his temper.

"What is it to thee, woman of ill-omen, where he goes?"

"Nothing—but something to thee, priest with a Sahib's face. Wilt thou carry him on thy shoulders?"

"I go to the Plains. None must hinder my return. I have wrestled with my soul till I am strengthless. The stupid body is spent, and we are far from the Plains."

"Behold!" she said simply, and drew aside to let Kim see his own utter helplessness. "Curse me. May be it will give him strength. Make a charm! Call on thy great God. Thou art a priest." She turned away.

The lama had squatted limply, still holding by the door-post. One cannot strike down an old man that he recovers again like a boy in a night. Weakness bowed him to the earth, but his eyes that hung on Kim were alive and imploring.

"It is all well," said Kim. "It is the thin air that weakens thee. In a little while we go! It is the mountain-sickness. I too am a little sick at stomach," . . . and he knelt and comforted with such poor words as came first to his lips. Then the woman returned, more erect than ever.

"Thy Gods useless, heh? Try mine. I am the Woman of Shamlegh." She hailed hoarsely, and there came out of a cow-pen her two husbands and three others with a dooli, the rude native litter of the Hills, that they use for carrying the sick and for visits of state. "These cattle," she did not condescend to look at them, "are thine for so long as thou shalt need."

"But we will not go Simla-way. We will not go near the Sahibs," cried the first husband.

"They will not run away as the others did, nor will they steal baggage. Two I know for weaklings. Stand to the rear-pole, Sonoo and Taree." They obeyed swiftly. "Lower now, and lift in that holy man. I will see to the village and your virtuous wives till ye return."

"When will that be?"

"Ask the priests. Do not pester me. Lay the food-bag at the foot, it balances better so."

"Oh, Holy One, thy Hills are kinder than our Plains!" cried Kim, relieved, as the lama tottered to the litter. "It is a very king's bed—a place of honour and ease. And we owe it to—"

"A woman of ill-omen. I need thy blessings as much as I do thy curses. It is my order and none of thine. Lift and away! Here! Hast thou money for the road?"

She beckoned Kim to her hut, and stooped above a battered English cash-box under her cot.

"I do not need anything," said Kim, angered where he should have been grateful. "I am already rudely loaded with favours."

She looked up with a curious smile and laid a hand on his shoulder. "At least, thank me. I am foul-faced and a hillwoman, but, as thy talk goes, I have acquired merit. Shall I show thee how the Sahibs render thanks?" and her hard eyes softened.

"I am but a wandering priest," said Kim, his eyes lighting in answer. "Thou needest neither my blessings nor my curses."

"Nay. But for one little moment—thou canst overtake the dooli in ten strides—if thou wast a Sahib, shall I show thee what thou wouldst do?"

"How if I guess, though?" said Kim, and putting his arm round her waist, he kissed her on the cheek, adding in English: "Thank you verree much, my dear."

Kissing is practically unknown among Asiatics, which may have been the reason that she leaned back with wide-open eyes and a face of panic.

"Next time," Kim went on, "you must not be so sure of your heathen priests. Now I say good-bye." He held out his hand English-fashion. She took it mechanically. "Good-bye, my dear."

"Good-bye, and—and"—she was remembering her English words one by one—"you will come back again? Good-bye, and—thee God bless you."

Half an hour later, as the creaking litter jolted up the hill path that leads south-easterly from Shamlegh, Kim saw a tiny figure at the hut door waving a white rag.

"She has acquired merit beyond all others," said the lama. "For to set a man upon the way to Freedom is half as great as though she had herself found it."

"Umm," said Kim thoughtfully, considering the past. "It may be that I have acquired merit also. . . . At least she did not treat me like a child." He hitched the front of his robe, where lay the slab of documents and maps, restowed the precious food-bag at the lama's feet, laid his hand on the litter edge, and buckled down to the slow pace of the grunting husbands.

"These also acquire merit," said the lama, after three miles.

"More than that, they shall be paid in silver," quoth Kim. The Woman of Shamlegh had given it to him; and it was only fair, he argued, that her men should earn it back again.

Chapter 15

I'd not give room for an Emperor—
I'd hold my road for a King.
To the Triple Crown I'd not bow down—
But this is a different thing!
I'll not fight with the Powers of Air—
Sentries pass him through!
Drawbridge let fall—He's the Lord of us all—
The Dreamer whose dream came true!
                                        "The Siege of the Fairies."

Two hundred miles north of Chini, on the blue shale of Ladakh, lies Yankling Sahib, the merry-minded man, spy-glassing wrathfully across the ridges for some sign of his pet tracker—a man from Ao-chung. But that renegade, with a new Mannlicher rifle and two hundred cartridges, is elsewhere, shooting musk-deer for the market, and Yankling Sahib will learn next season how very ill he has been.

Up the valleys of Bushahr—the far-beholding eagles of the Himalayas swerve at his new blue-and-white gored umbrella—hurries a Bengali, once fat and well-looking, now lean and weather-worn. He has received the thanks of two foreigners of distinction, piloted not unskilfully to Masho-bra tunnel which leads to the great and gay capital of India. It was not his fault that, blanketed by wet mists, he conveyed them past the telegraph-station and European colony of Kotgarh. It was not his fault, but that of the Gods, of whom he discoursed so engagingly, that he led them into the borders of Nahan, where the Rajah of that state mistook them for deserting British soldiery. Hurree Babu explained the greatness and glory, in their own country, of his companions, till the drowsy kinglet smiled. He explained it to every one who asked—many times—aloud—variously. He begged food, arranged accommodation, proved a skilful leech for an injury of the groin—such a blow as one may receive rolling down a rock-covered hillside in the dark—and in all things indispensable. The reason of his friendliness did him credit. With millions of fellow-serfs, he had learned to look upon Russia as the great deliverer from the North.

He was a fearful man. He had been afraid that he could not save his illustrious employers from the anger of an excited peasantry. He himself
would just as lief hit a holy man as not, but. . . . He was deeply grateful
and sincerely rejoiced that he had done his "little possible" towards bringing their venture to—barring the lost baggage—a successful issue. He had
forgotten the blows; denied that any blows had been dealt that unseemly
first night under the pines. He asked neither pension nor retaining fee,
but, if they deemed him worthy, would they write him a testimonial? It
might be useful to him later, if others, their friends, came over the Passes.
He begged them to remember him in their future greatnesses, for he
"opined subtly" that he, even he, Mohendro Lal Dutt, M. A. of Calcutta,
had "done the state some service."

They gave him a certificate praising his courtesy, helpfulness, and
unerring skill as a guide. He put it in his waist-belt and sobbed with
emotion; they had endured so many dangers together. He led them at
high noon along crowded Simla Mall to the Alliance Bank of Simla, where
they wished to establish their identity. Thence he vanished like a dawn-
cloud on Jakko.

Behold him, too fine drawn to sweat, too pressed to vaunt the drugs
in his little brass-bound box, ascending Shamlegh slope, a just man
made perfect. Watch him, all Babudom laid aside, smoking at noon on
a cot, while a woman with turquoise-studded head-gear points south-
easterly across the bare grass. Litters, she says, do not travel as fast as
single men, but his birds should now be in the Plains. The holy man
would not stay though Lispeth pressed him. The Babu groans heavily,
girds up his huge loins, and is off again. He does not care to travel after
dusk; but his days' marches—there is none to enter them in a book—
would astonish folk who mock at his race. Kindly villagers, remembering
the Dacca drug-vendor of two months ago, give him shelter against evil
spirits of the wood. He dreams of Bengali Gods, University text-books
of education, and the Royal Society, London, England. Next dawn the
bobbing blue-and-white umbrella goes forward.

On the edge of the Doon, Mussoorie well behind them and the Plains
spread out in golden dust before, rests a worn litter in which—all the
Hills know it—lies a sick lama who seeks a River for his healing. Villages
have almost come to blows over the honour of bearing it, for not only
has the lama given them blessings, but his disciple good money—full one-
third Sahibs' prices. Twelve miles a day has the dooli travelled, as the
greasy, rubbed pole-ends show, and by roads that few Sahibs use. Over
the Nilang Pass in storm when the driven snow-dust filled every fold of
the impassive lama's drapery; between the black horns of Raieng where
they heard the whistle of the wild goats through the clouds; pitching

and strained on the shale below; hard-held between shoulder and clenched jaw when they rounded the hideous curves of the Cut Road under Bhagirati; swinging and creaking to the steady jog-trot of the descent into the Valley of the Waters; pressed along the steamy levels of that locked valley; up, up and out again, to meet the roaring gusts off Kedarnath; set down of mid-days in the dun gloom of kindly oak-forests; passed from village to village in dawn-chill, when even devotees may be forgiven for swearing at impatient holy men; or by torch-light, when the least fearful think of ghosts—the dooli has reached her last stage. The little hill-folk sweat in the modified heat of the lower Sewaliks, and gather round the priests for their blessing and their wage.

"Ye have acquired merit," says the lama. "Merit greater than your knowing. And ye will return to the Hills," he sighs.

"Surely. The high Hills as soon as may be." The bearer rubs his shoulder, drinks water, spits it out again, and readjusts his grass sandal. Kim—his face is drawn and tired—pays very small silver from his belt, heaves out the food-bag, crams an oil-skin packet—they are holy writings—into his bosom, and helps the lama to his feet. The peace has come again into the old man's eyes, and he does not look for the hills to fall down and crush him as he did that terrible night when they were delayed by the flooded river.

The men pick up the dooli and swing out of sight between the scrub clumps.

The lama raises a hand toward the rampart of the Himalayas. "Not with you, O blessed among all hills, fell the Arrow of Our Lord! And never shall I breathe your air again!"

"But thou art ten times the stronger man in this good air," says Kim, for to his wearied soul appeal the well-cropped, kindly Plains. "Here, or hereabouts, fell the Arrow, yes. We will go very softly, perhaps a kos a day, for the Search is sure. But the bag weighs heavy."

"Ay, our Search is sure. I have come out of great temptation."

It was never more than a couple of miles a day now, and Kim's shoulders bore all the weight of it—the burden of an old man, the burden of the heavy food-bag with the locked books, the load of the writings on his heart, and the details of the daily routine. He begged in the dawn, set blankets for the lama's meditation, held the weary head on his lap through the noonday heats, fanning away the flies till his wrist ached, begged again in the evenings, and rubbed the lama's feet, who rewarded him with promise of Freedom—to-day, to-morrow, or, at furthest, the next day.

"Never was such a chela. I doubt at times whether Ananda more

faithfully nursed Our Lord. And thou art a Sahib? When I was a man—
a long time ago—I forgot that. Now I look upon thee often, and every
time I remember that thou art a Sahib. It is strange."

"Thou hast said there is neither black nor white. Why plague me with
this talk, Holy One? Let me rub the other foot. It vexes me. I am not
a Sahib. I am thy chela, and my head is heavy on my shoulders."

"Patience a little! We reach Freedom together. Then thou and I, upon
the far bank of the River, will look back upon our lives as in the Hills
we saw our days' marches laid out behind us. Perhaps I was once a Sahib."

" 'Was never a Sahib like thee, I swear it."

"I am certain the Keeper of the Images in the Wonder House was
in past life a very wise abbot. But even his spectacles do not maké my
eyes see. There fall shadows when I would look steadily. No matter—we
know the tricks of the poor stupid carcass—shadow changing to another
shadow. I am bound by the illusion of Time and Space. How far came
we to-day in the flesh?"

"Perhaps half a kos." Three-quarters of a mile, and it was a weary
march.

"Half a kos. Ha! I went ten thousand thousand in the spirit. How we
are all lapped and swathed and swaddled in these senseless things." He
looked at his thin blue-veined hand that found the beads so heavy. "Chela,
hast thou never a wish to leave me?"

Kim thought of the oilskin packet and the books in the food-bag. If
some one duly authorised would only take delivery of them the Great
Game might play itself for aught he then cared. He was tired and hot
in his head, and a cough that came from the stomach worried him.

"No," he said almost sternly. "I am not a dog or a snake to bite when
I have learned to love."

"Thou art too tender for me."

"Not that either. I have moved in one matter without consulting thee.
I have sent a message to the Kulu woman by that woman who gave us the
goat's milk this morn, saying that thou wast a little feeble and would
need a litter. I beat myself in my mind that I did not do it when we entered the Doon. We stay in this place till the litter returns."

"I am content. She is a woman with a heart of gold, as thou sayest,
but a talker—something of a talker."

"She will not weary thee. I have looked to that also. Holy One, my
heart is very heavy for my many carelessnesses towards thee." An hysterical catch rose in his throat. "I have walked thee too far; I have not
picked good food always for thee; I have not considered the heat; I have
talked to people on the road and left thee alone. . . . I have—I have
. . . Hai mai! But I love thee . . . and it is all too late. . . . I was a child.

. . . Oh why was I not a man! . . ." Overborne by strain, fatigue, and the weight beyond his years, Kim broke down and sobbed at the lama's feet.

"What a to-do is here," said the old man gently. "Thou has never stepped a hair's breadth from the Way of Obedience. Neglect me? Child, I have lived on thy strength as an old tree lives on the lime of a new wall. Day by day since Shamlegh down, I have stolen strength from thee. Therefore, not through any sin of thine art thou weakened. It is the Body—the silly, stupid Body—that speaks now. Not the assured Soul. Be comforted! Know at least the devils that thou fightest. They are earth-born—children of illusion. We will go to the woman from Kulu. She shall acquire merit in housing us, and specially in tending me. Thou shalt run free till strength returns. I had forgotten the stupid Body. If there be any blame, I bear it. But we are too close to the Gates of Deliverance to weigh blame. I could praise thee, but what need? In a little—in a very little—we shall sit beyond all needs."

And so he petted and comforted Kim with wise saws and grave texts on that little-understood beast, our Body, who, being but a delusion, insists on posing as the Soul, to the darkening of the Way, and the immense multiplication of unnecessary devils.

"Hai! hai! Let us talk of the woman from Kulu. Think you she will ask another charm for her grandsons? When I was a young man, a very long time ago, I was plagued with these vapours—and some others—and I went to an abbot—a very holy man and a seeker after truth, though then I knew it not. Sit up and listen, child of my soul! My tale was told. Said he to me, 'Chela, know this. There are many lies in the world, and not a few liars, but there are no liars like our bodies, except it be the sensations of our bodies.' Considering this I was comforted, and of his great favour he suffered me to drink tea in his presence. Suffer me now to drink tea, for I am thirsty."

With a laugh above his tears, Kim kissed the lama's feet, and went about tea-making.

"Thou leanest on me in the body, Holy One, but I lean on thee for some other things. Dost know it?"

"I have guessed maybe," and the lama's eyes twinkled. "We must change that."

So, when with scufflings and scrapings and a hot air of importance, paddled up nothing less than the Sahiba's pet palanquin sent twenty miles, with that same grizzled old Oorya servant in charge, and when they reached the disorderly order of the long white rambling house behind Saharunpore, the lama took his own measures.

Said the Sahiba cheerily from an upper window, after compliments: "What is the good of an old woman's advice to an old man? I told thee— I told thee, Holy One, to keep an eye upon the chela. How didst thou do it? Never answer me! I know. He has been running among the women. Look at his eyes—hollow and sunk—and the Betraying Line from the nose down! He has been sifted out! Fie! Fie! And a priest, too!"

Kim looked up over-weary to smile, shaking his head in denial.

"Do not jest," said the lama. "That time is done. We are here upon great matters. A sickness of soul took me in the Hills, and him a sickness of the body. Since then I have lived upon his strength—eating him."

"Children together—young and old," she sniffed, but forbore to make any new jokes. "May this present hospitality restore ye. Hold awhile and I will come to gossip of the high good Hills."

At evening time—her son-in-law was returned, so she did not need to go on inspection round the farm—she won to the meat of the matter, explained low-voicedly by the lama. The two old heads nodded wisely together. Kim had reeled to a room with a cot in it, and was dozing soddenly. The lama had forbidden him to set blankets or get food.

"I know—I know. Who but I?" she cackled. "We who go down to the burning-ghats clutch at the hands of those coming up from the River of Life with full water-jars—yes, brimming water-jars. I did the boy wrong. He lent thee his strength? It is true that the old eat the young daily. 'Stands now we must restore him."

"Thou hast many times acquired merit—"

"My merit. What is it? Old bag of bones making curries for men who do not ask 'Who cooked this?' Now if it were stored up for my grandson—"

"He that had the belly-pain?"

"To think the Holy One remembers that! I must tell his mother. It is most singular honour! 'He that had the belly-pain'—straightway the Holy One remembered. She will be proud."

"My chela is to me as a son to the unenlightened."

"Say grandson, rather. Mothers have not the wisdom of our years. If a child cries they say the heavens are falling. Now a grandmother is far enough separated from the pain of bearing and the pleasure of giving the breast to consider whether a cry is wickedness pure or the wind. And since thou speakest once again of wind, when last the Holy One was here, maybe I offended in pressing for charms."

"Sister," said the lama, using that form of address a Buddhist monk may sometimes employ towards a nun, "if charms comfort thee—"

"They are better than ten thousand doctors."

"I say, if they comfort thee, I who was Abbot of Suchzen will make as many as thou mayest desire. I have never seen thy face—"

"That even the monkeys who steal our loquats count for a gain. Hee! hee!"

"But as he who sleeps there said," he nodded at the shut door of the guest-chamber across the forecourt, "thou hast a heart of gold. . . . And he is in the spirit my very 'grandson' to me."

"Good! I am the Holy One's cow." This was pure Hinduism, but the lama never heeded. "I am old. I have borne sons in the body. Oh, once I could please men! Now I can cure them." He heard her armlets tinkle as though she bared arms for action. "I will take over the boy and dose him, and stuff him, and make him all whole. Hai! hai! We old people know something yet."

Wherefore when Kim, aching in every bone, opened his eyes, and would go to the cookhouse to get his master's food, he found strong coercion about him, and a veiled old figure at the door, flanked by the grizzled manservant, who told him precisely the very things that he was on no account to do.

"Thou must have? Thou shalt have nothing. What? A locked box in which to keep holy books? Oh, that is another matter. Heavens forbid I should come between a priest and his prayers! It shall be brought, and thou shalt keep the key."

They pushed the coffer under his cot, and Kim shut away Mahbub's pistol, the oil-skin packet of letters, and the locked books and diaries, with a groan of relief. For some absurd reason their weight on his shoulders was nothing to their weight on his poor mind. His neck ached under it of nights.

"Thine is a sickness uncommon in youth these days: since young folk have given up tending their betters. The remedy is sleep, and certain drugs," said the Sahiba; and he was glad to give himself up to the blankness that half menaced and half soothed him.

She brewed drinks, in some mysterious Asiatic equivalent to the still-room—drenches that smelt pestilently and tasted worse. She stood over Kim till they went down, and inquired exhaustively after they had come up. She laid a taboo upon the forecourt, and enforced it by means of an armed man. It is true he was seventy odd, that his scabbarded sword ceased at the hilt; but he represented the authority of the Sahiba, and loaded wains, chattering servants, calves, dogs, hens, and the like, fetched a wide compass by those parts. Best of all, when the body was cleared, she cut out from the mass of poor relations that crowded the back of the buildings—household dogs, we name them—a cousin's widow, skilled in what Europeans, who know nothing about it, call massage. And the two of them, laying him east and west, that the mysterious earth-currents which thrill the clay of our bodies might help and not hinder, took him to pieces all one long afternoon—bone by bone, muscle by muscle, ligament by ligament, and lastly, nerve by nerve. Kneaded to irresponsible pulp, half hypnotised by the perpetual flick and readjustment of the uneasy chudders that veiled their eyes, Kim slid ten thousand miles into slumber—thirty-six hours of it—sleep that soaked like rain after drought.

Then she fed him, and the house spun to her clamour. She caused fowls to be slain; she sent for vegetables, and the sober, slow-thinking gardener, nigh as old as she, sweated for it; she took spices, and milk, and onion, with little fish from the brooks—anon limes for sherbets, fat quails of the pit, then chicken-livers upon a skewer, with sliced ginger between.

"I have seen something of this world," she said over the crowded trays, "and there are but two sorts of women in it—those who take the strength out of a man and those who put it back. Once I was that one, and now I am this. Nay—do not play the priestling with me. Mine was but a jest. If it does not hold good now, it will when thou takest the road again. Cousin"—this to the poor relation, never wearied of extolling her patroness's charity—"he is getting a bloom on the skin of a new-curried horse. Our work is like polishing jewels to be thrown to a dance-girl—eh?"

Kim sat up and smiled. The terrible weakness had dropped from him like an old shoe. His tongue itched for free speech again, and but a week back the lightest word clogged it like ashes. The pain in his neck (he must have caught it from the lama) had gone with the heavy dengue-aches and the evil taste in the mouth. The two old women, a little, but not much, more careful about their veils now, clucked as merrily as the hens that had entered pecking through the open door.

"Where is my Holy One?" he demanded.

"Hear him! Thy Holy One is well," she snapped viciously. "Though that is none of his merit. Knew I a charm to make him wise, I'd sell my jewels and buy it. To refuse good food that I cooked myself—and go roving into the fields for two nights on an empty belly—and to tumble into a brook at the end of it—call you that holiness? Then, when he has nearly broken what thou hast left of my heart with anxiety, he tells me that he has acquired merit. Oh, how like are all men! No, that was not it—he tells me that he is freed from all sin. I could have told him that before he wetted himself all over. He is well now—this happened a week ago—but burn me such holiness! A babe of three would do better. Do not fret thyself for the Holy One. He keeps both eyes on thee when he is not wading our brooks."

"I do not remember to have seen him, I remember that the days and nights passed like bars of white and black, opening and shutting. I was not sick: I was only tired."

"A lethargy that comes by right some few score years later. But it is all done now."

"Maharanee," Kim began, but led by the look in her eye, changed it to the title of plain love—"Mother, I owe my life to thee. How shall I make thanks? Ten thousand blessings upon thy house and—"

"The house be unblessed." (It is impossible to give exactly the old lady's word.) "Thank the Gods as a priest if thou wilt, but thank me if thou carest as a son. Heavens above! Have I shifted thee and lifted thee and slapped and twisted thy ten toes to find texts flung at my head? Somewhere a mother must have borne thee to break her heart. What used thou to her—son?"

"I had no mother, my mother," said Kim. "She died, they tell me, when I was young."

"Hai mai! Then none can say I have robbed her of any right if—when thou takest the road again and this house is but one of a thousand used for shelter and forgotten, after an easy-flung blessing. No matter. I need no blessings, but—but—" She stamped her foot at the poor relation: "Take up the trays to the house. What is the good of stale food in the room, oh woman of ill-omen?"

"I ha—have borne a son in my time too, but he died," whimpered the bowed sister-figure behind the chudder. "Thou knowest he died! I only waited for the order to take away the tray."

"It is I that am the woman of ill-omen," cried the old lady penitently. "We that go down to the chattris (the big umbrellas above the burning-ghats where the priests take their last dues) clutch hard at the bearers of the chattis (water-jars—young folk full of the pride of life, she meant; but the pun is clumsy). When one cannot dance in the festival one must e'en look out of the window, and grandmothering takes all a woman's time. Thy master gives me all the charms I now desire for my daughter's eldest, by reason—is it?—that he is wholly free from sin. The hakim is brought very low these days. He goes about poisoning my servants for lack of their betters."

"What hakim, mother?"

"That very Dacca man who gave me the pill which rent me in three pieces. He cast up like a strayed camel a week ago, vowing that he and thou had been blood-brothers together up Kulu-way, and feigning great anxiety for thy health. He was very thin and hungry, so I gave orders to have him stuffed too—him and his anxiety!"

"I would see him if he is here."

"He eats five times a day, and lances boils for my hinds to save himself from an apoplexy. He is so full of anxiety for thy health that he sticks to the cook-house door and stays himself with scraps. He will keep. We shall never get rid of him."

"Send him here, mother"—the twinkle returned to Kim's eye for a flash— "and I will try."

"I'll send him, but to chase him off is an ill turn. At least he had the sense to fish the Holy One out of the brook; thus, as the Holy One did not say, acquiring merit."

"He is a very wise hakim. Send him, mother."

"Priest praising priest? A miracle! If he is any friend of thine (ye squabbled at your last meeting) I'll hale him here with horse-ropes and —and give him a caste-dinner afterwards, my son. . . . Get up and see the world! This lying abed is the mother of seventy devils . . . my son! my son!"

She trotted forth to raise a typhoon off the cook-house, and almost on her shadow rolled in the Babu, robed as to the shoulders like a Roman emperor, jowled like Titus, bareheaded, with new patent-leather shoes, in highest condition of fat, exuding joy and salutations.

"By Jove, Mister O'Hara, but I am jolly glad to see you. I will kindly shut the door. It is a pity you are sick. Are you very sick?"

"The papers—the papers from the kilta. The maps and the murasla!" He held out the key impatiently; for the present need on his soul was to get rid of the loot.

"You are quite right. That is correct departmental view to take. You have got everything?"

"All that was handwritten in the kilta I took. The rest I threw down the hill." He could hear the key's grate in the lock, the sticky pull of the slow-rending oil-cloth, and a quick shuffling of papers. He had been annoyed out of all reason by the knowledge that they lay below him through the sick idle days—a burden incommunicable. For that reason the blood tingled through his body, when Hurree, skipping elephantinely, shook hands again.

"This is fine! This is finest! Mister O'Hara! You have—ha! ha!—swiped the whole bag of tricks—locks, stocks, and barrels. They told me it was eight months' work gone up the spouts! By Jove, how they beat me! . . . Look, here is the letter from Hilas!" He intoned a line or two of Court Persian, which is the language of authorised and unauthorised diplomacy. "Mister Rajah Sahib has just about put his foot in the holes. He will have to explain offeecially how the deuce-an'-all he is writing love-letters to the Czar. And they are very clever maps . . . and there is three or four Prime Ministers of these parts implicated by the correspondence. By

Gad, Sar! The British Government will change the succession in Hi-las and Bunar, and nominate new heirs to the throne. 'Treason most base' . . . but you do not understand? Eh?"

"Are they in thy hands?" said Kim. It was all he cared for.

"Just you jolly well bet yourself they are." He stowed the entire trove about his body, as only Orientals can. "They are going up to the office, too. The old lady thinks I am permanent fixture here, but I shall go away with these straight off—immediately. Mr. Lurgan will be proud man. You are offeecially subordinate to me, but I shall embody your name in my verbal report. It is a pity we are not allowed written reports. We Bengalis excel in thee exact science." He tossed back the key and showed the box empty.

"Good. That is good. I was very tired. My Holy One was sick, too. And did he fall into—"

"Oah yess. I am his good friend, I tell you. He was behaving very strange when I came down after you, and I thought perhaps he might have the papers. I followed him on his meditations, and to discuss ethno-logical points also. You see, I am verree small person here nowadays, in comparison with all his charms. By Jove, O'Hara, do you know, he is af-flicted with infirmity of fits. Yess, I tell you. Cataleptic, too, if not also epileptic. I found him in such a state under a tree in articulo mortem, and he jumped up and walked into a brook and he was nearly drowned but for me. I pulled him out."

"Because I was not there!" said Kim. "He might have died."

"Yes, he might have died, but he is dry now, and asserts he has under-gone transfiguration." The Babu tapped his forehead knowingly. "I took notes of his statements for Royal Society—in posse. You must make haste and be quite well and come back to Simla, and I will tell you all my tale at Lurgan's. It was splendid. The bottoms of their trousers were quite torn, and old Nahan Rajah, he thought they were European soldiers deserting."

"Oh, the Russians? How long were they with thee?"

"One was a Frenchman. Oh, days and days and days! Now all the hill-people believe all Russians are all beggars. By Jove! they had not one dam-thing that I did not get them. And I told the common people—oah, such tales and anecdotes! I will tell you at old Lurgan's when you come up. We will have—ah—a night out! It is feather in both our caps! Yess, and they gave me a certificate.That is creaming joke. You should have seen them at the Alliance Bank identifying themselves! And thank Al-mighty God you got their papers so well! You do not laugh verree much, but you shall laugh when you are well. Now I will go straight to the railway and get out. You shall have all sorts of credits for your game.

When do you come along? We are very proud of you, though you gave
us great frights. And especially Mahbub."

"Ay, Mahbub. And where is he?"

"Selling horses in this vi-cinity, of course."

"Here! Why? Speak slowly. There is a thickness in my head still."

The Babu looked shyly down his nose. "Well, you see, I am fearful
man, and I do not like responsibility. You were sick, you see, and I did
not know where deuce-an'-all the papers were, and if so, how many.
So when I had come down here I slipped in private wire to Mahbub—he
was at Meerut for races—and I tell him how case stands. He comes up
with his men and he consorts with the lama, and then he calls me a fool,
and is very rude—"

"But wherefore—wherefore?"

"That is what I ask. I only suggest that if any one steals the papers
I should like some good strong, brave men to rob them back again. You
see they are vitally important, and Mahbub Ali he did not know where
you were."

"Mahbub Ali to rob the Sahiba's house? Thou art mad, Babu," said
Kim with indignation.

"I wanted the papers. Suppose she had stole them? It was only practical
suggestion, I think. You are not pleased, eh?"

A native proverb—unquotable—showed the blackness of Kim's disap-
proval.

"Well,"—Hurree shrugged his shoulders,—"there is no accounting for
thee taste. Mahbub was angry too. He has sold horses all about here, and
he says old lady is pukka (thorough) old lady and would not condescend
to such ungentlemanly things. I do not care. I have got the papers, and
I was very glad of moral support from Mahbub. I tell you I am fearful
man, but, somehow or other, the more fearful I am the more dam-tight
places I get into. So I was glad you came with me to Chini, and I am
glad Mahbub was close by. The old lady she is sometimes very rude to me
and my beautiful pills."

"Allah be merciful," said Kim on his elbow, rejoicing. "What a beast of
wonder is a Babu! And that man walked alone—if he did walk—with
robbed and angry foreigners!"

"Oah, thatt was nothing, after they had done beating me; but if I lost
the papers it was pretty jolly serious. Mahbub he nearly beat me too,
and he went and consorted with the lama no end. I shall stick to ethnological investigations henceforwards. Now good-bye, Mister O'Hara. I can
catch 4.25 p. m. to Umballa if I am quick. It will be good times when
we all tell thee tale up at Mister Lurgan's. I shall report you offeecially
better. Good-bye, my dear fallow, and when next you are under thee

emotions please do not use the Mohammedan terms with the Tibetan dress."

He shook hands twice—a Babu to his boot-heels—and opened the door. With the fall of the sunlight upon his still triumphant face he returned to the humble Dacca quack.

"He robbed them," thought Kim, forgetting his own share in the game. "He tricked them. He lied to them like a Bengali. They give him a chit (a testimonial). He makes them a mock at the risk of his life—I never would have gone down to them after the pistol-shots—and then he says he is a fearful man. . . . And he is a fearful man. I must get into the world again."

At first his legs bent like bad pipe-stems, and the flood and rush of the sunlit air dazzled him. He squatted by the white wall, the mind rummaging among the incidents of the long dooli journey, the lama's weaknesses, and, now that the stimulus of talk was removed, his own self-pity, of which, like the sick, he had great store. The unnerved brain edged away from all the outside, as a raw horse, once rowelled, sidles from the spur. It was enough, amply enough, that the spoil of the kilta was away—off his hands—out of his possession. He tried to think of the lama,—to wonder why he had tumbled into a brook,—but the bigness of the world, seen between the forecourt gates, swept linked thought aside. Then he looked upon the trees and the broad fields, with the thatched huts hidden among crops—looked with strange eyes unable to take up the size and proportion and use of things—stared for a still half-hour. All that while he felt, though he could not put it into words, that his soul was out of gear with its surroundings—a cog-wheel unconnected with any machinery, just like the idle cog-wheel of a cheap Beheea sugar-crusher laid by in a corner. The breezes fanned over him, the parrots shrieked at him, the noises of the populated house behind—squabbles, orders, and reproofs—hit on dead ears.

"I am Kim. I am Kim. And what is Kim?" His soul repeated it again and again.

He did not want to cry,—had never felt less like crying in his life,—but of a sudden easy, stupid tears trickled down his nose, and with an almost audible click he felt the wheels of his being lock up anew on the world without. Things that rode meaningless on the eyeball an instant before slid into proper proportion. Roads were meant to be walked upon, houses to be lived in, cattle to be driven, fields to be tilled, and men and women to be talked to. They were all real and true—solidly planted upon the feet—perfectly comprehensible—clay of his clay, neither more nor less. He shook himself like a dog with a flea in his ear, and rambled out of the gate. Said the Sahiba, to whom watchful eyes reported this move: "Let him go. I have done my share. Mother Earth must do the rest. When the Holy One comes back from meditation, tell him."

There stood an empty bullock-cart on a little knoll half a mile away, with a young banian tree behind—a look-out, as it were, above some new-ploughed levels; and his eyelids, bathed in soft air, grew heavy as he neared it. The ground was good clean dust—no new herbage that, living, is half-way to death already, but the hopeful dust that holds the seed of all life. He felt it between his toes, patted it with his palms, and joint by joint, sighing luxuriously, laid him down full length along in the shadow of the wooden-pinned cart. And Mother Earth was as faithful as the Sahiba. She breathed through him to restore the poise he had lost lying so long on a cot cut off from her good currents. His head lay powerless upon her breast, and his opened hands surrendered to her strength. The many-rooted tree above him, and even the dead man-handled wood beside, knew what he sought, as he himself did not know. Hour upon hour he lay deeper than sleep.

Towards evening, when the dust of returning kine made all the horizons smoke, came the lama and Mahbub Ali, both afoot, walking cautiously, for the house had told them where he had gone.

"Allah! What a fool's trick to play in open country," muttered the horse-dealer. "He could be shot a hundred times—but this is not the Border."

"And," said the lama, repeating a many-times-told tale, "never was such a chela. Temperate, kindly, wise, of ungrudging disposition, a merry heart upon the road, never forgetting, learned, truthful, courteous. Great is his reward!"

"I know the boy—as I have said."

"And he was all those things?"

"Some of them—but I have not yet found a Red Hat's charm for making him overly truthful. He has certainly been well nursed."

"The Sahiba is a heart of gold," said the lama earnestly. "She looks upon him as her son."

"Hmph! Half Hind seems that-way disposed. I only wished to see that the boy had come to no harm and was a free agent. As thou knowest, he and I were old friends in the first days of your pilgrimage together."

"That is a bond between us." The lama sat down. "We are at the end of the pilgrimage."

"No thanks to thee thine was not cut off for good and all a week back. I heard what the Sahiba said to thee when we bore thee up on the cot." Mahbub laughed, and tugged his newly-dyed beard.

"I was meditating upon other matters that tide. It was the hakim from Dacca broke my meditations."

"Otherwise"—this was in Pashtu for decency's sake—"thou wouldst have ended thy meditations upon the sultry side of Hell—being an unbeliever and an idolater for all thy child's simplicity. But now, Red Hat, what is to be done?"

"This very night,"—the words came slowly, vibrating with triumph,—"this very night he will be as free as I am from all taint of sin—assured as I am when he quits this body of Freedom from the Wheel of Things. I have a sign," he laid his hand above the torn chart in his bosom, "that my time is short; but I shall have safe-guarded him throughout the years. Remember, I have reached Knowledge, as I told thee only three nights back."

"It must be true, as the Tirah priest said when I stole his cousin's wife, that I am a sufi (a freethinker); for here I sit," said Mahbub to himself, "drinking in blasphemy unthinkable. . . . I remember the tale. On that, then, he goes to Jannatu l'Adn (the Gardens of Eden). But how? Wilt thou slay him or drown him in that wonderful river from which the Babu dragged thee?"

"I was dragged from no river," said the lama simply. "Thou hast forgotten what befell. I found it by knowledge."

"Oh, aye. True," stammered Mahbub, divided between high indignation and enormous mirth. "I had forgotten the exact run of what happened. Thou didst find it knowingly."

"And to say that I would take life is—not a sin, but a madness simple. My chela aided me to the River. It is his right to be cleansed from sin—with me."

"Ay, he needs cleansing. But afterwards, old man—afterwards?"

"What matter under all the heavens? He is sure of Nibban—enlightened —as I am."

"Well said. I had a fear he might mount Mohammed's Horse and fly away."

"Nay—he must go forth as a teacher."

"Aha! Now I see! That is the right gait for the colt. Certainly he must go forth as a teacher. He is somewhat urgently needed as a scribe by the State, for instance."

"To that end he was prepared. I acquired merit in that I gave alms for his sake. A good deed does not die. He aided me in my Search. I aided him in his. Just is the Wheel, O horse-seller from the North. Let him be a teacher; let him be a scribe—what matter? He will have attained Freedom at the end. The rest is illusion."

"What matter? When I must have him with me beyond Balkh in six months! I come up with ten lame horses and three strong-backed men— thanks to that chicken of a Babu—to break a sick boy by force out of an old trot's house. It seems that I stand by while a young Sahib is hoisted into Allah knows what of an idolater's heaven by means of old Red Hat. And I am reckoned something of a player of the Game myself! But the madman is fond of the boy; and I must be very reasonably mad too."

"What is the prayer?" said the lama, as the rough Pashtu rumbled into the red beard.

"No matter at all; but now I understand that the boy, sure of Paradise, can yet enter Government service, my mind is easier. I must get to my horses. It grows dark. Do not wake him. I have no wish to hear him call thee master."

"But he is my disciple. What else?"

"He has told me." Mahbub choked down his touch of spleen and rose laughing. "I am not altogether of thy faith, Red Hat—if so small a matter concern thee."

"It is nothing," said the lama.

"I thought not. Therefore it will not move thee sinless, new-washed and three parts drowned to boot, when I call thee a good man—a very good man. We have talked together some four or five evenings now, and for all I am a horse-coper I can still, as the saying is, see holiness beyond the legs of a horse. Yea, can see, too, how our Friend of all the World put his hand in thine at the first. Use him well, and suffer him to return to the world as a teacher, when thou hast—bathed his legs, if that be the proper medicine for the colt."

"Why not follow the Way thyself, and so accompany the boy?"

Mahbub stared stupefied at the magnificent insolence of the demand, which across the Border he would have paid with more than a blow. Then the humour of it touched his worldly soul.

"Softly—softly—one foot at a time, as the lame gelding went over the Umballa jumps. I may come to Paradise later—I have workings that way—great motions—and I owe them to thy simplicity. Thou hast never lied?"

"What need?"

"O Allah, hear him! 'What need' in this Thy world! Nor ever harmed a man?"

"Once—with a pencase—before I was wise."

"So? I think the better of thee. Thy teachings are good. Thou hast turned one man that I know from the path of strife." He laughed immensely. "He came here open-minded to commit a dacoity (a house-robbery with violence). Yes, to cut, rob, kill, and carry off what he desired."

"A great foolishness!"

"Oh! black shame too. So he thought after he had seen thee—and a

few others, male and female. So he abandoned it; and now he goes to
beat a big fat Babu man."

"I do not understand."

"Allah forbid it! Some men are strong in knowledge, Red Hat. Thy
strength is stronger still. Keep it—I think thou wilt. If the boy be not
a good servant, pull his ears off."

With a hitch of his broad Bokhariot belt the Pathan swaggered off into
the gloaming, and the lama came down from his clouds so far as to look
at the broad back.

"That person lacks courtesy, and is deceived by the shadow of appearances. But he spoke well of my chela, who now enters upon his reward.
Let me make the prayer! . . . Wake, O fortunate above all born of
women. Wake! It is found!"

Kim came up from those deep wells, and the lama attended his yawning pleasure; duly snapping fingers to head off evil spirits.

"I have slept a hundred years. Where—? Holy One, hast thou been
here long? I went out to look for thee, but"—he laughed drowsily—"I
slept by the way. I am all well now. Hast thou eaten? Let us go to the
house. It is many days since I tended thee. And the Sahiba fed thee
well? Who shampooed thy legs? What of the weaknesses—the belly and
the neck, and the beating in the ears?"

"Gone—all gone. Dost thou not know?"

"I know nothing, but that I have not seen thee in a monkey's age. Know
what?"

"Strange the knowledge did not reach out to thee, when all my thoughts
were theeward."

"I cannot see the face, but the voice is like a gong. Has the Sahiba
made a young man of thee by her cookery?"

He peered at the cross-legged figure, outlined jet-black against the
lemon-coloured drift of light. So does the stone Bodhisat sit who looks
down upon the patent self-registering turnstiles of the Lahore Museum.

The lama held his peace. Except for the click of the rosary and a faint
"clop-clop" of Mahbub's retreating feet, the soft, smoky silence of evening
in India wrapped them close.

"Hear me! I bring news."

"But let us—"

Out shot the long yellow hand compelling silence. Kim tucked his feet
under his robe-edge obediently.

"Hear me! I bring news! The Search is finished. Comes now the Reward. . . . Thus. When we were among the Hills, I lived on thy strength
till the young branch bowed and nigh broke. When we came out of
the Hills, I was troubled for thee and for other matters which I held

in my heart. The boat of my soul lacked direction; I could not see into the Cause of Things. So I gave thee over to the virtuous woman altogether. I took no food. I drank no water. Still I saw not the Way. They pressed food upon me and cried at my shut door. So I removed myself to a hollow under a tree. I took no food. I took no water. I sat in meditation two days and two nights, abstracting my mind; inbreathing and outbreathing in the required manner. . . . Upon the second night—so great was my reward—the wise Soul loosed itself from the silly Body and went free. This I have never before attained, though I have stood on the threshold of it. Consider, for it is a marvel!"

"A marvel indeed. Two days and two nights without food! Where was the Sahiba?" said Kim under his breath.

"Yea, my Soul went free, and, wheeling like an eagle, saw indeed that there was no Teshoo Lama nor any other soul. As a drop draws to water, so my soul drew near to the Great Soul which is beyond all things. At that point, exalted in contemplation, I saw all Hind, from Ceylon in the sea to the Hills, and my own Painted Rocks at Suchzen; I saw every camp and village, to the least, where we have ever rested. I saw them at one time and in one place; for they were within the Soul. By this I knew the Soul had passed beyond the illusion of Time and Space and of Things. By this I knew that I was free. I saw thee lying in thy cot, and I saw thee falling down hill under the idolater—at one time, in one place, in my Soul, which, as I say, had touched the Great Soul. Also I saw the stupid body of Teshoo Lama lying down, and the hakim from Dacca kneeled beside, shouting in its ear. Then my Soul was all alone, and I saw nothing, for I was all things, having reached the Great Soul. And I meditated a thousand thousand years, passionless, well aware of the Causes of all Things. Then a voice cried: 'What shall come to the boy if thou art dead?' and I was shaken back and forth in myself with pity for thee; and I said: 'I will return to my chela, lest he miss the Way.' Upon this my Soul, which is the soul of Teshoo Lama, withdrew itself from the Great Soul with strivings and yearnings and retchings and agonies not to be told. As the egg from the fish, as the fish from the water, as the water from the cloud, as the cloud from the thick air; so put forth, so leaped out, so drew away, so fumed up the soul of Teshoo Lama from the Great Soul. Then a voice cried: 'The River! Take heed to the River!' and I looked down upon all the world, which was as I had seen it before—one in time, one in place—and I saw plainly the River of the Arrow at my feet. At that hour my Soul was hampered by some evil or other whereof I was not wholly cleansed, and it lay upon my arms and coiled round my waist; but I put it aside, and I cast forth as an eagle in my flight for the very place of the River. I pushed aside world upon

world for thy sake. I saw the River below me—the River of the Arrow—
and, descending, the waters of it closed over me; and behold I was again
in the body of Teshoo Lama, but free from sin, and the hakim from
Dacca bore up my head in the waters of the River. It is here! It is behind
the mango-tope here—even here!"

"Allah Karim! Oh, well that the Babu was by! Wast thou very wet?"

"Why should I regard? I remember the hakim was concerned for the
body of Teshoo Lama. He haled it out of the holy water in his hands,
and there came afterwards thy horse-seller from the North with a cot
and men, and they put the body on the cot and bore it up to the Sahiba's
house."

"What said the Sahiba?"

"I was meditating in that body, and did not hear. So thus the Search
is ended. For the merit that I have acquired, the River of the Arrow is
here. It broke forth at our feet, as I have said. I have found it. Son of
my Soul, I have wrenched my Soul back from the Threshold of Freedom
to free thee from all sin—as I am free, and sinless. Just is the Wheel! Certain is our deliverance. Come!"

He crossed his hands on his lap and smiled, as a man may who has
won Salvation for himself and his beloved.

CAPTAINS COURAGEOUS

Chapter 1

THE WEATHER DOOR of the smoking-room had been left open to the North Atlantic fog, as the big liner rolled and lifted, whistling to warn the fishing-fleet.

'That Cheyne boy's the biggest nuisance aboard,' said a man in a frieze overcoat, shutting the door with a bang. 'He isn't wanted here. He's too fresh.'

A white-haired German reached for a sandwich, and grunted between bites: 'I know der breed. Ameriga is full of dot kind. I dell you you should imbort ropes' ends free under your dariff.'

'Pshaw! There isn't any real harm to him. He's more to be pitied than anything,' a man from New York drawled, as he lay at full length along the cushions under the wet skylight. 'They've dragged him around from hotel to hotel ever since he was a kid. I was talking to his mother this morning. She's a lovely lady, but she don't pretend to manage him. He's going to Europe to finish his education.'

'Education isn't begun yet.' This was a Philadelphian, curled up in a corner. 'That boy gets two hundred a month pocket-money, he told me. He isn't sixteen either.'

'Railroads, his father, aind't it?" said the German.

'Yep. That and mines and lumber and shipping. Built one place at San Diego, the old man has; another at Los Angeles; owns half a dozen railroads, half the lumber on the Pacific slope, and lets his wife spend the money,' the Philadelphian went on lazily. 'The West don't suit her, she says. She just tracks around with the boy and her nerves, trying to find out what'll amuse him, I guess. Florida, Adirondacks, Lakewood, Hot Springs, New York, and round again. He isn't much more than a second-hand hotel clerk now. When he's finished in Europe he'll be a holy terror.'

'What's the matter with the old man attending to him personally?' said a voice from the frieze ulster.

'Old man's piling up the rocks. 'Don't want to be disturbed, I guess. He'll find out his error a few years from now. Pity, because there's a heap of good in the boy if you could get at it.'

'Mit a rope's end, mit a rope's end!' growled the German.

Once more the door banged, and a slight, slim-built boy perhaps fifteen years old, a half-smoked cigarette hanging from one corner of his mouth, leaned in over the high footway. His pasty yellow complexion did not show well on a person of his years, and his look was a mixture of irresolution, bravado, and very cheap smartness. He was dressed in a cherry-coloured blazer, knickerbockers, red stockings, and bicycle shoes, with a red flannel cap at the back of the head. After whistling between his teeth, as he eyed the company, he said in a loud, high voice: 'Say, it's thick outside. You can hear the fish-boats squawking all around us. Say, wouldn't it be great if we ran down one?'

'Shut the door, Harvey,' said the New Yorker. 'Shut the door and stay outside. You're not wanted here.'

'Who'll stop me?' he answered deliberately. 'Did you pay for my passage, Mister Martin? 'Guess I've as good right here as the next man.'

He picked up some dice from a checker-board and began throwing, right hand against left.

'Say, gen'elmen, this is deader'n mud. Can't we make a game of poker between us?'

There was no answer, and he puffed his cigarette, swung his legs, and drummed on the table with rather dirty fingers. Then he pulled out a roll of bills as if to count them.

'How's your mamma this afternoon?' a man said. 'I didn't see her at lunch.'

'In her state-room, I guess. She's 'most always sick on the ocean. I'm going to give the stewardess fifteen dollars for looking after her. I don't go down more'n I can avoid. It makes me feel mysterious to pass that butler's pantry place. Say, this is the first time I've been on the ocean.'

'Oh, don't apologise, Harvey.'

'Who's apologising? This is the first time I've crossed the ocean, gen'elmen, and, except the first day, I haven't been sick one little bit. No, sir!' He brought down his fist with a triumphant bang, wetted his finger, and went on counting the bills.

'Oh, you're a high-grade machine, with the writing in plain sight,' the Philadelphian yawned. 'You'll blossom into a credit to your country if you don't take care.'

'I know it. I'm an American—first, last, and all the time. I'll show 'em that when I strike Europe. Pff! My cig's out. I can't smoke the truck the steward sells. Any gen'elman got a real Turkish cig on him?'

The chief engineer entered for a moment, red, smiling, and wet. 'Say, Mac,' cried Harvey cheerfully, 'how are we hitting it?'

'Vara much in the ordinary way,' was the grave reply. 'The young are as polite as ever to their elders, an' their elders are e'en tryin' to appreciate it.'

A low chuckle came from a corner. The German opened his cigar-case and handed a skinny black cigar to Harvey.

'Dot is der broper apparatus to smoke, my young friendt,' he said. 'You vill dry it? Yes? Den you vill be efer so happy.'

Harvey lit the unlovely thing with a flourish: he felt that he was getting on in grown-up society.

'It would take more'n this to keel me over,' he said, ignorant that he was lighting that terrible article, a 'Wheeling stogie.'

'Dot we shall bresently see,' said the German. 'Where are we now, Mr. Mactonal'?'

'Just there or thereabouts, Mr. Schaefer,' said the engineer. 'We'll be on the Grand Bank to-night; but in a general way o' speakin', we're all among the fishing-fleet now. We've shaved three dories an' near skelped the boom off a Frenchman since noon, an' that's close sailin', ye may say.'

'You like my cigar, eh?' the German asked, for Harvey's eyes were full of tears.

'Fine, full flavour,' he answered through shut teeth. 'Guess we've slowed down a little, haven't we? I'll skip out and see what the log says.'

'I might if I vhas you,' said the German.

Harvey staggered over the wet decks to the nearest rail. He was very unhappy; but he saw the deck-steward lashing chairs together, and since he had boasted before the man that he was never sea-sick, his pride made him go aft to the second-saloon deck at the stern which was finished in a turtle-back. The deck was deserted, and he crawled to the extreme end of it near the flag-pole. There he doubled up in limp agony, for the 'Wheeling stogie' joined with the surge and jar of the screw to sieve out his soul. His head swelled; sparks of fire danced before his eyes; his body seemed to lose weight, while his heels wavered in the breeze. He was fainting from sea-sickness, and a roll of the ship tilted him over the rail on to the smooth lip of the turtle-back. Then a low, gray mother-wave swung out of the fog, tucked Harvey under one arm, so to speak, and pulled him off and away to leeward; the great green closed over him, and he went quietly to sleep.

He was roused by the sound of a dinner-horn such as they used to blow at a summer-school he had once attended in the Adirondacks. Slowly he remembered that he was Harvey Cheyne, drowned and dead in mid-ocean, but was too weak to fit things together. A new smell filled his nostrils; wet and clammy chills ran down his back, and he was helplessly full of salt water. When he opened his eyes, he perceived that he was still on the top of the sea, for it was running round him in silver-coloured hills, and he was lying on a pile of half-dead fish, looking at a broad human back clothed in a blue jersey.

'It's no good,' thought the boy. 'I'm dead, sure enough, and this Thing is in charge.'

He groaned, and the figure turned its head, showing a pair of little gold rings half hidden in curly black hair.

'Aha! You feel some pretty well now?' it said. 'Lie still so; we trim better.'

With a swift jerk he sculled the flickering boat head-on to a foamless sea that lifted her twenty full feet only to slide her into a glassy pit beyond. But this mountain-climbing did not interrupt blue-jersey's talk. 'Fine good job, I say, that I catch you. Eh, wha-at? Better good job, I say, your boat not catch me. How you come to fall out?'

'I was sick,' said Harvey; 'sick, and couldn't help it.'

'Just in time I blow my horn, and your boat she yaw a little. Then I see you come all down. Eh, wha-at? I think you are cut into baits by the screw, but you dreeft—dreeft to me, and I make a big fish of you. So you shall not die this time.'

'Where am I?' said Harvey, who could not see that life was particularly safe where he lay.

'You are with me in the dory—Manuel my name, and I come from schooner "We're Here" of Gloucester. I live to Gloucester. By and by we get supper. Eh, wha-at?'

He seemed to have two pairs of hands and a head of cast-iron, for, not content with blowing through a big conch-shell, he must needs stand up to it, swaying with the sway of the flat-bottomed dory, and send a grinding, thuttering shriek through the fog. How long this entertainment lasted, Harvey could not remember, for he lay back terrified at the sight of the smoking swells. He fancied he heard a gun and a horn and shouting. Something bigger than the dory, but quite as lively, loomed alongside. Several voices talked at once; he was dropped into a dark, heaving hole, where men in oilskins gave him a hot drink, and took off his clothes, and he fell asleep.

When he waked he listened for the first breakfast-bell on the steamer, wondering why his state-room had grown so small. Turning, he looked into a narrow, triangular cave, lit by a lamp hung against a huge square beam. A three-cornered table within arm's reach ran from the angle of the bows to the foremast. At the after end, behind a well-used Plymouth stove, sat a boy about his own age, with a flat, red face and a pair of twinkling gray eyes. He was dressed in a blue jersey and high rubber boots. Several pairs of the same sort of foot-wear, an old cap, and some worn-out woollen socks lay on the floor, and black and yellow oilskins swayed to and fro beside the bunks. The place was packed as full of smells as a bale is of cotton. The oilskins had a peculiarly thick flavour of their own which made a sort of background to the smells of fried fish, burnt grease, paint, pepper, and stale tobacco; but these, again, were all hooped together by one encircling smell of ship and salt water. Harvey saw with disgust that there were no sheets on his bed-place. He was lying on a piece of dingy ticking full of lumps and nubbles. Then, too, the boat's motion was not that of a steamer. She was neither sliding nor rolling, but rather wriggling herself about in a silly, aimless way, like a colt at the end of a halter. Water-noises ran by close to his ear, and beams creaked and whined about him. All these things made him grunt despairingly and think of his mother.

'Feelin' better?' said the boy, with a grin. 'Hev some coffee?' He brought a tin cup full and sweetened it with molasses.

'Isn't there milk?' said Harvey, looking round the dark double tier of bunks as if he expected to find a cow there.

'Well, no,' said the boy. 'Ner there ain't likely to be till 'baout mid-September. 'Tain't bad coffee. I made it.'

Harvey drank in silence, and the boy handed him a plate full of pieces of crisp fried pork, which he ate ravenously.

'I've dried your clothes. Guess they've shrunk some,' said the boy. 'They ain't our style much—none of 'em. Twist round an' see ef you're hurt any.'

Harvey stretched himself in every direction, but could not report any injuries.

'That's good,' the boy said heartily. 'Fix yerself an' go on deck. Dad wants to see you. I'm his son—Dan, they call me—an' I'm cook's helper an' everything else aboard that's too dirty for the men. There ain't no boy here 'cep' me sence Otto went overboard—an' he was only a Dutchy, an' twenty year old at that. How d'you come to fall off in a dead flat ca'am?'

' 'Twasn't a calm,' said Harvey sulkily. 'It was a gale, and I was sea sick. Guess I must have rolled over the rail.'

'There was a little common swell yes'day an' last night,' said the boy. 'But ef thet's your notion of a gale—' He whistled. 'You'll know more 'fore you're through. Hurry! Dad's waitin'.'

Like many other unfortunate young people, Harvey had never in all his life received a direct order—never, at least, without long, and sometimes tearful, explanations of the advantages of obedience and the reasons for the request. Mrs. Cheyne lived in fear of breaking his spirit, which, perhaps, was the reason that she herself walked on the edge of nervous prostration. He could not see why he should be expected to hurry for any man's pleasure, and said so. 'Your dad can come down here if he's so anxious to talk to me. I want him to take me to New York right away. It'll pay him.'

Dan opened his eyes, as the size and beauty of this joke dawned on him. 'Say, dad,' he shouted up the foc'sle hatch, 'he says you kin slip down an' see him ef you're anxious that way. Hear, dad?'

The answer came back in the deepest voice Harvey had ever heard from a human chest: 'Quit foolin', Dan, and send him to me.'

Dan sniggered, and threw Harvey his warped bicycle shoes. There was something in the tones on the deck that made the boy dissemble his extreme rage and console himself with the thought of gradually unfolding the tale of his own and his father's wealth on the voyage home. This rescue would certainly make him a hero among his friends for life. He hoisted himself on deck up a perpendicular ladder, and stumbled aft, over a score of obstructions, to where a small, thick-set, clean-shaven man with gray eyebrows sat on a step that led up to the quarter-deck. The swell had passed in the night, leaving a long, oily sea, dotted round the horizon with the sails of a dozen fishing-boats. Between them lay little black specks, showing where the dories were out fishing. The schooner, with a triangular riding-sail on the mainmast, played easily at anchor, and except for the man by the cabin roof—'house,' they call it—she was deserted.

'Mornin'—good afternoon, I should say. You've nigh slep' the clock around, young feller,' was the greeting.

'Mornin',' said Harvey. He did not like being called 'young feller'; and, as one rescued from drowning, expected sympathy. His mother suffered agonies whenever he got his feet wet, but this mariner did not seem excited.

'Naow let's hear all abaout it. It's quite providential, first an' last, fer all concerned. What might be your name? Where from (we mistrust it's Noo York), an' where baound (we mistrust it's Europe)?'

Harvey gave his name, the name of the steamer, and a short history of the accident, winding up with a demand to be taken back immediately to New York, where his father would pay anything any one chose to name.

'H'm,' said the shaven man, quite unmoved by the end of Harvey's speech. 'I can't say we think special of any man, or boy even, that falls overboard from that kind o' packet in a flat ca'am. Least of all when his excuse is thet he's sea-sick.'

'Excuse!' cried Harvey. 'D'you suppose I'd fall overboard into your dirty little boat for fun?'

'Not knowin' what your notions o' fun may be, I can't rightly say, young feller. But if I was you, I wouldn't call the boat which, under Providence, was the means o' savin' ye, names. In the first place, it's blame irreligious. In the second, it's annoyin' to my feelin's—an' I'm Disko Troop o' the "We're Here" o' Gloucester, which you don't seem rightly to know.'

'I don't know and I don't care,' said Harvey. 'I'm grateful enough for being saved and all that of course; but I want you to understand that the sooner you take me back to New York the better it'll pay you.'

'Meanin'—haow?' Troop raised one shaggy eyebrow over a suspiciously mild blue eye.

'Dollars and cents,' said Harvey, delighted to think that he was making an impression. 'Cold dollars and cents.' He thrust a hand into a pocket, and threw out his stomach a little, which was his way of being grand. 'You've done the best day's work you ever did in your life when you pulled me in. I'm all the son Harvey Cheyne has.'

'He's bin favoured,' said Disko drily.

'And if you don't know who Harvey Cheyne is, you don't know much— that's all. Now turn her around and let's hurry.'

Harvey had a notion that the greater part of America was filled with people discussing and envying his father's dollars.

'Mebbe I do, an' mebbe I don't. Take a reef in your stummick, young feller. It's full o' my vittles.'

Harvey heard a chuckle from Dan, who was pretending to be busy by the stump-foremast, and the blood rushed to his face.

'We'll pay for that too,' he said. 'When do you suppose we shall get to New York?'

'I don't use Noo York any. Ner Boston. We may see Eastern Point abaout September, an' your pa—I'm real sorry I hain't heerd tell of him— may give me ten dollars efter all your talk. Then o' course he mayn't.'

'Ten dollars! Why, see here, I—' Harvey dived into his pocket for the wad of bills. All he brought up was a soggy packet of cigarettes.

'Not lawful currency, an' bad for the lungs. Heave 'em overboard, young feller, an' try agin.'

'It's been stole!' cried Harvey hotly.

'You'll hev to wait till you see your pa, to reward me, then?'

'A hundred and thirty-four dollars—all stolen,' said Harvey, hunting wildly through his pockets. 'Give them back.'

A curious change flitted across old Troop's hard face. 'What might you have been doin' at your time o' life with one hundred an' thirty-four dollars, young feller?'

'It was part of my pocket-money—for a month.' This Harvey thought would be a knock-down blow, and it was—indirectly.

'Oh! One hundred and thirty-four dollars is only part of his pocket-money—for one month only! You don't remember hittin' anything when you fell over, do you? Crack agin a stanchion, le's say? Old man Hasken o' the "East Wind" '—Troop seemed to be talking to himself—'he tripped on a hatch an' butted the mainmast with his head—hardish. 'Baout three weeks afterwards, old man Hasken he would hev it that the "East Wind" was a commerce-destroyin' man-o'-war, an' so he declared war on Sable Island because it was Bridish, an' the shoals run aout too far. They sewed him up in a bed-bag, his head an' feet appearin', fer the rest o' the trip, an' now he's to home in Essex playin' with little rag dolls.'

Harvey choked with rage, but Troop went on consolingly: 'We're sorry fer you. We're very sorry fer you—an' so young. We won't say no more abaout the money, I guess.'

''Course you won't. You stole it.'

'Suit yourself. We stole it ef it's any comfort to you. Naow, abaout goin' back. Allowin' we could do it, which we can't, you ain't in no fit state to go back to your home, an' we've jest come on to the Banks workin' fer our bread. We don't see the ha'af of a hundred dollars a month, let alone pocket-money; an' with good luck we'll be ashore again somewheres abaout the first weeks o' September.'

'But—but it's May now, and I can't stay here doin' nothing just because you want to fish. I can't, I tell you!'

'Right an' jest; jest an' right. No one asks you to do nothin'. There's a heap as you can do, for Otto he went overboard on Le Have. I mistrust he lost his grip in a gale we f'und there. Anyways he never come back to deny it. You've turned up, plain, plumb providential for all concerned. I mistrust, though, there's ruther few things you kin do. Ain't thet so?'

'I can make it lively for you and your crowd when we get ashore,' said Harvey, with a vicious nod, murmuring vague threats about 'piracy,' at which Troop almost—not quite—smiled.

'Excep' talk. I'd forgot that. You ain't asked to talk more'n you've a mind to aboard the "We're Here." Keep your eyes open, an' help Dan to do ez he's bid, an' sechlike, an' I'll give you—you ain't wuth it, but I'll give you—ten and a ha'af a month; say thirty-five at the end o' the trip. A little work will ease up your head, an' you kin tell us all abaout your dad an' your ma an' your money efterwards.'

'She's on the steamer,' said Harvey, his eyes filling with tears. 'Take me to New York at once.'

'Poor woman—poor woman! When she has you back she'll forgit it all, though. There's eight of us on the "We're Here," an' ef we went back naow—it's more'n a thousand mile—we'd lose the season. The men they wouldn't hev it—even allowin' I was agreeable.'

'But my father would make it all right.'

'He'd try. I don't doubt he'd try,' said Troop, 'but a whole season's catch is eight men's bread; an' you'll be better in your health when you see him in the fall. Go forward an' help Dan. It's ten an' a ha'af a month, ez I said, an', o' course, all f'und, same ez the rest o' us.'

'Do you mean I'm to clean pots and pans and things?' said Harvey.

'An' other things. You've no call to shout, young feller.'

'I won't! My father will give you enough to buy this dirty little fish-kettle'—Harvey stamped on the deck—'ten times over, if you take me to New York safe; and—and—you're ahead a hundred and thirty dollars by me, anyway.'

'Ha-ow?' said Troop, the iron face darkening.

'How? You know how, well enough. On top of all that, you want me to do menial work'—Harvey was very proud of that adjective—''till the fall. I tell you I will not. You hear?'

Troop regarded the top of the mainmast with deep interest for a while, as Harvey harangued fiercely all around him.

'Hsh!' he said at last. 'I'm figurin' out my responsibilities in my own mind. It's a matter o' jedgment.'

Dan stole up and plucked Harvey by the elbow. 'Don't go to tamperin' with dad any more,' he pleaded. 'You've called him a thief two or three times over, an' he don't take that from any livin' bein'.'

'I won't!' Harvey almost shrieked, disregarding the advice, and still Troop meditated.

'Seems kinder unneighbourly,' he said at last, his eye travelling down to Harvey. 'I don't blame you, not a mite, young feller, nor you won't blame me when the bile's out o' your systim. Be sure you sense what I say? Ten an' a ha'af fer second boy on the schooner—an' all f'und—fer to teach you an' fer the sake o' your health. Yes or no?'

'No!' said Harvey. 'Take me back to New York or I'll see you—'

He did not exactly remember what followed. He was lying in the scuppers, holding on to a nose that bled, while Troop looked down on him serenely.

'Dan,' he said to his son, 'I was sot agin this young feller when I first saw him, on account o' hasty jedgments. Never you be led astray by hasty jedgments, Dan. Naow I'm sorry for him, because he's clear dis-tracted in his upper works. He ain't responsible fer the names he's give me, nor fer his other statements—nor fer jumpin' overboard, which I'm abaout ha'af convinced he did. You be gentle with him, Dan, 'r I'll give you twice what I've give him. Them hemmeridges clears the head. Let him sluice it off!'

Troop went down solemnly into the cabin, where he and the older men bunked, leaving Dan to comfort the luckless heir to thirty millions.

Chapter 2

'I WARNED YE,' said Dan, as the drops fell thick and fast on the dark, oiled planking. 'Dad ain't noways hasty, but you fair earned it. Pshaw! there's no sense takin' on so.' Harvey's shoulders were rising and falling in spasms of dry sobbing. 'I know the feelin'. First time dad laid me out was the last—and that was my first trip. Makes ye feel sickish an' lonesome. I know.'

'It does,' moaned Harvey. 'That man's either crazy or drunk, and—and I can't do anything.'

'Don't say that to dad,' whispered Dan. 'He's set agin all liquor, an'—well, he told me you was the madman. What in creation made you call him a thief? He's my dad.'

Harvey sat up, mopped his nose, and told the story of the missing wad of bills. 'I'm not crazy,' he wound up. 'Only—your father has never seen more than a five-dollar bill at a time, and my father could buy up this boat once a week and never miss it.'

'You don't know what the "We're Here" 's worth. Your dad must hev a pile o' money. How did he git it? Dad sez loonies can't shake out a straight yarn. Go ahead.'

'In gold mines and things, West.'

'I've read o' that kind o' business. Out West, too? Does he go around with a pistol on a trick-pony, same ez the circus. They call that the Wild West, and I've heard that their spurs an' bridles was solid silver.'

'You are a chump!' said Harvey, amused in spite of himself. 'My father hasn't any use for ponies. When he wants to ride he takes his car.'

'Haow? Lobster-car?'

'No. His own private car, of course. You've seen a private car some time in your life?'

'Slatin Beeman he hez one,' said Dan cautiously. 'I saw her at the Union Depot in Boston, with three niggers hoggin' her run.' (Dan meant cleaning the windows.) 'But Slatin Beeman he owns 'baout every railroad on Long Island, they say; an' they say he's bought 'baout ha'af Noo Hampshire an' run a line fence around her, an' filled her up with lions an' tigers an' bears an' buffalo an' crocodiles an' such all. Slatin Beeman he's a millionaire. I've seen his car. Yes?'

'Well, my father's what they call a multi-millionaire; and he has two private cars. One's named for me, the "Harvey," and one for my mother, the "Constance."'

'Hold on,' said Dan. 'Dad don't ever let me swear, but I guess you can. 'Fore we go ahead, I want you to say hope you may die if you're lying.'

'Of course,' said Harvey.

'Thet ain't 'nuff. Say, "Hope I may die if I ain't speakin' truth."'

'Hope I may die right here,' said Harvey, 'if every word I've spoken isn't the cold truth.'

'Hundred an' thirty-four dollars an' all?' said Dan. 'I heard ye talkin' to dad, an' I ha'af looked you'd be swallered up, same's Jonah.'

Harvey protested himself red in the face. Dan was a shrewd young person along his own lines, and ten minutes' questioning convinced him that Harvey was not lying—much. Besides, he had bound himself by the most terrible oath known to boyhood, and yet he sat, alive, with a red-ended nose, in the scuppers, recounting marvels upon marvels.

'Gosh!' said Dan at last from the very bottom of his soul when Harvey had completed an inventory of the car named in his honour. Then a grin of mischievous delight overspread his broad face. 'I believe you, Harvey. Dad's made a mistake fer once in his life.'

'He has, sure,' said Harvey, who was meditating an early revenge.

'He'll be mad clear through. Dad jest hates to be mistook in his jedgments.' Dan lay back and slapped his thigh. 'Oh, Harvey, don't you spile the catch by lettin' on.'

'I don't want to be knocked down again. I'll get even with him, though.'

'Never heard any man ever got even with dad. But he'd knock ye down again sure. The more he was mistook the more he'd do it. But, gold mines and pistols—'

'I never said a word about pistols,' Harvey cut in, for he was on his oath.

'Thet's so; no more you did. Two private cars, then, one named fer you an' one fer her; an' two hundred dollars a month pocket-money, all knocked into the scuppers fer not workin' fer ten an' a ha'af a month! It's the top haul o' the season.' He exploded with noiseless chuckles.

'Then I was right?' said Harvey, who thought he had found a sympathiser.

'You was wrong; the wrongest kind o' wrong! You take right hold an' pitch in 'longside o' me, or you'll catch it, an' I'll catch it fer backin' you up. Dad always gives me double helps 'cause I'm his son, an' he hates favourin' folk. Guess you're kinder mad at dad. I've been that way time an' again. But dad's a mighty jest man; all the fleet says so.'

'Looks like justice, this, don't it?' Harvey pointed to his outraged nose. 'Thet's nothin'. Lets the shore blood outer you. Dad did it for yer health. Say, though, I can't have dealin's with a man that thinks me or dad or any one on the "We're Here" 's a thief. We ain't any common wharf-end crowd by any manner o' means. We're fishermen, an' we've shipped together for six years an' more. Don't you make any mistake on that! I told ye dad don't let me swear. He calls 'em vain oaths, and pounds me; but ef I could say what you said 'baout your pap an' his fixin's, I'd say that 'baout your dollars. I dunno what was in your pockets when I dried your kit, fer I didn't look to see; but I'd say, using the very same words ez you used jest now, neither me nor dad—an' we was the only two that teched you after you was brought aboard—knows anythin' 'baout the money. Thet's my say. Naow?'

The blood-letting had certainly cleared Harvey's brain, and may be the loneliness of the sea had something to do with it. 'That's all right,' he said. Then he looked down confusedly. 'Seems to me, that for a fellow just saved from drowning I haven't been over and above grateful, Dan.'

'Well, you was shook up and silly,' said Dan. 'Anyway, there was only dad an' me aboard to see it. The cook he don't count.'

'I might have thought about losing the bills that way,' Harvey said half to himself, 'instead of calling everybody in sight a thief. Where's your father?'

'In the cabin. What d'you want o' him again?'

'You'll see,' said Harvey, and he stepped, rather groggily, for his head was still singing, to the cabin steps, where the little ship's clock hung in plain sight of the wheel. Troop in the chocolate-and-yellow-painted cabin was busy with a note-book and an enormous black pencil, which he sucked hard from time to time.

'I haven't acted quite right,' said Harvey, surprised at his own meekness.

'What's wrong naow?' said the skipper. 'Walked into Dan, hev ye?'

'No; it's about you.'

'I'm here to listen.'

'Well I—I'm here to take things back,' said Harvey, very quickly. 'When a man's saved from drowning—' he gulped.

'Ey? You'll make a man yet ef you go on this way.'

'He oughtn't begin by calling people names.'

'Jest an' right—right an' jest,' said Troop, with the ghost of a dry smile.

'So I'm here to say I'm sorry.' Another big gulp.

Troop heaved himself slowly off the locker he was sitting on and held out an eleven-inch hand. 'I mistrusted 'twould do you sights o' good; an' this shows I weren't mistook in my jedgments.' A smothered chuckle on deck caught his ear. 'I am very seldom mistook in my jedgments.' The eleven-inch hand closed on Harvey's, numbing it to the elbow. 'We'll put a little more gristle to that 'fore we've done with you, young feller; an' I don't think any worse of ye fer anythin' thet's gone by. You wasn't fairly responsible. Go right abaout your business an' you won't take no hurt.'

'You're white,' said Dan, as Harvey regained the deck.

'I don't feel it,' said he, flushed to the tips of his ears.

'I didn't mean that way. I heard what dad said. When dad allows he don't think the worse of any man, dad's give himself away. He hates to be mistook in his jedgments too. Ho! ho! Onct dad has a jedgment, he'd sooner dip his colours to the British than change it. I'm glad it's settled right eend up. Dad's right when he says he can't take you back. It's all the livin' we make here—fishin'. The men'll be back like sharks after a dead whale in ha'af an hour.'

'What for?' said Harvey.

'Supper, o' course. Don't your stummick tell you? You've a heap to learn.'

'Guess I have,' said Harvey dolefully, looking at the tangle of ropes and blocks overhead.

'She's a daisy,' said Dan enthusiastically, misunderstanding the look. 'Wait till our mainsail's bent, an' she walks home with all her salt wet. There's some work first, though.' He pointed down into the darkness of the open main-hatch between the two masts.

'What's that for? It's all empty,' said Harvey.

'You an' me an' a few more hev got to fill it,' said Dan. 'That's where the fish goes.'

'Alive?' said Harvey.

'Well, no. They're so's to be ruther dead—an' flat—an' salt. There's a hundred hogshead o' salt in the bins; an' we hain't more'n covered our dunnage to now.'

'Where are the fish, though?'

'In the sea they say; in the boats we pray,' said Dan, quoting a fisherman's proverb. 'You come in last night with 'baout forty of 'em.'

He pointed to a sort of wooden pen just in front of the quarter-deck. 'You an' me we'll sluice that out when they're through. 'Send we'll hev full pens to-night! I've seen her down ha'af a foot with fish waitin' to clean, an' we stood to the tables till we was splittin' ourselves instid o' them, we was so sleepy. Yes, they're comin' in naow.' Dan looked over the low bulwarks at half a dozen dories rowing toward them over the shining, silky sea.

'I've never seen the sea from so low down,' said Harvey. 'It's fine.'

The low sun made the water all purple and pinkish, with golden lights on the barrels of the long swells, and blue and green mackerel shades in the hollows. Each schooner in sight seemed to be pulling her dories towards her by invisible strings, and the little black figures in the tiny boats pulled like clockwork toys.

'They've struck on good,' said Dan, between his half-shut eyes. 'Manuel hain't room fer another fish. Low ez a lily-pad in still water, ain't he?'

'Which is Manuel? I don't see how you can tell 'em 'way off, as you do.'

'Last boat to the south'ard. He f'und you last night,' said Dan, pointing. 'Manuel rows Portugoosey; ye can't mistake him. East o' him—he's a heap better'n he rows—is Pennsylvania. Loaded with saleratus, by the looks of him. East o' him—see how pretty they string out all along—with the humpy shoulders, is Long Jack. He's a Galway man inhabitin' South Boston, where they all live mostly, an' mostly them Galway men are good in a boat. North, away yonder—you'll hear him tune up in a minute—is Tom Platt. Man-o'-war's man he was on the old "Ohio"—first of our navy, he says, to go araound the Horn. He never talks of much else, 'cept when he sings, but he has fair fishin' luck. There! What did I tell you?'

A melodious bellow stole across the water from the northern dory. Harvey heard something about somebody's hands and feet being cold, and then:—

> 'Bring forth the chart, the doleful chart,
> See where them mountings meet!
> The clouds are thick around their heads,
> The mists around their feet.'

'Full boat,' said Dan with a chuckle. 'If he gives us "O Captain" it's toppin' full.'

The bellow continued:—

> 'And naow to thee, O Capting,
> Most earnestly I pray,
> That they shall never bury me
> In church or cloister gray.'

'Double game for Tom Platt. He'll tell you all about the old "Ohio" tomorrow. See that blue dory behind him? He's my uncle—dad's own brother—an' ef there's any bad luck loose on the Banks she'll fetch up agin Uncle Salters, sure. Look how tender he's rowin'. I'll lay my wage and share he's the only man stung up to-day—an' he's stung up good.'

'What'll sting him?' said Harvey, getting interested.

'Strawberries, mostly. Punkins, sometimes, an' sometimes lemons an' cucumbers. Yes, he's stung up from his elbows down. That man's luck's perfectly paralysin'. Naow we'll take a-holt o' the tackles an' hist 'em in. Is it true what you told me jest now, that you never done a hand's turn o' work in all your born life? Must feel kinder awful, don't it?'

'I'm going to try to work anyway,' Harvey replied stoutly. 'Only it's all dead new.'

'Lay a-holt o' that tackle, then. Behind ye!'

Harvey grabbed at a rope and long iron hook dangling from one of the stays of the mainmast, while Dan pulled down another that ran from something he called a 'topping lift,' as Manuel drew alongside in his loaded dory. The Portuguese smiled a brilliant smile that Harvey learned to know well later, and with a shorthandled fork began to throw fish into the pen on deck. 'Two hundred and thirty-one,' he shouted.

'Give him the hook,' said Dan, and Harvey ran it into Manuel's hands. He slipped it through a loop of rope at the dory's bow, caught Dan's tackle, hooked it to the stern-becket, and clambered into the schooner.

'Pull!' shouted Dan, and Harvey pulled, astonished to find how easily the dory rose.

'Hold on, she don't nest in the cross-trees!' Dan laughed; and Harvey held on, for the boat lay in the air above his head.

'Lower away,' Dan shouted, and as Harvey lowered, Dan swayed the light boat with one hand till it landed softly just behind the mainmast. 'They don't weigh nothin' empty. Thet was right smart fer a passenger. There's more trick to it in a sea-way.'

'Ah ha!' said Manuel, holding out a brown hand. 'You are some pretty well now? This time last night the fish they fish for you. Now you fish for fish. Eh, wha-at?'

'I'm—I'm ever so grateful,' Harvey stammered, and his unfortunate hand stole to his pocket once more, but he remembered that he had no money to offer. When he knew Manuel better the mere thought of the mistake he might have made would cover him with hot, uneasy blushes in his bunk.

'There is no to be thankful for to me!' said Manuel. 'How shall I leave you dreeft, dreeft all around the Banks? Now you are a fisherman—eh, wha-at? Ouh! Auh!' He bent backward and forward stiffly from the hips to get the kinks out of himself.

'I have not cleaned boat to-day. Too busy. They struck on queek. Danny, my son, clean for me.'

Harvey moved forward at once. Here was something he could do for the man who had saved his life.

Dan threw him a swab, and he leaned over the dory, mopping up the slime, clumsily, but with great goodwill. 'Hike out the footboards; they slide in them grooves,' said Dan. 'Swab 'em an' lay 'em down. Never let a footboard jam. Ye may want her bad some day. Here's Long Jack.'

A stream of glittering fish flew into the pen from a dory alongside.

'Manuel, you take the tackle. I'll fix the tables. Harvey, clear Manuel's boat. Long Jack's nestin' on the top of her.'

Harvey looked up from his swabbing at the bottom of another dory just above his head.

'Jest like the Injian puzzle-boxes, ain't they?' said Dan, as the one boat dropped into the other.

'Takes to ut like a duck to water,' said Long Jack, a grizzly-chinned, long-lipped Galway man, bending to and fro exactly as Manuel had done. Disko in the cabin growled up the hatchway, and they could hear him suck his pencil.

'Wan hunder an' forty-nine an' a half—bad luck to ye, Discobolus!' said Long Jack. 'I'm murderin' meself to fill your pockuts. Slate ut for a bad catch. The Portugee has bate me.'

Whack came another dory alongside, and more fish shot into the pen.

'Two hundred and three. Let's look at the passenger!' The speaker was even larger than the Galway man, and his face was made curious by a purple cut running slantways from his left eye to the right corner of his mouth.

Not knowing what else to do, Harvey swabbed each dory as it came down, pulled out the footboards, and laid them in the bottom of the boat.

'He's caught on good,' said the scarred man, who was Tom Platt, watching him critically. 'There are two ways o' doin' everything. One's fisher-fashion—any end first an' a slippery hitch over all—an' the other's—'

'What we did on the old "Ohio"!' Dan interrupted, brushing into the knot of men with a long board on legs. 'Git out o' here, Tom Platt, an' leave me fix the tables.'

He jammed one end of the board into two nicks in the bulwarks, kicked out the leg, and ducked just in time to avoid a swinging blow from the man-o'-war's man.

'An' they did that on the "Ohio," too, Danny. See?' said Tom Platt, laughing.

'Guess they was swivel-eyed, then, fer it didn't git home, and I know who'll find his boots on the main-truck ef he don't leave us alone. Haul ahead! I'm busy, can't ye see?'

'Danny, ye lie on the cable an' sleep all day,' said Long Jack. 'You're the hoight av impidence, an' I'm persuaded ye'll corrupt our supercargo in a week.'

'His name's Harvey,' said Dan, waving two strangely-shaped knives, 'an' he'll be worth five of any Sou' Boston clam-digger 'fore long.' He laid the knives tastefully on the table, cocked his head on one side, and admired the effect.

'I think it's forty-two,' said a small voice over-side, and there was a roar of laughter as another voice answered, 'Then my luck's turned fer onct, 'caze I'm forty-five, though I be stung outer all shape.'

'Forty-two or forty-five. I've lost count,' the small voice said.

'It's Penn an' Uncle Salters caountin' catch. This beats the circus any day,' said Dan. 'Jest look at 'em!'

'Come in—come in!' roared Long Jack. 'It's wet out yondher, children.'

'Forty-two, ye said.' This was Uncle Salters.

'I'll count again, then,' the voice replied meekly.

The two dories swung together and bunted into the schooner's side.

'Patience o' Jerusalem!' snapped Uncle Salters, backing water with a splash. 'What possest a farmer like you to set foot in a boat beats me. You've nigh stove me all up.'

'I am sorry, Mr. Salters. I came to sea on account of nervous dyspepsia. You advised me, I think.'

'You an' your nervis dyspepsy be drowned in the Whale-hole,' roared Uncle Salters, a fat and tubby little man. 'You're comin' down on me agin. Did ye say forty-two or forty-five?'

'I've forgotten, Mr. Salters. Let's count.'

'Don't see as it could be forty-five. I'm forty-five,' said Uncle Salters. 'You count keerful, Penn.'

Disko Troop came out of the cabin. 'Salters, you pitch your fish in naow at once,' he said in the tone of authority.

'Don't spile the catch, dad,' Dan murmured. 'Them two are on'y jest beginnin'.'

'Mother av delight! He's forkin' them wan by wan,' howled Long Jack, as Uncle Salters got to work laboriously; the little man in the other dory counting a line of notches on the gunwale.

'That was last week's catch,' he said, looking up plaintively, his forefinger where he had left off.

Manuel nudged Dan, who darted to the aftertackle, and, leaning far over-side, slipped the hook into the stern rope as Manuel made her fast forward. The others pulled gallantly and swung the boat in—man, fish, and all.

'One, two, four—nine,' said Tom Platt, counting with a practised eye. 'Forty-seven. Penn, you're it!' Dan let the aftertackle run and slid him out of the stern on to the deck amid a torrent of his own fish.

'Hold on!' roared Uncle Salters, bobbing by the waist. 'Hold on, I'm a bit mixed in my caount.'

He had no time to protest, but was hove inboard and treated like 'Pennsylvania.'

'Forty-one,' said Tom Platt. 'Beat by a farmer, Salters. An' you sech a sailor, too!'

''Tweren't fair caount,' said he, stumbling out of the pen; 'an' I'm stung up all to pieces.'

His thick hands were puffy and mottled purply white.

'Some folks will find strawberry-bottom,' said Dan, addressing the newly-risen moon, 'ef they hev to dive fer it, seems to me.'

'An' others,' said Uncle Salters, 'eats the fat o' the land in sloth, an' mocks their own blood-kin.'

'Seat ye! seat ye!' a voice Harvey had not heard called from the foc'sle. Disko Troop, Tom Platt, Long Jack, and Salters went forward on the word. Little Penn bent above his square deep-sea reel, and the tangled cod-lines. Manuel lay down full length on the deck, and Dan dropped into the hold, where Harvey heard him banging casks with a hammer.

'Salt,' he said, returning. 'Soon as we're through supper we git to dressing-down. You'll pitch to dad. Tom Platt an' dad they stow together, an' you'll hear 'em arguin'. We're second ha'af, you an' me an' Manuel an' Penn—the youth an' beauty o' the boat.'

'What's the good of that?' said Harvey. 'I'm hungry.'

'They'll be through in a minute. Snff! She smells good to-night. Dad ships a good cook ef he do suffer with his brother. It's a full catch to-day, ain't it?' He pointed at the pens piled high with cod. 'What water did ye hev, Manuel?'

'Twenty-fife father,' said the Portuguese sleepily. 'They strike on good an' queek. Some day I show you, Harvey.'

The moon was beginning to walk on the still sea before the elder men came aft. The cook had no need to cry 'second half.' Dan and Manuel were down the hatch and at table ere Tom Platt, last and most deliberate of the elders, had finished wiping his mouth with the back of his hand. Harvey followed Penn, and sat down before a tin pan of cods' tongues and sounds, mixed with scraps of pork and fried potato, a loaf of hot bread, and some black and powerful coffee. Hungry as they were, they waited while 'Pennsylvania' solemnly asked a blessing. Then they stoked in silence till Dan drew breath over his tin cup and demanded of Harvey how he felt.

'Most full, but there's just room for another piece.'

The cook was a huge jet-black negro, and, unlike all the negroes Harvey had met, did not talk, contenting himself with smiles and dumb-show invitations to eat more.

'See, Harvey,' said Dan, rapping with his fork on the table, 'it's jest as I said. The young an' handsome men—like me an' Pennsy an' you an' Manuel—we're second ha'af an' we eats when the first ha'af are through. They're the old fish; and they're mean an' humpy, an' their stummicks has to be humoured; so they come first, which they don't deserve. Ain't that so, doctor?'

The cook nodded.

'Can't he talk?' said Harvey in a whisper.

''Nough to git along. Not much o' anything we know. His natural tongue's kinder curious. Comes from the innards of Cape Breton, he does, where the farmers speak home-made Scotch. Cape Breton's full o' niggers whose folk run in there durin' aour war, an' they talk like the farmers—all huffy-chuffy.'

'That is not Scotch,' said 'Pennsylvania.' 'That is Gaelic. So I read in a book.'

'Penn reads a heap. Most of what he says is so—'cep' when it comes to a caount o' fish—eh?'

'Does your father just let them say how many they've caught without checking them?' said Harvey.

'Why, yes. Where's the sense of a man lyin' fer a few old cod?'

'Was a man once lied for his catch,' Manuel put in. 'Lied every day. Fife, ten, twenty-fife more fish than come he say there was.'

'Where was that?' said Dan. 'None o' aour folk?'

'Frenchman of Anguille.'

'Ah! Them West Shore Frenchmen don't caount anyway. Stands to reason they can't caount. Ef you run acrost any of their soft hooks, Harvey, you'll know why,' said Dan, with an awful contempt.

'Always more and never less,
Every time we come to dress,'

Long Jack roared down the hatch, and the 'second ha'af' scrambled up at once.

The shadow of the masts and rigging, with the never-furled riding-sail, rolled to and fro on the heaving deck in the moonlight, and the pile of fish by the stern shone like a dump of fluid silver. In the hold there were tramplings and rumblings where Disko Troop and Tom Platt moved among the salt-bins. Dan passed Harvey a pitchfork, and led him

to the inboard end of the rough table, where Uncle Salters was drumming
impatiently with a knife-haft. A tub of salt water lay at his feet.

'You pitch to dad an' Tom Platt down the hatch, an' take keer Uncle
Salters don't cut yer eye out,' said Dan, swinging himself into the hold.
'I'll pass salt below.'

Penn and Manuel stood knee-deep among cod in the pen, flourishing drawn knives. Long Jack, a basket at his feet and mittens on his
hands, faced Uncle Salters at the table, and Harvey stared at the pitchfork
and the tub.

'Hi!' shouted Manuel, stooping to the fish, and bringing one up with
a finger under its gill and a finger in its eye. He laid it on the edge of
the pen; the knife-blade glimmered with a sound of tearing, and the fish,
slit from throat to vent, with a nick on either side of the neck, dropped
at Long Jack's feet.

'Hi!' said Long Jack, with a scoop of his mittened hand. The cod's
liver dropped in the basket. Another wrench and scoop sent the head
and offal flying, and the empty fish slid across to Uncle Salters, who
snorted fiercely. There was another sound of tearing, the backbone flew
over the bulwarks, and the fish, headless, gutted, and open, splashed in
the tub, sending the salt water into Harvey's astonished mouth. After
the first yell, the men were silent. The cod moved along as though they
were alive, and long ere Harvey had ceased wondering at the miraculous
dexterity of it all, his tub was full.

'Pitch!' grunted Uncle Salters, without turning his head, and Harvey
pitched the fish by twos and threes down the hatch.

'Hi! Pitch 'em bunchy,' shouted Dan. 'Don't scatter! Uncle Salters is
the best splitter in the fleet. Watch him mind his book!'

Indeed, it looked a little as though the round uncle were cutting maga-
zine pages against time. Manuel's body, cramped over from the hips,
stayed like a statue; but his long arms grabbed the fish without ceasing.
Little Penn toiled valiantly, but it was easy to see he was weak. Once or
twice Manuel found time to help him without breaking the chain of supplies, and once Manuel howled because he had caught his finger in a
Frenchman's hook. These hooks are made of soft metal to be re-
bent after use; but the cod very often get away with them and are
hooked again elsewhere; and that is one of the many reasons why Gloucester boats despise the Frenchmen.

Down below, the rasping sound of rough salt rubbed on rough flesh
sounded like the whirring of a grindstone—a steady undertune to the
'click-nick' of the knives in the pen, the wrench and schloop of torn
heads, dropped livers, and flying offal; the 'caraaah' of Uncle Salters's

knife scooping away backbones; and the flap of wet, opened bodies falling into the tub.

At the end of an hour Harvey would have given the world to rest; for fresh, wet cod weigh more than you would think, and his back ached with the steady pitching. But he felt for the first time in his life that he was one of a working gang of men, took pride in the thought, and held on sullenly.

'Knife oh!' shouted Uncle Salters at last. Penn doubled up, gasping among the fish, Manuel bowed back and forth to supple himself, and Long Jack leaned over the bulwarks. The cook appeared, noiseless as a black shadow, collected a mass of backbones and heads, and retreated.

'Blood-ends for breakfast an' head-chowder,' said Long Jack, smacking his lips.

'Knife oh!' repeated Uncle Salters, waving the flat, curved splitter's weapon.

'Look by your foot, Harve,' cried Dan below.

Harvey saw half a dozen knives stuck in a cleat in the hatch combing. He dealt these around, taking over the dulled ones.

'Water!' said Disko Troop.

'Scuttle-butt's for'ard an' the dipper's alongside. Hurry, Harve,' said Dan.

He was back in a minute with a big dipperful of stale brown water which tasted like nectar, and loosed the jaws of Disko and Tom Platt.

'These are cod,' said Disko. 'They ain't Damarskus figs, Tom Platt, nor yet silver bars. I've told you that every single time sence we've sailed together.'

'A matter o' seven seasons,' returned Tom Platt coolly. 'Good stowin's good stowin' all the same, an' there's a right an' a wrong way o' stowin' ballast even. If you'd ever seen four hundred ton o' iron set into the—'

'Hi!' With a yell from Manuel the work began again, and never stopped till the pen was empty. The instant the last fish was down, Disko Troop rolled aft to the cabin with his brother; Manuel and Long Jack went forward; Tom Platt only waited long enough to slide home the hatch ere he too disappeared. In half a minute Harvey heard deep snores in the cabin, and he was staring blankly at Dan and Penn.

'I did a little better that time, Danny,' said Penn, whose eyelids were heavy with sleep. 'But I think it is my duty to help clean.'

'Wouldn't hev your conscience fer a thousand quintal,' said Dan. 'Turn in, Penn. You've no call to do boys' work. Draw a bucket, Harvey. Oh, Penn, dump these in the gurry-butt 'fore you sleep. Kin you keep awake that long?'

Penn took up the heavy basket of fish-livers, emptied them into a cask with a hinged top lashed by the foc'sle; then he too dropped out of sight in the cabin.

'Boys clean up after dressin'-down, an' first watch in ca'am weather is boys' watch on the "We're Here."' Dan sluiced the pen energetically, unshipped the table, set it up to dry in the moonlight, ran the red knife-blades through a wad of oakum, and began to sharpen them on a tiny grindstone as Harvey threw offal and backbones overboard under his direction.

At the first splash a silvery-white ghost rose bolt upright from the oily water and sighed a weird whistling sigh. Harvey started back with a shout, but Dan only laughed. 'Grampus,' said he. 'Beggin' fer fishheads. They up-eend thet way when they're hungry. Breath on him like the doleful tombs, hain't he?' A horrible stench of decayed fish filled the air as the pillar of white sank, and the water bubbled oilily. 'Hain't ye never seen a grampus up-eend before? You'll see 'em by hundreds 'fore ye're through. Say, it's good to hev a boy aboard again. Otto was too old, an' a Dutchy at that. Him an' me we fought consid'ble. Wouldn't ha' keered fer thet ef he'd hed a Christian tongue in his head. Sleepy?'

'Dead sleepy,' said Harvey, nodding forward.

'Mustn't sleep on watch. Rouse up an' see ef our anchor-light's bright an' shinin'. You're on watch now, Harve.'

'Pshaw! What's to hurt us? Bright's day. Sn—orrr!'

'Jest when things happen, dad says. Fine weather's goodsleepin', an' 'fore you know mebbe you're cut in two by a liner, an' seventeen brass-bound officers, all gen'elmen, lift their hand to it that your lights was aout an' there was a thick fog. Harve, I've kinder took to you, but ef you nod onct more I'll lay into you with a rope's end.'

The moon, who sees many strange things on the Banks, looked down on a slim youth in knickerbockers and a red jersey, staggering around the cluttered decks of a seventy-ton schooner, while behind him, waving a knotted rope, walked, after the manner of an executioner, a boy who yawned and nodded between the blows he dealt.

The lashed wheel groaned and kicked softly, the riding-sail slatted a little in the shifts of the light wind, the windlass creaked, and the miserable procession continued. Harvey expostulated, threatened, whimpered, and at last wept outright, while Dan, the words clotting on his tongue, spoke of the beauty of watchfulness and slashed away with the rope's end, punishing the dories as often as he hit Harvey. At last the clock in the cabin struck ten, and upon the tenth stroke little Penn crept on deck. He found two boys in two tumbled heaps side by side on the main hatch, so deeply asleep that he actually rolled them to their berths.

Chapter 3

IT WAS THE forty-fathom slumber that clears the soul and eye and heart, and sends you to breakfast ravening. They emptied a big tin dish of juicy fragments of fish—the blood-ends the cook had collected overnight. They cleaned up the plates and pans of the elder mess, who were out fishing, sliced pork for the midday meal, swabbed down the foc'sle, filled the lamps, drew coal and water for the cook, and investigated the fore-hold, where the boat's stores were stacked. It was another perfect day—soft, mild, and clear; and Harvey breathed to the very bottom of his lungs.

More schooners had crept up in the night, and the long blue seas were full of sails and dories. Far away on the horizon, the smoke of some liner, her hull invisible, smudged the blue, and to eastward a big ship's top-gallant sails, just lifting, made a square nick in it. Disko Troop was smoking by the roof of the cabin—one eye on the craft around, and the other on the little fly at the mainmast-head.

'When dad kerflummoxes that way,' said Dan in a whisper, 'he's doin' some high-line thinkin' fer all hands. I'll lay my wage an' share we'll make berth soon. Dad he knows the cod, an' the fleet they know dad knows. See 'em comin' up one by one, lookin' fer nothin' in particular, o' course, but scrowgin' on us all the time? There's the "Prince Leboo"; she's a Chatham boat. She's crep' up sence last night. An' see that big one with a patch in her foresail an' a new jib? She's the "Carrie Pitman" from West Chatham. She won't keep her canvas long onless her luck's changed since last season. She don't do much 'cep' drift. There ain't an anchor made 'll hold her. . . . When the smoke puffs up in little rings like that, dad's studyin' the fish. Ef we speak to him now, he'll git mad. Las' time I did, he jest took an' hove a boot at me.'

Disko Troop stared forward, the pipe between his teeth, with eyes that saw nothing. As his son said, he was studying the fish—pitting his knowledge and experience on the Banks against the roving cod in his own sea. He accepted the presence of the inquisitive schooners on the horizon as a compliment to his powers. But now that it was paid, he wished to draw away and make his berth alone, till it was time to go up to the Virgin and fish in the streets of that roaring town upon the waters. So

Disko Troop thought of recent weather, and gales, currents, food supplies, and other domestic arrangements, from the point of view of a
twenty-pound cod; was, in fact, for an hour, a cod himself, and looked
remarkably like one. Then he removed the pipe from his teeth.

'Dad,' said Dan, 'we've done our chores. Can't we go over-side a piece?
It's good catchin' weather.'

'Not in that cherry-coloured rig ner them ha'af-baked brown shoes.
Give him suthin' fit to wear.'

'Dad's pleased—that settles it,' said Dan delightedly, dragging Harvey
into the cabin, while Troop pitched a key down the steps. 'Dad keeps
my spare rig where he can overhaul it, 'cause ma sez I'm keerless.' He
rummaged through a locker, and in less than three minutes Harvey was
adorned with fisherman's rubber boots that came half up his thigh, a
heavy blue jersey well darned at the elbows, a pair of nippers, and a
sou'wester.

'Naow you look somethin' like,' said Dan. 'Hurry!'

'Keep nigh an' handy,' said Troop, 'an' don't go visitin' raound the fleet.
Ef any one asks you what I'm cal'latin to do, speak the truth an' say ye
don't know.'

A little red dory, labelled 'Hattie S.', lay astern of the schooner. Dan
hauled in the painter, and dropped lightly on to the bottom boards, while
Harvey tumbled clumsily after.

'That's no way o' gettin' into a boat,' said Dan. 'Ef there was any sea
you'd go to the bottom, sure. You've got to learn to meet her.'

Dan fitted the thole-pins, took the forward thwart, and watched Harvey's work. The boy had rowed, in a lady-like fashion, on the Adirondack
ponds; but there is a difference between squeaking pins and well-balanced
rullocks—light sculls and stubby, eight-foot sea-oars. They stuck in the
gentle swell, and Harvey grunted.

'Short! Row short!' said Dan. 'Ef you cramp your oar in any kind o'
sea you're liable to turn her over. Ain't she a daisy? Mine, too.'

The little dory was specklessly clean. In her bows lay a tiny anchor,
two jugs of water, and some seventy fathoms of thin brown dory-roding.
A tin dinner-horn rested in cleats just under Harvey's right hand, beside an ugly-looking maul, a short gaff, and a shorter wooden stick. A
couple of lines, with very heavy leads and double cod-hooks, all neatly
coiled on square reels, were stuck in their place by the gunwale.

'Where's the sail and mast?' said Harvey, for his hands were beginning
to blister.

Dan chuckled. 'Ye don't sail fishin'-dories much. Ye pull; but ye needn't
pull so hard. Don't you wish you owned her?'

'Well, I guess my father might give me one or two if I asked 'em,'

Harvey replied. He had been too busy to think much of his family till then.

'That's so. I forgot your dad's a millionaire. You don't act millionary any, naow. But a dory an' craft an' gear'—Dan spoke as though she were a whaleboat—'costs a heap. Think your dad 'ud give you one fer—fer a pet like?'

'Shouldn't wonder. It would be 'most the only thing I haven't stuck him for yet.'

''Must be an expensive kinder kid to home. Don't slitheroo thet way, Harve. Short's the trick, because no sea's ever dead still, an' the swells 'll—'

Crack! The loom of the oar kicked Harvey under the chin and knocked him backwards.

'That was what I was goin' to say. I hed to learn too, but I wasn't more than eight years old when I got my schoolin'.'

Harvey regained his seat with aching jaws and a frown.

'No good gettin' mad at things, dad says. It's our own fault ef we can't handle 'em, he says. Le's try here. Manuel 'll give us the water.'

The 'Portugee' was rocking fully a mile away, but when Dan up-ended an oar, he waved his left arm three times.

'Thirty fathom,' said Dan, stringing a salt clam on to the hook. 'Over with the doughboys. Bait same's I do, Harve, an' don't snarl your reel.'

Dan's line was out long before Harvey had mastered the mystery of baiting and heaving out the leads. The dory drifted along easily. It was not worth while to anchor till they were sure of good ground.

'Here we come!' Dan shouted, and a shower of spray rattled on Harvey's shoulders as a big cod flapped and kicked alongside. 'Muckle, Harvey, muckle! Under your hand! Quick!'

Evidently 'muckle' could not be the dinner-horn, so Harvey passed over the maul, and Dan scientifically stunned the fish before he pulled it inboard, and wrenched out the hook with the short wooden stick he called a 'gob-stick.' Then Harvey felt a tug, and pulled up zealously.

'Why, these are strawberries!' he shouted. 'Look!'

The hook had fouled among a bunch of strawberries, red on one side and white on the other—perfect reproductions of the land fruit, except that there were no leaves, and the stem was all pipy and slimy.

'Don't tech 'em! Slat 'em off. Don't—'

The warning came too late. Harvey had picked them from the hook, and was admiring them.

'Ouch!' he cried, for his fingers throbbed as though he had grasped many nettles.

'Naow ye know what strawberry-bottom means. Nothin' 'cep' fish should be teched with the naked fingers, dad says. Slat 'em off agin the gunnel, an' bait up, Harve. Lookin' won't help any. It's all in the wages.'

Harvey smiled at the thought of his ten and a half dollars a month, and wondered what his mother would say if she could see him hanging over the edge of a fishing-dory in mid-ocean. She suffered agonies whenever he went out on Saranac Lake; and, by the way, Harvey remembered distinctly that he used to laugh at her anxieties. Suddenly the line flashed through his hand, stinging even through the 'nippers,' the woollen circlets supposed to protect it.

'He's a logy. Give him room accordin' to his strength,' cried Dan. 'I'll help ye.'

'No, you won't,' Harvey snapped, as he hung on to the line. 'It's my first fish. Is—is it a whale?'

'Halibut, mebbe.' Dan peered down into the water alongside and flourished the big 'muckle,' ready for all chances. Something white and oval flickered and fluttered through the green. 'I'll lay my wage an' share he's over a hundred. Are you so everlastin' anxious to land him alone?'

Harvey's knuckles were raw and bleeding where they had been banged against the gunwale; his face was purple-blue between excitement and exertion; he dripped with sweat, and was half-blinded from staring at the circling sunlit ripples about the swiftly-moving line. The boys were tired long ere the halibut, who took charge of them and the dory for the next twenty minutes. But the big flat fish was gaffed and hauled in at last.

'Beginner's luck,' said Dan, wiping his forehead. 'He's all of a hundred.'

Harvey looked at the huge gray-and-mottled creature with unspeakable pride. He had seen halibut many times on marble slabs ashore, but it had never occurred to him to ask how they came inland. Now he knew; and every inch of his body ached with fatigue.

'Ef dad was along,' said Dan, hauling up, 'he'd read the signs plain's print. The fish are runnin' smaller an' smaller, an' you've took 'baout as logy a halibut's we're apt to find this trip. Yesterday's catch—did ye notice it?—was all big fish an' no halibut. Dad, he'd read them signs right off. Dad says everythin' on the Banks is signs, an' can be read wrong er right. Dad's deeper'n the Whale-hole.'

Even as he spoke some one fired a pistol on the 'We're Here,' and a potato-basket was run up in the fore-rigging.

'What did I say, naow? That's the call fer the whole crowd. Dad's onter something, er he'd never break fishin' this time o' day. Reel up, Harve, an' we'll pull back.'

They were to windward of the schooner, just ready to flirt the dory over the still sea, when sounds of woe half a mile off led them to Penn,

who was careering around a fixed point, for all the world like a gigantic
water-bug. The little man backed away and came down again with enormous energy, but at the end of each manœuvre his dory swung round
and snubbed herself on her rope.

'We'll hev to help him, else he'll root an' seed here,' said Dan.

'What's the matter?' said Harvey. This was a new world, where he could
not lay down the law to his elders, but had to ask questions humbly. And
the sea was horribly big and unexcited.

'Anchor's fouled. Penn's always losing 'em. Lost two this trip a'ready—
on sandy bottom too—an' dad says next one he loses, sure's fishin', he'll
give him the kelleg. That 'ud break Penn's heart.'

'What's a "kelleg"?' said Harvey, who had a vague idea it might be
some kind of marine torture, like keel-hauling in the story-books.

'Big stone instid of an anchor. You kin see a kelleg ridin' in the bows
fur's you can see a dory, an' all the fleet knows what it means. They'd
guy him dreadful. Penn couldn't stand that no more'n a dog with a dipper
to his tail. He's so everlastin' sensitive. Hello, Penn! Stuck again? Don't
try any more o' your patents. Come up on her, and keep your rodin'
straight up an' down.'

'It doesn't move,' said the little man, panting. 'It doesn't move at all,
and, indeed, I tried everything.'

'What's all this hurrah's-nest for'ard?' said Dan, pointing to a wild
tangle of spare oars and dory-roding, all matted together by the hand of
inexperience.

'Oh, that,' said Penn proudly, 'is a Spanish windlass. Mr. Salters showed
me how to make it; but even that doesn't move her.'

Dan bent low over the gunwale to hide a smile, twitched once or twice
on the roding, and, behold, the anchor drew at once.

'Haul up, Penn,' he said, laughing, 'er she'll git stuck again.'

They left him regarding the weed-hung flukes of the little anchor with
big, pathetic blue eyes, and thanking them profusely.

'Oh, say, while I think of it, Harve,' said Dan, when they were out of
ear-shot, 'Penn ain't quite all caulked. He ain't nowise dangerous, but his
mind's give out. See?'

'Is that so, or is it one of your father's judgments?' Harvey asked as he
bent to his oars. He felt he was learning to handle them more easily.

'Dad ain't mistook this time. Penn's a sure 'nuff loony. No, he ain't
thet exactly, so much ez a harmless ijjit. It was this way (you're rowin'
quite so, Harve), an' I tell you 'cause it's right you orter know. He was
a Moravian preacher once. Jacob Boller wuz his name, dad told me, an'
he lived with his wife an' four children somewheres out Pennsylvania
way. Well, Penn he took his folks along to a Moravian meetin'—camp-

meetin' most like—an' they stayed over jest one night in Johnstown. You've heerd talk o' Johnstown?'

Harvey considered. 'Yes, I have. But I don't know why. It sticks in my head same as Ashtabula.'

'Both was big accidents—that's why, Harve. Well, that one single night Penn and his folks was to the hotel Johnstown was wiped out. Dam bust an' flooded her, an' the houses struck adrift an' bumped into each other an' sunk. I've seen the pictures, an' they're dretful. Penn, he saw his folk drowned all 'n a heap 'fore he rightly knew what was comin'. His mind give out from that on. He mistrusted somethin' hed happened up to Johnstown, but for the poor life of him he couldn't remember what, an' he jest drifted araound smilin' an' wonderin'. He didn't know what he was, nor yit what he hed bin, an' thet way he run agin Uncle Salters, who was visitin' 'n Allegheny City. Ha'af my mother's folks they live scattered inside o' Pennsylvania, an' Uncle Salters he visits araound winters. Uncle Salters he kinder adopted Penn, well knowin' what his trouble wuz; an' he brought him East, an' he give him work on his farm.'

'Why, I heard him calling Penn a farmer last night when the boats bumped. Is your Uncle Salters a farmer?'

'Farmer!' shouted Dan. 'There ain't water enough 'tween here an' Hatt'rus to wash the furrer-mould off'n his boots. He's jest everlastin' farmer. Why, Harve, I've seen thet man hitch up a bucket, 'long towards sundown, an' set twiddlin' the spigot to the scuttle-butt same's ef 'twuz a cow's bag. He's thet much farmer! Well, Penn an' he they ran the farm—up Exeter way, 'twuz. Uncle Salters he sold it this spring to a jay from Boston as wanted to build a summer haouse, an' he got a heap for it. Well, them two loonies scratched along till, one day, Penn's church he'd belonged to—the Moravians—found out where he wuz drifted an' layin', an' wrote to Uncle Salters. Never heard what they said exactly; but Uncle Salters was mad. He's a 'piscopalian mostly—but he jest let 'em hev it both sides o' the bow, 's if he was a Baptist; an' sez he warn't goin' to give up Penn to any blame Moravian connection in Pennsylvania or anywheres else. Then he come to dad, towin' Penn,—that was two trips back,—an' sez he an' Penn must fish a trip fer their health. Guess he thought the Moravians wouldn't hunt the Banks fer Jacob Boller. Dad was agreeable, fer Uncle Salters he'd been fishin' off an' on fer thirty years, when he warn't inventin' patent manures, an' he took quarter-share in the "We're Here"; an' the trip done Penn so much good, dad made a habit o' takin' him. Some day, dad sez, he'll remember his wife an' kids an' Johnstown, an' then, like's not, he'll die, dad sez. Don't ye talk abaout Johnstown, ner such things to Penn, 'r Uncle Salters he'll heave ye overboard.'

'Poor Penn!' murmured Harvey. 'I shouldn't ever have thought Uncle Salters cared for him by the look of 'em together.'

'I like Penn though; we all do,' said Dan. 'We ought to ha' give him a tow, but I wanted to tell ye first.'

They were close to the schooner now, the other boats a little behind them.

'You needn't heave in the dories till after dinner,' said Troop from the deck. 'We'll dress-daown right off. Fix table, boys!'

'Deeper'n the Whale-deep,' said Dan, with a wink, as he set the gear for dressing-down. 'Look at them boats that hev edged up sence mornin'. They're all waitin' on dad. See 'em, Harve?'

'They are all alike to me.' And indeed, to a landsman, the nodding schooners around seemed run from the same mould.

'They ain't, though. That yaller, dirty packet with her bowsprit steeved that way, she's the "Hope of Prague." Nick Brady's her skipper, the meanest man on the Banks. We'll tell him so when we strike the Main Ledge. 'Way off yander's the "Day's Eye." The two Jeraulds own her. She's from Harwich; fastish, too, an' hez good luck; but dad, he'd find fish in a graveyard. Them other three, side along, they're the "Margie Smith," "Rose," and "Edith S. Walen," all from home. Guess we'll see the "Abbie M. Deering" to-morrer, dad, won't we? They're all slippin' over from the shoal o' 'Queereau.'

'You won't see many boats to-morrow, Danny.' When Troop called his son Danny, it was a sign that the old man was pleased. 'Boys, we're too crowded,' he went on, addressing the crew as they clambered inboard. 'We'll leave 'em to bait big an' catch small.' He looked at the catch in the pen, and it was curious to see how little and level the fish ran. Save for Harvey's halibut, there was nothing over fifteen pounds on deck.

'I'm waitin' on the weather,' he added.

'Ye'll have to make it yourself, Disko, for there's no sign I can see,' said Long Jack, sweeping the clear horizon.

And yet, half an hour later, as they were dressing-down, the Bank fog dropped on them, 'between fish and fish,' as they say. It drove steadily and in wreaths, curling and smoking along the colourless water. The men stopped dressing-down without a word. Long Jack and Uncle Salters slipped the windlass brakes into their sockets, and began to heave up the anchor; the windlass jarring as the wet hempen cable strained on the barrel. Manuel and Tom Platt gave a hand at the last. The anchor came up with a sob, and the riding-sail bellied as Troop steadied her at the wheel. 'Up jib and foresail,' said he.

'Slip 'em in the smother!' shouted Long Jack, making fast the jib-sheet, while the others raised the clacking, rattling rings of the foresail; and the foreboom creaked as the 'We're Here' looked up into the wind and dived off into blank, whirling white.

'There's wind behind this fog,' said Troop.

It was all wonderful beyond words to Harvey; and the most wonderful part was that he heard no orders except an occasional grunt from Troop, ending with, 'That's good, my son!'

'Never seen anchor weighed before?' said Tom Platt, to Harvey gaping at the damp canvas of the foresail.

'No. Where are we going?'

'Fish and make berth, as you'll find out 'fore you've bin a week aboard. It's all new to you, but we never know what may come to us. Now, take me—Tom Platt—I'd never ha' thought—'

'It's better than fourteen dollars a month an' a bullet in your belly,' said Troop, from the wheel. 'Ease your jumbo a grind.'

'Dollars an' cents better,' returned the man-o'-war's man, doing something to a big jib with a wooden spar tied to it. 'But we didn't think o' that when we manned the windlass brakes on the "Miss Jim Buck,"[1] outside Beaufort Harbour, with Fort Macon heavin' hot shot at our stern, an' a livin' gale atop of all. Where was you then, Disko?'

'Jest here, or hereabouts,' Disko replied, 'earnin' my bread on the deep waters, an' dodgin' Reb privateers. Sorry I can't accommodate you with red-hot shot, Tom Platt; but I guess we'll come aout all right on wind 'fore we see Eastern Point.'

There was an incessant slapping and chatter at the bows now, varied by a solid thud and a little spout of spray that clattered down on the foc'sle. The rigging dripped clammy drops, and the men lounged along the lee of the house—all save Uncle Salters, who sat stiffly on the main-hatch nursing his stung hands.

'Guess she'd carry stays'l,' said Disko, rolling one eye at his brother.

'Guess she wouldn't to any sorter profit. What's the sense o' wastin' canvas?' the farmer-sailor replied.

The wheel twitched almost imperceptibly in Disko's hands. A few seconds later a hissing wave-top slashed diagonally across the boat, smote Uncle Salters between the shoulders, and drenched him from head to foot. He rose sputtering, and went forward only to catch another.

'See dad chase him all around the deck,' said Dan. 'Uncle Salters he thinks his quarter-share's our canvas. Dad's put his duckin' act up on him two trips runnin'. Hi! That's found him where he feeds.' Uncle Salters had taken refuge by the foremast, but a wave slapped him over the knees. Disko's face was as blank as the circle of the wheel.

[1] The 'Gemsbok,' U.S.N.?

'Guess she'd lie easier under stays'l, Salters,' said Disko, as though he had seen nothing.

'Set your old kite, then,' roared the victim through a cloud of spray; 'only don't lay it to me if anything happens. Penn, you go below right off an' git your coffee. You ought to hev more sense than to bum araound on deck this weather.'

'Now they'll swill coffee an' play checkers till the cows come home,' said Dan, as Uncle Salters hustled Penn into the fore-cabin. 'Look's to me like's if we'd all be doin' so fer a spell. There's nothin' in creation deader-limpsey-idler 'n a Banker when she ain't on fish."

'I'm glad ye spoke, Danny,' cried Long Jack, who had been casting round in search of amusement. 'I'd clean forgot we'd a passenger under that T-wharf hat. There's no idleness for thim that don't know their ropes. Pass him along, Tom Platt, an' we'll larn him.'

' 'Tain't my trick this time,' grinned Dan. 'You've got to go it alone. Dad learned me with a rope's end.'

For an hour Long Jack walked his prey up and down, teaching, as he said, 'things at the sea that ivry man must know, blind, dhrunk, or asleep.' There is not much gear to a seventy-ton schooner with a stump foremast, but Long Jack had a gift of expression. When he wished to draw Harvey's attention to the peak halyards, he dug his knuckles into the back of the boy's neck and kept him at gaze for half a minute. He emphasised the difference between fore and aft generally by rubbing Harvey's nose along a few feet of the boom, and the lead of each rope was fixed in Harvey's mind by the end of the rope itself.

The lesson would have been easier had the deck been at all free; but there appeared to be a place for everything and anything except a man. Forward lay the windlass and its tackle, with the chain and hemp cables, all very unpleasant to trip over; the foc'sle stove-pipe, and the gurry-butts by the foc'sle hatch to hold the fish-livers. Aft of these the fore-boom and booby of the main-hatch took all the space that was not needed for the pumps and dressing-pens. Then came the nests of dories lashed to ring-bolts by the quarter-deck; the house, with tubs and oddments lashed all around it; and, last, the sixty-foot main-boom in its crutch, splitting things lengthwise, to duck and dodge under every time.

Tom Platt, of course, could not keep his oar out of the business, but ranged alongside with enormous and unnecessary descriptions of sails and spars on the old 'Ohio.'

'Niver mind fwhat he says; attind to me, Innocince. Tom Platt, this bally-hoo's not the "Ohio," an' you're mixing the bhoy bad.'

'He'll be ruined for life, beginnin' on a fore-an'-after this way,' Tom

Platt pleaded. 'Give him a chance to know a few leadin' principles. Sailin's an art, Harvey, as I'd show you if I had ye in the fore-top o' the—'

'I know ut. Ye'd talk him dead an' cowld. Silince, Tom Platt! Now, after all I've said, how'd you reef the foresail, Harve? Take your time answerin'.'

'Haul that in,' said Harvey, pointing to leeward.

'Fwhat? The North Atlantuc?'

'No, the boom. Then run that rope you showed me back there—'

'That's no way,' Tom Platt burst in.

'Quiet! He's larnin', an' has not the names good yet. Go on, Harve.'

'Oh, it's the reef-pennant. I'd hook the tackle on to the reef-pennant, and then let down—'

'Lower the sail, child! Lower!' said Tom Platt, in a professional agony.

'Lower the throat and peak halyards,' Harvey went on. Those names stuck in his head.

'Lay your hand on thim,' said Long Jack.

Harvey obeyed. 'Lower till that rope-loop—on the after-leach—kris—no, it's cringle—till the cringle was down on the boom. Then I'd tie her up the way you said, and then I'd hoist up the peak and throat halyards again.'

'You've forgot to pass the tack-earing, but wid time and help ye'll larn. There's good and just reason for ivry rope aboard, or else 'twould be overboard. D'ye follow me? 'Tis dollars an' cents I'm puttin' into your pocket, ye skinny little supercargo, so that fwhin ye've filled out ye can ship from Boston to Cuba an' tell thim Long Jack larned you. Now I'll chase ye around a piece, callin' the ropes, an' you'll lay your hand on thim as I call.'

He began, and Harvey, who was feeling rather tired, walked slowly to the rope named. A rope's end licked round his ribs, and nearly knocked the breath out of him.

'When you own a boat,' said Tom Platt, with severe eyes, 'you can walk. Till then, take all orders at the run. Once more—to make sure!'

Harvey was in a glow with the exercise, and this last cut warmed him thoroughly. Now, he was a singularly smart boy, the son of a very clever man and a very sensitive woman, with a fine resolute temper that systematic spoiling had nearly turned to mulish obstinacy. He looked at the other men, and saw that even Dan did not smile. It was evidently all in the day's work, though it hurt abominably. So he swallowed the hint with a gulp and a gasp and a grin. The same smartness that led him to take such advantage of his mother made him very sure that no one on the boat, except, maybe, Penn, would stand the least nonsense. One learns a great deal from a mere tone. Long Jack called over half a dozen more ropes, and

Harvey danced over the deck like an eel at ebb tide, one eye on Tom Platt.

'Ver' good. Ver' good done,' said Manuel. 'After supper I show you a little schooner I make with all her ropes. So we shall learn.'

'Fust-class fer—a passenger,' said Dan. 'Dad he's jest allowed you'll be wuth your salt maybe 'fore you're draownded. Thet's a heap fer dad. I'll learn you more our next watch together.'

'Taller!' grunted Disko, peering through the fog as it smoked over the bows. There was nothing to be seen ten feet beyond the surging jib-boom, while alongside rolled the endless procession of solemn, pale waves whispering and lipping one to the other.

'Now I'll learn you something Long Jack can't,' shouted Tom Platt, as from a locker by the stern he produced a battered deep-sea lead hollowed at one end, smeared the hollow from a saucer full of tallow, and went forward. 'I'll learn you how to fly the Blue Pigeon. Shooo!'

Disko did something to the wheel that checked the schooner's way, while Manuel, with Harvey to help (and a proud boy was Harvey), let down the jib in a lump on the boom. The lead sang a deep droning song as Tom Platt whirled it round and round.

'Go ahead, man,' said Long Jack impatiently. 'We're not drawin' twenty-five fut off Fire Island in a fog. There's no trick to ut.'

'Don't be jealous, Galway.' The released lead plopped into the sea far ahead as the schooner surged slowly forward.

'Soundin' is a trick, though,' said Dan, 'when your dipsey lead's all the eye you're like to hev for a week. What d'you make it, dad?'

Disko's face relaxed. His skill and honour were involved in the march he had stolen on the rest of the fleet, and he had his reputation as a master artist who knew the Banks blindfold. 'Sixty, mebbe—ef I'm any judge,' he replied, with a glance at the tiny compass in the window of the house.

'Sixty,' sang out Tom Platt, hauling in great wet coils.

The schooner gathered way once more. 'Heave!' said Disko, after a quarter of an hour.

'What d'you make it?' Dan whispered, and he looked at Harvey proudly. But Harvey was too proud of his own performances to be impressed just then.

'Fifty!' said the father. 'I mistrust we're right over the nick o' Green Bank on old Sixty-Fifty.'

'Fifty!' roared Tom Platt. They could scarcely see him through the fog. 'She's bust within a yard—like the shells at Fort Macon.'

'Bait up, Harve,' said Dan, diving for a line on the reel.

The schooner seemed to be straying promiscuously through the smother, her headsail banging wildly. The men waited and looked at the boys, who began fishing.

'Heugh!' Dan's lines twitched on the scored and scarred rail. 'Now haow in thunder did dad know? Help us here, Harve. It's a big un. Poke-hooked, too.' They hauled together, and landed a goggle-eyed twenty-pound cod. He had taken the bait right into his stomach.

'Why, he's all covered with little crabs,' cried Harvey, turning him over.

'By the great hook-block, they're lousy already,' said Long Jack. 'Disko, ye kape your spare eyes under the keel.'

Splash went the anchor, and they all heaved over the lines, each man taking his own place at the bulwarks.

'Are they good to eat?' Harvey panted, as he lugged in another crab-covered cod.

'Sure. When they're lousy it's a sign they've all been herdin' together by the thousand, and when they take the bait that way they're hungry. Never mind how the bait sets. They'll bite on the bare hook.'

'Say, this is great!' Harvey cried, as the fish came in gasping and splash-ing—nearly all poke-hooked, as Dan had said. 'Why can't we always fish from the boat instead of from the dories?'

'Allus can, till we begin to dress-daown. Efter thet, the heads and offals 'ud scare the fish to Fundy. Boat fishin' ain't reckoned progressive, though, unless ye know as much as dad knows. Guess we'll run aout aour trawl to-night. Harder on the back, this, than from the dory, ain't it?'

It was rather back-breaking work, for in a dory the weight of a cod is water-borne till the last minute, and you are, so to speak, abreast of him; but the few feet of a schooner's free-board make so much extra dead-hauling, and stooping over the bulwarks cramps the stomach. But it was wild and furious sport so long as it lasted; and a big pile lay aboard when the fish ceased biting.

'Where's Penn and Uncle Salters?' Harvey asked, slapping the slime off his oilskins, and reeling up the line in careful imitation of the others.

'Git's coffee and see.'

Under the yellow glare of the lamp on the pawl-post, the foc'sle table down and opened, utterly unconscious of fish or weather, sat the two men, a checker-board between them. Uncle Salters snarling at Penn's every move.

'What's the matter naow?' said the former, as Harvey, one hand in the leather loop at the head of the ladder, hung shouting to the cook.

'Big fish and lousy—heaps and heaps,' Harvey replied, quoting Long Jack. 'How's the game?'

Little Penn's jaw dropped. ''Tweren't none o' his fault,' snapped Uncle Salters. 'Penn's deef.'

'Checkers, weren't it?' said Dan, as Harvey staggered aft with the steaming coffee in a tin pail. 'That lets us out o' cleanin' up to-night. Dad's a jest man. They'll have to do it.'

'An' two young fellers I know'll bait up a tub or so o' trawl, while they're cleanin',' said Disko, lashing the wheel to his taste.

'Um! Guess I'd ruther clean up, dad.'

'Don't doubt it. Ye wun't, though. Dress-daown! Dress-daown! Penn'll pitch while you two bait up.'

'Why in thunder didn't them blame boys tell us you'd struck on?' said Uncle Salters, shuffling to his place at the table. 'This knife's gum-blunt, Dan.'

'Ef stickin' out cable don't wake ye, guess you'd better hire a boy o' your own,' said Dan, muddling about in the dusk over the tubs full of trawl-line lashed to windward of the house. 'Oh, Harve, don't ye want to slip down an' git's bait?'

'Bait ez we are,' said Disko. 'I mistrust shag-fishin' will pay better, ez things go.'

That meant the boys would bait with selected offal of the cod as the fish were cleaned—an improvement on paddling bare-handed in the little bait-barrels below. The tubs were full of neatly coiled line, carrying a big hook each few feet; and the testing and baiting of every single hook, with the stowage of the baited line so that it should run clear when shot from the dory, was a scientific business. Dan managed it in the dark, without looking, while Harvey caught his fingers on the barbs and bewailed his fate. But the hooks flew through Dan's fingers like tatting of an old maid's lap. 'I helped bait up trawl ashore 'fore I could well walk,' he said. 'But it's a putterin' job all the same. Oh, dad!' This shouted towards the hatch, where Disko and Tom Platt were salting. 'How many skates you reckon we'll need?'

''Baout three. Hurry!'

'There's three-hundred fathom to each tub,' Dan explained; 'more'n enough to lay out to-night. Ouch! Slipped up there, I did.' He stuck his finger in his mouth. 'I tell you, Harve, there ain't money in Gloucester 'ud hire me to ship on a reg'lar trawler. It may be progressive, but, barrin' that, it's the putterin'est, slim-jammest business top o' earth.'

'I don't know what this is, if 'tisn't regular trawling,' said Harvey sulkily. 'My fingers are all cut to frazzles.'

'Pshaw! This is jest one o' dad's blame experiments. He don't trawl 'less there's mighty good reason fer it. Dad knows. Thet's why he's baitin' ez he is. We'll hev her saggin' full when we take her up er we won't see a fin.'

Penn and Uncle Salters cleaned up as Disko had ordained, but the boys profited little. No sooner were the tubs furnished than Tom Platt and Long Jack, who had been exploring the inside of a dory with a lantern, snatched them away, loaded up the tubs and some small painted trawl-buoys, and hove the boat overboard into what Harvey regarded as an exceedingly rough sea. 'They'll be drowned! Why, the dory's loaded like a freight-car,' he cried.

'We'll be back,' said Long Jack, 'an' in case you'll not be lookin' for us we'll lay into you both if the trawl's snarled.'

The dory surged up on the crest of a wave, and just when it seemed impossible that she could avoid smashing against the schooner's side, slid over the ridge, and was swallowed up in the damp dusk.

'Take a-hold here, an' keep ringin' steady,' said Dan, passing Harvey the lanyard of a bell that hung just behind the windlass.

Harvey rang lustily, for he felt two lives depended on him. But Disko in the cabin, scrawling in the log-book, did not look like a murderer, and when he went to supper he even smiled drily at the anxious Harvey.

'This ain't no weather,' said Dan. 'Why, you an' me could set thet trawl! They've only gone out jest far 'nough so's not to foul our cable. They don't need no bell, reelly.'

'Clang! cling! clang!' Harvey kept it up, varied with occasional rub-a-dubs, for another half-hour. There was a bellow and a bump alongside. Manuel and Dan raced to the hooks of the dory-tackle; Long Jack and Tom Platt arrived on deck together, it seemed, one-half the North Atlantic at their backs, and the dory followed them in the air, landing with a clatter.

'Nary snarl,' said Tom Platt as he dripped. 'Danny, you'll do yet.'

'The pleasure av your comp'ny to the banquit,' said Long Jack, squelching the water from his boots as he capered like an elephant and stuck an oilskinned arm into Harvey's face. 'We do be condescending to honour the second half wid our presence.' And off they all four rolled to supper, where Harvey stuffed himself to the brim on fish-chowder and fried pies, and fell fast asleep just as Manuel produced from a locker a lovely two-foot model of the 'Lucy Holmes,' his first boat, and was going to show Harvey the ropes. Harvey never even twiddled his fingers as Penn pushed him into his bunk.

'It must be a sad thing—a very sad thing,' said Penn, watching the boy's face, 'for his mother and his father, who think he is dead. To lose a child—to lose a man-child!'

'Git out o' this, Penn,' said Dan. 'Go aft and finish your game with Uncle Salters. Tell dad I'll stand Harve's watch ef he don't keer. He's played aout.'

'Ver' good boy,' said Manuel, slipping out of his boots and disappearing into the black shadows of the lower bunk. 'Expec' he make good man, Danny. I no see he is any so mad as your parpa he says. Eh, wha-at?'

Dan chuckled, but the chuckle ended in a snore.

It was thick weather outside, with a rising wind, and the elder men stretched their watches. The hours struck clear in the cabin; the nosing bows slapped and scuffled with the seas; the foc'sle stove-pipe hissed and sputtered as the spray caught it; and the boys slept on, while Disko, Long Jack, Tom Platt, and Uncle Salters, each in turn, stumped aft to look at the wheel, forward to see that the anchor held, or to veer out a little more cable against chafing, with a glance at the dim anchor-light between each round.

Chapter 4

HARVEY WAKED to find the 'first half' at breakfast, the foc'sle door drawn to a crack, and every square inch of the schooner singing its own tune. The black bulk of the cook balanced behind the tiny galley over the glare of the stove, and the pots and pans in the pierced wooden board before it jarred and racketed to each plunge. Up and up the foc'sle climbed, yearning and surging and quivering, and then, with a clear, sickle-like swoop, came down into the seas. He could hear the flaring bows cut and squelch, and there was a pause ere the divided waters came down on the deck above, like a volley of buckshot. Followed the woolly sound of the cable in the hawse-hole; a grunt and squeal of the windlass; a yaw, a punt, and a kick, and the 'We're Here' gathered herself together to repeat the motions.

'Now, ashore,' he heard Long Jack saying; 'ye've chores, an' ye must do thim in any weather. Here we're well clear of the fleet, an' we've no chores—an' that's a blessin'. Good-night, all.' He passed like a big snake from the table to his bunk, and began to smoke. Tom Platt followed his example; Uncle Salters, with Penn, fought his way up the ladder to stand his watch, and the cook set for the 'second half.'

It came out of its bunks as the others had entered theirs, with a shake and a yawn. It ate till it could eat no more; and then Manuel filled his pipe with some terrible tobacco, crotched himself between the pawl-post and a forward bunk, cocked his feet up on the table, and smiled tender and indolent smiles at the smoke. Dan lay at length in his bunk, wrestling with a gaudy, gilt-stopped accordion, whose tunes went up and down with the pitching of the 'We're Here.' The cook, his shoulders against the locker, where he kept the fried pies (Dan was fond of fried pies), peeled potatoes, with one eye on the stove in event of too much water finding its way down the pipe; and the general smell and smother were past all description.

Harvey considered affairs, wondered that he was not deathly sick, and crawled into his bunk again, as the softest and safest place, while Dan struck up 'I don't want to play in your yard,' as accurately as the wild jerks allowed.

'How long is this for?' Harvey asked of Manuel.

'Till she get a little quiet, and we can row to trawl. Perhaps to-night. Perhaps two days more. You do not like? Eh, wha-at?'

'I should have been crazy sick a week ago, but it doesn't seem to upset me now—much.'

'That is because we make you fisherman, these days. If I was you, when I come to Gloucester, I would give two, three big candles for my good luck.'

'Give who?'

'To be sure—the Virgin of our Church on the Hill. She is very good to fishermen all the time. That is why so few of us Portugee men ever are drowned.'

'You're a Roman Catholic, then?'

'I am a Madeira man. I am not a Porto Pico boy. Shall I be Baptist, then? Eh, wha-at? I always give candles—two, three more when I come to Gloucester. The good Virgin she never forgets me, Manuel.'

'I don't sense it that way,' Tom Platt put in from his bunk; his scarred face lit up by the glare of a match as he sucked at his pipe. 'It stands to reason the sea's the sea; and you'll git jist about what's goin', candles or kerosene, fer that matter.'

' 'Tis a mighty good thing,' said Long Jack, 'to have a frind at coort, though. I'm o' Manuel's way o' thinkin'. About tin years back I was crew to a Sou' Boston market-boat. We was off Minot's Ledge wid a northeaster, butt first, atop of us, thicker'n burgoo. The ould man was dhrunk, his chin waggin' on the tiller, an' I sez to myself, "If iver I stick my boat-huk into T-wharf again, I'll show the saints fwhat manner o' craft they saved me out av." Now, I'm here, as ye can well see, an' the model of the dhirty ould "Kathleen" that took me a month to make, I gave ut to the priest, an' he hung ut up forninst the altar. There's more sense in givin' a model that's by way o' bein' a work av art than any candle. Ye can buy candles at store, but a model shows the good saints ye've tuk trouble an' are grateful.'

'D'you believe that, Irish?' said Tom Platt, turning on his elbow.

'Would I do ut if I did not, Ohio?'

'Wa-al, Enoch Fuller he made a model o' the old "Ohio," and she's to Salem museum now. Mighty pretty model, too, but I guess Enoch he never done it fer no sacrifice; an' the way I take it is—'

There were the makings of an hour-long discussion of the kind that fishermen love, where the talk runs in shouting circles, and no one proves anything at the end, had not Dan struck up this cheerful rhyme:

> 'Up jumped the mackerel with his striped back.
> Reef in the mainsail and haul on the tack;
> For it's windy weather—'

Here Long Jack joined in.

> 'And it's blowy weather;
> When the winds begin to blow, pipe all hands together!'

Dan went on, with a cautious look at Tom Platt, holding the accordion low in the bunk:

> 'Up jumped the cod with his chuckle-head,
> Went to the main-chains to heave at the lead,
> For it's windy weather,' etc.

Tom Platt seemed to be hunting for something. Dan crouched lower, but sang louder:

> 'Up jumped the flounder that swims to the ground.
> Chuckle-head! Chuckle-head! Mind where ye sound!'

Tom Platt's huge rubber boot whirled across the foc'sle and caught Dan's uplifted arm. There was war between the man and the boy ever since Dan had discovered that the mere whistling of that tune would make him angry as he heaved the lead.

'Thought I'd fetch yer,' said Dan, returning the gift with precision. 'Ef you don't like my music, git out your fiddle. I ain't goin' to lie here all day an' listen to you an' Long Jack arguin' 'baout candles. Fiddle, Tom Platt; or I'll learn Harve here the tune!'

Tom Platt leaned down to a locker and brought up an old white fiddle. Manuel's eye glistened, and from somewhere behind the pawl-post he drew out a tiny, guitar-like thing with wire strings, which he called a machette.

' 'Tis a concert,' said Long Jack, beaming through the smoke. 'A reg'lar Boston concert.'

There was a burst of spray as the hatch opened, and Disko, in yellow oilskins, descended.

'Ye're just in time, Disko. Fwhat's she doin' outside?'

'Jest this!' He dropped on to the lockers with the push and heave of the 'We're Here.'

'We're singin' to kape our breakfasts down. Ye'll lead, av course, Disko,' said Long Jack.

'Guess there ain't more'n 'baout two old songs I know, an' ye've heard them both.'

His excuses were cut short by Tom Platt launching into a most dolorous tune, like unto the moaning of winds and the creaking of masts. With his eyes fixed on the beams above, Disko began this ancient, ancient ditty, Tom Platt flourishing all round him to make the tune and words fit a little:

'There is a crack packet—crack packet o' fame,
She hails from Noo York, an' the "Dreadnought's" her name,
You may talk o' your fliers—Swallow-tail and Black Ball—
But the "Dreadnought's" the packet that can beat them all.

'Now the "Dreadnought" she lies in the River Mersey,
Because of the tug-boat to take her to sea;
But when she's off soundings you shortly will know:

(Chorus)
She's the Liverpool packet—O Lord, let her go.

'Now the "Dreadnought" she's howlin' 'crost the Banks o' Newfoundland,
Where the water's all shallow and the bottom's all sand.
Sez all the little fishes that swim to and fro:

(Chorus)
"She's the Liverpool packet—O Lord, let her go!" '

There were scores of verses, for he worked the 'Dreadnought' every mile of the way between Liverpool and New York as conscientiously as though he were on her deck, and the accordion pumped and the fiddle squeaked beside him. Tom Platt followed with something about 'the rough and tough M'Ginn, who would pilot the vessel in.' Then they called on Harvey, who felt very flattered, to contribute to the entertainment; but all that he could remember were some pieces of 'Skipper Ireson's Ride' that he had been taught at the camp-school in the Adirondacks. It seemed that they might be appropriate to the time and place, but he had no more than mentioned the title, when Disko brought down one foot with a bang, and cried, 'Don't go on, young feller! That's a mistaken jedgment—one o' the worst kind, too, becaze it's catchin' to the ear.'

'I orter ha' warned you,' said Dan. 'Thet allus fetches dad.'

'What's wrong?' said Harvey, surprised and a little angry.

'All you're goin' to say,' said Disko. 'All dead wrong from start to finish, an' Whittier he's to blame. I have no special call to right any Marblehead man, but 'tweren't no fault o' Ireson's. My father he told me the tale time an' again, an' this is the way 'twuz.'

'For the wan hundredth time,' put in Long Jack under his breath.

'Ben Ireson he was skipper o' the "Betty," young feller, comin' home from the Banks—that was before the war of 1812, but jestice is jestice at all times. They f'und the "Active" o' Portland, an' Gibbons o' that town he was her skipper; they f'und her leakin' off Cape Cod light. There was a terr'ble gale on, an' they was gettin' the "Betty" home's fast as they could craowd her. Well, Ireson he said there warn't any sense to reskin' a boat in that sea; the men they wouldn't hev it; and he laid it before them to stay by the "Active" till the sea run daown a piece. They wouldn't hev that either, hangin' araound the Cape in any sech weather, leak or no leak. They jest up stays'l an' quit, nat'rally takin' Ireson with 'em. Folks to Marblehead was mad at him not runnin' the risk, and becaez nex' day when the sea was ca'am (they never stopped to think o' that) some of the "Active's" folk was took off by a Truro man. They come into Marblehead with their own tale to tell, sayin' how Ireson had shamed his town, an' so forth an' so on; an' Ireson's men they was scared seein' public feelin' agin' 'em, an' they went back on Ireson, an' swore he was respons'ble for the hull act. 'Tweren't the women neither that tarred and feathered him—Marblehead women don't act that way—'twas a passel o' men an' boys, an' they carted him araound town in an old dory till the bottom fell aout an' Ireson he told 'em they'd be sorry for it some day. Well, the facts come aout later, same's they usually do, too late to be any ways useful to an honest man; an' Whittier he come along an' picked up the slack cend of a lyin' tale, an' tarred and feathered Ben Ireson all over onct more after he was dead. 'Twas the only time Whittier ever slipped up, an' 'tweren't fair. I whaled Dan good when he brought that piece back from school. You don't know no better, o' course; but I've give you the facts, hereafter an' evermore to be remembered. Ben Ireson weren't no sech kind o' man as Whittier makes aout; my father he knew him well, before an' after that business, an' you beware o' hasty jedgments, young feller. Next!'

Harvey had never heard Disko talk so long, and collapsed with burning cheeks; but, as Dan said promptly, a boy could only learn what he was taught at school, and life was too short to keep track of every lie along the coast.

Then Manuel touched the jangling, jarring little machette to a queer tune, and sang something in Portuguese about 'Nina, innocente!' ending with a full-handed sweep that brought the song up with a jerk. Then Disko obliged with his second song, to an old-fashioned creaky tune, and all joined in the chorus. This one stanza:

> 'Now Aprile is over and melted the snow,
> And outer Noo Bedford we shortly must tow;
> Yes, out o' Noo Bedford we shortly must clear,
> We're the whalers that never see wheat in the ear.'

Here the fiddle went very softly for a while by itself, and then:

> 'Wheat-in-the-ear, my true-love's posy blowin';
> Wheat-in-the-ear, we're goin' off to sea;
> Wheat-in-the-ear, I left you fit for sowin';
> When I come back a loaf o' bread you'll be!'

That made Harvey almost weep, though he could not tell why. But it was much worse when the cook dropped the potatoes and held out his hands for the fiddle. Still leaning against the locker door, he struck into a tune that was like something very bad but sure to happen whatever you did. After a little he sang, in an unknown tongue, his big chin down on the fiddletail, his white eyeballs glaring in the lamplight. Harvey swung out of his bunk to hear better; and amid the straining of the timbers and the wash of the waters the tune crooned and moaned on, like lee surf in a blind fog, till it ended with a wail.

'Jiminy Christmas! Thet gives me the blue creevles,' said Dan. 'What in thunder is it?'

'The song of Fin M'Coul,' said the cook, 'when he wass going to Norway.' His English was not thick, but all clear cut, as though it came from a gramophone.

'Faith, I've been to Norway, but I didn't make that unwholesim noise. 'Tis like some of the old songs, though,' said Long Jack, sighing.

'Don't let's hev another 'thout somethin' between,' said Dan; and the accordion struck up a rattling, catchy tune that ended:

> 'It's six an' twenty Sundays sence las' we saw the land,
>> With fifteen hunder quintal,
>> An' fifteen hunder quintal,
>> 'Teen hunder toppin' quintal,
>> 'Twixt old 'Queereau an' 'Grand!'

'Hold on!' roared Tom Platt. 'D'ye want to nail the trip, Dan? That's Jonah sure, 'less you sing it after all our salt's wet.'

'No, 'tain't. Is it, dad? Not unless you sing the very las' verse. You can't learn me anything on Jonahs!'

'What's that?' said Harvey. 'What's a Jonah?'

'A Jonah's anything that spoils the luck. Sometimes it's a man—sometimes it's a boy—or a bucket. I've known a splittin'-knife Jonah two trips till we was on to her,' said Tom Platt. 'There's all sorts o' Jonahs. Jim Bourke was one till he was drowned on Georges. I'd never ship with Jim Bourke, not if I was starvin'. There wuz a green dory on the "Ezra Flood." Thet was a Jonah too, the worst sort o' Jonah. Drowned four men she did, an' used to shine fiery o' nights, in the nest.'

'And you believe that?' said Harvey, remembering what Tom Platt had said about candles and models. 'Haven't we all got to take what's served?'

A mutter of dissent ran round the bunks. 'Outboard, yes; inboard, things can happen,' said Disko. 'Don't you go makin' a mock of Jonahs, young feller.'

'Well, Harve ain't no Jonah. Day after we catched him,' Dan cut in, 'we had a toppin' good catch.'

The cook threw up his head and laughed suddenly—a queer, thin laugh. He was a most disconcerting nigger.

'Murder!' said Long Jack. 'Don't do that again, doctor. We ain't used to ut.'

'What's wrong?' said Dan. 'Ain't he our mascot, an' didn't they strike on good after we'd struck him?'

'Oh yess,' said the cook. 'I know that, but the catch iss not finish yet.'

'He ain't goin' to do us any harm,' said Dan hotly. 'Where are ye hintin' an' edgin' to? He's all right.'

'No harm. No. But one day he will be your master, Danny.'

'That's all?' said Dan placidly. 'He wun't—not by a jugful.'

'Master!' said the cook, pointing to Harvey. 'Man!' and he pointed to Dan.

'That's news. Haow soon?' said Dan with a laugh.

'In some years, and I shall see it. Master and man—man and master.'

'How in thunder d'ye work that out?' said Tom Platt.

'In my head, where I can see.'

'Haow?' This from all the others at once.

'I do not know, but so it will be.' He dropped his head and went on peeling the potatoes, and not another word could they get out of him.

'Well,' said Dan, 'a heap o' things'll hev to come abaout 'fore Harve's any master o' mine; but I'm glad the doctor ain't choosen to mark him for a Jonah. Now, I mistrust Uncle Salters fer the Jonerest Jonah in the fleet regardin' his own special luck. Dunno ef it's spreadin' same's smallpox. He ought to be on the "Carrie Pitman." That boat's her own Jonah, sure—crews an' gear make no differ to her driftin'. Jiminy Christmas! She'll etch loose in a flat ca'am.'

'We're well clear o' the fleet, anyway,' said Disko. ' "Carrie Pitman" an' all.' There was a rapping on the deck.

'Uncle Salters has catched his luck,' said Dan, as his father departed.

'It's blowed clear,' Disko cried, and all the foc'sle tumbled up for a bit of fresh air. The fog had gone, but a sullen sea ran in great rollers behind it. The 'We're Here' slid, as it were, into long, sunk avenues and ditches which felt quite sheltered and homelike if they would only stay still; but they changed without rest or mercy, and flung up the schooner to crown one peak of a thousand gray hills, while the wind hooted through her rigging as she zigzagged down the slopes. Far away a sea would burst in a sheet of foam, and the others would follow suit as at a signal, till Harvey's eyes swam with the vision of interlacing whites and grays. Four or five Mother Carey's chickens stormed round in circles, shrieking as they swept past the bows. A rain-squall or two strayed aimlessly over the hopeless waste, ran down wind and back again, and melted away.

'Seems to me I saw somethin' flicker jest naow over yonder,' said Uncle Salters, pointing to the north-east.

'Can't be any of the fleet,' said Disko, peering under his eyebrows, a hand on the foc'sle gangway as the solid bows hatcheted into the troughs. 'Sea's oilin' over dretful fast. Danny, don't you want to skip up a piece an' see how aour trawl-buoy lays?'

Danny, in his big boots, trotted rather than climbed up the main rigging (this consumed Harvey with envy), hitched himself around the reeling cross-trees, and let his eye rove till it caught the tiny black buoy-flag on the shoulder of a mile-away swell.

'She's all right,' he hailed. 'Sail O! Dead to the no'th'ard, comin' down like smoke! Schooner she be, too.'

They waited yet another half-hour, the sky clearing in patches, with a flicker of sickly sun from time to time, that made patches of olive-green water. Then a stump-foremast lifted, ducked, and disappeared, to be followed on the next wave by a high stern with old-fashioned wooden snail's-horn davits. The sails were red tanned.

'Frenchman!' shouted Dan. 'No, 'tain't neither. Da-ad!'

'That's no French,' said Disko. 'Salters, your blame luck holds tighter'n a screw in a keg-head.'

'I've eyes. It's Uncle Abishai.'

'You can't nowise tell fer sure.'

'The head-king of all Jonahs,' groaned Tom Platt. 'Oh, Salters, Salters, why wasn't you abed an' asleep?'

'How could I tell?' said Poor Salters, as the schooner swung up.

She might have been the very 'Flying Dutchman,' so foul, draggled, and unkempt was every rope and stick aboard. Her old-style quarter-deck was some four or five feet high, and her rigging flew knotted and tangled like weed at a wharf-end. She was running before the wind—yawing frightfully—her staysail let down to act as a sort of extra foresail,—'scandalised,' they call it,—and her foreboom guyed out over the side. Her bowsprit cocked up like an old-fashioned frigate's; her jib-boom had been fished and spliced and nailed and clamped beyond further repair; and as she hove herself forward, and sat down on her broad tail, she looked for all the world like a blouzy, frouzy, bad old woman sneering at a decent girl.

'That's Abishai,' said Salters. 'Full o' gin an' Judique men, an' the judgments o' Providence layin' fer him an' never takin' good holt. He's run in to bait, Miquelon way.'

'He'll run her under,' said Long Jack. 'That's no rig fer this weather.'

'Not he, 'r he'd 'a' done it long ago,' Disko replied. 'Looks 's if he cal'lated to run us under. Ain't she daown by the head more'n natural, Tom Platt?'

'Ef it's his style o' loadin' her she ain't safe,' said the sailor slowly. 'Ef she's spewed her oakum, he'd better git to his pumps mighty quick.'

The creature threshed up, wore round with a clatter and rattle, and lay head to wind within earshot.

A gray-beard wagged over the bulwark, and a thick voice yelled something Harvey could not understand. But Disko's face darkened. 'He'd resk every stick he hez to carry bad news. Says we're in fer a shift o' wind. He's in fer worse. Abishai! Abishai!' He waved his arm up and down with the gesture of a man at the pumps, and pointed forward. The crew mocked him and laughed.

'Jounce ye, an' strip ye, an' trip ye!' yelled Uncle Abishai. 'A livin' gale —a livin' gale. Yah! Cast up fer your last trip, all you Gloucester haddocks. You won't see Gloucester no more, no more!'

'Crazy full—as usual,' said Tom Platt. 'Wish he hadn't spied us, though.'

She drifted out of hearing while the gray-head yelled something about a dance at the Bay of Bulls and a dead man in the foc'sle. Harvey shuddered. He had seen the slovenly tilted decks and the savage-eyed crew.

'An' that's a fine little floatin' hell fer her draught,' said Long Jack. 'I wondher what mischief he's been at ashore.'

'He's a trawler,' Dan explained to Harvey, 'an' he runs in fer bait all along the coast. Oh, no, not home, he don't go. He deals along the south an' east shore up yonder.' He nodded in the direction of the pitiless Newfoundland beaches. 'Dad won't never take me ashore there. They're a mighty tough crowd—an' Abishai's the toughest. You saw his boat? Well, she's nigh seventy year old, they say; the last o' the old Marblehead heeltappers. They don't make them quarter-decks any more. Abishai don't use Marblehead, though. He ain't wanted there. He jes' drif's araound, in debt, trawlin' an' cussin' like you've heard. Bin a Jonah fer years an' years, he hez. Gits liquor from the Feecamp boats fer makin' spells an' selling winds an' such truck. Crazy, I guess.'

' 'Twon't be any use underrunnin' the trawl to-night,' said Tom Platt, with quiet despair. 'He come alongside special to cuss us. I'd give my wage an' share to see him at the gangway o' the old "Ohio" 'fore we quit floggin'. Jest abaout six dozen, an' Sam Mocatta layin' 'em on criss-cross!'

The dishevelled 'heel-tapper' danced drunkenly down wind, and all eyes followed her. Suddenly the cook cried in his gramophone voice: 'It wass his own death made him speak so! He iss fey—fey, I tell you! Look!' She sailed into a patch of watery sunshine three or four miles distant. The patch dulled and faded out, and even as the light passed so did the schooner. She dropped into a hallow and—was not.

'Run under, by the Great Hook-Block!' shouted Disko, jumping aft. 'Drunk or sober, we've got to help 'em. Heave short and break her out! Smart!'

Harvey was thrown on the deck by the shock that followed the setting of the jib and foresail, for they hove short on the cable, and to save time, jerked the anchor bodily from the bottom, heaving in as they moved away. This is a bit of brute force seldom resorted to except in matters of life and death, and the little 'We're Here' complained like a human. They ran down to where Abishai's craft had vanished; found two or three trawl-tubs, a gin-bottle, and a stove-in dory, but nothing more. 'Let 'em go,' said Disko, though no one had hinted at picking them up. 'I wouldn't hev a match that belonged to Abishai aboard. Guess she run clear under. Must ha' been spewin' her oakum fer a week, an' they never thought to pump her. That's one more boat gone along o' leavin' port all hands drunk.'

'Glory be!' said Long Jack. 'We'd ha' been obliged to help 'em if they was top o' water.'

'Thinkin' o' that myself,' said Tom Platt.

'Fey! fey!' said the cook, rolling his eyes. 'He hass taken his own luck with him.'

'Ver' good thing, I think, to tell the fleet when we see. Eh, wha-at?'

said Manuel. 'If you runna that way before the wind, and she works open her seams—' He threw out his hands with an indescribable gesture, while Penn sat down on the house and sobbed at the sheer horror and pity of it all. Harvey could not realise that he had seen death on the open waters, but he felt very sick.

Then Dan went up the cross-trees, and Disko steered them back to within sight of their own trawl-buoys just before the fog blanketed the sea once again.

'We go mighty quick hereabouts when we do go,' was all he said to Harvey. 'You think on that fer a spell, young feller. That was liquor.'

After dinner it was calm enough to fish from the decks—Penn and Uncle Salters was very zealous this time—and the catch was large and large fish.

'Abishai has shorely took his luck with him,' said Salters. 'The wind hain't backed ner riz ner nothin'. How abaout the trawl? I despise superstition, anyway.'

Tom Platt insisted that they had much better haul the thing and make a new berth. But the cook said: 'The luck iss in two pieces. You will find it so when you look. I know.' This so tickled Long Jack that he overbore Tom Platt, and the two went out together.

Underrunning a trawl means pulling it in on one side of the dory, picking off the fish, rebaiting the hooks, and passing them back to the sea again—something like pinning and unpinning linen on a wash-line. It is a lengthy business and rather dangerous, for the long, sagging line may twitch a boat under in a flash. But when they heard: 'And naow to thee, O Capting' booming out of the fog, the crew of the 'We're Here' took heart. The dory swirled alongside well loaded; Tom Platt yelling for Manuel to act as relief-boat.

'The luck's cut square in two pieces,' said Long Jack, forking in the fish, while Harvey stood open-mouthed at the skill with which the plunging dory was saved from destruction. 'One half was jest punkins. Tom Platt wanted to haul her an' ha' done wid ut; but I said, "I'll back the doctor that has the second sight," an' the other half come up sagging full o' big uns. Hurry, Man'nle, an' bring 's a tub o' bait. There's luck afloat to-night.'

The fish bit at the newly-baited hooks from which their brethren had just been taken, and Tom Platt and Long Jack moved methodically up and down the length of the trawl, the boat's nose surging under the wet line of hooks, stripping the sea-cucumbers that they called pumpkins, slatting off the fresh-caught cod against the gunwale, rebaiting, and loading Manuel's dory till dusk.

'I'll take no risks,' said Disko then—'not with him floatin' around so near.

Abishai won't sink fer a week. Heave in the dories an' we'll dress-daown after supper.'

That was a mighty dressing-down, attended by three or four blowing grampuses. It lasted till nine o'clock, and Disko was thrice heard to chuckle as Harvey pitched the split fish into the hold.

'Say, you're haulin' ahead dretful fast,' said Dan, when they ground the knives after the men had turned in. 'There's somethin' of a sea to-night, an' I hain't heard you make no remarks on it.'

'Too busy,' Harvey replied, testing a blade's edge. 'Come to think of it, she is a high-kicker.'

The little schooner was gambolling all around her anchor among the silver-tipped waves. Backing with a start of affected surprise at the sight of the strained cable, she pounced on it like a kitten, while the spray of her descent burst through the hawse-holes with the report of a gun. Shaking her head, she would say: 'Well, I'm sorry I can't stay any longer with you. I'm going North,' and would sidle off, halting suddenly with a dramatic rattle of her rigging. 'As I was just going to observe,' she would begin, as gravely as a drunken man addressing a lamp-post. The rest of the sentence (she acted her words in dumb-show, of course) was lost in a fit of the fidgets, when she behaved like a puppy chewing a string, a clumsy woman in a side-saddle, a hen with her head cut off, or a cow stung by a hornet, exactly as the whims of the sea took her.

'See her sayin' her piece. She's Patrick Henry naow,' said Dan.

She swung sideways on a roller, and gesticulated with her jib-boom from port to starboard.

'But—ez—fer—me, give me liberty—er give me—death!'

Wop! She sat down in the moon-path on the water, curtseying with a flourish of pride impressive enough had not the wheel-gear sniggered mockingly in its box.

Harvey laughed aloud. 'Why, it's just as if she was alive,' he said.

'She's as stiddy as a haouse an' as dry as a herrin',' said Dan enthusiastically, as he slung across the deck in a batter of spray. 'Fends 'em off an' fends 'em off, an' "Don't ye come anigh me," she sez. Look at her—jest look at her! Sakes! You should see one o' them toothpicks histin' up her anchor on her spike outer fifteen-fathom water.'

'What's a toothpick, Dan?'

'Them new haddockers an' herrin' boats. Fine's a yacht forward, with yacht sterns to 'em an' a spike bowsprits, an' a haouse that 'ud take all our hold. I've heard that Burgess himself he made the models fer three or four of 'em. Dad's sot agin 'em on account o' their pitchin' an' joltin', but there's heaps o' money in 'em. Dad can find fish, but he ain't no ways progressive—he don't go with the march o' the times. They're chock-full o' labour-savin' jigs an' sech all. Ever seed the "Elector" o' Gloucester? She's a daisy, ef she is a toothpick.'

'What do they cost, Dan?'

'Hills o' dollars. Fifteen thousand, p'haps; more, mebbe. There's gold-leaf an' everything you kin think of.' Then to himself, half under his breath, 'Guess I'd call her "Hattie S.", too.'

Chapter 5

THAT WAS the first of many talks with Dan, who told Harvey why he would transfer his dory's name to the imaginary Burgess-modelled had-docker. Harvey heard a good deal about the real Hattie at Gloucester; saw a lock of her hair—which Dan, finding fair words of no avail, had 'hooked' as she sat in front of him at school that winter—and a photograph. Hattie was about fourteen years old, with an awful contempt for boys, and had been trampling on Dan's heart through the winter. All this was revealed under oath of solemn secrecy on moonlit decks, in the dead dark, or in choking fog; the whining wheel behind them, the climbing deck in front, and without, the unresting, clamorous sea. Once, of course, as the boys came to know each other, there was a fight, which raged from bow to stern till Penn came up and separated them, but promised not to tell Disko, who thought fighting on watch rather worse than sleeping. Harvey was no match for Dan physically, but it says a great deal for his new training that he took his defeat and did not try to get even with his conqueror by under-hand methods.

That was after he had been cured of a string of boils between his elbows and wrists, where the wet jersey and oilskins cut into the flesh. The salt water stung them unpleasantly, but when they were ripe, Dan treated them with Disko's razor, and assured Harvey that now he was a 'blooded Banker'; the affliction of gurry-sores being the mark of the caste that claimed him.

Since he was a boy and very busy, he did not bother his head with too much thinking. He was exceedingly sorry for his mother, and often longed to see her and above all to tell her of this wonderful new life, and how brilliantly he was acquitting himself in it. Otherwise he preferred not to wonder too much how she was bearing the shock of his supposed death. But one day, as he stood on the foc'sle ladder, guying the cook, who had accused him and Dan for hooking fried pies, it occurred to him that this was a vast improvement on being snubbed by strangers in the smoking-room of a hired liner.

He was a recognized part of the scheme of things on the 'We're Here'; had his place at the table and among the bunks; and could hold his own in the long talks on stormy days, when the others were always ready to listen to what they called his 'fairy tales' of his life ashore. It did not take him more than two days and a quarter to feel that if he spoke of his own life—it seemed very far away—no one except Dan (and even Dan's belief was sorely tried) credited him. So he invented a friend, a boy he had heard of, who drove a miniature four-pony drag in Toledo, Ohio, and ordered five suits of clothes at a time, and led things called 'germans' at parties where the oldest girl was not quite fifteen, but all the presents were of solid silver. Salters protested that this kind of yarn was desperately wicked, if not indeed positively blasphemous, but he listened as greedily as the others; and their criticisms at the end gave Harvey entirely new notions on 'germans,' clothes, cigarettes with gold-leaf tips, rings, watches, scent, small dinner-parties, champagne, card-playing, and hotel accommodation. Little by little he changed his tone when speaking of his 'friend,' whom Long Jack had christened 'the Crazy Kid,' 'the Gilt-edged Baby,' 'the Suckin' Vanderpoop,' and other pet names; and with his sea-booted feet cocked up on the table would even invent histories about silk pyjamas and specially imported neckwear, to the 'friend's' discredit. Harvey was a very adaptable person, with a keen eye and ear for every face and tone about him.

Before long he knew where Disko kept the old green-crusted quadrant that they called the 'hog-yoke'—under the bed-bag in his bunk. When he took the sun, and with the help of 'The Old Farmer's' almanac, found the latitude, Harvey would jump down into the cabin and scratch the reckoning and date with a nail on the rust of the stove-pipe. Now, the chief engineer of the liner could have done no more, and no engineer of thirty years' service could have assumed one half of the ancient-mariner air with which Harvey, first careful to spit over the side, made public the schooner's position for that day, and then, and not till then, relieved Disko of the quadrant. There is an etiquette in all these things.

The said 'hog-yoke,' an Eldridge chart, the farming almanac, Blunt's 'Coast Pilot,' and Bowditch's 'Navigator,' were all the weapons Disko needed to guide him, except the deep-sea lead that was his spare eye. Harvey nearly slew Penn with it when Tom Platt taught him first how to 'fly the blue pigeon'; and, though his strength was not equal to continuous sounding in any sort of a sea, for calm weather with a seven-pound lead on shoal water Disko used him freely. As Dan said: ' 'Tain't soundin's dad wants. It's samples. Grease her up good, Harve.' Harvey would tallow the cup at the end, and carefully bring the sand, shell, sludge, or whatever it might be, to Disko, who fingered and smelt it and gave judgment. As has been said, when Disko thought of cod he thought as a cod; and by some long-tested mixture of instinct and experience, moved the 'We're Here' from berth to berth, always with the fish, as a blindfolded chess-player moves on the unseen board.

But Disko's board was the Grand Bank—a triangle two hundred and fifty miles on each side—a waste of wallowing sea, cloaked with dank fog, vexed with gales, harried with drifting ice, scored by the tracks of the reckless liners, and dotted with the sails of the fishing-fleet.

For days they worked in fog—Harvey at the bell—till, grown familiar with the thick airs, he went out with Tom Platt, his heart rather in his mouth. But the fog would not lift, and the fish were biting, and no one can stay helplessly afraid for six hours at a time. Harvey devoted himself to his lines and the gaff or gob-stick as Tom Platt called for them; and they rowed back to the schooner guided by the bell and Tom's instinct; Manuel's conch sounding thin and faint beside them. But it was an unearthly experience, and, for the first time in a month, Harvey dreamed of the shifting, smoking floors of water round the dory, the lines that strayed away into nothing, and the air above that melted on the sea below ten feet from his straining eyes. A few days later he was out with Manuel on what should have been forty-fathom bottom, but the whole length of the roding ran out, and still the anchor found nothing, and Harvey grew mortally afraid, for that his last touch with earth was lost. 'Whale-hole,' said Manuel, hauling in. 'That is good joke on Disko. Come!' and he rowed to the schooner to find Tom Platt and the others jeering at the skipper because, for once, he had led them to the edge of the barren Whale-deep, the blank hole of the Grand Bank. They made another berth through the fog, and that time the hair of Harvey's head stood up when he went out in Manuel's dory. A whiteness moved in the whiteness of the fog with a breath like the breath of the grave, and there was a roaring, a plunging, and spouting. It was his first introduction to the dread summer berg of the Banks, and he cowered in the bottom of the boat while Manuel laughed. There were days, though, clear and soft and warm, when it seemed a sin to do anything but loaf over the hand-lines and spank the drifting 'sunscalds' with an oar; and there were days of light airs, when Harvey was taught how to steer the schooner from one berth to another.

It thrilled through him when he first felt the keel answer to his hand on the spokes and slide over the long hollows as the foresail scythed back and forth against the blue sky. That was magnificent, in spite of Disko saying that it would break a snake's back to follow his wake. But, as usual, pride ran before a fall. They were sailing on the wind with the staysail—an old one, luckily—set, and Harvey jammed her right into it to show Dan how completely he had mastered the art. The foresail went over with a bang, and the foregaff stabbed and ripped through the staysail, which was, of course, prevented from going over by the mainstay. They lowered the wreck in awful silence, and Harvey spent his leisure hours for the next few days under Tom Platt's lee, learning to use a needle and palm. Dan hooted with joy, for, as he said, he had made the very same blunder himself in his early days.

Boylike, Harvey imitated all the men by turns, till he had combined Disko's peculiar stoop at the wheel, Long Jack's swinging overhand when the lines were hauled, Manuel's round-shouldered but effective stroke in a dory, and Tom Platt's generous 'Ohio' stride along the deck.

''Tis beautiful to see how he takes to ut,' said Long Jack, when Harvey was looking out by the windlass one thick noon. 'I'll lay my wage an' share 'tis more'n half play-actin' to him, an' he consates himself he's a bowld mariner. Watch his little bit av a back now.'

'That's the way we all begin,' said Tom Platt. 'The boys they make believe all the time till they've cheated 'emselves into bein' men, an' so till they die—pretendin' an' pretendin'. I done it on the old "Ohio," I know. Stood my first watch—harbour watch—feelin' finer'n Farragut. Dan's full o' the same kind o' notions. See 'em now, actin' to be genewine moss-backs —every hair a rope-yarn an' blood Stockholm tar.' He spoke down the cabin stairs. 'Guess you're mistook in your judgments fer once, Disko. What in Rome made ye tell us all here the kid was crazy?'

'He wuz,' Disko replied. 'Crazy ez a loon when he come aboard; but I'll say he's sobered up consid'ble sence. I cured him.'

'He yarns good,' said Tom Platt. 'T'other night he told us abaout a kid of his own size steerin' a cunnin' little rig an' four ponies up an' down Toledo, Ohio, I think 'twas, an' givin' suppers to a crowd o' sim'lar kids. Cur'us kind o' fairy tale, but blame interestin'. He knows scores of 'em.'

'Guess he strikes 'em outen his own head,' Disko called from the cabin, where he was busy with the log-book. 'Stands to reason that sort is all made up. It don't take in no one but Dan, an' he laughs at it. I've heard him, behind my back.'

'Y'ever hear what Sim'on Peter Ca'houn said when they whacked up a match 'twix' his sister Hitty an' Lorin' Jerauld, an' the boys put up that joke on him daown to Georges?' drawled Uncle Salters, who was dripping peaceably under the lee of the starboard dory-nest.

Tom Platt puffed at his pipe in scornful silence: he was a Cape Cod man, and had not known that tale more than twenty years. Uncle Salters went on with a rasping chuckle:

'Sim'on Peter Ca'houn he said, an' he was jest right, abaout Lorin', "Ha'af on the taown," he said, "an' t'other ha'af blame fool; an' they told me she's married a 'ich man." Sim'on Peter Ca'houn he hedn't no roof to his mouth, an' talked that way.'

'He didn't talk any Pennsylvania Dutch,' Tom Platt replied. 'You'd better leave a Cape man to tell that tale. The Ca'houns was gipsies from 'way back.'

'Wal, I don't profess to be any elocutionist,' Salters said. 'I'm comin' to the moral o' things. That's jest abaout what aour Harve be! Ha'af on the taown, an' t'other ha'af blame fool; an' there's some'll believe he's a rich man. Yah!'

'Did ye ever think how sweet 'twould be to sail wid a full crew o' Salterses?' said Long Jack. 'Ha'af in the furrer an' other ha'af in the muckheap, as Ca'houn did not say, an' makes out he's a fisherman!'

A little laugh went round at Salters's expense.

Disko held his tongue and wrought over the log-book that he kept in a hatchet-faced, square hand; this was the kind of thing that ran on, page after soiled page:—

'17th July.— This day thick fog and few fish. Made berth to northward. So ends this day.

'18th July.— This day comes in with thick fog. Caught a few fish.

'19th July.— This day comes in with light breeze from N. E. and fine weather. Made a berth to eastward. Caught plenty fish.

'20th July.— This, the Sabbath, comes in with fog and light winds. So ends this day. Total fish caught this week, 3478.'

They never worked on Sundays, but shaved, and washed themselves if it were fine, and Pennsylvania sang hymns. Once or twice he suggested that, if it was not an impertinence, he thought he could preach a little. Uncle Salters nearly jumped down his throat at the mere notion, reminding him that he was not a preacher and mustn't think of such things. 'We'd hev him rememberin' Johnstown next,' Salters explained, 'an' what would happen then?' So they compromised on his reading aloud from a book called 'Josephus.' It was an old leather-bound volume, smelling of a hundred voyages, very solid and very like the Bible, but enlivened with accounts of battles and sieges; and they read it nearly from cover to cover. Otherwise Penn was a silent little body. He would not utter a word for three days on end sometimes, though he played checkers, listened to the songs, and laughed at the stories. When they tried to stir him up, he would answer: 'I don't wish to seem unneighbourly, but it is because I have nothing to say. My head feels quite empty. I've almost forgotten my name.' He would turn to Uncle Salters with an expectant smile.

'Why, Pennsylvania Pratt,' Salters would shout. 'You'll fergit me next.'

'No—never,' Penn would say, shutting his lips firmly. 'Pennsylvania Pratt, of course,' he would repeat over and over. Sometimes it was Uncle Salters who forgot, and told him he was Haskins or Rich or M'Vitty; but Penn was equally content—till next time.

He was always very tender with Harvey, whom he pitied both as a lost child and as a lunatic; and when Salters saw that Penn liked the boy, he relaxed too. Salters was not an amiable person (he esteemed it his business to keep the boys in order); and the first time Harvey, in fear and trembling, on a still day, managed to shin up to the main-truck (Dan was behind him ready to help), he esteemed it his duty to hang Salters's big sea-boots up there—a sight of shame and derision to the nearest schooner. With Disko, Harvey took no liberties; not even when the old man dropped direct orders, and treated him, like the rest of the crew, to 'Don't you want to do so and so?' and 'Guess you'd better,' and so forth. There was something about the clean-shaven lips and the puckered corners of the eyes that was mightily sobering to young blood.

Disko showed him the meaning of the thumbed and pricked Eldridge chart, which, he said, laid over any Government publication whatsoever; led him, pencil in hand, from berth to berth over the whole string of banks —Le Have, Western, Banquereau, St. Pierre, Green, and Grand—talking 'cod' meantime. Taught him, too, the principle on which the 'hog-yoke' was worked.

In this Harvey excelled Dan, for he had inherited a head for figures, and the notion of stealing information from one glimpse of the sullen Bank sun appealed to all his keen wits. In other sea-matters, his age handicapped him. As Disko said, he should have begun when he was ten. Dan could bait up trawl or lay his hand on any rope in the dark; and at a pinch, when Uncle Salters had a gurry-sore on his palm, could dress-down by sense of touch. He could steer in anything short of half a gale from the feel of the wind on his face, humouring the 'We're Here' just when she needed it. These things he did as automatically as he skipped about the rigging, or made his dory a part of his own will and body. But he could not communicate his knowledge to Harvey.

Still there was a good deal of general information flying about the schooner on stormy days, when they lay up in the foc'sle or sat on the cabin lockers, while spare eyebolts, leads, and rings rolled and rattled in the pauses of the talk. Disko spoke of whaling voyages in the Fifties; of great she-whales slain beside their young; of death agonies on the black, tossing seas, and blood that spurted forty feet in the air; of boats smashed to splinters; of patent rockets that went off wrong-end-first and bombarded the trembling crews; of cutting-in and boiling-down, and of that terrible 'nip' of '71, when twelve hundred men were made homeless on the ice in three days—wonderful tales, all true. But more wonderful still were his stories of the cod, and how they argued and reasoned on their private businesses deep down below the keel.

Long Jack's tastes ran more to the supernatural. He held them silent with ghastly stories of the 'Yo-hoes' on Monomoy Beach that mock and terrify lonely clam-diggers; of sand-walkers and dune-haunters who were never properly buried; of hidden treasure on Fire Island guarded by the spirits of Kidd's men; of ships that sailed in the fog straight over Truro township; of that harbour in Maine where no one but a stranger will lie at anchor twice in a certain place because of a dead crew who row along-side at midnight with the anchor in the bow of their old-fashioned boat, whistling—not calling, but whistling—for the soul of the man who broke their rest.

Harvey had a notion that the east coast of his native land, from Mount Desert south, was populated chiefly by people who took their horses there in the summer and entertained in country-houses with hardwood floors and Vantine portieres. He laughed at the ghost tales,—not as much as he would have done a month before,—but ended by sitting still and shuddering.

Tom Platt dealt with his interminable trip round the Horn on the old 'Ohio' in the flogging days; with a navy more extinct than the dodo—the navy that passed away in the great war. He told them how red-hot shot are dropped into a cannon, a wad of wet clay between them and the cartridge; how they sizzle and reek when they strike wood, and how the little ship-boys of the 'Miss Jim Buck' hove water over them and shouted to the fort to try again. And he told tales of blockade—long weeks of swaying at anchor, varied only by the departure and return of steamers that had used up their coal (there was no change for the sailing-ships); of gales and cold—cold that kept two hundred men, night and day, pounding and chopping at the ice on cable, blocks, and rigging, when the galley was as red-hot as the fort's shot, and men drank cocoa by the bucket. Tom Platt had no use for steam. His service closed when that thing was comparatively new. He admitted that it was a specious invention in time of peace, but looked hopefully for the day when sails should come back again on ten-thousand-ton frigates with hundred-and-ninety-foot booms.

Manuel's talk was slow and gentle—all about pretty girls in Madeira washing clothes in the dry beds of streams, by moonlight, under waving bananas; legends of saints, and tales of queer dances or fights away in the cold Newfoundland baiting-ports. Salters was mainly agricultural, for, though he read Josephus and expounded it, his mission in life was to prove the value of green manures, and specially of clover, against every form of phosphate whatsoever. He grew libellous about phosphates; he dragged greasy 'Orange Judd' books from his bunk and intoned them, wagging his finger at Harvey, to whom it was all Greek. Little Penn was so genuinely pained when Harvey made fun of Salters's lectures that the boy gave it up, and suffered in polite silence. That was very good for Harvey.

The cook naturally did not join in these conversations. As a rule, he spoke only when it was absolutely necessary; but at times a queer gift of speech descended on him, and he held forth, half in Gaelic, half in broken English, an hour at a time. He was specially communicative with the boys, and he never withdrew his prophecy that one day Harvey would be Dan's master, and that he would see it. He told them of mail-carrying in the winter up Cape Breton way, of the dog-train that goes to Coudray, and of the ram-steamer 'Arctic' that breaks the ice between the mainland and Prince Edward Island. Then he told them stories that his mother had told him, of life far to the southward where water never froze; and he said that when he died his soul would go to lie down on a warm white beach of sand with palm-trees waving above. That seemed to the boys a very odd idea for a man who had never seen a palm in his life. Then, too, regularly at each meal, he would ask Harvey, and Harvey alone, whether the cooking was to his taste; and this always made the 'second half' laugh. Yet they had a great respect for the cook's judgment, and in their hearts considered Harvey something of a mascot by consequence.

And while Harvey was taking in knowledge of new things at each pore and hard health with every gulp of the good air, the 'We're Here' went her ways and did her business on the Bank, and the silvery-gray kenches of well-pressed fish mounted higher and higher in the hold. No one day's work was out of the common, but the average days were many and close together.

Naturally a man of Disko's reputation was closely watched—'scrowged upon,' Dan called it—by his neighbours, but he had a very pretty knack of giving them the slip through the curdling, glidy fog-banks. Disko avoided company for two reasons. He wished to make his own experiments, in the first place; in the second, he objected to the mixed gatherings of a fleet of all nations. The bulk of them were mainly Gloucester boats, with a scattering from Provincetown, Harwich, Chatham, and some of the Maine ports, but the crews drew from goodness knows where. Risk breeds recklessness, and when greed is added, there are fine chances for every kind of accident in the crowded fleet, which, like a mob of sheep, is huddled round some unrecognized leader. 'Let the two Jeraulds lead 'em,' said Disko. 'We're baound to lay among 'em fer a spell on the Eastern Shoals, though, ef luck holds, we won't hev to lay long. Where we are naow, Harve, ain't considered noways good graound.'

'Ain't it?' said Harvey, who was drawing water (he had learned just how to wiggle the bucket properly), after an unusually long dressing-down. 'Shouldn't mind striking some poor ground for a change, then.'

'All the graound I want to see—don't want to strike her—is Eastern Point,' said Dan. 'Say, dad, it looks's if we wouldn't hev to lay more'n two weeks on the Shoals. You'll meet all the comp'ny you want then, Harve. That's the time we begin to work. No reg'lar meals fer no one then. 'Mug-up when ye're hungry, an' sleep when ye can't keep awake. Good job you wasn't picked up a month later than you was, or we'd never ha' had you dressed in shape fer the Old Virgin.'

Harvey understood from the Eldridge chart that the Old Virgin and a nest of curiously-named shoals were the turning-point of the cruise, and that with good luck they would wet the balance of their salt there; but seeing the size of the Virgin (it was one tiny dot), he wondered how even Disko with the hog-yoke and the lead could find her. He learned later that Disko was entirely equal to that and any other business, and could even help others. A big four-by-five blackboard hung in the cabin, and Harvey never understood the need of it till, after some blinding thick days, they heard the unmelodious tooting of a foot-power fog-horn—a machine whose note is that of a consumptive elephant.

They were making a short berth, towing the anchor under their foot to save trouble. 'Square-rigger bellowin' fer his latitude,' said Long Jack. The dripping red headsails of a bark glided out of the fog, and the 'We're Here' rang her bell thrice, using sea shorthand.

The larger boat backed her topsail, with shrieks and shoutings.

'Frenchman,' said Uncle Salters scornfully. 'Miquelon boat from St. Malo.' The farmer had a weatherly sea-eye. 'I'm most outer 'baccy, too, Disko.'

'Same here,' said Tom Platt. 'Hi! backez vous—backez vous! Standez awayez, you butt-ended mucho bono! Where you from—St. Malo, eh?'

'Ah, ha! mucho bono! Oui! oui! Clos Poulet—St. Malo! St. Pierre et Miquelon,' cried the other crowd, waving woollen caps and laughing. Then all together, 'Bord! Bord!'

'Bring up the board, Danny. Beats me how them Frenchmen fetch any-wheres, exceptin' America's fairish broadly. Forty-six Forty-nine's good enough fer them; an' I guess it's abaout right, too.'

Dan chalked the figures on the board, and they hung it in the main-rigging to a chorus of 'Mercis' from the bark.

'Seems kinder unneighbourly to let 'em swedge off like this,' Salters suggested, feeling in his pockets.

'Hev ye learned French then sence last trip?' said Disko. 'I don't want no more stone-ballast hove at us 'long o' your callin' Miquelon boats "footy cochins" same's you did off Le Have.'

'Harmon Rush he said that was the way to rise 'em. Plain United States is good enough fer me. We're all dretful short on terbakker. Young feller, don't you speak French?'

'Oh, yes,' said Harvey valiantly; and he bawled: 'Hi! Say! Arretez-vous! Attendez! Nous sommes venant pour tabac.'

'Ah, tabac, tabac!' they cried, and laughed again.

'That hit 'em. Let's heave a dory over, anyway,' said Tom Platt. 'I don't exactly hold no certificates on French, but I know another lingo that goes, I guess. Come on, Harve, an' interprut.'

The raffle and confusion when he and Harvey were hauled up the bark's black side was indescribable. Her cabin was all stuck round with glaring coloured prints of the Virgin—the Virgin of Newfoundland, they called her. Harvey found his French of no recognised Bank brand, and his conversation was limited to nods and grins. But Tom Platt waved his arms and got along swimmingly. The captain gave him a drink of un-speakable gin, and the opera-comique crew, with their hairy throats, red caps, and long knives, greeted him as a brother. Then the trade began. They had tobacco, plenty of it—American, that had never paid duty to France. They wanted chocolate and crackers. Harvey rowed back to ar-range with the cook and Disko, who owned the stores, and on his return the cocoa-tins and cracker-bags were counted out by the Frenchman's wheel. It looked like a piratical division of loot; but Tom Platt came out of it roped with black pigtail and stuffed with cakes of chewing and smoking tobacco. Then those jovial mariners swung off into the mist, and the last Harvey heard was a gay chorus:

> 'Par derriere chez ma tante,
> Il y a un bois joli,
> Et le rossignol y chante
> Et le jour et la nuit . . .
>
> Que donneriez-vous, belle,
> Qui l'amenerait ici?
> Je donnerai Quebec,
> Sorel et Saint Denis.'

'How was it my French didn't go, and your sign-talk did?' Harvey demanded when the barter had been distributed among the 'We're Heres.'

'Sign-talk!' Platt guffawed. 'Well, yes, 'twas sign-talk, but a heap older'n your French, Harve. Them French boats are chock-full o' Freemasons, an' that's why.'

'Are you a Freemason, then?'

'Looks that way, don't it?' said the man-o'-war's man, stuffing his pipe; and Harvey had another mystery of the deep sea to brood upon.

Chapter 6

THE THING that struck him most was the exceedingly casual way in which some craft loafed about the broad Atlantic. Fishing-boats, as Dan said, were naturally dependent on the courtesy and wisdom of their neighbours; but one expected better things of steamers. That was after another interesting interview, when they had been chased for three miles by a big lumbering old cattle-boat, all boarded over on the upper deck, that smelt like a thousand cattle-pens. A very excited officer yelled at them through a speaking-trumpet, and she lay and lollopped helplessly on the water while Disko ran the 'We're Here' under her lee and gave the skipper a piece of his mind. 'Where might ye be—eh? Ye don't deserve to be anywheres. You barn-yard tramps go hoggin' the road on the high seas with no blame considcration fer your neighbours, an' your eyes in your coffee-cups instid o' in your silly heads.'

At this the skipper danced on the bridge and said something about Disko's own eyes. 'We haven't had an observation for three days. D'you suppose we can run her blind?' he shouted.

'Wa-al, I can,' Disko retorted. 'What's come to your lead? Et it? Can't ye smell bottom, or are them cattle too rank?'

'What d'ye feed 'em?' said Uncle Salters with intense seriousness, for the smell of the pens woke all the farmer in him. 'They say they fall off dretful on a v'yage. Dunno as it's any o' my business, but I've a kind o' notion that oil-cake broke small an' sprinkled—'

'Thunder!' said a cattle-man in a red jersey as he looked over the side. 'What asylum did they let His Whiskers out of?'

'Young feller,' Salters began, standing up in the forerigging, 'let me tell yeou 'fore we go any further that I've—'

The officer on the bridge took off his cap with immense politeness. 'Excuse me,' he said, 'but I've asked for my reckoning. If the agricultural person with the hair will kindly shut his head, the sea-green barnacle with the wall eye may per-haps condescend to enlighten us.'

'Naow you've made a show o' me, Salters,' said Disko angrily. He could not stand up to that particular sort of talk, and snapped out the latitude and longitude without more lectures.

'Well, that's a boat-load of lunatics, sure,' said the skipper, as he rang up the engine-room and tossed a bundle of newspapers into the schooner.

'Of all the blamed fools, next to you, Salters, him an' his crowd are abaout the likeliest I've ever seen,' said Disko as the 'We're Here' slid away. 'I was jest givin' him my jedgment on lullsikin' round these waters like a lost child, an' you must cut in with your fool farmin'. Can't ye never keep things sep'rate?'

Harvey, Dan, and the others stood back, winking one to the other and full of joy; but Disko and Salters wrangled seriously till evening, Salters arguing that a cattle-boat was practically a barn on blue water, and Disko insisting that, even if this were the case, decency and fisher pride demanded that he should have kept 'things sep'rate.' Long Jack stood it in silence for a time—an angry skipper makes an unhappy crew—and then he spoke across the table after supper:

'Fwhat's the good o' bodderin' fwhat they'll say?' said he.

'They'll tell that tale agin us fer years—that's all,' said Disko. 'Oil-cake sprinkled!'

'With salt, o' course,' said Salters, impenitent, reading the farming reports from a week-old New York paper.

'It's plumb mortifyin' to all my feelin's,' the skipper went on.

'Can't see ut that way,' said Long Jack, the peacemaker. 'Look at here, Disko! Is there another packet afloat this day in this weather cud ha' met a tramp an', over an' above givin' her her reckonin',—over an' above that, I say,—cud ha' discoorsed wid her quite intelligent on the management av steers an' such at sea? Forgit ut! Av coorse they will not. 'Twas the most compenjus conversation that iver accrued. Double game an' twice runnin'—all to us.' Dan kicked Harvey under the table, and Harvey choked in his cup.

'Well,' said Salters, who felt that his honour had been somewhat plastered, 'I said I didn't know as 'twuz any business o' mine, 'fore I spoke.'

'An' right there,' said Tom Platt, experienced in discipline and etiquette —'right there, I take it, Disko, you should ha' asked him to stop ef the conversation wuz likely, in your jedgment, to be anyways—what it shouldn't.'

'Dunno but that's so,' said Disko, who saw his way to an honourable retreat from a fit of the dignities.

'Why, o' course it was so,' said Salters, 'you bein' skipper here; an' I'd cheerful hev stopped on a hint—not from any leadin' or conviction, but fer the sake o' bearin' an example to these two blame boys of aours.'

'Didn't I tell you, Harve, 'twould come araound to us 'fore we'd done? Always those blame boys. But I wouldn't have missed the show fer a half-share in a halibutter,' Dan whispered.

'Still, things should ha' been kep' sep'rate,' said Disko, and the light of new argument lit in Salters's eye as he crumbled cut plug into his pipe.

'There's a power av vartue in keepin' things sep'rate,' said Long Jack, intent on stilling the storm. 'That's fwhat Steyning of Steyning and Hare's f'und when he sent Counahan fer skipper on the "Marilla D. Kuhn," instid o' Cap. Newton that was took with inflam'try rheumatism, an' couldn't go. Counahan the Navigator we called him.'

'Nick Counahan he never went aboard fer a night 'thout a pond o' rum somewheres in the manifest,' said Tom Platt, playing up to the lead. 'He used to bum araound the c'mission houses to Boston lookin' fer the Lord to make him captain of a tow-boat on his merits. Sam Coy, up to Atlantic Avenoo, give him his board free fer a year or more on account of his stories. Counahan the Navigator! Tck! Tck! Dead these fifteen years, ain't he?'

'Seventeen, I guess,' said Long Jack. 'He died the year the "Caspar M'Veagh" was built; but he could niver keep things sep'rate. Steyning tuk him fer the reason the thief tuk the hot stove—bekaez there was nothin' else that season. The men was all to the Banks, and Counahan he whacked up an iverlastin' hard crowd fer crew. Rum! Ye cud ha' floated the "Marilla," insurance an' all, in fwhat they stowed aboard her. They lef' Boston Harbour for the great Grand Bank wid a roarin' nor'wester behind 'em an' all hands full to the bung. An' the hivens looked after thim, for divil a watch did they set, an' divil a rope did they lay hand to, till they'd seen the bottom av a fifteen-gallon cask o' bug-juice. That was about wan week, so far as Counahan remembered. (If I cud only tell the tale as he told ut!) All that whoile the wind blew like ould glory, an' the "Marilla"—'twas summer, and they'd give her a fore-topmast—struck her gait and kept ut. Then Counahan tuk the hog-yoke an' thrembled over it for a whoile, an' made out, betwix' that an' the chart an' the singin' in his head, that they was to the south'ard o' Sable Island, gettin' along glorious; but speakin' nothin'. Then they broached another keg, an' quit speculatin' about anythin' fer another spell. The "Marilla" she lay down whin she dropped Boston Light, and she never lufted her lee-rail up to that time—hustlin' on one an' the same slant. But they saw no weed, nor gulls, nor schooners; an' prisintly they obsarved they'd bin out a matter o' fourteen days, and they mistrusted the Bank had suspinded payment. So they sounded, an' got sixty fathom. "That's me," sez Counahan. "That's me iv'ry time! I've run her slap on the Bank fer you, an' when we get thirty fathom we'll turn in like little men. Counahan is the b'y," sez he. "Counahan the Navigator!"

'Nex' cast they got ninety. Sez Counahan: "Either the lead-line's tuk to stretchin' or else the Bank's sunk."

'They hauled ut up, bein' just about in that state when ut seemed right an' reasonable, and sat down on the deck countin' the knots, an' gettin' her snarled up hijjus. The "Marilla," she'd struck her gait, an' she hild ut, an' prisintly along come a tramp, an' Counahan spoke her.

' "Hev ye seen any fishin'-boats now?" sez he, quite casual.

' "There's lashin's av them off the Irish coast," sez the tramp.

' "Aah! go shake yerself," sez Counahan. "Fwhat have I to do wid the Irish coast?"

' "Then fwhat are ye doin' here?" sez the tramp.

' "Sufferin' Christianity!" sez Counahan (he always said that whin his pumps sucked, an' he was not feelin' good)—"Sufferin' Christianity!" he sez, "where am I at?"

' "Thirty-five mile west-sou'west o' Cape Clear," sez the tramp, "if that's any consolation to you."

'Counahan fetched wan jump, four feet sivin inches, measured by the cook.

' "Consolation!" sez he, bould as brass. "D'ye take me fer a dialect? Thirty-five mile from Cape Clear, an' fourteen days from Boston Light. Sufferin' Christianity, 'tis a record, an' by the same token I've a mother to Skibbereen!" Think av ut! The gall av um! But ye see he could niver keep things sep'rate.

'The crew was mostly Cork an' Kerry men, barrin' one Marylander that wanted to go back, but they called him a mutineer, an' they ran the ould "Marilla" into Skibbereen, an' they had an illigant time visitin' around with frinds on the ould sod fer a week. Thin they wint back, an' it cost 'em two-an'-thirty days to beat to the Banks again. 'Twas gettin' on towards fall, and grub was low, so Counahan ran her back to Boston, wid no more bones to ut.'

'And what did the firm say?' Harvey demanded.

'Fwhat could they? The fish was on the Banks, an' Counahan was at T-wharf talkin' av his record trip, east! They tuk their satisfaction out av that, an' ut all came av not keepin' the crew and the rum sep'rate in the first place; an' confusin' Skibbereen wid 'Queereau, in the second. Counahan the Navigator, rest his sowl! He was an imprompju citizen!'

'Once I was in the "Lucy Holmes,"' said Manuel, in his gentle voice. 'They not want any of her feesh in Gloucester. Eh, wha-at? Give us no price. So we go across the water, and think to sell to some Fayal man. Then it blow fresh, and we cannot see well. Eh, wha-at? Then it blow some more fresh, and we go down below and drive very fast—no one know where. By and by we see a land, and it get some hot. Then come two, three nigger in a brick. Eh, wha-at? We ask where we are, and they say—now, what you all think?'

'Grand Canary,' said Disko, after a moment. Manuel shook his head, smiling.

'Blanco,' said Tom Platt.

'No. Worse than that. We was below Bezagos, and the brick she was from Liberia! So we sell our feesh there! Not bad, so? Eh, wha-at?'

'Can a schooner like this go right across to Africa?' said Harvey.

'Go araound the Horn ef there's anythin' worth goin' fer, and the grub holds aout,' said Disko. 'My father he run his packet, an' she was a kind o' pinkey, abaout fifty ton, I guess,—the "Rupert,"—he run her over to Greenland's icy mountains the year ha'af our fleet was tryin' after cod there. An' what's more, he took my mother along with him,—to show her haow the money was earned, I presoom,—an' they was all iced up, an' I was born at Disko. Don't remember nothin' abaout it, o' course. We come back when the ice eased in the spring, but they named me fer the place. Kinder mean trick to put up on a baby, but we're all baound to make mistakes in aour lives.'

'Sure! Sure!' said Salters, wagging his head. 'All baound to make mistakes, an' I tell you two boys here thet after you've made a mistake—ye don't make fewer 'n a hundred a day—the next best thing's to own up to it, like men.'

Long Jack winked one tremendous wink that embraced all hands except Disko and Salters, and the incident was closed.

Then they made berth after berth to the northward, the dories out almost every day, running along the east edge of the Grand Bank in thirty to forty fathom water, and fishing steadily.

It was here Harvey first met the squid, who is one of the best cod-baits, but uncertain in his moods. They were waked out of their bunks one black night by yells of 'Squid O!' from Salters, and for an hour and a half every soul aboard hung over his squid-jig—a piece of lead painted red and armed at the lower end with a circle of pins bent backward like half-opened umbrella ribs. The squid—for some unknown reason—likes, and wraps himself round, this thing, and is hauled up ere he can escape from the pins. But as he leaves his home, he squirts first water and next ink into his captor's face; and it was curious to see the men waving their heads from side to side, to dodge the shot. They were as black as sweeps when the flurry ended; but a pile of fresh squid lay on the deck, and the larger cod thinks very well of a little shiny piece of squid-tentacle at the tip of a clam-baited hook. Next day they caught many fish, and met the 'Carrie Pitman,' to whom they shouted their luck, and she wanted to trade—seven cod for one fair-sized squid; but Disko would not agree at the price, and the 'Carrie' dropped sullenly to leeward and anchored half a mile away, in the hope of striking on to some for herself.

Disko said nothing till after supper, when he sent Dan and Manuel out to buoy the 'We're Here's' cable and announced his intention of turning in with the broadaxe. Dan naturally repeated these remarks to a dory from the 'Carrie,' who wanted to know why they were buoying their cable, since they were not on rocky bottom.

'Dad sez he wouldn't trust a ferryboat within five mile o' you,' Dan howled cheerfully.

'Why don't he git out, then? Who's hinderin'?' said the other.

'Cause you've jest the same ez lee-bowed him, an' he don't take that from any boat, not to speak o' sech a driftin' gurry-butt as you be.'

'She ain't driftin' any this trip,' said the man angrily, for the 'Carrie Pitman' had an unsavoury reputation for breaking her ground-tackle.

'Then haow d'you make berths?' said Dan. 'It's her best p'int o' sailin'. An' ef she's quit driftin', what in thunder are you doin' with a new jib-boom?' That shot went home.

'Hey, you Portugoosy organ-grinder, take your monkey back to Glouces-ter. Go back to school, Dan Troop,' was the answer.

'O-ver-alls! O-ver-alls!' yelled Dan, who knew that one of the 'Carrie's' crew had worked in an overall factory the winter before.

'Shrimp! Gloucester shrimp! Git aout, you Novy!'

To call a Gloucester man a Nova Scotian is not well received. Dan answered in kind.

'Novy yourself, ye Scrabble-towners—ye Chatham wreckers! Get aout with your brick in your stockin'!' And the forces separated, but Chatham had the worst of it.

'I knew haow 'twould be,' said Disko. 'She's drawed the wind raound already. Some one oughter put a dee-sist on thet packet. She'll snore till midnight an' jest when we're gittin' our sleep she'll strike adrift. Good job we ain't crowded with craft hereaways. But I ain't goin' to up anchor fer Chatham. She may hold.'

The wind, which had hauled round, rose at sundown and blew steadily. There was not enough sea, though, to disturb even a dory's tackle, but the 'Carrie Pitman' was a law unto herself. At the end of the boys' watch they heard the 'crack-crack-crack' of a huge muzzel-loading revolver aboard her.

'Glory, glory, hallelujah!' sang Dan. 'Here she comes, dad; butt-end first, walkin' in her sleep same's she done on 'Queereau.'

Had she been any other boat Disko would have taken his chances, but now he cut the cable as the 'Carrie Pitman,' with all the North Atlantic to play in, lurched down directly upon them. The 'We're Here,' under jib and riding-sail, gave her no more room than was absolutely necessary,— Disko did not wish to spend a week hunting for his cable,—but scuttled up into the wind as the 'Carrie' passed within easy hail, a silent and angry boat, at the mercy of a raking broadside of Bank chaff.

'Good evenin',' said Disko, raising his headgear, 'an' haow does your garden grow?'

'Go to Ohio an' hire a mule,' said Uncle Salters. 'We don't want no farmers here.'

'Will I lend you my dory-anchor?' cried Long Jack.

'Unship your rudder an' stick it in the mud,' said Tom Platt.

'Say!' Dan's voice rose shrill and high as he stood on the wheel-box. 'Sa-ay! Is there a strike in the o-ver-all factory; or hev they hired girls, ye Shackamaxons?'

'Veer out the tiller-lines,' cried Harvey, 'and nail 'em to the bottom.' That was a salt-flavoured jest he had been put up to by Tom Platt. Manuel leaned over the stern and yelled, 'Johnna Morgan play the organ! Ahaaaa!' He flourished his broad thumb with a gesture of unspeakable contempt and derision, while little Penn covered himself with glory by piping up: 'Gee a little. Hssh! Come here. Haw!'

They rode on their chain for the rest of the night, a short, snappy, uneasy motion, as Harvey found, and wasted half the forenoon recovering the cable. But the boys agreed the trouble was cheap at the price of triumph and glory, and they thought with grief over all the beautiful things that they might have said to the discomfited 'Carrie.'

Chapter 7

NEXT DAY they fell in with more sails, all circling slowly from the east northerly towards the west. But just when they expected to make the shoals by the Virgin the fog shut down, and they anchored, surrounded by the tinklings of invisible bells. There was not much fishing, but occasionally dory met dory in the fog and exchanged news.

That night, a little before dawn, Dan and Harvey, who had been sleeping most of the day, tumbled out to 'hook' fried pies. There was no reason why they should not have taken them openly; but they tasted better so, and it made the cook angry. The heat and smell below drove them on deck with their plunder, and they found Disko at the bell, which he handed over to Harvey.

'Keep her goin',' said he. 'I mistrust I hear somethin'. Ef it's anything, I'm best where I am so's to get at things.'

It was a forlorn little jingle; the thick air seemed to pinch it off; and in the pauses Harvey heard the muffled shriek of a liner's siren, and he knew enough of the Banks now to know what that meant. It came to him, with horrible distinctness, how a boy in a cherry-coloured jersey—he despised fancy blazers now with all a fisherman's contempt—how an ignorant, rowdy boy had once said it would be 'great' if a steamer ran down a fishing-boat. That boy had a state-room with a hot and cold bath, and spent ten minutes each morning picking over a gilt-edged bill of fare. And that same boy—no, his very much older brother—was up at four of the dim dawn in streaming, crackling oilskins, hammering, literally for the dear life, on a bell smaller than the steward's breakfast bell, while somewhere close at hand a thirty-foot steel stem was storming along at twenty miles an hour! The bitterest thought of all was that there were folks asleep in dry, upholstered cabins who would never learn that they had massacred a boat before breakfast. So Harvey rang the bell.

'Yes, they slow daown one turn o' their blame propeller,' said Dan, applying himself to Manuel's conch, 'fer to keep inside the law, an' that's consolin' when we're all at the bottom. Hark to her! She's a humper!'

'Aoooo—whoooo—whupp!' went the siren. 'Wingle—tingle—tink,' went the bell. 'Graaa—ouch!' went the conch, while sea and sky were all milled up in milky fog. Then Harvey felt that he was near a moving body, and found himself looking up and up at the wet edge of a cliff-like bow, leaping, it seemed, directly over the schooner. A jaunty little feather of water curled in front of it, and as it lifted it showed a long ladder of Roman numerals—XV. XVI. XVII. XVIII. and so forth—on a salmon-coloured, gleaming side. It tilted forward and downward with a heart-stilling 'Ssssooo'; the ladder disappeared; a line of brass-rimmed portholes flashed past; a jet of steam puffed in Harvey's helplessly uplifted hands; a spout of hot water roared along the rail of the 'We're Here,' and the little schooner staggered and shook in a rush of screw-torn water, as a liner's stern vanished in the fog. Harvey got ready to faint or be sick, or both, when he heard a crack like a trunk thrown on a sidewalk, and, all small in his ear, a far-away telephone voice drawling: 'Heave to! You've sunk us!'

'Is it us?' he gasped.

'No! Boat out yonder. Ring! We're goin' to look,' said Dan, running out a dory.

In half a minute all except Harvey, Penn, and the cook were over-side and away. Presently a schooner's stump-foremast, snapped clean across, drifted past the bows. Then an empty green dory came by, knocking on the 'We're Here's' side, as though she wished to be taken up. Then followed something, face down, in a blue jersey, but—it was not the whole of a man. Penn changed colour and caught his breath with a click. Harvey pounded despairingly at the bell, for he feared they might be sunk at any minute, and he jumped at Dan's hail as the crew came back.

'The "Jennie Cushman,"' said Dan hysterically, 'cut clean in half—graound up an' trompled on at that! Not a quarter of a mile away. Dad's got the old man. There ain't any one else, and—there was his son too. Oh, Harve, Harve, I can't stand it! I've seen—' He dropped his head on his arms and sobbed while the others dragged a gray-headed man aboard.

'What did you pick me up for?' the stranger groaned. 'Disko, what did you pick me up for?'

Disko dropped a heavy hand on his shoulder, for the man's eyes were wild and his lips trembled as he stared at the silent crew. Then up and spoke Pennsylvania Pratt, who was also Haskins or Rich or M'Vitty when Uncle Salters forgot; and his face was changed on him from the face of a fool to the countenance of an old, wise man, and he said in a strong voice: 'The Lord gave, and the Lord hath taken away; blessed be the name of the Lord! I was—I am a minister of the Gospel. Leave him to me.'

"Oh, you be, be you?' said the man. 'Then pray my son back to me! Pray back a nine-thousand-dollar boat an' a thousand quintal of fish. If you'd left me alone my widow could ha' gone on to the Provident an' worked fer her board, an' never known—an' never known. Now I'll hev to tell her.'

'There ain't nothin' to say,' said Disko. 'Better lie down a piece, Jason Olley.'

When a man has lost his only son, his summer's work, and his means of livelihood, in thirty counted seconds, it is hard to give consolation.

'All Gloucester men, wasn't they?' said Tom Platt, fiddling helplessly with a dory-becket.

'Oh, that don't make no odds,' said Jason, wringing the wet from his beard. 'I'll be rowin' summer boarders araound East Gloucester this fall.' He rolled heavily to the rail, singing:

> 'Happy birds that sing and fly
> Round thine altars, O Most High!'

'Come with me. Come below!' said Penn, as though he had a right to give orders. Their eyes met and fought for a quarter of a minute.

'I dunno who you be, but I'll come,' said Jason submissively. 'Mebbe I'll get back some o' the—some o' the—nine thousand dollars.' Penn led him into the cabin and slid the door behind.

'That ain't Penn,' cried Uncle Salters. 'It's Jacob Boller, an'—he's remembered Johnstown! I never seed such eyes in any livin' man's head. What's to do naow? What'll I do naow?'

They could hear Penn's voice and Jason's together. Then Penn's went on alone, and Salters slipped off his hat, for Penn was praying. Presently the little man came up the steps, huge drops of sweat on his face, and looked at the crew. Dan was still sobbing by the wheel.

'He don't know us,' Salters groaned. 'It's all to do over again, checkers and everything—an' what'll he say to me?'

Penn spoke; they could hear that it was to strangers. 'I have prayed,' said he. 'Our people believe in prayer. I have prayed for the life of this man's son. Mine were drowned before my eyes, she and my eldest and—the others. Shall a man be more wise than his Maker? I prayed never for their lives, but I have prayed for this man's son, and he will surely be sent him.'

Salters looked pleadingly at Penn to see if he remembered.

'How long have I been mad?' Penn asked suddenly. His mouth was twitching.

"Pshaw, Penn! You weren't never mad,' Salters began. 'Only a little distracted like.'

'I saw the houses strike the bridge before the fires broke out. I do not remember any more. How long ago is that?'

'I can't stand it! I can't stand it!' cried Dan, and Harvey whimpered in sympathy.

'Abaout five year,' said Disko, in a shaking voice.

'Then I have been a charge on some one for every day of that time. Who was the man?'

Disko pointed to Salters.

'Ye hain't—ye hain't!' cried the sea-farmer, twisting his hands together. 'Ye've more'n earned your keep twice-told; an' there's money owin' you, Penn, besides ha'af o' my quarter-share in the boat, which is yours fer value received.'

'You are good men. I can see that in your faces. But—'

'Mother av Mercy,' whispered Long Jack, 'an' he's been wid us all these trips! He's clean bewitched.'

A schooner's bell struck up alongside, and a voice hailed through the fog: 'O Disko! Heard abaout the "Jennie Cushman"?'

'They have found his son,' cried Penn. 'Stand you still and see the salvation of the Lord!'

'Got Jason aboard here,' Disko answered, but his voice quavered. 'There —warn't any one else?'

'We've f'und one, though. Run acrost him snarled up in a mess o' lumber thet might ha' bin a foc'sle. His head's cut some.'

'Who is he?'

The 'We're Heres' heart-beats answered one another.

'Guess it's young Olley,' the voice drawled.

Penn raised his hands and said something in German. Harvey could have sworn that a bright sun was shining upon his lifted face; but the drawl went on. 'Sa-ay! You fellers guyed us consid'rable t'other night.'

'We don't feel like guyin' any now,' said Disko.

'I know it; but to tell the honest truth we was kinder—kinder driftin' when we run agin young Olley.'

It was the irrepressible 'Carrie Pitman,' and a roar of unsteady laughter went up from the deck of the 'We're Here.'

'Hedn't you 'baout's well send the old man aboard? We're runnin' in fer more bait an' graound-tackle. Guess you won't want him, anyway, an' this blame windlass work makes us short-handed. We'll take care of him. He married my woman's aunt.'

'I'll give you anything in the boat,' said Troop.

'Don't want nothin', 'less, mebbe, an anchor that'll hold. Say! Young Olley's gittin' kinder baulky an' excited. Send the old man along.'

Penn waked him from his stupor of despair, and Tom Platt rowed him over. He went away without a word of thanks, not knowing what was to come; and the fog closed over all.

'And now,' said Penn, drawing a deep breath as though about to preach. 'And now'—the erect body sank like a sword driven home into the scabbard; the light faded from the over-bright eyes; the voice returned to its usual pitiful little titter—'and now,' said Pennsylvania Pratt, 'do you think it's too early for a little game of checkers, Mr. Salters?'

'The very thing—the very thing I was goin' to say myself,' cried Salters promptly. 'It beats all, Penn, how ye git on to what's in a man's mind.'

The little fellow blushed and meekly followed Salters forward.

'Up anchor! Hurry! Let's quit these crazy waters,' shouted Disko, and never was he more swiftly obeyed.

'Now what in creation d'ye suppose is the meanin' o' that all?' said Long Jack, when they were working through the fog once more, damp, dripping, and bewildered.

'The way I sense it,' said Disko, at the wheel, 'is this: The "Jennie Cushman" business comin' on an empty stummick—'

'He—we saw one of them go by,' sobbed Harvey.

'An' that, o' course, kinder hove him outer water, julluk runnin' a craft ashore; hove him right aout, I take it, to rememberin' Johnstown an' Jacob Boller an' such-like reminiscences. Well, consolin' Jason there held him up a piece, same's shorin' up a boat. Then, bein' weak, them props slipped an' slipped, an' he slided down the ways, an' naow he's water-borne agin. That's haow I sense it.'

They decided that Disko was entirely correct.

'''Twould ha' bruk Salters all up,' said Long Jack, 'if Penn had stayed Jacob Bollerin'. Did ye see his face when Penn asked who he'd been charged on all these years? How is ut, Salters?'

'Asleep—dead asleep. Turned in like a child,' Salters replied, tiptoeing aft. 'There won't be no grub till he wakes, natural. Did ye ever see sech a gift in prayer? He everlastin'ly hiked young Olley outer the ocean. Thet's my belief. Jason was tur'ble praoud of his boy, an' I mistrusted all along 'twas a jedgment on worshippin' vain idols.'

'There's others jest as sot,' said Disko.

'That's diff'runt,' Salters retorted quickly. 'Penn's not all caulked, an' I ain't only but doin' my duty by him.'

They waited, those hungry men, three hours, till Penn reappeared with a smooth face and a blank mind. He said he believed that he had been dreaming. Then he wanted to know why they were so silent, and they could not tell him.

Disko worked all hands mercilessly for the next three or four days; and when they could not go out, turned them into the hold to stack the ship's stores into smaller compass, to make more room for the fish. The packed mass ran from the cabin partition to the sliding door behind the foc'sle stove; and Disko showed how there is great art in stowing cargo so as to bring a schooner to her best draught. The crew were thus kept lively till they recovered their spirits; and Harvey was tickled with a rope's end by Long Jack for being, as the Galway man said, 'sorrowful as a sick cat over fwhat couldn't be helped.' He did a great deal of thinking in those dreary days; and told Dan what he thought, and Dan agreed with him— even to the extent of asking for fried pies instead of hooking them.

But a week later the two nearly upset the 'Hattie S.' in a wild attempt to stab a shark with an old bayonet tied to a stick. The grim brute rubbed alongside the dory begging for small fish, and between the three of them it was a mercy they all got off alive.

At last, after playing blind man's buff in the fog, there came a morning when Disko shouted down the foc'sle: 'Hurry, boys! We're in taown!'

Chapter 8

To THE END of his days, Harvey will never forget that sight. The sun was just clear of the horizon they had not seen for nearly a week, and his low red light struck into the riding-sails of three fleets of anchored schooners —one to the north, one to the westward, and one to the south. There must have been nearly a hundred of them, of every possible make and build, with, far away, a square-rigged Frenchman, all bowing and curtseying one to the other. From every boat dories were dropping away like bees from a crowded hive; and the clamour of voices, the rattling of ropes and blocks, and the splash of the oars carried for miles across the heaving water. The sails turned all colours, black, pearly-gray, and white, as the sun mounted; and more boats swung up through the mists to the southward.

The dories gathered in clusters, separated, re-formed, and broke again, all heading one way; while men hailed and whistled and cat-called and sang, and the water was speckled with rubbish thrown overboard.

'It's a town,' said Harvey. 'Disko was right. It is a town!'

'I've seen smaller,' said Disko. 'There's about a thousand men here; an' yonder's the Virgin.' He pointed to a vacant space of greenish sea where there were no dories.

The 'We're Here' skirted round the northern squadron, Disko waving his hand to friend after friend, and anchored as neatly as a racing yacht at the end of the season. The Bank fleet pass good seamanship in silence; but a bungler is jeered all along the line.

'Jest in time fer the caplin,' cried the 'Mary Chilton.'

'Salt 'most wet?' asked the 'King Philip.'

'Hey, Tom Platt! Come t' supper to-night?' said the 'Henry Clay'; and so questions and answers flew back and forth. Men had met one another before, dory-fishing in the fog, and there is no place for gossip like the Bank fleet. They all seemed to know about Harvey's rescue, and asked if he were worth his salt yet. The young bloods jested with Dan, who had a lively tongue of his own and inquired after their health by the town-nicknames they least liked. Manuel's countrymen jabbered at him in their own language; and even the silent cook was seen riding the jib-boom and shouting Gaelic to a friend as black as himself. After they had buoyed the cable—all around the Virgin is rocky bottom, and carelessness means chafed ground-tackle and danger from drifting—after they had buoyed the cable, their dories went forth to join the mob of boats anchored about a mile away. The schooners rocked and dipped at a safe distance, like mother ducks watching their brood, while the dories behaved like mannerless ducklings.

As they drove into the confusion, boat banging boat, Harvey's ears tingled at the comments on his rowing. Every dialect from Labrador to Long Island, with Portuguese, Neapolitan, Lingua Franca, French, and Gaelic, with songs and shoutings and new oaths, rattled round him, and he seemed to be the butt of it all. For the first time in his life he felt shy—perhaps that came from living so long with only the 'We're Heres'— among the scores of wild faces that rose and fell with the reeling small craft. A gentle, breathing swell, three furlongs from trough to barrel, would quietly shoulder up a string of variously painted dories. They hung for an instant, a wonderful frieze against the sky-line, and their men pointed and hailed. Next moment the open mouths, waving arms, and bare chests disappeared, while on another swell came up an entirely new line of characters like paper figures in a toy theatre. So Harvey stared. 'Watch out!' said Dan, flourishing a dip-net. 'When I tell you dip, you dip. The caplin' 'll school any time from naow on. Where'll we lay, Tom Platt?'

Pushing, shoving, and hauling, greeting old friends here and warning old enemies there, Commodore Tom Platt led his little fleet well to lee-ward of the general crowd, and immediately three or four men began to haul on their anchors with intent to lee-bow the 'We're Heres.' But a yell of laughter went up as a dory shot from her station with exceeding speed, its occupant pulling madly on the roding.

'Give her slack!' roared twenty voices. 'Let him shake it out.'

'What's the matter?' said Harvey, as the boat flashed away to the south-ward. 'He's anchored, isn't he?'

'Anchored, sure enough, but his graound-tackle's kinder shifty,' said Dan, laughing. 'Whale's fouled it. . . . Dip, Harve! Here they come!'

The sea round them clouded and darkened, and then frizzed up in showers of tiny silver fish, and over a space of five or six acres the cod began to leap like trout in May; while behind the cod, three or four broad gray-black backs broke the water into boils.

Then everybody shouted and tried to haul up his anchor to get among the school, and fouled his neighbour's line and said what was in his heart, and dipped furiously with his dip-net, and shrieked cautions and advice to his companions, while the deep fizzed like freshly-opened soda-water, and cod, men, and whales together flung in upon the luckless bait. Harvey was nearly knocked overboard by the handle of Dan's net. But in all the wild tumult he noticed, and never forgot, the wicked, set little eye—something like a circus-elephant's eye—of a whale that drove along almost level with the water, and, so he said, winked at him. Three boats found their rodings fouled by these reckless mid-sea hunters, and were towed half a mile ere their horses shook the line free.

Then the caplin moved off, and five minutes later there was no sound except the splash of the sinkers overside, the flapping of the cod, and the whack of the muckles as the men stunned them. It was wonderful fishing. Harvey could see the glimmering cod below, swimming slowly in droves, biting as steadily as they swam. Bank law strictly forbids more than one hook on one line when the dories are on the Virgin or the Eastern Shoals; but so close lay the boats that even single hooks snarled, and Harvey found himself in hot argument with a gentle, hairy Newfound-lander on one side and a howling Portuguese on the other.

Worse than any tangle of fishing-lines was the confusion of the dory-rodings below water. Each man had anchored where it seemed good to him, drifting and rowing round his fixed point. As the fish struck on less quickly, each man wanted to haul up and get to better ground; but every third man found himself intimately connected with some four or five neighbours. To cut another's roding is crime unspeakable on the Banks; yet it was done, and done without detection, three or four times that day. Tom Platt caught a Maine man in the black act and knocked him over the gunwale with an oar, and Manuel served a fellow-countryman in the same way. But Harvey's anchor-line was cut, and so was Penn's, and they were turned into relief-boats to carry fish to the 'We're Here' as the dories filled. The caplin schooled once more at twilight, when the mad clamour was repeated; and at dusk they rowed back to dress-down by the light of kerosene lamps on the edge of the pen.

It was a huge pile, and they went to sleep while they were dressing. Next day several boats fished right above the cap of the Virgin; and Harvey, with them, looked down on the very weed of that lonely rock, which rises to within twenty feet of the surface. The cod were there in legions, marching solemnly over the leathery kelp. When they bit, they bit all together, and so when they stopped. There was a slack time at noon, and the dories began to search for amusement. It was Dan who sighted the 'Hope of Prague' just coming up, and as her boats joined the company they were greeted with the question: 'Who's the meanest man in the fleet?'

Three hundred voices answered cheerily: 'Nick Bra-ady.' It sounded like an organ chant.

'Who stole the lamp-wicks?' That was Dan's contribution.

'Nick Bra-ady,' sang the boats.

'Who biled the salt bait fer soup?' This was an unknown backbiter a quarter of a mile away.

Again the joyful chorus. Now, Brady was not especially mean, but he had that reputation, and the fleet made the most of it. Then they discovered a man from a Truro boat, who, six years before, had been convicted of using a tackle with five or six hooks—a 'scrowger' they call it—on the Shoals. Naturally, he had been christened 'Scrowger Jim'; and though he had hidden himself on the Georges ever since, he found his honours waiting for him full blown. They took it up in a sort of fire-cracker chorus: 'Jim! O Jim! Jim! O Jim! Sssscrowger Jim!' That pleased everybody. And when a poetical Beverly man—he had been making it up all day, and talked about it for weeks—sang 'The "Carrie Pitman's" anchor doesn't hold her for a cent!' the dories felt that they were indeed fortunate. Then they had to ask that Beverly man how he was off for beans, because even poets must not have things all their own way. Every schooner and nearly every man got it in turn. Was there a careless or dirty cook anywhere? The dories sang about him and his food. Was a schooner badly found? The fleet was told at full length. Had a man hooked tobacco from a messmate? He was named in meeting; the name tossed from roller to roller. Disko's infallible judgments, Long Jack's market-boat that he had sold years ago, Dan's sweetheart (oh, but Dan was an angry boy!), Penn's bad luck with dory-anchors, Salters's views on manure, Manuel's little slips from virtue ashore, and Harvey's lady-like handling of the oar—all were laid before the public; and as the fog fell around them in silvery sheets beneath the sun, the voices sounded like a bench of invisible judges pronouncing sentence.

The dories roved and fished and squabbled till a swell underran the sea. Then they drew more apart to save their sides, and some one called that if the swell continued the Virgin would break. A reckless Galway man with his nephew denied this, hauled up anchor, and rowed over the very rock itself. Many voices called them to come away, while others dared them to hold on. As the smooth-backed rollers passed to the southward, they hove the dory high and high into the mist, and dropped her in ugly, sucking, dimpled water, where she spun round her anchor, within a foot or two of the hidden rock. It was playing with death for mere bravado; and the boats looked on in uneasy silence till Long Jack rowed up behind his countrymen and quietly cut their roding.

'Can't ye hear ut knockin'?' he cried. 'Pull for your miserable lives! Pull!'

The men swore and tried to argue as the boat drifted; but the next swell checked a little, like a man tripping on a carpet. There was a deep sob and a gathering roar, and the Virgin flung up a couple of acres of foaming water, white, furious, and ghastly over the shoal sea. Then all the boats greatly applauded Long Jack, and the Galway men held their tongue.

'Ain't it elegant?' said Dan, bobbing like a young seal at home. 'She'll break about once every ha'af hour now, 'less the swell piles up good. What's her reg'lar time when she's at work, Tom Platt?'

'Once ivry fifteen minutes, to the tick. Harve, you've seen the greatest thing on the Banks; an' but for Long Jack you'd seen some dead men too.'

There came a sound of merriment where the fog lay thicker and the schooners were ringing their bells. A big bark nosed cautiously out of the mist, and was received with shouts and cries of, 'Come along, darlin',' from the Irishry.

'Another Frenchman?' said Harvey.

'Hain't you eyes? She's a Baltimore boat, goin' in fear an' tremblin',' said Dan. 'We'll guy the very sticks out of her. Guess it's the fust time her skipper ever met up with the fleet this way.'

She was a black, buxom eight-hundred-ton craft. Her mainsail was looped up, and her topsail flapped undecidedly in what little wind was moving. Now a bark is feminine beyond all other daughters of the sea, and this tall, hesitating creature, with her white and gilt figurehead, looked just like a bewildered woman half lifting her skirts to cross a muddy street under the jeers of bad little boys. That was very much her situation. She knew she was somewhere in the neighbourhood of the Virgin, had caught the roar of it, and was, therefore, asking her way. This is a small part of what she heard from the dancing dories:

'The Virgin? Fwhat are you talkin' of? This is Le Have on a Sunday mornin'. Go home an' sober up.'

'Go home, ye tarrapin! Go home an' tell 'em we're comin'.'

Half a dozen voices together, in a most tuneful chorus, as her stern went down with a roll and a bubble into the troughs: 'Thay-aah—she—strikes!'

'Hard up! Hard up fer your life! You're on top of her now.'

'Daown! Hard daown! Let go everything!'

'All hands to the pumps!'

'Daown jib an' pole her!'

Here the skipper lost his temper and said things. Instantly fishing was suspended to answer him, and he heard many curious facts about his boat and her next port of call. They asked him if he were insured; and whence he had stolen his anchor, because, they said, it belonged to the 'Carrie Pitman'; they called his boat mud-scow, and accused him of dumping garbage to frighten the fish; they offered to tow him and charge it to his wife; and one audacious youth slipped almost under the counter, smacked it with his open palm, and yelled, 'Gid up, Buck!'

The cook emptied a pan of ashes on him, and he replied with cod-heads. The bark's crew fired small coal from the galley, and the dories threatened to come aboard and 'razee' her. They would have warned her at once had she been in real peril; but, seeing her well clear of the Virgin, they made the most of their chances. The fun was spoilt when the rock spoke again, a half-mile to windward, and the tormented bark set everything that would draw and went her ways; but the dories felt that the honours lay with them.

All that night the Virgin roared hoarsely; and next morning, over an angry, white-headed sea, Harvey saw the fleet with flickering masts waiting for a lead. Not a dory was hove out till ten o'clock, when the two Jeraulds of the 'Day's Eye,' imagining a lull which did not exist, set the example. In a minute half the boats were out and bobbing in the cockly swells, but Troop kept the 'We're Heres' at work dressing-down. He saw no sense in 'dares'; and as the storm grew that evening they had the pleasure of receiving wet strangers, only too glad to make any refuge in the gale. The boys stood by the dory-tackles with lanterns, the men ready to haul, one eye cocked for the sweeping wave that would make them drop everything and hold on for the dear life. Out of the dark would come a yell of 'Dory, dory!' They would hook up and haul in a drenched man and a half-sunk boat till their decks were littered down with nests of dories and the bunks were full. Five times in their watch did Harvey, with Dan, jump at the fore-gaff where it lay lashed on the boom, and cling with arms, legs, and teeth to rope and spar and sodden canvas as a big wave filled the decks. One dory was smashed to pieces and the sea pitched the man head first on to the decks, cutting his forehead open; and about dawn, the racing seas glimmered white all along their cold edges, another man, blue and ghastly, crawled in with a broken hand, asking news of his brother. Seven extra mouths sat down to breakfast—a Swede; a Chatham skipper; a boy from Hancock, Maine; one Duxbury, and three Province-town men.

There was a general sorting out among the fleet next day; and though no one said anything, all ate with better appetites when boat after boat reported full crews aboard. Only a couple of Portuguese and an old man from Gloucester were drowned, but many were cut or bruised; and two schooners had parted their tackle and been blown to the southward, three days' sail. A man died on a Frenchman—it was the same bark that had traded tobacco with the 'We're Heres.' She slipped away quite quietly one wet, white morning, moved to a patch of deep water, her sails all hanging anyhow, and Harvey saw the funeral through Disko's spy-glass. It was only an oblong bundle slid over-side. They did not seem to have any form of service, but in the night, at anchor, Harvey heard them across the star-powdered black water singing something that sounded like a hymn. It went to a very slow tune:

> 'La brigantine
> Qui va tourner,
> Roule et s'incline
> Pour m'entrainer.
> Oh, Vierge Marie,
> Pour moi priez Dieu!
> Adieu, patrie;
> Quebec, adieu!'

Tom Platt visited her, because, he said, the dead man was his brother as a Freemason. It came out that a wave had doubled the poor fellow over the heel of the bowsprit and broken his back. The news spread like a flash, for, contrary to general custom, the Frenchman held an auction of the dead man's kit,—he had no friends at St. Malo or Miquelon,—and everything was spread out on the top of the house, from his red knitted cap to the leather belt with the sheath-knife at the back. Dan and Harvey were out on twenty-fathom water in the 'Hattie S.', and naturally rowed over to join the crowd. It was a long pull, and they stayed some little time while Dan bought the knife, which had a curious brass handle. When they dropped over-side and pushed off into a drizzle of rain and a lop of sea, it occurred to them that they might get into trouble for neglecting the lines.

'Guess 'twon't hurt us any to be warmed up,' said Dan, shivering under his oilskins, and they rowed on into the heart of a white fog which, as usual, dropped on them without warning.

'There's too much blame tide hereabouts to trust to your instinks,' he said. 'Heave over the anchor, Harve, and we'll fish a piece till the thing lifts. Bend on your biggest lead. Three pound ain't any too much in this water. See how she's tightened on her rodin' already.'

There was quite a little bubble at the bows, where some irresponsible Bank current held the dory full stretch on her rope; but they could not see a boat's length in any direction. Harvey turned up his collar and bunched himself over his reel with the air of a wearied navigator. Fog had no special terrors for him now. They fished a while in silence, and found the cod struck on well. Then Dan drew the sheath-knife and tested the edge of it on the gunwale.

'That's a daisy,' said Harvey. 'How did you get it so cheap?'

'On account o' their blame Cath'lic superstitions,' said Dan, jabbing with the bright blade. 'They don't fancy takin' iron from off of a dead man, so to speak. See them Arichat Frenchmen step back when I bid?'

'But an auction ain't taking anything off a dead man. It's business.'

'We know it ain't, but there's no goin' in the teeth o' superstition. That's one o' the advantages o' livin' in a progressive country.' And Dan began whistling:

'Oh, Double Thatcher, how are you?
Now Eastern Point comes inter view.
The girls an' boys we soon shall see,
At anchor off Cape Ann!'

'Why didn't that Eastport man bid, then? He bought his boots. Ain't Maine progressive?'

'Maine? Pshaw! They don't know enough, or they hain't got money enough, to paint their haouses in Maine. I've seen 'em. The Eastport man he told me that the knife had been used—so the French captain told him —used up on the French coast last year.'

'Cut a man? Heave's the muckle.' Harvey hauled in his fish, rebaited, and threw over.

'Killed him! Course, when I heard that I was keener'n ever to get it.'

'Christmas! I didn't know it,' said Harvey, turning round. 'I'll give you a dollar for it when I—get my wages. Say, I'll give you two dollars.'

'Honest? D'you like it as much as all that?' said Dan, flushing. 'Well, to tell the truth, I kinder got it for you—to give; but I didn't let on till I saw how you'd take it. It's yours and welcome, Harve, because we're dory-mates, and so on and so forth, an' so followin'. Catch a-holt!'

He held it out, belt and all.

'But look at here. Dan, I don't see—'

'Take it. 'Tain't no use to me. I wish you to hev it.'

The temptation was irresistible. 'Dan, you're a white man,' said Harvey. 'I'll keep it as long as I live.'

'That's good hearin',' said Dan, with a pleasant laugh, and then, anxious to change the subject: 'Looks 's if your line was fast to somethin'.'

'Fouled, I guess,' said Harve, tugging. Before he pulled up he fastened the belt round him, and with deep delight heard the tip of the sheath click on the thwart. 'Con-cern the thing!' he cried. 'She acts as though she were on strawberry-bottom. It's all sand here, ain't it?'

Dan reached over and gave a judgmatic tweak. 'Holibut 'll act that way 'f he's sulky. Thet's not strawberry-bottom. Yank her once or twice. She gives, sure. Guess we'd better haul up an' make certain.'

They pulled together, making fast at each turn on the cleats, and the hidden weight rose sluggishly.

'Prize, oh! Haul!' shouted Dan, but the shout ended in a shrill, double shriek of horror, for out of the sea came—the body of the dead Frenchman buried two days before! The hook had caught him under the right arm-pit, and he swayed, erect and horrible, head and shoulders above water. His arms were tied to his side, and—he had no face. The boys fell over each other in a heap at the bottom of the dory, and there they lay while the thing bobbed alongside, held on the shortened line.

'The tide—the tide brought him!' said Harvey with quivering lips, as he fumbled at the clasp of the belt.

'Oh, Lord! oh, Harve!' groaned Dan, 'be quick. He's come for it. Let him have it. Take it off.'

'I don't want it! I don't want it!' cried Harvey. 'I can't find the bu-buckle.'

'Quick, Harve! He's on your line!'

Harvey sat up to unfasten the belt, facing the head that had no face under its streaming hair. 'He's fast still,' he whispered to Dan, who slipped out his knife and cut the line, as Harvey flung the belt far over-side. The body shot down with a plop, and Dan cautiously rose to his knees, whiter than the fog.

'He come for it. He come for it. I've seen a stale one hauled up on a trawl and I didn't much care, but he come to us special.'

'I wish—I wish I hadn't taken the knife. Then he'd have come on your line.'

'Dunno as thet would ha' made any differ. We're both scared out o' ten years' growth. Oh, Harve, did ye see his head?'

'Did I? I'll never forget it. But look at here, Dan; it couldn't have been meant. It was only the tide.'

'Tide! He come for it, Harve. Why, they sunk him six mile to south'ard o' the fleet, an' we're two miles from where she's lyin' now. They told me he was weighted with a fathom an' a half o' chain-cable.'

'Wonder what he did with the knife—up on the French coast?'

'Something bad. Guess he's bound to take it with him to the Judgment, an' so— What are you doin' with the fish?'

'Heaving 'em overboard,' said Harvey.

'What for? We shan't eat 'em.'

'I don't care. I had to look at his face while I was takin' the belt off. You can keep your catch if you like. I've no use for mine.'

Dan said nothing, but threw his fish over again.

'Guess it's best to be on the safe side,' he murmured at last. 'I'd give a month's pay if this fog 'ud lift. Things go abaout in a fog that ye don't see in clear weather—yo-hoes an' hollerers and such like. I'm sorter relieved he come the way he did instid o' walkin'. He might ha' walked.'

'Do-on't, Dan! We're right on top of him now. Wish I was safe aboard, bein' pounded by Uncle Salters.'

'They'll be lookin' fer us in a little. Gimme the tooter.' Dan took the tin dinner-horn, but paused before he blew.

'Go on,' said Harvey. 'I don't want to stay here all night.'

'Question is, haow he'd take it. There was a man from down the coast told me once he was in a schooner where they darsen't ever blow a horn to the dories, becaze the skipper—not the man he was with, but a captain that had run her five years before—he'd drownded a boy alongside in a drunk fit; an' ever after, that boy he'd row alongside too and shout, "Dory! dory!" with the rest.'

'Dory! dory!' a muffled voice cried through the fog. They cowered again, and the horn dropped from Dan's hand.

'Hold on!' cried Harvey, 'it's the cook.'

'Dunno what made me think o' thet fool tale, either,' said Dan. 'It's the doctor, sure enough.'

'Dan! Danny! Oooh, Dan! Harve! Harvey! Oooh, Haarveee!'

'We're here,' sung both boys together. They heard oars, but could see nothing till the cook, shining and dripping, rowed into them.

'What iss happened?' said he. 'You will be beat at home.'

'Thet's what we want. Thet's what we're sufferin' for,' said Dan. 'Anything homey's good enough fer us. We've had kinder depressin' company.' As the cook passed them a line, Dan told him the tale.

'Yess! He come for hiss knife,' was all he said at the end.

Never had the little rocking 'We're Here' looked so deliciously homelike as when the cook, born and bred in fogs, rowed them back to her. There was a warm glow of light from the cabin and a satisfying smell of food forward, and it was heavenly to hear Disko and the others, all quite alive and solid, leaning over the rail and promising them a first-class pounding. But the cook was a black master of strategy. He did not get the dories aboard till he had given the more striking points of the tale, explaining as he backed and bumped round the counter how Harvey was the mascot to destroy any possible bad luck. So the boys came over-side as rather uncanny heroes, and every one asked them questions instead of pounding them for making trouble. Little Penn delivered quite a speech on the folly of superstitions; but public opinion was against him and in favour of Long Jack, who told the most excruciating ghost-stories till nearly midnight. Under that influence no one except Salters and Penn said anything about 'idolatry' when the cook put a lighted candle, a cake of flour and water, and a pinch of salt on a shingle, and floated them out astern to keep the Frenchman quiet in case he was still restless. Dan lit the candle because he had bought the belt, and the cook grunted and muttered charms as long as he could see the ducking point of flame.

Said Harvey to Dan, as they turned in after watch, 'How about progress and Catholic superstitions?'

'Huh! I guess I'm as enlightened and progressive as the next man, but when it comes to a dead St. Malo deckhand scarin' a couple o' pore boys stiff fer the sake of a thirty-cent knife, why, then, the cook can take hold fer all o' me. I mistrust furriners, livin' or dead.'

Next morning all, except the cook, were rather ashamed of the cere-monies, and went to work double tides, speaking gruffly to one another.

The 'We're Here' was racing neck and neck for her last few loads against the 'Parry Norman'; and so close was the struggle that the fleet took sides and betted tobacco. All hands worked at the lines or dressing-down till they fell asleep where they stood—beginning before dawn and ending when it was too dark to see. They even used the cook as pitcher, and turned Harvey into the hold to pass salt, while Dan helped to dress-down. Luckily a 'Parry Norman' man sprained his wrist falling down the foc'sle, and the 'We're Heres' gained. Harvey could not see how one more fish could be crammed into her, but Disko and Tom Platt stowed and stowed, and planked the mass down with big stones from the ballast, and there was always 'jest another day's work.' Disko did not tell them when all the salt was wetted. He rolled to the lazarette aft the cabin and began hauling out the big mainsail. This was at ten in the morning. The riding-sail was down and the main- and topsail were up by noon, and dories came alongside with letters for home, envying their good fortune. At last she cleared decks, hoisted her flag,—as is the right

of the first boat off the Banks,—upanchored and began to move. Disko
pretended that he wished to accommodate folk who had not sent in their
mail, and so worked her gracefully in and out among the schooners. In
reality, that was his little triumphant procession, and for the fifth year
running it showed what kind of mariner he was. Dan's accordion and
Tom Platt's fiddle supplied the music of the magic verse you must not
sing till all the salt is wet:

> 'Hih! Yih! Yoho! Send your letters raound!
> All our salt is wetted, an' the anchor's off the ground!
> Bend, oh, bend your mains'l, we're back to Yankeeland—
>   With fifteen hunder' quintal,
>   An' fifteen hunder' quintal,
>   'Teen hunder' toppin' quintal,
> 'Twix' old 'Queereau an' Grand.'

The last letters pitched on deck wrapped round pieces of coal, and
the Gloucester men shouted messages to their wives and womenfolk and
owners, while the 'We're Here' finished the musical ride through the fleet,
her headsails quivering like a man's hand when he raises it to say good-bye.

Harvey very soon discovered that the 'We're Here' with her riding-sail,
strolling from berth to berth, and the 'We're Here' headed west by
south under home canvas, were two very different boats. There was a bite
and kick to the wheel even in 'boy's weather'; he could feel the dead
weight in the hold flung forward mightily across the surges, and the
streaming line of bubbles over-side made his eyes dizzy.

Disko kept them busy fiddling with the sails; and when those were
flattened like a racing yacht's, Dan had to wait on the big topsail, which
was put over by hand every time she went about. In spare moments
they pumped, for the packet fish dripped brine, which does not improve
a cargo. But since there was no fishing, Harvey had time to look at the
sea from another point of view. The low-sided schooner was naturally
on most intimate terms with her surroundings. They saw little of the
horizon save when she topped a swell; and usually she was elbowing,
fidgeting, and coaxing her steadfast way through gray, gray-blue, or black
hollows laced across and across with streaks of shivering foam; or rubbing
herself caressingly along the flank of some bigger water-hill. It was as if
she said: 'You wouldn't hurt me, surely? I'm only the little "We're Here."'
Then she would slide away chuckling softly to herself till she was brought
up by some fresh obstacle. The dullest of folk cannot see this kind of
thing hour after hour through long days without noticing it; and Harvey,
being anything but dull, began to comprehend and enjoy the dry chorus

of wave-tops turning over with a sound of incessant tearing; the hurry of the winds working across open spaces and herding the purple-blue cloud-shadows; the splendid upheaval of the red sunrise; the folding and packing away of the morning mists, wall after wall withdrawn across the white floors; the salty glare and blaze of noon; the kiss of rain falling over thousands of dead, flat square miles; the chilly blackening of everything at the day's end; and the million wrinkles of the sea under the moonlight, when the jib-boom solemnly poked at the low stars, and Harvey went down to get a doughnut from the cook.

But the best fun was when the boys were put on the wheel together, Tom Platt within hail, and she cuddled her lee-rail down to the crashing blue, and kept a little home-made rainbow arching unbroken over her windlass. Then the jaws of the booms whined against the mast, and the sheets creaked, and the sails filled with roaring; and when she slid into a hollow she trampled like a woman tripped in her own silk dress, and came out, her jib wet half-way up, yearning and peering for the tall twin lights of Thatcher's Island.

They left the cold gray of the Bank sea, saw the lumber ships making for Quebec by the Straits of St. Lawrence, with the Jersey salt-brigs from Spain and Sicily; found a friendly north-easter off Artimon Bank that drove them within view of the East light of Sable Island—a sight Disko did not linger over—and stayed with them past Western and Le Have, to the northern fringe of Georges. From there they picked up the deeper water, and let her go merrily.

'Hattie's pulling on the string,' Dan confided to Harvey. 'Hattie an' ma. Next Sunday you'll be hirin' a boy to throw water on the windows to make ye go to sleep. Guess you'll keep with us till your folks come. Do you know the best of gettin' ashore again?'

'Hot bath?' said Harvey. His eyebrows were all white with dried spray.

'That's good, but a night-shirt's better. I've been dreamin' o' night-shirts ever since we bent our mainsail. Ye can wiggle your toes then. Ma'll hev a new one fer me, all washed soft. It's home, Harve. It's home! Ye can sense it in the air. We're runnin' into the aidge of a hot wave naow, an' I can smell the bay-berries. Wonder if we'll get in fer supper. Port a trifle.'

The hesitating sails flapped and lurched in the close air as the deep smoothed out, blue and oily, round them. When they whistled for a wind only the rain came in spiky rods, bubbling and drumming, and behind the rain the thunder and the lightning of mid-August. They lay on the deck with bare feet and arms, telling one another what they would order at their first meal ashore; for now the land was in plain sight. A Gloucester sword-fish boat drifted alongside, a man in the little pulpit on the bowsprit flourishing his harpoon, his bare head plastered down with the wet. 'And all's well!' he sang cheerily, as though he were watch on a big liner. 'Wouverman's waiting fer you, Disko. What's the news o' the fleet?'

Disko shouted it and passed on, while the wild summer storm pounded overhead and the lightning flickered along the capes from four different quarters at once. It gave the low circle of hills round Gloucester Harbour, Ten Pound Island, the fish-sheds, with the broken line of house-roofs, and each spar and buoy on the water, in blinding photographs that came and went a dozen times to the minute as the 'We're Here' crawled in on half-flood, and the whistling-buoy moaned and mourned behind her. Then the storm died out in long, separated, vicious dags of blue-white flame, followed by a single roar like the roar of a mortar-battery, and the shaken air tingled under the stars, as it got back to silence.

'The flag, the flag,' said Disko suddenly, pointing upward.

'What is ut?' said Long Jack.

'Otto! Ha'af mast. They can see us from shore now.'

'I'd clean forgot. He's no folk to Gloucester, has he?'

'Girl he was goin' to be married to this fall.'

'Mary pity her!' said Long Jack, and lowered the little flag half-mast for the sake of Otto, swept overboard in a gale off Le Have three months before.

Disko wiped the wet from his eyes and led the 'We're Here' to Wouverman's wharf, giving his orders in whispers, while she swung round moored tugs, and night-watchmen hailed her from the ends of inky-black piers. Over and above the darkness and the mystery of the procession, Harvey could feel the land close round him once more, with its thousands of people asleep, and the smell of earth after rain, and the familiar noise of a switching-engine coughing to herself in a freight-yard; and all those things made his heart beat and his throat dry up as he stood by the foresheet. They heard the anchor-watch snoring on a lighthouse tug, nosed into a pocket of darkness where a lantern glimmered on either side; somebody waked with a grunt, threw them a rope, and they made fast to a silent wharf flanked with great iron-roofed sheds full of warm emptiness, and lay there without a sound.

Then Harvey sat down by the wheel, and sobbed and sobbed as though his heart would break, and a tall woman who had been sitting on a weight-scale dropped down into the schooner and kissed Dan once on the cheek; for she was his mother, and she had seen the 'We're Here' by the lightning flashes. She took no notice of Harvey till he had recovered himself a little, and Disko had told her his story. Then they went to Disko's house together as the dawn was breaking; and until the telegraph office was open and he could wire to his folk, Harvey Cheyne was perhaps the loneliest boy in all America. But the curious thing was that Disko and Dan seemed to think none the worse of him for crying.

Wouverman was not ready for Disko's prices till Disko, sure that the 'We're Here' was at least a week ahead of any other Gloucester boat, had given him a few days to swallow them; so all hands played about the streets, and Long Jack stopped the Rocky Neck trolley, on principle, as he said, till the conductor let him ride free. But Dan went about with his freckled nose in the air, bung-full of mystery and most haughty to his family.

'Dan, I'll hev to lay inter you ef you act this way,' said Troop pensively. 'Sence we've come ashore this time you've bin a heap too fresh.'

'I'd lay into him naow ef he was mine,' said Uncle Salters sourly. He and Penn boarded with the Troops.

'Oho!' said Dan, shuffling with the accordion round the back yard, ready to leap the fence if the enemy advanced. 'Dad, you're welcome to your own jedgment, but remember I've warned ye. Your own flesh an' blood ha' warned ye! 'Tain't any o' my fault ef you're mistook, but I'll be on deck to watch ye. An' ez fer yeou, Uncle Salters, Pharaoh's chief butler ain't in it 'longside o' you! You watch aout an' wait. You'll be ploughed under like your own blamed clover; but me—Dan Troop—I'll flourish like a green bay-tree because I warn't stuck on my own opinion.'

Disko was smoking in all his shore dignity and a pair of beautiful carpet slippers. 'You're gettin' ez crazy as poor Harve. You two go araound gigglin' an' squinchin' an' kickin' each other under the table till there's no peace in the haouse,' said he.

'There's goin' to be a heap less—fer some folks,' Dan replied. 'You wait an' see.'

He and Harvey went out on the trolley to East Gloucester, where they tramped through the bay-berry bushes to the lighthouse, and lay down on the big red boulders and laughed themselves hungry. Harvey had shown Dan a telegram, and the two swore to keep silence till the shell burst.

'Harve's folk?' said Dan, with an unruffled face after supper. 'Well, I guess they don't amount to much of anything, or we'd ha' heard from 'em by naow. His pop keeps a kind o' store out West. Maybe he'll give you's much as five dollars, dad.'

'What did I tell ye?' said Salters. 'Don't sputter over your vittles, Dan.'

Chapter 9

WHATEVER HIS PRIVATE sorrows may be, a multi-millionaire, like any other working man, should keep abreast of his business. Harvey Cheyne, senior, had gone East late in June to meet a woman broken down, half mad, who dreamed day and night of her son drowning in the gray seas. He had surrounded her with doctors, trained nurses, massage women, and even faith-cure companions, but they were useless. Mrs. Cheyne lay still and moaned, or talked of her boy by the hour together to any one who would listen. Hope she had none, and who could offer it? All she needed was assurance that drowning did not hurt; and her husband watched to guard lest she should make the experiment. Of his own sorrow he spoke little—hardly realised the depth of it till he caught himself asking the calendar on his writing-desk, 'What's the use of going on?'

There had always lain a pleasant notion at the back of his head that, some day, when he had rounded off everything and the boy had left college, he would take his son to his heart and lead him into his possessions. Then that boy, he argued, as busy fathers do, would instantly become his companion, partner, and ally, and there would follow splendid years of great works carried out together—the old head backing the young fire. Now his boy was dead—lost at sea, as it might have been a Swede sailor from one of Cheyne's big tea-ships; the wife was dying, or worse; he himself was trodden down by platoons of women and doctors and maids and attendants; worried almost beyond endurance by the shift and change of her poor restless whims; hopeless, with no heart to meet his many enemies.

He had taken the wife to his raw new palace in San Diego, where she and her people occupied a wing of great price, and Cheyne, in a veranda-room between a secretary and a typewriter, who was also a telegraphist, toiled along wearily from day to day. There was a war of rates among four Western railroads in which he was supposed to be interested; a devastating strike had developed in his lumber-camps in Oregon, and the legislature of the State of California, which has no love for its makers, was preparing open war against him.

Ordinarily he would have accepted battle ere it was offered, and have waged a pleasant and unscrupulous campaign. But now he sat limply, his soft black hat pushed forward on to his nose, his big body shrunk inside his loose clothes, staring at his boots or the Chinese junks in the bay, and assenting absently to the secretary's questions as he opened the Saturday mail.

Cheyne was wondering how much it would cost to drop everything and pull out. He carried huge insurances, could buy himself royal annuities, and between one of his places in Colorado and a little society (that would do the wife good), say in Washington and the South Carolina islands, a man might forget plans that had come to nothing. On the other hand. . . .

The click of the typewriter stopped; the girl was looking at the secretary, who had turned white.

He passed Cheyne a telegram repeated from San Francisco:—

'Picked up by fishing schooner "We're Here" having fallen off boat great times on Banks fishing all well waiting Gloucester Mass care Disko Troop for money or orders wire what shall do and how is mamma Harvey N. Cheyne.'

The father let it fall, laid his head down on the roller-top of the shut desk, and breathed heavily. The secretary ran for Mrs. Cheyne's doctor, who found Cheyne pacing to and fro.

'What—what d'you think of it? Is it possible? Is there any meaning to it? I can't quite make it out,' he cried.

'I can,' said the doctor. 'I lose seven thousand a year—that's all.' He thought of the struggling New York practice he had dropped at Cheyne's imperious bidding, and returned the telegram with a sigh.

'You mean you'd tell her? 'May be a fraud?'

'What's the motive?' said the doctor coolly. 'Detection's too certain. It's the boy sure enough.'

Enter a French maid, impudently, as an indispensable one who is kept on only by large wages.

'Mrs. Cheyne she say you must come at once. She think you are seek.'

The master of thirty millions bowed his head meekly and followed Suzanne; and a thin, high voice on the upper landing of the great whitewood square staircase cried, 'What is it? What has happened?'

No doors could keep out the shriek that rang through the echoing house a moment later, when her husband blurted out the news.

'And that's all right,' said the doctor serenely to the typewriter. 'About the only medical statement in novels with any truth to it is that joy don't kill, Miss Kinzey.'

'I know it; but we've a heap to do first.' Miss Kinzey was from Milwaukee, somewhat direct of speech, and as her fancy leaned towards the secretary, she divined there was work in hand. He was looking earnestly at the vast roller-map of America on the wall.

'Milsom, we're going right across. Private car—straight through—Boston. Fix the connections,' shouted Cheyne down the staircase.

'I thought so.'

The secretary turned to the typewriter, and their eyes met (out of that was born a story—nothing to do with this story). She looked inquiringly, doubtful of his resources. He signed to her to move to the Morse as a general brings brigades into action. Then he swept his hand musician-wise through his hair, regarded the ceiling, and set to work, while Miss Kinzey's white fingers called up the Continent of America.

'"K. H. Wade, Los Angeles—" The "Constance" is at Los Angeles, isn't she, Miss Kinzey?'

'Yep.' Miss Kinzey nodded between clicks as the secretary looked at his watch.

'Ready? "Send 'Constance,' private car, here, and arrange for special to leave here Sunday in time to connect with New York Limited at Sixteenth Street, Chicago, Tuesday next."'

Click—click—click! 'Couldn't you better that?' said Miss Kinzey.

'Not on those grades. That gives 'em sixty hours from here to Chicago. They won't gain anything by taking a special east of that. Ready? "Also arrange with Lake Shore and Michigan Southern to take 'Constance' on New York Central and Hudson River Buffalo to Albany, and B. and A. the same Albany to Boston. Indispensable I should reach Boston Wednesday evening. Be sure nothing prevents. Have also wired Canniff, Toucey, and Barnes.—Signed Cheyne."'

Miss Kinzey nodded, and the secretary went on.

'Now then. Canniff, Toucey, and Barnes, of course. Ready? "Canniff, Chicago. Please take my private car 'Constance' from Santa Fe at Sixteenth Street next Tuesday p.m. on N.Y. Limited through to Buffalo and deliver N.Y.C. for Albany."—Ever bin to N'York, Miss Kinzey? We'll go some day.—Ready? "Take 'Constance' car Buffalo to Albany on Limited Tuesday p.m." That's for Toucey.'

'Haven't bin to Noo York, but I know that!' with a toss of the head.

'Beg pardon. Now, Boston and Albany, Barnes, same instructions from Albany through to Boston. Leave three-five p.m. (you needn't wire that); arrive nine-five p.m. Wednesday. That covers everything Wade will do, but it pays to shake up the managers.'

'It's great,' said Miss Kinzey, with a look of admiration. This was the kind of man she understood and appreciated.

''Tisn't bad,' said Milsom modestly. 'Now, any one but me would have lost thirty hours and spent a week working out the run, instead of handing him over to the Santa Fe straight through to Chicago.'

'But see here, about that Noo York Limited. Chauncey Depew himself couldn't hitch his car to her,' Miss Kinzey suggested, recovering herself.

'Yes, but this isn't Chauncey. It's Cheyne—lightning. It goes.'

'Even so. 'Guess we'd better wire the boy. You've forgotten that, anyhow.'

'I'll ask.'

When he returned with the father's message bidding Harvey meet them in Boston at an appointed hour, he found Miss Kinzey laughing over the keys. Then Milsom laughed too, for the frantic clicks from Los Angeles ran: 'We want to know why—why—why? General uneasiness developed and spreading.'

Ten minutes later Chicago appealed to Miss Kinzey in these words: 'If crime of century is maturing please warn friends in time. We are all getting to cover here.'

This was capped by a message from Topeka (and wherein Topeka was concerned even Milsom could not guess): 'Don't shoot, Colonel. We'll come down.'

Cheyne smiled grimly at the consternation of his enemies when the telegrams were laid before him. 'They think we're on the war-path. Tell 'em we don't feel like fighting just now, Milsom. Tell 'em what we're going for. I guess you and Miss Kinzey had better come along, though it isn't likely I shall do any business on the road. Tell 'em the truth—for once.'

So the truth was told. Miss Kinzey clicked in the sentiment while the secretary added the memorable quotation, 'Let us have peace,' and in board-rooms two thousand miles away the representatives of sixty-three million dollars' worth of variously manipulated railroad interests breathed more freely. Cheyne was flying to meet the only son, so miraculously restored to him. The bear was seeking his cub, not the bulls. Hard men who had their knives drawn to fight for their financial lives put away the weapons and wished him God-speed, while half a dozen panic-smitten tinpot roads perked up their heads and spoke of the wonderful things they would have done had not Cheyne buried the hatchet.

It was a busy week-end among the wires: for, now that their anxiety was removed, men and cities hastened to accommodate. Los Angeles called to San Diego and Barstow that the Southern California engineers might know and be ready in their lonely roundhouses; Barstow passed the word to the Atlantic and Pacific; and Albuquerque flung it the whole length of the Atchison, Topeka, and Santa Fe management, even into Chicago. An engine, combination-car with crew, and the great and gilded 'Constance' private car were to be 'expedited' over those two thousand three hundred and fifty miles. The train would take precedence of one hundred and seventy-seven others meeting and passing; despatchers and crews of every one of those said trains must be notified. Sixteen locomotives, sixteen engineers, and sixteen firemen would be needed—each and every one the best available. Two and one-half minutes would be allowed for changing engines; three for watering and two for coaling. 'Warn the men, and arrange tanks and chutes accordingly; for Harvey Cheyne is in a hurry, a hurry—a hurry,' sang the wires. 'Forty miles an hour will be expected, and division superintendents will accompany this special over their respective divisions. From San Diego to Sixteenth Street, Chicago, let the magic carpet be laid down. Hurry! oh, hurry!'

'It will be hot,' said Cheyne, as they rolled out of San Diego in the dawn of Sunday. 'We're going to hurry, mamma, just as fast as ever we can; but I really don't think there's any good of your putting on your bonnet and gloves yet. You'd much better lie down and take your medicine. I'd play you a game o' dominoes, but it's Sunday.'

'I'll be good. Oh, I will be good. Only—taking off my bonnet makes me feel as if we'd never get there.'

'Try to sleep a little, mamma, and we'll be in Chicago before you know.'

'But it's Boston, father. Tell them to hurry.'

The six-foot drivers were hammering their way to San Bernardino and the Mohave wastes, but this was no grade for speed. That would come later. The heat of the desert followed the heat of the hills as they turned east to the Needles and the Colorado River. The car cracked in the utter drouth and glare, and they put crushed ice to Mrs. Cheyne's neck, and toiled up the long, long grades, past Ash Fork, towards Flagstaff, where the forests and quarries are, under the dry, remote skies. The needle of the speed-indicator flicked and wagged to and fro; the cinders rattled on the roof, and a whirl of dust sucked after the whirling wheels. The crew of the combination sat on their bunks, panting in their shirt-sleeves, and Cheyne found himself among them shouting old old stories of the railroad that every trainman knows, above the roar of the car. He told them about his son, and how the sea had given up its dead, and they nodded and spat and rejoiced with him; asked after 'her, back there,' and whether she could stand it if the engineer 'let her out a piece,' and Cheyne thought she could. Accordingly, the great fire-horse was 'let out' from Flagstaff to Winslow till a division superintendent protested.

But Mrs. Cheyne, in the boudoir state-room, where the French maid, sallow-white with fear, clung to the silver doorhandle, only moaned a little and begged her husband to bid them 'hurry.' And so they dropped the dry sands and moon-struck rocks of Arizona behind them, and grilled on till the crash of the couplings and the wheeze of the brake-hose told them they were at Coolidge by the Continental Divide.

Three bold and experienced men—cool, confident, and dry when they began; white, quivering, and wet when they finished their trick at those terrible wheels—swung her over the great lift from Albuquerque to Glorietta and beyond Springer, up and up to the Raton Tunnel on the State line, whence they dropped rocking into La Junta, had sight of the Arkansaw, and tore down the long slope to Dodge City, where Cheyne took comfort once again from setting his watch an hour ahead.

There was very little talk in the car. The secretary and typewriter sat together on the stamped Spanish leather cushions by the plate-glass observation window at the rear end, watching the surge and ripple of the ties crowded back behind them, and, it is believed, making notes of the scenery. Cheyne moved nervously between his own extravagant gorgeousness and the naked necessity of the combination, an unlit cigar in his teeth, till the pitying crews forgot that he was their tribal enemy, and did their best to entertain him.

At night the bunched electrics lit up that distressful palace of all the luxuries, and they fared sumptuously, swinging on through the emptiness of abject desolation. Now they heard the swish of a water-tank, and the guttural voice of a Chinaman, the clink-clink of hammers that tested the Krupp-steel wheels, and the oath of a tramp chased off the rear platform; now the solid crash of coal shot into the tender; and now a beating back of noises as they flew past a waiting train. Now they looked out into great abysses, a trestle purring beneath their tread, or up to rocks that barred out half the stars. Now scaur and ravine changed and rolled back to jagged mountains on the horizon's edge, and now broke into hills lower and lower, till at last came the true plains.

At Dodge City an unknown hand threw in a copy of a Kansas paper containing some sort of an interview with Harvey, who had evidently fallen in with an enterprising reporter, telegraphed on from Boston. The joyful journalese revealed that it was beyond question their boy, and it soothed Mrs. Cheyne for a while. Her one word 'hurry' was conveyed by the crews to the engineers at Nickerson, Topeka, and Marceline, where the grades are easy, and they brushed the continent behind them. Towns and villages were close together now, and a man could feel here that he moved among people.

'I can't see the dial, and my eyes ache so. What are we doing?'

'The very best we can, mamma. There's no sense in getting before the Limited. We'd only have to wait.'

'I don't care. I want to feel we're moving. Sit down and tell me the miles.'

Cheyne sat down and read the dial for her (there were some miles which stand for records to this day), but the seventy-foot car never changed its long steamer-like roll, moving through the heat with the hum of a giant bee. Yet the speed was not enough for Mrs. Cheyne; and the heat, the remorseless August heat, was making her giddy; the clock hands would not move, and when, oh, when would they be in Chicago?

It is not true, as they changed engines at Fort Madison, Cheyne passed over to the Amalgamated Brotherhood of Locomotive Engineers an endowment sufficient to enable them to fight him and his fellows on equal terms for evermore. He paid his obligations to engineers and firemen as he believed they deserved, and only his bank knows what he gave the crews who had sympathised with him. It is on record that the last crew took entire charge of switching operations at Sixteenth Street, because 'she' was in a doze at last, and Heaven was to help any one who bumped her.

Now the highly-paid specialist who conveys the Lake Shore and Michigan Southern Limited from Chicago to Elkhart is something of an autocrat, and he does not approve of being told how to back up to a car. None the less he handled the 'Constance' as if she might have been a load of dynamite, and when the crew rebuked him, they did it in whispers and dumb show.

'Pshaw!' said the Atchison, Topeka, and Santa Fe men, discussing life later; 'we weren't runnin' for a record. Harvey Cheyne's wife she were sick back, an' we didn't want to jounce her. Come to think of it, our runnin' time from San Diego to Chicago was 57.54. You can tell that to them Eastern way-trains. When we're tryin' for a record, we'll let you know.'

To the Western man (though this would not please either city), Chicago and Boston are cheek by jowl, and some railroads encourage the delusion. The Limited whirled the 'Constance' into Buffalo, and the arms of the New York Central and Hudson River (illustrious magnates with white whiskers and gold charms on their watch-chains boarded her here to talk a little business to Cheyne), who slid her gracefully into Albany, where the Boston and Albany completed the run from tide-water to tide-water—total time, eighty-seven hours and thirty-five minutes, or three days, fifteen hours and one-half. Harvey was waiting for them.

After violent emotion most people and all boys demand food. They feasted the returned prodigal behind drawn curtains, cut off in their great happiness, while the trains roared in and out around them. Harvey ate, drank, and enlarged on his adventures all in one breath, and when he had a hand free his mother fondled it. His voice was thickened with living in the open, salt air; his palms were rough and hard, his wrists dotted with the marks of gurry-sores; and a fine full flavour of cod-fish hung round rubber boots and blue jersey.

The father, well used to judging men, looked at him keenly. He did not know what enduring harm the boy might have taken. Indeed, he caught himself thinking that he knew very little whatever of his son; but he distinctly remembered an unsatisfied dough-faced youth who took delight in 'calling down the old man' and reducing his mother to tears—such a person as adds to the gaiety of public rooms and hotel piazzas where the ingenuous young of the wealthy play with or revile the bell-boys. But this well-set-up fisher youth did not wriggle, looked at him with eyes steady, clear, and unflinching, and spoke in a tone distinctly, even startlingly, respectful. There was that in his voice, too, which seemed to promise that the change might be permanent, and that the new Harvey had come to stay.

'Some one's been coercing him,' thought Cheyne. 'Now Constance would never have allowed that. Don't see as Europe could have done it any better.'

'But why didn't you tell this man, Troop, who you were?' the mother repeated, when Harvey had expanded his story at least twice.

'Disko Troop, dear. The best man that ever walked a deck. I don't care who the next is.'

'Why didn't you tell him to put you ashore? You know papa would have made it up to him ten times over.'

'I know it; but he thought I was crazy. I'm afraid I called him a thief because I couldn't find the bills in my pocket.'

'A sailor found them by the flagstaff that—that night,' sobbed Mrs. Cheyne.

'That explains it, then. I don't blame Troop any. I just said I wouldn't work—on a Banker, too—and of course he hit me on the nose, and, oh! I bled like a stuck hog.'

'My poor darling! They must have abused you horribly.'

'Dunno quite. Well, after that, I saw a light.'

Cheyne slapped his leg and chuckled. This was going to be a boy after his own hungry heart. He had never seen precisely that twinkle in Harvey's eye before.

'And the old man gave me ten and a half a month; he's paid me half now; and I took hold with Dan and pitched right in. I can't do a man's work yet. But I can handle a dory 'most as well as Dan, and I don't get rattled in a fog—much; and I can take my trick in light winds—that's steering, dear—and I can 'most bait up a trawl, and I know my ropes, of course; and I can pitch fish till the cows come home, and I'm great on old Josephus, and I'll show you how I can clear coffee with a piece of fish-skin and—I think I'll have another cup, please. Say, you've no notion what a heap of work there is in ten and a half a month!'

'I began with eight and a half, my son,' said Cheyne.

'That so? You never told me, sir.'

'You never asked, Harve. I'll tell you about it some day, if you care to listen. Try a stuffed olive.'

'Troop says the most interesting thing in the world is to find out how the next man gets his vittles. It's great to have a trimmed-up meal again. We were well fed, though. Best mug on the Banks. Disko fed us first-class. He's a great man. And Dan—that's his son—Dan's my partner. And there's Uncle Salters and his manures, an' he reads Josephus. He's sure I'm crazy yet. And there's poor little Penn, and he is crazy. You mustn't talk to him about Johnstown, because— And oh, you must know Tom Platt and Long Jack and Manuel. Manuel saved my life. I'm sorry he's a Portuguee. He can't talk much, but he's an everlasting musician. He found me struck adrift and drifting, and hauled me in.'

'I wonder your nervous system isn't completely wrecked,' said Mrs. Cheyne.

'What for, mamma? I worked like a horse and I ate like a hog and I slept like a dead man.'

That was too much for Mrs. Cheyne, who began to think of her visions of a corpse rocking on the salty seas. She went to her state-room, and Harvey curled up beside his father, explaining his indebtedness.

'You can depend upon me to do everything I can for the crowd, Harve. They seem to be good men on your showing.'

'Best in the fleet, sir. Ask at Gloucester,' said Harvey. 'But Disko believes still he's cured me of being crazy. Dan's the only one I've let on to about you, and our private cars and all the rest of it, and I'm not quite sure Dan believes. I want to paralyse 'em tomorrow. Say, can't they run the "Constance" over to Gloucester? Mamma don't look fit to be moved, anyway, and we're bound to finish cleaning out by tomorrow. Wouverman takes our fish. You see, we're first off the Banks this season, and it's four twenty-five a quintal. We held out till he paid it. They want it quick.'

'You mean you'll have to work to-morrow, then?'

'I told Troop I would. I'm on the scales. I've brought the tallies with me.' He looked at the greasy note-book with an air of importance that made his father choke. 'There isn't but three—no—two ninety-four or five quintal more by my reckoning.'

'Hire a substitute,' suggested Cheyne, to see what Harvey would say.

'Can't, sir. I'm tally-man for the schooner. Troop says I've a better head for figures than Dan. Troop's a mighty just man.'

'Well, suppose I don't move the "Constance" tonight, how'll you fix it?'
Harvey looked at the clock, which marked twenty past eleven.

'Then I'll sleep here till three and catch the four o'clock freight. They
let us men from the fleet ride free as a rule.'

'That's a notion. But I think we can get the "Constance" around about
as soon as your men's freight. Better go to bed now.'

Harvey spread himself on the sofa, kicked off his boots, and was asleep
before his father could shade the electrics. Cheyne sat watching the
young face under the shadow of the arm thrown over the forehead, and
among many things that occurred to him was the notion that he might
perhaps have been neglectful as a father.

'One never knows when one's taking one's biggest risks,' he said. 'It
might have been worse than drowning; but I don't think it has—I don't
think it has. If it hasn't, I haven't enough to pay Troop, that's all. And
I don't think it has.'

Morning brought a fresh sea breeze through the windows, the 'Constance' was side-tracked among freight-cars at Gloucester, and Harvey
had gone to his business.

'Then he'll fall overboard again and be drowned,' the mother said
bitterly.

'We'll go and look, ready to throw him a rope in case. You've never
seen him working for his bread,' said the father.

'What nonsense! As if any one expected—'

'Well, the man that hired him did. He's about right, too.'

They went down between the stores full of fishermen's oilskins to
Wouverman's wharf, where the 'We're Here' rode high, her Bank flag
still flying, all hands busy as beavers in the glorious morning light. Disko
stood by the main-hatch superintending Manuel, Penn, and Uncle Salters at the tackle. Dan was swinging the loaded baskets inboard as Long
Jack and Tom Platt filled them, and Harvey, with a note-book, represented the skipper's interests before the clerk of the scales on the salt-
sprinkled wharf-edge.

'Ready!' cried the voices below. 'Haul!' cried Disko. 'Hi!' said Manuel.
'Here!' said Dan, swinging the basket. Then they heard Harvey's voice,
clear and fresh, checking the weights.

The last of the fish had been whipped out, and Harvey leaped from
the string-piece six feet to a ratline, as the shortest way to hand Disko the
tally, shouting, 'Two ninety-seven, and an empty hold!'

'What's total, Harve?' said Disko.

'Eight sixty-five. Three thousand six hundred and seventy-six dollars
and a quarter. Wish I'd share as well as wage.'

'Well, I won't go so far as to say you hevn't deserved it, Harve. Don't you want to slip up to Wouverman's office, and take him our tallies?'

'Who's that boy?' said Cheyne to Dan, well used to all manner of questions from those idle imbeciles called summer boarders.

'Well, he's a kind o' supercargo,' was the answer. 'We picked him up struck adrift on the Banks. Fell overboard from a liner, he sez. He was a passenger. He's by way o' bein' a fisherman now.'

'Is he worth his keep?'

'Ye-ep. Dad, this man wants to know ef Harvey's worth his keep. Say, would you like to go aboard? We'll fix a ladder for her.'

'I should very much, indeed. 'Twon't hurt you, mamma, and you'll be able to see for yourself.'

The woman who could not lift her head a week ago scrambled down the ladder, and stood aghast amid the mess and tangle aft.

'Be you anyways interested in Harve?' said Disko.

'Well, ye-es.'

'He's a good boy, an' ketches right hold jest as he's bid. You've heard haow we found him? He was sufferin' from nervous prostration, I guess, 'r else his head had hit somethin', when we hauled him aboard. He's all over that naow. Yes, this is the cabin. 'Tain't anyways in order, but you're quite welcome to look round. Those are his figures on the stovepipe, where we keep the reckonin' mostly.'

'Did he sleep here?' said Mrs. Cheyne, sitting on a yellow locker and surveying the disorderly bunks.

'No. He berthed forward, madam, an' only fer him an' my boy hookin' fried pies an' muggin' up when they ought to ha' been asleep, I dunno as I've any special fault to find with him.'

'There weren't nothin' wrong with Harve,' said Uncle Salters, descending the steps. 'He hung my boots on the main-truck, and he ain't over an' above respectful to such as knows more'n he do, 'specially about farmin'; but he were mostly misled by Dan.'

Dan in the meantime, profiting by dark hints from Harvey early that morning, was executing a war-dance on deck. 'Tom, Tom!' he whispered down the hatch. 'His folks has come, an' dad hain't caught on yet, an' they're pow-wowin' in the cabin. She's a daisy, an' he's all Harve claimed he was, by the looks of him.'

'Howly Smoke!' said Long Jack, climbing out covered with salt and fish-skin. 'D'ye belave his tale av the kid an' the little four-horse rig was thrue?'

'I knew it all along,' said Dan. 'Come an' see dad mistook in his judgments.'

They came delightedly, just in time to hear Cheyne say, 'I'm glad he has a good character, because—he's my son.'

Disko's jaw fell—Long Jack always vowed that he heard the click of it,—and he stared alternately at the man and the woman.

'I got his telegram in San Diego four days ago, and we came over.'

'In a private car?' said Dan. 'He said ye might.'

'In a private car, of course.'

Dan looked at his father with a hurricane of irreverent winks.

'There was a tale he tould us av drivin' four little ponies in a rig av his own,' said Long Jack. 'Was that thrue now?'

'Very likely,' said Cheyne. 'Was it, mamma?'

'He had a little drag of his own when we were in Toledo, I think,' said the mother.

Long Jack whistled. 'Oh, Disko,' said he, and that was all.

'I wuz—I am mistook in my jedgments—worse'n the men o' Marble-head,' said Disko, as though the words were being windlassed out of him. 'I don't mind ownin' to you, Mister Cheyne, as I mistrusted the boy to be crazy. He talked kinder odd about money.'

'So he told me.'

'Did he tell ye anything else? 'Cause I pounded him once.' This with a somewhat anxious glance at Mrs. Cheyne.

'Oh, yes,' Cheyne replied. 'I should say it probably did him more good than anything else in the world.'

'I jedged 'twuz necessary, er I wouldn't ha' done it. I don't want you to think we abuse our boys any on this packet.'

'I don't think you do, Mr. Troop.'

Mrs. Cheyne had been looking at the faces—Disko's ivory-yellow, hairless, iron countenance; Uncle Salters's with its rim of agricultural hair; Penn's bewildered simplicity; Manuel's quiet smile; Long Jack's grin of delight, and Tom Platt's scar. Rough, by her standards, they certainly were; but she had a mother's wits in her eyes, and she rose with outstretched hands.

'Oh, tell me, which is who,' said she, half sobbing. 'I want to thank you and bless you—all of you.'

'Faith, that pays me a hunder time,' said Long Jack.

Disko introduced them all in due form. The captain of an old-time Chinaman could have done no better, and Mrs. Cheyne babbled incoherently. She nearly threw herself into Manuel's arms when she understood that he had first found Harvey.

'But how shall I leave him dreeft?' said poor Manuel. 'What do you yourself if you find him so? Eh, wha-at? We are in one good boy, and I am ever so pleased he come to be your son.'

'And he told me Dan was his partner!' she cried. Dan was already sufficiently pink, but he turned a rich crimson when Mrs. Cheyne kissed him on both cheeks before the assembly. Then they led her forward to show her the foc'sle, at which she wept again, and must needs go down to see Harvey's identical bunk, and there she found the nigger cook cleaning up the stove, and he nodded as though she were some one he had expected to meet for years. They tried, two at a time, to explain the boat's daily life to her, and she sat by the pawl-post, her gloved hands on the greasy table, laughing with trembling lips and crying with dancing eyes.

'And who's ever to use the "We're Here" after this?' said Long Jack to Tom Platt. 'I feel as if she'd made a cathedral av ut all.'

'Cathedral!' sneered Tom Platt. 'Oh, if it had bin even the Fish C'mission boat instid o' this bally-hoo o' blazes. Ef we only hed some decency an' order an' side-boys when she goes over. She'll have to climb that ladder like a hen, an' we—we ought to be mannin' the yards!'

'Then Harvey was not mad,' said Penn slowly to Cheyne.

'No, indeed—thank God,' the big millionaire replied, stooping down tenderly.

'It must be terrible to be mad. Except to lose your child, I do not know anything more terrible. But your child has come back? Let us thank God for that.'

'Hello!' said Harvey, looking down upon them benignly from the wharf.

'I wuz mistook, Harve. I wuz mistook,' said Disko swiftly, holding up a hand. 'I wuz mistook in my jedgments. Ye needn't rub it in any more.'

'Guess I'll take care o' that,' said Dan, under his breath.

'You'll be goin' off naow, won't ye?'

'Well, not without the balance of my wages 'less you want to have the "We're Here" attached.'

'Thet's so; I'd clean forgot,' and he counted out the remaining dollars. 'You done all you contracted to do, Harve; and you done it baout's well as ef you'd been brought up—' Here Disko brought himself up. He did not quite see where the sentence was going to end.

'Outside of a private car?' suggested Dan wickedly.

'Come on, and I'll show her to you,' said Harvey.

Cheyne stayed to talk to Disko, but the others made a procession to the depot, with Mrs. Cheyne at the head. The French maid shrieked at the invasion; and Harvey laid the glories of the 'Constance' before them without a word. They took them in in equal silence—stamped leather, silver doorhandles and rails, cut velvet, plateglass, nickel, bronze, hammered iron, and the rare woods of the continent inlaid.

'I told you,' said Harvey; 'I told you.' This was his crowning revenge, and a most ample one.

Mrs. Cheyne decreed a meal; and that nothing might be lacking to the tale Long Jack told afterwards in his boarding-house, she waited on them herself. Men who are accustomed to eat at tiny tables in howling gales have curiously neat and finished table-manners; but Mrs. Cheyne, who did not know this, was surprised. She longed to have Manuel for a butler; so silently and easily did he comport himself among the frail glass-ware and dainty silver. Tom Platt remembered great days on the 'Ohio,' and the manners of foreign potentates who dined with the officers; and Long Jack, being Irish, supplied the small talk till all were at their ease.

In the 'We're Here's' cabin the fathers took stock of each other behind their cigars. Cheyne knew well enough when he dealt with a man to whom he could not offer money; equally well he knew that no money could pay for what Disko had done. He kept his own counsel and waited for an opening.

'I hevn't done anything to your boy or fer your boy excep' make him work a piece an' learn him how to handle the hog-yoke,' said Disko. 'He has twice my boy's head for figgers.'

'By the way,' Cheyne answered casually, 'what d'you calculate to make of your boy?'

Disko removed his cigar and waved it comprehensively round the cabin. 'Dan's jest plain boy, an' he don't allow me to do any of his thinkin'. He'll hev this able little packet when I'm laid by. He ain't noways anxious to quit the business. I know that.'

'Mmm! Ever been West, Mr. Troop?'

'Bin's fer ez Noo York once in a boat. I've no use for railroads; no more hez Dan. Salt water's good enough fer the Troops. I've been 'most everywhere—in the nat'ral way, o' course.'

'I can give him all the salt water he's likely to need—till he's a skipper.'

'Haow's that? I thought you wuz a kinder railroad king. Harve told me so when—I was mistook in my jedgments.'

'We're all apt to be mistaken. I fancied perhaps you might know I own a line of tea-clippers—San Francisco to Yokohama. Six of 'em—iron-built, about seventeen hundred and eighty tons apiece.'

'Blame that boy! He never told. I'd ha' listened to that, instid o' his truck abaout railroads an' pony carriages.'

'He didn't know.'

'Little thing like that slipped his mind, I guess.'

'No, I only capt—took hold of the "Blue M." freighters—Morgan and M'Quade's old line—this summer.'

Disko collapsed where he sat, beside the stove.

'Great Cæsar Almighty! I mistrust I've bin fooled from one end to the other. Why, Phil Airheart he went from this very town six year back—no, seven—an' he's mate on the "San Jose" now—twenty-six days was her time out. His sister she's livin' here yet, an' she reads his letters to my woman. An' you own the "Blue M." freighters?'

Cheyne nodded.

'If I'd known that I'd ha' jerked the "We're Here" back to port all standin', on the word.'

'Perhaps that wouldn't have been so good for Harvey.'

'Ef I'd only known! If he'd only said about the cussed Line, I'd ha' understood! I'll never stand on my own jedgments again—never. They're well-found packets. Phil Airheart he says so.'

'I'm glad to have a recommend from that quarter. Airheart's skipper of the "San Jose" now. What I was getting at is to know whether you'd lend me Dan for a year or two, and we'll see if we can't make a mate of him. Would you trust him to Airheart?'

'It's a resk taking a raw boy—'

'I know a man who did more for me.'

'That's diff'runt. Look at here naow, I ain't recommendin' Dan special because he's my own flesh an' blood. I know Bank ways ain't clipper ways, but he hain't much to learn. Steer he can—no boy better, if I say it—an' the rest's in our blood an' get; but I could wish he warn't so cussed weak on navigation.'

'Airheart will attend to that. He'll ship as a boy for a voyage or two, and then we can put him in the way of doing better. Suppose you take him in hand this winter, and I'll send for him early in the spring. I know the Pacific's a long ways off—'

'Pshaw! We Troops, livin' an' dead, are all around the earth an' the seas thereof.'

'But I want you to understand—and I mean this—anytime you think you'd like to see him, tell me, and I'll attend to the transportation. 'Twon't cost you a cent.'

'Ef you'll walk a piece with me, we'll go to my house an' talk this to my woman. I've bin so crazy mistook in all my jedgments, it don't seem to me this was like to be real.'

They went over to Troop's eighteen-hundred-dollar, blue-trimmed white house, with a retired dory full of nasturtiums in the front yard and a shuttered parlour which was a museum of oversea plunder. There sat a large woman, silent and grave, with the dim eyes of those who look long to sea for the return of their beloved. Cheyne addressed himself to her, and she gave consent wearily.

'We lose one hundred a year from Gloucester only, Mr. Cheyne,' she said—'one hundred boys an' men; and I've come so's to hate the sea as if 'twuz alive an' listenin'. God never made it fer humans to anchor on. These packets o' yours, they go straight out, I take it, and straight home again?'

'As straight as the winds let 'em, and I give a bonus for record passages. Tea don't improve by being at sea.'

'When he wuz little he used to play at keeping store, an' I had hopes he might follow that up. But soon's he could paddle a dory, I knew that were goin' to be denied me.'

'They're square-riggers, mother; iron-built an' well found. Remember what Phil's sister reads you when she gits his letters.'

'I've never known as Phil told lies, but he's too venturesome (like most of 'em that use the sea). Ef Dan sees fit, Mr. Cheyne, he can go—fer all o' me.'

'She jest despises the ocean,' Disko explained, 'an' I—I dunno haow to act polite, I guess, er I'd thank you better.'

'My father—my own eldest brother—two nephews—an' my second sister's man,' she said, dropping her head on her hand. 'Would you care fer any one that took all those?'

Cheyne was relieved when Dan turned up and accepted with more delight than he was able to put into words. Indeed, the offer meant a plain and sure road to all desirable things; but Dan thought most of commanding watch on broad decks, and looking into faraway harbours.

Mrs. Cheyne had spoken privately to the unaccountable Manuel in the matter of Harvey's rescue. He seemed to have no desire for money. Pressed hard, he said that he would take five dollars, because he wanted to buy something for a girl. Otherwise—'How shall I take money when I make so easy my eats and smokes? You will giva some if I like or no? Eh, wha-at? Then you shall giva me money, but not that way. You shall giva all you can think.' He introduced her to a snuffy Portuguese priest with a list of semi-destitute widows as long as his cassock. As a strict Unitarian, Mrs. Cheyne could not sympathise with the creed, but she ended by respecting the brown, voluble little man.

Manuel, faithful son of the Church, appropriated all the blessings showered on her for her charity. 'That letta me out,' said he. 'I have now ver' good absolutions for six months'; and he strolled forth to get a handkerchief for the girl of the hour and to break the hearts of all the others.

Salters went West for a season with Penn, and left no address behind. He had a dread that these millionary people, with wasteful private cars, might take undue interest in his companion. It was better to visit inland relatives till the coast was clear. 'Never you be adopted by rich folk, Penn,' he said in the cars, 'or I'll take'n break this checker-board over your head. Ef you forgit your name agin—which is Pratt—you remember you belong with Salters Troop, an' set down right where you are till I come fer you. Don't go taggin' araound after them whose eyes bung out with fatness, accordin' to Scripcher.'

Chapter 10

BUT IT WAS otherwise with the 'We're Here's' silent cook, for he came up, his kit in a handkerchief, and boarded the 'Constance.' Pay was no particular object, and he did not in the least care where he slept. His business, as revealed to him in dreams, was to follow Harvey for the rest of his days. They tried argument and, at last, persuasion; but there is a difference between one Cape Breton and two Alabama negroes, and the matter was referred to Cheyne by the cook and porter. The millionaire only laughed. He presumed Harvey might need a body-servant some day or other, and was sure that one volunteer was worth five hirelings. Let the man stay, therefore; even though he called himself MacDonald and swore in Gaelic. The car could go back to Boston, whence, if he were still of the same mind, they would take him West.

With the 'Constance,' which in his heart of hearts he loathed, departed the last remnant of Cheyne's millionairedom, and he gave himself up to an energetic idleness. This Gloucester was a new town in a new land, and he purposed to 'take it in,' as of old he had taken in all the cities from Snohomish to San Diego of that world whence he hailed. They made money along the crooked street which was half wharf and half ship's store: as a leading professional he wished to learn how the noble game was played. Men said that four out of every five fish-balls served at New England's Sunday breakfast came from Gloucester, and overwhelmed him with figures in proof—statistics of boats, gear, wharf-frontage, capital invested, salting, packing, factories, insurance, wages, repairs, and profits. He talked with the owners of the large fleets whose skippers were little more than hired men, and whose crews were almost all Swedes or Portuguese. Then he conferred with Disko, one of the few who owned their craft, and compared notes in his vast head. He coiled himself away on chain-cables in marine junk-shops, asking questions with cheerful, un-slaked Western curiosity till all the water-front wanted to know 'what in thunder that man was after, anyhow.' He prowled into the Mutual Insurance rooms, and demanded explanations of the mysterious remarks chalked up on the blackboard day by day; and that brought down upon him secretaries of every Fisherman's Widow and Orphan Aid Society within the city limits. They begged shamelessly, each man anxious to beat the other institution's record, and Cheyne tugged at his beard and handed them all over to Mrs. Cheyne.

She was resting in a boarding-house near Eastern Point—a strange establishment, managed apparently by the boarders, where the tablecloths were red and white checkered, and the population, who seemed to have known one another intimately for years, rose up at midnight to make Welsh rarebits if it felt hungry. On the second morning of her stay Mrs. Cheyne put away her diamond solitaires before she came down to break-fast.

'They're most delightful people,' she confided to her husband; 'so friendly and simple, too, though they are all Boston, nearly.'

'That isn't simpleness, mamma,' he said, looking across the boulders behind the apple-trees where the hammocks were slung. 'It's the other thing, that we—that I haven't got.'

'It can't be,' said Mrs. Cheyne quietly. 'There isn't a woman here owns a dress that cost a hundred dollars. Why, we—'

'I know it, dear. We have—of course we have. I guess it's only the style they wear East. Are you having a good time?'

'I don't see very much of Harvey; he's always with you; but I ain't near as nervous as I was.'

'I haven't had such a good time since Willie died. I never rightly under-stood that I had a son before this. Harve's got to be a great boy. Anything I can fetch you, dear? Cushion under your head? Well, we'll go down to the wharf again and look around.'

Harvey was his father's shadow in those days, and the two strolled along side by side, Cheyne using the grades as an excuse for laying his hand on the boy's square shoulder. It was then that Harvey noticed and admired what had never struck him before—his father's curious power of getting at the heart of new matters as learned from men in the street.

'How d'you make 'em tell you everything without opening your head?' demanded the son, as they came out of a rigger's loft.

'I've dealt with quite a few men in my time, Harve, and one sizes 'em up somehow, I guess. I know something about myself, too.' Then, after a pause, as they sat down on a wharf-edge, 'Men can 'most always tell when a man has handled things for himself, and then they treat him as one of themselves.'

'Same as they treat me down at Wouverman's wharf. I'm one of the crowd now. Disko has told every one I've earned my pay.' Harvey spread out his hands and rubbed the palms together. 'They're all soft again,' he said dolefully.

'Keep 'em that way for the next few years, while you're getting your education. You can harden 'em up after.'

'Ye-es, I suppose so,' was the reply, in no delighted voice.

'It rests with you, Harve. You can take cover behind your mamma, of course, and put her on to fussing about your nerves and your high-strungness and all that kind of poppy-cock.'

'Have I ever done that?' said Harvey uneasily.

His father turned where he sat and thrust out a long hand. 'You know as well as I do that I can't make anything of you if you don't act straight by me. I can handle you alone if you'll stay alone, but I don't pretend to manage both you and mamma. Life's too short, anyway.'

'Don't make me out much of a fellow, does it?'

'I guess it was my fault a good deal; but if you want the truth, you haven't been much of anything up to date. Now, have you?'

'Umm! Disko thinks. . . . Say, what d'you reckon it's cost you to raise me from the start—first, last, and all over?'

Cheyne smiled. 'I've never kept track, but I should estimate, in dollars and cents, nearer fifty than forty thousand; maybe sixty. The young generation comes high. It has to have things, and it tires of 'em, and—the old man foots the bill.'

Harve whistled, but at heart he was rather pleased to think that his upbringing had cost so much. 'And all that's sunk capital, isn't it?'

'Invested, Harve. Invested, I hope.'

'Making it only thirty thousand, the thirty I've earned is about ten cents on the hundred. That's a mighty poor catch.' Harvey wagged his head solemnly.

Cheyne laughed till he nearly fell off the pile into the water.

'Disko has got a heap more than that out of Dan since he was ten; and Dan's at school half the year, too.'

'Oh, that's what you're after, is it?'

'No, I'm not after anything. I'm not stuck on myself any just now—that's all. . . . I ought to be kicked.'

'I can't do it, old man; or I would, I presume, if I'd been made that way.'

'Then I'd have remembered it to the last day I lived—and never forgiven you,' said Harvey, his chin on his doubled fists.

'Exactly. That's about what I'd do. You see?'

'I see. The fault's with me and no one else. All the samey, something's got to be done about it.'

Cheyne drew a cigar from his vest pocket, bit off the end, and fell to smoking. Father and son were very much alike; for the beard hid Cheyne's mouth, and Harvey had his father's slightly aquiline nose, close-set black eyes, and narrow, high cheek-bones. With a touch of brown paint he would have made up very picturesquely as a Red Indian of the story-books.

'Now you can go on from here,' said Cheyne slowly, 'costing me between six and eight thousand a year till you're a voter. Well, we'll call you a man then. You can go right on from that, living on me to the tune of forty or fifty thousand, besides what your mother will give you, with a valet and a yacht or a fancy ranch where you can pretend to raise trotting stock and play cards with your own crowd.'

'Like Torry Tuck?' Harvey put in.

'Yep; or the two De Vitre boys or old man M'Quade's son. California's full of 'em, and here's an Eastern sample while we're talking.'

A shiny black steam yacht, with mahogany deckhouse, nickel-plated binnacles, and pink and white striped awnings, puffed up the harbour, flying the burgee of some New York club. Two young men in what they conceived to be sea costumes were playing cards by the saloon skylight, and a couple of women with red and blue parasols looked on and laughed noisily.

'Shouldn't care to be caught out in her in any sort of a breeze. No beam,' said Harvey critically, as the yacht slowed to pick up her mooring-buoy.

'They're having what stands them for a good time. I can give you that, and twice as much as that, Harve. How d'you like it?'

'Cæsar! That's no way to get a dinghy over-side,' said Harvey, still intent on the yacht. 'If I couldn't slip a tackle better than that I'd stay ashore. . . . What if I don't?'

'Stay ashore—or what?'

'Yacht and ranch and live on "the old man," and—get behind mamma when there's trouble,' said Harvey, with a twinkle in his eye.

'Why, in that case, you come right in with me, my son.'

'Ten dollars a month?' Another twinkle.

'Not a cent more until you're worth it, and you won't begin to touch that for a few years.'

'I'd sooner begin sweeping out the office—isn't that how the big bugs start?—and touch something now than—'

'I know it; we all feel that way. But I guess we can hire any sweeping we need. I made the same mistake myself of starting in too soon.'

'Thirty million dollars' worth o' mistake, wasn't it? I'd risk it for that.'
'I lost some; and I gained some. I'll tell you.'

Cheyne pulled his beard, and smiled as he looked over the still water, and spoke away from Harvey, who presently began to be aware that his father was telling the story of his life. He talked in a low, even voice, without gesture and without expression, and it was a history for which a dozen leading journals would cheerfully have paid many dollars—the story of forty years that was at the same time the story of the New West, whose story is yet to be written.

It began with a kinless boy turned loose in Texas, and went on fantastically through a hundred changes and chops of life, the scenes shifting from State after Western State, from cities that sprang up in a month and in a season utterly withered away, to wild ventures in wilder camps that are now laborious paved municipalities. It covered the building of three railroads and the deliberate wreck of a fourth. It told of steamers, townships, forests, and mines, and the men of every nation under heaven, manning, creating, hewing, and digging these. It touched on chances of gigantic wealth flung before eyes that could not see, or missed by the merest accident of time and travel; and through the mad shift of things, sometimes on horseback, more often afoot, now rich, now poor, in and out, and back and forth, deck-hand, train-hand, contractor, boarding-house keeper, journalist, engineer, drummer, real-estate agent, politician, dead-beat, rum-seller, mine-owner, speculator, cattleman, or tramp, moved Harvey Cheyne, alert and quiet, seeking his own ends, and, so he said, the glory and advancement of his country.

He told of the faith that never deserted him, even when he hung on the ragged edge of despair—the faith that comes of knowing men and things. He enlarged, as though he were talking to himself, on his very great courage and resource at all times. The thing was so evident in the man's mind that he never even changed his tone. He described how he had bested his enemies, or forgiven them, exactly as they had bested or forgiven him in those careless days; how he had entreated, cajoled, and bullied towns, companies, and syndicates, all for their enduring good; crawled round, through, or under mountains and ravines, dragging a string and hoop-iron railroad after him, and in the end, how he had sat still while promiscuous communities tore the last fragments of his character to shreds.

The tale held Harvey almost breathless, his head a little cocked to one side, his eyes fixed on his father's face, as the twilight deepened and the red cigar-end lit up the furrowed cheeks and heavy eyebrows. It seemed to him like watching a locomotive storming across country in the dark—a mile between each glare of the opened fire-door; but this locomotive could talk, and the words shook and stirred the boy to the core of his soul. At last Cheyne pitched away the cigar-butt, and the two sat in the dark over the lapping water.

'I've never told that to any one before,' said the father.

Harvey gasped. 'It's just the greatest thing that ever was!' said he.

'That's what I got. Now I'm coming to what I didn't get. It won't sound much of anything to you, but I don't wish you to be as old as I am before you find out. I can handle men, of course, and I'm no fool along my own lines, but—but—I can't compete with the man who has been taught! I've picked up as I went along, and I guess it sticks out all over me.'

'I've never seen it,' said the son indignantly.

'You will, though, Harve. You will—just as soon as you're through college. Don't I know it? Don't I know the look on men's faces when they think me a—a "mucker," as they call it out here? I can break them to little pieces—yes—but I can't get back at 'em to hurt 'em where they live. I don't say they're 'way 'way up, but I feel I'm 'way, 'way, 'way off, somehow. Now you've got your chance. You've got to soak up all the learning that's around, and you'll live with a crowd that are doing the same thing. They'll be doing it for a few thousand dollars a year at most: but remember you'll be doing it for millions. You'll learn law enough to look after your own property when I'm out o' the light, and you'll have to be solid with the best men in the market (they are useful later); and above all, you'll have to stow away the plain, common, sit-down-with-your-chin-on-your-elbows book-learning. Nothing pays like that, Harve, and it's bound to pay more and more each year in our country—in business and in politics. You'll see.'

'There's no sugar my end of the deal,' said Harvey. 'Four years at college! Wish I'd chosen the valet and the yacht!'

'Never mind, my son,' Cheyne insisted. 'You're investing your capital where it'll bring in the best returns; and I guess you won't find our property shrunk any when you're ready to take hold. Think it over, and let me know in the morning. Hurry! We'll be late for supper!'

As this was a business talk, there was no need for Harvey to tell his mother about it; and Cheyne naturally took the same point of view. But Mrs. Cheyne saw and feared, and was a little jealous. Her boy, who rode rough-shod over her, was gone, and in his stead reigned a keen-faced youth, abnormally silent, who addressed most of his conversation to his father. She understood it was business, and therefore a matter beyond her premises. If she had any doubts, they were resolved when Cheyne went to Boston and brought back a new diamond marquise ring.

'What have you two men been doing now?' she said, with a weak little smile, as she turned it in the light.

'Talking—just talking, mamma; there's nothing mean about Harvey.'

There was not. The boy had made a treaty on his own account. Railroads, he explained gravely, interested him as little as lumber, real estate, or mining. What his soul yearned after was control of his father's newly-purchased sailing-ships. If that could be promised him within what he conceived to be a reasonable time, he, for his part, guaranteed diligence and sobriety at college for four or five years. In vacation he was to be allowed full access to all details connected with the line,—he had asked not more than two thousand questions about it,—from his father's most private papers in the safe to the tug in San Francisco harbour.

'It's a deal,' said Cheyne at the last. 'You'll alter your mind twenty times before you leave college, o' course; but if you take hold of it in proper shape, and if you don't tie it up before you're twenty-three, I'll make the thing over to you. How's that, Harve?'

'Nope; never pays to split up a going concern. There's too much competition in the world anyway, and Disko says "blood-kin hev to stick together." His crowd never go back on him. That's one reason, he says, why they make such big fares. Say, the "We're Here" goes off to the Georges on Monday. They don't stay long ashore, do they?'

'Well, we ought to be going too, I guess. I've left my business hung up at loose ends between two oceans, and it's time to connect again. I just hate to do it, though; haven't had a holiday like this for twenty years.'

'We can't go without seeing Disko off,' said Harvey; 'and Monday's Memorial Day. Let's stay over that, anyway.'

'What is this memorial business? They were talking about it at the boarding-house,' said Cheyne weakly. He, too, was not anxious to spoil the golden days.

'Well, as far as I can make out, this business is a sort of song-and-dance act, whacked up for the summer boarders. Disko don't think much of it, he says, because they take up a collection for the widows and orphans. Disko's independent. Haven't you noticed that?'

'Well—yes. A little. In spots. It is a town show, then?'

'The summer convention is. They read out the names of the fellows drowned or gone astray since last time, and they make speeches, and recite, and all. Then, Disko says, the secretaries of the Aid Societies go into the back yard and fight over the catch. The real show, he says, is in the spring. The ministers all take a hand then, and there aren't any summer boarders around.'

'I see,' said Cheyne, with the brilliant and perfect comprehension of one born into and bred up to city pride. 'We'll stay over for Memorial Day, and get off in the afternoon.'

'Guess I'll go down to Disko's and make him bring his crowd up before they sail. I'll have to stand with them, of course.'

'Oh, that's it, is it?' said Cheyne. 'I'm only a poor summer boarder, and you're—'

'A Banker—full-blooded Banker,' Harvey called back as he boarded a trolley, and Cheyne went on with his blissful dreams for the future.

Disko had no use for public functions where appeals were made for charity, but Harvey pleaded that the glory of the day would be lost, so far as he was concerned, if the 'We're Heres' absented themselves. Then Disko made conditions. He had heard—it was astonishing how all the world knew all the world's business along the water-front—he had heard that a 'Philadelphia actress-woman' was going to take part in the exercises; and he mistrusted that she would deliver 'Skipper Ireson's Ride.' Personally, he had as little use for actresses as for summer boarders; but justice was justice, and though he himself (here Dan giggled) had once slipped up on a matter of judgment, this thing must not be. So Harvey came back to East Gloucester and spent half a day explaining to an amused actress with a royal reputation on two seaboards the inwardness of the mistake she contemplated; and she admitted that it was justice, even as Disko had said.

Cheyne knew by old experience what would happen; but anything of the nature of a public palaver was meat and drink to the man's soul. He saw the trolleys hurrying west, in the hot, hazy morning, full of women in light summer dresses, and white-faced, straw-hatted men fresh from Boston desks; the stack of bicycles outside the post office; the come-and-go of busy officials, greeting one another; the slow flick and swash of bunting in the heavy air; and the important man with a hose sluicing the brick sidewalk.

'Mother,' he said suddenly, 'don't you remember—after Seattle was burned out—and they got her going again?'

Mrs. Cheyne nodded, and looked critically down the crooked street. Like her husband, she understood these gatherings, all the West over, and compared them one against another. The fishermen began to mingle with the crowd about the town-hall doors—blue-jowled Portuguese, their women bare-headed or shawled for the most part; clear-eyed Nova Scotians, and men of the Maritime Provinces; French, Italians, Swedes, and Danes, with outside crews of coasting schooners; and everywhere women in black, who saluted one another with a gloomy pride, for this was their day of great days. And there were ministers of many creeds—pastors of great, gilt-edged congregations, at the seaside for a rest, with shepherds of the regular work,—from the priests of the Church on the Hill to bush-bearded ex-sailor Lutherans, hail-fellow with the men of a score of boats. There were owners of lines of schooners, large contributors to the societies, and small men, their few craft pawned to the mastheads, with bankers and marine-insurance agents, captains of tugs and water-boats, riggers, fitters, lumpers, salters, boat-builders, and coopers, and all the mixed population of the water-front.

They drifted along the line of seats made gay with the dresses of the summer boarders, and one of the town officials patrolled and perspired till he shone all over with pure civic pride. Cheyne had met him for five minutes a few days before, and between the two there was entire under-standing.

'Well, Mr. Cheyne, and what d'you think of our city?—Yes, madam, you can sit anywhere you please.—You have this kind of thing out West, I presume?'

'Yes, but we aren't as old as you.'

'That's so, of course. You ought to have been at the exercises when we celebrated our two hundred and fiftieth birthday. I tell you, Mr. Cheyne, the old city did herself credit.'

'So I heard. It pays, too. What's the matter with the town that it don't have a first-class hotel, though?'

'—Right over there to the left, Pedro. Heaps o' room for you and your crowd.— Why, that's what I tell 'em all the time, Mr. Cheyne. There's big money in it, but I presume that don't affect you any. What we want is—'

A heavy hand fell on his broadcloth shoulder, and the flushed skipper of a Portland coal-and-ice coaster spun him half round. 'What in thunder do you fellows mean by clappin' the law on the town when all decent men are at sea this way? Heh? Town's dry's a bone, an' smells a sight worse sence I quit. 'Might ha' left us one saloon, anyway.'

'Don't seem to have hindered your nourishment this morning, Carsen. I'll go into the politics of it later. Sit down by the door and think over your arguments till I come back.'

'What good's arguments to me? In Miquelon champagne's eighteen dollars a case, and—' The skipper lurched into his seat as an organ-prelude silenced him.

'Our new organ,' said the official proudly to Cheyne. 'Cost us four thousand dollars, too. We'll have to get back to high-license next year to pay for it. I wasn't going to let the ministers have all the religion at their convention. Those are some of our orphans standing up to sing. My wife taught 'em. See you again later, Mr. Cheyne. I'm wanted on the platform.'

High, clear, and true, children's voices bore down the last noise of those settling into their places.

'O all ye Works of the Lord, bless ye the Lord: praise Him, and magnify Him for ever!'

The women throughout the hall leaned forward to look as the reiterated cadences filled the air. Mrs. Cheyne, with some others, began to breathe short; she had hardly imagined there were so many widows in the world; and instinctively searched for Harvey. He had found the 'We're Heres' at the back of the audience, and was standing, as by right, between Dan and Disko. Uncle Salters, returned the night before with Penn, from Pamlico Sound, received him suspiciously.

'Hain't your folk gone yet?' he grunted. 'What are you doin' here, young feller?'

'O ye Seas and Floods, bless ye the Lord: praise Him, and magnify Him for ever!'

'Hain't he good right?' said Dan. 'He's bin there, same as the rest of us.'

'Not in them clothes,' Salters snarled.

'Shut your head, Salters,' said Disko. 'Your bile's gone back on you. Stay right where ye are, Harve.'

Then up and spoke the orator of the occasion, another pillar of the municipality, bidding the world welcome to Gloucester, and incidentally pointing out wherein Gloucester excelled the rest of the world. Then he turned to the sea-wealth of the city, and spoke of the price that must be paid for the yearly harvest. They would hear later the names of their lost dead—one hundred and seventeen of them. (The widows stared a little, and looked at one another here.) Gloucester could not boast any overwhelming mills or factories. Her sons worked for such wage as the sea gave; and they all knew that neither Georges nor the Banks were cow-pastures. The utmost that folk ashore could accomplish was to help the widows and the orphans; and after a few general remarks he took his opportunity of thanking, in the name of the city, those who had so public-spiritedly consented to participate in the exercises of the occasion.

'I jest despise the beggin' pieces in it,' growled Disko. 'It don't give folk a fair notion of us.'

'Ef folk won't be fore-handed an' put by when they've the chance,' returned Salters, 'it stands in the nature o' things they hev to be 'shamed.

You take warnin' by that, young feller. Riches endureth but for a season, ef you scatter them araound on lugsuries—'

'But to lose everything—everything,' said Penn. 'What can you do then? Once I'—the watery-blue eyes stared up and down, as if looking for something to steady them—'once I read—in a book, I think—of a boat where everyone was run down—except some one—and he said to me—'

'Shucks!' said Salters, cutting in. 'You read a little less an' take more int'rust in your vittles, and you'll come nearer earnin' your keep, Penn.'

Harvey, jammed among the fishermen, felt a creepy, crawly, tingling thrill that began in the back of his neck and ended at his boots. He was cold, too, though it was a stifling day.

''That the actress from Philadelphia?' said Disko Troop, scowling at the platform. 'You've fixed it about old man Ireson, hain't ye, Harve? Ye know why naow.'

It was not 'Ireson's Ride' that the woman delivered, but some sort of poem about a fishing-port called Brixham and a fleet of trawlers beating in against storm by night, while the women made a guiding fire at the head of the quay with everything they could lay hands on.

> 'They took the grandam's blanket,
>   Who shivered and bade them go;
> They took the baby's cradle,
>   Who could not say them no.'

'Whew!' said Dan, peering over Long Jack's shoulder. 'That's great! Must ha' bin expensive, though.'

'Ground-hog case,' said the Galway man. 'Badly lighted port, Danny.'

> '   .   .   .
>   And knew not all the while
> If they were lighting a bonfire
>   Or only a funeral pile.'

The wonderful voice took hold of the people by their heartstrings; and when she told how the drenched crews were flung ashore, living and dead, and they carried the bodies to the glare of the fires, asking: 'Child, is this your father?' or 'Wife, is this your man?' you could hear hard breathing all over the benches.

> 'And when the boats of Brixham
>   Go out to face the gales,
> Think of the love that travels
>   Like light upon their sails!'

There was very little applause when she finished. The women were looking for their handkerchiefs, and many of the men stared at the ceiling with shiny eyes.

'H'm,' said Salters; 'that 'ud cost ye a dollar to hear at any theater—maybe two. Some folk, I presoom, can afford it. Seems downright waste to me. . . . Naow, how in Jerusalem did Cap Bart Edwardes strike adrift here?'

'No keepin' him under,' said an Eastport man behind. 'He's a poet, an' he's baound to say his piece. Comes from daown aour way, too.'

He did not say that Captain B. Edwardes had striven for five consecutive years to be allowed to recite a piece of his own composition on Gloucester Memorial Day. An amused and exhausted committee had at last given him his desire. The simplicity and utter happiness of the old man, as he stood up in his very best Sunday clothes, won the audience ere he opened his mouth. They sat unmurmuring through seven-and-thirty hatchet-made verses describing at fullest length the loss of the schooner 'Joan Hasken' off the Georges in the gale of 1867, and when he came to an end they shouted with one kindly throat.

A far-sighted Boston reporter slid away for a full copy of the epic and an interview with the author; so that earth had nothing more to offer Captain Bart Edwardes, ex-whaler, shipwright, master-fisherman, and poet, in the seventy-third year of his age.

'Naow, I call that sensible,' said the Eastport man. 'I've bin over that graound with his writin' jest as he read it, in my two hands, and I can testify that he's got it all in.'

'If Dan here couldn't do better'n that with one hand before breakfast, he ought to be switched,' said Salters, upholding the honour of Massachusetts on general principles. 'Not but what I'm free to own he's considerable litt'ery—fer Maine. Still—'

'Guess Uncle Salters goin' to die this trip. Fust compliment he's ever paid me,' Dan sniggered. 'What's wrong with you, Harve? You act all quiet and you look greenish. Feelin' sick?'

'Don't know what's the matter with me,' Harvey replied. ''Seems if my insides were too big for my outsides. I'm all crowded up and shivery.'

'Dispepsy? Pshaw—too bad. We'll wait for the readin', an' then we'll quit, an' catch the tide.'

The widows—they were nearly all of that season's making—braced themselves rigidly like people going to be shot in cold blood, for they knew what was coming. The summer-boarder girls in pink and blue shirt-waists stopped tittering over Captain Edwardes's wonderful poem, and looked back to see why all was silent. The fishermen pressed forward as that town official who had talked with Cheyne bobbed up on the platform and began to read the year's list of losses, dividing them into months. Last September's casualties were mostly single men and strangers, but his voice rang very loud in the stillness of the hall:

'9th September.—Schooner "Florrie Anderson" lost, with all aboard, off the Georges:

Reuben Pitman, master, 50, single, Main Street, City.

Emil Olsen, 19, single, 329 Hammond Street, City; Denmark.

Oscar Stanberg, single, 25, Sweden.

Carl Stanberg, single, 28 Main Street, City.

Pedro, supposed Madeira, single, Keene's boarding house, City.

Joseph Welsh, alias Joseph Wright, 30, St. John's, Newfoundland.'

'No—Augusty, Maine,' a voice cried from the body of the hall.

'He shipped from St. John's,' said the reader, looking to see.

'I know it. He belongs in Augusty. My nevvy.'

The reader made a pencilled correction on the margin of the list, and resumed:

'Same schooner, Charlie Ritchie, Liverpool, Nova Scotia, 33, single. Albert May, 267 Rogers Street, City, 27, single.

27th September.—Orvin Dollard, 30, married, drowned in dory off Eastern Point.'

That shot went home, for one of the widows flinched where she sat, clasping and unclasping her hands. Mrs. Cheyne, who had been listening with wide-opened eyes, threw up her head and choked. Dan's mother, a few seats to the right, saw and heard and quickly moved to her side. The reading went on. By the time they reached the January and February wrecks the shots were falling thick and fast, and the widows drew breath between their teeth:

'14th February.—Schooner "Harry Randolph" dismasted on the way home from Newfoundland; Asa Musie, married, 32, Main Street, City, lost overboard.

23rd February.—Schooner "Gilbert Hope"; went astray in dory, Robert Beavon, 29, married, native of Pubnico, Nova Scotia.'

But his wife was in the hall. They heard a low cry, as though a little animal had been hit. It was stifled at once, and a girl staggered out of the hall. She had been hoping against hope for months, because some who have gone adrift in dories have been miraculously picked up by deep-sea sailing-ships. Now she had her certainty, and Harvey could see the policeman on the sidewalk hailing a hack for her. 'It's fifty cents to the depot'—the driver began, but the policeman held up his hand—'but I'm goin' there anyway. Jump right in. Look at here, Alf; you don't pull me next time my lamps ain't lit. See?'

The side-door closed on the patch of bright sunshine, and Harvey's eyes turned again to the reader and his endless list.

'19th April.—Schooner "Mamie Douglas" lost on the Banks with all hands.

Edward Canton, 43, master, married, City.

D. Hawkins, alias Williams, 34, married, Shelbourne, Nova Scotia.

G. W. Clay, coloured, 28, married, City.'

And so on, and so on. Great lumps were rising in Harvey's throat, and his stomach reminded him of the day when he fell from the liner.

'10th May.—Schooner "We're Here" [the blood tingled all over him]. Otto Svendson, 20, single, City, lost overboard.'

Once more a low, tearing cry from somewhere at the back of the hall.

'She shouldn't ha' come. She shouldn't ha' come,' said Long Jack, with a cluck of pity.

'Don't scrowge, Harve,' grunted Dan. Harvey heard that much, but the rest was all darkness spotted with fiery wheels. Disko leaned forward and spoke to his wife, where she sat with one arm round Mrs. Cheyne, and the other holding down the snatching, catching, ringed hands.

'Lean your head daown—right daown!' she whispered. 'It'll go off in a minute.'

'I ca-an't! I do-don't! Oh, let me—' Mrs. Cheyne did not at all know what she said.

'You must,' Mrs. Troop repeated. 'Your boy's jest fainted dead away. They do that some when they're gettin' their growth. Wish to tend to him? We can git aout this side. Quite quiet. You come right along with me. Psha', my dear, we're both women, I guess. We must tend to aour men-folk. Come!'

The 'We're Heres' promptly went through the crowd as a bodyguard, and it was a very white and shaken Harvey that they propped up on a bench in an anteroom.

'Favours his ma,' was Mrs. Troop's only comment, as the mother bent over her boy.

'How d'you suppose he could ever stand it?' she cried indignantly to Cheyne, who had said nothing at all. 'It was horrible—horrible! We shouldn't have come. It's wrong and wicked! It—it isn't right! Why—why couldn't they put these things in the papers, where they belong? Are you better, darling?'

That made Harvey very properly ashamed. 'Oh, I'm all right, I guess,' he said, struggling to his feet, with a broken giggle. 'Must ha' been something I ate for breakfast.'

'Coffee, perhaps,' said Cheyne, whose face was all in hard lines, as though it had been cut out of bronze. 'We won't go back again.'

'Guess 'twould be 'baout's well to git daown to the wharf,' said Disko. 'It's close in along with them Dagoes, an' the fresh air will fresh Mrs. Cheyne up.'

Harvey announced that he never felt better in his life; but it was not till he saw the 'We're Here,' fresh from the lumper's hands, at Wouverman's wharf, that he lost his all-overish feelings in a queer mixture of pride and sorrowfulness. Other people—summer boarders and such-like—played about in catboats or looked at the sea from pierheads; but he understood things from the inside—more things than he could begin to think about. None the less, he could have sat down and howled because the little schooner was going off. Mrs. Cheyne simply cried and cried every step of the way, and said most extraordinary things to Mrs. Troop, who 'babied' her till Dan, who had not been 'babied' since he was six, whistled aloud.

And so the old crowd—Harvey felt like the most ancient of mariners—dropped into the old schooner among the battered dories, while Harvey slipped the stern-fast from the pierhead, and they slid her along the wharfside with their hands. Every one wanted to say so much that no one said anything in particular. Harvey bade Dan take care of Uncle Salters's sea-boots and Penn's dory-anchor, and Long Jack entreated Harvey to remember his lessons in seamanship; but the jokes fell flat in the presence of the two women, and it is hard to be funny with green harbour-water widening between good friends.

'Up jib and fores'l!' shouted Disko, getting to the wheel, as the wind took her. 'See you later, Harve. Dunno but I come near thinkin' a heap o' you an' your folks.'

Then she glided beyond earshot, and they sat down to watch her up the harbour. And still Mrs. Cheyne wept.

'Psha', my dear,' said Mrs. Troop; 'we're both women, I guess. Like's not it'll ease your heart to hev your cry aout. God He knows it never done me a mite o' good; but then He knows I've had something to cry fer!'

Now it was a few years later, and upon the other edge of America, that a young man came through the clammy sea-fog up a windy street which is flanked with most expensive houses built of wood to imitate stone. To him, as he was standing by a hammered iron gate, entered on horseback—and the horse would have been cheap at a thousand dollars—another young man. And this is what they said:

'Hello, Dan!'

'Hello, Harve!'

'What's the best with you?'

'Well, I'm so's to be that kind o' animal called second mate this trip. Ain't you most through with that triple-invoiced college o' yours?'

'Getting that way. I tell you, the Leland Stanford Junior isn't a circumstance to the old "We're Here"; but I'm coming into the business for keeps next fall.'

'Meanin' aour packets?'

'Nothing else. You just wait till I get my knife into you, Dan. I'm going to make the old line lie down and cry when I take hold.'

'I'll resk it,' said Dan, with a brotherly grin, as Harvey dismounted and asked whether he were coming in.

'That's what I took the cable fer; but, say, is the doctor anywheres araound? I'll draown that crazy nigger some day, his one cussed joke an' all.'

There was a low, triumphant chuckle as the ex-cook of the 'We're Here' came out of the fog to take the horse's bridle. He allowed no one but himself to attend to any of Harvey's wants.

'Thick as the Banks, ain't it, doctor?' said Dan propitiatingly.

But the coal-black Celt with the second-sight did not see fit to reply till he had tapped Dan on the shoulder, and for the twentieth time croaked the old, old prophecy in his ear:

'Master—man. Man—master,' said he. 'You remember, Dan Troop, what I said? On the "We're Here"?'

'Well, I won't go so far as to deny that it do look like it as things stand at present,' said Dan. 'She was an able packet, and one way an' another I owe her a heap—her and dad.'

'Me too,' quoth Harvey Cheyne.

Without Benefit of Clergy
"They"
The Man Who Would Be King

WITHOUT BENEFIT OF CLERGY

Before my Spring I garnered Autumn's gain,
Out of her time my field was white with grain,
The year gave up her secrets to my woe.
Forced and deflowered each sick season lay,
In mystery of increase and decay;
I saw the sunset ere men saw the day,
Who am too wise in that I should not know.

Bitter Waters

I

'But if it be a girl?'

'Lord of my life, it cannot be. I have prayed for so many nights, and sent gifts to Sheikh Badl's shrine so often, that I know God will give us a son—a man-child that shall grow into a man. Think of this and be glad. My mother shall be his mother till I can take him again, and the mullah of the Pattan mosque shall cast his nativity—God send he be born in an auspicious hour!—and then, and then thou wilt never weary of me, thy slave.'

'Since when hast thou been a slave, my queen?'

'Since the beginning—till this mercy came to me. How could I be sure of thy love when I knew that I had been bought with silver?'

'Nay, that was the dowry. I paid it to thy mother.'

'And she has buried it, and sits upon it all day long like a hen. What talk is yours of dower! I was bought as though I had been a Lucknow dancing-girl instead of a child.'

'Art thou sorry for the sale?'

'I have sorrowed; but to-day I am glad. Thou wilt never cease to love me now?—answer, my king.'

'Never—never. No.'

'Not even though the *mem-log*—the white women of thy own blood— love thee? And remember, I have watched them driving in the evening; they are very fair.'

'I have seen fire-balloons by the hundred. I have seen the moon, and—then I saw no more fire-balloons.'

Ameera clapped her hands and laughed. 'Very good talk,' she said. Then with an assumption of great stateliness, 'It is enough. Thou hast my permission to depart,—if thou wilt.'

The man did not move. He was sitting on a low red-lacquered couch in a room furnished only with blue and white floor-cloth, some rugs, and a very complete collection of native cushions. At his feet sat a woman of sixteen, and she was all but all the world in his eyes. By every rule and law she should have been otherwise, for he was an Englishman, and she a Mussulman's daughter bought two years before from her mother, who, being left without money, would have sold Ameera shrieking to the Prince of Darkness if the price had been sufficient.

It was a contract entered into with a light heart; but even before the girl had reached her bloom she came to fill the greater portion of John Holden's life. For her, and the withered hag her mother, he had taken a little house overlooking the great red-walled city, and found,—when the marigolds had sprung up by the well in the courtyard and Ameera had established herself according to her own ideas of comfort, and her mother had ceased grumbling at the inadequacy of the cooking-places, the distance from the daily market, and at matters of house-keeping in general,—that the house was to him his home. Any one could enter his bachelor's bungalow by day or night, and the life that he led there was an unlovely one. In the house in the city his feet only could pass beyond the outer courtyard to the women's rooms; and when the big wooden gate was bolted behind him he was king in his own territory, with Ameera for queen. And there was going to be added to this kingdom a third person whose arrival Holden felt inclined to resent. It interfered with his perfect happiness. It disarranged the orderly peace of the house that was his own. But Ameera was wild with delight at the thought of it, and her mother not less so. The love of a man, and particularly a white man, was at the best an inconstant affair, but it might, both women argued, be held fast by a baby's hands. 'And then,' Ameera would always say, 'then he will never care for the white *mem-log*. I hate them all—I hate them all.'

'He will go back to his own people in time,' said the mother; 'but by the blessing of God that time is yet afar off.'

Holden sat silent on the couch thinking of the future, and his thoughts were not pleasant. The drawbacks of a double life are manifold. The Government, with singular care, had ordered him out of the station for a fortnight on special duty in the place of a man who was watching by the bedside of a sick wife. The verbal notification of the transfer had been edged by a cheerful remark that Holden ought to think himself lucky in being a bachelor and a free man. He came to break the news to Ameera.

'It is not good,' she said slowly, 'but it is not all bad. There is my mother here, and no harm will come to me—unless indeed I die of pure joy. Go thou to thy work and think no troublesome thoughts. When the days are done I believe . . . nay, I am sure. And—and then I shall lay *him* in thy arms, and thou wilt love me for ever. The train goes to-night, at midnight is it not? Go now, and do not let they heart be heavy by cause of me. But thou wilt not delay in returning? Thou wilt not stay on the road to talk to the bold white *mem-log*. Come back to me swiftly, my life.'

As he left the courtyard to reach his horse that was tethered to the gate-post, Holden spoke to the white-haired old watchman who guarded the house, and bade him under certain contingencies despatch the filled-up telegraph-form that Holden gave him. It was all that could be done, and with the sensations of a man who has attended his own funeral Holden went away by the night mail to his exile. Every hour of the day he dreaded the arrival of the telegram, and every hour of the night he pictured to himself the death of Ameera. In consequence his work for the State was not of first-rate quality, nor was his temper towards his colleagues of the most amiable. The fortnight ended without a sign from his home, and, torn to pieces by his anxieties, Holden returned to be swallowed up for two precious hours by a dinner at the club, wherein he heard, as a man hears in a swoon, voices telling him how execrably he had performed the other man's duties, and how he had endeared himself to all his associates. Then he fled on horseback through the night with his heart in his mouth. There was no answer at first to his blows on the gate, and he had just wheeled his horse round to kick it in when Pir Khan appeared with a lantern and held his stirrup.

'Has aught occurred?' said Holden.

'The news does not come from my mouth, Protector of the Poor, but——'

He held out his shaking hand as befitted the bearer of good news who is entitled to a reward.

Holden hurried through the courtyard. A light burned in the upper room. His horse neighed in the gateway, and he heard a shrill little wail that sent all the blood into the apple of his throat. It was a new voice, but it did not prove that Ameera was alive.

'Who is there?' he called up the narrow brick staircase.

There was a cry of delight from Ameera, and then the voice of the mother, tremulous with old age and pride—'We be two women and—the —man—thy—son.'

On the threshold of the room Holden stepped on a naked dagger, that was laid there to avert ill-luck, and it broke at the hilt under his impatient heel.

'God is great!' cooed Ameera in the half-light. 'Thou hast taken his misfortunes on thy head.'

'Ay, but how is it with thee, life of my life? Old woman, how is it with her?'

'She has forgotten her sufferings for joy that the child is born. There is no harm; but speak softly,' said the mother.

'It only needed thy presence to make me all well,' said Ameera. 'My king, thou hast been very long away. What gifts hast thou for me? Ah, ah! It is I that bring gifts this time. Look, my life, look. Was there ever such a babe? Nay, I am too weak even to clear my arm from him.'

'Rest then, and do not talk. I am here, *bachari* [little woman].'

'Well said, for there is a bond and a heel-rope [*peecharee*] between us now that nothing can break. Look—canst thou see in this light? He is without spot or blemish. Never was such a man-child. *Ya illah!* he shall be a pundit—no, a trooper of the Queen. And, my life, dost thou love me as well as ever, though I am faint and sick and worn? Answer truly.'

'Yea. I love as I have loved, with all my soul. Lie still, pearl, and rest.'

'Then do not go. Sit by my side here—so. Mother, the lord of this house needs a cushion. Bring it.' There was an almost imperceptible movement on the part of the new life that lay in the hollow of Ameera's arm. 'Aho!' she said, her voice breaking with love. 'The babe is a champion from his birth. He is kicking me in the side with mighty kicks. Was there ever such a babe! And he is ours to us—thine and mine. Put thy hand on his head, but carefully, for he is very young, and men are unskilled in such matters.'

Very cautiously Holden touched with the tips of his fingers the downy head.

'He is of the faith,' said Ameera; 'for lying here in the night-watches I whispered the call to prayer and the profession of faith into his ears. And it is most marvellous that he was born upon a Friday, as I was born. Be careful of him, my life; but he can almost grip with his hands.'

Holden found one helpless little hand that closed feebly on his finger. And the clutch ran through his body till it settled about his heart. Till then his sole thought had been for Ameera. He began to realise that there was some one else in the world, but he could not feel that it was a veritable son with a soul. He sat down to think, and Ameera dozed lightly.

'Get hence, *sahib*,' said her mother under her breath. 'It is not good that she should find you here on waking. She must be still.'

'I go,' said Holden submissively. 'Here be rupees. See that my *baba* gets fat and finds all that he needs.'

The chink of the silver roused Ameera. 'I am his mother, and no hireling,' she said weakly. 'Shall I look to him more or less for the sake of money? Mother, give it back. I have born my lord a son.'

The deep sleep of weakness came upon her almost before the sentence was completed. Holden went down to the courtyard very softly with his heart at ease. Pir Khan, the old watchman, was chuckling with delight. 'This house is now complete,' he said, and without further comment thrust into Holden's hands the hilt of a sabre worn many years ago when he, Pir Khan, served the Queen in the police. The bleat of a tethered goat came from the well-kerb.

'There be two,' said Pir Khan, 'two goats of the best. I bought them, and they cost much money; and since there is no birth-party assembled their flesh will be all mine. Strike craftily, *sahib!* 'Tis an ill-balanced sabre at the best. Wait till they raise their heads from cropping the marigolds.'

'And why?' said Holden, bewildered.

'For the birth-sacrifice. What else? Otherwise the child being unguarded from fate may die. The Protector of the Poor knows the fitting words to be said.'

Holden had learned them once with little thought that he would ever speak them in earnest. The touch of the cold sabre-hilt in his palm turned suddenly to the clinging grip of the child upstairs—the child that was his own son—and a dread of loss filled him.

'Strike!' said Pir Khan. 'Never life came into the world but life was paid for it. See, the goats have raised their heads. Now! With a drawing cut!'

Hardly knowing what he did Holden cut twice as he muttered the Mahomedan prayer that runs: 'Almighty! In place of this my son I offer life for life, blood for blood, head for head, bone for bone, hair for hair, skin for skin.' The waiting horse snorted and bounded in his pickets at the smell of the raw blood that spirted over Holden's riding-boots.

'Well smitten!' said Pir Khan, wiping the sabre. 'A swordsman was lost in thee. Go with a light heart, Heaven-born. I am thy servant, and the servant of thy son. May the Presence live a thousand years and . . . the flesh of the goats is all mine?' Pir Khan drew back richer by a month's pay. Holden swung himself into the saddle and rode off through the low-hanging wood-smoke of the evening. He was full of riotous exultation, alternating with a vast vague tenderness directed towards no particular object, that made him choke as he bent over the neck of his uneasy horse. 'I never felt like this in my life,' he thought. 'I'll go to the club and pull myself together.'

A game of pool was beginning, and the room was full of men. Holden entered, eager to get to the light and the company of his fellows, singing at the top of his voice—

In Baltimore a-walking, a lady I did meet!

'Did you?' said the club-secretary from his corner. 'Did she happen to tell you that your boots were wringing wet? Great goodness, man, it's blood!'

'Bosh!' said Holden, picking his cue from the rack. 'May I cut in? It's dew. I've been riding through high crops. My faith! my boots are in a mess though!

'And if it be a girl she shall wear a wedding-ring,
And if it be a boy he shall fight for his king,
With his dirk, and his cap, and his little jacket blue,
He shall walk the quarter-deck—'

'Yellow on blue—green next player,' said the marker monotonously.

'*He shall walk the quarter-deck,*—Am I green, marker? *He shall walk the quarter-deck,*—eh! that's a bad shot,—*As his daddy used to do!*'

'I don't see that you have anything to crow about,' said a zealous junior civilian acidly. 'The Government is not exactly pleased with your work when you relieved Sanders.'

'Does that mean a wigging from headquarters?' said Holden with an abstracted smile. 'I think I can stand it.'

The talk beat up round the ever-fresh subject of each man's work, and steadied Holden till it was time to go to his dark empty bungalow, where his butler received him as one who knew all his affairs. Holden remained awake for the greater part of the night, and his dreams were pleasant ones.

II

'How old is he now?'

'*Ya illah!* What a man's question! He is all but six weeks old; and on this night I go up to the housetop with thee, my life, to count the stars. For that is auspicious. And he was born on a Friday under the sign of the Sun, and it has been told to me that he will outlive us both and get wealth. Can we wish for aught better, beloved?'

'There is nothing better. Let us go up to the roof, and thou shalt count the stars—but a few only, for the sky is heavy with cloud.'

'The winter rains are late, and maybe they come out of season. Come, before all the stars are hid. I have put on my richest jewels.'

'Thou hast forgotten the best of all.'

'*Ai!* Ours. He comes also. He has never yet seen the skies.'

Ameera climbed the narrow staircase that led to the flat roof. The child, placid and unwinking, lay in the hollow of her right arm, gorgeous in silver-fringed muslin with a small skull-cap on his head. Ameera wore all that she valued most. The diamond nose-stud that takes the place of the Western patch in drawing attention to the curve of the nostril, the gold ornament in the centre of the forehead studded with tallow-drop emeralds and flawed rubies, the heavy circlet of beaten gold that was fastened around her neck by the softness of the pure metal, and the chinking curb-patterned silver anklets hanging low over the rosy ankle-bone. She was dressed in jade-green muslin as befitted a daughter of the Faith, and from shoulder to elbow and elbow to wrist ran bracelets of silver tied with floss silk, frail glass bangles slipped over the wrist in proof of the slenderness of the hand, and certain heavy gold bracelets that had no part in her country's ornaments but, since they were Holden's gift and fastened with a cunning European snap, delighted her immensely.

They sat down by the low white parapet of the roof, overlooking the city and its lights.

'They are happy down there,' said Ameera. 'But I do not think that they are as happy as we. Nor do I think the white *mem-log* are as happy. And thou?'

'I know they are not.'

'How dost thou know?'

'They give their children over to the nurses.'

'I have never seen that,' said Ameera with a sigh, 'nor do I wish to see. *Ahi!*—she dropped her head on Holden's shoulder,—'I have counted forty stars, and I am tired. Look at the child, love of my life, he is counting too.'

The baby was staring with round eyes at the dark of the heavens. Ameera placed him in Holden's arms, and he lay there without a cry.

'What shall we call him among ourselves?' she said. 'Look! Art thou ever tired of looking? He carries thy very eyes. But the mouth——'

'Is thine, most dear. Who should know better than I?'

'*'*Tis such a feeble mouth. Oh, so small! And yet it holds my heart between its lips. Give him to me now. He has been too long away.'

'Nay, let him lie; he has not yet begun to cry.'

'When he cries thou wilt give him back—eh? What a man of mankind thou art! If he cried he were only the dearer to me. But, my life, what little name shall we give him?'

The small body lay close to Holden's heart. It was utterly helpless and very soft. He scarcely dared to breathe for fear of crushing it. The caged green parrot that is regarded as a sort of guardian-spirit in most native households moved on its perch and fluttered a drowsy wing.

'There is the answer,' said Holden. 'Mian Mittu has spoken. He shall be the parrot. When he is ready he will talk mightily and run about. Mian Mittu is the parrot in thy—in the Mussulman tongue, is it not?'

'Why put me so far off?' said Ameera fretfully. 'Let it be like unto some English name—but not wholly. For he is mine.'

'Then call him Tota, for that is likest English.'

'Ay, Tota, and that is still the parrot. Forgive me, my lord, for a minute ago, but in truth he is too little to wear all the weight of Mian Mittu for name. He shall be Tota—our Tota to us. Hearest thou, O small one? Littlest, thou art Tota.' She touched the child's cheek, and he waking wailed, and it was necessary to return him to his mother, who soothed him with the wonderful rhyme of *Aré koko, Jaré koko!* which says:

> Oh crow! Go crow! Baby's sleeping sound,
> And the wild plums grow in the jungle, only a penny a pound.
> Only a penny a pound, *baba*, only a penny a pound.

Reassured many times as to the price of those plums, Tota cuddled himself down to sleep. The two sleek, white well-bullocks in the court-yard were steadily chewing the cud of their evening meal; old Pir Khan squatted at the head of Holden's horse, his police sabre across his knees, pulling drowsily at a big water-pipe that croaked like a bull-frog in a pond. Ameera's mother sat spinning in the lower verandah, and the wooden gate was shut and barred. The music of a marriage-procession came to the roof above the gentle hum of the city, and a string of flying-foxes crossed the face of the low moon.

'I have prayed,' said Ameera after a long pause, 'I have prayed for two things. First, that I may die in thy stead if thy death is demanded, and in the second that I may die in the place of the child. I have prayed to the Prophet and to Beebee Miriam [the Virgin Mary]. Thinkest thou either will hear?'

'From thy lips who would not hear the lightest word?'

'I asked for straight talk, and thou hast given me sweet talk. Will my prayers be heard?'

'How can I say? God is very good.'

'Of that I am not sure. Listen now. When I die, or the child dies, what is thy fate? Living, thou wilt return to the bold white *mem-log*, for kind calls to kind.'

'Not always.'

'With a woman, no; with a man it is otherwise. Thou wilt in this life, later on, go back to thine own folk. That I could almost endure, for I should be dead. But in thy very death thou wilt be taken away to a strange place and a paradise that I do not know.'

'Will it be paradise?'

'Surely, for who would harm thee? But we two—I and the child—shall be elsewhere, and we cannot come to thee, nor canst thou come to us. In the old days, before the child was born, I did not think of these things; but now I think of them always. It is very hard talk.'

'It will fall as it will fall. To-morrow we do not know, but to-day and love we know well. Surely we are happy now.'

'So happy that it were well to make our happiness assured. And thy Beebee Miriam should listen to me; for she is also a woman. But then she would envy me! It is not seemly for men to worship a woman.'

Holden laughed aloud at Ameera's little spasm of jealousy.

'Is it not seemly? Why didst thou not turn me from worship of thee, then?'

'Thou a worshipper! And of me? My king, for all thy sweet words, well I know that I am thy servant and thy slave, and the dust under thy feet. And I would not have it otherwise. See!'

Before Holden could prevent her she stooped forward and touched his feet; recovering herself with a little laugh she hugged Tota closer to her bosom. Then, almost savagely—

'Is it true that the bold white *mem-log* live for three times the length of my life? Is it true that they make their marriages not before they are old women?'

'They marry as do others—when they are women.'

'That I know, but they wed when they are twenty-five. Is that true?'

'That is true.'

'*Ya illah!* At twenty-five! Who would of his own will take a wife even of eighteen? She is a woman—aging every hour. Twenty-five! I shall be an old woman at that age, and—— Those *mem-log* remain young for ever. How I hate them!'

'What have they to do with us?'

'I cannot tell. I know only that there may now be alive on this earth a woman ten years older than I who may come to thee and take thy love ten years after I am an old woman, gray-headed, and the nurse of Tota's son. That is unjust and evil. They should die too.'

'Now, for all thy years thou art a child, and shalt be picked up and carried down the staircase.'

'Tota! Have a care for Tota, my lord! Thou at least art as foolish as any babe!' Ameera tucked Tota out of harm's way in the hollow of her neck, and was carried downstairs laughing in Holden's arms, while Tota opened his eyes and smiled after the manner of the lesser angels.

He was a silent infant, and, almost before Holden could realise that he was in the world, developed into a small gold-coloured little god and unquestioned despot of the house overlooking the city. Those were months of absolute happiness to Holden and Ameera—happiness withdrawn from the world, shut in behind the wooden gate that Pir Khan guarded. By day Holden did his work with an immense pity for such as were not so fortunate as himself, and a sympathy for small children that amazed and amused many mothers at the little station-gatherings. At nightfall he returned to Ameera,—Ameera, full of the wondrous doings of Tota; how he had been seen to clap his hands together and move his fingers with intention and purpose—which was manifestly a miracle—how later, he had of his own initiative crawled out of his low bedstead on to the floor and swayed on both feet for the space of three breaths.

'And they were long breaths, for my heart stood still with delight,' said Ameera.

Then Tota took the beasts into his councils—the well-bullocks, the little gray squirrels, the mongoose that lived in a hole near the well, and especially Mian Mittu, the parrot, whose tail he grievously pulled, and Mian Mittu screamed till Ameera and Holden arrived.

'O villain! Child of strength! This to thy brother on the house-top! *Tobah, tobah!* Fie! Fie! But I know a charm to make him wise as Suleiman and Aflatoun [Solomon and Plato]. Now look,' said Ameera. She drew from an embroidered bag a handful of almonds. 'See! we count seven. In the name of God!'

She placed Mian Mittu, very angry and rumpled, on the top of his cage, and seating herself between the babe and the bird she cracked and peeled an almond less white than her teeth. 'This is a true charm, my life, and do not laugh. See! I give the parrot one half and Tota the other.' Mian Mittu with careful beak took his share from between Ameera's lips, and she kissed the other half into the mouth of the child, who ate it slowly with wondering eyes. 'This I will do each day of seven, and without doubt he who is ours will be a bold speaker and wise. Eh, Tota, what wilt thou be when thou art a man and I am gray-headed?' Tota tucked his fat legs into adorable creases. He could crawl, but he was not going to waste the spring of his youth in idle speech. He wanted Mian Mittu's tail to tweak.

When he was advanced to the dignity of a silver belt—which, with a magic square engraved on silver and hung round his neck, made up the greater part of his clothing—he staggered on a perilous journey down the garden to Pir Khan and proffered him all his jewels in exchange for one little ride on Holden's horse, having seen his mother's mother chaffering with pedlars in the verandah. Pir Khan wept and set the untried feet on his own gray head in sign of fealty, and brought the bold adventurer to his mother's arms, vowing that Tota would be a leader of men ere his beard was grown.

One hot evening, while he sat on the roof between his father and mother watching the never-ending warfare of the kites that the city boys flew, he demanded a kite of his own with Pir Khan to fly it, because he had a fear of dealing with anything larger than himself, and when Holden called him a 'spark,' he rose to his feet and answered slowly in defence of his new-found individuality, 'Hum'park nahin hai. Hum admi hai [I am no spark, but a man].'

The protest made Holden choke and devote himself very seriously to a consideration of Tota's future. He need hardly have taken the trouble. The delight of that life was too perfect to endure. Therefore it was taken away as many things are taken away in India—suddenly and without warning. The little lord of the house, as Pir Khan called him, grew sorrowful and complained of pains who had never known the meaning of pain. Ameera, wild with terror, watched him through the night, and in the dawning of the second day the life was shaken out of him by fever—the seasonal autumn fever. It seemed altogether impossible that he could die, and neither Ameera nor Holden at first believed the evidence of the little body on the bedstead. Then Ameera beat her head against the wall and would have flung herself down the well in the garden had Holden not restrained her by main force.

One mercy only was granted to Holden. He rode to his office in broad daylight and found waiting him an unusually heavy mail that demanded concentrated attention and hard work. He was not, however, alive to this kindness of the gods.

III

The first shock of a bullet is no more than a brisk pinch. The wrecked body does not send in its protest to the soul till ten or fifteen seconds later. Holden realised his pain slowly, exactly as he had realised his happiness, and with the same imperious necessity for hiding all trace of it. In the beginning he only felt that there had been a loss, and that Ameera needed comforting, where she sat with her head on her knees shivering as Mian Mittu from the house-top called, Tota! Tota! Tota! Later all his world and the daily life of it rose up to hurt him. It was an outrage that any one of the children at the band-stand in the evening should be alive and clamorous, when his own child lay dead. It was more than mere pain when one of them touched him, and stories told by over-fond fathers of their children's latest performances cut him to the quick. He could not declare his pain. He had neither help, comfort, nor sympathy; and Ameera at the end of each weary day would lead him through the hell of self-questioning reproach which is reserved for those who have lost a child, and believe that with a little—just a little—more care it might have been saved.

'Perhaps,' Ameera would say, 'I did not take sufficient heed. Did I, or did I not? The sun on the roof that day when he played so long alone and I was—*ahi!* braiding my hair—it may be that the sun then bred the fever. If I had warned him from the sun he might have lived. But, oh my life, say that I am guiltless! Thou knowest that I loved him as I love thee. Say that there is no blame on me, or I shall die—I shall die!'

'There is no blame,—before God, none. It was written and how could we do aught to save? What has been, has been. Let it go, beloved.'

'He was all my heart to me. How can I let the thought go when my arm tells me every night that he is not here? *Ahi! Ahi!* O Tota, come back to me—come back again, and let us be all together as it was before!'

'Peace, peace! For thine own sake, and for mine also, if thou lovest me—rest.'

'By this I know thou dost not care; and how shouldst thou? The white men have hearts of stone and souls of iron. Oh, that I had married a man of mine own people—though he beat me—and had never eaten the bread of an alien!'

'Am I an alien—mother of my son?'

'What else—*Sahib?* . . . Oh, forgive me—forgive! The death has driven me mad. Thou art the life of my heart, and the light of my eyes, and the breath of my life, and—and I have put thee from me, though it was but for a moment. If thou goest away, to whom shall I look for help? Do not be angry. Indeed, it was the pain that spoke and not thy slave.'

'I know, I know. We be two who were three. The greater need therefore that we should be one.'

They were sitting on the roof as of custom. The night was a warm one in early spring, and sheet-lightning was dancing on the horizon to a broken tune played by far-off thunder. Ameera settled herself in Holden's arms.

'The dry earth is lowing like a cow for the rain, and I—I am afraid. It was not like this when we counted the stars. But thou lovest me as much as before, though a bond is taken away? Answer!'

'I love more because a new bond has come out of the sorrow that we have eaten together, and that thou knowest.'

'Yea, I knew,' said Ameera in a very small whisper. 'But it is good to hear thee say so, my life, who art so strong to help. I will be a child no more, but a woman and an aid to thee. Listen! Give me my *sitar* and I will sing bravely.'

She took the light silver-studded *sitar* and began a song of the great hero Rajah Rasalu. The hand failed on the strings, the tune halted, checked, and at a low note turned off to the poor little nursery-rhyme about the wicked crow—

> And the wild plums grow in the jungle, only a penny a pound.
> Only a penny a pound, *baba*—only . . .

Then came the tears, and the piteous rebellion against fate till she slept, moaning a little in her sleep, with the right arm thrown clear of the body as though it protected something that was not there. It was after this night that life became a little easier for Holden. The ever-present pain of loss drove him into his work, and the work repaid him by filling up his mind for nine or ten hours a day. Ameera sat alone in the house and brooded, but grew happier when she understood that Holden was more at ease, according to the custom of women. They touched happiness again, but this time with caution.

'It was because we loved Tota that he died. The jealousy of God was upon us,' said Ameera. 'I have hung up a large black jar before our window to turn the evil eye from us, and we must make no protestations of delight, but go softly underneath the stars, lest God find us out. Is that not good talk, worthless one?'

She had shifted the accent on the word that means 'beloved,' in proof of the sincerity of her purpose. But the kiss that followed the new christening was a thing that any deity might have envied. They went about henceforward saying, 'It is naught, it is naught'; and hoping that all the Powers heard.

The Powers were busy on other things. They had allowed thirty million people four years of plenty wherein men fed well and the crops were certain, and the birthrate rose year by year; the districts reported a purely agricultural population varying from nine hundred to two thousand to the square mile of the overburdened earth; and the Member for Lower Tooting, wandering about India in pot-hat and frock-coat, talked largely of the benefits of British rule and suggested as the one thing needful the establishment of a duly qualified electoral system and a general bestowal of the franchise. His long-suffering hosts smiled and made him welcome, and when he paused to admire, with pretty picked words, the blossom of the blood-red *dhak*-tree that had flowered untimely for a sign of what was coming, they smiled more than ever.

It was the Deputy Commissioner of Kot-Kumharsen, staying at the club for a day, who lightly told a tale that made Holden's blood run cold as he overheard the end.

'He won't bother any one any more. Never saw a man so astonished in my life. By Jove, I thought he meant to ask a question in the House about it. Fellow-passenger in his ship—dined next him—bowled over by cholera and died in eighteen hours. You needn't laugh, you fellows. The Member for Lower Tooting is awfully angry about it; but he's more scared. I think he's going to take his enlightened self out of India.'

'I'd give a good deal if he were knocked over. It might keep a few vestrymen of his kidney to their own parish. But what's this about cholera? It's full early for anything of that kind,' said the warden of an unprofitable salt-lick.

'Don't know,' said the Deputy Commissioner reflectively. 'We've got locusts with us. There's sporadic cholera all along the north—at least we're calling it sporadic for decency's sake. The spring crops are short in five districts, and nobody seems to know where the rains are. It's nearly March now. I don't want to scare anybody, but it seems to me that Nature's going to audit her accounts with a big red pencil this summer.'

'Just when I wanted to leave, too!' said a voice across the room.

'There won't be much leave this year, but there ought to be a great deal of promotion. I've come in to persuade the Government to put my pet canal on the list of famine-relief works. It's an ill-wind that blows no good. I shall get that canal finished at last.'

'Is it the old programme then,' said Holden; 'famine, fever, and cholera?'

'Oh no. Only local scarcity and an unusual prevalence of seasonal sickness. You'll find it all in the reports if you live till next year. You're a lucky chap. *You* haven't got a wife to send out of harm's way. The hill-stations ought to be full of women this year.'

'I think you're inclined to exaggerate the talk in the *bazars*,' said a young civilian in the Secretariat. 'Now I have observed——'

'I daresay you have,' said the Deputy Commissioner, 'but you've a great deal more to observe, my son. In the meantine, I wish to observe to you——' and he drew him aside to discuss the construction of the canal that was so dear to his heart. Holden went to his bungalow and began to understand that he was not alone in the world, and also that he was afraid for the sake of another,—which is the most soul-satisfying fear known to man.

Two months later, as the Deputy had foretold, Nature began to audit her accounts with a red pencil. On the heels of the spring-reapings came a cry for bread, and the Government, which had decreed that no man should die of want, sent wheat. Then came the cholera from all four quarters of the compass. It struck a pilgrim-gathering of half a million at a sacred shrine. Many died at the feet of their god; the others broke down and ran over the face of the land carrying the pestilence with them. It smote a walled city and killed two hundred a day. The people crowded the trains, hanging on to the footboards and squatting on the roofs of the carriages, and the cholera followed them, for at each station they dragged out the dead and the dying. They died by the roadside, and the horses of the Englishmen shied at the corpses in the grass. The rains did not come, and the earth turned to iron lest man should escape death by hiding in her. The English sent their wives away to the hills and went about their work, coming forward as they were bidden to fill the gaps in the fighting-line. Holden, sick with fear of losing his chiefest treasure on earth, had done his best to persuade Ameera to go away with her mother to the Himalayas.

'Why should I go,' she said one evening on the roof.

'There is sickness, and people are dying, and all the white *mem-log* have gone.'

'All of them?'

'All—unless perhaps there remain some old scald-head who vexes her husband's heart by running risk of death.'

'Nay; who stays is my sister, and thou must not abuse her, for I will be a scald-head too. I am glad all the bold *mem-log* are gone.'

'Do I speak to a woman or a babe? Go to the hills and I will see to it that thou goest like a queen's daughter. Think, child. In a red-lacquered bullock-cart, veiled and curtained, with brass peacocks upon the pole and red cloth hangings. I will send two orderlies for guard, and——'

'Peace! Thou art the babe in speaking thus. What use are those toys to me? *He* would have patted the bullocks and played with the housings. For his sake, perhaps,—thou hast made me very English—I might have gone. Now I will not. Let the *mem-log* run.'

'Their husbands are sending them, beloved.'

'Very good talk. Since when hast thou been my husband to tell me what to do? I have but borne thee a son. Thou art only all the desire of my soul to me. How shall I depart when I know that if evil befall thee by the breadth of so much as my littlest finger-nail—is that not small?—I should be aware of it though I were in paradise. And here, this summer thou mayest die—*ai, janee*, die! and in dying they might call to tend thee a white woman, and she would rob me in the last of thy love!'

'But love is not born in a moment or on a death-bed!'

'What dost thou know of love, stoneheart? She would take thy thanks at least and, by God and the Prophet and Beebee Miriam the mother of thy Prophet, that I will never endure. My lord and my love, let there be no more foolish talk of going away. Where thou art, I am. It is enough.' She put an arm round his neck and a hand on his mouth.

There are not many happinesses so complete as those that are snatched under the shadow of the sword. They sat together and laughed, calling each other openly by every pet name that could move the wrath of the gods. The city below them was locked up in its own torments. Sulphur fires blazed in the streets; the conches in the Hindu temples screamed and bellowed, for the gods were inattentive in those days. There was a service in the great Mahomedan shrine, and the call to prayer from the minarets was almost unceasing. They heard the wailing in the houses of the dead, and once the shriek of a mother who had lost a child and was calling for its return. In the gray dawn they saw the dead borne out through the city gates, each litter with its own little knot of mourners. Wherefore they kissed each other and shivered.

It was a red and heavy audit, for the land was very sick and needed a little breathing-space ere the torrent of cheap life should flood it anew. The children of immature fathers and undeveloped mothers made no resistance. They were cowed and sat still, waiting till the sword should be sheathed in November if it were so willed. There were gaps among the English, but the gaps were filled. The work of superintending famine-relief, cholera-sheds, medicine-distribution, and what little sanitation was possible, went forward because it was so ordered.

Holden had been told to keep himself in readiness to move to replace the next man who should fall. There were twelve hours in each day when he could not see Ameera, and she might die in three. He was considering what his pain would be if he could not see her for three months, or if she died out of his sight. He was absolutely certain that her death would be demanded—so certain that when he looked up from the telegram and saw Pir Khan breathless in the doorway, he laughed aloud. 'And?' said he,——

'When there is a cry in the night and the spirit flutters into the throat, who has a charm that will restore? Come swiftly, Heaven-born! It is the black cholera.'

Holden galloped to his home. The sky was heavy with clouds, for the long-deferred rains were near and the heat was stifling. Ameera's mother met him in the courtyard, whimpering, 'She is dying. She is nursing herself into death. She is all but dead. What shall I do, sahib?'

Ameera was lying in the room in which Tota had been born. She made no sign when Holden entered, because the human soul is a very lonely thing and, when it is getting ready to go away, hides itself in a misty borderland where the living may not follow. The black cholera does its work quietly and without explanation. Ameera was being thrust out of life as though the Angel of Death had himself put his hand upon her. The quick breathing seemed to show that she was either afraid or in pain, but neither eyes nor mouth gave any answer to Holden's kisses. There was nothing to be said or done. Holden could only wait and suffer. The first drops of the rain began to fall on the roof, and he could hear shouts of joy in the parched city.

The soul came back a little and the lips moved. Holden bent down to listen. 'Keep nothing of mine,' said Ameera. 'Take no hair from my head. *She* would make thee burn it later on. That flame I should feel. Lower! Stoop lower! Remember only that I was thine and bore thee a son. Though thou wed a white woman to-morrow, the pleasure of receiving in thy arms thy first son is taken from thee for ever. Remember me when thy son is born—the one that shall carry thy name before all men. His misfortunes be on my head. I bear witness—I bear witness'—the lips were forming the words on his ear—'that there is no God but—thee, beloved!'

Then she died. Holden sat still, and all thought was taken from him,—till he heard Ameera's mother lift the curtain.

'Is she dead, *sahib?*'

'She is dead.'

'Then I will mourn, and afterwards take an inventory of the furniture in this house. For that will be mine. The *sahib* does not mean to resume it? It is so little, so very little, *sahib*, and I am an old woman. I would like to lie softly.'

'For the mercy of God be silent a while. Go out and mourn where I cannot hear.'

'*Sahib*, she will be buried in four hours.'

'I know the custom. I shall go ere she is taken away. That matter is in thy hands. Look to it, that the bed on which—on which she lies——'

'Aha! That beautiful red-lacquered bed. I have long desired——'

'That the bed is left here untouched for my disposal. All else in the house is thine. Hire a cart, take everything, go hence, and before sunrise let there be nothing in this house but that which I have ordered thee to respect.'

'I am an old woman. I would stay at least for the days of mourning, and the rains have just broken. Whither shall I go?'

'What is that to me? My order is that there is a going. The house-gear is worth a thousand rupees and my orderly shall bring thee a hundred rupees to-night.'

'That is very little. Think of the cart-hire.'

'It shall be nothing unless thou goest, and with speed. O woman, get hence and leave me with my dead!'

The mother shuffled down the staircase, and in her anxiety to take stock of the house-fittings forgot to mourn. Holden stayed by Ameera's side and the rain roared on the roof. He could not think connectedly by reason of the noise, though he made many attempts to do so. Then four sheeted ghosts glided dripping into the room and stared at him through their veils. They were the washers of the dead. Holden left the room and went out to his horse. He had come in a dead, stifling calm through ankle-deep dust. He found the courtyard a rain-lashed pond alive with frogs; a torrent of yellow water ran under the gate, and a roaring wind drove the bolts of the rain like buckshot against the mud-walls. Pir Khan was shivering in his little hut by the gate, and the horse was stamping uneasily in the water.

'I have been told the *sahib's* order,' said Pir Khan. 'It is well. This house is now desolate. I go also, for my monkey-face would be a reminder of that which has been. Concerning the bed, I will bring that to thy house yonder in the morning; but remember, *sahib*, it will be to thee a knife turning in a green wound. I go upon a pilgrimage, and I will take no money. I have grown fat in the protection of the Presence whose sorrow is my sorrow. For the last time I hold his stirrup.'

He touched Holden's foot with both hands and the horse sprang out into the road, where the creaking bamboos were whipping the sky and all the frogs were chuckling. Holden could not see for the rain in his face. He put his hands before his eyes and muttered—

'Oh you brute! You utter brute!'

The news of his trouble was already in his bungalow. He read the knowledge in his butler's eyes when Ahmed Khan brought in food, and for the first and last time in his life laid a hand upon his master's shoulder, saying, 'Eat, *sahib*, eat. Meat is good against sorrow. I also have known. Moreover the shadows come and go, *sahib*; the shadows come and go. These be curried eggs.'

Holden could neither eat nor sleep. The heavens sent down eight inches of rain in that night and washed the earth clean. The waters tore down walls, broke roads, and scoured open the shallow graves on the Mahom-edan burying-ground. All next day it rained, and Holden sat still in his house considering his sorrow. On the morning of the third day he received a telegram which said only, 'Ricketts, Myndonie. Dying. Holden relieve. Immediate.' Then he thought that before he departed he would look at the house wherein he had been master and lord. There was a break in the weather, and the rank earth steamed with vapour.

He found that the rains had torn down the mud pillars of the gate-way, and the heavy wooden gate that had guarded his life hung lazily from one hinge. There was grass three inches high in the courtyard; Pir Khan's lodge was empty, and the sodden thatch sagged between the beams. A gray squirrel was in possession of the verandah, as if the house had been untenanted for thirty years instead of three days. Ameera's mother had removed everything except some mildewed matting. The *tick-tick* of the little scorpions as they hurried across the floor was the only sound in the house. Ameera's room and the other one where Tota had lived were heavy with mildew; and the narrow staircase leading to the roof was streaked and stained with rain-borne mud. Holden saw all these things, and came out again to meet in the road Durga Dass, his landlord,— portly, affable, clothed in white muslin, and driving a Cee-spring buggy. He was overlooking his property to see how the roofs stood the stress of the first rains.

'I have heard,' said he, 'you will not take this place any more, *sahib?*'

'What are you going to do with it?'

'Perhaps I shall let it again.'

'Then I will keep it on while I am away.'

Durga Dass was silent for some time. 'You shall not take it on, *sahib,*' he said. 'When I was a young man I also——, but to-day I am a member of the Municipality. Ho! Ho! No. When the birds have gone what need to keep the nest? I will have it pulled down—the timber will sell for something always. It shall be pulled down, and the Municipality shall make a road across, as they desire, from the burning-ghat to the city wall, so that no man may say where this house stood.'

"THEY"

A Short Story

"THEY"

ONE view called me to another; one hill top to its fellow, half across the county, and since I could answer at no more trouble than the snapping forward of a lever, I let the country flow under my wheels. The orchid-studded flats of the East gave way to the thyme, ilex, and grey grass of the Downs; these again to the rich cornland and fig-trees of the lower coast, where you carry the beat of the tide on your left hand for fifteen level miles; and when at last I turned inland through a huddle of rounded hills and woods I had run myself clean out of my known marks. Beyond that precise hamlet which stands godmother to the capital of the United States, I found hidden villages where bees, the only things awake, boomed in eighty-foot lindens that overhung grey Norman churches; miraculous brooks diving under stone bridges built for heavier traffic than would ever vex them again; tithe-barns larger than their churches, and an old smithy that cried out aloud how it had once been a hall of the Knights of the Temple. Gipsies I found on a common where the gorse, bracken, and heath fought it out together up a mile of Roman road; and a little farther on I disturbed a red fox rolling dog-fashion in the naked sunlight.

As the wooded hills closed about me I stood up in the car to take the bearings of that great Down whose ringed head is a landmark for fifty miles across the low countries. I judged that the lie of the country would bring me across some westward running road that went to his feet, but I did not allow for the confusing veils of the woods. A quick turn plunged me first into a green cutting brimful of liquid sunshine, next into a gloomy tunnel where last year's dead leaves whispered and scuffled about my tyres. The strong hazel stuff meeting overhead had not been cut for a couple of generations at least, nor had any axe helped the moss-cankered oak and beech to spring above them. Here the road changed frankly into a carpeted ride on whose brown velvet spent prim-rose-clumps showed like jade, and a few sickly, white-stalked blue-bells nodded together. As the slope favoured I shut off the power and slid over the whirled leaves, expecting every moment to meet a keeper; but I only heard a jay, far off, arguing against the silence under the twilight of the trees.

Still the track descended. I was on the point of reversing and working my way back on the second speed ere I ended in some swamp, when I saw sunshine through the tangle ahead and lifted the brake.

It was down again at once. As the light beat across my face my fore-wheels took the turf of a great still lawn from which sprang horsemen ten feet high with levelled lances, monstrous peacocks, and sleek round-headed maids of honour—blue, black, and glistening—all of clipped yew. Across the lawn—the marshalled woods besieged it on three sides—stood an ancient house of lichened and weather-worn stone, with mullioned windows and roofs of rose-red tile. It was flanked by semi-circular walls, also rose-red, that closed the lawn on the fourth side, and at their feet a box hedge grew man-high. There were doves on the roof about the slim brick chimneys, and I caught a glimpse of an octagonal dove-house behind the screening wall.

Here, then, I stayed; a horseman's green spear laid at my breast; held by the exceeding beauty of that jewel in that setting.

"If I am not packed off for a trespasser, or if this knight does not ride a wallop at me," thought I, "Shakespeare and Queen Elizabeth at least must come out of that half-open garden door and ask me to tea."

A child appeared at an upper window, and I thought the little thing waved a friendly hand. But it was to call a companion, for presently an-other bright head showed. Then I heard a laugh among the yew-peacocks, and turning to make sure (till then I had been watching the house only) I saw the silver of a fountain behind a hedge thrown up against the sun. The doves on the roof cooed to the cooing water; but between the two notes I caught the utterly happy chuckle of a child absorbed in some light mischief.

The garden door—heavy oak sunk deep in the thickness of the wall—opened further: a woman in a big garden hat set her foot slowly on the time-hollowed stone step and as slowly walked across the turf. I was form-ing some apology when she lifted up her head and I saw that she was blind.

"I heard you," she said. "Isn't that a motor car?"

"I'm afraid I've made a mistake in my road. I should have turned off up above—I never dreamed"—I began.

"But I'm very glad. Fancy a motor car coming into the garden! It will be such a treat——" She turned and made as though looking about her. "You—you haven't seen any one have you—perhaps?"

"No one to speak to, but the children seemed interested at a distance."

"Which?"

"I saw a couple up at the window just now, and I think I heard a little chap in the grounds."

"Oh, lucky you!" she cried, and her face brightened. "I hear them, of course, but that's all. You've seen them and heard them?"

"Yes," I answered. "And if I know anything of children one of them's having a beautiful time by the fountain yonder. Escaped, I should imagine."

"You're fond of children?"

I gave her one or two reasons why I did not altogether hate them.

"Of course, of course," she said. "Then you understand. Then you won't think it foolish if I ask you to take your car through the gardens, once or twice—quite slowly. I'm sure they'd like to see it. They see so little, poor things. One tries to make their life pleasant, but——" she threw out her hands towards the woods. "We're so out of the world here."

"That will be splendid," I said. "But I can't cut up your grass."

She faced to the right. "Wait a minute," she said. "We're at the South gate, aren't we? Behind those peacocks there's a flagged path. We call it the Peacock's Walk. You can't see it from herc, they tell me, but if you squeeze along by the edge of the wood you can turn at the first peacock and get on to the flags."

It was a sacrilege to wake that dreaming house-front with the clatter of machinery, but I swung the car to clear the turf, brushed along the edge of the wood and turned in on the broad stone path where the fountain-basin lay like one star-sapphire.

"May I come too?" she cried. "No, please don't help me. They'll like it better if they see me."

She felt her way lightly to the front of the car, and with one foot on the step she called: "Children, oh, children! Look and see what's going to happen!"

The voice would have drawn lost souls from the Pit, for the yearning that underlay its sweetness, and I was not surprised to hear an answering shout behind the yews. It must have been the child by the fountain, but he fled at our approach, leaving a little toy boat in the watcr. I saw the glint of his blue blouse among the still horsemen.

Very disposedly we paraded the length of the walk and at her request backed again. This time the child had got the better of his panic, but stood far off and doubting.

"The little fellow's watching us," I said. "I wonder if he'd like a ride."

"They're very shy still. Very shy. But, oh, lucky you to be able to see them! Let's listen."

I stopped the machine at once, and the humid stillness, heavy with the scent of box, cloaked us deep. Shears I could hear where some gardener was clipping; a mumble of bees and broken voices that might have been the doves.

"Oh, unkind!" she said weariedly.

"Perhaps they're only shy of the motor. The little maid at the window looks tremendously interested."

"Yes?" She raised her head. "It was wrong of me to say that. They are really fond of me. It's the only thing that makes life worth living—when they're fond of you, isn't it? I daren't think what the place would be without them. By the way, is it beautiful?"

"I think it is the most beautiful place I have ever seen."

"So they all tell me. I can feel it, of course, but that isn't quite the same thing."

"Then have you never——?" I began, but stopped abashed.

"Not since I can remember. It happened when I was only a few months old, they tell me. And yet I must remember something, else how could I dream about colours. I see light in my dreams, and colours, but I never see *them*. I only hear them just as I do when I'm awake."

"It's difficult to see faces in dreams. Some people can, but most of us haven't the gift," I went on, looking up at the window where the child stood all but hidden.

"I've heard that too," she said. "And they tell me that one never sees a dead person's face in a dream. Is that true?"

"I believe it is—now I come to think of it."

"But how is it with yourself—yourself?" The blind eyes turned towards me.

"I have never seen the faces of my dead in any dream," I answered.

"Then it must be as bad as being blind."

The sun had dipped behind the woods and the long shades were possessing the insolent horsemen one by one. I saw the light die from off the top of a glossy-leaved lance and all the brave hard green turn to soft black. The house, accepting another day at end, as it had accepted an hundred thousand gone, seemed to settle deeper into its rest among the shadows.

"Have you ever wanted to?" she said after the silence.

"Very much sometimes," I replied. The child had left the window as the shadows closed upon it.

"Ah! So've I, but I don't suppose it's allowed. . . . Where d'you live?"

"Quite the other side of the county—sixty miles and more, and I must be going back. I've come without my big lamp."

"But it's not dark yet. I can feel it."

"I'm afraid it will be by the time I get home. Could you lend me someone to set me on my road at first? I've utterly lost myself."

"I'll send Madden with you to the cross-roads. We are so out of the world, I don't wonder you were lost! I'll guide you round to the front of the house; but you will go slowly, won't you, till you're out of the grounds? It isn't foolish, do you think?"

"I promise you I'll go like this," I said, and let the car start herself down the flagged path.

We skirted the left wing of the house, whose elaborately cast lead guttering alone was worth a day's journey; passed under a great rose-grown gate in the red wall, and so round to the high front of the house which in beauty and stateliness as much excelled the back as that all others I had seen.

"Is it so very beautiful?" she said wistfully when she heard my raptures. "And you like the lead-figures too? There's the old azalea garden behind. They say that this place must have been made for children. Will you help me out, please? I should like to come with you as far as the cross-roads, but I mustn't leave them. Is that you, Madden? I want you to show this gentleman the way to the cross-roads. He has lost his way but—he has seen them."

A butler appeared noiselessly at the miracle of old oak that must be called the front door, and slipped aside to put on his hat. She stood looking at me with open blue eyes in which no sight lay, and I saw for the first time that she was beautiful.

"Remember," she said quietly, "if you are fond of them you will come again," and disappeared within the house.

The butler in the car said nothing till we were nearly at the lodge gates, where catching a glimpse of a blue blouse in a shrubbery I swerved amply lest the devil that leads little boys to play should drag me into child-murder.

"Excuse me," he asked of a sudden, "but why did you do that, Sir?"

"The child yonder."

"Our young gentleman in blue?"

"Of course."

"He runs about a good deal. Did you see him by the fountain, Sir?"

"Oh, yes, several times. Do we turn here?"

"Yes, Sir. And did you 'appen to see them upstairs too?"

"At the upper window? Yes."

"Was that before the mistress come out to speak to you, Sir?"

"A little before that. Why d'you want to know?"

He paused a little. "Only to make sure that—that they had seen the car, Sir, because with children running about, though I'm sure you're driving particularly careful, there might be an accident. That was all, Sir. Here are the cross-roads. You can't miss your way from now on. Thank you, Sir, but that isn't *our* custom, not with——"

"I beg your pardon," I said, and thrust away the British silver.

"Oh, it's quite right with the rest of 'em as a rule. Goodbye, Sir."

He retired into the armour-plated conning tower of his caste and walked away. Evidently a butler solicitous for the honour of his house, and interested, probably through a maid, in the nursery.

Once beyond the signposts at the cross-roads I looked back, but the crumpled hills interlaced so jealously that I could not see where the house had lain. When I asked its name at a cottage along the road, the fat woman who sold sweetmeats there gave me to understand that people with motor cars had small right to live—much less to "go about talking like carriage folk." They were not a pleasant-mannered community.

When I retraced my route on the map that evening I was little wiser. Hawkin's Old Farm appeared to be the survey title of the place, and the old County Gazeteer, generally so ample, did not allude to it. The big house of those parts was Hodnington Hall, Georgian with early Victorian embellishments, as an atrocious steel engraving attested. I carried my difficulty to a neighbour—a deep-rooted tree of that soil—and he gave me a name of a family which conveyed no meaning.

A month or so later—I went again, or it may have been that my car took the road of her own volition. She over-ran the fruitless Downs, threaded every turn of the maze of lanes below the hills, drew through the high-walled woods, impenetrable in their full leaf, came out at the cross-roads where the butler had left me, and a little further on developed an internal trouble which forced me to turn her in on a grass way-waste that cut into a summer-silent hazel wood. So far as I could make sure by the sun and a six-inch Ordnance map, this should be the road flank of that wood which I had first explored from the heights above. I made a mighty serious business of my repairs and a glittering shop of my repair kit, spanners, pump, and the like, which I spread out orderly upon a rug. It was a trap to catch all childhood, for on such a day, I argued, the children would not be far off. When I paused in my work I listened, but the wood was so full of the noises of summer (though the birds had mated) that I could not at first distinguish these from the tread of small cautious feet stealing across the dead leaves. I rang my bell in an alluring manner, but the feet fled, and I repented, for to a child a sudden noise is very real terror. I must have been at work half an hour when I heard in the wood the voice of the blind woman crying: "Children, oh children, where are you?" and the stillness made slow to close on the perfection of that cry. She came towards me, half feeling her way between the tree boles, and though a child it seemed clung to her skirt, it swerved into the leafage like a rabbit as she drew nearer.

"Is that you?" she said, "from the other side of the county?"

"Yes, it's me from the other side of the county."

"Then why didn't you come through the upper woods? They were there just now."

"They were here a few minutes ago. I expect they knew my car had broken down, and came to see the fun."

"Nothing serious, I hope? How do cars break down?"

"In fifty different ways. Only mine has chosen the fifty first."

She laughed merrily at the tiny joke, cooed with delicious laughter, and pushed her hat back.

"Let me hear," she said.

"Wait a moment," I cried, "and I'll get you a cushion."

She set her foot on the rug all covered with spare parts, and stooped above it eagerly. "What delightful things!" The hands through which she saw glanced in the chequered sunlight. "A box here—another box! Why you've arranged them like playing shop!"

"I confess now that I put it out to attract them. I don't need half those things really."

"How nice of you! I heard your bell in the upper wood. You say they were here before that?"

"I'm sure of it. Why are they so shy? That little fellow in blue who was with you just now ought to have got over his fright. He's been watching me like a Red Indian."

"It must have been your bell," she said. "I heard one of them go past me in trouble when I was coming down. They're shy—so shy even with me." She turned her face over her shoulder and cried again: "Children! Oh, children! Look and see!"

"They must have gone off together on their own affairs," I suggested, for there was a murmur behind us of lowered voices broken by the sudden squeaking giggles of childhood. I returned to my tinkerings and she leaned forward, her chin on her hand, listening interestedly.

"How many are they?" I said at last. The work was finished, but I saw no reason to go.

Her forehead puckered a little in thought. "I don't quite know," she said simply. "Sometimes more—sometimes less. They come and stay with me because I love them, you see."

"That must be very jolly," I said, replacing a drawer, and as I spoke I heard the inanity of my answer.

"You—you aren't laughing at me," she cried. "I—I haven't any of my own. I never married. People laugh at me sometimes about them because —because——"

"Because they're savages," I returned. "It's nothing to fret for. That sort laugh at everything that isn't in their own fat lives."

"I don't know. How should I? I only don't like being laughed at about *them.* It hurts; and when one can't see. . . . I don't want to seem silly," her chin quivered like a child's as she spoke, "but we blindies have only one skin, I think. Everything outside hits straight at our souls. It's different with you. You've such good defences in your eyes—looking out—before anyone can really pain you in your soul. People forget that with us."

I was silent reviewing that inexhaustible matter—the more than inherited (since it is also carefully taught) brutality of the Christian peoples, beside which the mere heathendom of the West Coast nigger is clean and restrained. It led me a long distance into myself.

"Don't do that!" she said of a sudden, putting her hands before her eyes. "What?"

She made a gesture with her hand.

"That! It's—it's all purple and black. Don't! That colour hurts."

"But, how in the world do you know about colours?" I exclaimed, for here was a revelation indeed.

"Colours as colours?" she asked.

"No. *Those* Colours which you saw just now."

"You know as well as I do," she laughed, "else you wouldn't have asked that question. They aren't in the world at all. They're in *you*—when you went so angry."

"D'you mean a dull purplish patch, like port-wine mixed with ink?" I said.

"I've never seen ink or port-wine, but the colours aren't mixed. They are separate—all separate."

"Do you mean black streaks and jags across the purple?"

She nodded. "Yes—if they are like this," and zig-zagged her finger again, "but it's more red than purple—that bad colour."

"And what are the colours at the top of the—whatever you see?"

Slowly she leaned forward and traced on the rug the figure of the Egg itself.

"I see them so," she said, pointing with a grass stem, "white, green, yellow, red, purple, and when people are angry or bad, black across the red—as you were just now."

"Who told you anything about it—in the beginning?" I demanded.

"About the colours? No one. I used to ask what colours were when I was little—in table-covers and curtains and carpets, you see—because some colours hurt me and some made me happy. People told me; and when I got older that was how I saw people." Again she traced the outline of the Egg which it is given to very few of us to see.

"All by yourself?" I repeated.

"All by myself. There wasn't anyone else. I only found out afterwards that other people did not see the Colours."

She leaned against the tree-bole plaiting and unplaiting chance-plucked grass stems. The children in the wood had drawn nearer. I could see them with the tail of my eye frolicking like squirrels.

"Now I am sure you will never laugh at me," she went on after a long silence. "Nor at *them*."

"Goodness! No!" I cried, jolted out of my train of thought. "A man who laughs at a child—unless the child is laughing too—is a heathen!"

"I didn't mean that of course. You'd never laugh *at* children, but I thought—I used to think—that perhaps you might laugh about *them*. So now I beg your pardon. . . . What are you going to laugh at?"

I had made no sound, but she knew.

"At the notion of your begging my pardon. If you had done your duty as a pillar of the state and a landed proprietress you ought to have summoned me for trespass when I barged through your woods the other day. It was disgraceful of me—inexcusable."

She looked at me, her head against the tree trunk—long and steadfastly —this woman who could see the naked soul.

"How curious," she half whispered. "How very curious."

"Why, what have I done?"

"You don't understand . . . and yet you understood about the Colours. Don't you understand?"

She spoke with a passion that nothing had justified, and I faced her bewilderedly as she rose. The children had gathered themselves in a roundel behind a bramble bush. One sleek head bent over something smaller, and the set of the little shoulders told me that fingers were on lips. They too, had some child's tremendous secret. I alone was hopelessly astray there in the broad sunlight.

"No," I said, and shook my head as though the dead eyes could note. "Whatever it is, I don't understand yet. Perhaps I shall later—if you'll let me come again."

"You will come again," she answered. "You will surely come again and walk in the wood."

"Perhaps the children will know me well enough by that time to let me play with them—as a favour. You know what children are like."

"It isn't a matter of favour but of right," she replied, and while I wondered what she meant, a dishevelled woman plunged round the bend of the road, loose-haired, purple, almost lowing with agony as she ran. It was my rude, fat friend of the sweetmeat shop. The blind woman heard and stepped forward. "What is it, Mrs. Madehurst?" she asked.

The woman flung her apron over her head and literally grovelled in the dust, crying that her grandchild was sick to death, that the local doctor was away fishing, that Jenny the mother was at her wit's end, and so forth, with repetitions and bellowings.

"Where's the next nearest doctor?" I asked between paroxysms.

"Madden will tell you. Go round to the house and take him with you. I'll attend to this. Be quick!" She half-supported the fat woman into the shade. In two minutes I was blowing all the horns of Jericho under the front of the House Beautiful, and Madden, in the pantry, rose to the crisis like a butler and a man.

A quarter of an hour at illegal speeds caught us a doctor five miles away. Within the half-hour we had decanted him, much interested in motors, at the door of the sweetmeat shop, and drew up the road to await the verdict.

"Useful things cars," said Madden, all man and no butler. "If I'd had one when mine took sick she wouldn't have died."

"How was it?" I asked.

"Croup. Mrs. Madden was away. No one knew what to do. I drove eight miles in a tax cart for the doctor. She was choked when we came back. This car 'd ha' saved her. She'd have been close on ten now."

"I'm sorry," I said. "I thought you were rather fond of children from what you told me going to the cross-roads the other day."

"Have you seen 'em again, Sir—this mornin'?"

"Yes, but they're well broke to cars. I couldn't get any of them within twenty yards of it."

He looked at me carefully as a scout considers a stranger—not as a menial should lift his eyes to his divinely appointed superior.

"I wonder why," he said just above the breath that he drew.

We waited on. A light wind from the sea wandered up and down the long lines of the woods, and the wayside grasses, whitened already with summer dust, rose and bowed in sallow waves.

A woman, wiping the suds off her arms, came out of the cottage next the sweetmeat shop.

"I've be'n listenin' in de back-yard," she said cheerily. "He says Arthur's unaccountable bad. Did ye hear him shruck just now? Unaccountable bad. I reckon t'will come Jenny's turn to walk in de wood nex' week along Mr. Madden."

"Excuse me, Sir, but your lap-robe is slipping," said Madden deferentially. The woman started, dropped a curtsey, and hurried away.

"What does she mean by 'walking in the wood'?" I asked.

"It must be some saying they use hereabouts. I'm from Norfolk myself," said Madden. "They're an independent lot in this county. She took you for a chauffeur, Sir."

I saw the Doctor come out of the cottage followed by a draggle-tailed wench who clung to his arm as though he could make treaty for her with Death. "Dat sort," she wailed—"dey're just as much to us dat has 'em as if dey was lawful born. Just as much—just as much! An' God he'd be just as pleased if you saved 'un, Doctor. Don't take it from me. Miss Florence will tell ye de very same. Don't leave 'im, Doctor!"

"I know. I know," said the man, "but he'll be quiet for a while now. We'll get the nurse and the medicine as fast as we can." He signalled me to come forward with the car, and I strove not to be privy to what followed; but I saw the girl's face, blotched and frozen with grief, and I felt the hand without a ring clutching at my knees when we moved away.

The Doctor was a man of some humour, for I remember he claimed my car under the Oath of Æsculapius, and used it and me without mercy. First we convoyed Mrs. Madehurst and the blind woman to wait by the sick bed till the nurse should come. Next we invaded a neat county town for prescriptions (the Doctor said the trouble was cerebro-spinal meningitis), and when the County Institute, banked and flanked with scared market cattle, reported itself out of nurses for the moment we literally flung ourselves loose upon the county. We conferred with the owners of great houses—magnates at the ends of overarching avenues whose big-boned womenfolk strode away from their tea-tables to listen to the imperious Doctor. At last a whitehaired lady sitting under a cedar of Lebanon and surrounded by a court of magnificent Borzois—all hostile to motors—gave the Doctor, who received them as from a princess, written orders which we bore many miles at top speed, through a park, to a French nunnery, where we took over in exchange a pallid-faced and trembling Sister. She knelt at the bottom of the tonneau telling her beads without pause till, by short cuts of the Doctor's invention, we had her to the sweet-meat shop once more. It was a long afternoon crowded with mad episodes that rose and dissolved like the dust of our wheels; cross-sections of remote and incomprehensible lives through which we raced at right angles; and I went home in the dusk, wearied out, to dream of the clashing horns of cattle; round-eyed nuns walking in a garden of graves; pleasant tea-parties beneath shaded trees; the carbolic-scented, grey-painted corridors of the County Institute; the steps of shy children in the wood, and the hands that clung to my knees as the motor began to move.

I had intended to return in a day or two, but it pleased Fate to hold me from that side of the county, on many pretexts, till the elder and the wild rose had fruited. There came at last a brilliant day, swept clear from the south-west, that brought the hills within hand's reach—a day of unstable airs and high filmy clouds. Through no merit of my own I was free, and set the car for the third time on that known road. As I reached the crest of the Downs I felt the soft air change, saw it glaze under the sun; and, looking down at the sea, in that instant beheld the blue of the Channel turn through polished silver and dulled steel to dingy pewter. A laden collier hugging the coast steered outward for deeper water and, across copper-coloured haze, I saw sails rise one by one on the anchored fishing-fleet. In a deep dene behind me an eddy of sudden wind drummed through sheltered oaks, and spun aloft the first day sample of autumn leaves. When I reached the beach road the sea-fog fumed over the brick-fields, and the side was telling all the groins of the gale beyond Ushant. In less than an hour summer England vanished in chill grey. We were again the shut island of the North, all the ships of the world bellowing at our perilous gates; and between their outcries ran the piping of bewildered gulls. My cap dripped moisture, the folds of the rug held it in pools or sluiced it away in runnels, and the salt-rime stuck to my lips.

Inland the smell of autumn loaded the thickened fog among the trees, and the drip became a continuous shower. Yet the late flowers—mallow of the wayside, scabious of the field, and dahlia of the garden—showed gay in the midst, and beyond the sea's breath there was little sign of decay in the leaf. Yet in the villages the house doors were all open, and bare-legged, bare-headed children sat at ease on the damp doorsteps to shout "pip-pip" at the stranger.

I made bold to call at the sweetmeat shop, where Mrs. Madehurst met me with a fat woman's hospitable tears. Jenny's child, she said, had died two days after the nun had come. It was, she felt, best out of the way, even though insurance offices, for reasons which she did not pretend to follow, would not willingly insure such stray lives. "Not but what Jenny didn't tend to Arthur as though he'd come all proper at de end of de first year—like Jenny herself." Thanks to Miss Florence, the child had been buried with a pomp which, in Mrs. Madehurst's opinion, more than covered the small irregularity of its birth. She described the coffin, within and without, the glass hearse, and the evergreen lining of the grave.

"But how's the mother?" I asked.

"Jenny? Oh, she'll get over it. I've felt dat way with one or two o' my own. She'll get over. She's walkin' in de wood now."

"In this weather?"

Mrs. Madehurst looked at me with narrowed eyes across the counter.

"I dunno but it opens de 'eart like. Yes, it opens de 'eart. Dat's where losin' and bearin' comes so alike in de long run, we do say."

Now the wisdom of the old wives is greater than that of all the Fathers, and this last oracle sent me thinking so extendedly as I went up the road, that I nearly ran over a woman and a child at the wooded corner by the lodge gates of the House Beautiful.

"Awful weather!" I cried, as I slowed dead for the turn.

"Not so bad," she answered placidly out of the fog. "Mine's used to 'un. You'll find yours indoors, I reckon."

Indoors, Madden received me with professional courtesy, and kind inquiries for the health of the motor, which he would put under cover.

I waited in a still, nut-brown hall, pleasant with late flowers and warmed with a delicious wood fire—a place of good influence and great peace. (Men and women may sometimes, after great effort, achieve a creditable lie; but the house, which is their temple, cannot say anything save the truth of those who have lived in it.) A child's cart and a doll lay on the black-and-white floor, where a rug had been kicked back. I felt that the children had only just hurried away—to hide themselves, most like—in the many turns of the great adzed staircase that climbed statelily out of the hall, or to crouch at gaze behind the lions and roses of the carven gallery above. Then I heard her voice above me, singing as the blind sing—from the soul:—

> In the pleasant orchard-closes.

And all my early summer came back at the call.

> In the pleasant orchard-closes,
> God bless all our gains say we—
> But may God bless all our losses,
> Better suits with our degree.

She dropped the marring fifth line, and repeated—

> Better suits with our degree!

I saw her lean over the gallery, her linked hands white as pearl against the oak.

"Is that you—from the other side of the county?" she called.

"Yes, me—from the other side of the county," I answered laughing.

"What a long time before you had to come here again." She ran down the stairs, one hand lightly touching the broad rail. "It's two months and four days. Summer's gone!"

"I meant to come before, but Fate prevented."

"I knew it. Please do something to that fire. They won't let me play with it, but I can feel it's behaving badly. Hit it!"

I looked on either side of the deep fireplace, and found but a half-charred hedge-stake with which I punched a black log into flame.

"It never goes out, day or night," she said, as though explaining. "In case any one comes in with cold toes, you see."

"It's even lovelier inside than it was out," I murmured. The red light poured itself along the age-polished dusky panels till the Tudor roses and lions of the gallery took colour and motion. An old eagle-topped convex mirror gathered the picture into its mysterious heart, distorting afresh the distorted shadows, and curving the gallery lines into the curves of a ship. The day was shutting down in half a gale as the fog turned to stringy scud. Through the uncurtained mullions of the broad window I could see valiant horsemen of the lawn rear and recover against the wind that taunted them with legions of dead leaves.

"Yes, it must be beautiful," she said. "Would you like to go over it? There's still light enough upstairs."

I followed her up the unflinching, wagon-wide staircase to the gallery whence opened the thin fluted Elizabethan doors.

"Feel how they put the latch low down for the sake of the children." She swung a light door inward.

"By the way, where are they?" I asked. "I haven't even heard them to-day."

She did not answer at once. Then, "I can only hear them," she replied softly. "This is one of their rooms—everything ready, you see."

She pointed into a heavily-timbered room. There were little low gate tables and children's chairs. A doll's house, its hooked front half open, faced a great dappled rocking-horse, from whose padded saddle it was but a child's scramble to the broad window-seat overlooking the lawn. A toy gun lay in a corner beside a gilt wooden cannon.

"Surely they've only just gone," I whispered. In the failing light a door creaked cautiously. I heard the rustle of a frock and the patter of feet— quick feet through a room beyond.

"I heard that," she cried triumphantly. "Did you? Children, O children, where are you?"

The voice filled the walls that held it lovingly to the last perfect note, but there came no answering shout such as I had heard in the garden. We hurried on from room to oak-floored room; up a step here, down three steps there; among a maze of passages; always mocked by our quarry. One might as well have tried to work an unstopped warren with a single ferret. There were bolt-holes innumerable—recesses in walls, embrasures of deep slitten windows now darkened, whence they could start up behind us; and abandoned fireplaces, six feet deep in the masonry, as well as the tangle of communicating doors. Above all, they had the twilight for their helper in our game. I had caught one or two joyous chuckles of evasion, and once or twice had seen the silhouette of a child's frock against some darkening window at the end of a passage; but we returned empty-handed to the gallery, just as a middle-aged woman was setting a lamp in its niche.

"No, I haven't seen her either this evening, Miss Florence," I heard her say, "but that Turpin he says he wants to see you about his shed."

"Oh, Mr. Turpin must want to see me very badly. Tell him to come to the hall, Mrs. Madden."

I looked down into the hall whose only light was the dulled fire, and deep in the shadow I saw them at last. They must have slipped down while we were in the passages, and now thought themselves perfectly hidden behind an old gilt leather screen. By child's law, my fruitless chase was as good as an introduction, but since I had taken so much trouble I resolved to force them to come forward later by the simple trick, which children detest, of pretending not to notice them. They lay close, in a little huddle, no more than shadows except when a quick flame betrayed an outline.

"And now we'll have some tea," she said. "I believe I ought to have offered it you at first, but one doesn't arrive at manners somehow when one lives alone and is considered—h'm—peculiar." Then with very pretty scorn, "would you like a lamp to see to eat by?"

"The firelight's much pleasanter, I think." We descended into that delicious gloom and Madden brought tea.

I took my chair in the direction of the screen ready to surprise or be surprised as the game should go, and at her permission, since a hearth is always sacred, bent forward to play with the fire.

"Where do you get these beautiful short faggots from?" I asked idly. "Why, they are tallies!"

"Of course," she said. "As I can't read or write I'm driven back on the early English tally for my accounts. Give me one and I'll tell you what it meant."

I passed her an unburned hazel-tally, about a foot long, and she ran her thumb down the nicks.

"This is the milk-record for the home farm for the month of April last year, in gallons," said she. "I don't know what I should have done without tallies. An old forester of mine taught me the system. It's out of date now for every one else; but my tenants respect it. One of them's coming now to see me. Oh, it doesn't matter. He has no business here out of office hours. He's a greedy, ignorant man—very greedy or—he wouldn't come here after dark."

"Have you much land then?"

"Only a couple of hundred acres in hand, thank goodness. The other six hundred are nearly all let to folk who knew my folk before me, but this Turpin is quite a new man—and a highway robber."

"But are you sure I sha'n't be——?"

"Certainly not. You have the right. He hasn't any children."

"Ah, the children!" I said, and slid my low chair back till it nearly touched the screen that hid them. "I wonder whether they'll come out for me."

There was a murmur of voices—Madden's and a deeper note—at the low, dark side door, and a ginger-headed, canvas-gaitered giant of the unmistakable tenant farmer type stumbled or was pushed in.

"Come to the fire, Mr. Turpin," she said.

"If—if you please, Miss, I'll—I'll be quite as well by the door." He clung to the latch as he spoke like a frightened child. Of a sudden I realised that he was in the grip of some almost overpowering fear.

"Well?"

"About that new shed for the young stock—that was all. These first autumn storms settin' in . . . but I'll come again, Miss." His teeth did not chatter much more than the door latch.

"I think not," she answered levelly. "The new shed—m'm. What did my agent write you on the 15th?"

"I—fancied p'raps that if I came to see you—ma—man to man like, Miss. But——"

His eyes rolled into every corner of the room wide with horror. He half opened the door through which he had entered, but I noticed it shut again —from without and firmly.

"He wrote what I told him," she went on. "You are overstocked already. Dunnett's Farm never carried more than fifty bullocks—even in Mr. Wright's time. And *he* used cake. You've sixty-seven and you don't cake. You've broken the lease in that respect. You're dragging the heart out of the farm."

"I'm—I'm getting some minerals—superphosphates—next week. I've as good as ordered a truck-load already. I'll go down to the station to-morrow about 'em. Then I can come and see you man to man like, Miss, in the daylight. . . . That gentleman's not going away, is he?" He almost shrieked.

I had only slid the chair a little further back, reaching behind me to tap on the leather of the screen, but he jumped like a rat.

"No. Please attend to me, Mr. Turpin." She turned in her chair and faced him with his back to the door. It was an old and sordid little piece of scheming that she forced from him—his plea for the new cowshed at his landlady's expense, that he might with the covered manure pay his next year's rent out of the valuation after, as she made clear, he had bled the enriched pastures to the bone. I could not but admire the intensity of his greed, when I saw him out-facing for its sake whatever terror it was that ran wet on his forehead.

I ceased to tap the leather—was, indeed, calculating the cost of the shed —when I felt my relaxed hand taken and turned softly between the soft hands of a child. So at last I had triumphed. In a moment I would turn and acquaint myself with those quick-footed wanderers. . . .

The little brushing kiss fell in the centre of my palm—as a gift on which the fingers were, once, expected to close: as the all faithful half-reproachful signal of a waiting child not used to neglect even when grown-ups were busiest—a fragment of the mute code devised very long ago.

Then I knew. And it was as though I had known from the first day when I looked across the lawn at the high window.

I heard the door shut. The woman turned to me in silence, and I felt that she knew.

What time passed after this I cannot say. I was roused by the fall of a log, and mechanically rose to put it back. Then I returned to my place in the chair very close to the screen.

"Now you understand," she whispered, across the packed shadows.

"Yes, I understand—now. Thank you."

"I—I only hear them." She bowed her head in her hands. "I have no right, you know—no other right. I have neither borne nor lost—neither borne nor lost!"

"Be very glad then," said I, for my soul was torn open within me.

"Forgive me!"

She was still, and I went back to my sorrow and my joy.

"It was because I loved them so," she said at last, brokenly. "*That* was why it was, even from the first—even before I knew that they—they were all I should ever have. And I loved them so!"

She stretched out her arms to the shadows and the shadows within the shadow.

"They came because I loved them—because I needed them. I—I must have made them come. Was that wrong, think you?"

"No—no."

"I—I grant you that the toys and—and all that sort of thing were nonsense, but—but I used to so hate empty rooms myself when I was little." She pointed to the gallery. "And the passages all empty. . . . And how could I ever bear the garden door shut? Suppose——"

"Don't! For pity's sake, don't!" I cried. The twilight had brought a cold rain with gusty squalls that plucked at the leaded windows.

"And the same thing with keeping the fire in all night. *I* don't think it so foolish—do you?"

I looked at the broad brick hearth, saw, through tears I believe, that there was no unpassable iron on or near it, and bowed my head.

"I did all that and lots of other things—just to make believe. Then they came. I heard them, but I didn't know that they were not mine by right till Mrs. Madden told me——"

"The butler's wife? What?"

"One of them—I heard—she saw. And knew. Hers! *Not* for me. I didn't know at first. Perhaps I was jealous. Afterwards, I began to understand that it was only because I loved them, not because—— . . . Oh, you *must* bear or lose," she said piteously. "There is no other way—and yet they love me. They must! Don't they?"

There was no sound in the room except the lapping voices of the fire, but we two listened intently, and she at least took comfort from what she heard. She recovered herself and half rose. I sat still in my chair by the screen.

"Don't think me a wretch to whine about myself like this, but—but I'm all in the dark, you know, and *you* can see."

In truth I could see, and my vision confirmed me in my resolve, though that was like the very parting of spirit and flesh. Yet a little longer I would stay since it was the last time.

"You think it is wrong, then?" she cried sharply, though I had said nothing.

"Not for you. A thousand times no. For you it is right. . . . I am grateful to you beyond words. For me it would be wrong. For me only. . . ."

"Why?" she said, but passed her hand before her face as she had done at our second meeting in the wood. "Oh, I see," she went on simply as a child. "For you it would be wrong." Then with a little indrawn laugh, "and, d'you remember, I called you lucky—once—at first. You who must never come here again!"

She left me to sit a little longer by the screen, and I heard the sound of her feet die out along the gallery above.

THE MAN WHO WOULD BE KING

A Short Story

THE MAN WHO WOULD BE KING

Brother to a Prince and fellow to a beggar if he be found worthy.

The law, as quoted, lays down a fair conduct of life, and one not easy to follow. I have been fellow to a beggar again and again under circumstances which prevented either of us finding out whether the other was worthy. I have still to be brother to a Prince, though I once came near to kinship with what might have been a veritable King and was promised the reversion of a Kingdom—army, law-courts, revenue and policy all complete. But, to-day, I greatly fear that my King is dead, and if I want a crown I must go hunt it for myself.

The beginning of everything was in a railway train upon the road to Mhow from Ajmir. There had been a Deficit in the Budget, which necessitated travelling, not Second-class, which is only half as dear as First-class, but by Intermediate, which is very awful indeed. There are no cushions in the Intermediate class, and the population are either Intermediate, which is Eurasian, or native, which for a long night journey is nasty, or Loafer, which is amusing though intoxicated. Intermediates do not buy from refreshment-rooms. They carry their food in bundles and pots, and buy sweets from the native sweetmeat-sellers, and drink the roadside water. That is why in hot weather Intermediates are taken out of the carriages dead, and in all weathers are most properly looked down upon.

My particular Intermediate happened to be empty till I reached Nasirabad, when a big black-browed gentleman in shirt-sleeves entered, and, following the custom of Intermediates, passed the time of day. He was a wanderer and a vagabond like myself, but with an educated taste for whiskey. He told tales of things he had seen and done, of out-of-the-way corners of the Empire into which he had penetrated, and of adventures in which he risked his life for a few days' food.

'If India was filled with men like you and me, not knowing more than the crows where they'd get their next day's rations, it isn't seventy millions of revenue the land would be paying—it's seven hundred millions,' said he; and as I looked at his mouth and chin I was disposed to agree with him.

We talked politics—the politics of Loaferdom that sees things from the underside where the lath and plaster is not smoothed off—and we talked postal arrangements because my friend wanted to send a telegram back from the next station to Ajmir, the turning-off place from the Bombay to the Mhow line as you travel westward. My friend had no money beyond eight annas which he wanted for dinner, and I had no money at all, owing to the hitch in the Budget before mentioned. Further, I was going into a wilderness where, though I should resume touch with the Treasury, there were no telegraph offices. I was, therefore, unable to help him in any way.

'We might threaten a Station-master, and make him send a wire on tick,' said my friend, 'but that'd mean enquiries for you and for me, and I've got my hands full these days. Did you say you were travelling back along this line within any days?'

'Within ten,' I said.

'Can't you make it eight?' said he. 'Mine is rather urgent business.'

'I can send your telegram within ten days if that will serve you,' I said.

'I couldn't trust the wire to fetch him now I think of it. It's this way. He leaves Delhi on the 23rd for Bombay. That means he'll be running through Ajmir about the night of the 23rd.'

'But I'm going into the Indian Desert,' I explained.

'Well *and* good,' said he. 'You'll be changing at Marwar Junction to get into Jodhpore territory—you must do that—and he'll be coming through Marwar Junction in the early morning of the 24th by the Bombay Mail. Can you be at Marwar Junction on that time? 'Twon't be inconveniencing you because I know that there's precious few pickings to be got out of these Central India States—even though you pretend to be correspondent of the *Backwoodsman*.'

'Have you ever tried that trick?' I asked.

'Again and again, but the Residents find you out, and then you get escorted to the Border before you've time to get your knife into them. But about my friend here. I *must* give him a word o' mouth to tell him what's come to me or else he won't know where to go. I would take it more than kind of you if you was to come out of Central India in time to catch him at Marwar Junction, and say to him: "He has gone South for the week." He'll know what that means. He's a big man with a red beard, and a great swell he is. You'll find him sleeping like a gentleman with all his luggage round him in a Second-class apartment. But don't you be afraid. Slip down the window and say: "He has gone South for the week," and

THE MAN WHO WOULD BE KING

he'll tumble. It's only cutting your time of stay in those parts by two days. I ask you as a stranger—going to the West,' he said with emphasis.

'Where have *you* come from?' said I.

'From the East,' said he, 'and I am hoping that you will give him the message on the Square—for the sake of my Mother as well as your own.'

Englishmen are not usually softened by appeals to the memory of their mothers; but for certain reasons, which will be fully apparent, I saw fit to agree.

'It's more than a little matter,' said he, 'and that's why I asked you to do it—and now I know that I can depend on you doing it. A Second-class carriage at Marwar Junction, and a red-haired man asleep in it. You'll be sure to remember. I get out at the next station, and I must hold on there till he comes or sends me what I want.'

'I'll give the message if I catch him,' I said, 'and for the sake of your Mother as well as mine I'll give you a word of advice. Don't try to run the Central India States just now as the correspondent of the *Backwoodsman*. There's a real one knocking about here, and it might lead to trouble.'

'Thank you,' said he simply, 'and when will the swine be gone? I can't starve because he's ruining my work. I wanted to get hold of the Degumber Rajah down here about his father's widow, and give him a jump.'

'What did he do to his father's widow, then?'

'Filled her up with red pepper and slippered her to death as she hung from a beam. I found that out myself and I'm the only man that would dare going into the State to get hush-money for it. They'll try to poison me, same as they did in Chortumna when I went on the loot there. But you'll give the man at Marwar Junction my message?'

He got out at a little roadside station, and I reflected. I had heard, more than once, of men personating correspondents of newspapers and bleeding small Native States with threats of exposure, but I had never met any of the caste before. They lead a hard life, and generally die with great suddenness. The Native States have a wholesome horror of English newspapers, which may throw light on their peculiar methods of government, and do their best to choke correspondents with champagne, or drive them out of their mind with four-in-hand barouches. They do not understand that nobody cares a straw for the internal administration of Native States so long as oppression and crime are kept within decent limits, and the ruler is not drugged, drunk, or diseased from one end of the year to the other. They are the dark places of the earth, full of unimaginable cruelty, touching the railway and the Telegraph on one side, and, on the other, the days of Harun-al-Raschid. When I left the train I did business with divers Kings, and in eight days passed through many changes of life. Sometimes I wore dress-clothes and consorted with Princes and Politicals, drinking from crystal and eating from silver. Sometimes I lay out upon the ground and devoured what I could get, from a plate made of leaves, and drank the running water, and slept under the same rug as my servant. It was all in the day's work.

Then I headed for the Great Indian Desert upon the proper date, as I had promised, and the night Mail set me down at Marwar Junction, where a funny little, happy-go-lucky, native-managed railway runs to Jodhpore. The Bombay Mail from Delhi makes a short halt at Marwar. She arrived as I got in, and I had just time to hurry to her platform and go down the carriages. There was only one Second-class on the train. I slipped the window and looked down upon a flaming red beard, half covered by a railway rug. That was my man, fast asleep, and I dug him gently in the ribs. He woke with a grunt and I saw his face in the light of the lamps. It was a great and shining face.

'Tickets again?' said he.

'No,' said I. 'I am to tell you that he is gone South for the week. He has gone South for the week!'

The train had begun to move out. The red man rubbed his eyes. 'He has gone South for the week,' he repeated. 'Now that's just like his impidence. Did he say that I was to give you anything? 'Cause I won't.'

'He didn't,' I said and dropped away, and watched the red lights die out in the dark. It was horribly cold because the wind was blowing off the sands. I climbed into my own train—not an Intermediate carriage this time—and went to sleep.

If the man with the beard had given me a rupee I should have kept it as a memento of a rather curious affair. But the consciousness of having done my duty was my only reward.

Later on I reflected that two gentlemen like my friends could not do any good if they foregathered and personated correspondents of newspapers, and might, if they black-mailed one of the little rat-trap states of Central India or Southern Rajputana, get themselves into serious difficulties. I therefore took some trouble to describe them as accurately as I could remember to people who would be interested in deporting them: and succeeded, so I was later informed, in having them headed back from the Degumber borders.

Then I became respectable, and returned to an Office where there were no Kings and no incidents outside the daily manufacture of a newspaper. A newspaper office seems to attract every conceivable sort of person, to the prejudice of discipline. Zenana-mission ladies arrive, and beg that the Editor will instantly abandon all his duties to describe a Christian prize-giving in a back-slum of a perfectly inaccessible village; Colonels who have been overpassed for command sit down and sketch the outline of a series of ten, twelve, or twenty-four leading articles on Seniority *versus* Selection; missionaries wish to know why they have not been permitted to escape from their regular vehicles of abuse and swear at a brother-missionary under special patronage of the editorial We; stranded theatrical companies troop up to explain that they cannot pay for their advertisements, but on their return from New Zealand or Tahiti will do so with interest; inventors of patent punkah-pulling machines, carriage couplings and unbreakable swords and axle-trees call with specifications in their pockets and hours at their disposal; tea-companies enter and elaborate their prospectuses with the office pens; secretaries of ball-committees clamour to have the glories of their last dance more fully described; strange ladies rustle in and say: 'I want a hundred lady's cards printed *at once, please,*' which is manifestly part of an Editor's duty; and every dissolute ruffian that ever tramped the Grand Trunk Road makes it his business to ask for employment as a proof-reader. And, all the time, the telephone-bell is ringing madly, and Kings are being killed on the Continent, and Empires are saying—'You're another,' and Mister Gladstone is calling down brimstone upon the British Dominions, and the little black copy-boys are whining, *'kaa-pi chay-ha-yeh'* (copy wanted) like tired bees, and most of the paper is as blank as Modred's shield.

But that is the amusing part of the year. There are six other months when none ever come to call, and the thermometer walks inch by inch up to the top of the glass, and the office is darkened to just above reading-light, and the press-machines are red-hot of touch, and nobody writes anything but accounts of amusements in the Hill-stations or obituary notices. Then the telephone becomes a tinkling terror, because it tells you of the sudden deaths of men and women that you knew intimately, and the prickly-heat covers you with a garment, and you sit down and write: 'A slight increase of sickness is reported from the Khuda Janta Khan District. The outbreak is purely sporadic in its nature, and, thanks to the energetic efforts of the District authorities, is now almost at an end. It is, however, with deep regret we record the death,' etc.

Then the sickness really breaks out, and the less recording and reporting the better for the peace of the subscribers. But the Empires and the Kings continue to divert themselves as selfishly as before, and the Foreman thinks that a daily paper really ought to come out once in twenty-four hours, and all the people at the Hill-stations in the middle of their amusements say: 'Good gracious! Why can't the paper be sparkling? I'm sure there's plenty going on up here.'

That is the dark half of the moon, and, as the advertisements say, 'must be experienced to be appreciated.'

It was in that season, and a remarkably evil season, that the paper began running the last issue of the week on Saturday night, which is to say Sunday morning, after the custom of a London paper. This was a great convenience, for immediately after the paper was put to bed, the dawn would lower the thermometer from 96° to almost 84° for half an hour, and in that chill—you have no idea how cold is 84° on the grass until you begin to pray for it—a very tired man could get off to sleep ere the heat roused him.

One Saturday night it was my pleasant duty to put the paper to bed alone. A King or courtier or a courtesan or a Community was going to die or get a new Constitution, or do something that was important on the other side of the world, and the paper was to be held open till the latest possible minute in order to catch the telegram.

It was a pitchy black night, as stifling as a June night can be, and the *loo*, the red-hot wind from the westward, was booming among the tinder-dry trees and pretending that the rain was on its heels. Now and again a spot of almost boiling water would fall on the dust with the flop of a frog, but all our weary world knew that was only pretence. It was a shade cooler in the press-room than the office, so I sat there, while the type ticked and clicked, and the night-jars hooted at the windows, and the all but naked compositors wiped the sweat from their foreheads, and called for water. The thing that was keeping us back, whatever it was, would not come off, though the *loo* dropped and the last type was set, and the whole round earth stood still in the choking heat, with its finger on its lip, to wait the event. I drowsed, and wondered whether the telegraph was a blessing, and whether this dying man, or struggling people, might be aware of the inconvenience the delay was causing. There was no special reason beyond the heat and worry to make tension, but, as the clock-hands crept up to three o'clock and the machines spun their fly-wheels two and three times to see that all was in order, before I said the word that would set them off, I could have shrieked aloud.

Then the roar and rattle of the wheels shivered the quiet into little bits. I rose to go away, but two men in white clothes stood in front of me. The first one said: 'It's him!' The second said: 'So it is!' And they both laughed almost as loudly as the machinery roared, and mopped their foreheads. 'We seed there was a light burning across the road and we were sleeping in that ditch there for coolness, and I said to my friend here, The office is open. Let's come along and speak to him as turned us back from the Degumber State,' said the smaller of the two. He was the man I had met in the Mhow train, and his fellow was the red-bearded man of Marwar Junction. There was no mistaking the eyebrows of the one or the beard of the other.

I was not pleased, because I wished to go to sleep, not to squabble with loafers. 'What do you want?' I asked.

'Half an hour's talk with you, cool and comfortable, in the office,' said the red-bearded man. 'We'd *like* some drink—the Contrack doesn't begin yet, Peachey, so you needn't look—but what we really want is advice. We don't want money. We ask you as a favour, because we found out you did us a bad turn about Degumber State.'

I led from the press-room to the stifling office with the maps on the walls, and the red-haired man rubbed his hands. 'That's something like,' said he. 'This was the proper shop to come to. Now, Sir, let me introduce to you Brother Peachey Carnehan, that's him, and Brother Daniel Dravot, that is *me*, and the less said about our professions the better, for we have been most things in our time. Soldier, sailor, compositor, photographer, proof-reader, street-preacher, and correspondents of the *Backwoodsman* when we thought the paper wanted one. Carnehan is sober, and so am I. Look at us first, and see that's sure. It will save you cutting into my talk. We'll take one of your cigars apiece, and you shall see us light up.'

I watched the test. The men were absolutely sober, so I gave them each a tepid whiskey and soda.

'Well *and* good,' said Carnehan of the eyebrows, wiping the froth from his moustache. 'Let me talk now, Dan. We have been all over India, mostly on foot. We have been boiler-fitters, engine-drivers, petty contractors, and all that, and we have decided that India isn't big enough for such as us.'

They certainly were too big for the office. Dravot's beard seemed to fill half the room and Carnehan's shoulders the other half, as they sat on the big table. Carnehan continued: 'The country isn't half worked out because they that governs it won't let you touch it. They spend all their blessed time in governing it, and you can't lift a spade, nor chip a rock, nor look for oil, nor anything like that without all the Government saying—"Leave it alone, and let us govern." Therefore, such *as* it is, we will let it alone, and go away to some other place where a man isn't crowded and can come to his own. We are not little men, and there is nothing we are afraid of except Drink, and we have signed a Contrack on that. *Therefore*, we are going away to be Kings.'

'Kings in our own right,' muttered Dravot.

'Yes, of course,' I said. 'You've been tramping in the sun, and it's a very warm night, and hadn't you better sleep over the notion? Come tomorrow.'

'Neither drunk nor sunstruck,' said Dravot. 'We have slept over the notion half a year, and require to see Books and Atlases, and we have decided that there is only one place now in the world that two strong men can Sar-a-*whack*. They call it Kafiristan. By my reckoning it's the top

right-hand corner of Afghanistan, not more than three hundred miles
from Peshawar. They have two-and-thirty heathen idols there, and we'll
be the thirty-third and fourth. It's a mountaineous country, and the
women of those parts are very beautiful.'

'But that is provided against in the Contrack,' said Carnehan. 'Neither
Woman nor Liqu-or, Daniel.'

'And that's all we know, except that no one has gone there, and they
fight, and in any place where they fight a man who knows how to drill
men can always be a King. We shall go to those parts and say to any King
we find—"D'you want to vanquish your foes?" and we will show him how
to drill men; for that we know better than anything else. Then we will
subvert that King and seize his Throne and establish a Dy-nasty.'

'You'll be cut to pieces before you're fifty miles across the Border,' I
said. 'You have to travel through Afghanistan to get to that country. It's
one mass of mountains and peaks and glaciers, and no Englishman has
been through it. The people are utter brutes, and even if you reached
them you couldn't do anything.'

'That's more like,' said Carnehan. 'If you could think us a little more
mad we would be more pleased. We have come to you to know about this
country, to read a book about it, and to be shown maps. We want you to
tell us that we are fools and to show us your books.' He turned to the book-
cases.

'Are you at all in earnest?' I said.

'A little,' said Dravot sweetly. 'As big a map as you have got, even if it's
all blank where Kafiristan is, and any books you've got. We can read,
though we aren't very educated.'

I uncased the big thirty-two-miles-to-the-inch map of India, and two
smaller Frontier maps, hauled down volume INF-KAN of the *Encyclopædia Britannica,* and the men consulted them.

'See here!' said Dravot, his thumb on the map. 'Up to Jagdallak, Peachey
and me know the road. We was there with Roberts' Army. We'll have to
turn off to the right at Jagdallak through Laghmann territory. Then we
get among the hills—fourteen thousand feet—fifteen thousand—it will be
cold work there, but it don't look very far on the map.'

I handed him Wood on the *Sources of the Oxus.* Carnehan was deep in
the *Encyclopædia.*

'They're a mixed lot,' said Dravot reflectively; 'and it won't help us
to know the names of their tribes. The more tribes the more they'll fight,
and the better for us. From Jagdallak to Ashang. H'mm!'

'But all the information about the country is as sketchy and inaccurate
as can be,' I protested. 'No one knows anything about it really. Here's
the file of the *United Services' Institute.* Read what Bellew says.'

'Blow Bellew!' said Carnehan. 'Dan, they're a stinkin' lot of heathens, but this book here says they think they're related to us English.'

I smoked while the men pored over *Raverty, Wood*, the maps, and the *Encyclopædia*.

'There is no use your waiting,' said Dravot politely. 'It's about four o'clock now. We'll go before six o'clock if you want to sleep, and we won't steal any of the papers. Don't you sit up. We're two harmless lunatics, and if you come to-morrow evening down to the Serai we'll say good-bye to you.'

'You *are* two fools,' I answered. 'You'll be turned back at the Frontier or cut up the minute you set foot in Afghanistan. Do you want any money or a recommendation down-country? I can help you to the chance of work next week.'

'Next week we shall be hard at work ourselves, thank you,' said Dravot. 'It isn't so easy being a King as it looks. When we've got our Kingdom in going order we'll let you know, and you can come up and help us to govern it.'

'Would two lunatics make a Contrack like that?' said Carnehan, with subdued pride, showing me a greasy half-sheet of notepaper on which was written the following. I copied it, then and there, as a curiosity—

This Contract between me and you persuing witnesseth in the name of God—Amen and so forth.

> *(One) That me and you will settle this matter together; i.e., to be Kings of Kafiristan.*
>
> *(Two) That you and me will not, while this matter is being settled, look at any Liquor, nor any Woman black, white, or brown, so as to get mixed up with one or the other harmful.*
>
> *(Three) That we conduct ourselves with Dignity and Discretion, and if one of us gets into trouble the other will stay by him.*

> *Signed by you and me this day.*
> *Peachey Taliaferro Carnehan.*
> *Daniel Dravot.*
> *Both Gentlemen at Large.*

'There was no need for the last article,' said Carnehan, blushing modestly; 'but it looks regular. Now you know the sort of men that loafers are— we *are* loafers, Dan, until we get out of India—and *do* you think that we would sign a Contrack like that unless we was in earnest? We have kept away from the two things that make life worth having.'

'You won't enjoy your lives much longer if you are going to try this idiotic adventure. Don't set the office on fire,' I said, 'and go away before nine o'clock.'

I left them still poring over the maps and making notes on the back of the 'Contrack.' 'Be sure to come down to the Serai to-morrow,' were their parting words.

The Kumharsen Serai is the great four-square sink of humanity where the strings of camels and horses from the North load and unload. All the nationalities of Central Asia may be found there, and most of the folk of India proper. Balkh and Bokhara there meet Bengal and Bombay, and try to draw eye-teeth. You can buy ponies, turquoises, Persian pussy-cats, saddlebags, fat-tailed sheep and musk in the Kumharsen Serai, and get many strange things for nothing. In the afternoon I went down to see whether my friends intended to keep their word or were lying there drunk.

A priest attired in fragments of ribbons and rags stalked up to me, gravely twisting a child's paper whirligig. Behind him was his servant bending under the load of a crate of mud toys. The two were loading up two camels, and the inhabitants of the Serai watched them with shrieks of laughter.

'The priest is mad,' said a horse-dealer to me. 'He is going up to Kabul to sell toys to the Amir. He will either be raised to honour or have his head cut off. He came in here this morning and has been behaving madly ever since.'

'The witless are under the protection of God,' stammered a flat-cheeked Usbeg in broken Hindi. 'They foretell future events.'

'Would they could have foretold that my caravan would have been cut up by the Shinwaris almost within shadow of the Pass!' grunted the Eusufzai agent of a Rajputana trading-house whose goods had been diverted into the hands of other robbers just across the Border, and whose misfortunes were the laughing-stock of the bazar. 'Ohé, priest, whence come you and whither do you go?'

'From Roum have I come,' shouted the priest, waving his whirligig; 'from Roum, blown by the breath of a hundred devils across the sea! O thieves, robbers, liars, the blessing of Pir Khan on pigs, dogs, and per-jurers! Who will take the protected of God to the North to sell charms that are never still to the Amir? The camels shall not gall, the sons shall not fall sick, and the wives shall remain faithful while they are away, of the men who give me place in their caravan. Who will assist me to slipper the King of the Roos with a golden slipper with a silver heel? The protec-tion of Pir Khan be upon his labours!' He spread out the skirts of his gaberdine and pirouetted between the lines of tethered horses.

'There starts a caravan from Peshawar to Kabul in twenty days, *Huzrut,*' said the Eusufzai trader. 'My camels go therewith. Do thou also go and bring us good-luck.'

'I will go even now!' shouted the priest. 'I will depart upon my winged camels, and be at Peshawar in a day! Ho! Hazar Mir Khan,' he yelled to his servant, 'drive out the camels, but let me first mount my own.'

He leaped on the back of his beast as it knelt, and, turning round to me, cried: 'Come thou also, Sahib, a little along the road, and I will sell thee a charm—an amulet that shall make thee King of Kafiristan.'

Then the light broke upon me, and I followed the two camels out of the Serai till we reached open road and the priest halted.

'What d'you think o' that?' said he in English. 'Carnehan can't talk their patter, so I've made him my servant. He makes a handsome servant. 'Tisn't for nothing that I've been knocking about the country for four-teen years. Didn't I do that talk neat? We'll hitch on to a caravan at Peshawar till we get to Jagdallak, and then we'll see if we can get donkeys for our camels, and strike into Kafiristan. Whirligigs for the Amir, O Lor! Put your hand under the camel-bags and tell me what you feel.'

I felt the butt of a Martini, and another and another.

'Twenty of 'em,' said Dravot placidly. 'Twenty of 'em and ammuni-tion to correspond, under the whirligigs and the mud dolls.'

'Heaven help you if you are caught with those things!' I said. 'A Martini is worth her weight in silver among the Pathans.'

'Fifteen hundred rupees of capital—every rupee we could beg, borrow, or steal—are invested on these two camels,' said Dravot. 'We won't get caught. We're going through the Khaiber with a regular caravan. Who'd touch a poor mad priest?'

'Have you got everything you want?' I asked, overcome with astonish-ment.

'Not yet, but we shall soon. Give us a memento of your kindness, *Brother.* You did me a service, yesterday, and that time in Marwar. Half my Kingdom shall you have, as the saying is.' I slipped a small charm compass from my watch chain and handed it up to the priest.

'Good-bye,' said Dravot, giving me hand cautiously. 'It's the last time we'll shake hands with an Englishman these many days. Shake hands with him, Carnehan,' he cried, as the second camel passed me.

Carnehan leaned down and shook hands. Then the camels passed away along the dusty road, and I was left alone to wonder. My eye could de-tect no failure in the disguises. The scene in the Serai proved that they were complete to the native mind. There was just the chance, therefore, that Carnehan and Dravot would be able to wander through Afghanistan without detection. But, beyond, they would find death—certain and awful death.

Ten days later a native correspondent giving me the news of the day from Peshawar, wound up his letter with: 'There has been much laughter here on account of a certain mad priest who is going in his estimation to sell petty gauds and insignificant trinkets which he ascribes as great charms to H.H. the Amir of Bokhara. He passed through Peshawar and associated himself to the Second Summer caravan that goes to Kabul. The merchants are pleased because through superstition they imagine that such mad fellows bring good-fortune.'

The two, then, were beyond the Border. I would have prayed for them, but, that night, a real King died in Europe, and demanded an obituary notice.

The wheel of the world swings through the same phases again and again. Summer passed and winter thereafter, and came and passed again. The daily paper continued and I with it, and upon the third summer there fell a hot night, a night-issue, and a strained waiting for something to be telegraphed from the other side of the world, exactly as had happened before. A few great men had died in the past two years, the machines worked with more clatter, and some of the trees in the Office garden were a few feet taller. But that was all the difference.

I passed over to the press-room, and went through just such a scene as I have already described. The nervous tension was stronger than it had been two years before, and I felt the heat more acutely. At three o'clock I cried, 'Print off,' and turned to go, when there crept to my chair what was left of a man. He was bent into a circle, his head was sunk between his shoulders, and he moved his feet one over the other like a bear. I could hardly see whether he walked or crawled—this rag-wrapped, whining cripple who addressed me by name, crying that he was come back. 'Can you give me a drink?' he whimpered. 'For the Lord's sake, give me a drink!'

I went back to the office, the man following with groans of pain, and I turned up the lamp.

'Don't you know me?' he gasped, dropping into a chair and he turned his drawn face, surmounted by a shock of gray hair, to the light.

I looked at him intently. Once before had I seen eyebrows that met over the nose in an inch-broad black band, but for the life of me I could not tell where.

'I don't know you,' I said, handing him the whiskey. 'What can I do for you?'

He took a gulp of the spirit raw, and shivered in spite of the suffocating heat.

'I've come back,' he repeated; 'and I was the King of Kafiristan—me and Dravot—crowned Kings we was! In this office we settled it—you setting there and giving us the books. I am Peachey—Peachey Taliaferro Carnehan, and you've been setting here ever since—O Lord!'

I was more than a little astonished, and expressed my feelings accordingly.

'It's true,' said Carnehan, with a dry cackle, nursing his feet, which were wrapped in rags. 'True as gospel. Kings we were, with crowns upon our heads—me and Dravot—poor Dan—oh, poor, poor Dan, that would never take advice, not though I begged of him!'

'Take the whiskey,' I said, 'and take your own time. Tell me all you can recollect of everything from beginning to end. You got across the border on your camels, Dravot dressed as a mad priest and you his servant. Do you remember that?'

'I ain't mad—yet, but I shall be that way soon. Of course I remember. Keep looking at me, or maybe my words will go all to pieces. Keep looking at me in my eyes and don't say anything.'

I leaned forward and looked into his face as steadily as I could. He dropped one hand upon the table and I grasped it by the wrist. It was twisted like a bird's claw, and upon the back was a ragged, red, diamond-shaped scar.

'No, don't look there. Look at *me*,' said Carnehan. 'That comes afterwards, but for the Lord's sake don't distrack me. We left with that caravan, me and Dravot playing all sorts of antics to amuse the people we were with. Dravot used to make us laugh in the evenings when all the people was cooking their dinners—cooking their dinners, and . . . what did they do then? They lit little fires with sparks that went into Dravot's beard, and we all laughed—fit to die. Little red fires they was, going into Dravot's big red beard—so funny.' His eyes left mine and he smiled foolishly.

'You went as far as Jagdallak with that caravan,' I said at a venture, 'after you had lit those fires. To Jagdallak, where you turned off to try to get into Kafiristan.'

'No, we didn't, neither. What are you talking about? We turned off before Jagdallak, because we heard the roads was good. But they wasn't good enough for our two camels—mine and Dravot's. When we left the caravan, Dravot took off all his clothes and mine too, and said we would be heathen, because the Kafirs didn't allow Mohammedans to talk to them. So we dressed betwixt and between, and such a sight as Daniel Dravot I never saw yet nor expect to see again. He burned half his beard, and slung a sheep-skin over his shoulder, and shaved his head into patterns. He shaved mine, too, and made me wear outrageous things to look like a heathen. That was in a most mountaineous country, and our camels couldn't go along any more because of the mountains. They were tall and black, and coming home I saw them fight like wild goats—there are lots of goats in Kafiristan. And these mountains, they never keep still, no more than the goats. Always fighting they are, and don't let you sleep at night.'

'Take some more whiskey,' I said very slowly. 'What did you and Daniel Dravot do when the camels could go no further because of the rough roads that led into Kafiristan?'

'What did which do? There was a party called Peachey Taliaferro Carnehan that was with Dravot. Shall I tell you about him? He died out there in the cold. Slap from the bridge fell old Peachey, turning and twisting in the air like a penny whirligig that you can sell to the Amir. —No; they was two for three ha'pence, those whirligigs, or I am much mistaken and woeful sore. . . . And then these camels were no use, and Peachey said to Dravot—"For the Lord's sake let's get out of this before our heads are chopped off," and with that they killed the camels all among the mountains, not having anything in particular to eat, but first they took off the boxes with the guns and the ammunition, till two men came along driving four mules. Dravot up and dances in front of them, sing-ing—"Sell me four mules." Says the first man—"If you are rich enough to buy, you are rich enough to rob;" but before ever he could put his hand to his knife, Dravot breaks his neck over his knee, and the other party runs away. So Carnehan loaded the mules with the rifles that was taken off the camels, and together we starts forward into those bitter cold mountaineous parts, and never a road broader than the back of your hand.'

He paused for a moment, while I asked him if he could remember the nature of the country through which he had journeyed.

'I am telling you as straight as I can, but my head isn't as good as it might be. They drove nails through it to make me hear better how Dravot died. The country was mountaineous and the mules were most contrary, and the inhabitants was dispersed and solitary. They went up and up, and down and down, and that other party, Carnehan, was imploring of Dravot not to sing and whistle so loud, for fear of bringing down the tremenjus avalanches. But Dravot says that if a King couldn't sing it wasn't worth being King, and whacked the mules over the rump, and never took no heed for ten cold days. We came to a big level valley all among the moun-tains, and the mules were near dead, so we killed them, not having any-thing in special for them or us to eat. We sat upon the boxes, and played odd and even with the cartridges that was jolted out.

'Then ten men with bows and arrows ran down that valley, chasing twenty men with bows and arrows, and the row was tremenjus. They was fair men—fairer than you or me—with yellow hair and remarkable well built. Says Dravot, unpacking the guns—"This is the beginning of the business. We'll fight for the ten men," and with that he fires two rifles at the twenty men, and drops one of them at two hundred yards from the rock where he was sitting. The other men began to run, but Carnehan and Dravot sits on the boxes picking them off at all ranges, up and down the valley. Then we goes up to the ten men that had run across the snow too, and they fires a footy little arrow at us. Dravot he shoots above their heads and they all falls down flat. Then he walks over them and kicks them, and then he lifts them up and shakes hands all round to make them friendly like. He calls them and gives them the boxes to carry, and waves his hand for all the world as though he was King already. They takes the boxes and him across the valley and up the hill into a pine wood on the top, where there was half a dozen big stone idols. Dravot he goes to the biggest—a fellow they call Imbra—and lays a rifle and a cartridge at his feet, rubbing his nose respectful with his own nose, patting him on the head, and saluting in front of it. He turns round to the men and nods his head, and says—"That's all right. I'm in the know too, and all these old jim-jams are my friends." Then he opens his mouth and points down it, and when the first man brings him food, he says—"No;" and when the second man brings him food he says—"No;" but when one of the old priests and the boss of the village brings him food, he says—"Yes;" very haughty, and eats it slow. That was how he came to our first village, without any trouble, just as though we had tumbled from the skies. But we tumbled from one of those damned rope-bridges, you see and—you couldn't expect a man to laugh much after that?'

'Take some more whiskey and go on,' I said. 'That was the first village you came into. How did you get to be King?'

'I wasn't King,' said Carnehan. 'Dravot he was the King, and a handsome man he looked with the gold crown on his head and all. Him and the other party stayed in that village, and every morning Dravot sat by the side of old Imbra, and the people came and worshipped. That was Dravot's order. Then a lot of men came into the valley, and Carnehan and Dravot picks them off with the rifles before they knew where they was, and runs down into the valley and up again the other side and finds another village, same as the first one, and the people all falls down flat on their faces, and Dravot says—"Now what is the trouble between you two villages?" and the people points to a woman, as fair as you or me, that was carried off, and Dravot takes her back to the first village and counts up the dead—eight there was. For each dead man Dravot pours a little milk on the ground and waves his arms like a whirligig and "That's all right," says he. Then he and Carnehan takes the big boss of each village by the arm and walks them down into the valley, and shows them how to scratch a

line with a spear right down the valley, and gives each a sod of turf from
both sides of the line. Then all the people comes down and shouts like
the devil and all, and Dravot says—"Go and dig the land, and be fruitful
and multiply," which they did, though they didn't understand. Then we
asks the names of things in their lingo—bread and water and fire and
idols and such, and Dravot leads the priest of each village up to the idol,
and says he must sit there and judge the people, and if anything goes
wrong he is to be shot.

'Next week they was all turning up the land in the valley as quiet as
bees and much prettier, and the priests heard all the complaints and told
Dravot in dumb show what it was about. "That's just the beginning," says
Dravot. "They think we're Gods." He and Carnehan picks out twenty
good men and shows them how to click off a rifle, and form fours, and
advance in line, and they was very pleased to do so, and clever to see the
hang of it. Then he takes out his pipe and his baccy-pouch and leaves one
at one village, and one at the other, and off we two goes to see what was
to be done in the next valley. That was all rock, and there was a little village there, and Carnehan says—"Send 'em to the old valley to plant," and
takes 'em there and gives 'em some land that wasn't took before. They
were a poor lot, and we blooded 'em with a kid before letting 'em into the
new Kingdom. That was to impress the people, and then they settled down
quiet, and Carnehan went back to Dravot who had got into another valley,
all snow and ice and most mountaineous. There was no people there and
the Army got afraid, so Dravot shoots one of them, and goes on till he
finds some people in a village, and the Army explains that unless the
people wants to be killed they had better not shoot their little matchlocks;
for they had matchlocks. We makes friends with the priest and I stays
there alone with two of the Army, teaching the men how to drill, and a
thundering big Chief comes across the snow with kettle-drums and horns
twanging, because he heard there was a new God kicking about. Carnehan sights for the brown of the men half a mile across the snow and wings
one of them. Then he sends a message to the Chief that, unless he wished
to be killed, he must come and shake hands with me and leave his arms
behind. The Chief comes alone first, and Carnehan shakes hands with him
and whirls his arms about, same as Dravot used, and very much surprised
that Chief was, and strokes my eyebrows. Then Carnehan goes alone to
the Chief, and asks him in dumb show if he had an enemy he hated. "I
have," says the Chief. So Carnehan weeds out the pick of his men, and
sets the two of the Army to show them drill and at the end of two weeks
the men can manœuvre about as well as Volunteers. So he marches with
the Chief to a great big plain on the top of a mountain, and the Chief's
men rushes into a village and takes it; we three Martinis firing into the

brown of the enemy. So we took that village too, and I gives the Chief a rag from my coat and says, "Occupy till I come;" which was scriptural. By way of a reminder, when me and the Army was eighteen hundred yards away, I drops a bullet near him standing on the snow, and all the people falls flat on their faces. Then I sends a letter to Dravot wherever he be by land or by sea.'

At the risk of throwing the creature out of train I interrupted—'How could you write a letter up yonder?'

'The letter?—Oh!—The letter! Keep looking at me between the eyes, please. It was a string-talk letter, that we'd learned the way of it from a blind beggar in the Punjab.'

I remember that there had once come to the office a blind man with a knotted twig and a piece of string which he wound round the twig according to some cipher of his own. He could, after the lapse of days or hours, repeat the sentence which he had reeled up. He had reduced the alphabet to eleven primitive sounds; and tried to teach me his method, but I could not understand.

'I sent that letter to Dravot,' said Carnehan; 'and told him to come back because this Kingdom was growing too big for me to handle, and then I struck for the first valley, to see how the priests were working. They called the village we took along with the Chief, Bashkai, and the first village we took, Er-Heb. The priests at Er-Heb was doing all right, but they had a lot of pending cases about land to show me, and some men from another village had been firing arrows at night. I went out and looked for that village, and fired four rounds at it from a thousand yards. That used all the cartridges I cared to spend, and I waited for Dravot, who had been away two or three months, and I kept my people quiet.

'One morning I heard the devil's own noise of drums and horns, and Dan Dravot marches down the hill with his Army and a tail of hundreds of men, and, which was the most amazing, a great gold crown on his head. "My Gord, Carnehan," says Daniel, "this is a tremenjus business, and we've got the whole country as far as it's worth having. I am the son of Alexander by Queen Semiramis, and you're my younger brother and a God too! It's the biggest thing we've ever seen. I've been marching and fighting for six weeks with the Army, and every footy little village for fifty miles has come in rejoiceful; and more than that, I've got the key of the whole show, as you'll see, and I've got a crown for you! I told 'em to make two of 'em at a place called Shu, where the gold lies in the rock like suet in mutton. Gold I've seen, and turquoise I've kicked out of the cliffs, and there's garnets in the sands of the river, and here's a chunk of amber that a man brought me. Call up all the priests, and, here, take your crown."

'One of the men opens a black hair bag, and I slips the crown on. It was too small and too heavy, but I wore it for the glory. Hammered gold it was —five pound weight, like a hoop of a barrel.

"Peachey," says Dravot, "we don't want to fight no more. The Craft's the trick so help me!" and he brings forward that same Chief that I left at Bashkai—Billy Fish we called him afterwards, because he was so like Billy Fish that drove the big tank-engine at Mach on the Bolan in the old days. "Shake hands with him," says Dravot, and I shook hands and nearly dropped, for Billy Fish gave me the Grip. I said nothing, but tried him with the Fellow Craft Grip. He answers, all right, and I tried the Master's Grip, but that was a slip. "A Fellow Craft he is!" I says to Dan. "Does he know the word?"—"He does," says Dan, "and all the priests know. It's a miracle! The Chiefs and the priests can work a Fellow Craft Lodge in a way that's very like ours, and they've cut the marks on the rocks, but they don't know the Third Degree, and they've come to find out. It's Gord's Truth. I've known these long years that the Afghans knew up to the Fellow Craft Degree, but this is a miracle. A God and a Grand-Master of the Craft am I, and a Lodge in the Third Degree I will open, and we'll raise the head priests and the Chiefs of the villages."

'"It's against all the law," I says, "holding a Lodge without warrant from any one; and you know we never held office in any Lodge."

'"It's a master-stroke o' policy," says Dravot. "It means running the country as easy as a four-wheeled bogie on a down grade. We can't stop to enquire now, or they'll turn against us. I've forty Chiefs at my heel, and passed and raised according to their merit they shall be. Billet these men on the villages, and see that we run up a Lodge of some kind. The temple of Imbra will do for the Lodge-room. The women must make aprons as you show them. I'll hold a levee of Chief's to-night and Lodge to-morrow."

'I was fair run off my legs, but I wasn't such a fool as not to see what a pull this Craft business gave us. I showed the priests' families how to make aprons of the degrees, but for Dravot's apron the blue border and marks was made of turquoise lumps on white hide, not cloth. We took a great square stone in the temple for the Master's chair, and little stones for the officers' chairs, and painted the black pavement with white squares, and did what we could to make things regular.

'At the levee which was held that night on the hillside with big bon-fires, Dravot gives out that him and me were Gods and sons of Alexander, and Past Grand-Masters in the Craft, and was come to make Kafiristan a country where every man should eat in peace and drink in quiet, and specially obey us. Then the Chiefs come round to shake hands, and they were so hairy and white and fair it was just shaking hands with old friends. We gave them names according as they was like men we had known in India—Billy Fish, Holly Dilworth, Pikky Kergan, that was Bazar-master when I was at Mhow, and so on, and so on.

'The most amazing miracles was at Lodge next night. One of the old priests was watching us continuous, and I felt uneasy, for I knew we'd have to fudge the Ritual, and I didn't know what the men knew. The old priest was a stranger come in from beyond the village of Bashkai. The minute Dravot puts on the Master's apron that the girls had made for him, the priest fetches a whoop and a howl, and tries to overturn the stone that Dravot was sitting on. "It's all up now," I says. "That comes of meddling with the Craft without warrant!" Dravot never winked an eye, not when ten priests took and tilted over the Grand-Master's chair—which was to say the stone of Imbra. The priest begins rubbing the bottom end of it to clear away the black dirt, and presently he shows all the other priests the Master's Mark, same as was on Dravot's apron, cut into the stone. Not even the priests of the temple of Imbra knew it was there. The old chap falls flat on his face at Dravot's feet and kisses 'em. "Luck again," said Dravot, across the Lodge to me, "they say it's the missing Mark that no one could understand the why of. We're more than safe now." Then he bangs the butt of his gun for a gavel and says: "By virtue of the authority vested in me by my own right hand and the help of Peachey, I declare myself Grand-Master of all Freemasonry in Kafiristan in this the Mother Lodge o' the country, and King of Kafiristan equally with Peachey!" At that he puts on his crown and I puts on mine—I was doing Senior Warden—and we opens the Lodge in most ample form. It was a amazing miracle! The priests moved in Lodge through the first two degrees almost without telling, as if the memory was coming back to them. After that, Peachey and Dravot raised such as was worthy—high priests and Chiefs of far-off villages. Billy Fish was the first, and I can tell you we scared the soul out of him. It was not in any way according to Ritual, but it served our turn. We didn't raise more than ten of the biggest men, because we didn't want to make the Degree common. And they was clamouring to be raised.

'"In another six months," said Dravot, "we'll hold another Communication, and see how you are working." Then he asks them about their villages, and learns that they was fighting one against the other, and were sick and tired of it. And when they wasn't doing that they was fighting with the Mohammedans. "You can fight those when they come into our country," says Dravot. "Tell off every tenth man of your tribes for a Frontier guard, and send two hundred at a time to this valley to be drilled. Nobody is going to be shot or speared any more so long as he does well, and I know that you won't cheat me, because you're white people—sons of Alexander—and not like common, black Mohammedans. You are *my* people,

and by God," says he, running off into English at the end—"I'll make a
damned fine Nation of you, or I'll die in the making!"

'I can't tell all we did for the next six months, because Dravot did a lot
I couldn't see the hang of, and he learned their lingo in a way I never
could. My work was to help the people plough, and now and again go out
with some of the Army and see what the other villages were doing, and
make 'em throw rope-bridges across the ravines which cut up the country
horrid. Dravot was very kind to me, but when he walked up and down in
the pine wood pulling that bloody red beard of his with both fists I knew
he was thinking plans I could not advise about, and I just waited for
orders.

'But Dravot never showed me disrespect before the people. They were
afraid of me and the Army, but they loved Dan. He was the best of
friends with the priests and the Chiefs; but any one could come across
the hills with a complaint, and Dravot would hear him out fair, and call
four priests together and say what was to be done. He used to call in
Billy Fish from Bashkai, and Pikky Kergan from Shu, and an old Chief
we called Kafuzelum—it was like enough to his real name—and hold
councils with 'em when there was any fighting to be done in small villages. That was his Council of War, and the four priests of Bashkai, Shu,
Khawak, and Madora was his Privy Council. Between the lot of 'em they
sent me, with forty men and twenty rifles, and sixty men carrying turquoises, into the Ghorband country to buy those hand-made Martini
rifles, that come out of the Amir's workshops at Kabul, from one of the
Amir's Herati regiments that would have sold the very teeth out of their
mouths for turquoises.

'I stayed in Ghorband a month, and gave the Governor there the pick
of my baskets for hush-money, and bribed the Colonel of the regiment
some more, and, between the two and the tribes-people, we got more
than a hundred hand-made Martinis, a hundred good Kohat Jezails that'll
throw to six hundred yards, and forty man-loads of very bad ammuni-
tion for the rifles. I came back with what I had, and distributed 'em
among the men that the Chiefs sent into me to drill. Dravot was too
busy to attend to those things, but the old Army that we first made helped
me, and we turned out five hundred men that could drill, and two hundred that knew how to hold arms pretty straight. Even those cork-screwed,
hand-made guns was a miracle to them. Dravot talked big about powder-
shops and factories, walking up and down in the pine wood when the
winter was coming on.

'"I won't make a Nation," says he. "I'll make an Empire! These men
aren't niggers; they're English! Look at their eyes—look at their mouths.
Look at the way they stand up. They sit on chairs in their own houses.

They're the Lost Tribes, or something like it, and they've grown to be English. I'll take a census in the spring if the priests don't get frightened. There must be a fair two million of 'em in these hills. The villages are full o' little children. Two million people—two hundred and fifty thousand fighting men—and all English! They only want the rifles and a little drilling. Two hundred and fifty thousand men, ready to cut in on Russia's right flank when she tries for India! Peachey, man," he says, chewing his beard in great hunks, "we shall be Emperors—Emperors of the Earth! Rajah Brooke will be a suckling to us. I'll treat with the Viceroy on equal terms. I'll ask him to send me twelve picked English—twelve that I know of—to help us govern a bit. There's Mackray, Sergeant-pensioner at Segowli—many's the good dinner he's given me, and his wife a pair of trousers. There's Donkin, the Warder of Tounghoo Jail; there's hundreds that I could lay my hand on if I was in India. The Viceroy shall do it for me, I'll send a man through in the spring for those men, and I'll write for a dispensation from the Grand Lodge for what I've done as Grand-Master. That—and all the Sniders that'll be thrown out when the native troops in India take up the Martini. They'll be worn smooth, but they'll do for fighting in these hills. Twelve English, a hundred thousands Sniders run through the Amir's country in driblets—I'd be content with twenty thousand in one year—and we'd be an Empire. When everything was shipshape, I'd hand over the crown—this crown I'm wearing now—to Queen Victoria on my knees, and she'd say: 'Rise up, Sir Daniel Dravot.' Oh, it's big! It's big, I tell you! But there's so much to be done in every place—Bashkai, Khawak, Shu, and everywhere else."

'"What is it?" I says. "There are no more men coming in to be drilled this autumn. Look at those, fat, black clouds. They're bringing the snow."

'"It isn't that," says Daniel, putting his hand very hard on my shoulder; "and I don't wish to say anything that's against you, for no other living man would have followed me and made me what I am as you have done. You're a first-class Commander-in-Chief, and the people know you; but—it's a big country, and somehow you can't help me, Peachey, in the way I want to be helped."

'"Go to your blasted priests, then!" I said, and I was sorry when I made that remark, but it did hurt me sore to find Daniel talking so superior when I'd drilled all the men, and done all he told me.

'"Don't let's quarrel, Peachey," says Daniel without cursing. "You're a King too, and the half of this Kingdom is yours; but can't you see, Peachey, we want cleverer men than us now—three or four of 'em, that we can scatter about for our Deputies. It's a hugeous great State, and I can't always tell the right thing to do, and I haven't time for all I want to do, and here's the winter coming on and all." He put half his beard into his mouth, all red like the gold of his crown.

'"I'm sorry, Daniel," says I. "I've done all I could. I've drilled the men and shown the people how to stack their oats better; and I've brought in those tinware rifles from Ghorband—but I know what you're driving at. I take it Kings always feel oppressed that way."

'"There's another thing too," says Dravot, walking up and down. "The winter's coming and these people won't be giving much trouble, and if they do we can't move about. I want a wife."

'"For Gord's sake leave the women alone!" I says. "We've both got all the work we can, though I *am* a fool. Remember the Contrack, and keep clear o' women."

'"The Contrack only lasted till such time as we was Kings; and Kings we have been these months past," says Dravot, weighing his crown in his hand. "You go get a wife too, Peachey—a nice, strappin', plump girl that'll keep you warm in the winter. They're prettier than English girls, and we can take the pick of 'em. Boil 'em once or twice in hot water, and they'll come out like chicken and ham."

'"Don't tempt me!" I says. "I will not have any dealings with a woman not till we are a dam' sight more settled than we are now. I've been doing the work o' two men, and you've been doing the work o' three. Let's lie off a bit, and see if we can get some better tobacco from Afghan country and run in some good liquor; but no women."

'"Who's talking o' *women?*" says Dravot. "I said *wife*—a Queen to breed a King's son for the King. A Queen out of the strongest tribe, that'll make them your blood-brothers, and that'll lie by your side and tell you all the people thinks about you and their own affairs. That's what I want."

'"Do you remember that Bengali woman I kept at Mogul Serai when I was a plate-layer?" says I. "A fat lot o' good she was to me. She taught me the lingo and one or two other things; but what happened? She ran away with the Station Master's servant and half my month's pay. Then she turned up at Dadur Junction in tow of a half-caste, and had the impidence to say I was her husband—all among the drivers in the running-shed too!"

'"We've done with that," says Dravot, "these women are whiter than you or me, and a Queen I will have for the winter months."

'"For the last time o' asking, Dan, do *not*," I says. "It'll only bring us harm. The Bible says that Kings ain't to waste their strength on women, 'specially when they've got a new raw Kingdom to work over."

'"For the last time of answering I will," said Dravot, and he went away through the pine-trees looking like a big red devil, the sun being on his crown and beard and all.

'But getting a wife was not as easy as Dan thought. He put it before the Council, and there was no answer till Billy Fish said that he'd better ask the girls. Dravot damned them all round. "What's wrong with me?" he shouts, standing by the idol Imbra. "Am I a dog or am I not enough of a man for your wenches? Haven't I put the shadow of my hand over this country? Who stopped the last Afghan raid?" It was me really, but Dravot was too angry to remember. "Who bought your guns? Who repaired the bridges? Who's the Grand-Master of the sign cut in the stone?" says he, and he thumped his hand on the block that he used to sit on in Lodge, and at Council, which opened like Lodge always. Billy Fish said nothing and no more did the others. "Keep your hair on, Dan," said I; "and ask the girls. That's how it's done at Home, and these people are quite English."

'"The marriage of the King is a matter of State," says Dan, in a white-hot rage, for he could feel, I hope, that he was going against his better mind. He walked out of the Council-room, and the others sat still, looking at the ground.

'"Billy Fish," says I to the Chief of Bashkai, "what's the difficulty here? A straight answer to a true friend."

'"You know," says Billy Fish. "How should a man tell you who knows everything? How can daughters of men marry Gods or Devils? It's not proper."

'I remembered something like that in the Bible; but if, after seeing us as long as they had, they still believed we were Gods, it wasn't for me to undeceive them.

'"A God can do anything," says I. "If the King is fond of a girl he'll not let her die."—"She'll have to," said Billy Fish. "There are all sorts of Gods and Devils in these mountains, and now and again a girl marries one of them and isn't seen any more. Besides, you two know the Mark cut in the stone. Only the Gods knows that. We thought you were men till you showed the sign of the Master."

'I wished then that we had explained about the loss of the genuine secrets of a Master-Mason at the first go-off; but I said nothing. All that night there was a blowing of horns in a little dark temple half-way down the hill, and I heard a girl crying fit to die. One of the priests told us that she was being prepared to marry the King.

'"I'll have no nonsense of that kind," says Dan. "I don't want to interfere with your customs, but I'll take my own wife."—"The girl's a little bit afraid," says the priest. "She thinks she's going to die, and they are a-heartening of her up down in the temple."

' "Hearten her very tender, then," says Dravot, "or I'll hearten you with the butt of a gun so you'll never want to be heartened again." He licked his lips, did Dan, and stayed up walking about more than half the night, thinking of the wife that he was going to get in the morning. I wasn't any means comfortable, for I knew that dealings with a woman in foreign parts, though you was a crowned King twenty times over, could not but be risky. I got up very early in the morning while Dravot was asleep, and I saw the priests talking together in whispers, and the Chiefs talking together too, and they looked at me out of the corners of their eyes.

' "What is up, Fish?" I say to the Bashkai man, who was wrapped up in his furs and looking splendid to behold.

' "I can't rightly say," says he; "but if you can make the King drop all this nonsense about marriage, you'll be doing him and me and yourself a great service."

' "That I do believe," says I. "But sure, you know, Billy, as well as me, having fought against and for us, that the King and me are nothing more than two of the finest men that God Almighty ever made. Nothing more, I do assure you."

' "That may be," says Billy Fish, "and yet I should be sorry if it was." He sinks his head upon his great fur cloak for a minute and thinks. "King," says he, "be you man or God or Devil, I'll stick by you to-day. I have twenty of my men with me, and they will follow me. We'll go to Bashkai until the storm blows over."

'A little snow had fallen in the night, and everything was white except the greasy fat clouds that blew down and down from the north. Dravot came out with his crown on his head, swinging his arms and stamping his feet, and looking more pleased than Punch.

' "For the last time, drop it, Dan," says I in a whisper, "Billy Fish here says that there will be a row."

' "A row among my people!" says Dravot. "Not much. Peachey, you're a fool not to get a wife too. Where's the girl?" says he with a voice as loud as the braying of a jackass. "Call up all the Chiefs and priests, and let the Emperor see if his wife suits him."

'There was no need to call any one. They were all there leaning on their guns and spears round the clearing in the centre of the pine wood. A lot of priests went down to the little temple to bring up the girl, and the horns blew fit to wake the dead. Billy Fish saunters round and gets as close to Daniel as he could, and behind him stood his twenty men with matchlocks. Not a man of them under six feet. I was next to Dravot, and behind me was twenty men of the regular Army. Up comes the girl, and a strapping wench she was, covered with silver and turquoises but white as death, and looking back every minute at the priests.

' "She'll do," said Dan, looking her over. "What's to be afraid of, lass? Come and kiss me." He puts his arm round her. She shuts her eyes, gives a bit of a squeak, and down goes her face in the side of Dan's flaming red beard.

' "The slut's bitten me!" says he, clapping his hand to his neck, and sure enough, his hand was red with blood. Billy Fish and two of his match-lock-men catches hold of Dan by the shoulders and drags him into the Bashkai lot, while the priests howls in their lingo,—"Neither God nor Devil but a man!" I was all taken aback, for a priest cut at me in front, and the Army behind began firing into the Bashkai men.

' "God A'mighty!" says Dan. "What is the meaning o' this?"

' "Come back! Come away!" says Billy Fish. "Ruin and Mutiny is the matter. We'll break for Bashkai if we can."

'I tried to give some sort of orders to my men—the men o' the regular Army—but it was no use, so I fired into the brown of 'em with an English Martini and drilled three beggars in a line. The valley was full of shouting, howling creatures, and every soul was shrieking, "Not a God nor a Devil but only a man!" The Bashkai troops stuck to Billy Fish all they were worth, but their matchlocks wasn't half as good as the Kabul breech-loaders, and four of them dropped. Dan was bellowing like a bull, for he was very wrathy; and Billy Fish had a hard job to prevent him running out at the crowd.

' "We can't stand," says Billy Fish. "Make a run for it down the valley! The whole place is against us." The matchlock-men ran, and we went down the valley in spite of Dravot. He was swearing horrible and crying out he was a King. The priests rolled great stones on us, and the regular Army fired hard, and there wasn't more than six men, not counting Dan, Billy Fish, and Me, that came down to the bottom of the valley alive.

'Then they stopped firing and the horns in the temple blew again. "Come away—for Gord's sake come away!" says Billy Fish. "They'll send runners out to all the villages before ever we get to Bashkai. I can protect you there, but I can't do anything now."

'My own notion is that Dan began to go mad in his head from that hour. He stared up and down like a stuck pig. Then he was all for walking back alone and killing the priests with his bare hands; which he could have done. "An Emperor am I," says Daniel, "and next year I shall be a Knight of the Queen."

' "All right, Dan," says I; "but come along now while there's time."

' "It's your fault," says he, "for not looking after your Army better. There was mutiny in the midst, and you didn't know—you damned engine-driving, plate-laying, missionary's-pass-hunting hound!" He sat upon a rock and called me every foul name he could lay tongue to. I was too heart-sick to care, though it was all his foolishness that brought the smash.

'"I'm sorry, Dan," says I, "but there's no accounting for natives. This business is our Fifty-Seven. Maybe we'll make something out of it yet, when we've got to Bashkai."

'"Let's get to Bashkai, then," says Dan, "and, by God, when I come back here again I'll sweep the valley so there isn't a bug in a blanket left!"

'We walked all that day, and all that night Dan was stumping up and down on the snow, chewing his beard and muttering to himself.

'"There's no hope o' getting clear," said Billy Fish. "The priests will have sent runners to the villages to say that you are only men. Why didn't you stick on as Gods till things was more settled? I'm a dead man," says Billy Fish, and he throws himself down on the snow and begins to pray to his Gods.

'Next morning we was in a cruel bad country—all up and down, no level ground at all, and no food either. The six Bashkai men looked at Billy Fish hungry-way as if they wanted to ask something, but they said never a word. At noon we came to the top of a flat mountain all covered with snow, and when we climbed up into it, behold, there was an Army in position waiting in the middle!

'"The runners have been very quick," says Billy Fish, with a little bit of a laugh. "They are waiting for us."

'Three or four men began to fire from the enemy's side, and a chance shot took Daniel in the calf of the leg. That brought him to his senses. He looks across the snow at the Army, and sees the rifles that we had brought into the country.

'"We're done for," says he. "They are Englishmen, these people,—and it's my blasted nonsense that has brought you to this. Get back, Billy Fish, and take your men away; you've done what you could, and now cut for it. Carnehan," says he, "shake hands with me and go along with Billy. Maybe they won't kill you. I'll go and meet 'em alone. It's me that did it. Me, the King!"

'"Go!" says I. "Go to Hell, Dan. I'm with you here. Billy Fish, you clear out, and we two will meet those folk."

'"I'm a Chief," says Billy Fish, quite quiet. "I stay with you. My men can go."

'The Bashkai fellows didn't wait for a second word but ran off, and Dan and Me and Billy Fish walked across to where the drums were drumming and the horns were horning. It was cold—awful cold. I've got that cold in the back of my head now. There's a lump of it there.'

The punkah-coolies had gone to sleep. Two kerosene lamps were blazing in the office, and the perspiration poured down my face and splashed on the blotter as I leaned forward. Carnehan was shivering, and I feared that his mind might go. I wiped my face, took a fresh grip of the piteously mangled hands, and said: 'What happened after that?'

The momentary shift of my eyes had broken the clear current.

'What was you pleased to say?' whined Carnehan. 'They took them without any sound. Not a little whisper all along the snow, not though the King knocked down the first man that set hand on him—not though old Peachey fired his last cartridge into the brown of 'em. Not a single solitary sound did those swines make. They just closed up tight, and I tell you their furs stunk. There was a man called Billy Fish, a good friend of us all, and they cut his throat, Sir, then and there, like a pig; and the King kicks up the bloody snow and says: "We've had a dashed fine run for our money. What's coming next?" But Peachey, Peachey Taliaferro, I tell you, Sir, in confidence as betwixt two friends, he lost his head, Sir. No, he didn't neither. The King lost his head, so he did, all along o' one of those cunning rope-bridges. Kindly let me have the paper-cutter, Sir. It tilted this way. They marched him a mile across that snow to a rope-bridge over a ravine with a river at the bottom. You may have seen such. They prodded him behind like an ox. "Damn your eyes!" says the King. "D'you suppose I can't die like a gentleman?" He turns to Peachey—Peachey that was crying like a child. "I've brought you to this, Peachey," says he. "Brought you out of your happy life to be killed in Kafiristan, where you was late Commander-in-Chief of the Emperor's forces. Say you forgive me, Peachey."—"I do," says Peachey. "Fully and freely do I forgive you, Dan."—"Shake hands, Peachey," says he. "I'm going now." Out he goes, looking neither right nor left, and when he was plumb in the middle of those dizzy dancing ropes,—"Cut, you beggars," he shouts; and they cut, and old Dan fell, turning round and round and round, twenty thousand miles, for he took half an hour to fall till he struck the water, and I could see his body caught on a rock with the gold crown close beside.

'But do you know what they did to Peachey between two pine-trees? They crucified him, Sir, as Peachey's hand will show. They used wooden pegs for his hands and his feet; and he didn't die. He hung there and screamed, and they took him down next day, and said it was a miracle that he wasn't dead. They took him down—poor old Peachey that hadn't done them any harm—that hadn't done them any——'

He rocked to and fro and wept bitterly, wiping his eyes with the back of his scarred hands and moaning like a child for some ten minutes.

'They was cruel enough to feed him up in the temple, because they said he was more of a God than old Daniel that was a man. Then they turned him out on the snow, and told him to go home, and Peachey came home in about a year, begging along the roads quite safe; for Daniel

Dravot he walked before and said: "Come along, Peachey. It's a big thing we're doing." The mountains they danced at night, and the mountains they tried to fall on Peachey's head, but Dan he held up his hand, and Peachey came along bent double. He never let go of Dan's hand, and he never let go of Dan's head. They gave it to him as a present in the temple, to remind him not to come again, and though the crown was pure gold, and Peachey was starving, never would Peachey sell the same. You knew Dravot, Sir! You knew Right Worshipful Brother Dravot! Look at him now!'

He fumbled in the mass of rags round his bent waist; brought out a black horsehair bag embroidered with silver thread; and shook therefrom on to my table—the dried, withered head of Daniel Dravot! The morning sun that had long been paling the lamps struck the red beard and blind sunken eyes; struck, too, a heavy circlet of gold studded with raw turquoises, that Carnehan placed tenderly on the battered temples.

'You be'old now,' said Carnehan, 'the Emperor in his 'abit as he lived— the King of Kafiristan with his crown upon his head. Poor old Daniel that was a monarch once!'

I shuddered, for, in spite of defacements manifold, I recognised the head of the man of Marwar Junction. Carnehan rose to go. I attempted to stop him. He was not fit to walk abroad. 'Let me take away the whiskey, and give me a little money,' he gasped. 'I was a King once. I'll go to the Deputy Commissioner and ask to set in the Poorhouse till I get my health. No, thank you, I can't wait till you get a carriage for me. I've urgent private affairs—in the south—at Marwar.'

He shambled out of the office and departed in the direction of the Deputy Commissioner's house. That day at noon I had occasion to go down the blinding hot Mall, and I saw a crooked man crawling along the white dust of the roadside, his hat in his hand, quavering dolorously after the fashion of street-singers at Home. There was not a soul in sight, and he was out of all possible earshot of the houses. And he sang through his nose, turning his head from right to left:—

> 'The Son of Man goes forth to war,
> A golden crown to gain;
> His blood-red banner streams afar—
> Who follows in his train?'

I waited to hear no more, but put the poor wretch into my carriage and drove him off to the nearest missionary for eventual transfer to the Asylum. He repeated the hymn twice while he was with me whom he did not in the least recognise, and I left him singing it to the missionary.

Two days later I enquired after his welfare of the Superintendent of the Asylum.

'He was admitted suffering from sun-stroke. He died early yesterday morning,' said the Superintendent. 'Is it true that he was half an hour bareheaded in the sun at midday?'

'Yes,' said I, 'but do you happen to know if he had anything upon him by any chance when he died?'

'Not to my knowledge,' said the Superintendent.

And there the matter rests.

BARRACK-ROOM
BALLADS

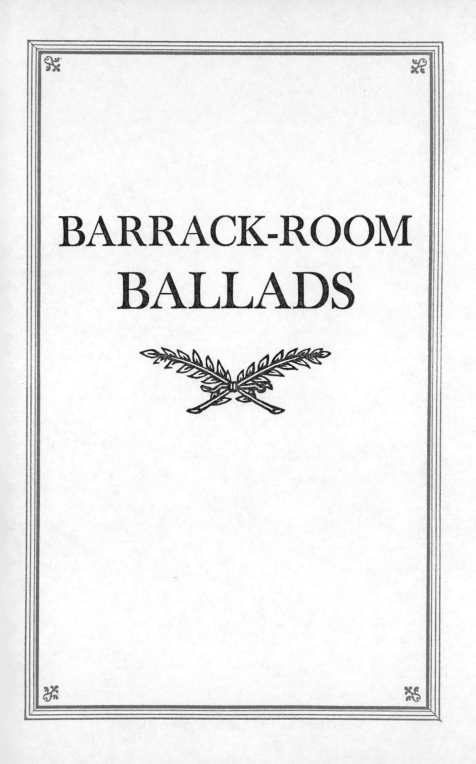

TO THOMAS ATKINS

PRELUDE TO "BARRACK-ROOM BALLADS" WHICH FOLLOW

I have made for you a song,
And it may be right or wrong,
But only you can tell me if it's true.
I have tried for to explain
Both your pleasure and your pain,
And, Thomas, here's my best respects to you!

O there'll surely come a day
When they'll give you all your pay,
And treat you as a Christian ought to do;
So, until that day comes round,
Heaven keep you safe and sound,
And, Thomas, here's my best respects to you!

"BOBS"

1898

FIELD-MARSHAL LORD ROBERTS OF KANDAHAR: DIED IN FRANCE 1914

There's a little red-faced man,
      Which is Bobs,
Rides the tallest 'orse 'e can—
      Our Bobs.
If it bucks or kicks or rears,
'E can sit for twenty years
With a smile round both 'is ears—
      Can't yer, Bobs?

Then 'ere's to Bobs Bahadur—little Bobs, Bobs, Bobs!
'E's our pukka Kandaharder—
      Fightin' Bobs, Bobs, Bobs!
'E's the Dook of *Aggy Chel*;[1]
'E's the man that done us well,
An' we'll follow 'im to 'ell—
      Won't we, Bobs?

If a limber's slipped a trace,
      'Ook on Bobs.
If a marker's lost 'is place,
      Dress by Bobs.
For 'e's eyes all up 'is coat,
An' a bugle in 'is throat,
An' you will not play the goat
      Under Bobs.

'E's a little down on drink,
      Chaplain Bobs;
But it keeps us outer Clink—
      Don't it, Bobs?
So we will not complain
Tho' 'e's water on the brain,
If 'e leads us straight again—
      Blue-light[2] Bobs.

If you stood 'im on 'is head,
      Father Bobs,
You could spill a quart of lead
      Outer Bobs.
'E's been at it thirty years,
An-amassin' souveneers
In the way o' slugs an' spears—
      Ain't yer, Bobs?

What 'e does not know o' war,
      Gen'ral Bobs,
You can arst the shop next door—
      Can't they, Bobs?

[1] Get ahead.   [2] Temperance.

Oh, 'e's little but he's wise,
'E's terror for 'is size,
An'—'e—does—not—advertise—
  Do yer, Bobs?

Now they've made a bloomin' Lord
  Outer Bobs,
Which was but 'is fair reward—
  Weren't it, Bobs?
So 'e'll wear a coronet
Where 'is helmet used to set;
But we know you won't forget—
  Will yer, Bobs?

Then 'ere's to Bobs Bahadur—little Bobs, Bobs, Bobs,
Pocket-Wellin'ton an' *arder*[1]—
  Fightin' Bobs, Bobs, Bobs!
This ain't no bloomin' ode,
But you've 'elped the soldier's load,
An' for benefits bestowed,
  Bless yer, Bobs!

DANNY DEEVER

"What are the bugles blowin' for?" said Files-on-Parade.
"To turn you out, to turn you out," the Colour-Sergeant said.
"What makes you look so white, so white?" said Files-on-Parade.
"I'm dreadin' what I've got to watch," the Colour-Sergeant said.
 For they're hangin' Danny Deever, you can hear the Dead March
  play,
 The Regiment's in 'ollow square—they're hangin' him to-day;
 They've taken of his buttons off an' cut his stripes away,
 An' they're hangin' Danny Deever in the mornin'.

"What makes the rear-rank breathe so 'ard?" said Files-on-Parade.
"It's bitter cold, it's bitter cold," the Colour-Sergeant said.
"What makes that front-rank man fall down?" said Files-on-Parade.
"A touch o' sun, a touch o' sun," the Colour-Sergeant said.

[1] And a half.

They are hangin' Danny Deever, they are marchin' of 'im round,
They 'ave 'alted Danny Deever by 'is coffin on the ground;
An' 'e'll swing in 'arf a minute for a sneakin' shootin' hound—
O they're hangin' Danny Deever in the mornin'!

" 'Is cot was right-'and cot to mine," said Files-on-Parade.
" 'E's sleepin' out an' far to-night," the Colour-Sergeant said.
"I've drunk 'is beer a score o' times," said Files-on-Parade.
" 'E's drinkin' bitter beer alone," the Colour-Sergeant said.
They are hangin' Danny Deever, you must mark 'im to 'is place,
For 'e shot a comrade sleepin'—you must look 'im in the face;
Nine 'undred of 'is county an' the Regiment's disgrace,
While they're hangin' Danny Deever in the mornin'.

"What's that so black agin the sun?" said Files-on-Parade.
"It's Danny fightin' 'ard for life," the Colour-Sergeant said.
"What's that that whimpers over'ead?" said Files-on-Parade.
"It's Danny's soul that's passin' now," the Colour-Sergeant said.
For they're done with Danny Deever, you can 'ear the quickstep play,
The Regiment's in column, an' they're marchin' us away;
Ho! the young recruits are shakin', an' they'll want their beer to-day,
After hangin' Danny Deever in the mornin'!

TOMMY

I went into a public-'ouse to get a pint o' beer,
The publican 'e up an' sez, "We serve no red-coats here."
The girls be'ind the bar they laughed an' giggled fit to die,
I outs into the street again an' to myself sez I:
O it's Tommy this, an' Tommy that, an' "Tommy, go away";
But it's "Thank you, Mister Atkins," when the band begins to play—
The band begins to play, my boys, the band begins to play,
O it's "Thank you, Mister Atkins," when the band begins to play.

I went into a theatre as sober as could be,
They gave a drunk civilian room, but 'adn't none for me;
They sent me to the gallery or round the music-'alls,
But when it comes to fightin', Lord! they'll shove me in the stalls!

For it's Tommy this, an' Tommy that, an' "Tommy, wait outside";
But it's "Special train for Atkins" when the trooper's on the tide—
The troopship's on the tide, my boys, the troopship's on the tide,
O it's "Special train for Atkins" when the trooper's on the tide.

Yes, makin' mock o' uniforms that guard you while you sleep
Is cheaper than them uniforms, an' they're starvation cheap;
An' hustlin' drunken soldiers when they're goin' large a bit
Is five times better business than paradin' in full kit.
    Then it's Tommy this, an' Tommy that, an' "Tommy, 'ow's yer soul?"
    But it's "Thin red line of 'eroes" when the drums begin to roll—
    The drums begin to roll, my boys, the drums begin to roll,
    O it's "Thin red line of 'eroes" when the drums begin to roll.

We aren't no thin red 'eroes, nor we aren't no blackguards too,
But single men in barricks, most remarkable like you;
An' if sometimes our conduck isn't all your fancy paints,
Why, single men in barricks don't grow into plaster saints;
    While it's Tommy this, an' Tommy that, an' "Tommy, fall be'ind,"
    But it's "Please to walk in front, sir," when there's trouble in the
        wind—
    There's trouble in the wind, my boys, there's trouble in the wind,
    O it's "Please to walk in front, sir," when there's trouble in the wind.

You talk o' better food for us, an' schools, an' fires, an' all:
We'll wait for extry rations if you treat us rational.
Don't mess about the cook-room slops, but prove it to our face
The Widow's Uniform is not the soldier-man's disgrace.
    For it's Tommy this, an' Tommy that, an' "Chuck him out, the brute!"
    But it's "Saviour of 'is country" when the guns begin to shoot;
    An' it's Tommy this, an' Tommy that, an' anything you please;
    An' Tommy ain't a bloomin' fool—you bet that Tommy sees!

"FUZZY-WUZZY"

SOUDAN EXPEDITIONARY FORCE. EARLY CAMPAIGNS

We've fought with many men acrost the seas,
    An' some of 'em was brave an' some was not:
The Paythan an' the Zulu an' Burmese;
    But the Fuzzy was the finest o' the lot.

We never got a ha'porth's change of 'im:
  'E squatted in the scrub an' 'ocked our 'orses,
'E cut our sentries up at Sua*kim,*
    An' 'e played the cat an' banjo with our forces.
      So 'ere's *to* you, Fuzzy-Wuzzy, at your 'ome in the Soudan;
      You're a pore benighted 'eathen but a first-class fightin' man;
      We gives you your certificate, an' if you want it signed
      We'll come an' 'ave a romp with you whenever you're inclined.

We took our chanst among the Kyber 'ills,
  The Boers knocked us silly at a mile,
The Burman give us Irriwaddy chills,
  An' a Zulu *impi* dished us up in style:
But all we ever got from such as they
  Was pop to what the Fuzzy made us swaller;
We 'eld our bloomin' own, the papers say,
  But man for man the Fuzzy knocked us 'oller.
    Then 'ere's *to* you, Fuzzy-Wuzzy, an' the missis and the kid;
    Our orders was to break you, an' of course we went an' did.
    We sloshed you with Martinis, an' it wasn't 'ardly fair;
    But for all the odds agin' you, Fuzzy-Wuz, you broke the square.

'E 'asn't got no papers of 'is own,
  'E 'asn't got no medals nor rewards,
So *we* must certify the skill 'e's shown
  In usin' of 'is long two-'anded swords:
When 'e's 'oppin' in an' out among the bush
  With 'is coffin-'eaded shield an' shovel-spear,
An 'appy day with Fuzzy on the rush
  Will last an 'ealthy Tommy for a year.
    So 'ere's *to* you, Fuzzy-Wuzzy, an' your friends which are no more,
    If we 'adn't lost some messmates we would 'elp you to deplore.
    But give an' take's the gospel, an' we'll call the bargain fair,
    For if you 'ave lost more than us, you crumpled up the square!

'E rushes at the smoke when we let drive,
  An', before we know, 'e's 'ackin' at our 'ead;
'E's all 'ot sand an' ginger when alive,
  An' 'e's generally shammin' when 'e's dead.
'E's a daisy, 'e's a ducky, 'e's a lamb!
  E's a injia-rubber idiot on the spree,

'E's the on'y thing that doesn't give a damn
  For a Regiment o' British Infantree!
    So 'ere's *to* you, Fuzzy-Wuzzy, at your 'ome in the Soudan;
    You're a pore benighted 'eathen but a first-class fightin' man;
    An' 'ere's *to* you, Fuzzy-Wuzzy, with your 'ayrick 'ead of 'air—
    You big black boundin' beggar—for you broke a British square!

SOLDIER, SOLDIER

Soldier, soldier come from the wars,
  "Why don't you march with my true love?"
"We're fresh from off the ship an' 'e's, maybe, give the slip,
  "An' you'd best go look for a new love."

    New love! True love!
    Best go look for a new love,
    The dead they cannot rise, an' you'd better dry your eyes,
    An' you'd best go look for a new love.

"Soldier, soldier come from the wars,
  "What did you see o' my true love?"
"I seen 'im serve the Queen in a suit o' rifle-green,
  "An' you'd best go look for a new love."

"Soldier, soldier come from the wars,
  "Did ye see no more o' my true love?"
"I seen 'im runnin' by when the shots begun to fly—
  "But you'd best go look for a new love."

"Soldier, soldier come from the wars,
  "Did aught take 'arm to my true love?"
"I couldn't see the fight, for the smoke it lay so white—
  "And you'd best go look for a new love."

"Soldier, soldier come from the wars,
  "I'll up an' tend to my true love!"
" 'E's lying on the dead with a bullet through 'is 'ead,
  "An' you'd best go look for a new love."

"Soldier, soldier come from the wars,
  "I'll down an' die with my true love!"

"The pit we dug'll 'ide 'im an' the twenty more beside 'im—
"An' you'd best go look for a new love."

"Soldier, soldier come from the wars,
"Do you bring no sign from my true love?"
"I bring a lock of 'air that 'e allus used to wear,
"An' you'd best go look for a new love."

"Soldier, soldier come from the wars,
"O then I know it's true I've lost my true love!"
"An' I tell you truth again—when you've lost the feel o' pain
"You'd best take me for your new love."

    True love! New love!
    Best take 'im for a new love,
    The dead they cannot rise, an' you'd better dry your eyes
    An' you'd best take 'im for your new love.

SCREW-GUNS

Smokin' my pipe on the mountings, sniffin' the mornin'-cool,
I walks in my old brown gaiters along o' my old brown mule,
With seventy gunners be'ind me, an' never a beggar forgets
It's only the pick of the Army that handles the dear little pets —'Tss! 'Tss!
    For you all love the screw-guns—the screw-guns they all love you!
    So when we call round with a few guns, o' course you will know
        what to do—hoo! hoo!
    Jest send in your Chief an' surrender—it's worse if you fights or you
        runs:
    You can go where you please, you can skid up the trees, but you
        don't get away from the guns!

They sends us along where the roads are, but mostly we goes where
        they ain't.
We'd climb up the side of a sign-board an' trust to the stick o' the paint:
We've chivied the Naga an' Looshai; we've give the Afreedeeman fits;
For we fancies ourselves at two thousand, we guns that are built in two
        bits—'Tss! 'Tss!
    For you all love the screw-guns . . .

If a man doesn't work, why, we drills 'im an' teaches 'im 'ow to behave.
If a beggar can't march, why, we kills 'im an' rattles 'im into 'is grave.
You've got to stand up to our business an' spring without snatchin' or
    fuss.
D'you say that you sweat with the field-guns? By God, you must lather
    with us—'Tss! 'Tss!
    For you all love the screw-guns . . .

The eagles is screamin' around us, the river's a-moanin' below,
We're clear o' the pine an' the oak-scrub, we're out on the rocks an' the
    snow,
An' the wind is as thin as a whip-lash what carries away to the plains
The rattle an' stamp o' the lead-mules—the jinglety-jink o' the chains—
    'Tss! 'Tss!
    For you all love the screw-guns . . .

There's a wheel on the Horns o' the Mornin', an' a wheel on the edge
    o' the Pit,
An' a drop into nothin' beneath you as straight as a beggar can spit:
With the sweat runnin' out o' your shirt-sleeves, an' the sun off the snow
    in your face,
An' 'arf o' the men on the drag-ropes to hold the gun in 'er place—'Tss!
    'Tss!
    For you all love the screw-guns . . .

Smokin' my pipe on the mountings, sniffin' the mornin'-cool,
I climbs in my old brown gaiters along o' my old brown mule.
The monkey can say what our road was—the wild-goat 'e knows where
    we passed.
Stand easy, you long-eared old darlin's! Out drag-ropes! With shrapnel!
    Hold fast—'Tss! 'Tss!
    For you all love the screw-guns—the screw-guns they all love you!
    So when we take tea with a few guns, o' course you will know what
      to do—hoo! hoo!
    Jest send in your Chief an' surrender—it's worse if you fights or you
      runs:
    You may hide in the caves, they'll be only your graves, but you can't
      get away from the guns!

CELLS

I've a head like a concertina, I've a tongue like a buttonstick,
I've a mouth like an old potato, and I'm more than a little sick,
But I've had my fun o' the Corp'ral's Guard; I've made the cinders fly,
And I'm here in the Clink for a thundering drink and blacking the
    Corporal's eye.
        With a second-hand overcoat under my head,
        And a beautiful view of the yard,
    O it's pack-drill for me and a fortnight's C.B.
        For "drunk and resisting the Guard!"
        Mad drunk and resisting the Guard—
        'Strewth, but I socked it them hard!
    So it's pack-drill for me and a fortnight's C.B.
        For "drunk and resisting the Guard."

I started o' canteen porter, I finished o' canteen beer,
But a dose o' gin that a mate slipped in, it was that that brought me here.
'Twas that and an extry double Guard that rubbed my nose in the dirt—
But I fell away with the Corp'ral's stock and the best of the Corp'ral's shirt.

I left my cap in a public-house, my boots in the public road,
And Lord knows where—and I don't care—my belt and my tunic goed.
They'll stop my pay, they'll cut away the stripes I used to wear,
But I left my mark on the Corp'ral's face, and I think he'll keep it there!

My wife she cries on the barrack-gate, my kid in the barrack-yard.
It ain't that I mind the Ord'ly-room—it's *that* that cuts so hard.
I'll take my oath before them both that I will sure abstain,
But as soon as I'm in with a mate and gin, I know I'll do it again!

        With a second-hand overcoat under my head,
        And a beautiful view of the yard,
    Yes, it's pack-drill for me and a fortnight's C.B.
        For "drunk and resisting the Guard!"
        Mad drunk and resisting the Guard—
        'Strewth, but I socked it them hard!
    So it's pack-drill for me and a fortnight's C.B.
        For "drunk and resisting the Guard."

GUNGA DIN

You may talk o' gin and beer
When you're quartered safe out 'ere,
An' you're sent to penny-fights an' Aldershot it;
But when it comes to slaughter
You will do your work on water,
An' you'll lick the bloomin' boots of 'im that's got it.
Now in Injia's sunny clime,
Where I used to spend my time
A-servin' of 'Er Majesty the Queen,
Of all them blackfaced crew
The finest man I knew
Was our regimental bhisti, Gunga Din.
      He was "Din! Din! Din!
   "You limpin' lump o' brick-dust, Gunga Din!
     "Hi! Slippy *hitherao!*
     "Water, get it! *Panee lao,*[1]
   "You squidgy-nosed old idol, Gunga Din."

The uniform 'e wore
Was nothin' much before,
An' rather less than 'arf o' that be'ind,
For a piece o' twisty rag
An' a goatskin water-bag
Was all the field-equipment 'e could find.
When the sweatin' troop-train lay
In a sidin' through the day,
Where the 'eat would make your bloomin' eyebrows crawl,
We shouted "Harry By!"[2]
Till our throats were bricky-dry,
Then we wopped 'im 'cause 'e couldn't serve us all.
      It was "Din! Din! Din!
   "You 'eathen, where the mischief 'ave you been?
     "You put some *juldee*[3] in it
     "Or I'll *marrow*[4] you this minute
   "If you don't fill up my helmet, Gunga Din!"

---

[1] Bring water swiftly.   [2] O brother.   [3] Be quick.   [4] Hit you.

'E would dot an' carry one
Till the longest day was done;
An' 'e didn't seem to know the use o' fear.
If we charged or broke or cut,
You could bet your bloomin' nut,
'E'd be waitin' fifty paces right flank rear.
With 'is mussick[1] on 'is back,
'E would skip with our attack,
An' watch us till the bugles made "Retire,"
An' for all 'is dirty 'ide
'E was white, clear white, inside
When 'e went to tend the wounded under fire!
      It was "Din! Din! Din!"
  With the bullets kickin' dust-spots on the green.
      When the cartridges ran out,
      You could hear the front-ranks shout,
  "Hi! ammunition-mules an' Gunga Din!"

I shan't forgit the night
When I dropped be'ind the fight
With a bullet where my belt-plate should 'a' been.
I was chokin' mad with thirst,
An' the man that spied me first
Was our good old grinnin', gruntin' Gunga Din.
'E lifted up my 'ead,
An' he plugged me where I bled,
An' 'e guv me 'arf-a-pint o' water green.
It was crawlin' and it stunk,
But of all the drinks I've drunk,
I'm gratefullest to one from Gunga Din.
      It was "Din! Din! Din!
  " 'Ere's a beggar with a bullet through 'is spleen;
    " 'E's chawin' up the ground,
    "An' 'e's kickin' all around:
  "For Gawd's sake git the water, Gunga Din!"

'E carried me away
To where a dooli lay,
An' a bullet come an' drilled the beggar clean.

      [1] Water-skin.

'E put me safe inside,
An' just before 'e died,
"I 'ope you liked your drink," sez Gunga Din.
So I'll meet 'im later on
At the place where 'e is gone—
Where it's always double drill and no canteen.
'E'll be squattin' on the coals
Givin' drink to poor damned souls,
An' I'll get a swig in hell from Gunga Din!
            Yes, Din! Din! Din!
    You Lazarushian-leather Gunga Din!
        Though I've belted you and flayed you,
        By the livin' Gawd that made you,
    You're a better man than I am, Gunga Din!

OONTS

NORTHERN INDIA TRANSPORT TRAIN

Wot makes the soldier's 'eart to penk, wot makes 'im to perspire?
It isn't standin' up to charge nor lyin' down to fire;
But it's everlastin' waitin' on a everlastin' road
For the commissariat camel an' 'is commissariat load.
    O the oont,[1] O the oont, O the commissariat oont!
        With 'is silly neck a-bobbin' like a basket full o' snakes;
    We packs 'im like an idol, an' you ought to 'ear 'im grunt,
        An' when we get 'im loaded up 'is blessed girth-rope breaks.

Wot makes the rear-guard swear so 'ard when night is drorin' in,
An' every native follower is shiverin' for 'is skin?
It ain't the chanst o' being rushed by Paythans from the 'ills,
It's the commissariat camel puttin' on 'is bloomin' frills!
    O the oont, O the oont, O the hairy scary oont!
        A-trippin' over tent-ropes when we've got the night alarm!
    We socks 'im with a stretcher-pole an' 'eads 'im off in front,
        An' when we've saved 'is bloomin' life 'e chaws our bloomin' arm.

[1] Camel:—*oo* is pronounced like *u* in "bull," but by Mr. Atkins to rhyme with "front."

The 'orse 'e knows above a bit, the bullock's but a fool,
The elephant's a gentleman, the battery-mule's a mule;
But the commissariat cam-u-el, when all is said an' done,
'E's a devil an' a ostrich an' a orphan-child in one.
    O the oont, O the oont, O the Gawd-forsaken oont!
      The lumpy-'umpy 'ummin'-bird a-singin' where 'e lies,
    'E's blocked the whole division from the rear-guard to the front,
      An' when we get him up again—the beggar goes an' dies!

'E'll gall an' chafe an' lame an' fight—'e smells most awful vile.
'E'll lose 'isself for ever if you let 'im stray a mile.
'E's game to graze the 'ole day long an' 'owl the 'ole night through,
An' when 'e comes to greasy ground 'e splits 'isself in two.
    O the oont, O the oont, O the floppin', droppin' oont,
      When 'is long legs give from under an' 'is meltin' eye is dim!
    The Tribes is up be'ind us, and the Tribes is out in front—
      It ain't no jam for Tommy, but it's kites an' crows for 'im.

So when the cruel march is done, an' when the roads is blind,
An' when we sees the camp in front an' 'ears the shots be'ind,
Ho! then we strips 'is saddle off, and all 'is woes is past.
'E thinks on us that used 'im so, and gets revenge at last.
    O the oont, O the oont, O the floatin', bloatin' oont!
      The late lamented camel in the water-cut 'e lies;
    We keeps a mile be'ind 'im an' we keeps a mile in front,
      But 'e gets into the drinkin'-casks, and then o' course we dies!

LOOT

If you've ever stole a pheasant-egg be'ind the keeper's back,
    If you've ever snigged the washin' from the line,
If you've ever crammed a gander in your bloomin' 'aversack,
    You will understand this little song o' mine.
But the service rules are 'ard, an' from such we are debarred,
    For the same with English morals does not suit.
        (*Cornet*: Toot! toot!)
Why, they call a man a robber if 'e stuffs 'is marchin' clobber[1]
    With the—

---

[1] Clothes.

(*Chorus*) Loo! loo! Lulu! lulu! Loo! loo! Loot! loot! loot!
        Ow, the loot!
        Bloomin' loot!
    That's the thing to make the boys git up an' shoot!
        It's the same with dogs an' men,
        If you'd make 'em come again
      Clap 'em forward with a Loo! loo! Lulu! Loot!
(*ff*)   Whoopee! Tear 'im, puppy! Loo! loo! Lulu! Loot! loot! loot!

If you've knocked a nigger edgeways when 'e's thrustin' for your life,
    You must leave 'im very careful where 'e fell;
An' may thank your stars an' gaiters if you didn't feel 'is knife
    That you ain't told off to bury 'im as well.
Then the sweatin' Tommies wonder as they spade the beggars under
    Why lootin' should be entered as a crime.
So, if my song you'll 'ear, I will learn you plain an' clear
    'Ow to pay yourself for fightin' overtime.
        (*Chorus*) With the loot, . . .

Now remember when you're 'acking round a gilded Burma god
    That 'is eyes is very often precious stones;
An' if you treat a nigger to a dose o' cleanin'-rod
    'E's like to show you everything 'e owns.
When 'e won't prodooce no more, pour some water on the floor
    Where you 'ear it answer 'ollow to the boot
        (*Cornet:* Toot! toot!)—
When the ground begins to sink, shove your baynick down the chink,
    An' you're sure to touch the—
(*Chorus*) Loo! loo! Lulu! Loot! loot! loot!
        Ow, the loot! . . .
When from 'ouse to 'ouse you're 'unting, you must always work in pairs—
    It 'alves the gain, but safer you will find—
For a single man gets bottled on them twisty-wisty stairs,
    An' a woman comes and clobs 'im from be'ind.
When you've turned 'em inside out, an' it seems beyond a doubt
    As if there weren't enough to dust a flute
        (*Cornet:* Toot! toot!)—
Before you sling your 'ook, at the 'ousetops take a look,
    For it's underneath the tiles they 'ide the loot.
        (*Chorus*) Ow, the loot! . . .

You can mostly square a Sergint an' a Quartermaster too,
　If you only take the proper way to go.
I could never keep my pickin's, but I've learned you all I knew—
　But don't you never say I told you so.
An' now I'll bid good-bye, for I'm gettin' rather dry,
　An' I see another tunin' up to toot
　　　　(*Cornet:* Toot! toot!)—
So 'ere's good-luck to those that wears the Widow's clo'es,
　An' the Devil send 'em all they want o' loot!
　　　　(*Chorus*) Yes, the loot,
　　　　　　　Bloomin' loot!
　　　　In the tunic an' the mess-tin an' the boot!
　　　　　It's the same with dogs an' men,
　　　　　If you'd make 'em come again
(*fff*)　Whoop 'em forward with a Loo! loo! Lulu! Loot! loot! loot!
　　　　Heeya! Sick 'im, puppy! Loo! loo! Lulu! Loot! loot! loot!

"SNARLEYOW"

This 'appened in a battle to a batt'ry of the corps
Which is first among the women an' amazin' first in war;
An' what the bloomin' battle was I don't remember now,
But Two's off-lead[1] 'e answered to the name o' *Snarleyow*.
　　　　Down in the Infantry, nobody cares;
　　　　Down in the Cavalry, Colonel 'e swears;
　　　　But down in the lead with the wheel at the flog
　　　　Turns the bold Bombardier to a little whipped dog!

They was movin' into action, they was needed very sore,
To learn a little schoolin' to a native army-core,
They 'ad nipped against an uphill, they was tuckin' down the brow,
When a tricky trundlin' roundshot give the knock to *Snarleyow*.

They cut 'im loose an' left 'im—'e was almost tore in two—
But he tried to follow after as a well-trained 'orse should do;
'E went an' fouled the limber, an' the Driver's Brother squeals:
"Pull up, pull up for *Snarleyow*—'is head's between 'is 'eels!"

　　　　[1] The leading right-hand horse of No. 2 gun.

The Driver 'umped 'is shoulder, for the wheels was goin' round,
An' there ain't no "Stop, conductor!" when a batt'ry's changin' ground;
Sez 'e: "I broke the beggar in, an' very sad I feels,
"But I couldn't pull up, not for *you*—your 'ead between your 'eels!"

'E 'adn't 'ardly spoke the word, before a droppin' shell
A little right the batt'ry an' between the sections fell;
An' when the smoke 'ad cleared away, before the limber-wheels,
There lay the Driver's Brother with 'is 'ead between 'is 'eels.

Then sez the Driver's Brother, an' 'is words was very plain,
"For Gawd's own sake get over me, an' put me out o' pain."
They saw 'is wounds was mortial, an' they judged that it was best,
So they took an' drove the limber straight across 'is back an' chest.

The Driver 'e give nothin' 'cept a little coughin' grunt,
But 'e swung 'is 'orses 'andsome when it came to "Action Front!"
An' if one wheel was juicy, you may lay your Monday head
'Twas juicier for the niggers when the case begun to spread.

The moril of this story, it is plainly to be seen:
You 'aven't got no families when servin' of the Queen—
You 'aven't got no brothers, fathers, sisters, wives, or sons—
If you want to win your battles take an' work your bloomin' guns!
     Down in the Infantry, nobody cares;
     Down in the Cavalry, Colonel 'e swears;
     But down in the lead with the wheel at the flog
     Turns the bold Bombardier to a little whipped dog!

THE WIDOW AT WINDSOR

    'Ave you 'eard o' the Widow at Windsor
      With a hairy gold crown on 'er 'ead?
    She 'as ships on the foam—she 'as millions at 'ome,
      An' she pays us poor beggars in red.
      (Ow, poor beggars in red!)
    There's 'er nick on the cavalry 'orses,
      There's 'er mark on the medical stores—

An' 'er troopers you'll find with a fair wind be'ind
  That takes us to various wars.
     (Poor beggars!—barbarious wars!)
        Then 'ere's to the Widow at Windsor,
          An' 'ere's to the stores an' the guns,
        The men an' the 'orses what makes up the forces
          O' Missis Victorier's sons.
        (Poor beggars! Victorier's sons!)

Walk wide o' the Widow at Windsor,
  For 'alf o' Creation she owns:
We 'ave bought 'er the same with the sword an' the flame,
  An' we've salted it down with our bones.
     (Poor beggars!—it's blue with our bones!)
Hands off o' the sons o' the Widow,
  Hands off o' the goods in 'er shop,
For the Kings must come down an' the Emperors frown
  When the Widow at Windsor says "Stop!"
     (Poor beggars!—we're sent to say "Stop!")
        Then 'ere's to the Lodge o' the Widow,
          From the Pole to the Tropics it runs—
          To the Lodge that we tile with the rank an' the file,
          An' open in form with the guns.
        (Poor beggars!—it's always they guns!)

We 'ave 'eard o' the Widow at Windsor,
  It's safest to leave 'er alone:
For 'er sentries we stand by the sea an' the land
  Wherever the bugles are blown.
     (Poor beggars!—an' don't we get blown!)
Take 'old o' the Wings o' the Mornin',
  An' flop round the earth till you're dead;
But you won't get away from the tune that they play
  To the bloomin' old rag over'ead.
     (Poor beggars!—it's 'ot over'ead!)
        Then 'ere's to the Sons o' the Widow,
          Wherever, 'owever they roam.
        'Ere's all they desire, an' if they require
          A speedy return to their 'ome.
        (Poor beggars!—they'll never see 'ome!)

BELTS

There was a row in Silver Street that's near to Dublin Quay,
Between an Irish regiment an' English cavalree;
It started at Revelly an' it lasted on till dark:
The first man dropped at Harrison's, the last forninst the Park.
    For it was:—"Belts, belts, belts, an' that's one for you!"
    An' it was "Belts, belts, belts, an' that's done for you!"
    O buckle an' tongue
    Was the song that we sung
    From Harrison's down to the Park!

There was a row in Silver Street—the regiments was out,
They called us "Delhi Rebels," an' we answered "Threes about!"
That drew them like a hornets' nest—we met them good an' large,
The English at the double an' the Irish at the charge.
    Then it was:—"Belts, &c."

There was a row in Silver Street—an' I was in it too;
We passed the time o' day, an' then the belts went whirraru!
I misremember what occurred, but, subsequint the storm,
A *Freeman's Journal Supplemint* was all *my* uniform.
    O it was:—"Belts, &c."

There was a row in Silver Street—they sent the Polis there,
The English were too drunk to know, the Irish didn't care;
But when they grew impertinent we simultaneous rose,
Till half o' them was Liffey mud an' half was tatthered clo'es.
    For it was:—"Belts, &c."

There was a row in Silver Street—it might ha' raged till now,
But some one drew his side-arm clear, an' nobody knew how;
'Twas Hogan took the point an' dropped; we saw the red blood run:
An' so we all was murderers that started out in fun.
    While it was: "Belts, &c."

There was a row in Silver Street—but that put down the shine,
Wid each man whisperin' to his next:—" 'Twas never work o' mine!"

We went away like beaten dogs, an' down the street we bore him,
The poor dumb corpse that couldn't tell the bhoys were sorry for him.
    When it was:—"Belts, &c."

There was a row in Silver Street—it isn't over yet,
For half of us are under guard wid punishments to get;
'Tis all a merricle to me as in the Clink I lie:
There was a row in Silver Street—begod, I wonder why!
        But it was:—"Belts, belts, belts, an' that's one for you!"
        An' it was "Belts, belts, belts, an' that's done for you!"
        O buckle an' tongue
        Was the song that we sung
        From Harrison's down to the Park!

THE YOUNG BRITISH SOLDIER

When the 'arf-made recruity goes out to the East
'E acts like a babe an' 'e drinks like a beast,
An' 'e wonders because 'e is frequent deceased
        Ere 'e's fit for to serve as a soldier.
            Serve, serve, serve as a soldier,
            Serve, serve, serve as a soldier,
            Serve, serve, serve as a soldier,
                So-oldier *of* the Queen!

Now all you recruities what's drafted to-day,
You shut up your rag-box an' 'ark to my lay,
An' I'll sing you a soldier as far as I may:
        A soldier what's fit for a soldier.
            Fit, fit, fit for a soldier . . .

First mind you steer clear o' the grog-sellers' huts,
For they sell you Fixed Bay'nets that rots out your guts—
Ay, drink that 'ud eat the live steel from your butts—
        An' it's bad for the young British soldier.
            Bad, bad, bad for the soldier . . .

When the cholera comes—as it will past a doubt—
Keep out of the wet and don't go on the shout,
For the sickness gets in as the liquor dies out,
        An' it crumples the young British soldier.
            Crum-, crum-, crumples the soldier . . .

But the worst o' your foes is the sun over'ead:
You *must* wear your 'elmet for all that is said:
If 'e finds you uncovered 'e'll knock you down dead,
    An' you'll die like a fool of a soldier.
        Fool, fool, fool of a soldier . . .

If you're cast for fatigue by a sergeant unkind,
Don't grouse like a woman nor crack on nor blind;
Be handy and civil, and then you will find
    That it's beer for the young British soldier.
        Beer, beer, beer for the soldier . . .

Now, if you must marry, take care she is old—
A troop-sergeant's widow's the nicest, I'm told,
For beauty won't help if your rations is cold,
    Nor love ain't enough for a soldier.
        'Nough, 'nough, 'nough for a soldier . . .

If the wife should go wrong with a comrade, be loth
To shoot when you catch 'em—you'll swing, on my oath!—
Make 'im take 'er and keep 'er: that's Hell for them both,
    An' you're shut o' the curse of a soldier.
        Curse, curse, curse of a soldier . . .

When first under fire an' you're wishful to duck
Don't look nor take 'eed at the man that is struck.
Be thankful you're livin', and trust to your luck
    And march to your front like a soldier.
        Front, front, front like a soldier . . .

When 'arf of your bullets fly wide in the ditch,
Don't call your Martini a cross-eyed old bitch;
She's human as you are—you treat her as sich,
    An' she'll fight for the young British soldier.
        Fight, fight, fight for the soldier . . .

When shakin' their bustles like ladies so fine,
The guns o' the enemy wheel into line,
Shoot low at the limbers an' don't mind the shine,
    For noise never startles the soldier.
        Start-, start-, startles the soldier . . .

If your officer's dead and the sergeants look white,
Remember it's ruin to run from a fight:
So take open order, lie down, and sit tight,
    And wait for supports like a soldier.
        Wait, wait, wait like a soldier . . .

When you're wounded and left on Afghanistan's plains,
And the women come out to cut up what remains,
Jest roll to your rifle and blow out your brains
    An' go to your Gawd like a soldier.
        Go, go, go like a soldier,
        Go, go, go like a soldier,
        Go, go, go like a soldier,
          So-oldier *of* the Queen!

MANDALAY

By the old Moulmein Pagoda, lookin' lazy at the sea,
There's a Burma girl a-settin', and I know she thinks o' me;
For the wind is in the palm-trees, and the temple-bells they say:
"Come you back, you British soldier; come you back to Mandalay!"
    Come you back to Mandalay,
    Where the old Flotilla lay:
    Can't you 'ear their paddles chunkin' from Rangoon to Manda-
        lay?
    On the road to Mandalay,
    Where the flyin'-fishes play,
    An' the dawn comes up like thunder outer China 'crost the Bay!

'Er petticoat was yaller an' 'er little cap was green,
An' 'er name was Supi-yaw-lat—jes' the same as Theebaw's Queen,
An' I seed her first a-smokin' of a whackin' white cheroot,
An' a-wastin' Christian kisses on an 'eathen idol's foot:
    Bloomin' idol made o' mud—
    Wot they called the Great Gawd Budd—
    Plucky lot she cared for idols when I kissed 'er where she stud!
    On the road to Mandalay . . .

When the mist was on the rice-fields an' the sun was droppin' slow,
She'd git 'er little banjo an' she'd sing "*Kulla-lo-lo!*"
With 'er arm upon my shoulder an' 'er cheek again my cheek
We useter watch the steamers an' the *hathis* pilin' teak.
      Elephints a-pilin' teak
      In the sludgy, squdgy creek,
      Where the silence 'ung that 'eavy you was 'arf afraid to speak!
      On the road to Mandalay . . .

But that's all shove be'ind me—long ago an' fur away,
An' there ain't no 'buses runnin' from the Bank to Mandalay;
An' I'm learnin' 'ere in London what the ten-year soldier tells:
"If you've 'eard the East a-callin', you won't never 'eed naught else."
      No! you won't 'eed nothin' else
      But them spicy garlic smells,
      An' the sunshine an' the palm-trees an' the tinkly temple-bells;
      On the road to Mandalay . . .

I am sick o' wastin' leather on these gritty pavin'-stones,
An' the blasted English drizzle wakes the fever in my bones;
Tho' I walks with fifty 'ousemaids outer Chelsea to the Strand,
An' they talks a lot o' lovin', but wot do they understand?
      Beefy face an' grubby 'and—
      Law! wot do they understand?
      I've a neater, sweeter maiden in a cleaner, greener land!
      On the road to Mandalay . . .

Ship me somewheres east of Suez, where the best is like the worst,
Where there aren't no Ten Commandments an' a man can raise a thirst;
For the temple-bells are callin', an' it's there that I would be—
By the old Moulmein Pagoda, looking lazy at the sea;
      On the road to Mandalay,
      Where the old Flotilla lay,
      With our sick beneath the awnings when we went to Mandalay!
      On the road to Mandalay,
      Where the flyin'-fishes play,
      An' the dawn comes up like thunder outer China 'crost the Bay!

TROOPIN'

OLD ENGLISH ARMY IN THE EAST

Troopin', troopin', troopin' to the sea:
'Ere's September come again—the six-year men are free.
O leave the dead be'ind us, for they cannot come away
To where the ship's a-coalin' up that takes us 'ome to-day.
        We're goin' 'ome, we're goin' 'ome,
            Our ship is *at* the shore,
        An' you must pack your 'aversack,
            For we won't come back no more.
        Ho, don't you grieve for me,
            My lovely Mary-Ann!
        For I'll marry you yit on a fourp'ny bit
            As a time-expired man.

The *Malabar's* in 'arbour with the fumner at 'er tail,
An' the time-expired's waitin' of 'is orders for to sail.
Ho! the weary waitin' when on Khyber 'ills we lay,
But the time-expired's waitin' of 'is orders 'ome to-day.

They'll turn us out at Portsmouth wharf in cold an' wet an' rain,
All wearin' Injian cotton kit, but we will not complain.
They'll kill us of pneumonia—for that's their little way—
But damn the chills and fever, men, we're goin' 'ome to-day!

Troopin', troopin', winter's round again!
See the new draf's pourin' in for the old campaign;
Ho, you poor recruities, but you've got to earn your pay—
What's the last from Lunnon, lads? We're goin' there to-day.

Troopin', troopin', give another cheer—
'Ere's to English women an' a quart of English beer.
The Colonel an' the Regiment an' all who've got to stay,
Gawd's Mercy strike 'em gentle! Whoop! we're goin' 'ome to-day.
        We're goin' 'ome, we're goin' 'ome,
            Our ship is *at* the shore,
        An' you must pack your 'aversack,
            For we won't come back no more.

Ho, don't you grieve for me,
   My lovely Mary-Ann!
For I'll marry you yit on a fourp'ny bit
   As a time-expired man.

THE WIDOW'S PARTY

"Where have you been this while away,
        Johnnie, Johnnie?"
Out with the rest on a picnic lay.
        Johnnie, my Johnnie, aha!
They called us out of the barrack-yard
To Gawd knows where from Gosport Hard,
And you can't refuse when you get the card,
        And the Widow gives the party.
          (*Bugle:* Ta—rara—ra-ra-rara!)

"What did you get to eat and drink,
        Johnnie, Johnnie?"
Standing water as thick as ink,
        Johnnie, my Johnnie, aha!
A bit o' beef that were three year stored,
A bit o' mutton as tough as a board,
And a fowl we killed with a sergeant's sword,
        When the Widow give the party.

"What did you do for knives and forks,
        Johnnie, Johnnie?"
We carries 'em with us wherever we walks,
        Johnnie, my Johnnie, aha!
And some was sliced and some was halved,
And some was crimped and some was carved,
And some was gutted and some was starved,
        When the Widow give the party.

"What ha' you done with half your mess,
        Johnnie, Johnnie?"
They couldn't do more and they wouldn't do less.
        Johnnie, my Johnnie, aha!

They ate their whack and they drank their fill,
And I think the rations has made them ill,
For half my comp'ny's lying still
                        Where the Widow give the party.

"How did you get away—away,
                        Johnnie, Johnnie?"
On the broad o' my back at the end o' the day,
                        Johnnie, my Johnnie, aha!
I comed away like a bleedin' toff,
For I got four niggers to carry me off,
As I lay in the bight of a canvas trough,
                        When the Widow give the party.

"What was the end of all the show,
                        Johnnie, Johnnie?"
Ask my Colonel, for I don't know,
                        Johnnie, my Johnnie, aha!
We broke a King and we built a road—
A court-house stands where the Reg-ment goed.
And the river's clean where the raw blood flowed
                        When the Widow give the party.
                        (*Bugle:* Ta—rara—ra-ra-rara!)

FORD O' KABUL RIVER

Kabul town's by Kabul river—
  Blow the trumpet, draw the sword—
There I lef' my mate for ever,
  Wet an' drippin' by the ford.
    Ford, ford, ford o' Kabul river,
      Ford o' Kabul river in the dark!
    There's the river up and brimmin', an' there's 'arf a squadron
      swimmin'
      'Cross the ford o' Kabul river in the dark.

Kabul town's a blasted place—
  Blow the trumpet, draw the sword—
'Strewth I shan't forget 'is face
  Wet an' drippin' by the ford!

Ford, ford, ford o' Kabul river,
 Ford o' Kabul river in the dark!
Keep the crossing-stakes beside you, an' they will surely guide you
 'Cross the ford o' Kabul river in the dark.

Kabul town is sun and dust—
 Blow the trumpet, draw the sword—
I'd ha' sooner drownded fust
 'Stead of 'im beside the ford.
 Ford, ford, ford o' Kabul river,
  Ford o' Kabul river in the dark!
 You can 'ear the 'orses threshin'; you can 'ear the men a-splashin',
  'Cross the ford o' Kabul river in the dark.

Kabul town was ours to take—
 Blow the trumpet, draw the sword—
I'd ha' left it for 'is sake—
 'Im that left me by the ford.
 Ford, ford, ford o' Kabul river,
  Ford o' Kabul river in the dark!
 It's none so bloomin' dry there; ain't you never comin' nigh there,
  'Cross the ford o' Kabul river in the dark?

Kabul town'll go to hell—
 Blow the trumpet, draw the sword—
'Fore I see him 'live an' well—
 'Im the best beside the ford.
 Ford, ford, ford o' Kabul river,
  Ford o' Kabul river in the dark!
 Gawd 'elp 'em if they blunder, for their boots'll pull 'em under,
  By the ford o' Kabul river in the dark.

Turn your 'orse from Kabul town—
 Blow the trumpet, draw the sword—
'Im an' 'arf my troop is down,
 Down and drownded by the ford.
 Ford, ford, ford o' Kabul river,
  Ford o' Kabul river in the dark!
 There's the river low an' fallin', but it ain't no use a-callin'
  'Cross the ford o' Kabul river in the dark!

GENTLEMEN-RANKERS

To the legion of the lost ones, to the cohort of the damned,
    To my brethren in their sorrow overseas,
Sings a gentleman of England cleanly bred, machinely crammed,
    And a trooper of the Empress, if you please.
Yes, a trooper of the forces who has run his own six horses,
    And faith he went the pace and went it blind,
And the world was more than kin while he held the ready tin,
    But to-day the Sergeant's something less than kind.
        We're poor little lambs who've lost our way,
           Baa! Baa! Baa!
        We're little black sheep who've gone astray,
           Baa—aa—aa!
        Gentlemen-rankers out on the spree,
        Damned from here to Eternity,
        God ha' mercy on such as we,
           Baa! Yah! Bah!

Oh, it's sweet to sweat through stables, sweet to empty kitchen slops,
    And it's sweet to hear the tales the troopers tell,
To dance with blowzy housemaids at the regimental hops
    And thrash the cad who says you waltz too well.
Yes, it makes you cock-a-hoop to be "Rider" to your troop,
    And branded with a blasted worsted spur,
When you envy, O how keenly, one poor Tommy living cleanly
    Who blacks your boots and sometimes calls you "Sir."

If the home we never write to, and the oaths we never keep,
    And all we know most distant and most dear,
Across the snoring barrack-room return to break our sleep,
    Can you blame us if we soak ourselves in beer?
When the drunken comrade mutters and the great guard-lantern gutters
    And the horror of our fall is written plain,
Every secret, self-revealing on the aching whitewashed ceiling,
    Do you wonder that we drug ourselves from pain?

We have done with Hope and Honour, we are lost to Love and Truth,
    We are dropping down the ladder rung by rung,

And the measure of our torment is the measure of our youth.
    God help us, for we knew the worst too young!
Our shame is clean repentance for the crime that brought the sentence,
    Our pride it is to know no spur of pride,
And the Curse of Reuben holds us till an alien turf enfolds us
    And we die, and none can tell Them where we died.
        We're poor little lambs who've lost our way,
           Baa! Baa! Baa!
        We're little black sheep who've gone astray,
           Baa—aa—aa!
        Gentlemen-rankers out on the spree,
        Damned from here to Eternity,
        God ha' mercy on such as we,
           Baa! Yah! Bah!

ROUTE MARCHIN'

We're marchin' on relief over Injia's sunny plains,
A little front o' Christmas-time an' just be'ind the Rains;
Ho! get away, you bullock-man, you've 'eard the bugle blowed,
There's a regiment a-comin' down the Grand Trunk Road;
        With its best foot first
        And the road a-sliding past,
        An' every bloomin' campin'-ground exactly like the last;
        While the Big Drum says,
        With 'is *"rowdy-dowdy-dow!"*—
        "Kiko kissywarsti don't you *hamsher argy jow?"*[1]

Oh, there's them Injian temples to admire when you see.
There's the peacock round the corner an' the monkey up the tree,
An' there's that rummy silver-grass a-wavin' in the wind,
An' the old Grand Trunk a-trailin' like a rifle-sling be'ind.
        While it's best foot first, . . .

At half-past five's Revelly, an' our tents they down must come,
Like a lot of button-mushrooms when you pick 'em up at 'ome.
But it's over in a minute, an' at six the column starts,
While the women and the kiddies sit an' shiver in the carts.
        An' it's best foot first, . . .

[1] Why don't you get on?

Oh, then it's open order, an' we lights our pipes an' sings,
An' we talks about our rations an' a lot of other things,
An' we thinks o' friends in England, an' we wonders what they're at,
An' 'ow they would admire for to hear us sling the *bat*.[2]
      An' it's best foot first, . . .

It's none so bad o' Sundays, when you're lyin' at your ease,
To watch the kites a-wheelin' round them feather-'eaded trees,
For although there ain't no women, yet there ain't no barrick-yards,
So the orficers goes shootin' an' the men they plays at cards.
      Till it's best foot first, . . .

So 'ark an' 'eed, you rookies, which is always grumblin' sore,
There's worser things than marchin' from Umballa to Cawnpore;
An' if your 'eels are blistered an' they feels to 'urt like 'ell,
You drop some tallow in your socks an' that will make 'em well.
      For it's best foot first, . . .

We're marchin' on relief over Injia's coral strand,
Eight 'undred fightin' Englishmen, the Colonel, and the Band;
Ho! get away, you bullock-man, you've 'eard the bugle blowed,
There's a regiment a-comin' down the Grand Trunk Road;
        With its best foot first
        And the road a-sliding past,
        An' every bloomin' campin'-ground exactly like the last;
        While the Big Drum says,
        With 'is *"rowdy-dowdy-dow!"*—
        "Kiko kissywarsti don't you *hamsher argy jow?"*

PRIVATE ORTHERIS'S SONG

"THE COURTING OF DINAH SHADD."—LIFE'S HANDICAP

    My girl she give me the go onest,
      When I was a London lad;
    An' I went on the drink for a fortnight,
      An' then I went to the bad.

---

[2] Language. Thomas's first and firmest conviction is that he is a profound Orientalist and a fluent speaker of Hindustani. As a matter of fact, he depends largely on the sign-language.

The Queen she give me a shillin'
To fight for 'er over the seas;
But Guv'ment built me a fever-trap,
An' Injia give me disease.

(*Chorus*) Ho! don't you 'eed what a girl says,
An' don't you go for the beer;
But I was an ass when I was at grass,
An' that is why I'm 'ere.

I fired a shot at a Afghan,
The beggar 'e fired again,
An' I lay on my bed with a 'ole in my 'ed,
An' missed the next campaign!
I up with my gun at a Burman
Who carried a bloomin' *dah,*
But the cartridge stuck and the bay'nit bruk,
An' all I got was the scar.

(*Chorus*) Ho! don't you aim at a Afghan,
When you stand on the skyline clear;
An' don't you go for a Burman
If none o' your friends is near.

I served my time for a Corp'ral,
An' wetted my stripes with pop,
For I went on the bend with a intimate friend,
An' finished the night in the 'shop.'
I served my time for a Sergeant;
The Colonel 'e sez 'No!
The most you'll see is a full C.B.'
An'. . . . very next night 'twas so!

(*Chorus*) Ho! don't you go for a Corp'ral
Unless your 'ed is clear;
But I was an ass when I was at grass,
An' that is why I'm 'ere.

I've tasted the luck o' the Army
In barrack an' camp an' clink,
An' I lost my tip through the bloomin' trip
Along o' the women an' drink.

I'm down at the heel o' my service,
  An' when I am laid on the shelf,
My very worst friend from beginning to end
  By the blood of a mouse was myself!

  (*Chorus*) Ho! don't you 'eed what a girl says,
      An' don't you go for the beer;
      But I was an ass when I was at grass,
      An' that is why I'm 'ere!

SHILLIN' A DAY

My name is O'Kelly, I've heard the Revelly
From Birr to Bareilly, from Leeds to Lahore,
Hong-Kong and Peshawur,
Lucknow and Etawah,
And fifty-five more all endin' in "pore."
Black Death and his quickness, the depth and the thickness
Of sorrow and sickness I've known on my way,
But I'm old and I'm nervis,
I'm cast from the Service,
And all I deserve is a shillin' a day.

    (*Chorus*) Shillin' a day,
        Bloomin' good pay—
        Lucky to touch it, a shillin' a day!

Oh, it drives me half crazy to think of the days I
Went slap for the Ghazi, my sword at my side,
When we rode Hell-for-leather
Both squadrons together,
That didn't care whether we lived or we died.
But it's no use despairin', my wife must go charin'
An' me commissairin', the pay-bills to better,
So if me you be'old
In the wet and the cold,
By the Grand Metropold, won't you give me a letter?

(*Full chorus*) Give 'im a letter—
'Can't do no better,
Late Troop-Sergeant-Major an'—runs with a letter!
Think what 'e's been,
Think what 'e's seen.
Think of his pension an'—
GAWD SAVE THE QUEEN!

"BACK TO THE ARMY AGAIN"

I'm 'ere in a ticky ulster an' a broken billycock 'at,
A-layin' on to the sergeant I don't know a gun from a bat;
My shirt's doin' duty for jacket, my sock's stickin' out o' my boots,
An' I'm learnin' the damned old goose-step along o' the new recruits!

      Back to the Army again, sergeant,
        Back to the Army again.
      Don't look so 'ard, for I 'aven't no card,
        I'm back to the Army again!

I done my six years' service. 'Er Majesty sez: "Good day—
You'll please to come when you're rung for, an' 'ere's your 'ole back-pay:
An' fourpence a day for baccy—an' bloomin' gen'rous, too;
An' now you can make your fortune—the same as your orf'cers do."

      Back to the Army again, sergeant,
        Back to the Army again.
      'Ow did I learn to do right-about-turn?
        I'm back to the Army again!

A man o' four-an'-twenty that 'asn't learned of a trade—
Beside "Reserve" agin' him—'e'd better be never made.
I tried my luck for a quarter, an' that was enough for me,
An' I thought of 'Er Majesty's barricks, an' I thought I'd go an' see.

      Back to the Army again, sergeant,
        Back to the Army again.
      'Tisn't my fault if I dress when I 'alt—
        I'm back to the Army again!

The sergeant arst no questions, but 'e winked the other eye,
'E sez to me, " 'Shun!" an' I shunted, the same as in days gone by;
For 'e saw the set o' my shoulders, an' I couldn't 'elp 'oldin' straight
When me an' the other rookies come under the barrick-gate.

> Back to the Army again, sergeant,
>   Back to the Army again.
> 'Oo would ha' thought I could carry an' port?[1]
>   I'm back to the Army again!

I took my bath, an' I wallered—for, Gawd, I needed it so!
I smelt the smell o' the barricks, I 'eard the bugles go.
I 'eard the feet on the gravel—the feet o' the men what drill—
An' I sez to my flutterin' 'eart-strings, I sez to 'em, "Peace, be still!"

> Back to the Army again, sergeant,
>   Back to the Army again.
> 'Oo said I knew when the troopship was due?
>   I'm back to the Army again!

I carried my slops to the tailor; I sez to 'im, "None o' your lip!
You tight 'em over the shoulders, an' loose 'em over the 'ip,
For the set o' the tunic's 'orrid." An' 'e sez to me, "Strike me dead,
But I thought you was used to the business!" an' so 'e done what I said.

> Back to the Army again, sergeant,
>   Back to the Army again.
> Rather too free with my fancies? Wot—me?
>   I'm back to the Army again!

Next week I'll 'ave 'em fitted; I'll buy me a swagger-cane;
They'll let me free o' the barricks to walk on the Hoe again,
In the name o' William Parsons, that used to be Edward Clay,
An'—any pore beggar that wants it can draw my fourpence a day!

> Back to the Army again, sergeant,
>   Back to the Army again.
> Out o' the cold an' the rain, sergeant,
>   Out o' the cold an' the rain.
>   'Oo's there?

[1] Carry and port his rifle.

A man that's too good to be lost you,
  A man that is 'andled an' made—
A man that will pay what 'e cost you
  In learnin' the others their trade—parade!
You're droppin' the pick o' the Army
  Because you don't 'elp 'em remain,
But drives 'em to cheat to get out o' the street
  An' back to the Army again!

"BIRDS OF PREY" MARCH

TROOPS FOR FOREIGN SERVICE

March! The mud is cakin' good about our trousies.
  Front!—eyes front, an' watch the Colour-casin's drip.
Front! The faces of the women in the 'ouses
  Ain't the kind o' things to take aboard the ship.

Cheer! An' we'll never march to victory.
Cheer! An' we'll never live to 'ear the cannon roar!
    The Large Birds o' Prey
    They will carry us away,
An' you'll never see your soldiers any more!

Wheel! Oh, keep your touch; we're goin' round a corner.
  Time!—mark time, an' let the men be'ind us close.
Lord! The transport's full, an' 'alf our lot not on 'er—
  Cheer, Oh, cheer! We're going off where no one knows.

March! The Devil's none so black as 'e is painted!
  Cheer! We'll 'ave some fun before we're put away.
'Alt an' 'and 'er out—a woman's gone and fainted!
  Cheer! Get on!—Gawd 'elp the married men to-day!

Hoi! Come up, you 'ungry beggars, to yer sorrow.
  ('Ear them say they want their tea, an' want it quick!)
You won't have no mind for slingers,[1] not to-morrow—
  No; you'll put the 'tween-decks stove out, bein' sick!

[1] Bread soaked in tea.

'Alt! The married kit 'as all to go before us!
'Course it's blocked the bloomin' gangway up again!
Cheer, Oh, cheer the 'Orse Guards watchin' tender o'er us,
Keepin' us since eight this mornin' in the rain!

Stuck in 'eavy marchin'-order, sopped and wringin'—
Sick, before our time to watch 'er 'eave an' fall,
'Ere's your 'appy 'ome at last, an' stop your singin'.
'Alt! Fall in along the troop-deck! Silence all!

Cheer! For we'll never live to see no bloomin' victory!
Cheer! An' we'll never live to 'ear the cannon roar!
   (One cheer more!)
    The jackal an' the kite
    'Ave an 'ealthy appetite,
An' you'll never see your soldiers any more! ('Ip! Urroar!)
    The eagle an' the crow
    They are waitin' ever so,
An' you'll never see your soldiers any more! ('Ip! Urroar!)
    Yes, the Large Birds o' Prey
    They will carry us away,
An' you'll never see your soldiers any more!

"SOLDIER AN' SAILOR TOO"

THE ROYAL REGIMENT OF MARINES

As I was spittin' into the Ditch aboard o' the *Crocodile,*
I seed a man on a man-o'-war got up in the Reg'lars' style.
'E was scrapin' the paint from off of 'er plates, an' I sez to 'im, " 'Oo are
    you?"
Sez 'e, "I'm a Jolly—'Er Majesty's Jolly—soldier an' sailor too!"
Now 'is work begins by Gawd knows when, and 'is work is never through;
'E isn't one o' the reg'lar Line, nor 'e isn't one of the crew.
'E's kind of a giddy harumfrodite—soldier an' sailor too!

An', after, I met 'im all over the world, a-doin' all kinds of things,
Like landin' 'isself with a Gatlin' gun to talk to them 'eathen kings;
'E sleeps in an 'ammick instead of a cot, an' 'e drills with the deck on a
    slew,

An' 'e sweats like a Jolly—'Er Majesty's Jolly—soldier an' sailor too!
For there isn't a job on the top o' the earth the beggar don't know, nor do—
You can leave 'im at night on a bald man's 'ead, to paddle 'is own canoe—
'E's sort of a bloomin' cosmopolouse—soldier an' sailor too.

We've fought 'em in trooper, we've fought 'em in dock, and drunk with
    'em in betweens,
When they called us the seasick scull'ry-maids, an' we called 'em the Ass-
    Marines;
But, when we was down for a double fatigue, from Woolwich to Ber-
    nardmyo,
We sent for the Jollies—'Er Majesty's Jollies—soldier an' sailor too!
They think for 'emselves, an' they steal for 'emselves, and they never ask
    what's to do,
But they're camped an' fed an' they're up an' fed before our bugle's blew.
Ho! they ain't no limpin' procrastitutes—soldier an' sailor too.

You may say we are fond of an 'arness-cut, or 'ootin' in barrick-yards,
Or startin' a Board School mutiny along o' the Onion Guards;[1]
But once in a while we can finish in style for the ends of the earth to view,
The same as the Jollies—'Er Majesty's Jollies—soldier an' sailor too!
They come of our lot, they was brothers to us; they was beggars we'd met
    an' knew;
Yes, barrin' an inch in the chest an' the arm, they was doubles o' me an'
    you;
For they weren't no special chrysanthemums—soldier an' sailor too!

To take your chance in the thick of a rush, with firing all about,
Is nothing so bad when you've cover to 'and an' leave an' likin' to shout;
But to stand an' be still to the *Birken'ead* drill[2] is a damn' tough bullet to
    chew,
An' they done it, the Jollies—'Er Majesty's Jollies—soldier an' sailor too!
Their work was done when it 'adn't begun; they was younger nor me an'
    you;
Their choice it was plain between drownin' in 'eaps an' bein' mopped by
    the screw,
So they stood an' was still to the *Birken'ead* drill, soldier an' sailor too!

[1] Long ago, a battalion of the Guards was sent to Bermuda as a punishment for riotous conduct in barracks.
[2] In 1852 the *Birkenhead* transport was sunk off Simon's Bay. The Marines aboard her went down as drawn up on her deck.

We're most of us liars, we're 'arf of us thieves, an' the rest are as rank as can be,
But once in a while we can finish in style (which I 'ope it won't 'appen to me).
But it makes you think better o' you an' your friends, an' the work you may 'ave to do,
When you think o' the sinkin' *Victorier's*[1] Jollies—soldier an' sailor too!
Now there isn't no room for to say ye don't know—they 'ave proved it plain and true—
That, whether it's Widow, or whether it's ship, *Victorier's* work is to do,
An' they done it, the Jollies—'Er Majesty's Jollies—soldier an' sailor too!

SAPPERS

ROYAL ENGINEERS

When the Waters were dried an' the Earth did appear,
    ("It's all one," says the Sapper),
The Lord He created the Engineer,
    Her Majesty's Royal Engineer,
    With the rank and pay of a Sapper!

When the Flood came along for an extra monsoon,
'Twas Noah constructed the first pontoon
    To the plans of Her Majesty's, etc.

But after fatigue in the wet an' the sun,
Old Noah got drunk, which he wouldn't ha' done
    If he'd trained with, etc.

When the Tower o' Babel had mixed up men's *bat*,[1]
Some clever civilian was managing that,
    An' none of, etc.

When the Jews had a fight at the foot of a hill,
Young Joshua ordered the sun to stand still,
    For he was a Captain of Engineers, etc.

[1] Admiral Tryon's flagship, sunk in collision in 1893.
[1] Talk.

When the Children of Israel made bricks without straw,
They were learnin' the regular work of our Corps,
　　The work of, etc.

For ever since then, if a war they would wage,
Behold us a-shinin' on history's page—
　　First page for, etc.

We lay down their sidings an' help 'em entrain,
An' we sweep up their mess through the bloomin' campaign,
　　In the style of, etc.

They send us in front with a fuse an' a mine
To blow up the gates that are rushed by the Line,
　　But bent by, etc.

They send us behind with a pick an' a spade,
To dig for the guns of a bullock-brigade
　　Which has asked for, etc.

We work under escort in trousers and shirt,
An' the heathen they plug us tail-up in the dirt,
　　Annoying, etc.

We blast out the rock an' we shovel the mud,
We make 'em good roads an'—they roll down the *khud*,[2]
　　Reporting, etc.

We make 'em their bridges, their wells, an' their huts,
An' the telegraph-wire the enemy cuts,
　　An' it's blamed on, etc.

An' when we return, an' from war we would cease,
They grudge us adornin' the billets of peace,
　　Which are kept for, etc.

We build 'em nice barracks—they swear they are bad.
That our Colonels are Methodist, married or mad,
　　Insultin', etc.

[2] Hillside.

They haven't no manners nor gratitude too,
For the more that we help 'em, the less will they do,
   But mock at, etc.

Now the Line's but a man with a gun in his hand,
An' Cavalry's only what horses can stand,
   When helped by, etc.

Artillery moves by the leave o' the ground,
But *we* are the men that do something all round,
   For *we* are, etc.

I have stated it plain, an' my argument's thus
   ("It's all one," says the Sapper)
There's only one Corps which is perfect—that's us;
   An' they call us Her Majesty's Engineers,
   Her Majesty's Royal Engineers,
   With the rank and pay of a Sapper!

THAT DAY

It got beyond all orders an' it got beyond all 'ope;
   It got to shammin' wounded an' retirin' from the 'alt.
'Ole companies was lookin' for the nearest road to slope;
   It were just a bloomin' knock-out—an' our fault!

   Now there ain't no chorus 'ere to give,
   Nor there ain't no band to play;
   An' I wish I was dead 'fore I done what I did,
   Or seen what I seed that day!

We was sick o' bein' punished, an' we let 'em know it, too;
   An' a company-commander up an' 'it us with a sword,
An' some one shouted "'Ook it!" an' it come to *sove-ki-poo,*
   An' we chucked our rifles from us—O my Gawd!

There was thirty dead an' wounded on the ground we wouldn't keep—
   No, there wasn't more than twenty when the front begun to go—
But, Christ! along the line o' flight they cut us up like sheep,
   An' that was all we gained by doin' so!

I 'eard the knives be'ind me, but I dursn't face my man,
  Nor I don't know where I went to, 'cause I didn't 'alt to see,
Till I 'eard a beggar squealin' out for quarter as 'e ran,
  An' I thought I knew the voice an'—it was me!

We was 'idin' under bedsteads more than 'arf a march away:
  We was lyin' up like rabbits all about the country-side;
An' the Major cursed 'is Maker 'cause 'e'd lived to see that day,
  An' the Colonel broke 'is sword acrost, an' cried.

We was rotten 'fore we started—we was never disciplined;
  We made it out a favour if an order was obeyed.
Yes, every little drummer 'ad 'is rights an' wrongs to mind,
  So we had to pay for teachin'—an' we paid!

The papers 'id it 'andsome, but you know the Army knows;
  We was put to groomin' camels till the regiments withdrew,
An' they gave us each a medal for subduin' England's foes,
  An' I 'ope you like my song—because it's true!

> *An' there ain't no chorus 'ere to give,*
>   *Nor there ain't no band to play;*
> *But I wish I was dead 'fore I done what I did,*
>   *Or seen what I seed that day!*

"THE MEN THAT FOUGHT AT MINDEN"

IN THE LODGE OF INSTRUCTION

The men that fought at Minden, they was rookies in their time—
  So was them that fought at Waterloo!
All the 'ole command, yuss, from Minden to Maiwand,
  They was once dam' sweeps like you!

> *Then do not be discouraged, 'Eaven is your 'elper,*
>   *We'll learn you not to forget;*
> *An' you mustn't swear an' curse, or you'll only catch it worse,*
>   *For we'll make you soldiers yet!*

The men that fought at Minden, they 'ad stocks beneath their chins,
  Six inch 'igh an' more;

But fatigue it was their pride, and they *would* not be denied
    To clean the cook-'ouse floor.

The men that fought at Minden, they had anarchistic bombs
    Served to 'em by the name of 'and-grenades;
But they got it in the eye (same as you will by-an'-by)
    When they clubbed their field-parades.

The men that fought at Minden, they 'ad buttons up an' down,
    Two-an'-twenty dozen of 'em told;
But they didn't grouse an' shirk at an hour's extry work,
    They kept 'em bright as gold.

The men that fought at Minden, they was armed with musketoons,
    Also, they was drilled by 'alberdiers.
I don't know what they were, but the sergeants took good care
    They washed be'ind their ears.

The men that fought at Minden, they 'ad ever cash in 'and
    Which they did not bank nor save,
But spent it gay an' free on their betters—such as me—
    For the good advice I gave.

The men that fought at Minden, they was civil—yuss, they was—
    Never didn't talk o' rights an' wrongs,
But they got it with the toe (same as you will git it—so!)—
    For interrupting songs.

The men that fought at Minden, they was several other things
    Which I don't remember clear;
But *that's* the reason why, now the six-year men are dry,
    The rooks will stand the beer!

   Then do not be discouraged, 'Eaven is your 'elper,
    We'll learn you not to forget.
   An' you mustn't swear an' curse, or you'll only catch it worse,
    An' we'll make you soldiers yet!

   Soldiers yet, if you've got it in you—
    All for the sake of the Core;
   Soldiers yet, if we 'ave to skin you—
    Run an' get the beer, Johnny Raw—Johnny Raw!
    Ho! run an' get the beer, Johnny Raw!

CHOLERA CAMP

INFANTRY IN INDIA

We've got the cholera in camp—it's worse than forty fights;
We're dyin' in the wilderness the same as Isrulites.
It's before us, an' be'ind us, an' we cannot get away,
An' the doctor's just reported we've ten more to-day!

   Oh, strike your camp an' go, the bugle's callin',
      The Rains are fallin'—
The dead are bushed an' stoned to keep 'em safe below.
The Band's a-doin' all she knows to cheer us;
The Chaplain's gone and prayed to Gawd to 'ear us—
      To 'ear us—
O Lord, for it's a-killin' of us so!

Since August, when it started, it's been stickin' to our tail,
Though they've 'ad us out by marches an' they've 'ad us back by rail;
But it runs as fast as troop trains, and we cannot get away,
An' the sick-list to the Colonel makes ten more to-day.

There ain't no fun in women nor there ain't no bite to drink;
It's much too wet for shootin', we can only march and think;
An' at evenin', down the *nullahs*, we can 'ear the jackals say,
"Get up, you rotten beggars, you've ten more to-day!"

'Twould make a monkey cough to see our way o' doin' things—
Lieutenants takin' companies an' Captains takin' wings,
An' Lances actin' Sergeants—eight file to obey—
For we've lots o' quick promotion on ten deaths a day!

Our Colonel's white an' twitterly—'e gets no sleep nor food,
But mucks about in 'orspital where nothing does no good.
'E sends us 'eaps o' comforts, all bought from 'is pay—
But there aren't much comfort 'andy on ten deaths a day.

Our Chaplain's got a banjo, an' a skinny mule 'e rides,
An' the stuff he says an' sings us, Lord, it makes us split our sides!
With 'is black coat-tails a-bobbin' to *Ta-ra-ra Boom-der-ay!*
'E's the proper kind o' *padre* for ten deaths a day.

An' Father Victor 'elps 'im with our Roman Catholicks—
He knows an 'eap of Irish songs an' rummy conjurin'-tricks;
An' the two they works together when it comes to play or pray.
So we keep the ball a-rollin' on ten deaths a day.

We've got the cholerer in camp—we've got it 'ot an' sweet.
It ain't no Christmas dinner, but it's 'elped an' we must eat.
We've gone beyond the funkin', 'cause we've found it doesn't pay,
An' we're rockin' round the districk on ten deaths a day!

> Then strike your camp an' go, the Rains are fallin',
>   The Bugle's callin'!
> The dead are bushed an' stoned to keep 'em safe below!
> An' them that do not like it they can lump it,
> An' them that cannot stand it they can jump it;
> We've got to die somewhere—some way—some 'ow—
> We might as well begin to do it now!
> Then, Number One, let down the tent-pole slow,
> Knock out the pegs an' 'old the corners—so!
> Fold in the flies, furl up the ropes, an' stow!
> Oh, strike—oh, strike your camp an' go!
>   (Gawd 'elp us!)

THE LADIES

> I've taken my fun where I've found it;
>   I've rogued an' I've ranged in my time;
> I've 'ad my pickin' o' sweethearts,
>   An' four o' the lot was prime.
> One was an 'arf-caste widow,
>   One was a woman at Prome,
> One was the wife of a *jemadar-sais*[1]
>   An' one is a girl at 'ome.
>
> Now I aren't no 'and with the ladies,
>   For, takin' 'em all along,
> You never can say till you've tried 'em,
>   An' then you are like to be wrong.

[1] Head-groom.

There's times when you'll think that you mightn't,
  There's times when you'll know that you might;
But the things you will learn from the Yellow an' Brown,
  They'll 'elp you a lot with the White!

I was a young un at 'Oogli,
  Shy as a girl to begin;
Aggie de Castrer she made me,
  An' Aggie was clever as sin;
Older than me, but my first un—
  More like a mother she were—
Showed me the way to promotion an' pay,
  An' I learned about women from 'er!

Then I was ordered to Burma,
  Actin' in charge o' Bazar,
An' I got me a tiddy live 'eathen
  Through buyin' supplies off 'er pa.
Funny an' yellow an' faithful—
  Doll in a teacup she were—
But we lived on the square, like a true-married pair,
  An' I learned about women from 'er!

Then we was shifted to Neemuch
  (Or I might ha' been keepin' 'er now),
An' I took with a shiny she-devil,
  The wife of a nigger at Mhow;
Taught me the gipsy-folks' *bolee*;[1]
  Kind o' volcano she were,
For she knifed me one night 'cause I wished she was white,
  And I learned about women from 'er!

Then I come 'ome in a trooper,
  'Long of a kid o' sixteen—
'Girl from a convent at Meerut,
  The straightest I ever 'ave seen.
Love at first sight was 'er trouble,
  She didn't know what it were;
An' I wouldn't do such, 'cause I liked 'er too much,
  But—I learned about women from 'er!

[1] Slang.

I've taken my fun where I've found it,
   An' now I must pay for my fun,
For the more you 'ave known o' the others
   The less will you settle to one;
An' the end of it's sittin' and thinkin',
   An' dreamin' Hell-fires to see;
So be warned by my lot (which I know you will not),
   An' learn about women from me!

   What did the Colonel's Lady think?
     Nobody never knew.
   Somebody asked the Sergeant's Wife,
     An' she told 'em true!
   When you get to a man in the case,
     They're like as a row of pins—
   For the Colonel's Lady an' Judy O'Grady
     Are sisters under their skins!

BILL 'AWKINS

" 'As anybody seen Bill 'Awkins?"
   "Now 'ow in the devil would I know?"
" 'E's taken my girl out walkin',
   An' I've got to tell 'im so—
     Gawd—bless—'im!
   I've got to tell 'im so."

"D'yer know what 'e's like, Bill 'Awkins?"
   "Now what in the devil would I care?"
" 'E's the livin', breathin' image of an organ-grinder's monkey,
   With a pound of grease in 'is 'air—
     Gawd—bless—'im!
   An' a pound o' grease in 'is 'air."

"An' s'pose you met Bill 'Awkins,
   Now what in the devil 'ud ye do?"
"I'd open 'is cheek to 'is chin-strap buckle,
   An' bung up 'is both eyes, too—
     Gawd—bless—'im!
   An' bung up 'is both eyes, too!"

"Look 'ere, where 'e comes, Bill 'Awkins!
  Now, what in the devil will you say?"
"It isn't fit an' proper to be fightin' on a Sunday,
  So I'll pass 'im the time o' day—
      Gawd—bless—'im!
  I'll pass 'im the time o' day!"

THE MOTHER-LODGE

There was Rundle, Station Master,
    An' Beazeley of the Rail,
An' 'Ackman, Commissariat,
    An' Donkin o' the Jail;
An' Blake, Conductor-Sergeant,
    Our Master twice was 'e,
With 'im that kept the Europe-shop,
    Old Framjee Eduljee.

Outside—"Sergeant! Sir! Salute! Salaam!"
Inside—"Brother," an' it doesn't do no 'arm.
We met upon the Level an' we parted on the Square,
An' I was Junior Deacon in my Mother-Lodge out there!

We'd Bola Nath, Accountant,
    An' Saul the Aden Jew,
An' Din Mohammed, draughtsman
    Of the Survey Office too;
There was Babu Chuckerbutty,
    An' Amir Singh the Sikh,
An' Castro from the fittin'-sheds,
    The Roman Catholick!

We 'adn't good regalia,
    An' our Lodge was old an' bare,
But we knew the Ancient Landmarks,
    An' we kep' 'em to a hair;
An' lookin' on it backwards
    It often strikes me thus,
There ain't such things as infidels,
    Excep', per'aps, it's us.

For monthly, after Labour,
    We'd all sit down and smoke
(We dursn't give no banquets,
    Lest a Brother's caste were broke),
An' man on man got talkin'
    Religion an' the rest,
An' every man comparin'
    Of the God 'e knew the best.

So man on man got talkin',
    An' not a Brother stirred
Till mornin' waked the parrots
    An' that dam' brain-fever-bird;
We'd say 'twas 'ighly curious,
    An' we'd all ride 'ome to bed,
With Mo'ammed, God, an' Shiva
    Changin' pickets in our 'ead.

Full oft on Guv'ment service
    This rovin' foot 'ath pressed,
An' bore fraternal greetin's
    To the Lodges east an' west,
Accordin' as commanded,
    From Kohat to Singapore,
But I wish that I might see them
    In my Mother-Lodge once more!

I wish that I might see them,
    My Brethren black an' brown,
With the trichies smellin' pleasant
    An' the *hog-darn*[1] passin' down;
An' the old khansamah[2] snorin'
    On the bottle-khana[3] floor,
Like a Master in good standing
    With my Mother-Lodge once more.

Outside—"Sergeant! Sir! Salute! Salaam!"
Inside—"Brother," an' it doesn't do no 'arm.
We met upon the Level an' we parted on the Square,
An' I was Junior Deacon in my Mother-Lodge out there!

  [1] Cigar-lighter.   [2] Butler.   [3] Pantry.

"FOLLOW ME 'OME"

There was no one like 'im, 'Orse or Foot,
 Nor any o' the Guns I knew;
An' because it was so, why, o' course 'e went an' died,
 Which is just what the best men do.

 So it's knock out your pipes an' follow me!
 An' it's finish up your swipes an' follow me!
 Oh, 'ark to the big drum callin',
 Follow me—follow me 'ome!

'Is mare she neighs the 'ole day long,
 She paws the 'ole night through,
An' she won't take 'er feed 'cause o' waitin' for 'is step,
 Which is just what a beast would do.

'Is girl she goes with a bombardier
 Before 'er month is through;
An' the banns are up in church, for she's got the beggar hooked,
 Which is just what a girl would do.

We fought 'bout a dog—last week it were—
 No more than a round or two;
But I strook 'im cruel 'ard, an' I wish I 'adn't now,
 Which is just what a man can't do.

'E was all that I 'ad in the way of a friend,
 An' I've 'ad to find one new;
But I'd give my pay an' stripe for to get the beggar back,
 Which it's just too late to do!

 So it's knock out your pipes an' follow me!
 An' it's finish up your swipes an' follow me!
 Oh, 'ark to the fifes a-crawlin'!
 Follow me—follow me 'ome!

 Take 'im away! 'E's gone where the best men go.
 Take 'im away! An' the gun-wheels turnin' slow.

Take 'im away! There's more from the place 'e come.
Take 'im away, with the limber an' the drum.

For it's "Three rounds blank" an' follow me,
An' it's "Thirteen rank" an' follow me;
  Oh, passin' the love o' women,
    Follow me—follow me 'ome!

THE SERGEANT'S WEDDIN'

'E was warned agin 'er—
  That's what made 'im look;
She was warned agin' 'im—
  That is why she took.
'Wouldn't 'ear no reason,
  'Went an' done it blind;
We know all about 'em,
  They've got all to find!

Cheer for the Sergeant's weddin'—
  Give 'em one cheer more!
Grey gun-'orses in the lando,
  An' a rogue is married to, etc.

What's the use o' tellin'
  'Arf the lot she's been?
'E's a bloomin' robber,
  An' 'e keeps canteen.
'Ow did 'e get 'is buggy?
  Gawd, you needn't ask!
'Made 'is forty gallon
  Out of every cask!

Watch 'im, with 'is 'air cut,
  Count us filin' by—
Won't the Colonel praise 'is
  Pop—u—lar—i—ty!
We 'ave scores to settle—
  Scores for more than beer;
She's the girl to pay 'em—
  That is why we're 'ere!

See the Chaplain thinkin'?
  See the women smile?
Twig the married winkin'
  As they take the aisle?
Keep your side-arms quiet,
  Dressin' by the Band.
Ho! You 'oly beggars,
  Cough be'ind your 'and!

Now it's done an' over,
  'Ear the organ squeak,
" 'Voice that breathed o'er Eden"—
  Ain't she got the cheek!
White an' laylock ribbons,
  'Think yourself so fine!
I'd pray Gawd to take yer
  'Fore I made yer mine!

Escort to the kerridge,
  Wish 'im luck, the brute!
Chuck the slippers after—
  (Pity 'tain't a boot!)
Bowin' like a lady,
  Blushin' like a lad—
'Oo would say to see 'em
  Both is rotten bad?

Cheer for the Sergeant's weddin'—
  Give 'em one cheer more!
Grey gun-'orses in the lando,
  An' a rogue is married to, etc.

THE JACKET

ROYAL HORSE ARTILLERY

Through the Plagues of Egyp' we was chasin' Arabi,
  Gettin' down an' shovin' in the sun;
An' you might 'ave called us dirty, an' you might ha' called us dry,
  An' you might 'ave 'eard us talkin' at the gun.

But the Captain 'ad 'is jacket, an' the jacket it was new—
    ('Orse Gunners, listen to my song!)
An' the wettin' of the jacket is the proper thing to do,
    Nor we didn't keep 'im waiting very long.

One day they gave us orders for to shell a sand redoubt,
    Loadin' down the axle-arms with case;
But the Captain knew 'is dooty, an' he took the crackers out
    An' he put some proper liquor in its place.
An' the Captain saw the shrapnel, which is six-an'-thirty clear.
    ('Orse Gunners, listen to my song!)
"Will you draw the weight," sez 'e, "or will you draw the beer?"
    An' we didn't keep 'im waiting very long.

    For the Captain, etc.

Then we trotted gentle, not to break the bloomin' glass,
    Though the Arabites 'ad all their ranges marked;
But we dursn't 'ardly gallop, for the most was bottled Bass,
    An' we'd dreamed of it since we was disembarked.
So we fired economic with the shells we 'ad in 'and,
    ('Orse Gunners, listen to my song!)
But the beggars under cover 'ad the impidence to stand,
    An' we couldn't keep 'em waitin' very long.

    And the Captain, etc.

So we finished 'arf the liquor (an' the Captain took champagne),
    An' the Arabites was shootin' all the while;
An' we left our wounded 'appy with the empties on the plain,
    An' we used the bloomin' guns for proje*tile!*
We limbered up an' galloped—there was nothin' else to do—
    ('Orse Gunners, listen to my song!)
An' the Battery come a-boundin' like a boundin' kangaroo,
    But they didn't watch us comin' very long.

    As the Captain, etc.

We was goin' most extended—we was drivin' very fine,
    An' the Arabites were losin' 'igh an' wide,
Till the Captain took the glacis with a rattlin' "right incline,"
    An' we dropped upon their 'eads the other side.

Then we give 'em quarter—such as 'adn't up and cut
('Orse Gunners, listen to my song!)
An' the Captain stood a limberful of fizzy somethin' Brutt,
But we didn't leave it fizzing very long.

For the Captain, etc.

We might ha' been court-martialled, but it all come out all right.
When they signalled us to join the main command,
There was every round expended, there was every gunner tight,
An' the Captain waved a corkscrew in 'is 'and!

But the Captain 'ad 'is jacket, etc.

THE 'EATHEN

The 'eathen in 'is blindness bows down to wood an' stone;
'E don't obey no orders unless they is 'is own;
'E keeps 'is side-arms awful: 'e leaves 'em all about,
An' then comes up the Regiment an' pokes the 'eathen out.

All along o 'dirtiness, all along o' mess,
All along o 'doin' things rather-more-or-less,
All along of abby-nay,[1] kul,[2] an' hazar-ho,[3]
Mind you keep your rifle an' yourself jus' so!

The young recruit is 'aughty—'e draf's from Gawd knows where;
They bid 'im show 'is stockin's an' lay 'is mattress square;
'E calls it bloomin' nonsense—'e doesn't know, no more—
An' then up comes 'is Company an' kicks 'im round the floor!

The young recruit is 'ammered—'e takes it very hard;
'E 'angs 'is 'ead an' mutters—'e sulks about the yard;
'E talks o' "cruel tyrants" which 'e'll swing for by-an'-by,
An' the others 'ears an' mocks 'im, an' the boy goes orf to cry.

The young recruit is silly—'e thinks o' suicide.
'E's lost 'is gutter-devil; 'e 'asn't got 'is pride;

[1] Not now.   [2] To-morrow.   [3] Wait a bit.

But day by day they kicks 'im, which 'elps 'im on a bit,
Till 'e finds 'isself one mornin' with a full an' proper kit.

　Gettin' clear o' dirtiness, gettin' done with mess,
　Gettin' shut o' doin' things rather-more-or-less;
　Not so fond of abby-nay, kul, nor hazar-ho,
　Learns to keep 'is rifle an' 'isself jus' so!

The young recruit is 'appy—'e throws a chest to suit;
You see 'im grow mustaches; you 'ear 'im slap 'is boot.
'E learns to drop the "bloodies" from every word 'e slings,
An' 'e shows an 'ealthy brisket when 'e strips for bars an' rings.

The cruel-tyrant-sergeants they watch 'im 'arf a year;
They watch 'im with 'is comrades, they watch 'im with 'is beer;
They watch 'im with the women at the regimental dance,
And the cruel-tyrant-sergeants send 'is name along for "Lance."

An' now 'e's 'arf o' nothin', an' all a private yet,
'Is room they up an' rags 'im to see what they will get.
They rags 'im low an' cunnin', each dirty trick they can,
But 'e learns to sweat 'is temper an' 'e learns to sweat 'is man.

An', last, a Colour-Sergeant, as such to be obeyed,
'E schools 'is men at cricket, 'e tells 'em on parade;
They sees 'im quick an' 'andy, uncommon set an' smart,
An' so 'e talks to orficers which 'ave the Core at 'eart.

'E learns to do 'is watchin' without it showin' plain;
'E learns to save a dummy, an' shove 'im straight again;
'E learns to check a ranker that's buyin' leave to shirk;
An' 'e learns to make men like 'im so they'll learn to like their work.

An' when it comes to marchin' he'll see their socks are right,
An' when it comes to action 'e shows 'em how to sight.
'E knows their ways of thinkin' and just what's in their mind;
'E knows when they are takin' on an' when they've fell be'ind.

'E knows each talkin' corp'ral that leads a squad astray;
'E feels 'is innards 'eavin', 'is bowels givin' way;
'E sees the blue-white faces all tryin' 'ard to grin,
An' 'e stands an' waits an' suffers till it's time to cap 'em in.

An' now the hugly bullets come peckin' through the dust,
An' no one wants to face 'em, but every beggar must;
So, like a man in irons, which isn't glad to go,
They moves 'em off by companies uncommon stiff an' slow.

Of all 'is five years' schoolin' they don't remember much
Excep' the not retreatin', the step an' keepin' touch.
It looks like teachin' wasted when they duck an' spread an' 'op—
But if 'e 'adn't learned 'em they'd be all about the shop.

An' now it's " 'Oo goes backward?" an' now it's " 'Oo comes on?"
And now it's "Get the doolies," an' now the Captain's gone;
An' now it's bloody murder, but all the while they 'ear
'Is voice, the same as barrick-drill, a-shepherdin' the rear.

'E's just as sick as they are, 'is 'eart is like to split,
But 'e works 'em, works 'em, works 'em till he feels 'em take the bit;
The rest is 'oldin' steady till the watchful bugles play,
An' 'e lifts 'em, lifts 'em, lifts 'em through the charge that wins the day!

   The 'eathen in 'is blindness bows down to wood an' stone;
   'E don't obey no orders unless they is 'is own.
   The 'eathen in 'is blindness must end where 'e began,
   But the backbone of the Army is the Non-commissioned Man!

   Keep away from dirtiness—keep away from mess,
   Don't get into doin' things rather-more-or-less!
   Let's ha' done with abby-nay, kul, and hazar-ho;
   Mind you keep your rifle an' yourself jus' so!

THE SHUT-EYE SENTRY

   Sez the Junior Orderly Sergeant
     To the Senior Orderly Man:
   "Our Orderly Orf'cer's *hokee-mut,*[1]
     "You 'elp 'im all you can.
   "For the wine was old and the night is cold,
     "An' the best we may go wrong;
   "So, 'fore 'e gits to the sentry-box,
     "You pass the word along."

           [1] Very drunk.

So it was "Rounds! What Rounds?" at two of a frosty night,
  'E's 'oldin' on by the sergeant's sash, but, sentry, shut your eye.
An' it was "Pass! All's well! Oh, ain't 'e drippin' tight!
  'E'll need an affidavit pretty badly by-an'-by."

> The moon was white on the barricks,
>   The road was white an' wide,
> An' the Orderly Orf'cer took it all,
>   An' the ten-foot ditch beside.
> An' the corporal pulled an' the sergeant pushed,
>   An' the three they danced along,
> But I'd shut my eyes in the sentry-box,
>   So I didn't see nothin' wrong.

Though it was "Rounds! What Rounds?" O corporal, 'old 'im up!
  'E's usin' 'is cap as it shouldn't be used, but, sentry, shut your eye,
An' it was "Pass! All's well! Ho, shun the foamin' cup!
  'E'll need," etc.

> 'Twas after four in the mornin';
>   We 'ad to stop the fun,
> An' we sent 'im 'ome on a bullock-cart,
>   With 'is belt an' stock undone;
> But we sluiced 'im down an' we washed 'im out,
>   An' a first-class job we made,
> When we saved 'im, smart as a bombardier,
>   For six o'clock parade.

It 'ad been "Rounds! What Rounds? Oh, shove 'im straight again!
  'E's usin' 'is sword for a bicycle, but, sentry, shut your eye."
An' it was "Pass! All's well! 'E's called me 'Darlin' Jane!'
  'E'll need," etc.

> The drill was long an' 'eavy,
>   The sky was 'ot an' blue.
> An' 'is eye was wild an' 'is 'air was wet,
>   But 'is sergeant pulled 'im through.
> Our men was good old trusties—
>   They'd done it on their 'ead—
> But you ought to 'ave 'eard 'em markin' time
>   To 'ide the things 'e said!

For it was "Right flank—wheel!" for "'Alt, an' stand at ease!"
 An' "Left extend!" for "Centre close!" O marker, shut your eye!
An' it was, "'Ere, sir, 'ere! before the Colonel sees!"
 So he needed affidavits pretty badly by-an'-by.

There was two-an'-thirty sergeants,
    There was corp'rals forty-one,
There was just nine 'undred rank an' file
    To swear to a touch o' sun.
There was me 'e'd kissed in the sentry-box,
    As I 'ave not told in my song,
But I took my oath, which were Bible-truth,
    I 'adn't seen nothin' wrong.

There's them that's 'ot an' 'aughty,
    There's them that's cold an' 'ard,
But there comes a night when the best gets tight,
    And then turns out the Guard.
I've seen them 'ide their liquor
    In every kind o' way,
But most depends on makin' friends
    With Privit Thomas A.!

When it is "Rounds! What Rounds? 'E's breathin' through 'is nose.
 'E's reelin', rollin', roarin', tight, but, sentry, shut your eye."
An' it is "Pass! All's well!" An' that's the way it goes:
 We'll 'elp 'im for 'is mother, an' 'e'll 'elp us by-an'-by!

"MARY, PITY WOMEN!"

You call yourself a man,
    For all you used to swear,
An' leave me, as you can,
    My certain shame to bear?
I 'ear! You do not care—
You done the worst you know.
    I 'ate you, grinnin' there. . . .
Ah, Gawd, I love you so!

Nice while it lasted, an' now it is over—
Tear out your 'eart an' good-bye to your lover!
What's the use o' grievin', when the mother that bore you
(Mary, pity women!) knew it all before you?

It aren't no false alarm,
   The finish to your fun;
You—you 'ave brung the 'arm,
   An' I'm the ruined one!
   An' now you'll off an' run
With some new fool in tow.
   Your 'eart? You 'aven't none. . . .
Ah, Gawd, I love you so!

When a man is tired there is naught will bind 'im;
All 'e solemn promised 'e will shove be'ind 'im.
What's the good o' prayin' for the Wrath to strike 'im
(Mary, pity women!), when the rest are like 'im?

What 'ope for me or—it?
   What's left for us to do?
I've walked with men a bit,
   But this—but this is you.
   So 'elp me, Christ, it's true!
Where can I 'ide or go?
   You coward through and through! . . .
Ah, Gawd, I love you so!

All the more you give 'em the less are they for givin'—
Love lies dead, an' you cannot kiss 'im livin'.
Down the road 'e led you there is no returnin'
(Mary, pity women!), but you're late in learnin'!

You'd like to treat me fair?
   You can't, because we're pore?
We'd starve? What do I care!
   We might, but *this* is shore!
   I want the name—no more—
The name, an' lines to show,
   An' not to be an 'ore. . . .
Ah, Gawd, I love you so!

What's the good o' pleadin', when the mother that bore you
(Mary, pity women!) knew it all before you?
Sleep on 'is promises an' wake to your sorrow
(Mary, pity women!), for we sail to-morrow!

"FOR TO ADMIRE"

The Injian Ocean sets an' smiles
    So sof', so bright, so bloomin' blue;
There aren't a wave for miles an' miles
    Excep' the jiggle from the screw.
The ship is swep', the day is done,
    The bugle's gone for smoke and play;
An' black ag'in the settin' sun
    The Lascar sings, *"Hum deckty hai!"*[1]

For to admire an' for to see,
    For to be'old this world so wide—
It never done no good to me,
    But I can't drop it if I tried!

I see the sergeants pitchin' quoits,
    I 'ear the women laugh an' talk,
I spy upon the quarter-deck
    The orficers an' lydies walk.
I thinks about the things that was,
    An' leans an' looks acrost the sea,
Till, spite of all the crowded ship,
    There's no one lef' alive but me.

The things that was which I 'ave seen,
    In barrick, camp, an' action too,
I tells them over by myself,
    An' sometimes wonders if they're true;
For they was odd—most awful odd—
    But all the same, now they are o'er,
There must be 'eaps o' plenty such,
    An' if I wait I'll see some more.

[1] I'm looking out.

Oh, I 'ave come upon the books,
  An' frequent broke a barrick-rule,
An' stood beside an' watched myself
  Be'avin' like a bloomin' fool.
I paid my price for findin' out,
  Nor never grutched the price I paid,
But sat in Clink without my boots,
  Admirin' 'ow the world was made.

Be'old a cloud upon the beam,
  An' 'umped above the sea appears
Old Aden, like a barrick-stove
  That no one's lit for years an' years.
I passed by that when I began,
  An' I go 'ome the road I came,
A time-expired soldier-man
  With six years' service to 'is name.

My girl she said, "Oh, stay with me!"
  My mother 'eld me to 'er breast.
They've never written none, an' so
  They must 'ave gone with all the rest—
With all the rest which I 'ave seen
  An' found an' known an' met along.
I cannot say the things I feel,
  And so I sing my evenin' song:

For to admire an' for to see,
  For to be'old this world so wide—
It never done no good to me,
  But I can't drop it if I tried!

The Light That Failed

Chapter 1

So we settled it all when the storm was done
  As comf'y as comf'y could be;
And I was to wait in the barn, my dears,
  Because I was only three,
And Teddy would run to the rainbow's foot,
  Because he was five and a man.
And that's how it all began, my dears,
  And that's how it all began.

'Big Barn Stories.'

'WHAT DO YOU think she'd do if she caught us? We oughtn't to have it, you know,' said Maisie.

'Beat me, and lock you up in your bedroom,' Dick answered, without hesitation. 'Have you got the cartridges?'

'Yes; they're in my pocket, but they are joggling horribly. Do pin-fire cartridges go off of their own accord?'

'Don't know. Take the revolver, if you are afraid, and let me carry them.'

'I'm not afraid.' Maisie strode forward swiftly, a hand in her pocket and her chin in the air. Dick followed with a small pin-fire revolver.

The children had discovered that their lives would be unendurable without pistol-practice. After much forethought and self-denial, Dick had saved seven shillings and sixpence, the price of a badly-constructed Belgian revolver. Maisie could only contribute half a crown to the syndicate for the purchase of a hundred cartridges. 'You can save better than I can, Dick,' she explained; 'I like nice things to eat, and it doesn't matter to you. Besides, boys ought to do these things.'

Dick grumbled a little at the arrangement, but went out and made the purchases, which the children were then on their way to test. Revolvers did not lie in the scheme of their daily life as decreed for them by the guardian who was incorrectly supposed to stand in the place of a mother to these two orphans. Dick had been under her care for six years, during which time she had made her profit of the allowances supposed to be expended on his clothes, and, partly through thoughtlessness, partly through a natural desire to pain,—she was a widow of some years anxious to marry again,—had made his days burdensome on his young shoulders. Where he had looked for love, she gave him first aversion and then hate. Where he growing older had sought a little sympathy, she gave him ridicule. The many hours that she could spare from the ordering of her small house she devoted to what she called the home-training of Dick Heldar. Her religion, manufactured in the main by her own intelligence and a keen study of the Scriptures, was an aid to her in this matter. At such times as she herself was not personally displeased with Dick, she left him to understand that he had a heavy account to settle with his Creator; wherefore Dick learned to loathe his God as intensely as he loathed Mrs. Jennett; and this is not a wholesome frame of mind for the young. Since she chose to regard him as a hopeless liar, when dread of pain drove him to his first untruth, he naturally developed into a liar, but an economical and self-contained one, never throwing away the least unnecessary fib, and never hesitating at the blackest, were it only plausible, that might make his life a little easier. The treatment taught him at least the power of living alone,—a power that was of service to him when he went to a public school and the boys laughed at his clothes, which were poor in quality and much mended. In the holidays he returned to the teachings of Mrs. Jennett, and, that the chain of discipline might not be weakened by association with the world, was generally beaten, on one count or another, before he had been twelve hours under her roof.

The autumn of one year brought him a companion in bondage, a long-haired, gray-eyed little atom, as self-contained as himself, who moved about the house silently, and for the first few weeks spoke only to the goat that was her chiefest friend on earth and lived in the back-garden. Mrs. Jennett objected to the goat on the grounds that he was un-Christian,—which he certainly was. 'Then,' said the atom, choosing her words very deliberately, 'I shall write to my lawyer-people and tell them that you are a very bad woman. Amomma is mine, mine, mine!' Mrs. Jennett made a movement to the hall, where certain umbrellas and canes stood in a rack. The atom understood as clearly as Dick what this meant. 'I have been beaten before,' she said, still in the same passionless voice; 'I have been beaten worse than you can ever beat me. If you beat me I shall write to my lawyer-people and tell them that you do not give me enough to eat. I am not afraid of you.' Mrs. Jennett did not go into the hall, and the atom, after a pause to assure herself that all danger of war was past, went out, to weep bitterly on Amomma's neck.

Dick learned to know her as Maisie, and at first mistrusted her profoundly, for he feared that she might interfere with the small liberty of action left to him. She did not, however; and she volunteered no friendliness until Dick had taken the first steps. Long before the holidays were over, the stress of punishment shared in common drove the children together, if it were only to play into each other's hands as they prepared lies for Mrs. Jennett's use. When Dick returned to school, Maisie whispered, 'Now I shall be all alone to take care of myself; but,' and she nodded her head bravely, 'I can do it. You promised to send Amomma a grass collar. Send it soon.' A week later she asked for that collar by return of post, and was not pleased when she learned that it took time to make. When at last Dick forwarded the gift she forgot to thank him for it.

Many holidays had come and gone since that day, and Dick had grown into a lanky hobbledehoy more than ever conscious of his bad clothes. Not for a moment had Mrs. Jennett relaxed her tender care of him, but the average canings of a public school—Dick fell under punishment about three times a month—filled him with contempt for her powers. 'She doesn't hurt,' he explained to Maisie, who urged him to rebellion, 'and she is kinder to you after she has whacked me.' Dick shambled through the days unkept in body and savage in soul, as the smaller boys of the school learned to know, for when the spirit moved him he would hit them, cunningly and with science. The same spirit made him more than once try to tease Maisie, but the girl refused to be made unhappy. 'We are both miserable as it is,' said she. 'What is the use of trying to make things worse? Let's find things to do, and forget things.'

The pistol was the outcome of that search. It could only be used on the muddiest foreshore of the beach, far away from bathing-machines and pier-heads, below the grassy slopes of Fort Keeling. The tide ran out nearly two miles on that coast, and the many-coloured mud-banks, touched by the sun, sent up a lamentable smell of dead weed. It was late in the afternoon when Dick and Maisie arrived on their ground, Amomma trotting patiently behind them.

'Mf!' said Maisie, sniffing the air. 'I wonder what makes the sea so smelly. I don't like it.'

'You never like anything that isn't made just for you,' said Dick bluntly. 'Give me the cartridges, and I'll try first shot. How far does one of these little revolvers carry?'

'Oh, half a mile,' said Maisie promptly. 'At least it makes an awful noise. Be careful with the cartridges; I don't like those jagged stick-up things on the rim. Dick, do be careful.'

'All right. I know how to load. I'll fire at the breakwater out there.'

He fired, and Amomma ran away bleating. The bullet threw up a spurt of mud to the right of the weed-wreathed piles.

'Throws high and to the right. You try, Maisie. Mind, it's loaded all round.'

Maisie took the pistol and stepped delicately to the verge of the mud, her hand firmly closed on the butt, her mouth and left eye screwed up. Dick sat down on a tuft of bank and laughed. Amomma returned very cautiously. He was accustomed to strange experiences in his afternoon walks, and, finding the cartridge-box unguarded, made investigations with his nose. Maisie fired, but could not see where the bullet went.

'I think it hit the post,' she said, shading her eyes and looking out across the sailless sea.

'I know it has gone out to the Marazion Bell Buoy,' said Dick, with a chuckle. 'Fire low and to the left; then perhaps you'll get it. Oh, look at Amomma!—he's eating the cartridges!'

Maisie turned, the revolver in her hand, just in time to see Amomma scampering away from the pebbles Dick threw after him. Nothing is sacred to a billy-goat. Being well fed and the adored of his mistress, Amomma had naturally swallowed two loaded pin-fire cartridges. Maisie hurried up to assure herself that Dick had not miscounted the tale.

'Yes, he's eaten two.'

'Horrid little beast! Then they'll joggle about inside him and blow up, and serve him right. . . . Oh, Dick! have I killed you?'

Revolvers are tricky things for young hands to deal with. Maisie could not explain how it had happened, but a veil of reeking smoke separated her from Dick, and she was quite certain that the pistol had gone off in his face. Then she heard him sputter, and dropped on her knees beside him, crying, 'Dick, you aren't hurt, are you? I didn't mean it.'

'Of course you didn't,' said Dick, coming out of the smoke and wiping his cheek. 'But you nearly blinded me. That powder stuff stings awfully.' A neat little splash of gray lead on a stone showed where the bullet had gone. Maisie began to whimper.

'Don't,' said Dick, jumping to his feet and shaking himself. 'I'm not a bit hurt.'

'No, but I might have killed you,' protested Maisie, the corners of her mouth drooping. 'What should I have done then?'

'Gone home and told Mrs. Jennett.' Dick grinned at the thought; then, softening, 'Please don't worry about it. Besides, we are wasting time. We've got to get back to tea. I'll take the revolver for a bit.'

Maisie would have wept on the least encouragement, but Dick's indifference, albeit his hand was shaking as he picked up the pistol, restrained her. She lay panting on the beach while Dick methodically bombarded the breakwater. 'Got it at last!' he exclaimed, as a lock of weed flew from the wood.

'Let me try,' said Maisie imperiously. 'I'm all right now.'

They fired in turns till the rickety little revolver nearly shook itself to pieces, and Amomma the outcast—because he might blow up at any moment—browsed in the background and wondered why stones were thrown at him. Then they found a balk of timber floating in a pool which was commanded by the seaward slope of Fort Keeling, and they sat down together before this new target.

'Next holidays,' said Dick, as the now thoroughly fouled revolver kicked wildly in his hand, 'we'll get another pistol,—central fire,—that will carry farther.'

'There won't be any next holidays for me,' said Maisie. 'I'm going away.'

'Where to?'

'I don't know. My lawyers have written to Mrs. Jennett, and I've got to be educated somewhere,—in France, perhaps,—I don't know where; but I shall be glad to go away.'

'I shan't like it a bit. I suppose I shall be left. Look here, Maisie, is it really true you're going? Then these holidays will be the last I shall see anything of you; and I go back to school next week. I wish—'

The young blood turned his cheeks scarlet. Maisie was picking grass-tufts and throwing them down the slope at a yellow sea-poppy nodding all by itself to the illimitable levels of the mud-flats and the milk-white sea beyond.

'I wish,' she said, after a pause, 'that I could see you again some time. You wish that too?'

'Yes, but it would have been better if—if—you had—shot straight over there—down by the breakwater.'

Maisie looked with large eyes for a moment. And this was the boy who only ten days before had decorated Amomma's horns with cut-paper ham-frills and turned him out, a bearded derision, among the public ways! Then she dropped her eyes: this was not the boy.

'Don't be stupid,' she said reprovingly, and with swift instinct attacked the side-issue. 'How selfish you are! Just think what I should have felt if that horrid thing had killed you! I'm quite miserable enough already.'

'Why? Because you're going away from Mrs. Jennett?'

'No.'

'From me, then?'

No answer for a long time. Dick dared not look at her. He felt, though he did not know, all that the past four years had been to him, and this the more acutely since he had no knowledge to put his feelings in words.

'I don't know,' she said. 'I suppose it is.'

'Maisie, you must know. I'm not supposing.'

'Let's go home,' said Maisie weakly.

But Dick was not minded to retreat.

'I can't say things,' he pleaded, 'and I'm awfully sorry for teasing you about Amomma the other day. It's all different now, Maisie, can't you see? And you might have told me that you were going, instead of leaving me to find out.'

'You didn't. I did tell. Oh, Dick, what's the use of worrying?'

'There isn't any; but we've been together years and years, and I didn't know how much I cared.'

'I don't believe you ever did care.'

'No, I didn't; but I do,—I care awfully now. Maisie,' he gulped,— 'Maisie, darling, say you care too, please.'

'I do; indeed I do; but it won't be any use.'

'Why?'

'Because I am going away.'

'Yes, but if you promise before you go. Only say—will you?' A second 'darling' came to his lips more easily than the first. There were few endearments in Dick's home or school life; he had to find them by instinct. Dick caught the little hand blackened with the escaped gas of the revolver.

'I promise,' she said solemnly; 'but if I care there is no need for promising.'

'And you do care?' For the first time in the past few minutes their eyes met and spoke for them who had no skill in speech. . . .

'Oh, Dick, don't! please don't! It was all right when we said goodmorning; but now it's all different!' Amomma looked on from afar. He had seen his property quarrel frequently, but he had never seen kisses exchanged before. The yellow sea-poppy was wiser, and nodded its head approvingly. Considered as a kiss, that was a failure, but since it was the first, other than those demanded by duty, in all the world that either had ever given or taken, it opened to them new worlds, and every one of them glorious, so that they were lifted above the consideration of any worlds at all, especially those in which tea is necessary, and sat still, holding each other's hands and saying not a word.

'You can't forget now,' said Dick at last. There was that on his cheek that stung more than gunpowder.

'I shouldn't have forgotten anyhow,' said Maisie, and they looked at each other and saw that each was changed from the companion of an hour ago to a wonder and a mystery they could not understand. The sun began to set, and a night-wind thrashed along the bents of the foreshore.

'We shall be awfully late for tea,' said Maisie. 'Let's go home.'

'Let's use the rest of the cartridges first,' said Dick; and he helped Maisie down the slope of the fort to the sea,—a descent that she was quite capable of covering at full speed. Equally gravely Maisie took the grimy hand. Dick bent forward clumsily; Maisie drew the hand away, and Dick blushed.

'It's very pretty,' he said.

'Pooh!' said Maisie, with a little laugh of gratified vanity. She stood close to Dick as he loaded the revolver for the last time and fired over the sea, with a vague notion at the back of his head that he was protecting Maisie from all the evils in the world. A puddle far across the mud caught the last rays of the sun and turned into a wrathful red disc. The light held Dick's attention for a moment, and as he raised his revolver there fell upon him a renewed sense of the miraculous, in that he was standing by Maisie who had promised to care for him for an indefinite length of time till such date as—A gust of the growing wind drove the girl's long black hair across his face as she stood with her hand on his shoulder calling Amomma 'a little beast,' and for a moment he was in the dark,—a darkness that stung. The bullet went singing out to the empty sea.

'Spoilt my aim,' said he, shaking his head. 'There aren't any more cartridges; we shall have to run home.' But they did not run. They walked very slowly, arm in arm. And it was a matter of indifference to them whether the neglected Amomma with two pin-fire cartridges in his inside blew up or trotted beside them; for they had come into a golden heritage and were disposing of it with all the wisdom of all their years.

'And I shall be—' quoth Dick valiantly. Then he checked himself: 'I don't know what I shall be. I don't seem to be able to pass any exams., but I can make awful caricatures of the masters. Ho! ho!'

'Be an artist, then,' said Maisie. 'You're always laughing at my trying to draw; and it will do you good.'

'I'll never laugh at anything you do,' he answered. 'I'll be an artist, and I'll do things.'

'Artists always want money, don't they?'

'I've got a hundred and twenty pounds a year of my own. My guardians tell me I'm to have it when I come of age. That will be enough to begin with.'

'Ah, I'm rich,' said Maisie. 'I've got three hundred a year all my own when I'm twenty-one. That's why Mrs. Jennett is kinder to me than she is to you. I wish, though, that I had somebody that belonged to me,—just a father or a mother.'

'You belong to me,' said Dick, 'for ever and ever.'

'Yes, we belong—for ever. It's very nice.' She squeezed his arm. The kindly darkness hid them both, and, emboldened because he could only just see the profile of Maisie's cheek with the long lashes veiling the gray eyes, Dick at the front door delivered himself of the words he had been boggling over for the last two hours.

'And I—love you, Maisie,' he said, in a whisper that seemed to him to ring across the world,—the world that he would to-morrow or the next day set out to conquer.

There was a scene, not, for the sake of discipline, to be reported, when Mrs. Jennett would have fallen upon him, first for disgraceful unpunctuality, and secondly, for nearly killing himself with a forbidden weapon. 'I was playing with it, and it went off by itself,' said Dick, when the powder-pocked cheek could no longer be hidden, 'but if you think you're going to lick me you're wrong. You are never going to touch me again. Sit down and give me my tea. You can't cheat us out of that, anyhow.' Mrs. Jennett gasped and became livid. Maisie said nothing, but encouraged Dick with her eyes, and he behaved abominably all that evening. Mrs. Jennett prophesied an immediate judgment of Providence and a descent into Tophet later, but Dick walked in Paradise and would not hear. Only when he was going to bed Mrs. Jennett recovered and asserted herself. He had bidden Maisie good-night with down-dropped eyes and from a distance.

'If you aren't a gentleman you might try to behave like one,' said Mrs. Jennett spitefully. 'You've been quarrelling with Maisie again.'

This meant that the usual good-night kiss had been omitted. Maisie, white to the lips, thrust her cheek forward with a fine air of indifference, and was duly pecked by Dick, who tramped out of the room red as fire. That night he dreamed a wild dream. He had won all the world and brought it to Maisie in a cartridge-box, but she turned it over with her foot, and, instead of saying, 'Thank you,' cried—

'Where is the grass collar you promised for Amomma? Oh, how selfish you are!'

Chapter 2

Then we brought the lances down, then the bugles blew
When we went to Kandahar, ridin' two an' two,
Ridin', ridin', ridin' two an' two,
Ta-ra-ra-ra-ra-ra-ra,
All the way to Kandahar, ridin' two an' two.
                                                    'Barrack-Room Ballad.'

I'M NOT ANGRY with the British public, but I wish we had a few thousand of them scattered among these rocks. They wouldn't be in such a hurry to get at their morning papers then. Can't you imagine the regulation householder—Lover of Justice, Constant Reader, Paterfamilias, and all that lot—frizzling on hot gravel?'

'With a blue veil over his head, and his clothes in strips. Has any man here a needle? I've got a piece of sugar-sack.'

'I'll lend you a packing-needle for six square inches of it then. Both my knees are worn through.'

'Why not six square acres, while you're about it? But lend me the needle, and I'll see what I can do with the selvage. I don't think there's enough to protect my royal body from the cold blast as it is. What are you doing with that everlasting sketch-book of yours, Dick?'

'Study of our Special Correspondent repairing his wardrobe,' said Dick gravely, as the other man kicked off a pair of sorely-worn riding-breeches and began to fit a square of coarse canvas over the most obvious open space. He grunted disconsolately as the vastness of the void developed itself.

'Sugar-bags, indeed! Hi! you pilot-man there! lend me all the sails of that whale-boat.'

A fez-crowned head bobbed up in the stern-sheets, divided itself into exact halves with one flashing grin, and bobbed down again. The man of the tattered breeches, clad only in a Norfolk jacket and a gray flannel shirt, went on with his clumsy sewing, while Dick chuckled over the sketch.

Some twenty whale-boats were nuzzling a sand-bank which was dotted with English soldiery of half a dozen corps, bathing or washing their clothes. A heap of boat-rollers, commissariat-boxes, sugar-bags, and flour- and small-arm-ammunition-cases showed where one of the whale-boats had been compelled to unload hastily; and a regimental carpenter was swearing aloud as he tried, on a wholly insufficient allowance of white lead, to plaster up the sun-parched gaping seams of the boat herself.

'First the bloomin' rudder snaps,' said he to the world in general; 'then the mast goes; an' then, s' 'elp me, when she can't do nothin' else, she opens 'erself out like a cock-eyed Chinese lotus.'

'Exactly the case with my breeches, whoever you are,' said the tailor, without looking up. 'Dick, I wonder when I shall see a decent shop again.'

There was no answer, save the incessant angry murmur of the Nile as it raced round a basalt-walled bend and foamed across a rock-ridge half a mile up-stream. It was as though the brown weight of the river would drive the white men back to their own country. The indescrib- able scent of Nile mud in the air told that the stream was falling and that the next few miles would be no light thing for the whale-boats to over- pass. The desert ran down almost to the banks, where, among gray, red, and black hillocks, a camel-corps was encamped. No man dared even for a day lose touch of the slow-moving boats; there had been no fighting for weeks past, and throughout all that time the Nile had never spared them. Rapid had followed rapid, rock rock, and island-group island- group, till the rank and file had long since lost all count of direction and very nearly of time. They were moving somewhere, they did not know why, to do something, they did not know what. Before them lay the Nile, and at the other end of it was one Gordon, fighting for the dear life, in a town called Khartoum. There were columns of British troops in the desert, or in one of the many deserts; there were columns on the river; there were yet more columns waiting to embark on the river; there were fresh drafts waiting at Assioot and Assuan; there were lies and rumours running over the face of the hopeless land from Suakin to the Sixth Cataract, and men supposed generally that there must be some one in authority to direct the general scheme of the many movements. The duty of that particular river-column was to keep the whale-boats afloat in the water, to avoid trampling on the villagers' crops when the gangs 'tracked' the boats with lines thrown from midstream, to get as much sleep and food as was possible, and, above all, to press on without delay in the teeth of the churning Nile.

With the soldiers sweated and toiled the correspondents of the news- papers, and they were almost as ignorant as their companions. But it was above all things necessary that England at breakfast should be amused and thrilled and interested, whether Gordon lived or died, or half the British army went to pieces in the sands. The Soudan campaign was a picturesque one, and lent itself to vivid word-painting. Now and again a 'Special' managed to get slain,—which was not altogether a disadvantage to the paper that employed him,—and more often the hand-to-hand nature of the fighting allowed of miraculous escapes which were worth telegraphing home at eighteenpence the word. There were many correspondents with many corps and columns,—from the veterans who had followed on the heels of the cavalry that occupied Cairo in '82, what time Arabi Pasha called himself king, who had seen the first miserable work round Suakin when the sentries were cut up nightly and the scrub swarmed with spears, to youngsters jerked into the business at the end of a telegraph-wire to take the place of their betters killed or invalided.

Among the seniors—those who knew every shift and change in the perplexing postal arrangements, the value of the seediest, weediest Egyptian garron offered for sale in Cairo or Alexandria, who could talk a telegraph clerk into amiability and soothe the ruffled vanity of a newly-appointed staff-officer when press regulations became burdensome—was the man in the flannel shirt, the black-browed Torpenhow. He represented the Central Southern Syndicate in the campaign, as he had represented it in the Egyptian war, and elsewhere. The syndicate did not concern itself greatly with criticisms of attack and the like. It supplied the masses, and all it demanded was picturesqueness and abundance of detail; for there is more joy in England over a soldier who insubordinately steps out of square to rescue a comrade than over twenty generals slaving even to baldness at the gross details of transport and commissariat.

He had met at Suakin a young man, sitting on the edge of a recently-abandoned redoubt about the size of a hat-box, sketching a clump of shell-torn bodies on the gravel plain.

'What are you for?' said Torpenhow. The greeting of the correspondent is that of the commercial traveller on the road.

'My own hand,' said the young man, without looking up. 'Have you any tobacco?'

Torpenhow waited till the sketch was finished, and when he had looked at it said, 'What's your business here?'

'Nothing; there was a row, so I came. I'm supposed to be doing something down at the painting-slips among the boats, or else I'm in charge of the condenser on one of the water-ships. I've forgotten which.'

'You've cheek enough to build a redoubt with,' said Torpenhow, and took stock of the new acquaintance. 'Do you always draw like that?'

The young man produced more sketches. 'Row on a Chinese pig-boat,' said he sententiously, showing them one after another.—'Chief mate

dirked by a comprador.—Junk ashore off Hakodate.—Somali muleteer
being flogged.—Star-shell bursting over camp at Berbera.—Slave-dhow being chased round Tajurrah Bay.—Soldier lying dead in the moonlight
outside Suakin,—throat cut by Fuzzies.'

'H'm!' said Torpenhow, 'can't say I care for Verestchagin-and-water
myself, but there's no accounting for tastes. Doing anything now, are
you?'

'No. I'm amusing myself here.'

Torpenhow looked at the aching desolation of the place. ''Faith, you've
queer notions of amusement. 'Got any money?'

'Enough to go on with. Look here: do you want me to do war-work?'

'I don't. My syndicate may, though. You can draw more than a little,
and I don't suppose you care much what you get, do you?'

'Not this time. I want my chance first.'

Torpenhow looked at the sketches again, and nodded. 'Yes, you're right
to take your first chance when you can get it.'

He rode away swiftly through the Gate of the Two War-Ships, rattled
across the causeway into the town, and wired to his syndicate, 'Got man
here, picture-work. Good and cheap. Shall I arrange? Will do letterpress
with sketches.'

The man on the redoubt sat swinging his legs and murmuring, 'I
knew the chance would come, sooner or later. By Gad, they'll have to
sweat for it if I come through this business alive!'

In the evening Torpenhow was able to announce to his friend that
the Central Southern Agency was willing to take him on trial, paying
expenses for three months. 'And, by the way, what's your name?' said
Torpenhow.

'Heldar. Do they give me a free hand?'

'They've taken you on chance. You must justify the choice. You'd better stick to me. I'm going up country with a column, and I'll do what
I can for you. Give me some of your sketches taken here, and I'll send
'em along.' To himself he said, 'That's the best bargain the Central Southern has ever made; and they got me cheaply enough.'

So it came to pass that, after some purchase of horse-flesh and arrangements financial and political, Dick was made free of the New and Honourable Fraternity of war correspondents, who all possess the inalienable
right of doing as much work as they can and getting as much for it as
Providence and their owners shall please. To these things are added in
time, if the brother be worthy, the power of glib speech that neither man
nor woman can resist when a meal or a bed is in question, the eye of
a horse-coper, the skill of a cook, the constitution of a bullock, the digestion of an ostrich, and an infinite adaptability to all circumstances.

But many die before they attain to this degree, and the past-masters in the craft appear for the most part in dress-clothes when they are in England, and thus their glory is hidden from the multitude.

Dick followed Torpenhow wherever the latter's fancy chose to lead him, and between the two they managed to accomplish some work that almost satisfied themselves. It was not an easy life in any way, and under its influence the two were drawn very closely together, for they ate from the same dish, they shared the same water-bottle, and, most binding tie of all, their mails went off together. It was Dick who managed to make gloriously drunk a telegraph-clerk in a palm hut far beyond the Second Cataract, and, while the man lay in bliss on the floor, possessed himself of some laboriously acquired exclusive information, forwarded by a confiding correspondent of an opposition syndicate, made a careful duplicate of the matter, and brought the result to Torpenhow, who said that all was fair in love or war correspondence, and built an excellent descriptive article from his rival's riotous waste of words. It was Torpenhow who —but the tale of their adventures, together and apart, from Philæ to the waste wilderness of Herawi and Muella, would fill many books. They had been penned into a square side by side, in deadly fear of being shot by overexcited soldiers; they had fought with baggage-camels in the chill dawn; they had jogged along in silence under blinding sun on indefatigable little Egyptian horses; and they had floundered on the shallows of the Nile when the whale-boat in which they had found a berth chose to hit a hidden rock and rip out half her bottom-planks.

Now they were sitting on the sand-bank, and the whale-boats were bringing up the remainder of the column.

'Yes,' said Torpenhow, as he put the last rude stitches into his over-long-neglected gear, 'it has been a beautiful business.'

'The patch or the campaign?' said Dick. 'Don't think much of either myself.'

'You want the "Eurylas" brought up above the Third Cataract, don't you? and eighty-one-ton guns at Jakdul? Now, I'm quite satisfied with my breeches.' He turned round gravely to exhibit himself, after the manner of a clown.

'It's very pretty. Specially the lettering on the sack. G. B. T. Government Bullock Train. That's a sack from India.'

'It's my initials,—Gilbert Belling Torpenhow. I stole the cloth on purpose. What the mischief are the camel-corps doing yonder?' Torpenhow shaded his eyes and looked across the scrub-strewn gravel.

A bugle blew furiously, and the men on the bank hurried to their arms and accoutrements.

' "Pisan soldiery surprised while bathing," ' remarked Dick calmly. 'D'you remember the picture? It's by Michael Angelo. All beginners copy it. That scrub's alive with enemy.'

The camel-corps on the bank yelled to the infantry to come to them, and a hoarse shouting down the river showed that the remainder of the column had wind of the trouble and was hastening to take share in it. As swiftly as a reach of still water is crisped by the wind, the rock-strewn ridges and scrub-topped hills were troubled and alive with armed men. Mercifully, it occurred to these to stand far off for a time, to shout and gesticulate joyously. One man even delivered himself of a long story. The camel-corps did not fire. They were only too glad of a little breathing-space, until some sort of square could be formed. The men on the sand-bank ran to their side; and the whale-boats, as they toiled up within shouting distance, were thrust into the nearest bank and emptied of all save the sick and a few men to guard them. The Arab orator ceased his outcries, and his friends howled.

'They look like the Mahdi's men,' said Torpenhow, elbowing himself into the crush of the square; 'But what thousands of 'em there are! The tribes hereabout aren't against us, I know.'

'Then the Mahdi's taken another town,' said Dick, 'and set all these yelping devils free to chaw us up. Lend us your glass.'

'Our scouts should have told us of this. We've been trapped,' said a subaltern. 'Aren't the camel-guns ever going to begin? Hurry up, you men!'

There was no need for any order. The men flung themselves panting against the sides of the square, for they had good reason to know that whoso was left outside when the fighting began would very probably die in an extremely unpleasant fashion. The little hundred-and-fifty pound camel-guns posted at one corner of the square opened the ball as the square moved forward by its right to get possession of a knoll of rising ground. All had fought in this manner many times before, and there was no novelty in the entertainment: always the same hot and stifling formation, the smell of dust and leather, the same boltlike rush of the enemy, the same pressure on the weakest side of the square, the few minutes of desperate hand-to-hand scuffle, and then the silence of the desert, broken only by the yells of those whom the handful of cavalry attempted to pursue. They had grown careless. The camel-guns spoke at intervals, and the square slouched forward amid the protests of the camels. Then came the attack of three thousand men who had not learned from books that it is impossible for troops in close order to attack against breech-loading fire. A few dropping shots heralded their approach, and a few horsemen led, but the bulk of the force was naked humanity, mad with rage, and armed with the spear and the sword. The instinct of the desert, where there is always much war, told them that the right flank of the square was the weakest, for they swung clear of the front. The camel-guns shelled them as they passed, and opened for an instant lanes through their midst, most like those quick-closing vistas in a Kentish hop-garden seen when the train races by at full speed; and the infantry fire, held till the opportune moment, dropped them in close-packed hundreds. No civilised troops in the world could have endured the hell through which they came, the living leaping high to avoid the dying who clutched at their heels, the wounded cursing and staggering forward, till they fell—a torrent black as the sliding water above a mill-dam—full on the right flank of the square. Then the line of the dusty troops and the faint blue desert sky overhead went out in rolling smoke, and the little stones on the heated ground and the tinder-dry clumps of scrub became matters of surpassing interest, for men measured their agonised retreat and re-covery by these things, counting mechanically and hewing their way back to chosen pebble and branch. There was no semblance of any concerted fighting. For aught the men knew, the enemy might be attempting all four sides of the square at once. Their business was to destroy what lay in front of them, to bayonet in the back those who passed over them, and, dying, to drag down the slayer till he could be knocked on the head by some avenging gun-butt. Dick waited quietly with Torpenhow and a young doctor till the stress became unendurable. There was no hope of attending to the wounded till the attack was repulsed, so the three moved forward gingerly towards the weakest side. There was a rush from without, the short 'hough-hough' of the stabbing spears, and a man on a horse, followed by thirty or forty others, dashed through, yelling and hacking. The right flank of the square sucked in after them, and the other sides sent help. The wounded, who knew that they had but a few hours more to live, caught at the enemy's feet and brought them down, or, staggering to a discarded rifle, fired blindly into the scuffle that raged in the centre of the square. Dick was conscious that somebody had cut him violently across his helmet, that he had fired his revolver into a black, foam-flecked face which forthwith ceased to bear any resemblance to a face, and that Torpenhow had gone down under an Arab whom he had tried to 'collar low,' and was turning over and over with his captive, feeling for the man's eyes. The doctor was jabbing at a venture with a bayonet, and a helmetless soldier was firing over Dick's shoulder: the flying grains of powder stung his cheek. It was to Torpenhow that Dick turned by instinct. The representative of the Central Southern Syndicate had shaken himself clear of his enemy, and rose, wiping his thumb on his trousers. The Arab, both hands to his forehead, screamed aloud, then snatched up his spear and rushed at Torpenhow, who was panting under shelter of Dick's revolver. Dick fired twice, and the man dropped limply. His upturned face lacked one eye. The musketry-fire redoubled, but cheers mingled with it. The rush had failed, and the enemy were flying. If the heart of the square were shambles, the ground beyond was a butcher's shop. Dick thrust his way forward between the maddened men. The remnant of the enemy were retiring, as the few—the very few—English cavalry rode down the laggards.

Beyond the lines of the dead, a broad blood-stained Arab spear cast aside in the retreat lay across a stump of scrub, and beyond this again the illimitable dark levels of the desert. The sun caught the steel and turned it into a savage red disc. Some one behind him was saying, 'Ah, get away, you brute!' Dick raised his revolver and pointed towards the desert. His eye was held by the red splash in the distance, and the clamour about him seemed to die down to a very far-away whisper, like the whisper of a level sea. There was the revolver and the red light, . . . and the voice of some one scaring something away, exactly as had fallen somewhere before,—probably in a past life. Dick waited for what should happen afterwards. Something seemed to crack inside his head, and for an instant he stood in the dark,—a darkness that stung. He fired at random, and the bullet went out across the desert as he muttered, 'Spoilt my aim. There aren't any more cartridges. We shall have to run home.' He put his hand to his head and brought it away covered with blood.

'Old man, you're cut rather badly,' said Torpenhow. 'I owe you something for this business. Thanks. Stand up! I say, you can't be ill here.'

Dick had fallen stiffly on Torpenhow's shoulder, and was muttering something about aiming low and to the left. Then he sank to the ground and was silent. Torpenhow dragged him off to a doctor and sat down to work out an account of what he was pleased to call 'a sanguinary battle, in which our arms had acquitted themselves,' etc.

All that night, when the troops were encamped by the whale-boats, a black figure danced in the strong moonlight on the sand-bar and shouted that Gordon the accursed one was dead,—was dead,—was dead,—that two steamers were rock-staked on the Nile outside the city, and that of all their crews there remained not one; and Gordon was dead,—was dead,—was dead!

But Torpenhow took no heed. He was watching Dick, who was calling aloud to the restless Nile for Maisie,—and again Maisie!

'Behold a phenomenon,' said Torpenhow, rearranging the blanket.

'Here is a man, presumably human, who mentions the name of one woman only. And I've seen a good deal of delirium, too.—Dick, here's some fizzy drink.'

'Thank you, Maisie,' said Dick.

Chapter 3

So he thinks he shall take to the sea again
For one more cruise with his buccaneers,
To singe the beard of the King of Spain,
And capture another Dean of Jaen
And sell him in Algiers.

'A Dutch Picture.'

THE SOUDAN campaign and Dick's broken head had been some months
ended and mended, and the Central Southern Syndicate had paid Dick
a certain sum on account for work done, which work they were careful
to assure him was not altogether up to their standard. Dick heaved the
letter into the Nile at Cairo, cashed the draft in the same town, and bade
a warm farewell to Torpenhow at the station.

'I am going to lie up for a while and rest,' said Torpenhow. 'I don't
know where I shall live in London, but if God brings us to meet, we shall
meet. Are you staying here on the off-chance of another row? There will
be none till the Southern Soudan is reoccupied by our troops. Mark that.
Good-bye; bless you; come back when your money's spent; and give me
your address.'

Dick loitered in Cairo, Alexandria, Ismailia, and Port Said,—especially
Port Said. There is iniquity in many parts of the world, and vice in all,
but the concentrated essence of all the iniquities and all the vices in all
the continents finds itself at Port Said. And through the heart of that
sand-bordered hell, where the mirage flickers day long above the Bitter
Lakes, move, if you will only wait, most of the men and women you have
known in this life. Dick established himself in quarters more riotous than
respectable. He spent his evenings on the quay, and boarded many ships,
and saw very many friends,—gracious Englishwomen with whom he had
talked not too wisely in the veranda of Shepheard's Hotel, hurrying war
correspondents, skippers of the contract troop-ships employed in the campaign, army officers by the score, and others of less reputable trades. He
had choice of all the races of the East and West for studies, and the
advantage of seeing his subjects under the influence of strong excite-

ment at the gaming-tables, saloons, dancing-hells, and elsewhere. For recreation there was the straight vista of the Canal, the blazing sands, the procession of shipping, and the white hospitals where the English soldiers lay. He strove to set down in black and white and colour all that Providence sent him, and when that supply was ended sought about for fresh material. It was a fascinating employment, but it ran away with his money, and he had drawn in advance the hundred and twenty pounds to which he was entitled yearly. 'Now I shall have to work and starve!' thought he, and was addressing himself to this new fate when a mysterious telegram arrived from Torpenhow in England, which said, 'Come back, quick: you have caught on. Come.'

A large smile overspread his face. 'So soon! that's good hearing,' said he to himself. 'There will be an orgie to-night. I'll stand or fall by my luck. 'Faith, it's time it came!' He deposited half of his funds in the hands of his well-known friends Monsieur and Madame Binat, and ordered himself a Zanzibar dance of the finest. Monsieur Binat was shaking with drink, but Madame smiled sympathetically—

'Monsieur needs a chair, of course, and of course Monsieur will sketch: Monsieur amuses himself strangely.'

Binat raised a blue-white face from a cot in the inner room. 'I understand,' he quavered. 'We all know Monsieur. Monsieur is an artist, as I have been.' Dick nodded. 'In the end,' said Binat, with gravity, 'Monsieur will descend alive into hell, as I have descended.' And he laughed.

'You must come to the dance, too,' said Dick; 'I shall want you.'

'For my face? I knew it would be so. For my face? My God! and for my degradation so tremendous! I will not. Take him away. He is a devil. Or at least do thou. Celeste, demand of him more.' The excellent Binat began to kick and scream.

'All things are for sale in Port Said,' said Madame. 'If my husband comes it will be so much more. Eh, 'ow you call—'alf a sovereign.'

The money was paid, and the mad dance was held at night in a walled courtyard at the back of Madame Binat's house. The lady herself, in faded mauve silk always about to slide from her yellow shoulders, played the piano, and to the tin-pot music of a Western waltz the naked Zanzibari girls danced furiously by the light of kerosene lamps. Binat sat upon a chair and stared with eyes that saw nothing, till the whirl of the dance and the clang of the rattling piano stole into the drink that took the place of blood in his veins, and his face glistened. Dick took him by the chin brutally and turned that face to the light. Madame Binat looked over her shoulder and smiled with many teeth. Dick leaned against the wall and sketched for an hour, till the kerosene lamps began to smell, and the girls threw themselves panting on the hard-beaten ground. Then he shut his book with a snap and moved away, Binat pluck-ing feebly at his elbow. 'Show me,' he whimpered. 'I too was once an artist, even I!' Dick showed him the rough sketch. 'Am I that?' he screamed. 'Will you take that away with you and show all the world that it is I,—Binat?' He moaned and wept.

'Monsieur has paid for all,' said Madame. 'To the pleasure of seeing Monsieur again.'

The courtyard gate shut, and Dick hurried up the sandy street to the nearest gambling-hell, where he was well known. 'If the luck holds, it's an omen; if I lose, I must stay here.' He placed his money picturesquely about the board, hardly daring to look at what he did. The luck held. Three turns of the wheel left him richer by twenty pounds, and he went down to the shipping to make friends with the captain of a decayed cargo-steamer, who landed him in London with fewer pounds in his pocket than he cared to think about.

A thin gray fog hung over the city, and the streets were very cold; for summer was in England.

'It's a cheerful wilderness, and it hasn't the knack of altering much,' Dick thought, as he tramped from the Docks westward. 'Now, what must I do?'

The packed houses gave no answer. Dick looked down the long light-less streets and at the appalling rush of traffic. 'Oh, you rabbit-hutches!' said he, addressing a row of highly respectable semi-detached residences. 'Do you know what you've got to do later on? You have to supply me with men-servants and maid-servants,'—here he smacked his lips,—'and the peculiar treasure of kings. Meantime I'll get clothes and boots, and presently I will return and trample on you.' He stepped forward ener-getically; he saw that one of his shoes was burst at the side. As he stooped to make investigations, a man jostled him into the gutter. 'All right,' he said. 'That's another nick in the score. I'll jostle you later on.'

Good clothes and boots are not cheap, and Dick left his last shop with the certainty that he would be respectably arrayed for a time, but with only fifty shillings in his pocket. He returned to streets by the Docks, and lodged himself in one room, where the sheets on the bed were almost audibly marked in case of theft, and where nobody seemed to go to bed at all. When his clothes arrived he sought the Central Southern Syndi-cate for Torpenhow's address, and got it, with the intimation that there was still some money owing to him.

'How much?' said Dick, as one who habitually dealt in millions.

'Between thirty and forty pounds. If it would be any convenience to you, of course we could let you have it at once; but we usually settle accounts monthly.'

'If I show that I want anything now, I'm lost,' he said to himself. 'All I need I'll take later on.' Then, aloud, 'It's hardly worth while; and I'm going into the country for a month, too. Wait till I come back, and I'll see about it.'

'But we trust, Mr. Heldar, that you do not intend to sever your connection with us?'

Dick's business in life was the study of faces, and he watched the speaker keenly. 'That man means something,' he said. 'I'll do no business till I've seen Torpenhow. There's a big deal coming.' So he departed, making no promises, to his one little room by the Docks. And that day was the seventh of the month, and that month, he reckoned with awful distinctness, had thirty-one days in it!

It is not easy for a man of catholic tastes and healthy appetites to exist for twenty-four days on fifty shillings. Nor is it cheering to begin the experiment alone in all the loneliness of London. Dick paid seven shillings a week for his lodging, which left him rather less than a shilling a day for food and drink. Naturally, his first purchase was of the materials of his craft; he had been without them too long. Half a day's investigation and comparison brought him to the conclusion that sausages and mashed potatoes, twopence a plate, were the best food. Now, sausages once or twice a week for breakfast are not unpleasant. As lunch, even, with mashed potatoes, they become monotonous. As dinner they are impertinent. At the end of three days Dick loathed sausages, and, going forth, pawned his watch to revel on sheep's head, which is not as cheap as it looks, owing to the bones and the gravy. Then he returned to sausages and mashed potatoes. Then he confined himself entirely to mashed potatoes for a day, and was unhappy because of pain in his inside. Then he pawned his waistcoat and his tie, and thought regretfully of money thrown away in times past. There are few things more edifying unto Art than the actual belly-pinch of hunger, and Dick in his few walks abroad—he did not care for exercise, it raised desires that could not be satisfied—found himself dividing mankind into two classes,—those who looked as if they might give him something to eat, and those who looked otherwise. 'I never knew what I had to learn about the human face before,' he thought; and, as a reward for his humility, Providence caused a cab-driver at a sausage-shop where Dick fed that night to leave half eaten a great chunk of bread. Dick took it,—would have fought all the world for its possession,—and it cheered him.

The month dragged through at last, and, nearly prancing with impatience, he went to draw his money. Then he hastened to Torpenhow's address and smelt the smell of cooking meats all along the corridors of the chambers. Torpenhow was on the top floor, and Dick burst into his room, to be received with a hug which nearly cracked his ribs, as Torpenhow dragged him to the light and spoke of twenty different things in the same breath.

'But you're looking tucked up,' he concluded.

'Got anything to eat?' said Dick, his eye roaming round the room.

'I shall be having breakfast in a minute. What do you say to sausages?'

'No, anything but sausages! Torp, I've been starving on that accursed horse-flesh for thirty days and thirty nights.'

'Now, what lunacy has been your latest?'

Dick spoke of the last few weeks with unbridled speech. Then he opened his coat; there was no waistcoat below. 'I ran it fine, awfully fine, but I've just scraped through.'

'You haven't much sense, but you've got a backbone anyhow. Eat, and talk afterwards.' Dick fell upon eggs and bacon and gorged till he could gorge no more. Torpenhow handed him a filled pipe, and he smoked as men smoke who for three weeks have been deprived of good tobacco.

'Ouf!' said he. 'That's heavenly! Well?'

'Why in the world didn't you come to me?'

'Couldn't; I owe you too much already, old man. Besides, I had a sort of superstition that this temporary starvation—that's what it was, and it hurt—would bring me more luck later. It's over and done with now, and none of the Syndicate know how hard up I was. Fire away. What's the exact state of affairs as regards myself?'

'You had my wire? You've caught on here. People like your work immensely. I don't know why, but they do. They say you have a fresh touch and a new way of drawing things. And, because they're chiefly home-bred English, they say you have insight. You're wanted by half a dozen papers; you're wanted to illustrate books.'

Dick grunted scornfully.

'You're wanted to work up your smaller sketches and sell them to the dealers. They seem to think the money sunk in you is a good investment. Good Lord! who can account for the fathomless folly of the public?'

'They're a remarkably sensible people.'

'They are subject to fits, if that's what you mean; and you happen to be the object of the latest fit among those who are interested in what they call Art. Just now you're a fashion, a phenomenon, or whatever you please. I appeared to be the only person who knew anything about you here, and I have been showing the most useful men a few of the sketches you gave me from time to time. Those coming after your work on the

Central Southern Syndicate appear to have done your business. You're in luck.'

'Huh! call it luck! Do call it luck, when a man has been kicking about the world like a dog, waiting for it to come! I'll luck 'em later on. I want a place to work in first.'

'Come here,' said Torpenhow, crossing the landing. 'This place is a big box room really, but it will do for you. There's your skylight, or your north light, or whatever window you call it, and plenty of room to thrash about in, and a bedroom beyond. What more do you need?'

'Good enough,' said Dick, looking round the large room that took up a third of a top story in the rickety chambers overlooking the Thames. A pale yellow sun shone through the skylight and showed the much dirt of the place. Three steps led from the door to the landing, and three more to Torpenhow's room. The well of the staircase disappeared into darkness, pricked by tiny gas-jets, and there were sounds of men talking, and doors slamming seven flights below, in the warm gloom.

'Do they give you a free hand here?' said Dick cautiously. He was Ishmael enough to know the value of liberty.

'Anything you like: latch-keys and license unlimited. We are permanent tenants for the most part here. 'Tisn't a place I would recommend for a Young Men's Christian Association, but it will serve. I took these rooms for you when I wired.'

'You're a great deal too kind, old man.'

'You didn't suppose you were going away from me, did you?' Torpenhow put his hand on Dick's shoulder, and the two walked up and down the room, henceforward to be called the studio, in sweet and silent communion. They heard rapping at Torpenhow's door. 'That's some ruffian come up for a drink,' said Torpenhow; and he raised his voice cheerily. There entered no one more ruffianly than a portly middle-aged gentleman in a satin-faced frockcoat. His lips were parted and pale, and there were deep pouches under the eyes.

'Weak heart,' said Dick to himself, and, as he shook hands, 'very weak heart. His pulse is shaking his fingers.'

The man introduced himself as the head of the Central Southern Syndicate and 'one of the most ardent admirers of your work, Mr. Heldar. I assure you, in the name of the syndicate, that we are immensely indebted to you; and I trust, Mr. Heldar, you won't forget that we were largely instrumental in bringing you before the public.' He panted because of the seven flights of stairs.

Dick glanced at Torpenhow, whose left eyelid lay for a moment dead on his cheek.

'I shan't forget,' said Dick, every instinct of defence roused in him.

'You've paid me so well that I couldn't, you know. By the way, when I am settled in this place I should like to send and get my sketches. There must be nearly a hundred and fifty of them with you.'

'That is er—is what I came to speak about. I fear we can't allow it exactly, Mr. Heldar. In the absence of any specified agreement the sketches are our property, of course.'

'Do you mean to say that you are going to keep them?'

'Yes; and we hope to have your help, on your own terms, Mr. Heldar, to assist us in arranging a little exhibition, which, backed by our name and the influence we naturally command among the press, should be of material service to you. Sketches such as yours—'

'Belong to me. You engaged me by wire, you paid me the lowest rates you dared. You can't mean to keep them! Good God alive, man, they're all I've got in the world!'

Torpenhow watched Dick's face and whistled.

Dick walked up and down, thinking. He saw the whole of his little stock in trade, the first weapon of his equipment, annexed at the outset of his campaign by an elderly gentleman whose name Dick had not caught aright, who said that he represented a syndicate, which was a thing for which Dick had not the least reverence. The injustice of the proceedings did not much move him; he had seen the strong hand prevail too often in other places to be squeamish over the moral aspects of right and wrong. But he ardently desired the blood of the gentleman in the frockcoat, and when he spoke again it was with a strained sweetness that Torpenhow knew well for the beginning of strife.

'Forgive me, sir, but you have no—no younger man who can arrange this business with me?'

'I speak for the syndicate. I see no reason for a third party to—'

'You will in a minute. Be good enough to give back my sketches.'

The man stared blankly at Dick, and then at Torpenhow, who was leaning against the wall. He was not used to ex-employees who ordered him to be good enough to do things.

'Yes, it is rather a cold-blooded steal,' said Torpenhow critically; 'but I'm afraid, I am very much afraid, you've struck the wrong man. Be careful, Dick: remember, this isn't the Soudan.'

'Considering what services the syndicate have done you in putting your name before the world—'

This was not a fortunate remark; it reminded Dick of certain vagrant years lived out in loneliness and strife and unsatisfied desires. The memory did not contrast well with the prosperous gentleman who proposed to enjoy the fruit of those years.

'I don't know quite what to do with you,' began Dick meditatively. 'Of course, you're a thief, and you ought to be half killed, but in your case you'd probably die. I don't want you dead on this floor, and, besides, it's unlucky just as one's moving in. Don't hit, sir; you'll only excite yourself.' He put one hand on the man's forearm and ran the other down the plump body beneath the coat. 'My goodness!' said he to Torpenhow, 'and this gray beast dares to be a thief! I have seen an Esneh camel-driver have the black hide taken off his body in strips for stealing half a pound of wet dates, and he was as tough as whipcord. This thing's soft all over—like a woman.'

There are few things more poignantly humiliating than being handled by a man who does not intend to strike. The head of the syndicate began to breathe heavily. Dick walked round him, pawing him, as a cat paws a soft hearth-rug. Then he traced with his forefinger the leaden pouches underneath the eyes, and shook his head. 'You were going to steal my things,—mine, mine, mine!—you, who don't know when you may die. Write a note to your office,—you say you're the head of it,—and order them to give Torpenhow my sketches,—every one of them. Wait a minute: your hand's shaking. Now!' He thrust a pocket-book before him. The note was written. Torpenhow took it and departed without a word, while Dick walked round and round the spellbound captive, giving him such advice as he conceived best for the welfare of his soul. When Torpenhow returned with a gigantic portfolio, he heard Dick say, almost soothingly, 'Now, I hope this will be a lesson to you; and if you worry me when I have settled down to work with any nonsense about actions for assault, believe me, I'll catch you and manhandle you, and you'll die. You haven't very long to live, anyhow. Go! Imshi! Bootsak!—Get out!' The man departed, staggering and dazed. Dick drew a long breath: 'Phew! what a lawless lot these people are! The first thing a poor orphan meets is gang robbery, organised burglary! Think of the hideous blackness of that man's mind! Are my sketches all right, Torp?'

'Yes; one hundred and forty-seven of them. Well, I must say, Dick, you've begun well.'

'He was interfering with me. It only meant a few pounds to him, but it was everything to me. I don't think he'll bring an action. I gave him some medical advice gratis about the state of his body. It was cheap at the little flurry it cost him. Now, let's look at my things.'

Two minutes later Dick had thrown himself down on the floor and was deep in the portfolio, chuckling lovingly as he turned the drawings over and thought of the price at which they had been bought.

The afternoon was well advanced when Torpenhow came to the door and saw Dick dancing a wild saraband under the skylight.

'I builded better than I knew, Torp,' he said, without stopping the dance. 'They're good! They're damned good! They'll go like flame! I shall have an exhibition of them on my own brazen hook. And that man would have cheated me out of it! Do you know that I'm sorry now that I didn't actually hit him?'

'Go out,' said Torpenhow,—'go out and pray to be delivered from the sin of arrogance, which you never will be. Bring your things up from whatever place you're staying in, and we'll try to make this barn a little more shipshape.'

'And then—oh, then,' said Dick, still capering, 'we will spoil the Egyptians!'

Chapter 4

The wolf-cub at even lay hid in the corn,
When the smoke of the cooking hung gray:
He knew where the doe made a couch for her fawn,
And he looked to his strength for his prey.
But the moon swept the smoke-wreaths away.
And he turned from his meal in the villager's close,
And he bayed to the moon as she rose.

'In Seonee.'

'WELL, and how does success taste?' said Torpenhow, some three months later. He had just returned to chambers after a holiday in the country.

'Good,' said Dick, as he sat licking his lips before the easel in the studio. 'I want more,—heaps more. The lean years have passed, and I approve of these fat ones.'

'Be careful, old man. That way lies bad work.'

Torpenhow was sprawling in a long chair with a small fox-terrier asleep on his chest, while Dick was preparing a canvas. A dais, a background, and a lay-figure were the only fixed objects in the place. They rose from a wreck of oddments that began with felt-covered water-bottles, belts, and regimental badges, and ended with a small bale of second-hand uniforms and a stand of mixed arms. The mark of muddy feet on the dais showed that a military model had just gone away. The watery autumn sunlight was failing, and shadows sat in the corners of the studio.

'Yes,' said Dick deliberately, 'I like the power; I like the fun; I like the fuss; and above all I like the money. I almost like the people who make the fuss and pay the money. Almost. But they're a queer gang,— an amazingly queer gang!'

'They have been good enough to you, at any rate. That tin-pot exhibition of your sketches must have paid. Did you see that the papers called it the "Wild Work Show"?'

'Never mind. I sold every shred of canvas I wanted to; and, on my word, I believe it was because they believed I was a self-taught flagstone artist. I should have got better prices if I had worked my things on wool or scratched them on camel-bone instead of using mere black and white and colour. They are a queer gang, these people. Limited isn't the word to describe 'em. I met a fellow the other day who told me that it was impossible that shadows on white sand should be blue,—ultramarine, —as they are. I found out, later, that that man had been as far as Brighton beach; but he knew all about Art, confound him. He gave me a lecture on it, and recommended me to go to school to learn technique. I wonder what old Kami would have said to that.'

'When were you under Kami, man of extraordinary beginnings?'

'I studied with him for two years in Paris. He taught by personal magnetism. All he ever said was, "Continuez, mes enfants," and you had to make the best you could of that. He had a divine touch, and he knew something about colour. Kami used to dream colour. I swear he could never have seen the genuine article; but he evolved it, and it was good.'

'Recollect some of those views in the Soudan?' said Torpenhow, with a provoking drawl.

Dick squirmed in his place. 'Don't! It makes me want to get out there again. What colour that was! Opal and umber and amber and claret and brick-red and sulphur—cockatoo-crest sulphur—against brown, with a nigger-black rock sticking up in the middle of it all, and a decorative frieze of camels festooning in front of a pure pale turquoise sky.' He began to walk up and down. 'And yet, you know, if you try to give these people the thing as God gave it keyed down to their comprehension and according to the powers He has given you—'

'Modest man! Go on.'

'Half a dozen epicene young pagans who haven't even been to Algiers will tell you, first, that your notion is borrowed, and, secondly, that it isn't Art.'

'This comes of my leaving town for a month. Dickie, you've been promenading among the toy-shops and hearing people talk.'

'I couldn't help it,' said Dick penitently. 'You weren't here, and it was lonely these long evenings. A man can't work for ever.'

'A man might have gone to a pub, and got decently drunk.'

'I wish I had; but I forgathered with some men of sorts. They said they were artists, and I knew some of them could draw,—but they wouldn't draw. They gave me tea,—tea at five in the afternoon!—and talked about Art and the state of their souls. As if their souls mattered. I've heard more about Art and seen less of her in the last six months than in the whole of my life. Do you remember Cassavetti, who worked for some continental syndicate, out with the desert column? He was a regular

Christmas-tree of contraptions when he took the field in full fig, with his water-bottle, lanyard, revolver, writing-case, housewife, gig-lamps, and the Lord knows what all. He used to fiddle about with 'em and show us how they worked; but he never seemed to do much except fudge his reports from the Nilghai. See?'

'Dear old Nilghai! He's in town, fatter than ever. He ought to be up here this evening. I see the comparison perfectly. You should have kept clear of all that man-millinery. Serves you right; and I hope it will unsettle your mind.'

'It won't. It has taught me what Art—holy sacred Art—means.'

'You've learnt something while I've been away. What is Art?'

'Give 'em what they know, and when you've done it once do it again.' Dick dragged forward a canvas laid face to the wall. 'Here's a sample of real Art. It's going to be a facsimile reproduction for a weekly. I called it "His Last Shot." It's worked up from the little water-colour I made outside El Maghrib. Well, I lured my model, a beautiful rifleman, up here with drink. I drored him, and I redrored him, and I tredrored him, and I made him a flushed, dishevelled, bedevilled scallawag, with his helmet at the back of his head, and the living fear of death in his eye, and the blood oozing out of a cut over his ankle-bone. He wasn't pretty, but he was all soldier and very much man.'

'Once more, modest child!'

Dick laughed. 'Well, it's only to you I'm talking. I did him just as well as I knew how, making allowance for the slickness of oils. Then the art-manager of that abandoned paper said that his subscribers wouldn't like it. It was brutal and coarse and violent,—man being naturally gentle when he's fighting for his life. They wanted something more restful, with a little more colour. I could have said a good deal, but you might as well talk to a sheep as an art-manager. I took my "Last Shot" back. Behold the result! I put him into a lovely red coat without a speck on it. That is Art. I polished his boots,—observe the high light on the toe. That is Art. I cleaned his rifle,—rifles are always clean on service,—because that is Art. I pipeclayed his helmet,—pipeclay is always used on active service, and is indispensable to Art. I shaved his chin, I washed his hands, and gave him an air of fatted peace. Result, military tailor's pattern-plate. Price, thank Heaven, twice as much as for the first sketch, which was moderately decent.'

'And do you suppose you're going to give that thing out as your work?'

'Why not? I did it. Alone I did it, in the interests of sacred, home-bred Art and "Dickenson's Weekly."'

Torpenhow smoked in silence for a while. Then came the verdict, delivered from rolling clouds: 'If you were only a mass of blathering vanity, Dick, I wouldn't mind,—I'd let you go to the deuce on your own mahlstick; but when I consider what you are to me, and when I find that to vanity you add the twopenny-halfpenny pique of a twelve-year-old girl, then I bestir myself in your behalf. Thus!'

The canvas ripped as Torpenhow's booted foot shot through it, and the terrier jumped down, thinking rats were about.

'If you have any bad language to use, use it. You have not. I continue. You are an idiot, because no man born of woman is strong enough to take liberties with his public, even though they be—which they ain't —all you say they are.'

'But they don't know any better. What can you expect from creatures born and bred in this light?' Dick pointed to the yellow fog. 'If they want furniture-polish, let them have furniture-polish, so long as they pay for it. They are only men and women. You talk as though they were gods.'

'That sounds very fine, but it has nothing to do with the case. They are the people you have to work for, whether you like it or not. They are your masters. Don't be deceived, Dickie; you aren't strong enough to trifle with them,—or with yourself, which is more important. Moreover,— Come back, Binkie: that red daub isn't going anywhere,—unless you take precious good care you will fall under the damnation of the cheque-book, and that's worse than death. You will get drunk—you're half drunk already —on easily-acquired money. For that money and your own infernal vanity you are willing to deliberately turn out bad work. You'll do quite enough bad work without knowing it. And, Dickie, as I love you and as I know you love me, I am not going to let you cut off your nose to spite your face for all the gold in England. That's settled. Now swear.'

'Don't know,' said Dick. 'I've been trying to make myself angry, but I can't, you're so abominably reasonable. There will be a row on "Dickenson's Weekly," I fancy.'

'Why the Dickenson do you want to work on a weekly paper? It's slow bleeding of power.'

'It brings in the very desirable dollars,' said Dick, his hands in his pockets.

Torpenhow watched him with large contempt. 'Why, I thought it was a man!' said he. 'It's a child.'

'No, it isn't,' said Dick, wheeling quickly. 'You've no notion what the certainty of cash means to a man who has always wanted it badly. Nothing will pay me for some of my life's joys; on that Chinese pig-boat, for instance, when we ate bread and jam for every meal, because Ho-Wang wouldn't allow us anything better, and it all tasted of pig,—Chinese pig. I've worked for this, I've sweated and I've starved for this, line on line and month after month. And now I've got it I am going to make the most of it while it lasts. Let them pay—they've no knowledge.'

'What does Your Majesty please to want? You can't smoke more than you do; you won't drink; you're a gross feeder; and you dress in the dark, by the look of you. You wouldn't keep a horse the other day when I suggested, because, you said, it might fall lame, and whenever you cross the street you take a hansom. Even you are not foolish enough to suppose that theatres and all the live things you can buy thereabouts mean Life. What earthly need have you for money?'

'It's there, bless its golden heart,' said Dick. 'It's there all the time. Providence has sent me nuts while I have teeth to crack 'em with. I haven't yet found the nut I wish to crack, but I'm keeping my teeth filed. Perhaps some day you and I will go for a walk round the wide earth.'

'With no work to do, nobody to worry us, and nobody to compete with? You would be unfit to speak to in a week. Besides, I shouldn't go. I don't care to profit by the price of a man's soul,—for that's what it would mean. Dick, it's no use arguing. You're a fool.'

'Don't see it. When I was on that Chinese pig-boat our captain got enormous credit for saving about twenty-five thousand very sea-sick little pigs, when our old tramp of a steamer fell foul of a timber-junk. Now, taking those pigs as a parallel—'

'Oh, confound your parallels! Whenever I try to improve your soul you always drag in some irrelevant anecdote from your shady past. Pigs aren't the British public; credit on the high seas isn't credit here; and self-respect is self-respect all the world over. Go out for a walk and try to catch some self-respect. And I say, if the Nilghai comes up this evening can I show him your diggings?'

'Surely. You'll be asking whether you must knock at my door, next.' And Dick departed, to take counsel with himself in the rapidly-gathering London fog.

Half an hour after he had left the Nilghai laboured up the staircase. He was the chiefest, as he was the hugest, of the war correspondents, and his experiences dated from the birth of the needle-gun. Saving only his ally, Keneu the Great War Eagle, there was no man mightier in the craft than he, and he always opened his conversation with the news that there would be trouble in the Balkans in the spring. Torpenhow laughed as he entered.

'Never mind the trouble in the Balkans. Those little states are always screeching. You've heard about Dick's luck?'

'Yes; he has been called up to notoriety, hasn't he? I hope you keep him properly humble. He wants suppressing from time to time.'

'He does. He's beginning to take liberties with what he thinks is his reputation.'

'Already! By Jove, he has cheek! I don't know about his reputation, but he'll come a cropper if he tries that sort of thing.'

'So I told him. I don't think he believes it.'

'They never do when they first start off. What's that wreck on the ground there?'

'Specimen of his latest impertinence.' Torpenhow thrust the torn edges of the canvas together and showed the well-groomed picture to the Nilghai, who looked at it for a moment and whistled.

'It's a chromo,' said he,—'a chromo-litholeo-margarine fake! What possessed him to do it? And yet how thoroughly he has caught the note that catches a public who think with their boots and read with their elbows! The cold-blooded insolence of the work almost saves it; but he mustn't go on with this. Hasn't he been praised and cockered up too much? You know these people here have no sense of proportion. They'll call him a second Detaille and a third-hand Meissonier while his fashion lasts. It's windy diet for a colt.'

'I don't think it affects Dick much. You might as well call a young wolf a lion and expect him to take the compliment in exchange for a shin-bone. Dick's soul is in the bank. He's working for cash.'

'Now he has thrown up war work, I suppose he doesn't see that the obligations of the service are just the same, only the proprietors are changed.'

'How should he know? He thinks he is his own master.'

'Does he? I could undeceive him for his good if there's any virtue in print. He wants the whip-lash.'

'Lay it on with science, then. I'd flay him myself, but I like him too much.'

'I've no scruples. He had the audacity to try to cut me out with a woman at Cairo once. I forgot that, but I remember now.'

'Did he cut you out?'

'You'll see when I have dealt with him. But, after all, what's the good? Leave him alone and he'll come home, if he has any stuff in him, dragging or wagging his tail behind him. There's more in a week of life than in a lively weekly. None the less I'll slate him. I'll slate him ponderously in the "Cataclysm."'

'Good luck to you; but I fancy nothing short of a crowbar would make Dick wince. His soul seems to have been fired before we came across him. He's intensely suspicious and utterly lawless.'

'Matter of temper,' said the Nilghai. 'It's the same with horses. Some you wallop and they work, some you wallop and they jib, and some you wallop and they go out for a walk with their hands in their pockets.'

'That's exactly what Dick has done,' said Torpenhow. 'Wait till he comes back. In the meantime you can begin your slating here. I'll show you some of his last and worst work in his studio.'

Dick had instinctively sought running water for a comfort to his mood of mind. He was leaning over the Embankment wall, watching the rush of the Thames, through the arches of Westminster Bridge. He began by thinking of Torpenhow's advice, but, as of custom, lost himself in the study of the faces flocking past. Some had death written on their features, and Dick marvelled that they could laugh. Others, clumsy and coarse-built for the most part, were alight with love; others were merely drawn and lined with work; but there was something, Dick knew, to be made out of them all. The poor at least should suffer that he might learn, and the rich should pay for the output of his learning. Thus his credit in the world and his cash balance at the bank would be increased. So much the better for him. He had suffered. Now he would take toll of the ills of others.

The fog was driven apart for a moment, and the sun shone, a blood-red wafer, on the water. Dick watched the spot till he heard the voice of the tide between the piers die down like the wash of the sea at low tide. A girl hard pressed by her lover shouted shamelessly, 'Ah, get away, you beast!' and a shift of the same wind that had opened the fog drove across Dick's face the black smoke of a river-steamer at her berth below the wall. He was blinded for the moment, then spun round and found himself face to face with—Maisie.

There was no mistaking. The years had turned the child to a woman, but they had not altered the dark-gray eyes, the thin scarlet lips, or the firmly-modelled mouth and chin; and, that all should be as it was of old, she wore a closely-fitting gray dress.

Since the human soul is finite and not in the least under its own command, Dick, advancing, said, 'Halloo!' after the manner of schoolboys, and Maisie answered, 'Oh, Dick, is that you?' Then against his will, and before the brain, newly released from considerations of the cash balance, had time to dictate to the nerves, every pulse of Dick's body throbbed furiously and his palate dried in his mouth. The fog shut down again, and Maisie's face was pearl-white through it. No word was spoken, but Dick fell into step at her side, and the two paced the Embankment together, keeping the step as perfectly as in their afternoon excursions to the mud-flats. Then Dick, a little hoarsely—

'What has happened to Amomma?'

'He died, Dick. Not cartridges; over-eating. He was always greedy. Isn't it funny?'

'Yes. No. Do you mean Amomma?'

'Ye—es. No. This. Where have you come from?'

'Over there.' He pointed eastward through the fog. 'And you?'

'Oh, I'm in the north,—the black north, across all the Park. I am very busy.'

'What do you do?'

'I paint a great deal. That's all I have to do.'

'Why, what's happened? You had three hundred a year.'

'I have that still. I am painting; that's all.'

'Are you alone, then?'

'There's a girl living with me. Don't walk so fast, Dick; you're out of step.'

'Then you noticed it too?'

'Of course I did. You're always out of step.'

'So I am. I'm sorry. You went on with the painting?'

'Of course. I said I should. I was at the Slade, then at Merton's in St. John's Wood, the big studio, then I pepper-potted,—I mean I went to the National,—and now I'm working under Kami.'

'But Kami is in Paris surely?'

'No; he has his teaching studio at Vitry-sur-Marne. I work with him in the summer, and I live in London in the winter. I'm a householder.'

'Do you sell much?'

'Now and again, but not often. There is my 'bus, I must take it or lose half an hour. Good-bye, Dick.'

'Good-bye, Maisie. Won't you tell me where you live? I must see you again; and perhaps I could help you. I—I paint a little myself.'

'I may be in the Park to-morrow if there is no working light. I walk from the Marble Arch down and back again; that is my little excursion. But of course I shall see you again.' She stepped into the omnibus and was swallowed up by the fog.

'Well—I—am—damned!' exclaimed Dick, and returned to the chambers.

Torpenhow and the Nilghai found him sitting on the steps to the studio door, repeating the phrase with an awful gravity.

'You'll be more damned when I've done with you,' said the Nilghai, upheaving his bulk from behind Torpenhow's shoulder and waving a sheaf of half-dry manuscript. 'Dick, it is of common report that you are suffering from swelled head.'

'Halloo, Nilghai. Back again? How are the Balkans and all the little Balkans? One side of your face is out of drawing, as usual.'

'Never mind that. I am commissioned to smite you in print. Torpenhow refuses from false delicacy. I've been overhauling the pot-boilers in your studio. They are simply disgraceful.'

'Oho! that's it, is it? If you think you can slate me, you're wrong. You can only describe, and you need as much room to turn in, on paper, as a P. and O. cargo-boat. But continue, and be swift. I'm going to bed.'

'H'm! h'm! h'm! The first part only deals with your pictures. Here's the peroration: "For work done without conviction, for power wasted on trivialities, for labour expended with levity for the deliberate purpose of winning the easy applause of a fashion-driven public—"'

'That's "His Last Shot," second edition. Go on.'

'—"public, there remains but one end,—the oblivion that is preceded by toleration and cenotaphed with contempt. From that fate Mr. Heldar has yet to prove himself out of danger."'

'Wow—wow—wow—wow—wow!' said Dick profanely. 'It's a clumsy ending and vile journalese, but it's quite true. And yet,'—he sprang to his feet and snatched at the manuscript,—'you scarred, deboshed, battered old gladiator! you're sent out when a war begins, to minister to the blind, brutal, British public's bestial thirst for blood. They have no arenas now, but they must have special correspondents. You're a fat gladiator who comes up through a trap-door and talks of what he's seen. You stand on precisely the same level as an energetic bishop, an affable actress, a devastating cyclone, or—mine own sweet self. And you presume to lecture me about my work! Nilghai, if it were worth while I'd caricature you in four papers!'

The Nilghai winced. He had not thought of this.

'As it is, I shall take this stuff and tear it small—so!' The manuscript fluttered in slips down the dark well of the staircase. 'Go home, Nilghai,' said Dick; 'go home to your lonely little bed, and leave me in peace. I am about to turn in till to-morrow.'

'Why, it isn't seven yet!' said Torpenhow, with amazement.

'It shall be two in the morning, if I choose,' said Dick, backing to the studio door. 'I go to grapple with a serious crisis, and I shan't want any dinner.'

The door shut and was locked.

'What can you do with a man like that?' said the Nilghai.

'Leave him alone. He's as mad as a hatter.'

At eleven there was kicking on the studio door. 'Is the Nilghai with

you still?' said a voice from within. 'Then tell him he might have condensed the whole of his lumbering nonsense into an epigram: "Only the
free are bond, and only the bond are free." Tell him he's one idiot, Torp,
and tell him I'm another.'

'All right. Come out and have supper. You're smoking on an empty
stomach.'

There was no answer.

Chapter 5

'I have a thousand men,' said he,
'To wait upon my will,
And towers nine upon the Tyne,
And three upon the Till.'

'And what care I for your men,' said she,
'Or towers from Tyne to Till,
Sith you must go with me,' she said,
'To wait upon my will?'

'Sir Hoggie and the Fairies.'

NEXT MORNING Torpenhow found Dick sunk in deepest repose of tobacco.

'Well, madman, how d'you feel?'

'I don't know. I'm trying to find out.'

'You had much better do some work.'

'Maybe; but I'm in no hurry. I've made a discovery. Torp, there's too much Ego in my Cosmos.'

'Not really! Is this revelation due to my lectures, or the Nilghai's?'

'It came to me suddenly, all on my own account. Much too much Ego; and now I'm going to work.'

He turned over a few half-finished sketches, drummed on a new canvas, cleaned three brushes, set Binkie to bite the toes of the lay-figure, rattled through his collection of arms and accoutrements, and then went out abruptly, declaring that he had done enough for the day.

'This is positively indecent,' said Torpenhow, 'and the first time that Dick has ever broken up a light morning. Perhaps he has found out that he has a soul, or an artistic temperament, or something equally valuable. That comes of leaving him alone for a month. Perhaps he has been going out of evenings. I must look to this.' He rang for the bald-headed old housekeeper, whom nothing could astonish or annoy.

'Beeton, did Mr. Heldar dine out at all while I was out of town?'

'Never laid 'is dress-clothes out once, sir, all the time. Mostly 'e dined in; but 'e brought some most remarkable fancy young gentlemen up 'er after theatres once or twice. Remarkable fancy they was. You gentlemen on the top floor does very much as you likes, but it do seem to me, sir, droppin' a walkin'-stick down five flights o' stairs an' then goin' down four abreast to pick it up again at half-past two in the mornin', singin', "Bring back the whisky, Willie darlin',"—not once or twice, but scores o' times,—isn't charity to the other tenants. What I say is, "Do as you would be done by." That's my motto.'

'Of course! of course! I'm afraid the top floor isn't the quietest in the house.'

'I make no complaints, sir. I have spoke to Mr. Heldar friendly, an' he laughed, an' did me a picture of the missis that is as good as a coloured print. It 'asn't the 'igh shine of a photograph, but what I say is, "Never look a gift-horse in the mouth." Mr. Heldar's dress-clothes 'aven't been on him for weeks.'

'Then it's all right,' said Torpenhow to himself. 'Orgies are healthy, and Dick has a head of his own, but when it comes to women making eyes I'm not so certain.—Binkie, never you be a man, little dorglums. They're contrary brutes, and they do things without any reason.'

Dick had turned northward across the Park, but he was walking in the spirit on the mud-flats with Maisie. He laughed aloud as he remembered the day when he had decked Amomma's horns with the ham-frills, and Maisie, white with rage, had cuffed him. How long those four years seemed in review, and how closely Maisie was connected with every hour of them! Storm across the sea, and Maisie in a gray dress on the beach, sweeping her drenched hair out of her eyes and laughing at the home-ward race of the fishing-smacks; hot sunshine on the mud-flats, and Maisie sniffing scornfully, with her chin in the air; Maisie flying before the wind that threshed the foreshore and drove the sand like small shot about her ears; Maisie, very composed and independent, telling lies to Mrs. Jennett while Dick supported her with coarser perjuries; Maisie picking her way delicately from stone to stone, a pistol in her hand and her teeth firm-set; and Maisie in a gray dress sitting on the grass between the mouth of a cannon and a nodding yellow sea-poppy. The pictures passed before him one by one, and the last stayed the longest. Dick was perfectly happy with a quiet peace that was as new to his mind as it was foreign to his experience. It never occurred to him that there might be other calls upon his time than loafing across the Park in the forenoon.

'There's a good working light now,' he said, watching his shadow placidly. 'Some poor devil ought to be grateful for this. And there's Maisie!'

She was walking towards him from the Marble Arch, and he saw that no mannerism of her gait had been changed. It was good to find her still Maisie, and, so to speak, his next-door neighbour. No greeting passed between them, because there had been none in the old days.

'What are you doing out of your studio at this hour?' said Dick, as one who was entitled to ask.

'Idling. Just idling. I got angry with a chin and scraped it out. Then I left it in a little heap of paint-chips and came away.'

'I know what palette-knifing means. What was the piccy?'

'A fancy head that wouldn't come right,—horrid thing!'

'I don't like working over scraped paint when I'm doing flesh. The grain comes up woolly as the paint dries.'

'Not if you scrape properly.' Maisie waved her hand to illustrate her methods. There was a dab of paint on the white cuff. Dick laughed.

'You're as untidy as ever.'

'That comes well from you. Look at your own cuff.'

'By Jove, yes! It's worse than yours. I don't think we've much altered in anything. Let's see, though.' He looked at Maisie critically. The pale blue haze of an autumn day crept between the tree-trunks of the Park and made a background for the gray dress, the black velvet toque above the black hair, and the resolute profile.

'No, there's nothing changed. How good it is! D'you remember when I fastened your hair into the snap of a handbag?'

Maisie nodded, with a twinkle in her eyes, and turned her full face to Dick.

'Wait a minute,' said he. 'That mouth is down at the corners a little. Who's been worrying you, Maisie?'

'No one but myself. I never seem to get on with my work, and yet I try hard enough, and Kami says—'

'"Continuez, mesdemoiselles. Continuez toujours, mes enfants." Kami is depressing. I beg your pardon.'

'Yes, that's what he says. He told me last summer that I was doing better and he'd let me exhibit this year.'

'Not in this place, surely?'

'Of course not. The Salon.'

'You fly high.'

'I've been beating my wings long enough. Where do you exhibit, Dick?'

'I don't exhibit. I sell.'

'What is your line, then?'

'Haven't you heard?' Dick's eyes opened. Was this thing possible? He cast about for some means of conviction. They were not far from the Marble Arch. 'Come up Oxford Street a little and I'll show you.'

A small knot of people stood round a print-shop that Dick knew well. 'Some reproduction of my work inside,' he said, with suppressed triumph. Never before had success tasted so sweet upon the tongue. 'You see the sort of things I paint. D'you like it?'

Maisie looked at the wild whirling rush of a field-battery going into action under fire. Two artillerymen stood behind her in the crowd.

'They've chucked the off lead-'orse,' said one to the other. ''E's tore up awful, but they're makin' good time with the others. That lead-driver drives better nor you, Tom. See 'ow cunnin' e's nursin' 'is 'orse.'

'Number Three'll be off the limber, next jolt,' was the answer.

'No, 'e won't. See 'ow 'is foot's braced against the iron? 'E's all right.'

Dick watched Maisie's face and swelled with joy—fine, rank, vulgar triumph. She was more interested in the little crowd than in the picture. That was something that she could understand.

'And I wanted it so! Oh, I did want it so!' she said at last, under her breath.

'Me,—all me!' said Dick placidly. 'Look at their faces. It hits 'em. They don't know what makes their eyes and mouths open; but I know. And I know my work's right.'

'Yes. I see. Oh, what a thing to have come to one!'

'Come to one, indeed! I had to go out and look for it. What do you think?'

'I call it success. Tell me how you got it.'

They returned to the Park, and Dick delivered himself of the saga of his own doings, with all the arrogance of a young man speaking to a woman. From the beginning he told the tale, the I—I—I's flashing through the records as telegraph-poles fly past the traveller. Maisie listened and nodded her head. The histories of strife and privation did not move her a hair's-breadth. At the end of each canto he would conclude, 'And that gave me some notion of handling colour,' or light, or whatever it might be that he had set out to pursue and understand. He led her breathless across half the world, speaking as he had never spoken in his life before. And in the flood-tide of his exaltation there came upon him a great desire to pick up this maiden who nodded her head and said, 'I understand. Go on,'—to pick her up and to carry her away with him, because she was Maisie, and because she understood, and because she was his right, and a woman to be desired above all women.

Then he checked himself abruptly. 'And so I took all I wanted,' he said, 'and I had to fight for it. Now you tell.'

Maisie's tale was almost as gray as her dress. It covered years of patient toil backed by savage pride that would not be broken though dealers laughed, and fogs delayed work, and Kami was unkind and even sar-

THE LIGHT THAT FAILED

castic, and girls in other studios were painfully polite. It had a few bright spots, in pictures accepted at provincial exhibitions, but it wound up with the oft-repeated wail, 'And so you see, Dick, I had no success, though I worked so hard.'

Then pity filled Dick. Even thus had Maisie spoken when she could not hit the breakwater, half an hour before she had kissed him. And that had happened yesterday.

'Never mind,' he said. 'I'll tell you something, if you'll believe it.' The words were shaping themselves of their own accord. 'The whole thing, lock, stock, and barrel, isn't worth one big yellow sea-poppy below Fort Keeling.'

Maisie flushed a little. 'It's all very well for you to talk, but you've had the success and I haven't.'

'Let me talk, then. I know you'll understand. Maisie, dear, it sounds a bit absurd, but those ten years never existed, and I've come back again. It really is just the same. Can't you see? You're alone now and I'm alone. What's the use of worrying? Come to me instead, darling.'

Maisie poked the gravel with her parasol. They were sitting on a bench. 'I understand,' she said slowly. 'But I've got my work to do, and I must do it.'

'Do it with me, then, dear. I won't interrupt.'

'No, I couldn't. It's my work,—mine,—mine,—mine! I've been alone all my life in myself, and I'm not going to belong to anybody except myself. I remember things as well as you do, but that doesn't count. We were babies then, and we didn't know what was before us. Dick, don't be selfish. I think I see my way to a little success next year. Don't take it away from me.'

'I beg your pardon, darling. It's my fault for speaking stupidly. I can't expect you to throw up all your life just because I'm back. I'll go to my own place and wait a little.'

'But, Dick, I don't want you to—go—out of—my life, now you've just come back.'

'I'm at your orders; forgive me.' Dick devoured the troubled little face with his eyes. There was triumph in them, because he could not conceive that Maisie should refuse sooner or later to love him, since he loved her.

'It's wrong of me,' said Maisie, more slowly than before; 'it's wrong and selfish; but, oh, I've been so lonely! No, you misunderstand. Now I've seen you again,—it's absurd, but I want to keep you in my life.'

'Naturally. We belong.'

'We don't; but you always understood me, and there is so much in my work that you could help me in. You know things and the ways of doing things. You must.'

'I do, I fancy, or else I don't know myself. Then I suppose you won't care to lose sight of me altogether, and you want me to help you in your work?'

'Yes; but remember, Dick, nothing will ever come of it. That's why I feel so selfish. Let things stay as they are. I do want your help.'

'You shall have it. But let's consider. I must see your pics first, and overhaul your sketches, and find out about your tendencies. You should see what the papers say about my tendencies! Then I'll give you good advice, and you shall paint according. Isn't that it, Maisie?'

Again there was unholy triumph in Dick's eye.

'It's too good of you,—much too good. Because you are consoling yourself with what will never happen, and I know that, and yet I wish to keep you. Don't blame me later, please.'

'I'm going into the matter with my eyes open. Moreover, the queen can do no wrong. It isn't your selfishness that impresses me. It's your audacity in proposing to make use of me.'

'Pooh! You're only Dick,—and a print-shop.'

'Very good: that's all I am. But, Maisie, you believe, don't you, that I love you? I don't want you to have any false notions about brothers and sisters.'

Maisie looked up for a moment and dropped her eyes.

'It's absurd, but—I believe. I wish I could send you away before you get angry with me. But—but the girl that lives with me is red-haired, and an impressionist, and all our notions clash.'

'So do ours, I think. Never mind. Three months from to-day we shall be laughing at this together.'

Maisie shook her head mournfully. 'I knew you wouldn't understand, and it will only hurt you more when you find out. Look at my face, Dick, and tell me what you see.'

They stood up and faced each other for a moment. The fog was gathering, and it stifled the roar of the traffic of London beyond the railings. Dick brought all his painfully-acquired knowledge of faces to bear on the eyes, mouth, and chin underneath the black velvet toque.

'It's the same Maisie, and it's the same me,' he said. 'We've both nice little wills of our own, and one or other of us has to be broken. Now about the future. I must come and see your pictures some day,—I suppose when the red-haired girl is on the premises.'

'Sundays are my best times. You must come on Sundays. There are such heaps of things I want to talk about and ask your advice about. Now I must get back to work.'

'Try to find out before next Sunday what I am,' said Dick. 'Don't take my word for anything I've told you. Good-bye, darling, and bless you.'

Maisie stole away like a little gray mouse. Dick watched her till she was out of sight, but he did not hear her say to herself, very soberly, 'I'm a wretch,—a horrid, selfish wretch. But it's Dick, and Dick will understand.'

No one has yet explained what actually happens when an irresistible force meets the immovable post, though many have thought deeply, even as Dick thought. He tried to assure himself that Maisie would be led in a few weeks by his mere presence and discourse to a better way of thinking. Then he remembered much too distinctly her face and all that was written on it.

'If I know anything of heads,' he said, 'there's everything in that face but love. I shall have to put that in myself; and that chin and mouth won't be won for nothing. But she's right. She knows what she wants, and she's going to get it. What insolence! Me! Of all the people in the wide world, to use me! But then she's Maisie. There's no getting over that fact; and it's good to see her again. This business must have been simmering at the back of my head for years. . . . She'll use me as I used Binat at Port Said. She's quite right. It will hurt a little. I shall have to see her every Sunday,—like a young man courting a housemaid. She's sure to come round; and yet—that mouth isn't a yielding mouth. I shall be wanting to kiss her all the time, and I shall have to look at her pictures,— I don't even know what sort of work she does yet,—and I shall have to talk about Art,—Woman's Art! Therefore, particularly and perpetually, damn all varieties of Art! It did me a good turn once, and now it's in my way. I'll go home and do some Art.'

Half-way to the studio Dick was smitten with a terrible thought. The figure of a solitary woman in the fog suggested it.

'She's all alone in London, with a red-haired impressionist girl, who probably has the digestion of an ostrich. Most red-haired people have. Maisie's a bilious little body. They'll eat like lone women,—meals at all hours and tea with all meals. I remember how the students in Paris used to pig along. She may fall ill at any minute, and I shan't be able to help. Whew! This is ten times worse than owning a wife.'

Torpenhow came into the studio at dusk, and looked at Dick with his eyes full of the austere love that springs up between men who have tugged at the same oar together and are yoked by custom and use and the intimacies of toil. This is a good love, and, since it allows, and even encourages, strife, recrimination, and the most brutal sincerity, does not die, but increases, and is proof against any absence and evil conduct.

Dick was silent after he handed Torpenhow the filled pipe of council.

He thought of Maisie and her possible needs. It was a new thing to think of anybody but Torpenhow, who could think for himself. Here at last was an outlet for that cash balance. He could adorn Maisie barbarically with jewelry,—a thick gold necklace round that little neck, bracelets upon the rounded arms, and rings of price upon her hands,—the cool, temperate, ringless hands that he had taken between his own. It was an absurd thought, for Maisie would not even allow him to put one ring on one finger, and she would laugh at golden trappings. It would be better to sit with her quietly in the dusk, his arm round her neck and her face on his shoulder, as befitted husband and wife. Torpenhow's boots creaked that night, and his strong voice jarred. Dick's brows contracted and he murmured an evil word because he had taken all his success as a right and part payment for past discomfort, and now he was checked in his stride by a woman who admitted all the success and did not instantly care for him.

'I say, old man,' said Torpenhow, who had made one or two vain attempts at conversation, 'I haven't put your back up by anything I've said lately, have I?'

'You! No. How could you?'

''Liver out of order?'

'The truly healthy man doesn't know he has a liver. I'm only a bit worried about things in general. I suppose it's my soul.'

'The truly healthy man doesn't know he has a soul. What business have you with luxuries of that kind?'

'It came of itself. Who's the man that says that we're all islands shouting lies to each other across seas of misunderstanding?'

'He's right, whoever he is,—except about the misunderstanding. I don't think we could misunderstand each other.'

The blue smoke curled back from the ceiling in clouds. Then Torpenhow, insinuatingly—

'Dick, is it a woman?'

'Be hanged if it's anything remotely resembling a woman; and if you begin to talk like that, I'll hire a red-brick studio with white paint trimmings and begonias and petunias and blue Hungarias to play among three-and-sixpenny pot-palms, and I'll mount all my pics in aniline-dye plush plasters, and I'll invite every woman who yelps and maunders and moans over what her guidebooks tell her is Art, and you shall receive 'em, Torp,—in a snuff-brown velvet coat with yellow trousers and an orange tie. You'll like that.'

'Too thin, Dick. A better man than you denied with cursing and swearing on a memorable occasion. You've overdone it, just as he did. It's no business of mine, of course, but it's comforting to think that somewhere under the stars there's saving up for you a tremendous thrashing. Whether it'll come from heaven or earth I don't know, but it's bound to come and break you up a little. You want hammering.'

Dick shivered. 'All right,' said he. 'When this island is disintegrated it will call for you.'

'I shall come round the corner and help to disintegrate it some more. We're talking nonsense. Come along to a theatre.'

Chapter 6

'And you may lead a thousand men,
Nor ever draw the rein,
But ere ye lead the Faery Queen
'Twill burst your heart in twain.'

He has slipped his foot from the stirrup-bar,
The bridle from his hand,
And he is bound by hand and foot
To the Queen o' Faery-land.
                                        'Sir Hoggie and the Fairies.'

SOME WEEKS LATER, on a very foggy Sunday, Dick was returning across the Park to his studio. 'This,' he said, 'is evidently the thrashing that Torp meant. It hurts more than I expected; but the queen can do no wrong. And she certainly has some notion of drawing.'

He had just finished a Sunday visit to Maisie,—always under the green eyes of the red-haired impressionist girl, whom he learned to hate at sight,—and was tingling with a keen sense of shame. Sunday after Sunday, putting on his best clothes, he had walked over to the untidy house north of the Park, first to see Maisie's pictures, and then to criticise and advise upon them as he realised that they were productions on which advice would not be wasted. Sunday after Sunday, and his love grew with each visit, he had been compelled to cram his heart back from between his lips when it prompted him to kiss Maisie several times and very much indeed. Sunday after Sunday, the head above the heart had warned him that Maisie was not yet attainable, and that it would be better to talk as connectedly as possible upon the mysteries of the craft that was all in all to her. Therefore it was his fate to endure weekly torture in the studio built out over the clammy back-garden of a frail stuffy little villa where nothing was ever in its right place and nobody ever called,—to endure and to watch Maisie moving to and fro with the teacups. He abhorred tea, but, since it gave him a little longer time in her presence, he drank it devoutly, and the red-haired girl sat in an untidy heap and eyed him without speaking. She was always watching him. Once, and only once, when she had left the studio Maisie showed him an album that held a few poor cuttings from provincial papers,—the briefest of hurried notes on some of her pictures sent to outlying exhibitions. Dick stooped and kissed the paint-smudged thumb on the open page. 'Oh, my love, my love,' he muttered, 'do you value these things? Chuck 'em into the waste-paper basket!'

'Not till I get something better,' said Maisie, shutting the book.

Then Dick, moved by no respect for his public and a very deep regard for the maiden, did deliberately propose, in order to secure more of these coveted cuttings, that he should paint a picture which Maisie should sign.

'That's childish,' said Maisie, 'and I didn't think it of you. It must be my work. Mine,—mine,—mine!'

'Go and design decorative medallions for rich brewers' houses. You are thoroughly good at that.' Dick was sick and savage.

'Better things than medallions, Dick,' was the answer in tones that recalled a gray-eyed atom's fearless speech to Mrs. Jennett. Dick would have abased himself utterly, but that the other girl trailed in.

Next Sunday he laid at Maisie's feet small gifts of pencils that could almost draw of themselves and colours in whose permanence he believed, and he was ostentatiously attentive to the work in hand. It demanded, among other things, an exposition of the faith that was in him. Torpenhow's hair would have stood on end had he heard the fluency with which Dick preached his own gospel of Art.

A month before, Dick would have been equally astonished; but it was Maisie's will and pleasure, and he dragged his words together to make plain to her comprehension all that had been hidden to himself of the whys and wherefores of work. There is not the least difficulty in doing a thing if you only know how to do it; the trouble is to explain your method.

'I could put this right if I had a brush in my hand,' said Dick despairingly, over the modelling of a chin that Maisie complained would not 'look flesh,'—it was the same chin that she had scraped out with the palette-knife,—'but I find it almost impossible to teach you. There's a queer grim Dutch touch about your painting that I like; but I've a notion that you're weak in drawing. You foreshorten as though you never used the model, and you've caught Kami's pasty way of dealing with flesh in shadow. Then, again, though you don't know it yourself, you shirk hard work. Suppose you spend some of your time on line alone. Line doesn't allow of shirking. Oils do, and three square inches of flashy, tricky stuff in the corner of a pic sometimes carry a bad thing off,—as I know. That's immoral. Do line-work for a little while, and then I can tell more about your powers, as old Kami used to say.'

Maisie protested: she did not care for the pure line.

'I know,' said Dick. 'You want to do your fancy heads with a bunch of flowers at the base of the neck to hide bad modelling.' The red-haired girl laughed a little. 'You want to do landscapes with cattle knee-deep in grass to hide bad drawing. You want to do a great deal more than you can do. You have sense of colour, but you want form. Colour's a gift,—put it aside and think no more about it,—but form you can be drilled into. Now, all your fancy heads—and some of them are very good—will keep you exactly where you are. With line you must go forward or backward, and it will show up all your weaknesses.'

'But other people—' began Maisie.

'You mustn't mind what other people do. If their souls were your soul it would be different. You stand and fall by your own work, remember, and it is waste of time to think of any one else in this battle.'

Dick paused, and the longing that had been so resolutely put away came back into his eyes. He looked at Maisie, and the look asked as plainly as words, Was it not time to leave all this barren wilderness of canvas and counsel and join hands with Life and Love?

Maisie assented to the new programme of schooling so adorably that Dick could hardly restrain himself from picking her up then and there and carrying her off to the nearest registrar's office. It was the implicit obedience to the spoken word and the blank indifference to the unspoken desire that baffled and buffeted his soul. He held authority in that house,—authority limited, indeed, to one-half of one afternoon in seven, but very real while it lasted. Maisie had learned to appeal to him on many subjects, from the proper packing of pictures to the condition of a smoky chimney. The red-haired girl never consulted him about anything. On the other hand she accepted his appearances without protest, and watched him always. He discovered that the meals of the establishment were irregular and fragmentary. They depended chiefly on tea, pickles, and biscuit, as he had suspected from the beginning. The girls were supposed to market week and week about, but they lived, with the help of a charwoman, as casually as the young ravens. Maisie spent most of her income on models, and the other girl revelled in apparatus as refined as her work was rough. Armed with knowledge dear-bought from the Docks, Dick warned Maisie that the end of semi-starvation meant the crippling of power to work, which was considerably worse than death. Maisie took the warning, and gave more thought to what she ate and drank. When this trouble returned upon him, as it generally did in the long winter twilights, the remembrance of that little act of domestic authority and his coercion with a hearth-brush of the smoky drawing-room chimney stung Dick like a whip-lash.

He conceived that this memory would be the extreme of his sufferings, till, one Sunday, the red-haired girl announced that she would make a study of Dick's head, and that he would be good enough to sit still, and—quite as an afterthought—look at Maisie. He sat, because he could not well refuse, and for the space of half an hour he reflected on all the people in the past whom he had laid open for the purposes of his own craft. He remembered Binat most distinctly,—that Binat who had once been an artist and talked about degradation.

It was the merest monochrome roughing-in of a head, but it presented the dumb waiting, the longing, and, above all, the hopeless enslavement of the man, in a spirit of bitter mockery.

'I'll buy it,' said Dick promptly, 'at your own price.'

'My price is too high, but I daresay you'll be as grateful if—' The wet sketch fluttered from the girl's hand and fell into the ashes of the studio stove. When she picked it up it was hopelessly smudged.

'Oh, it's all spoiled!' said Maisie. 'And I never saw it. Was it like?'

'Thank you,' said Dick under his breath to the red-haired girl, and he removed himself swiftly.

'How that man hates me!' said the girl. 'And how he loves you, Maisie!'

'What nonsense! I know Dick's very fond of me, but he has his work to do, and I have mine.'

'Yes, he is fond of you, and I think he knows there is something in impressionism, after all. Maisie, can't you see?'

'See? See what?'

'Nothing; only, I know that if I could get any man to look at me as that man looks at you, I'd—I don't know what I'd do! But he hates me. Oh, how he hates me!'

She was not altogether correct. Dick's hatred was tempered with gratitude for a few moments, and then he forgot the girl entirely. Only the sense of shame remained, and he was nursing it across the Park in the fog. 'There'll be an explosion one of these days,' he said wrathfully. 'But it isn't Maisie's fault; she's right, quite right, as far as she knows, and I can't blame her. This business has been going on for three months nearly. Three months!—and it cost me ten years' knocking about to get at the notion, the merest raw notion, of my work. That's true; but then I didn't have pins, drawing-pins and palette-knives, stuck into me every Sunday. Oh, my little darling, if ever I break you, somebody will have a very bad time of it. No, she won't. I'd be as big a fool about her as I am now. I'll poison that red-haired girl on my wedding-day,—she's unwholesome,—and now I'll pass on these present bad times to Torp.'

Torpenhow had been moved to lecture Dick more than once lately on the sin of levity, and Dick had listened and replied not a word. In the weeks between the first few Sundays of his discipline he had flung himself savagely into his work, resolved that Maisie should at least know the full stretch of his powers. Then he had taught Maisie that she must not pay the least attention to any work outside her own, and Maisie had obeyed him all too well. She took his counsels, but was not interested in his pictures.

'Your things smell of tobacco and blood,' she said once. 'Can't you do anything except soldiers?'

'I could do a head of you that would startle you,' thought Dick,—this was before the red-haired girl had brought him under the guillotine,—but he only said, 'I am very sorry,' and harrowed Torpenhow's soul that evening with blasphemies against Art. Later, insensibly and to a large extent against his own will, he ceased to interest himself in his own work. For Maisie's sake, and to soothe the self-respect that it seemed to him he lost each Sunday, he would not consciously turn out bad stuff, but, since Maisie did not care even for his best, it were better not to do anything at all save wait and mark time between Sunday and Sunday. Torpenhow was disgusted as the weeks went by fruitless, and then attacked him one Sunday evening when Dick felt utterly exhausted after three hours' biting self-restraint in Maisie's presence. There was Language, and Torpenhow withdrew to consult the Nilghai, who had come in to talk continental politics.

'Bone-idle, is he? Careless, and touched in the temper?' said the Nilghai. 'It isn't worth worrying over. Dick is probably playing the fool with a woman.'

'Isn't that bad enough?'

'No. She may throw him out of gear and knock his work to pieces for a while. She may even turn up here some day and make a scene on the staircase: one never knows. But until Dick speaks of his own accord you had better not touch him. He is no easy-tempered man to handle.'

'No; I wish he were. He is such an aggressive, cock-sure, you-be-damned fellow.'

'He'll get that knocked out of him in time. He must learn that he can't storm up and down the world with a box of moist tubes and a slick brush. You're fond of him?'

'I'd take any punishment that's in store for him if I could; but the worst of it is, no man can save his brother.'

'No, and the worser of it is, there is no discharge in this war. Dick must learn his lesson like the rest of us. Talking of war, there'll be trouble in the Balkans in the spring.'

'That trouble is long coming. I wonder if we could drag Dick out there when it comes off?'

Dick entered the room soon afterwards, and the question was put to him. 'Not good enough,' he said shortly. 'I'm too comf'y where I am.'

'Surely you aren't taking all the stuff in the papers seriously?' said the Nilghai. 'Your vogue will be ended in less than six months,—the public will know your touch and go on to something new,—and where will you be then?'

'Here, in England.'

'When you might be doing decent work among us out there? Nonsense! I shall go, The Keneu will be there, Torp will be there, Cassavetti will be there, and the whole lot of us will be there, and we shall have as much as ever we can do, with unlimited fighting and the chance for you of seeing things that would make the reputation of three Verestchagins.'

'Um!' said Dick, pulling at his pipe.

'You prefer to stay here and imagine that all the world is gaping at your pictures? Just think how full an average man's life is of his own pursuits and pleasures. When twenty thousand of him find time to look up between mouthfuls and grunt something about something they aren't the least interested in, the net result is called fame, reputation, or notoriety, according to the taste and fancy of the speller my lord.'

'I know that as well as you do. Give me credit for a little gumption.'

'Be hanged if I do!'

'Be hanged, then; you probably will be,—for a spy, by excited Turks. Heigh-ho! I'm weary, dead weary, and virtue has gone out of me.' Dick dropped into a chair, and was fast asleep in a minute.

'That's a bad sign,' said the Nilghai, in an undertone.

Torpenhow picked the pipe from the waistcoat where it was beginning to burn, and put a pillow behind the head. 'We can't help; we can't help,' he said. 'It's a good ugly sort of old cocoa-nut, and I'm fond of it. There's the scar of the wipe he got when he was cut over in the square.'

'Shouldn't wonder if that has made him a trifle mad.'

'I should. He's a most businesslike madman.'

Then Dick began to snore furiously.

'Oh, here, no affection can stand this sort of thing. Wake up, Dick, and go and sleep somewhere else, if you intend to make a noise about it.'

'When a cat has been out on the tiles all night,' said the Nilghai in his beard, 'I notice that she usually sleeps all day. This is natural history.'

Dick staggered away rubbing his eyes and yawning. In the night-watches he was overtaken with an idea, so simple and so luminous that he wondered he had never conceived it before. It was full of craft. He would seek Maisie on a week-day,—would suggest an excursion, and would take her by train to Fort Keeling, over the very ground that they two had trodden together ten years ago.

'As a general rule,' he explained to his chin-lathered reflection in the morning, 'it isn't safe to cross an old trail twice. Things remind one of things, and a cold wind gets up, and you feel sad; but this is an exception to every rule that ever was. I'll go to Maisie at once.'

Fortunately, the red-haired girl was out shopping when he arrived, and Maisie in a paint-spattered blouse was warring with her canvas. She was not pleased to see him; for week-day visits were a stretch of the bond; and it needed all his courage to explain his errand.

'I know you've been working too hard,' he concluded, with an air of authority. 'If you do that you'll break down. You had much better come.'

'Where to?' said Maisie wearily. She had been standing before her easel too long, and was very tired.

'Anywhere you please. We'll take a train to-morrow and see where it stops. We'll have lunch somewhere, and I'll bring you back in the evening.'

'If there's a good working light to-morrow I lose a day.' Maisie balanced the heavy white chestnut palette irresolutely.

Dick bit back an oath that was hurrying to his lips. He had not yet learned patience with the maiden to whom her work was all in all.

'You'll lose ever so many more, dear, if you use every hour of working light. Overwork's only murderous idleness. Don't be unreasonable. I'll call for you to-morrow after breakfast early.'

'But surely you are going to ask—'

'No, I am not. I want you and nobody else. Besides, she hates me as much as I hate her. She won't care to come. To-morrow, then; and pray that we get sunshine.'

Dick went away delighted, and by consequence did no work whatever. He strangled a wild desire to order a special train, but bought a great gray kangaroo cloak lined with glossy black marten, and then retired into himself to consider things.

'I'm going out for the day to-morrow with Dick,' said Maisie to the red-haired girl when the latter returned, tired, from marketing in the Edgware Road.

'He deserves it. I shall have the studio floor thoroughly scrubbed while you're away. It's very dirty.'

Maisie had enjoyed no sort of holiday for months, and looked forward to the little excitement, but not without misgivings.

'There's nobody nicer than Dick when he talks sensibly,' she thought, 'but I'm sure he'll be silly and worry me, and I'm sure I can't tell him anything he'd like to hear. If he'd only be sensible I should like him so much better.'

Dick's eyes were full of joy when he made his appearance next morning and saw Maisie, gray-ulstered and black-velvet-hatted, standing in the hall-way. Palaces of marble, and not sordid imitations of grained wood, were surely the fittest background for such a divinity. The red-haired girl drew her into the studio for a moment and kissed her hurriedly. Maisie's eyebrows climbed to the top of her forehead; she was altogether unused to these demonstrations. 'Mind my hat,' she said, hurrying away, and ran down the steps to Dick waiting by the hansom.

'Are you quite warm enough? Are you sure you wouldn't like some more breakfast? Put this cloak over your knees.'

'I'm quite comf'y, thanks. Where are we going, Dick? Oh, do stop singing like that. People will think we're mad.'

'Let 'em think,—if the exertion doesn't kill them. They don't know who we are, and I'm sure I don't care who they are. My faith, Maisie, you're looking lovely!'

Maisie stared directly in front of her and did not reply. The wind of a keen, clear winter morning had put colour into her cheeks. Overhead, the creamy-yellow smoke-clouds were thinning away one by one against a pale-blue sky, and the improvident sparrows broke off from water-spout committees and cab-rank cabals to clamour of the coming of spring.

'It will be lovely weather in the country,' said Dick.

'But where are we going?'

'Wait and see.'

They stopped at Victoria, and Dick sought tickets. For less than half the fraction of an instant it occurred to Maisie, comfortably settled by the waiting-room fire, that it was much more pleasant to send a man to the booking-office than to elbow one's way through the crowd. Dick put her into a Pullman,—solely on account of the warmth there; and she regarded the extravagance with grave scandalised eyes as the train moved out into the country.

'I wish I knew where we are going,' she repeated for the twentieth time. The name of a well-remembered station flashed by, towards the end of the run, and Maisie was enlightened.

'Oh, Dick, you villain!'

'Well, I thought you might like to see the place again. You haven't been here since old times, have you?'

'No. I never cared to see Mrs. Jennett again; and she was all that was ever there.'

'Not quite. Look out a minute. There's the windmill above the potato-fields; they haven't built villas there yet; d'you remember when I shut you up in it?'

'Yes. How she beat you for it! I never told it was you.'

'She guessed. I jammed a stick under the door and told you that I was burying Amomma alive in the potatoes, and you believed me. You had a trusting nature in those days.'

They laughed and leaned to look out, identifying ancient landmarks with many reminiscences. Dick fixed his weather eye on the curve of Maisie's cheek, very near his own, and watched the blood rise under the clear skin. He congratulated himself upon his cunning, and looked that the evening would bring him a great reward.

When the train stopped they went out to look at an old town with new eyes. First, but from a distance, they regarded the house of Mrs. Jennett.

'Suppose she should come out now, what would you do?' said Dick, with mock terror.

'I should make a face.'

'Show then,' said Dick, dropping into the speech of childhood.

Maisie made that face in the direction of the mean little villa, and Dick laughed aloud.

'"This is disgraceful,"' said Maisie, mimicking Mrs. Jennett's tone. '"Maisie, you run in at once, and learn the collect, gospel, and epistle for the next three Sundays. After all I've taught you, too, and three helps every Sunday at dinner! Dick's always leading you into mischief. If you aren't a gentleman, Dick, you might at least—"'

The sentence ended abruptly. Maisie remembered when it had last been used.

'"Try to behave like one,"' said Dick promptly. 'Quite right. Now we'll get some lunch and go on to Fort Keeling,—unless you'd rather drive there?'

'We must walk, out of respect to the place. How little changed it all is!'

They turned in the direction of the sea through unaltered streets, and the influence of old things lay upon them. Presently they passed a con-fectioner's shop much considered in the days when their joint pocket-money amounted to a shilling a week.

'Dick, have you any pennies?' said Maisie, half to herself.

'Only three; and if you think you're going to have two of 'em to buy peppermints with, you're wrong. She says peppermints aren't ladylike.'

Again they laughed, and again the colour came into Maisie's cheeks as the blood boiled through Dick's heart. After a large lunch they went down to the beach and to Fort Keeling across the waste, wind-bitten

THE LIGHT THAT FAILED

land that no builder had thought it worth his while to defile. The winter
breeze came in from the sea and sang about their ears.

'Maisie,' said Dick, 'your nose is getting a crude Prussian blue at the
tip. I'll race you as far as you please for as much as you please.'

She looked round cautiously, and with a laugh set off, swiftly as the
ulster allowed, till she was out of breath.

'We used to run miles,' she panted. 'It's absurd that we can't run now.'

'Old age, dear. This it is to get fat and sleek in town. When I
wished to pull your hair you generally ran for three miles, shrieking at
the top of your voice. I ought to know, because those shrieks were meant
to call up Mrs. Jennett with a cane and—'

'Dick, I never got you a beating on purpose in my life.'

'No, of course you never did. Good Heavens! look at the sea.'

'Why, it's the same as ever!' said Maisie.

Torpenhow had gathered from Mr. Beeton that Dick, properly dressed
and shaved, had left the house at half-past eight in the morning with a
travelling-rug over his arm. The Nilghai rolled in at mid-day for chess
and polite conversation.

'It's worse than anything I imagined,' said Torpenhow.

'Oh, the everlasting Dick, I suppose! You fuss over him like a hen with
one chick. Let him run riot if he thinks it'll amuse him. You can whip a
young pup off feather, but you can't whip a young man.'

'It isn't a woman. It's one woman; and it's a girl.'

'Where's your proof?'

'He got up and went out at eight this morning,—got up in the middle
of the night, by Jove! a thing he never does except when he's on service.
Even then, remember, we had to kick him out of his blankets before the
fight began at El-Maghrib. It's disgusting.'

'It looks odd; but maybe he's decided to buy a horse at last. He might
get up for that, mightn't he?'

'Buy a blazing wheelbarrow! He'd have told us if there was a horse in
the wind. It's a girl.'

'Don't be certain. Perhaps it's only a married woman.'

'Dick has some sense of humour, if you haven't. Who gets up in the
gray dawn to call on another man's wife? It's a girl.'

'Let it be a girl, then. She may teach him that there's somebody else
in the world besides himself.'

'She'll spoil his hand. She'll waste his time, and she'll marry him, and
ruin his work for ever. He'll be a respectable married man before we can
stop him, and—he'll never go on the long trail again.'

'All quite possible, but the earth won't spin the other way when it happens. . . . Ho! ho! I'd give something to see Dick "go wooing with the boys." Don't worry about it. These things be with Allah, and we can only look on. Get the chessmen.'

The red-haired girl was lying down in her own room, staring at the ceiling. The footsteps of people on the pavement sounded, as they grew indistinct in the distance, like a many-times-repeated kiss that was all one long kiss. Her hands were by her side, and they opened and shut savagely from time to time.

The charwoman in charge of the scrubbing of the studio knocked at her door: 'Beg y' pardon, miss, but in cleanin' of a floor there's two, not to say three, kind of soap, which is yaller, an' mottled, an' disinfectink. Now, jist before I took my pail into the passage I thought it would be pre'aps jest as well if I was to come up 'ere an' ask you what sort of soap you was wishful that I should use on them boards. The yaller soap, miss—'

There was nothing in the speech to have caused the paroxysm of fury that drove the red-haired girl into the middle of the room, almost shouting—

'Do you suppose I care what you use? Any kind will do!—any kind!'

The woman fled, and the red-haired girl looked at her own reflection in the glass for an instant and covered her face with her hands. It was as though she had shouted some shameless secret aloud.

Chapter 7

Roses red and roses white
Plucked I for my love's delight.
She would none of all my posies,—
Bade me gather her blue roses.

Half the world I wandered through,
Seeking where such flowers grew;
Half the world unto my quest
Answered but with laugh and jest.

It may be beyond the grave
She shall find what she would have.
Mine was but an idle quest,—
Roses white and red are best!

'Blue Roses.'

INDEED THE SEA had not changed. Its waters were low on the mud-banks, and the Marazion bell-buoy clanked and swung in the tide-way. On the white beach-sand dried stumps of sea-poppy shivered and chattered together.

'I don't see the old breakwater,' said Maisie under her breath.

'Let's be thankful that we have as much as we have. I don't believe they've mounted a single new gun on the fort since we were here. Come and look.'

They came to the glacis of Fort Keeling, and sat down in a nook sheltered from the wind under the tarred throat of a forty-pounder cannon.

'Now, if Amomma were only here!' said Maisie.

For a long time both were silent. Then Dick took Maisie's hand and called her by her name.

She shook her head and looked out to sea.

'Maisie, darling, doesn't it make any difference?'

'No!' between clenched teeth. 'I'd—I'd tell you if it did; but it doesn't. Oh, Dick, please be sensible.'

'Don't you think that it ever will?'

'No, I'm sure it won't.'

'Why?'

Maisie rested her chin on her hand, and, still regarding the sea, spoke hurriedly—

'I know what you want perfectly well, but I can't give it you, Dick. It isn't my fault; indeed it isn't. If I felt that I could care for any one— But I don't feel that I care. I simply don't understand what the feeling means.'

'Is that true, dear?'

'You've been very good to me, Dickie; and the only way I can pay you back is by speaking the truth. I daren't tell a fib. I despise myself quite enough as it is.'

'What in the world for?'

'Because—because I take everything that you give me and I give you nothing in return. It's mean and selfish of me, and whenever I think of it it worries me.'

'Understand once for all, then, that I can manage my own affairs, and if I choose to do anything you aren't to blame. You haven't a single thing to reproach yourself with, darling.'

'Yes, I have, and talking only makes it worse.'

'Then don't talk about it.'

'How can I help myself? If you find me alone for a minute you are always talking about it; and when you aren't you look it. You don't know how I despise myself sometimes.'

'Great goodness!' said Dick, nearly jumping to his feet. 'Speak the truth now, Maisie, if you never speak it again! Do I—does this worrying bore you?'

'No. It does not.'

'You'd tell me if it did?'

'I should let you know, I think.'

'Thank you. The other thing is fatal. But you must learn to forgive a man when he's in love. He's always a nuisance. You must have known that?'

Maisie did not consider the last question worth answering, and Dick was forced to repeat it.

'There were other men, of course. They always worried just when I was in the middle of my work, and wanted me to listen to them.'

'Did you listen?'

'At first; and they couldn't understand why I didn't care. And they used to praise my pictures; and I thought they meant it. I used to be proud of the praise, and tell Kami, and—I shall never forget—once Kami laughed at me.'

'You don't like being laughed at, Maisie, do you?'

'I hate it. I never laugh at other people unless—unless they do bad work. Dick, tell me honestly what you think of my pictures generally —of everything of mine that you've seen.'

'"Honest, honest, and honest over!"' quoted Dick from a catchword of long ago. 'Tell me what Kami always says.'

Maisie hesitated. 'He—he says that there is feeling in them.'

'How dare you tell me a fib like that? Remember I was under Kami for two years. I know exactly what he says.'

'It isn't a fib.'

'It's worse; it's a half-truth. Kami says, when he puts his head on one side,—so,—"Il y a du sentiment, mais il n'y a pas de parti pris."' He rolled the 'r' threateningly, as Kami used to do.

'Yes, that is what he says; and I'm beginning to think that he is right.'

'Certainly he is.' Dick admitted that two people in the world could do and say no wrong. Kami was the man.

'And now you say the same thing. It's so disheartening.'

'I'm sorry, but you asked me to speak the truth. Besides, I love you too much to pretend about your work. It's strong, it's patient some-times,—not always,—and sometimes there's power in it, but there's no special reason why it should be done at all. At least, that's how it strikes me.'

'There's no special reason why anything in the world should ever be done. You know that as well as I do. I only want success.'

'You're going the wrong way to get it, then. Hasn't Kami ever told you so?'

'Don't quote Kami to me. I want to know what you think. My work's bad, to begin with.'

'I didn't say that, and I don't think it.'

'It's amateurish, then.'

'That it most certainly is not. You're a workwoman, darling, to your boot-heels, and I respect you for that.'

'You don't laugh at me behind my back?'

'No, dear. You see, you are more to me than any one else. Put this cloak thing round you, or you'll get chilled.'

Maisie wrapped herself in the soft marten skins, turning the gray kan-garoo fur to the outside.

'This is delicious,' she said, rubbing her chin thoughtfully along the fur. 'Well? Why am I wrong in trying to get a little success?'

'Just because you try. Don't you understand, darling? Good work has nothing to do with—doesn't belong to—the person who does it. It's put into him or her from outside.'

'But how does that affect—'

'Wait a minute. All we can do is to learn how to do our work, to be masters of our materials instead of servants, and never to be afraid of anything.'

'I understand that.'

'Everything else comes from outside ourselves. Very good. If we sit down quietly to work out notions that are sent to us, we may or we may not do something that isn't bad. A great deal depends on being master of the bricks and mortar of the trade. But the instant we begin to think about success and the effect of our work—to play with one eye on the gallery—we lose power and touch and everything else. At least that's how I have found it. Instead of being quiet and giving every power you possess to your work, you're fretting over something which you can neither help nor hinder by a minute. See?'

'It's so easy for you to talk in that way. People like what you do. Don't you ever think about the gallery?'

'Much too often; but I'm always punished for it by loss of power. It's as simple as the Rule of Three. If we make light of our work by using it for our own ends, our work will make light of us, and, as we're the weaker, we shall suffer.'

'I don't treat my work lightly. You know that it's everything to me.'

'Of course; but, whether you realise it or not, you give two strokes for yourself to one for your work. It isn't your fault, darling. I do exactly the same thing, and know that I'm doing it. Most of the French schools, and all the schools here, drive the students to work for their own credit, and for the sake of their pride. I was told that all the world was interested in my work, and everybody at Kami's talked turpentine, and I honestly believed that the world needed elevating and influencing and all manner of impertinences, by my brushes. By Jove, I actually believed that! When my little head was bursting with a notion that I couldn't handle because I hadn't sufficient knowledge of my craft, I used to run about wondering at my own magnificence and getting ready to astonish the world.'

'But surely one can do that sometimes?'

'Very seldom with malice aforethought, darling. And when it's done it's such a tiny thing, and the world's so big, and all but a millionth part of it doesn't care. Maisie, come with me and I'll show you something of the size of the world. One can no more avoid working than eating,—that goes on by itself,—but try to see what you are working for.

I know such little heavens that I could take you to,—islands tucked away under the Line. You sight them after weeks of crashing through water as black as black marble because it's so deep, and you sit in the fore-chains day after day and see the sun rise almost afraid because the sea's so lonely.'

'Who is afraid?—you, or the sun?'

'The sun, of course. And there are noises under the sea, and sounds overhead in a clear sky. Then you find your island alive with hot moist orchids that make mouths at you, and can do everything except talk. There's a waterfall in it three hundred feet high, just like a sliver of green jade laced with silver; and millions of wild bees live up in the rocks; and you can hear the fat cocoa-nuts falling from the palms; and you order an ivory-white servant to sling you a long yellow hammock with tassels on it like ripe maize, and you put up your feet and hear the bees hum and the water fall till you go to sleep.'

'Can one work there?'

'Certainly. One must do something always. You hang your canvas up in a palm-tree and let the parrots criticise. When they scuffle you heave a ripe custard-apple at them, and it bursts in a lather of cream. There are hundreds of places. Come and see them.'

'I don't quite like that place. It sounds lazy. Tell me another.'

'What do you think of a big, red, dead city built of red sandstone, with raw green aloes growing between the stones, lying out neglected on honey-coloured sands? There are forty dead kings there, Maisie, each in a gorgeous tomb finer than all the others. You look at the palaces and streets and shops and tanks, and think that men must live there, till you find a wee gray squirrel rubbing its nose all alone in the market-place, and a jewelled peacock struts out of a carved doorway and spreads its tail against a marble screen as fine pierced as point-lace. Then a monkey —a little black monkey—walks through the main square to get a drink from a tank forty feet deep. He slides down the creepers to the water's edge, and a friend holds him by the tail in case he should fall in.'

'Is all that true?'

'I've been there and seen. Then evening comes, and the lights change till it's just as though you stood in the heart of a king-opal. A little before sundown, as punctually as clockwork, a big bristly wild boar, with all his family following, trots through the city gate, churning the foam on his tusks. You climb on the shoulder of a blind black stone god and watch that pig choose himself a palace for the night and stump in wag-ging his tail. Then the night-wind gets up, and the sands move, and you hear the desert outside the city singing, "Now I lay me down to sleep," and everything is dark till the moon rises. Maisie, darling, come with me and see what the world is really like. It's very lovely, and it's very horrible,—but I won't let you see anything horrid,—and it doesn't care your life or mine for pictures or anything else except doing its own work and making love. Come and I'll show you how to brew sangaree, and sling a hammock, and—oh, thousands of things, and you'll see for yourself what colour means, and we'll find out together what love means, and then, maybe, we shall be allowed to do some good work. Come away!'

'Why?' said Maisie.

'How can you do anything until you have seen everything, or as much as you can? And besides, darling, I love you. Come along with me. You have no business here; you don't belong to this place; you're half a gipsy,—your face tells that; and I—even the smell of open water makes me restless. Come across the sea and be happy!'

He had risen to his feet, and stood in the shadow of the gun, looking down at the girl. The very short winter afternoon had worn away, and, before they knew, the winter moon was walking the untroubled sea. Long ruled lines of silver showed where a ripple of the rising tide was turning over the mud-banks. The wind had dropped, and in the intense stillness they could hear a donkey cropping the frosty grass many yards away. A faint beating like that of a muffled drum came out of the moon-haze.

'What's that?' said Maisie quickly. 'It sounds like a heart beating. Where is it?'

Dick was so angry at this sudden wrench to his pleadings that he could not trust himself to speak, and in this silence caught the sound. Maisie from her seat under the gun watched him with a certain amount of fear. She wished so much that he would be sensible and cease to worry her with over-sea emotion that she both could and could not understand. She was not prepared, however, for the change in his face as he listened.

'It's a steamer,' he said,—'a twin-screw steamer, by the beat. I can't make her out, but she must be standing very close in-shore. Ah!' as the red of a rocket streaked the haze, 'she's standing in to signal before she clears the Channel.'

'Is it a wreck?' said Maisie, to whom these words were as Greek.

Dick's eyes were turned to the sea. 'Wreck! What nonsense! She's only reporting herself. Red rocket forward—there's a green light aft now, and two red rockets from the bridge.'

'What does that mean?'

'It's the signal of the Cross Keys Line running to Australia. I wonder which steamer it is.' The note of his voice had changed; he seemed to be talking to himself, and Maisie did not approve of it. The moonlight broke the haze for a moment, touching the black sides of a long steamer working down Channel. 'Four masts and three funnels—she's in deep draught, too. That must be the "Barralong," or the "Bhutia." No, the "Bhutia" has a clipper bow. It's the "Barralong," to Australia. She'll lift the Southern Cross in a week,—lucky old tub!—oh, lucky old tub!'

He stared intently, and moved up the slope of the fort to get a better view, but the mist on the sea thickened again, and the beating of the screws grew fainter. Maisie called to him a little angrily, and he returned, still keeping his eyes to seaward. 'Have you ever seen the Southern Cross blazing right over your head?' he asked. 'It's superb!'

'No,' she said shortly, 'and I don't want to. If you think it's so lovely why don't you go and see it yourself?'

She raised her face from the soft blackness of the marten skins about her throat, and her eyes shone like diamonds. The moonlight on the gray kangaroo fur turned it to frosted silver of the coldest.

'By Jove, Maisie, you look like a little heathen idol tucked up there.' The eyes showed that they did not appreciate the compliment. 'I'm sorry,' he continued. 'The Southern Cross isn't worth looking at unless some one helps you to see. That steamer's out of hearing.'

'Dick,' she said quietly, 'suppose I were to come to you now,—be quiet a minute,—just as I am, and caring for you just as much as I do.'

'Not as a brother, though? You said you didn't—in the Park.'

'I never had a brother. Suppose I said, "Take me to those places, and in time, perhaps, I might really care for you," what would you do?'

'Send you straight back to where you came from, in a cab. No, I wouldn't; I'd let you walk. But you couldn't do it, dear. And I wouldn't run the risk. You're worth waiting for till you can come without reservation.'

'Do you honestly believe that?'

'I have a hazy sort of idea that I do. Has it never struck you in that light?'

'Ye—es. I feel so wicked about it.'

'Wickeder than usual?'

'You don't know all I think. It's almost too awful to tell.'

'Never mind. You promised to tell me the truth—at least.'

'It's so ungrateful of me, but—but, though I know you care for me, and I like to have you with me, I'd—I'd even sacrifice you, if that would bring me what I want.'

'My poor little darling! I know that state of mind. It doesn't lead to good work.'

'You aren't angry? Remember, I do despise myself.'

'I'm not exactly flattered,—I had guessed as much before,—but I'm not angry. I'm sorry for you. Surely you ought to have left a littleness like that behind you years ago.'

'You've no right to patronise me! I only want what I have worked for so long. It came to you without any trouble, and—and I don't think it's fair.'

'What can I do? I'd give ten years of my life to get you what you want. But I can't help you; even I can't help.'

A murmur of dissent from Maisie. He went on—

'And I know by what you have just said that you're on the wrong road to success. It isn't got at by sacrificing other people,—I've had that much knocked into me; you must sacrifice yourself, and live under orders, and never think for yourself, and never have real satisfaction in your work except just at the beginning, when you're reaching out after a notion.'

'How can you believe all that?'

'There's no question of belief or disbelief. That's the law, and you take it or refuse it as you please. I try to obey, but I can't, and then my work turns bad on my hands. Under any circumstances, remember, four-fifths of everybody's work must be bad. But the remnant is worth the trouble for its own sake.'

'Isn't it nice to get credit even for bad work?'

'It's much too nice. But—May I tell you something? It isn't a pretty tale, but you're so like a man that I forget when I'm talking to you.'

'Tell me.'

'Once when I was out in the Soudan I went over some ground that we had been fighting on for three days. There were twelve hundred dead; and we hadn't time to bury them.'

'How ghastly!'

'I had been at work on a big double-sheet sketch, and I was wondering what people would think of it at home. The sight of that field taught me a good deal. It looked just like a bed of horrible toadstools in all colours, and—I'd never seen men in bulk go back to their beginnings before. So I began to understand that men and women were only material to work with, and that what they said or did was of no consequence. See? Strictly speaking, you might just as well put your ear down to the palette to catch what your colours are saying.'

'Dick, that's disgraceful!'

'Wait a minute. I said strictly speaking. Unfortunately, everybody must be either a man or a woman.'

'I'm glad you allow that much.'

'In your case I don't. You aren't a woman. But ordinary people, Maisie, must behave and work as such. That's what makes me so savage.' He hurled a pebble towards the sea as he spoke. 'I know that it is outside my business to care what people say; I can see that it spoils my output if I listen to 'em; and yet, confound it all,'—another pebble flew seaward, —'I can't help purring when I'm rubbed the right way. Even when I can see on a man's forehead that he is lying his way through a clump of pretty speeches, those lies make me happy and play the mischief with my hand.'

'And when he doesn't say pretty things?'

'Then, belovedest,'—Dick grinned,—'I forget that I am the steward of these gifts, and I want to make that man love and appreciate my work with a thick stick. It's too humiliating altogether; but I suppose even if one were an angel and painted humans altogether from outside, one would lose in touch what one gained in grip.'

Maisie laughed at the idea of Dick as an angel.

'But you seem to think,' she said, 'that everything nice spoils your hand.'

'I don't think. It's the law,—just the same as it was at Mrs. Jennett's. Everything that is nice does spoil your hand. I'm glad you see so clearly.'

'I don't like the view.'

'Nor I. But—have got orders: what can do? Are you strong enough to face it alone?'

'I suppose I must.'

'Let me help, darling. We can hold each other very tight and try to walk straight. We shall blunder horribly, but it will be better than stumbling apart. Maisie, can't you see reason?'

'I don't think we should get on together. We should be two of a trade, so we should never agree.'

'How I should like to meet the man who made that proverb! He lived in a cave and ate raw bear, I fancy. I'd make him chew his own arrow-heads. Well?'

'I should be only half married to you. I should worry and fuss about my work as I do now. Four days out of the seven I'm not fit to speak to.'

'You talk as if no one else in the world had ever used a brush. D'you suppose that I don't know the feeling of worry and bother and can't-get-at-ness? You're lucky if you only have it four days out of the seven. What difference would that make?'

'A great deal—if you had it too.'

'Yes, but I could respect it. Another man might not. He might laugh at you. But there's no use talking about it. If you can think in that way you can't care for me—yet.'

The tide had nearly covered the mud-banks, and twenty little ripples broke on the beach before Maisie chose to speak.

'Dick,' she said slowly, 'I believe very much that you are better than I am.'

'This doesn't seem to bear on the argument—but in what way?'

'I don't quite know, but in what you said about work and things; and then you're so patient. Yes, you're better than I am.'

Dick considered rapidly the murkiness of an average man's life. There was nothing in the review to fill him with a sense of virtue. He lifted the hem of the cloak to his lips.

'Why,' said Maisie, making as though she had not noticed, 'can you see things that I can't? I don't believe what you believe; but you're right, I believe.'

'If I've seen anything, God knows I couldn't have seen it but for you, and I know that I couldn't have said it except to you. You seemed to make everything clear for a minute; but I don't practise what I preach. You would help me. . . . There are only us two in the world for all purposes, and—and you like to have me with you?'

'Of course I do. I wonder if you can realise how utterly lonely I am!'

'Darling, I think I can.'

'Two years ago, when I first took the little house, I used to walk up and down the back-garden trying to cry. I never can cry. Can you?'

'It's some time since I tried. What was the trouble? Overwork?'

'I don't know; but I used to dream that I had broken down, and had no money, and was starving in London. I thought about it all day, and it frightened me—oh, how it frightened me!'

'I know that fear. It's the most terrible of all. It wakes me up in the night sometimes. You oughtn't to know anything about it.'

'How do you know?'

'Never mind. Is your three hundred a year safe?'

'It's in Consols.'

'Very well. If any one comes to you and recommends a better investment,—even if I should come to you,—don't you listen. Never shift the money for a minute, and never lend a penny of it,—even to the red-haired girl.'

'Don't scold me so! I'm not likely to be foolish.'

'The earth is full of men who'd sell their souls for three hundred a year; and women come and talk, and borrow a five-pound note here and a ten-pound note there; and a woman has no conscience in a money debt. Stick to your money, Maisie; for there's nothing more ghastly in the world than poverty in London. It's scared me. By Jove, it put the fear into me! And one oughtn't to be afraid of anything.'

To each man is appointed his particular dread,—the terror that, if he does not fight against it, must cow him even to the loss of his manhood.

Dick's experience of the sordid misery of want had entered into the deeps of him, and, lest he might find virtue too easy, that memory stood behind him, tempting to shame, when dealers came to buy his wares. As the Nilghai quaked against his will at the still green water of a lake or a mill-dam, as Torpenhow flinched before any white arm that could cut or stab and loathed himself for flinching, Dick feared the poverty he had once tasted half in jest. His burden was heavier than the burdens of his companions.

Maisie watched the face working in the moonlight.

'You've plenty of pennies now,' she said soothingly.

'I shall never get enough,' he began, with vicious emphasis. Then laughing, 'I shall always be threepence short in my accounts.'

'Why threepence?'

'I carried a man's bag once from Liverpool Street Station to Blackfriars Bridge. It was a sixpenny job,—you needn't laugh; indeed it was, —and I wanted the money desperately. He only gave me threepence; and he hadn't even the decency to pay in silver. Whatever money I make I shall never get that odd threepence out of the world.'

This was not language befitting the man who had preached of the sanctity of work. It jarred on Maisie, who preferred her payment in applause, which, since all men desire it, must be of the right. She hunted for her little purse and gravely took out a threepenny bit.

'There it is,' she said. 'I'll pay you, Dickie; and don't worry any more; it isn't worth while. Are you paid?'

'I am,' said the very human apostle of fair craft, taking the coin. 'I'm paid a thousand times, and we'll close that account. It shall live on my watch-chain; and you're an angel, Maisie.'

'I'm very cramped, and I'm feeling a little cold. Good gracious! the cloak is all white, and so is your moustache! I never knew it was so chilly.'

A light frost lay white on the shoulder of Dick's ulster. He, too, had forgotten the state of the weather. They laughed together, and with that laugh ended all serious discourse.

They ran inland across the waste to warm themselves, then turned to look at the glory of the full tide under the moonlight and the intense black shadows of the furze-bushes. It was an additional joy to Dick that Maisie could see colour even as he saw it,—could see the blue in the white of the mist, the violet that is in gray palings, and all things else as they are,—not of one hue, but a thousand. And the moonlight came into Maisie's soul, so that she, usually reserved, chattered of herself and of the things she took interest in,—of Kami, wisest of teachers, and of the girls in the studio,—of the Poles, who will kill themselves with overwork if they are not checked; of the French, who talk at great length of much more than they will ever accomplish; of the slovenly English, who toil hopelessly and cannot understand that inclination does not imply power; of the Americans, whose rasping voices in the hush of a hot afternoon strain tense-drawn nerves to breaking-point, and whose suppers lead to indigestion; of tempestuous Russians, neither to hold nor to bind, who tell the girls ghost-stories till the girls shriek; of stolid Germans, who come to learn one thing, and, having mastered that much, stolidly go away and copy pictures for evermore. Dick listened enraptured because it was Maisie who spoke. He knew the old life.

'It hasn't changed much,' he said. 'Do they still steal colours at lunch-time?'

'Not steal. Attract is the word. Of course they do. I'm good—I only attract ultramarine; but there are students who'd attract flake-white.'

'I've done it myself. You can't help it when the palettes are hung up. Every colour is common property once it runs down,—even though you do start it with a drop of oil. It teaches people not to waste their tubes.'

'I should like to attract some of your colours, Dick. Perhaps I might catch your success with them.'

'I mustn't say a bad word, but I should like to. What in the world, which you've just missed a lovely chance of seeing, does success or want of success, or a three-storied success, matter compared with—No, I won't open that question again. It's time to go back to town.'

'I'm sorry, Dick, but—'

'You're much more interested in that than you are in me.'

'I don't know. I don't think I am.'

'What will you give me if I tell you a sure short-cut to everything you want,—the trouble and the fuss and the tangle and all the rest? Will you promise to obey me?'

'Of course.'

'In the first place, you must never forget a meal because you happen to be at work. You forgot your lunch twice last week,' said Dick, at a venture, for he knew with whom he was dealing.

'No, no,—only once, really.'

'That's bad enough. And you mustn't take a cup of tea and a biscuit in place of a regular dinner, because dinner happens to be a trouble.'

'You're making fun of me!'

'I never was more in earnest in my life. Oh, my love, my love, hasn't it dawned on you yet what you are to me? Here's the whole earth in a conspiracy to give you a chill, or run over you, or drench you to the skin, or cheat you out of your money, or let you die of overwork and underfeeding, and I haven't the mere right to look after you. Why, I don't even know if you have sense enough to put on warm things when the weather's cold.'

'Dick, you're the most awful boy to talk to—really! How do you suppose I managed when you were away?'

'I wasn't here, and I didn't know. But now I'm back I'd give everything I have for the right of telling you to come in out of the rain.'

'Your success too?'

This time it cost Dick a severe struggle to refrain from bad words. 'As Mrs. Jennett used to say, you're a trial, Maisie! You've been cooped up in the schools too long, and you think every one is looking at you. There aren't twelve hundred people in the world who understand pictures. The others pretend and don't care. Remember, I've seen twelve hundred men dead in toadstool-beds. It's only the voice of the tiniest little fraction of people that makes success. The real world doesn't care a tinker's—doesn't care a bit. For aught you or I know, every man in the world may be arguing with a Maisie of his own.'

'Poor Maisie!'

'Poor Dick, I think. Do you believe while he's fighting for what's dearer than his life he wants to look at a picture? And even if he did, and if all the world did, and a thousand million people rose up and shouted hymns to my honour and glory, would that make up to me for the knowledge that you were out shopping in the Edgware Road on a rainy day without an umbrella? Now we'll go to the station.'

'But you said on the beach—' persisted Maisie with a certain fear.

Dick groaned aloud: 'Yes, I know what I said. My work is everything I have, or am, or hope to be, to me, and I believe I've learnt the law that governs it; but I've some lingering sense of fun left,—though you've nearly knocked it out of me. I can just see that it isn't everything to all the world. "Do what I say, and not what I do."'

Maisie was careful not to reopen debatable matters, and they returned to London joyously. The terminus stopped Dick in the midst of an eloquent harangue on the beauties of exercise. He would buy Maisie a horse,—such a horse as never yet bowed head to bit,—would stable it, with a companion, some twenty miles from London, and Maisie, solely for her health's sake, should ride with him twice or thrice a week.

'That's absurd,' said she. 'It wouldn't be proper.'

'Now, who in all London to-night would have sufficient interest or audacity to call us two to account for anything we chose to do?'

Maisie looked at the lamps, the fog, and the hideous turmoil. Dick was right; but horse-flesh did not make for Art as she understood it.

'You're very nice sometimes, but you're very foolish more times. I'm not going to let you give me horses, or take you out of your way to-night.

I'll go home by myself. Only I want you to promise me something. You won't think any more about that extra threepence, will you? Remember, you've been paid; and I won't allow you to be spiteful and do bad work for a little thing like that. You can be so big that you mustn't be tiny.'

This was turning the tables with a vengeance. There remained only to put Maisie into her hansom.

'Good-bye,' she said simply. 'You'll come on Sunday. It has been a beautiful day, Dick. Why can't it be like this always?'

'Because love's like line-work: you must go forward or backward; you can't stand still. By the way, go on with your line-work. Good-night, and, for my—for any sake, take care of yourself.'

He turned to walk home, meditating. The day had brought him nothing that he hoped for, but—surely this was worth many days—it had brought him nearer to Maisie. The end was only a question of time now, and the prize well worth the waiting. By instinct, once more, he turned to the river.

'And she understood at once,' he said, looking at the water. 'She found out my pet besetting sin on the spot and paid it off. My God, how she understood! And she said I was better than she was! Better than she was!' He laughed at the absurdity of the notion. 'I wonder if girls guess at one-half a man's life. They can't, or—they wouldn't marry us.' He took her gift out of his pocket, and considered it in the light of a miracle and a pledge of the comprehension that, one day, would lead to perfect happiness. Meantime Maisie was alone in London, with none to save her from danger. And the packed wilderness was very full of danger.

Dick made his prayer to Fate disjointedly after the manner of the heathen as he threw the piece of silver into the river. If any evil were to befall, let him bear the burden and let Maisie go unscathed, since the threepenny piece was dearest to him of all his possessions. It was a small coin in itself, but Maisie had given it, and the Thames held it, and surely the Fates would be bribed for this once.

The drowning of the coin seemed to cut him free from thought of Maisie for the moment. He took himself off the bridge and went whistling to his chambers with a strong yearning for some man-talk and tobacco after his first experience of an entire day spent in the society of a woman. There was a stronger desire at his heart when there rose before him an unsolicited vision of the 'Barralong' dipping deep and sailing free for the Southern Cross.

Chapter 8

And these two, as I have told you,
Were the friends of Hiawatha,
Chibiabos, the musician,
And the very strong man, Kwasind.

'Hiawatha.'

TORPENHOW WAS PAGING the last sheets of some manuscript, while the Nilghai, who had come for chess and remained to talk tactics, was reading through the first part, commenting scornfully the while.

'It's picturesque enough and it's sketchy,' said he; 'but as a serious consideration of affairs in Eastern Europe, it's not worth much.'

'It's off my hands at any rate. . . . Thirty-seven, thirty-eight, thirty-nine slips altogether, aren't there? That should make between eleven and twelve pages of valuable misinformation. Heigho!' Torpenhow shuffled the writing together and hummed—

'Young lambs to sell, young lambs to sell,
If I'd as much money as I could tell,
I never would cry, Young lambs to sell!'

Dick entered, self-conscious and a little defiant, but in the best of tempers with all the world.

'Back at last?' said Torpenhow.

'More or less. What have you been doing?'

'Work. Dickie, you behave as though the Bank of England were behind you. Here's Sunday, Monday, and Tuesday gone and you haven't done a line. It's scandalous.'

'The notions come and go, my children—they come and go like our 'baccy,' he answered, filling his pipe. 'Moreover,' he stooped to thrust a spill into the grate, 'Apollo does not always stretch his—Oh, confound your clumsy jests, Nilghai!'

'This is not the place to preach the theory of direct inspiration,' said the Nilghai, returning Torpenhow's large and workmanlike bellows to their nail on the wall. 'We believe in cobblers' wax. La!—where you sit down.'

'If you weren't so big and fat,' said Dick, looking round for a weapon, 'I'd—'

'No skylarking in my rooms. You two smashed half my furniture last time you threw cushions about. You might have the decency to say How d'you do? to Binkie. Look at him.'

Binkie had jumped down from the sofa and was fawning round Dick's knee, and scratching at his boots.

'Dear man!' said Dickie, snatching him up, and kissing him on the black patch above his right eye. 'Did ums was, Binks? Did that ugly Nilghai turn you off the sofa? Bite him, Mr. Binkle.' He pitched him on the Nilghai's stomach, as the big man lay at ease, and Binkie pretended to destroy the Nilghai inch by inch, till a sofa-cushion extinguished him, and panting he stuck out his tongue at the company.

'The Binkie-boy went for a walk this morning before you were up, Torp. I saw him making love to the butcher at the corner when the shutters were being taken down—just as if he hadn't enough to eat in his own proper house,' said Dick.

'Binks, is that a true bill?' said Torpenhow severely. The little dog retreated under the sofa-cushion, and showed by the fat white back of him that he really had no further interest in the discussion.

''Strikes me that another disreputable dog went for a walk, too,' said the Nilghai. 'What made you get up so early? Torp said you might be buying a horse?'

'He knows it would need three of us for a serious business like that. No, I felt lonesome and unhappy, so I went out to look at the sea, and watch the pretty ships go by.'

'Where did you go?'

'Somewhere on the Channel. Progly or Snigly, or some one-horse watering-place was its name; I've forgotten; but it was only two hours' run from London and the ships went by.'

'Did you see anything you knew?'

'Only the "Barralong" outwards to Australia, and an Odessa grain-boat loaded down by the head. It was a thick day, but the sea smelt good.'

'Wherefore put on one's best trousers to see the "Barralong"?' said Torpenhow, pointing.

'Because I've nothing except these things and my painting duds. Besides, I wanted to do honour to the sea.'

'Did she make you feel restless?' asked the Nilghai keenly.

'Crazy. Don't speak of it. I'm sorry I went.'

Torpenhow and the Nilghai exchanged a look as Dick, stooping, busied himself among the former's boots and trees.

'These will do,' he said at last; 'I can't say I think much of your taste in slippers, but the fit's the thing.' He slipped his feet into a pair of socklike sambhur-skin foot coverings, found a long chair, and lay at length.

'They're my own pet pair,' Torpenhow said. 'I was just going to put them on myself.'

''All your reprehensible selfishness. Just because you see me happy for a minute you want to worry me and stir me up. Find another pair.'

'Good for you that Dick can't wear your clothes, Torp. You two live communistically,' said the Nilghai. 'Dick never has anything that I can wear. He's only useful to sponge upon.'

'Confound you, have you been rummaging round among my caches, then?' said Dick. 'I put a sovereign in the tobacco-jar yesterday. How do you expect a man to keep his accounts properly if you—'

Here the Nilghai began to laugh, and Torpenhow joined him.

'Hid a sovereign yesterday! You're no sort of a financier. You lent me a fiver about a month back. Do you remember?' Torpenhow said.

'Yes, of course.'

'Do you remember that I paid it you ten days later, and you put it at the bottom of the tobacco?'

'By Jove, did I? I thought it was in one of my colour boxes.'

'You thought! About a week ago I went into your studio to get some 'baccy and found it.'

'What did you do with it?'

'Took the Nilghai to a theatre and fed him.'

'You couldn't feed the Nilghai under twice the money—not though you gave him Army beef. Well, I suppose I should have found it out sooner or later. What is there to laugh at?'

'You're a most amazing cuckoo in many directions,' said the Nilghai, still chuckling over the thought of the dinner. 'Never mind. We had both been working very hard, and it was your unearned increment we spent, and as you're only a loafer it didn't matter.'

'That's pleasant—from the man who is bursting with my meat, too. I'll get that dinner back one of these days. Suppose we go to a theatre now.'

''Put our boots on,—and dress,—and wash?' The Nilghai spoke very lazily.

'I withdraw the motion.'

'Suppose, just for a change—as a startling variety, you know—we, that is to say we, get our charcoal and our canvas and go on with our work.' Torpenhow spoke pointedly, but Dick only wriggled his toes inside the soft leather moccasins.

'What a one-idea'd clucker it is! If I had any unfinished figures on hand, I haven't any model; if I had my model, I haven't any spray, and I never leave charcoal unfixed over night; and if I had my spray and twenty photographs of backgrounds, I couldn't do anything tonight. I don't feel that way.'

'Binkie-dog, he's a lazy hog, isn't he?' said the Nilghai.

'Very good, I will do some work,' said Dick, rising swiftly. 'I'll fetch the Nungapunga Book, and we'll add another picture to the Nilghai Saga.'

'Aren't you worrying him a little too much?' asked the Nilghai, when Dick had left the room.

'Perhaps, but I know what he can turn out if he likes. It makes me savage to hear him praised for past work when I know what he ought to do. You and I are arranged for—'

'By Kismet and our own powers, more's the pity. I have dreamed of a good deal.'

'So have I, but we know our limitations now. I'm dashed if I know what Dick's may be when he gives himself to his work. That's what makes me so keen about him.'

'And when all's said and done, you will be put aside—quite rightly— for a female girl.'

'I wonder . . . Where do you think he has been to-day?'

'To the sea. Didn't you see the look in his eyes when he talked about her? He's as restless as a swallow in autumn.'

'Yes; but did he go alone?'

'I don't know, and I don't care, but he has the beginnings of the go-fever upon him. He wants to up-stakes and move out. There's no mistaking the signs. Whatever he may have said before, he has the call upon him now.'

'It might be his salvation,' Torpenhow said.

'Perhaps—if you care to take the responsibility of being a saviour: I'm averse to tampering with souls myself.'

Dick returned with a great clasped sketch-book that the Nilghai knew well and did not love too much. In it Dick had drawn in his playtime all manner of moving incidents, experienced by himself or related to him by the others, of all the four corners of the earth. But the wider range of the Nilghai's body and life attracted him most. When truth failed here he fell back on fiction of the wildest, and represented incidents in the Nilghai's career that were unseemly,—his marriages with many African princesses, his shameless betrayal, for Arab wives, of army corps to the Mahdi, his tattooment by skilled operators in Burmah, his interview (and his fears) with the yellow headsman in the blood-stained execution-ground of Canton, and finally, the passings of his spirit into the bodies of whales, elephants, and toucans. Torpenhow from time to time had added rhymed descriptions, and the whole was a curious piece of art, because Dick decided, having regard to the name of the book, which being interpreted means 'naked,' that it would be wrong to draw the Nilghai with any clothes on, under any circumstances. Consequently the last sketch, representing that much-enduring man calling on the War Office to press his claims to the Egyptian medal, was hardly delicate. He settled himself comfortably at Torpenhow's table and turned over the pages.

'What a fortune you would have been to Blake, Nilghai!' he said. 'There's a succulent pinkness about some of these sketches that's more than lifelike. "The Nilghai surrounded while bathing by the Mahdieh"—that was founded on fact, eh?'

'It was very nearly my last bath, you irreverent dauber. Has Binkie come into the Saga yet?'

'No; the Binkie-boy hasn't done anything except eat and kill cats. Let's see. Here you are as a stained-glass saint in a church. 'Deuced decorative lines about your anatomy; you ought to be grateful for being handed down to posterity in this way. Fifty years hence you'll exist in rare and curious facsimiles at ten guineas each. What shall I try this time? The domestic life of the Nilghai?'

''Hasn't got any.'

'The undomestic life of the Nilghai, then. Of course. Mass-meeting of his wives in Trafalgar Square. That's it. They came from the ends of the earth to attend Nilghai's wedding to an English bride. This shall be in sepia. It's a sweet material to work with.'

'It's a scandalous waste of time,' said Torpenhow.

'Don't worry; it keeps one's hand in—specially when you begin without the pencil.' He set to work rapidly. 'That's Nelson's Column. Presently the Nilghai will appear shinning up it.'

'Give him some clothes this time.'

'Certainly—a veil and an orange-wreath, because he's been married.'

'Gad, that's clever enough!' said Torpenhow over his shoulder, as Dick brought out of the paper with three twirls of the brush a very fat back and labouring shoulder pressed against the stone.

'Just imagine,' Dick continued, 'if we could publish a few of these dear little things every time the Nilghai subsidises a man who can write, to give the public an honest opinion of my pictures.'

'Well, you'll admit I always tell you when I have done anything of that kind. I know I can't hammer you as you ought to be hammered, so I give the job to another. Young Maclagan, for instance—'

'No-o—one half-minute, old man; stick your hand out against the dark of the wall-paper—you only burble and call me names. That left shoulder's out of drawing. I must literally throw a veil over that. Where's my pen-knife? Well, what about Maclagan?'

'I only gave him his riding-orders to—to lambast you on general principles for not producing work that will last.'

'Whereupon that young fool,'—Dick threw back his head and shut one eye as he shifted the page under his hand,—'being left alone with an ink-pot and what he conceived were his own notions, went and spilt them both over me in the papers. You might have engaged a grown man for the business, Nilghai. How do you think the bridal veil looks now, Torp?'

'How the deuce do three dabs and two scratches make the stuff stand away from the body as it does?' said Torpenhow, to whom Dick's methods were always new.

'It just depends on where you put 'em. If Maclagan had known that much about his business he might have done better.'

'Why don't you put the damned dabs into something that will stay, then?' insisted the Nilghai, who had really taken considerable trouble in hiring for Dick's benefit the pen of a young gentleman who devoted most of his waking hours to an anxious consideration of the aims and ends of Art, which, he wrote, was One and Indivisible.

'Wait a minute till I see how I am going to manage my procession of wives. You seem to have married extensively, and I must rough 'em in with the pencil—Medes, Parthians, Edomites. . . . Now, setting aside the weakness and the wickedness and—and the fat-headedness of deliberately trying to do work that will live, as they call it, I'm content with the knowledge that I've done my best up to date, and I shan't do anything like it again for some hours at least—probably years. Most probably never.'

'What! 'Any stuff you have in stock your best work?' said Torpenhow.

'Anything you've sold?' said the Nilghai.

'Oh, no. It isn't here and it isn't sold. Better than that, it can't be sold, and I don't think any one knows where it is. I'm sure I don't. . . . And yet more and more wives, on the north side of the square. Observe the virtuous horror of the lions!'

'You may as well explain,' said Torpenhow, and Dick lifted his head from the paper.

'The sea reminded me of it,' he said slowly. 'I wish it hadn't. It weighs some few thousand tons—unless you cut it out with a cold chisel.'

'Don't be an idiot. You can't pose with us here,' said the Nilghai.

'There's no pose in the matter at all. It's a fact. I was loafing from Lima to Auckland in a big, old, condemned passenger-ship turned into a cargo-boat and owned by a second-hand Italian firm. She was a crazy basket. We were cut down to fifteen ton of coal a day, and we thought ourselves lucky when we kicked seven knots an hour out of her. Then we used to stop and let the bearings cool down, and wonder whether the crack in the shaft was spreading.'

'Were you a steward or a stoker in those days?'

'I was flush for the time being, so I was a passenger, or else I should have been a steward, I think,' said Dick with perfect gravity, returning to the procession of angry wives. 'I was the only other passenger from Lima, and the ship was half empty, and full of rats and cockroaches and scorpions.'

'But what has this to do with the picture?'

'Wait a minute. She had been in the China passenger trade and her lower deck had bunks for two thousand pigtails. Those were all taken down, and she was empty up to her nose, and the lights came through the port-holes—most annoying lights to work in till you got used to them. I hadn't anything to do for weeks. The ship's charts were in pieces and our skipper daren't run south for fear of catching a storm. So he did his best to knock all the Society Islands out of the water one by one, and I went into the lower deck, and did my picture on the port side as far forward in her as I could go. There was some brown paint and some green paint that they used for the boats, and some black paint for iron-work, and that was all I had.'

'The passengers must have thought you mad.'

'There was only one, and it was a woman; but it gave me the notion of my picture.'

'What was she like?' said Torpenhow.

'She was a sort of Negroid-Jewess-Cuban; with morals to match. She couldn't read or write, and she didn't want to, but she used to come down and watch me paint, and the skipper didn't like it, because he was paying her passage and had to be on the bridge occasionally.'

'I see. That must have been cheerful.'

'It was the best time I ever had. To begin with, we didn't know whether we should go up or go down any minute when there was a sea on; and when it was calm it was paradise; and the woman used to mix the paints and talk broken English, and the skipper used to steal down every few minutes to the lower deck, because he said he was afraid of fire. So, you see, we could never tell when we might be caught, and I had a splendid notion to work out in only three keys of colour.'

'What was the notion?'

'Two lines in Poe—'

'Neither the angels in Heaven above nor the demons down under the sea,
Can ever dissever my soul from the soul of the beautiful Annabel Lee.

'It came out of the sea—all by itself. I drew that fight, fought out in green water over the naked, choking soul, and the woman served as the model for the devils and the angels both—sea-devils and sea-angels, and the soul half drowned between them. It doesn't sound much, but when there was a good light on the lower deck it looked very fine and creepy. It was seven by fourteen feet, all done in shifting light for shifting lights.'

'Did the woman inspire you much?' said Torpenhow.

'She and the sea between them—immensely. There was a heap of bad drawing in that picture. I remember I went out of my way to foreshorten for sheer delight of doing it, and I foreshortened damnably, but for all that it's the best thing I've ever done; and now I suppose the ship's broken up or gone down. Whew! What a time that was!'

'What happened after all?'

'It all ended. They were loading her with wool when I left the ship, but even the stevedores kept the picture clear to the last. The eyes of the demons scared them, I honestly believe.'

'And the woman?'

'She was scared too when it was finished. She used to cross herself before she went down to look at it. Just three colours and no chance of getting any more, and the sea outside and unlimited love-making inside, and the fear of death atop of everything else, O Lord!' He had ceased to look at the sketch, but was staring straight in front of him across the room.

'Why don't you try something of the same kind now?' said the Nilghai.

'Because those things come not by fasting and prayer. When I find a cargo-boat and a Jewess-Cuban and another notion and the same old life, I may.'

'You won't find them here,' said the Nilghai.

'No, I shall not.' Dick shut the sketch-book with a bang. 'This room's as hot as an oven. Open the window, some one.'

He leaned into the darkness, watching the greater darkness of London below him. The chambers stood much higher than the other houses, commanding a hundred chimneys—crooked cowls that looked like sitting cats as they swung round, and other uncouth brick and zinc mysteries supported by iron stanchions and clamped by S-pieces. Northward the lights of Piccadilly Circus and Leicester Square threw a copper-coloured glare above the black roofs, and southward lay all the orderly lights of the Thames. A train rolled out across one of the railway bridges, and its thunder drowned for a minute the dull roar of the streets. The Nilghai looked at his watch and said shortly, 'That's the Paris night-mail. You can book from here to St. Petersburg if you choose.'

Dick crammed head and shoulders out of the window and looked across the river. Torpenhow came to his side, while the Nilghai passed over quietly to the piano and opened it. Binkie, making himself as large as possible, spread out upon the sofa with the air of one who is not to be lightly disturbed.

'Well,' said the Nilghai to the two pairs of shoulders, 'have you never seen this place before?'

A steam-tug on the river hooted as she towed her barges to wharf. Then the boom of the traffic came into the room. Torpenhow nudged Dick. 'Good place to bank in—bad place to bunk in, Dickie, isn't it?'

Dick's chin was in his hand as he answered, in the words of a general not without fame, still looking out on the darkness—' "My God, what a city to loot!" '

Binkie found the night air tickling his whiskers and sneezed plaintively.

'We shall give the Binkie-dog a cold,' said Torpenhow. 'Come in,' and they withdrew their heads. 'You'll be buried in Kensal Green, Dick, one of these days, if it isn't closed by the time you want to go there—buried within two feet of some one else, his wife and his family.'

'Allah forbid! I shall get away before that time comes. Give a man room to stretch his legs, Mr. Binkle.' Dick flung himself down on the sofa and tweaked Binkie's velvet ears, yawning heavily the while.

'You'll find that wardrobe-case very much out of tune,' Torpenhow said to the Nilghai. 'It's never touched except by you.'

'A piece of gross extravagance,' Dick grunted. 'The Nilghai only comes when I'm out.'

'That's because you're always out. Howl, Nilghai, and let him hear.'

'The life of the Nilghai is fraud and slaughter,
His writings are watered Dickens and water;
But the voice of the Nilghai raised on high
Makes even the Mahdieh glad to die!'

Dick quoted from Torpenhow's letterpress in the Nungapunga Book. 'How do they call moose in Canada, Nilghai?'

The man laughed. Singing was his one polite accomplishment, as many Press-tents in far-off lands had known.

'What shall I sing?' said he, turning in the chair.

' "Moll Roe in the Morning," ' said Torpenhow at a venture.

'No,' said Dick sharply, and the Nilghai opened his eyes. The old chanty whereof he, among a very few, possessed all the words was not a pretty one, but Dick had heard it many times before without wincing. Without prelude he launched into that stately tune that calls together and troubles the hearts of the gipsies of the sea—

> 'Farewell and adieu to you, Spanish ladies,
> Farewell and adieu to you, ladies of Spain.'

Dick turned uneasily on the sofa, for he could hear the bows of the 'Barralong' crashing into the green seas on her way to the Southern Cross. Then came the chorus—

> 'We'll rant and we'll roar like true British sailors,
> We'll rant and we'll roar across the salt seas,
> Until we take soundings in the Channel of Old England
> From Ushant to Scilly 'tis forty-five leagues.'

'Thirty-five—thirty-five,' said Dick petulantly. 'Don't tamper with Holy Writ. Go on, Nilghai.'

> 'The first land we made it was called the Deadman,'

and they sang to the end very vigorously.

'That would be a better song if her head were turned the other way— to the Ushant light, for instance,' said the Nilghai.

'Flinging its arms about like a mad windmill,' said Torpenhow. 'Give us something else, Nilghai. You're in fine fog-horn form to-night.'

'Give us the "Ganges Pilot": you sang that in the square the night before El-Maghrib. By the way, I wonder how many of the chorus are alive to-night,' said Dick.

Torpenhow considered for a minute. 'By Jove! I believe only you and I. Raynor, Vickery, and Deenes—all dead; Vincent caught smallpox in Cairo, carried it here and died of it. Yes, only you and I and the Nilghai.'

'Umph! And yet the men here who've done their work in a well-warmed studio all their lives, with a policeman at each corner, say that I charge too much for my pictures.'

'They are buying your work, not your insurance policies, dear child,' said the Nilghai.

'I gambled with one to get at the other. Don't preach. Go on with the "Pilot." Where in the world did you get that song?'

'On a tombstone,' said the Nilghai. 'On a tombstone in a distant land. I made it an accompaniment with heaps of bass chords.'

'Oh, Vanity! Begin.' And the Nilghai began—

'I have slipped my cable, messmates, I'm drifting down with the tide,
I have my sailing orders, while ye at anchor ride.
And never on fair June morning have I put out to sea
With clearer conscience or better hope, or a heart more light and free.

'Shoulder to shoulder, Joe, my boy, into the crowd like a wedge
Strike with the hangers, messmates, but do not cut with the edge.
Cries Charnock, "Scatter the faggots, double that Brahmin in two,
The tall pale widow for me, Joe, the little brown girl for you!"

'Young Joe (you're nearing sixty), why is your hide so dark?
Katie has soft fair blue eyes, who blackened yours?—Why, hark!'

They were all singing now, Dick with the roar of the wind of the open
sea about his ears as the deep bass voice let itself go.

'The morning gun—Ho, steady!—the arquebuses to me!
I ha' sounded the Dutch High Admiral's heart as my lead doth sound the sea.

'Sounding, sounding the Ganges, floating down with the tide,
Moor me close to Charnock, next to my nut-brown bride.
My blessing to Kate at Fairlight—Holwell, my thanks to you;
Steady! We steer for Heaven, through sand-drifts cold and blue.'

'Now what is there in that nonsense to make a man restless?' said Dick,
hauling Binkie from his feet to his chest.

'It depends on the man,' said Torpenhow.

'The man who has been down to look at the sea,' said the Nilghai.

'I didn't know she was going to upset me in this fashion.'

'That's what men say when they go to say good-bye to a woman. It's
more easy, though, to get rid of three women than a piece of one's life and
surroundings.'

'But a woman can be—' began Dick unguardedly.

'A piece of one's life,' continued Torpenhow. 'No, she can't.' His face
darkened for a moment. 'She says she wants to sympathise with you and
help you in your work, and everything else that clearly a man must do for
himself. Then she sends round five notes a day to ask why the dickens you
haven't been wasting your time with her.'

'Don't generalise,' said the Nilghai. 'By the time you arrive at five notes
a day you must have gone through a good deal and behaved accordingly.
'Shouldn't begin these things, my son.'

'I shouldn't have gone down to the sea,' said Dick, just a little anxious to
change the conversation. 'And you shouldn't have sung.'

'The sea isn't sending you five notes a day,' said the Nilghai.

'No, but I'm fatally compromised. She's an enduring old hag, and I'm sorry I ever met her. Why wasn't I born and bred and dead in a three-pair back?'

'Hear him blaspheming his first love! Why in the world shouldn't you listen to her?' said Torpenhow.

Before Dick could reply the Nilghai lifted up his voice with a shout that shook the windows, in 'The Men of the Sea,' that begins, as all know, 'The sea is a wicked old woman,' and after racing through eight lines whose imagery is truthful, ends in a refrain, slow as the clacking of a capstan when the boat comes unwillingly up to the bars where the men sweat and tramp in the shingle.

> ' "Ye that bore us, O restore us!
> She is kinder than ye;
> For the call is on our heart-strings!"
> Said The Men of the Sea.'

The Nilghai sang that verse twice, with simple craft, intending that Dick should hear. But Dick was waiting for the farewell of the men to their wives.

> ' "Ye that love us, can ye move us?
> She is dearer than ye;
> And your sleep will be the sweeter,"
> Said The Men of the Sea.'

The rough words beat like the blows of the waves on the bows of the rickety boat from Lima in the days when Dick was mixing paints, making love, drawing devils and angels in the half dark, and wondering whether the next minute would place the Italian captain's knife between his shoulder-blades. And the go-fever, which is more real than many doctors' diseases, waked and raged, urging him who loved Maisie beyond anything in the world to go away and taste the old hot, unregenerate life again,—to scuffle, swear, gamble, and love light loves with his fellows; to take ship and know the sea once more, and by her beget pictures; to talk to Binat among the sands of Port Said while Yellow 'Tina mixed the drinks; to hear the crackle of musketry, and see the smoke roll outward, thin and thicken again till the shining black faces came through, and in that hell every man was strictly responsible for his own head, and his own alone, and struck with an unfettered arm. It was impossible, utterly impossible, but—

' "Oh, our fathers, in the churchyard,
She is older than ye,
And our graves will be the greener,"
Said The Men of the Sea.'

'What is there to hinder?' said Torpenhow, in the long hush that followed the song.

'You said a little time since that you wouldn't come for a walk round the world, Torp.'

'That was months ago, and I only objected to your making money for travelling expenses. You've shot your bolt here and it has gone home. Go away and do some work, and see some things.'

'Get some of the fat off you; you're disgracefully out of condition,' said the Nilghai, making a plunge from the chair and grasping a handful of Dick generally over the right ribs. 'Soft as putty—pure tallow born of over-feeding. Train it off, Dickie.'

'We're all equally gross, Nilghai. Next time you have to take the field you'll sit down, wink your eyes, gasp, and die in a fit.'

'Never mind. You go away on a ship. Go to Lima again, or to Brazil. There's always trouble in South America.'

'Do you suppose I want to be told where to go? Great Heavens, the only difficulty is to know where I'm to stop. But I shall stay here, as I told you before.'

'Then you'll be buried in Kensal Green and turn into adipocere with the others,' said Torpenhow. 'Are you thinking of commissions in hand? Pay forfeit and go. You've money enough to travel as a king if you please.'

'You've the grisliest notions of amusement, Torp. I think I see myself shipping first class on a six-thousand-ton hotel, and asking the third engineer what makes the engines go round, and whether it isn't very warm in the stokehold. Ho! ho! I should ship as a loafer if ever I shipped at all, which I'm not going to do. I shall compromise, and go for a small trip to begin with.'

'That's something at any rate. Where will you go?' said Torpenhow. 'It would do you all the good in the world, old man.'

The Nilghai saw the twinkle in Dick's eye and refrained from speech.

'I shall go in the first place to Rathray's stable, where I shall hire one horse, and take him very carefully as far as Richmond Hill. Then I shall walk him back again, in case he should accidentally burst into a lather and make Rathray angry. I shall do that to-morrow for the sake of air and exercise.'

'Bah!' Dick had barely time to throw up his arm and ward off the cushion that the disgusted Torpenhow heaved at his head.

'Air and exercise indeed,' said the Nilghai, sitting down heavily on Dick. 'Let's give him a little of both. Get the bellows, Torp.'

At this point the conference broke up in disorder, because Dick would not open his mouth till the Nilghai held his nose fast, and there was some trouble in forcing the nozzle of the bellows between his teeth; and even when it was there he weakly tried to puff against the force of the blast, and his cheeks blew up with a great explosion; and the enemy becoming helpless with laughter he so beat them over the head with a soft sofa-cushion that that became unsewn and distributed its feathers, and Binkie, interfering in Torpenhow's interests, was bundled into the half-empty bag and advised to scratch his way out, which he did after a while, travelling rapidly up and down the floor in the shape of an agitated green haggis, and when he came out looking for satisfaction, the three pillars of his world were picking feathers out of their hair.

'A prophet has no honour in his own country,' said Dick ruefully, dusting his knees. 'This filthy fluff will never brush off my bags.'

'It was all for your good,' said the Nilghai. ''Nothing like air and exercise.'

'All for your good,' said Torpenhow, not in the least with reference to past clowning. 'It would let you focus things at their proper worth and prevent your becoming slack in this hothouse of a town. Indeed it would, old man. I shouldn't have spoken if I hadn't thought so. Only, you make a joke of everything.'

'Before God I do no such thing,' said Dick quickly and earnestly. 'You don't know me if you think that.'

'I don't think it,' said the Nilghai.

'How can fellows like ourselves, who know what life and death really mean, dare to make a joke of anything? I know we pretend it, to save ourselves from breaking down or going to the other extreme. Can't I see, old man, how you're always anxious about me, and try to advise me to make my work better? Do you suppose I don't think about that myself? But you can't help me—you can't help me—not even you. I must play my own hand alone in my own way.'

'Hear, hear,' from the Nilghai.

'What's the one thing in the Nilghai Saga that I've never drawn in the Nungapunga Book?' Dick continued to Torpenhow, who was a little astonished at the outburst.

Now there was one blank page in the book given over to the sketch that Dick had not drawn of the crowning exploit in the Nilghai's life; when that man, being young and forgetting that his body and bones belonged to the paper that employed him, had ridden over sunburned slippery grass in the rear of Bredow's brigade on the day that the troopers flung themselves at Canrobert's artillery, and for aught they knew twenty battalions in front, to save the battered 24th German Infantry, to give time to decide the fate of Vionville, and to learn ere their remnant came back to Flavigny that cavalry can attack and crumple and break unshaken infantry. Whenever he was inclined to think over a life that might have been better, an income that might have been larger, and a soul that might have been considerably cleaner, the Nilghai would comfort himself with the thought, 'I rode with Bredow's brigade at Vionville,' and take heart for any lesser battle the next day might bring.

'I know,' he said very gravely. 'I was always glad that you left it out.'

'I left it out because Nilghai taught me what the German army learned then, and what Schmidt taught their cavalry. I don't know German. What is it? "Take care of the time and the dressing will take care of itself." I must ride my own line to my own beat, old man.'

'Tempo ist Richtung. You've learned your lesson well,' said the Nilghai. 'He must go alone. He speaks truth, Torp.'

'Maybe I'm as wrong as I can be—hideously wrong. I must find that out for myself, as I have to think things out for myself, but I daren't turn my head to dress by the next man. It hurts me a great deal more than you know not to be able to go, but I cannot, that's all. I must do my own work and live my own life in my own way, because I'm responsible for both. Only don't think I frivol about it, Torp. I have my own matches and sulphur, and I'll make my own hell, thanks.'

There was an uncomfortable pause. Then Torpenhow said blandly, 'What did the Governor of North Carolina say to the Governor of South Carolina?'

'Excellent notion. It is a long time between drinks. There are the makings of a very fine prig in you, Dick,' said the Nilghai.

'I've liberated my mind, estimable Binkie, with the feathers in his mouth.' Dick picked up the still indignant one and shook him tenderly. 'You're tied up in a sack and made to run about blind, Binkie-wee, without any reason, and it has hurt your little feelings. Never mind. Sic volo, sic jubeo, stet pro ratione voluntas, and don't sneeze in my eye because I talk Latin. Good-night.'

He went out of the room.

'That's distinctly one for you,' said the Nilghai. 'I told you it was hopeless to meddle with him. He's not pleased.'

'He'd swear at me if he weren't. I can't make it out. He has the go-fever upon him and he won't go. I only hope that he mayn't have to go some day when he doesn't want to,' said Torpenhow.

•   •   •   •   •   •   •

In his own room Dick was settling a question with himself—and the question was whether all the world, and all that was therein, and a burning desire to exploit both, was worth one threepenny piece thrown into the Thames.

'It came of seeing the sea, and I'm a cur to think about it,' he decided. 'After all the honeymoon will be that tour—with reservations; only . . . only I didn't realise that the sea was so strong. I didn't feel it so much when I was with Maisie. These damnable songs did it. He's beginning again.'

But it was only Herrick's Nightpiece to Julia that the Nilghai sang, and before it was ended Dick reappeared on the threshold, not altogether clothed indeed, but in his right mind, thirsty and at peace.

The mood had come and gone with the rising and the falling of the tide by Fort Keeling.

Chapter 9

'If I have taken the common clay
And wrought it cunningly
In the shape of a god that was digged a clod,
The greater honour to me.'

'If thou hast taken the common clay,
And thy hands be not free
From the taint of the soil, thou hast made thy spoil
The greater shame to thee.'

'The Two Potters.'

HE DID no work of any kind for the rest of the week. Then came another Sunday. He dreaded and longed for the day always, but since the red-haired girl had sketched him there was rather more dread than desire in his mind.

He found that Maisie had entirely neglected his suggestions about line-work. She had gone off at score filled with some absurd notion for a 'fancy head.' It cost Dick something to command his temper.

'What's the good of suggesting anything?' he said pointedly.

'Ah, but this will be a picture,—a real picture; and I know that Kami will let me send it to the Salon. You don't mind, do you?'

'I suppose not. But you won't have time for the Salon.'

Maisie hesitated a little. She even felt uncomfortable.

'We're going over to France a month sooner because of it. I shall get the idea sketched out here and work it up at Kami's.'

Dick's heart stood still, and he came very near to being disgusted with his queen who could do no wrong. 'Just when I thought I had made some headway, she goes off chasing butterflies. It's too maddening!'

There was no possibility of arguing, for the red-haired girl was in the studio. Dick could only look unutterable reproach.

'I'm sorry,' he said, 'and I think you make a mistake. But what's the idea of your new picture?'

'I took it from a book.'

'That's bad, to begin with. Books aren't the places for pictures. And—'

'It's this,' said the red-haired girl behind him. 'I was reading it to Maisie the other day from "The City of Dreadful Night." D'you know the book?'

'A little. I am sorry I spoke. There are pictures in it. What has taken her fancy?'

'The description of the Melancolia—

> 'Her folded wings as of a mighty eagle,
> But all too impotent to lift the regal
> Robustness of her earth-born strength and pride.

And here again. (Maisie, get the tea, dear.)

> 'The forehead charged with baleful thoughts and dreams,
> The household bunch of keys, the housewife's gown,
>   Voluminous indented, and yet rigid
>   As though a shell of burnished metal frigid,
> Her feet thick-shod to tread all weakness down.'

There was no attempt to conceal the scorn of the lazy voice. Dick winced.

'But that has been done already by an obscure artist of the name of Durer,' said he. 'How does the poem run?—

> 'Three centuries and threescore years ago,
> With phantasies of his peculiar thought.

You might as well try to rewrite "Hamlet." It will be waste of time.'

'No, it won't,' said Maisie, putting down the teacups with clatter to reassure herself. 'And I mean to do it. Can't you see what a beautiful thing it would make?'

'How in perdition can one do work when one hasn't had the proper training? Any fool can get a notion. It needs training to drive the thing through,—training and conviction; not rushing after the first fancy.' Dick spoke between his teeth.

'You don't understand,' said Maisie. 'I think I can do it.'

Again the voice of the girl behind him—

> 'Baffled and beaten back, she works on still;
>   Weary and sick of soul, she works the more.
> Sustained by her indomitable will,
>   The hands shall fashion, and the brain shall pore,
> And all her sorrow shall be turned to labour—

I fancy Maisie means to embody herself in the picture.'

'Sitting on a throne of rejected pictures? No, I shan't, dear. The notion in itself has fascinated me.—Of course you don't care for fancy heads, Dick. I don't think you could do them. You like blood and bones.'

'That's a direct challenge. If you can do a Melancolia that isn't merely a sorrowful female head, I can do a better one; and I will, too. What d'you know about Melancolias?' Dick firmly believed that he was even then tasting three-quarters of all the sorrow in the world.

'She was a woman,' said Maisie, 'and she suffered a great deal,—till she could suffer no more. Then she began to laugh at it all, and then I painted her and sent her to the Salon.'

The red-haired girl rose up and left the room, laughing.

Dick looked at Maisie humbly and hopelessly.

'Never mind about the picture,' he said. 'Are you really going back to Kami's a month before your time?'

'I must, if I want to get the picture done.'

'And that's all you want?'

'Of course. Don't be stupid, Dick.'

'You haven't the power. You have only the ideas—the ideas and the little cheap impulses. How you could have kept at your work for ten years steadily is a mystery to me. So you are really going,—a month before you need?'

'I must do my work.'

'Your work—bah! . . . No, I didn't mean that. It's all right, dear. Of course you must do your work, and—I think I'll say good-bye for this week.'

'Won't you even stay for tea?'

'No, thank you. Have I your leave to go, dear? There's nothing more you particularly want me to do, and the line-work doesn't matter.'

'I wish you could stay, and then we could talk over my picture. If only one single picture's a success it draws attention to all the others. I know some of my work is good, if only people could see. And you needn't have been so rude about it.'

'I'm sorry. We'll talk the Melancolia over some one of the other Sundays. There are four more—yes, one, two, three, four—before you go. Good-bye, Maisie.'

Maisie stood by the studio window, thinking, till the red-haired girl returned, a little white at the corners of her lips.

'Dick's gone off,' said Maisie. 'Just when I wanted to talk about the picture. Isn't it selfish of him?'

Her companion opened her lips as if to speak, shut them again, and went on reading 'The City of Dreadful Night.'

Dick was in the Park, walking round and round a tree that he had chosen as his confidante for many Sundays past. He was swearing audibly, and when he found that the infirmities of the English tongue hemmed in his rage, he sought consolation in Arabic, which is expressly designed for the use of the afflicted. He was not pleased with the reward of his patient service; nor was he pleased with himself; and it was long before he arrived at the proposition that the queen could do no wrong.

'It's a losing game,' he said. 'I'm worth nothing when a whim of hers is in question. But in a losing game at Port Said we used to double the stakes and go on. She do a Melancolia! She hasn't the power, or the insight, or the training. Only the desire. She's cursed with the curse of Reuben. She won't do line-work, because it means real work; and yet she's stronger than I am. I'll make her understand that I can beat her on her own Melancolia. Even then she wouldn't care. She says I can only do blood and bones. I don't believe she has blood in her veins. All the same I love her; and I must go on loving her; and if I can humble her vanity I will. I'll do a Melancolia that shall be something like a Melancolia,— "the Melancolia that transcends all wit." I'll do it at once, con—bless her.'

He discovered that the notion would not come to order, and that he could not free his mind for an hour from the thought of Maisie's departure. He took very small interest in her rough studies for the Melancolia when she showed them next week. The Sundays were racing past, and the time was at hand when all the church bells in London could not ring Maisie back to him. Once or twice he said something to Binkie about 'hermaphroditic futilities,' but the little dog received so many confidences both from Torpenhow and Dick that he did not trouble his tulip-ears to listen.

Dick was permitted to see the girls off. They were going by the Dover night-boat; and they hoped to return in August. It was then February, and Dick felt that he was being hardly used. Maisie was so busy stripping the small house across the Park, and packing her canvases, that she had no time for thought. Dick went down to Dover and wasted a day there fretting over a wonderful possibility. Would Maisie at the very last allow him one small kiss? He reflected that he might capture her by the strong arm, as he had seen women captured in the Southern Soudan, and lead her away; but Maisie would never be led. She would turn her gray eyes upon him and say, 'Dick, how selfish you are!' Then his courage would fail him. It would be better, after all, to beg for that kiss.

Maisie looked more than usually kissable as she stepped from the night-mail on to the windy pier, in a gray waterproof and a little gray cloth travelling-cap. The red-haired girl was not so lovely. Her green eyes were hollow and her lips were dry. Dick saw the trunks aboard, and went to

Maisie's side in the darkness under the bridge. The mail-bags were thundering into the forehold, and the red-haired girl was watching them.

'You'll have a rough passage to-night,' said Dick. 'It's blowing outside. I suppose I may come over and see you if I'm good?'

'You mustn't. I shall be busy. At least, if I want you I'll send for you. But I shall write from Vitry-sur-Marne. I shall have heaps of things to consult you about. Oh, Dick, you have been so good to me!—so good to me!'

'Thank you for that, dear. It hasn't made any difference, has it?'

'I can't tell a fib. It hasn't—in that way. But don't think I'm not grateful.'

'Damn the gratitude!' said Dick huskily to the paddle-box.

'What's the use of worrying? You know I should ruin your life, and you'd ruin mine, as things are now. You remember what you said when you were so angry that day in the Park? One of us has to be broken. Can't you wait till that day comes?'

'No, love. I want you unbroken—all to myself.'

Maisie shook her head. 'My poor Dick, what can I say?'

'Don't say anything. Give me a kiss? Only one kiss, Maisie. I'll swear I won't take any more. You might as well, and then I can be sure you're grateful.'

Maisie put her cheek forward, and Dick took his reward in the darkness. It was only one kiss, but, since there was no time-limit specified, it was a long one. Maisie wrenched herself free angrily, and Dick stood abashed and tingling from head to heel.

'Good-bye, darling. I didn't mean to scare you. I'm sorry. Only—keep well and do good work,—specially the Melancolia. I'm going to do one, too. Remember me to Kami, and be careful what you drink. Country drinking-water is bad everywhere, but it's worse in France. Write to me if you want anything, and good-bye. Say good-bye to the what-you-call-um girl, and—can't I have another kiss? No. You're quite right. Good-bye.'

A shout told him that it was not seemly to charge up the mail-bag incline. He reached the pier as the steamer began to move off, and he followed her with his heart.

'And there's nothing—nothing in the wide world—to keep us apart except her obstinacy. These Calais night-boats are much too small. I'll get Torp to write to the papers about it. She's beginning to pitch already.'

Maisie stood where Dick had left her till she heard a little gasping cough at her elbow. The red-haired girl's eyes were alight with cold flame.

'He kissed you!' she said. 'How could you let him, when he wasn't anything to you? How dared you take a kiss from him? Oh, Maisie, let's go to the ladies' cabin. I'm sick,—deadly sick.'

'We aren't into open water yet. Go down, dear, and I'll stay here. I don't like the smell of the engines. . . . Poor Dick! He deserved one,—only one. But I didn't think he'd frighten me so.'

Dick returned to town next day just in time for lunch, for which he had telegraphed. To his disgust, there were only empty plates in the studio. He lifted up his voice like the bears in the fairy-tale, and Torpenhow entered, looking very guilty.

'H'sh!' said he. 'Don't make such a noise. I took it. Come into my rooms, and I'll show you why.'

Dick paused amazed at the threshold, for on Torpenhow's sofa lay a girl asleep and breathing heavily. The little cheap sailor-hat, the blue-and-white dress, fitter for June than for February, dabbled with mud at the skirts, the jacket trimmed with imitation Astrakhan and ripped at the shoulder-seams, the one-and-eleven-penny umbrella, and, above all, the disgraceful condition of the kid-topped boots, declared all things.

'Oh, I say, old man, this is too bad! You mustn't bring this sort up here. They steal things from the rooms.'

'It looks bad, I admit, but I was coming in after lunch, and she staggered into the hall. I thought she was drunk at first, but it was collapse. I couldn't leave her as she was, so I brought her up here and gave her your lunch. She was fainting from want of food. She went fast asleep the minute she had finished.'

'I know something of that complaint. She's been living on sausages, I suppose. Torp, you should have handed her over to a policeman for presuming to faint in a respectable house. Poor little wretch. Look at that face! There isn't an ounce of immorality in it. Only folly,—slack, fatuous, feeble, futile folly. It's a typical head. D'you notice how the skull begins to show through the flesh padding on the face and cheek-bone?'

'What a cold-blooded barbarian it is! Don't hit a woman when she's down. Can't we do anything? She was simply dropping with starvation. She almost fell into my arms, and when she got to the food she ate like a wild beast. It was horrible.'

'I can give her money, which she would probably spend in drinks. Is she going to sleep for ever?'

The girl opened her eyes and glared at the men between terror and effrontery.

'Feeling better?' said Torpenhow.

'Yes. Thank you. There aren't many gentlemen that are as kind as you are. Thank you.'

'When did you leave service?' said Dick, who had been watching the scarred and chapped hands.

'How did you know I was in service? I was. General servant. I didn't like it.'

'And how do you like being your own mistress?'

'Do I look as if I liked it?'

'I suppose not. One moment. Would you be good enough to turn your face to the window?'

The girl obeyed, and Dick watched her face keenly,—so keenly that she made as if to hide behind Torpenhow.

'The eyes have it,' said Dick, walking up and down. 'They are superb eyes for my business. And, after all, every head depends on the eyes. This has been sent from heaven to make up for—what was taken away. Now the weekly strain's off my shoulders, I can get to work in earnest. Evidently sent from heaven. Yes. Raise your chin a little, please.'

'Gently, old man, gently. You're scaring somebody out of her wits,' said Torpenhow, who could see the girl trembling.

'Don't let him hit me! Oh, please don't let him hit me. I've been hit cruel to-day because I spoke to a man. Don't let him look at me like that! He's reg'lar wicked, that one. Don't let him look at me like that, neither! Oh, I feel as if I hadn't nothing on when he looks at me like that!'

The overstrained nerves in the frail body gave way, and the girl wept like a little child and began to scream. Dick threw open the window, and Torpenhow flung the door back.

'There you are,' said Dick soothingly. 'My friend here can call for a policeman, and you can run through that door. Nobody is going to hurt you.'

The girl sobbed convulsively for a few minutes, and then tried to laugh.

'Nothing in the world to hurt you. Now listen to me for a minute. I'm what they call an artist by profession. You know what artists do?'

'They draw the things in red and black ink on the pop-shop labels.'

'I daresay. I haven't risen to pop-shop labels yet. Those are done by the Academicians. I want to draw your head.'

'What for?'

'Because it's pretty. That is why you will come to the room across the landing three times a week at eleven in the morning, and I'll give you three quid a week just for sitting still and being drawn. And there's a quid on account.'

'For nothing? Oh, my!' The girl turned the sovereign in her hand, and with more foolish tears: 'Ain't neither o' you two gentlemen afraid of my bilking you?'

'No. Only ugly girls do that. Try and remember this place. And, by the way, what's your name?'

'I'm Bessie,—Bessie—It's no use giving the rest. Bessie Broke,—Stone-broke if you like. What's your names? But there,—no one ever gives the real ones.'

Dick consulted Torpenhow with his eyes.

'My name's Heldar, and my friend's called Torpenhow; and you must be sure to come here. Where do you live?'

'South-the-water,—one room,—five and sixpence a week. Aren't you making fun of me about that three quid?'

'You'll see later on. And, Bessie, next time you come, remember, you needn't wear that paint. It's bad for the skin, and I have all the colours you'll be likely to need.'

Bessie withdrew, scrubbing her cheek with a ragged pocket-handkerchief. The two men looked at each other.

'You're a man,' said Torpenhow.

'I'm afraid I've been a fool. It isn't our business to run about the earth reforming Bessie Brokes. And a woman of any kind has no right on this landing.'

'Perhaps she won't come back.'

'She will if she thinks she can get food and warmth here. I know she will, worse luck. But remember, old man, she isn't a woman: she's my model; and be careful.'

'The idea! She's a dissolute little scarecrow,—a gutter-snippet and nothing more.'

'So you think. Wait till she has been fed a little and freed from fear. That fair type recovers itself very quickly. You won't know her in a week or two, when that abject fear has died out of her eyes. She'll be too happy and smiling for my purposes.'

'But surely you're taking her out of charity?—to please me?'

'I am not in the habit of playing with hot coals to please anybody. She has been sent from heaven, as I may have remarked before, to help me with my Melancolia.'

''Never heard a word about the lady before.'

'What's the use of having a friend if you must sling your notions at him in words? You ought to know what I'm thinking about. You've heard me grunt lately?'

'Even so; but grunts mean anything in your language from bad 'baccy to wicked dealers. And I don't think I've been much in your confidence for some time.'

'It was a high and soulful grunt. You ought to have understood that it meant the Melancolia.' Dick walked Torpenhow up and down the room, keeping silence. Then he smote him in the ribs. 'Now don't you see it? Bessie's abject futility, and the terror in her eyes, welded on to one or two details in the way of sorrow that have come under my experience lately. Likewise some orange and black,—two keys of each. But I can't explain on an empty stomach.'

'It sounds mad enough. You'd better stick to your soldiers, Dick, instead of maundering about heads and eyes and experiences.'

'Think so?' Dick began to dance on his heels, singing—

'They're as proud as a turkey when they hold the ready cash,
    You ought to 'ear the way they laugh an' joke;
They are tricky an' they're funny when they've got the ready money,—
    Ow! but see 'em when they're all stone-broke.'

Then he sat down to pour out his heart to Maisie in a four-sheet letter of counsel and encouragement, and registered an oath that he would get to work with an undivided heart as soon as Bessie should reappear.

The girl kept her appointment unpainted and unadorned, afraid and overbold by turns. When she found that she was merely expected to sit still, she grew calmer, and criticised the appointments of the studio with freedom and some point. She liked the warmth and the comfort and the release from fear of physical pain. Dick made two or three studies of her head in monochrome, but the actual notion of the Melancolia would not arrive.

'What a mess you keep your things in!' said Bessie, some days later, when she felt herself thoroughly at home. 'I s'pose your clothes are just as bad. Gentlemen never think what buttons and tape are made for.'

'I buy things to wear, and wear 'em till they go to pieces. I don't know what Torpenhow does.'

Bessie made diligent inquiry in the latter's room, and unearthed a bale of disreputable socks. 'Some of these I'll mend now,' she said, 'and some I'll take home. D'you know, I sit all day long at home doing nothing, just like a lady, and no more noticing them other girls in the house than if they was so many flies? I don't have any unnecessary words, but I put 'em down quick, I can tell you, when they talk to me. No; it's quite nice these days. I lock my door, and they can only call me names through the keyhole, and I sit inside, just like a lady, mending socks. Mr. Torpenhow wears his socks out both ends at once.'

'Three quid a week from me, and the delights of my society. No socks mended. Nothing from Torp except a nod on the landing now and again, and all his socks mended. Bessie is very much a woman,' thought Dick; and he looked at her between half-shut eyes. Food and rest had transformed the girl, as Dick knew they would.

'What are you looking at me like that for?' she said quickly. 'Don't. You look reg'lar bad when you look that way. You don't think much o' me, do you?'

'That depends on how you behave.'

Bessie behaved beautifully. Only it was difficult at the end of a sitting to bid her go out into the gray streets. She very much preferred the studio and a big chair by the stove, with some socks in her lap as an excuse for delay. Then Torpenhow would come in, and Bessie would be moved to tell strange and wonderful stories of her past, and still stranger ones of her present improved circumstances. She would make them tea as though she had a right to make it; and once or twice on these occasions Dick caught Torpenhow's eyes fixed on the trim little figure, and because Bessie's flittings about the room made Dick ardently long for Maisie, he realised whither Torpenhow's thoughts were tending. And Bessie was exceedingly careful of the condition of Torpenhow's linen. She spoke very little to him, but sometimes they talked together on the landing.

'I was a great fool,' Dick said to himself. 'I know what red firelight looks like when a man's trampling through a strange town; and ours is a lonely, selfish sort of life at the best. I wonder Maisie doesn't feel that sometimes. But I can't order Bessie away. That's the worst of beginning things. One never knows where they stop.'

One evening, after a sitting prolonged to the last limit of the light, Dick was roused from a nap by a broken voice in Torpenhow's room. He jumped to his feet. 'Now what ought I to do? It looks foolish to go in. —Oh, bless you, Binkie!' The little terrier thrust Torpenhow's door open with his nose and came out to take possession of Dick's chair. The door swung wide unheeded, and Dick across the landing could see Bessie in the half-light making her little supplication to Torpenhow. She was kneeling by his side, and her hands were clasped across his knee.

'I know,—I know,' she said thickly. ''Tisn't right o' me to do this, but I can't help it; and you were so kind,—so kind; and you never took any notice o' me. And I've mended all your things so carefully,—I did. Oh, please, 'tisn't as if I was asking you to marry me. I wouldn't think of it. But you —couldn't you take and live with me till Miss Right comes along? I'm only Miss Wrong, I know, but I'd work my hands to the bare bone for you. And I'm not ugly to look at. Say you will?'

Dick hardly recognised Torpenhow's voice in reply—

'But look here. It's no use. I'm liable to be ordered off anywhere at a minute's notice if a war breaks out. At a minute's notice—dear.'

'What does that matter? Until you go, then. Until you go. 'Tisn't much I'm asking, and—you don't know how good I can cook.' She put an arm round his neck and was drawing his head down.

'Until—I—go, then.'

'Torp,' said Dick across the landing. He could hardly steady his voice. 'Come here a minute, old man. I'm in trouble.'—'Heaven send he'll listen to me!' There was something very like an oath from Bessie's lips. She was afraid of Dick, and disappeared down the staircase in panic, but it seemed an age before Torpenhow entered the studio. He went to the mantelpiece, buried his head on his arms, and groaned like a wounded bull.

'What the devil right have you to interfere?' he said, at last.

'Who's interfering with which? Your own sense told you long ago you couldn't be such a fool. It was a tough rack, St. Anthony, but you're all right now.'

'I oughtn't to have seen her moving about these rooms as if they belonged to her. That's what upset me. It gives a lonely man a sort of hankering, doesn't it?' said Torpenhow piteously.

'Now you talk sense. It docs. But, since you aren't in a condition to discuss the disadvantages of double housekeeping, do you know what you're going to do?'

'I don't. I wish I did.'

'You're going away for a season on a brilliant tour to regain tone. You're going to Brighton, or Scarborough, or Prawle Point, to see the ships go by. And you're going at once. Isn't it odd? I'll take care of Binkie, but out you go immediately. Never resist the devil. He holds the bank. Fly from him. Pack your things and go.'

'I believe you're right. Where shall I go?'

'And you call yourself a special correspondent! Pack first and inquire afterwards.'

An hour later Torpenhow was despatched into the night in a hansom. 'You'll probably think of some place to go to while you're moving,' said Dick. 'Go to Euston, to begin with, and—oh yes—get drunk to-night.'

He returned to the studio, and lighted more candles, for he found the room very dark.

'Oh, you Jezebel! you futile little Jezebel! Won't you hate me to-morrow? —Binkie, come here.'

Binkie turned over on his back on the hearth-rug, and Dick stirred him with a meditative foot.

'I said she was not immoral. I was wrong. She said she could cook. That showed premeditated sin. Oh, Binkie, if you are a man you will go to perdition; but if you are a woman, and say that you can cook, you will go to a much worse place.'

Chapter 10

What's yon that follows at my side?—
The foe that ye must fight, my lord.—
That hirples swift as I can ride?—
The shadow of your might, my lord.—
Then wheel my horse against the foe!—
He's down and overpast, my lord.
Ye war against the sunset glow:
The darkness gathers fast, my lord.
'The Fight of Heriot's Ford.'

'THIS IS A cheerful life,' said Dick, some days later. 'Torp's away; Bessie hates me; I can't get at the notion of the Melancolia; Maisie's letters are scrappy; and I believe I have indigestion. What gives a man pains across his head and spots before his eyes, Binkie? Shall us take some liver pills?'

Dick had just gone through a lively scene with Bessie. She had for the fiftieth time reproached him for sending Torpenhow away. She explained her enduring hatred for Dick, and made it clear to him that she only sat for the sake of his money. 'And Mr. Torpenhow's ten times a better man than you,' she concluded.

'He is. That's why he went away. I should have stayed and made love to you.'

The girl sat with her chin on her hand, scowling. 'To me! I'd like to catch you! If I wasn't afraid o' being hung I'd kill you. That's what I'd do. D'you believe me?'

Dick smiled wearily. It is not pleasant to live in the company of a notion that will not work out, a fox-terrier that cannot talk, and a woman who talks too much. He would have answered, but at that moment there unrolled itself from one corner of the studio a veil, as it were, of the filmiest gauze. He rubbed his eyes, but the gray haze would not go.

'This is disgraceful indigestion. Binkie, we will go to a medicine-man. We can't have our eyes interfered with, for by these we get our bread; also mutton-chop bones for little dogs.'

The doctor was an affable local practitioner with white hair, and he said nothing till Dick began to describe the gray film in the studio.

'We all want a little patching and repairing from time to time,' he chirped. 'Like a ship, my dear sir,—exactly like a ship. Sometimes the hull is out of order, and we consult the surgeon; sometimes the rigging, and then I advise; sometimes the engines, and we go to the brain-specialist; sometimes the look-out on the bridge is tired, and then we see an oculist. I should recommend you to see an oculist. A little patching and repairing from time to time is all we want. An oculist, by all means.'

Dick sought an oculist,—the best in London. He was certain that the local practitioner did not know anything about his trade, and more certain that Maisie would laugh at him if he were forced to wear spectacles.

'I've neglected the warnings of my lord the stomach too long. Hence these spots before the eyes, Binkie. I can see as well as I ever could.'

As he entered the dark hall that led to the consulting-room a man cannoned against him. Dick saw the face as it hurried out into the street.

'That's the writer-type. He has the same modelling of the forehead as Torp. He looks very sick. Probably heard something he didn't like.'

Even as he thought, a great fear came upon Dick, a fear that made him hold his breath as he walked into the oculist's waiting-room, with the heavy carved furniture, the dark-green paper, and the sober-hued prints on the wall. He recognised a reproduction of one of his own sketches.

Many people were waiting their turn before him. His eye was caught by a flaming red-and-gold Christmas-carol book. Little children came to that eye-doctor, and they needed large-type amusement.

'That's idolatrous bad Art,' he said, drawing the book towards himself. 'From the anatomy of the angels, it has been made in Germany.' He opened it mechanically, and there leaped to his eyes a verse printed in red ink—

'The next good joy that Mary had,
    It was the joy of three,
To see her good Son Jesus Christ
    Making the blind to see;
Making the blind to see, good Lord,
    And happy may we be.
Praise Father, Son, and Holy Ghost
    To all eternity!'

Dick read and re-read the verse till his turn came, and the doctor was bending above him seated in an armchair. The blaze of a gas-microscope in his eyes made him wince. The doctor's hand touched the scar of the sword-cut on Dick's head, and Dick explained briefly how he had come by it. When the flame was removed, Dick saw the doctor's face, and the fear came upon him again. The doctor wrapped himself in a mist of words. Dick caught allusions to 'scar,' 'frontal bone,' 'optic nerve,' 'extreme caution,' and the 'avoidance of mental anxiety.'

'Verdict?' he said faintly. 'My business is painting, and I daren't waste time. What do you make of it?'

Again the whirl of words, but this time they conveyed a meaning.

'Can you give me anything to drink?'

Many sentences were pronounced in that darkened room, and the prisoners often needed cheering. Dick found a glass of liqueur brandy in his hand.

'As far as I can gather,' he said, coughing above the spirit, 'you call it decay of the optic nerve, or something, and therefore hopeless. What is my time-limit, avoiding all strain and worry?'

'Perhaps one year.'

'My God! And if I don't take care of myself?'

'I really could not say. One cannot ascertain the exact amount of injury inflicted by the sword-cut. The scar is an old one, and—exposure to the strong light of the desert, did you say?—with excessive application to fine work? I really could not say.'

'I beg your pardon, but it has come without any warning. If you will let me, I'll sit here for a minute, and then I'll go. You have been very good in telling me the truth. . . . Without any warning . . . without any warning. Thanks.'

Dick went into the street, and was rapturously received by Binkie. 'We've got it very badly, little dog! Just as badly as we can get it. We'll go to the Park to think it out.'

They headed for a certain tree that Dick knew well, and they sat down to think, because his legs were trembling under him and there was cold fear at the pit of his stomach.

'How could it have come without any warning? It's as sudden as being shot. It's the living death, Binkie. We're to be shut up in the dark in one year if we're careful, and we shan't see anybody, and we shall never have anything we want, not though we live to be a hundred.' Binkie wagged his tail joyously. 'Binkie, we must think. Let's see how it feels to be blind.' Dick shut his eyes, and flaming commas and Catherine-wheels floated inside the lids. Yet when he looked across the Park the scope of his vision was not contracted. He could see perfectly, until a procession of slow-wheeling fireworks defiled across his eyeballs.

'Little dorglums, we aren't at all well. Let's go home. If only Torp were back, now!'

But Torpenhow was in the South of England, inspecting dockyards in the company of the Nilghai. His letters were brief and full of mystery.

Dick had never asked anybody to help him in his joys or his sorrows. He argued, in the loneliness of the studio, henceforward to be decorated with a film of gray gauze in one corner, that, if his fate were blindness, all the Torpenhows in the world could not save him. 'I can't call him off his trip to sit down and sympathise with me. I must pull through the business alone,' he said. He was lying on the sofa eating his moustache and wondering what the darkness of the night would be like. Then came to his mind the memory of a quaint scene in the Soudan. A soldier had been nearly hacked in two by a broad-bladed Arab spear. For one instant the man felt no pain. Looking down, he saw that his life-blood was going from him. The stupid bewilderment on his face was so intensely comic that both Dick and Torpenhow, still panting and unstrung from a fight for life, had roared with laughter, in which the man seemed as if he would join, but, as his lips parted in a sheepish grin, the agony of death came upon him, and he pitched grunting at their feet. Dick laughed again, remembering the horror. It seemed so exactly like his own case. 'But I have a little more time allowed me,' he said. He paced up and down the room, quietly at first, but afterwards with the hurried feet of fear. It was as though a black shadow stood at his elbow and urged him to go forward; and there were only weaving circles and floating pin-dots before his eyes.

'We must be calm, Binkie; we must be calm.' He talked aloud for the sake of distraction. 'This isn't nice at all. What shall we do? We must do something. Our time is short. I shouldn't have believed that this morning; but now things are different. Binkie, where was Moses when the light went out?'

Binkie smiled from ear to ear, as a well-bred terrier should, but made no suggestion.

'"Were there but world enough and time, This coyness, Binkie, were no crime. . . . But at my back I always hear—"' He wiped his forehead, which was unpleasantly damp. 'What can I do? What can I do? I haven't any notions left, and I can't think connectedly, but I must do something, or I shall go off my head.'

The hurried walk recommenced, Dick stopping every now and again to drag forth long-neglected canvases and old note-books; for he turned to his work by instinct as a thing that could not fail. 'You won't do, and you won't do,' he said, at each inspection. 'No more soldiers. I couldn't paint 'em. Sudden death comes home too nearly, and this is battle and murder both for me.'

The day was failing, and Dick thought for a moment that the twilight of the blind had come upon him unawares. 'Allah Almighty!' he cried despairingly, 'help me through the time of waiting, and I won't whine when my punishment comes. What can I do now, before the light goes?' There was no answer. Dick waited till he could regain some sort of control over himself. His hands were shaking, and he prided himself on their steadiness; he could feel that his lips were quivering, and the sweat was running down his face. He was lashed by fear, driven forward by the desire to get to work at once and accomplish something, and maddened by the refusal of his brain to do more than repeat the news that he was about to go blind. 'It's a humiliating exhibition,' he thought, 'and I'm glad Torp isn't here to see. The doctor said I was to avoid mental worry. Come here and let me pet you, Binkie.'

The little dog yelped because Dick nearly squeezed the bark out of him. Then he heard the man speaking in the twilight and, doglike, understood that his trouble stood off from him—

'Allah is good, Binkie. Not quite so gentle as we could wish, but we'll discuss that later. I think I see my way to it now. All those studies of Bessie's head were nonsense, and they nearly brought your master into a scrape. I hold the notion now as clear as crystal,—"the Melancolia that transcends all wit." There shall be Maisie in that head, because I shall never get Maisie; and Bess, of course, because she knows all about Melancolia, though she doesn't know she knows; and there shall be some drawing in it, and it shall all end up with a laugh. That's for myself. Shall she giggle or grin? No, she shall laugh right out of the canvas, and every man and woman that ever had a sorrow of their own shall—what is it the poem says?—

'Understand the speech and feel a stir
Of fellowship in all disastrous fight.

"In all disastrous fight"? That's better than painting the thing merely to pique Maisie. I can do it now because I have it inside me. Binkie, I'm going to hold you up by your tail. You're an omen. Come here.'

Binkie swung head downward for a moment without speaking.

''Rather like holding a guinea-pig; but you're a brave little dog, and you don't yelp when you're hung up. It is an omen.'

Binkie went to his own chair, and as often as he looked, saw Dick walking up and down, rubbing his hands and chuckling. That night Dick wrote a letter to Maisie full of the tenderest regard for her health, but saying very little about his own, and dreamed of the Melancolia to be born. Not till morning did he remember that something might happen to him in the future.

He fell to work, whistling softly, and was swallowed up in the clean, clear joy of creation, which does not come to man too often, lest he should consider himself the equal of his God, and so refuse to die at the appointed time. He forgot Maisie, Torpenhow, and Binkie at his feet, but remembered to stir Bessie, who needed very little stirring, into a tremendous rage, that he might watch the smouldering lights in her eyes. He threw himself without reservation into his work, and did not think of the doom that was to overtake him, for he was possessed with his notion, and the things of this world had no power upon him.

'You're pleased to-day,' said Bessie.

Dick waved his mahl-stick in mystic circles and went to the sideboard for a drink. In the evening, when the exaltation of the day had died down, he went to the sideboard again, and after some visits became convinced that the eye-doctor was a liar, since he still could see everything very clearly. He was of opinion that he would even make a home for Maisie, and that whether she liked it or not she should be his wife. The mood passed next morning, but the sideboard and all upon it remained for his comfort. Again he set to work, and his eyes troubled him with spots and dashes and blurs till he had taken counsel with the sideboard, and the Melancolia both on the canvas and in his own mind appeared lovelier than ever. There was a delightful sense of irresponsibility upon him, such as they feel who walking among their fellow-men know that the death-sentence of disease is upon them, and, since fear is but waste of the little time left, are riotously happy. The days passed without event. Bessie arrived punctually always, and, though her voice seemed to Dick to come from a distance, her face was always very near, and the Melancolia began to flame on the canvas, in the likeness of a woman who had known all the sorrow in the world and was laughing at it. It was true that the corners of the studio draped themselves in gray film and retired into the darkness, that the spots in his eyes and the pains across his head were very troublesome, and that Maisie's letters were hard to read and harder still to answer. He could not tell her of his trouble, and he could not laugh at her accounts of her own Melancolia which was always going to be finished. But the furious days of toil and the nights of wild dreams made amends for all, and the sideboard was his best friend on earth. Bessie was singularly dull. She used to shriek with rage when Dick stared at her between half-closed eyes. Now she sulked or watched him with disgust, saying very little.

Torpenhow had been absent for six weeks. An incoherent note heralded his return. 'News! great news!' he wrote. 'The Nilghai knows, and so does The Keneu. We're all back on Thursday. Get lunch and clean your accoutrements.'

Dick showed Bessie the letter, and she abused him for that he had ever sent Torpenhow away and ruined her life.

'Well,' said Dick brutally, 'you're better as you are, instead of making love to some drunken beast in the street.' He felt that he had rescued Torpenhow from great temptation.

'I don't know if that's any worse than sitting to a drunken beast in a studio. You haven't been sober for three weeks. You've been soaking the whole time; and yet you pretend you're better than me!'

'What d'you mean?' said Dick.

'Mean! You'll see when Mr. Torpenhow comes back.'

It was not long to wait. Torpenhow met Bessie on the staircase without a sign of feeling. He had news that was more to him than many Bessies, and The Keneu and the Nilghai were trampling behind him, calling for Dick.

'Drinking like a fish,' Bessie whispered. 'He's been at it for nearly a month.' She followed the men stealthily to hear judgment done.

They came into the studio, rejoicing, to be welcomed over-effusively by a drawn, lined, shrunken, haggard wreck,—unshaven, blue-white about the nostrils, stooping in the shoulders, and peering under his eyebrows nervously. The drink had been at work as steadily as Dick.

'Is this you?' said Torpenhow.

'All that's left of me. Sit down. Binkie's quite well, and I've been doing some good work.' He reeled where he stood.

'You've done some of the worst work you've ever done in your life. Man alive, you're—'

Torpenhow turned to his companions appealingly, and they left the room to find lunch elsewhere. Then he spoke; but, since the reproof of a friend is much too sacred and intimate a thing to be printed, and since Torpenhow used figures and metaphors which were unseemly, and contempt untranslatable, it will never be known what was actually said to Dick, who blinked and winked and picked at his hands. After a time the culprit began to feel the need of a little self-respect. He was quite sure that he had not in any way departed from virtue, and there were reasons, too, of which Torpenhow knew nothing. He would explain.

He rose, tried to straighten his shoulders, and spoke to the face he could hardly see.

'You are right,' he said. 'But I am right, too. After you went away I had some trouble with my eyes. So I went to an oculist, and he turned a gasogene—I mean a gas-engine—into my eye. That was very long ago. He said, "Scar on the head,—sword-cut and optic nerve." Make a note of that. So I am going blind. I have some work to do before I go blind, and I suppose that I must do it. I cannot see much now, but I can see best when I am drunk. I did not know I was drunk till I was told, but I must go on with my work. If you want to see it, there it is.' He pointed to the all but finished Melancolia and looked for applause.

Torpenhow said nothing, and Dick began to whimper feebly, for joy at seeing Torpenhow again, for grief at misdeeds—if indeed they were misdeeds—that made Torpenhow remote and unsympathetic, and for childish vanity hurt, since Torpenhow had not given a word of praise to his wonderful picture.

Bessie looked through the keyhole after a long pause, and saw the two walking up and down as usual, Torpenhow's hand on Dick's shoulder. Hereat she said something so improper that it shocked even Binkie, who was dribbling patiently on the landing in the hope of seeing his master again.

Chapter 11

The lark will make her hymn to God,
The partridge call her brood,
While I forget the heath I trod,
The fields wherein I stood.
'Tis dule to know not night from morn,
But deeper dule to know
I can but hear the hunter's horn
That once I used to blow.

'The Only Son.'

IT WAS the third day after Torpenhow's return, and his heart was heavy.

'Do you mean to tell me that you can't see to work without whisky? It's generally the other way about.'

'Can a drunkard swear on his honour?' said Dick.

'Yes, if he has been as good a man as you.'

'Then I give you my word of honour,' said Dick, speaking hurriedly through parched lips. 'Old man, I can hardly see your face now. You've kept me sober for two days,—if I ever was drunk,—and I've done no work. Don't keep me back any more. I don't know when my eyes may give out. The spots and dots and the pains and things are crowding worse than ever. I swear I can see all right when I'm—when I'm moderately screwed, as you say. Give me three more sittings from Bessie and all the—stuff I want, and the picture will be done. I can't kill myself in three days. It only means a touch of D. T. at the worst.'

'If I give you three days more will you promise me to stop work and—the other thing, whether the picture's finished or not?'

'I can't. You don't know what that picture means to me. But surely you could get the Nilghai to help you, and knock me down and tie me up. I shouldn't fight for the whisky, but I should for the work.'

'Go on, then. I give you three days; but you're nearly breaking my heart.'

Dick returned to his work, toiling as one possessed; and the yellow devil of whisky stood by him and chased away the spots in his eyes. The Melancolia was nearly finished, and was all or nearly all that he had hoped she would be. Dick jested with Bessie, who reminded him that he was 'a drunken beast'; but the reproof did not move him.

'You can't understand, Bess. We are in sight of land now, and soon we shall lie back and think about what we've done. I'll give you three months' pay when the picture's finished, and next time I have any more work in hand—but that doesn't matter. Won't three months' pay make you hate me less?'

'No, it won't! I hate you, and I'll go on hating you. Mr. Torpenhow won't speak to me any more. He's always looking at map-things and red-backed books.'

Bessie did not say that she had again laid siege to Torpenhow, or that he had at the end of her passionate pleading picked her up, given her a kiss, and put her outside the door with a recommendation not to be a little fool. He spent most of his time in the company of the Nilghai, and their talk was of war in the near future, the hiring of transports, and secret preparations among the dockyards. He did not care to see Dick till the picture was finished.

'He's doing first-class work,' he said to the Nilghai, 'and it's quite out of his regular line. But, for the matter of that, so's his infernal drinking.'

'Never mind. Leave him alone. When he has come to his senses again we'll carry him off from this place and let him breathe clean air. Poor Dick! I don't envy you, Torp, when his eyes fail.'

'Yes, it will be a case of "God help the man who's chained to our Davie." The worst is that we don't know when it will happen; and I believe the uncertainty and the waiting have sent Dick to the whisky more than anything else.'

'How the Arab who cut his head open would grin if he knew!'

'He's at perfect liberty to grin if he can. He's dead. That's poor consolation now.'

In the afternoon of the third day Torpenhow heard Dick calling for him. 'All finished!' he shouted. 'I've done it! Come in! Isn't she a beauty? Isn't she a darling? I've been down to hell to get her; but isn't she worth it?'

Torpenhow looked at the head of a woman who laughed,—a full-lipped, hollow-eyed woman who laughed from out of the canvas as Dick had intended she should.

'Who taught you how to do it?' said Torpenhow. 'The touch and notion have nothing to do with your regular work. What a face it is! What eyes, and what insolence!' Unconsciously he threw back his head and laughed with her. 'She's seen the game played out,—I don't think she had a good time of it,—and now she doesn't care. Isn't that the idea?'

'Exactly.'

'Where did you get the mouth and chin from? They don't belong to Bess.'

'They're—some one else's. But isn't it good? Isn't it thundering good? Wasn't it worth the whisky? I did it. Alone I did it, and it's the best I can do.' He drew his breath sharply, and whispered, 'Just God! what could I not do ten years hence, if I can do this now!—By the way, what do you think of it, Bess?'

The girl was biting her lips. She loathed Torpenhow because he had taken no notice of her.

'I think it's just the horridest, beastliest thing I ever saw,' she answered, and turned away.

'More than you will be of that way of thinking, young woman.—Dick, there's a sort of murderous, viperine suggestion in the poise of the head that I don't understand,' said Torpenhow.

'That's trick-work,' said Dick, chuckling with delight of being completely understood. 'I couldn't resist one little bit of sheer swagger. It's a French trick, and you wouldn't understand; but it's got at by slewing round the head a trifle, and a tiny, tiny foreshortening of one side of the face from the angle of the chin to the top of the left ear. That, and deepening the shadow under the lobe of the ear. It was flagrant trick-work; but, having the notion fixed, I felt entitled to play with it.—Oh, you beauty!'

'Amen! She is a beauty. I can feel it.'

'So will every man who has any sorrow of his own,' said Dick, slapping his thigh. 'He shall see his trouble there, and, by the Lord Harry, just when he's feeling properly sorry for himself he shall throw back his head and laugh,—as she is laughing. I've put the life of my heart and the light of my eyes into her, and I don't care what comes. . . . I'm tired,—awfully tired. I think I'll get to sleep. Take away the whisky, it has served its turn, and give Bessie thirty-six quid, and three over for luck. Cover the picture.'

He dropped asleep in the long chair, his face white and haggard almost before he had finished the sentence. Bessie tried to take Torpenhow's hand. 'Aren't you never going to speak to me any more?' she said; but Torpenhow was looking at Dick.

'What a stock of vanity the man has! I'll take him in hand to-morrow and make much of him. He deserves it.—Eh! what was that, Bess?'

'Nothing. I'll put things tidy here a little, and then I'll go. You couldn't give me that three months' pay now, could you? He said you were to.'

Torpenhow gave her a cheque and went to his own rooms. Bessie faithfully tidied up the studio, set the door ajar for flight, emptied half a bottle of turpentine on a duster, and began to scrub the face of the Melancolia viciously. The paint did not smudge quickly enough. She took a palette-knife and scraped, following each stroke with the wet duster. In five minutes the picture was a formless, scarred muddle of colours. She threw the paint-stained duster into the studio stove, stuck out her tongue at the sleeper, and whispered, 'Bilked!' as she turned to run down the staircase. She would never see Torpenhow any more, but she had at least done harm to the man who had come between her and her desire and who used to make fun of her. Cashing the cheque was the very cream of the jest to Bessie. Then the little privateer sailed across the Thames, to be swallowed up in the gray wilderness of South-the-water.

Dick slept till late into the evening, when Torpenhow dragged him off to bed. His eyes were as bright as his voice was hoarse. 'Let's have another look at the picture,' he said, insistently as a child.

'You—go—to—bed,' said Torpenhow. 'You aren't at all well, though you mayn't know it. You're as jumpy as a cat.'

'I reform to-morrow. Good-night.'

As he repassed through the studio, Torpenhow lifted the cloth above the picture, and almost betrayed himself by outcries: 'Wiped out!—scraped out and turped out! If Dick knows this to-night he'll go perfectly mad. He's on the verge of jumps as it is. That's Bess,—the little fiend! Only a woman could have done that!—with the ink not dry on the cheque, too! Dick will be raving mad to-morrow. It was all my fault for trying to help gutter-devils. Oh, my poor Dick, the Lord is hitting you very hard!'

Dick could not sleep that night, partly for pure joy, and partly because the well-known Catherine-wheels inside his eyes had given place to crackling volcanoes of many-coloured fire. 'Spout away,' he said aloud. 'I've done my work, and now you can do what you please.' He lay still, staring at the ceiling, the long-pent-up delirium of drink in his veins, his brain on fire with racing thoughts that would not stay to be considered, and his hands crisped and dry. He had just discovered that he was painting the face of the Melancolia on a revolving dome ribbed with millions of lights, and that all his wondrous thoughts stood embodied hundreds of feet below his tiny swinging plank, shouting together in his honour, when something cracked inside his temples like an overstrained bow-string, the glittering dome broke inward, and he was alone in the thick night.

'I'll go to sleep. The room's very dark. Let's light a lamp and see how the Melancolia looks. There ought to have been a moon.'

It was then that Torpenhow heard his name called by a voice that he did not know,—in the rattling accents of deadly fear.

'He's looked at the picture,' was his first thought, as he hurried into the bedroom and found Dick sitting up and beating the air with his hands.

'Torp! Torp! Where are you? For pity's sake, come to me!'

'What's the matter?'

Dick clutched at his shoulder. 'Matter! I've been lying here for hours in the dark, and you never heard me. Torp, old man, don't go away. I'm all in the dark. In the dark, I tell you!'

Torpenhow held the candle within a foot of Dick's eyes, but there was no light in those eyes. He lit the gas, and Dick heard the flame catch. The grip of his fingers on Torpenhow's shoulder made Torpenhow wince.

'Don't leave me. You wouldn't leave me alone now, would you? I can't see. D'you understand? It's black,—quite black,—and I feel as if I was falling through it all.'

'Steady does it.' Torpenhow put his arm round Dick and began to rock him gently to and fro.

'That's good. Now don't talk. If I keep very quiet for a while this darkness will lift. It seems just on the point of breaking. H'sh!' Dick knit his brows and stared desperately in front of him. The night air was chilling Torpenhow's toes.

'Can you stay like that a minute?' he said. 'I'll get my dressing-gown and some slippers.'

Dick clutched the bed-head with both hands and waited for the darkness to clear away. 'What a time you've been!' he cried, when Torpenhow returned. 'It's as black as ever. What are you banging about in the doorway?'

'Long chair,—horse-blanket,—pillow. Going to sleep by you. Lie down now; you'll be better in the morning.'

'I shan't!' The voice rose to a wail. 'My God! I'm blind! I'm blind, and the darkness will never go away.' He made as if to leap from the bed, but Torpenhow's arms were round him, and Torpenhow's chin was on his shoulder, and his breath was squeezed out of him. He could only gasp, 'Blind!' and wriggle feebly.

'Steady, Dickie, steady!' said the deep voice in his ear, and the grip tightened. 'Bite on the bullet, old man, and don't let them think you're afraid.' The grip could draw no closer. Both men were breathing heavily. Dick threw his head from side to side and groaned.

'Let me go,' he panted. 'You're cracking my ribs. We—we mustn't let them think we're afraid, must we,—all the Powers of Darkness and that lot?'

'Lie down. It's all over now.'

'Yes,' said Dick obediently. 'But would you mind letting me hold your hand? I feel as if I wanted something to hold on to. One drops through the dark so.'

Torpenhow thrust out a large and hairy paw from the long chair. Dick clutched it tightly, and in half an hour had fallen asleep. Torpenhow withdrew his hand, and, stooping over Dick, kissed him lightly on the forehead, as men do sometimes kiss a wounded comrade in the hour of death, to ease his departure.

In the gray dawn Torpenhow heard Dick talking to himself. He was adrift on the shoreless tides of delirium, speaking very quickly—

'It's a pity,—a great pity; but it's helped, and it must be eaten, Master George. . . . Sufficient unto the day is the blindness thereof, and, further, putting aside all Melancolias and false humours, it is of obvious notoriety—such as mine was—that the queen can do no wrong. Torp doesn't know that. I'll tell him when we're a little farther into the desert. . . . What a bungle those boatmen are making of the steamer-ropes! They'll have that four-inch hawser chafed through in a minute. I told you so—there she goes! . . . White foam on green water, and the steamer slewing round. How good that looks! I'll sketch it. No, I can't. I'm afflicted with ophthalmia. That was one of the ten plagues of Egypt, and it extends up the Nile in the shape of cataract. Ha! that's a joke, Torp. Laugh, you graven image, and stand clear of the hawser. . . . It'll knock you into the water and make your dress all dirty, Maisie dear.'

'Oh!' said Torpenhow. 'This happened before. That night on the river.'

'She'll be sure to say it's my fault if you get muddy, and you're quite near enough to the breakwater. . . . Maisie, that's not fair. Ah! I knew you'd miss. Low and to the left, dear. But you've no conviction. Everything in the world except conviction. Don't be angry, darling. I'd cut my hand off if it would give you anything more than obstinacy. My right hand, if it would serve.'

'Now we mustn't listen. Here's an island shouting across seas of misunderstanding with a vengeance. But it's shouting truth, I fancy,' said Torpenhow.

The babble continued. It all bore upon Maisie. Sometimes Dick lectured at length on his craft, then he cursed himself for his folly in being enslaved. He pleaded to Maisie for a kiss—only one kiss—before she went away, and called to her to come back from Vitry-sur-Marne, if she would; but through all his ravings he bade heaven and earth witness that the queen could do no wrong.

Torpenhow listened attentively, and learned every detail of Dick's life that had been hidden from him. For three days Dick raved through his past, and then slept a natural sleep. 'What a strain he has been running under, poor chap!' said Torpenhow. 'Dick, of all men, handing himself over like a dog. And I was lecturing him on arrogance! I ought to have known that it was no use to judge a man. But I did it. What a demon that girl must be! Dick's given her his life,—confound him!—and she's given him one kiss apparently.'

'Torp,' said Dick from the bed, 'go out for a walk. You've been here too long. I'll get up. Hi! This is annoying. I can't dress myself. Oh, it's too absurd!'

Torpenhow helped him into his clothes and led him to the big chair in the studio. He sat quietly waiting under strained nerves for the darkness to lift. It did not lift that day, nor the next. Dick adventured on a voyage round the walls. He hit his shins against the stove, and this suggested to him that it would be better to crawl on all-fours, one hand in front of him. Torpenhow found him on the floor.

'I'm trying to get the geography of my new possessions,' said he. 'D'you remember that nigger you gouged in the square? Pity you didn't keep the odd eye. It would have been useful. Any letters for me? Give me all the ones in fat gray envelopes with a sort of crown thing outside. They're of no importance.'

Torpenhow gave him a letter with a black M on the envelope flap. Dick put it into his pocket. There was nothing in it that Torpenhow might not have read, but it belonged to himself and to Maisie, who would never belong to him.

'When she finds that I don't write she'll stop writing. It's better so. I couldn't be any use to her now,' Dick argued, and the tempter suggested that he should make known his condition. Every nerve in him revolted. 'I have fallen low enough already. I'm not going to beg for pity. Besides, it would be cruel to her.' He strove to put Maisie out of his thoughts; but the blind have many opportunities for thinking, and as the tides of his strength came back to him in the long employless days of dead darkness, Dick's soul was troubled to the core. Another letter, and another, came from Maisie. Then there was silence, and Dick sat by the window, the pulse of summer in the air, and pictured her being won by another man, stronger than himself. His imagination, the keener for the dark background it worked against, spared him no single detail that might send him raging up and down the studio, to stumble over the stove that seemed to be in four places at once. Worst of all, tobacco would not taste in the darkness. The arrogance of the man had disappeared, and in its place were settled despair that Torpenhow knew, and blind passion that Dick confided to his pillow at night. The intervals between the paroxysms were filled with intolerable waiting and the weight of intolerable darkness.

'Come out into the Park,' said Torpenhow. 'You haven't stirred out since the beginning of things.'

'What's the use? There's no movement in the dark; and, besides,'—he paused irresolutely at the head of the stairs;—'something will run over me.'

'Not if I'm with you. Proceed gingerly.'

The roar of the streets filled Dick with nervous terror, and he clung to Torpenhow's arm. 'Fancy having to feel for a gutter with your foot!' he said petulantly, as he turned into the Park. 'Let's curse God and die.'

'Sentries are forbidden to pay unauthorised compliments. By Jove, there are the Guards!'

Dick's figure straightened. 'Let's get near 'em. Let's go in and look. Let's get on the grass and run. I can smell the trees.'

'Mind the low railing. That's all right!' Torpenhow kicked out a tuft of grass with his heel. 'Smell that,' he said. 'Isn't it good?' Dick snuffed luxuriously. 'Now pick up your feet and run.' They approached as near to the regiment as was possible. The clank of bayonets being unfixed made Dick's nostrils quiver.

'Let's get nearer. They're in column, aren't they?'

'Yes. How did you know?'

'Felt it. Oh, my men!—my beautiful men!' He edged forward as though he could see. 'I could draw those chaps once. Who'll draw 'em now?'

'They'll move off in a minute. Don't jump when the band begins.'

'Huh! I'm not a new charger. It's the silences that hurt. Nearer, Torp! —nearer! Oh, my God, what wouldn't I give to see 'em for a minute!—one half minute!'

He could hear the armed life almost within reach of him, could hear the slings tighten across the bandsman's chest as he heaved the big drum from the ground.

'Sticks crossed above his head,' whispered Torpenhow.

'I know. I know! Who should know if I don't? H'sh!'

The drumsticks fell with a boom, and the men swung forward to the crash of the band. Dick felt the wind of the massed movement in his face, heard the maddening tramp of feet and the friction of the pouches on the belts. The big drum pounded out the tune. It was a music-hall refrain that made a perfect quickstep—

> 'He must be a man of decent height,
>   He must be a man of weight,
> He must come home on a Saturday night
>   In a thoroughly sober state;
> He must know how to love me,
>   And he must know how to kiss;
> And if he's enough to keep us both
>   I can't refuse him bliss.'

'What's the matter?' said Torpenhow, as he saw Dick's head fall when the last of the regiment had departed.

'Nothing. I feel a little bit out of the running,—that's all. Torp, take me back. Why did you bring me out?'

Chapter 12

There were three friends that buried the fourth,
*   The mould in his mouth and the dust in his eyes;*
And they went south, and east, and north,—
*   The strong man fights, but the sick man dies.*

There were three friends that spoke of the dead,—
*   The strong man fights, but the sick man dies.—*
'And would he were here with us now,' they said,
*   'The sun in our face and the wind in our eyes.'*

Ballad.

THE NILGHAI was angry with Torpenhow. Dick had been sent to bed, —blind men are ever under the orders of those who can see,—and since he had returned from the Park had fluently sworn at Torpenhow because he was alive, and all the world because it was alive and could see, while he, Dick, was dead in the death of the blind, who, at the best, are only burdens upon their associates. Torpenhow had said something about a Mrs. Gummidge, and Dick had retired in a black fury to handle and re-handle three unopened letters from Maisie.

The Nilghai, fat, burly, and aggressive, was in Torpenhow's rooms. Behind him sat The Keneu, the Great War Eagle, and between them lay a large map embellished with black and white-headed pins.

'I was wrong about the Balkans,' said the Nilghai. 'But I'm not wrong about this business. The whole of our work in the Southern Soudan must be done over again. The public doesn't care, of course, but the Government does, and they are making their arrangements quietly. You know that as well as I do.'

'I remember how the people cursed us when our troops withdrew from Omdurman. It was bound to crop up sooner or later. But I can't go,' said Torpenhow. He pointed through the open door; it was a hot night. 'Can you blame me?'

The Keneu purred above his pipe like a large and very happy cat—
'Don't blame you in the least. It's uncommonly good of you, and all the

rest of it, but every man—even you, Torp—must consider his work. I know it sounds brutal, but Dick's out of the race,—down,—gastados, expended, finished, done for. He has a little money of his own. He won't starve, and you can't pull out of your stride for his sake. Think of your own reputation.'

'Dick's was five times bigger than mine and yours put together.'

'That was because he signed his name to everything he did. It's all ended now. You must hold yourself in readiness to move out. You can command your own prices, and you do better work than any three of us.'

'Don't tell me how tempting it is. I'll stay here to look after Dick for a while. He's as cheerful as a bear with a sore head, but I think he likes to have me near him.'

The Nilghai said something uncomplimentary about soft-headed fools who throw away their careers for other fools. Torpenhow flushed angrily. The constant strain of attendance on Dick had worn his nerves thin.

'There remains a third fate,' said The Keneu thoughtfully. 'Consider this, and be not larger fools than is necessary. Dick is—or rather was—an able-bodied man of moderate attractions and a certain amount of audacity.'

'Oho!' said the Nilghai, who remembered an affair at Cairo. 'I begin to see.—Torp, I'm sorry.'

Torpenhow nodded forgiveness: 'You were more sorry when he cut you out, though.—Go on, Keneu.'

'I've often thought, when I've seen men die out in the desert, that if the news could be sent through the world, and the means of transport were quick enough, there would be one woman at least at each man's bedside.'

'There would be some mighty quaint revelations. Let us be grateful things are as they are,' said the Nilghai.

'Let us rather reverently consider whether Torp's three-cornered ministrations are exactly what Dick needs just now.—What do you think yourself, Torp?'

'I know they aren't. But what can I do?'

'Lay the matter before the Board. We are all Dick's friends here. You've been most in his life.'

'But I picked it up when he was off his head.'

'The greater chance of its being true. I thought we should arrive. Who is she?'

Then Torpenhow told a tale in plain words, as a special correspondent who knows how to make a verbal precis should tell it. The men listened without interruption.

'Is it possible that a man can come back across the years to his calf-love?' said Keneu. 'Is it possible?'

'I give the facts. He says nothing about it now, but he sits fumbling three letters from her when he thinks I'm not looking. What am I to do?'

'Speak to him,' said the Nilghai.

'Oh yes! Write to her,—I don't know her full name, remember,—and ask her to accept him out of pity. I believe you once told Dick you were sorry for him, Nilghai. You remember what happened, eh? Go into the bedroom and suggest full confession and an appeal to this Maisie girl, whoever she is. I honestly believe he'd try to kill you; and the blindness has made him rather muscular.'

'Torpenhow's course is perfectly clear,' said The Keneu. 'He will go to Vitry-sur-Marne, which is on the Bezieres-Landes Railway,—single track from Tourgas. The Prussians shelled it out in '70 because there was a poplar on the top of a hill eighteen hundred yards from the church spire. There's a squadron of cavalry quartered there,—or ought to be. Where this studio Torp spoke about may be I cannot tell. That is Torp's business. I have given him his route. He will dispassionately explain the situation to the girl, and she will come back to Dick,—the more especially because, to use Dick's words, "there is nothing but her damned obstinacy to keep them apart."'

'And they have four hundred and twenty pounds a year between 'em. Dick never lost his head for figures, even in his delirium. You haven't the shadow of an excuse for not going,' said the Nilghai.

Torpenhow looked very uncomfortable. 'But it's absurd and impossible. I can't drag her back by the hair.'

'Our business—the business for which we draw our money—is to do absurd and impossible things,—generally with no reason whatever except to amuse the public. Here we have a reason. The rest doesn't matter. I shall share these rooms with the Nilghai till Torpenhow returns. There will be a batch of unbridled "specials" coming to town in a little while, and these will serve as their headquarters. Another reason for sending Torpenhow away. Thus Providence helps those who help others, and'— here The Keneu dropped his measured speech—'we can't have you tied by the leg to Dick when the trouble begins. It's your only chance of getting away; and Dick will be grateful.'

'He will,—worse luck! I can but go and try. I can't conceive a woman in her senses refusing Dick.'

'Talk that out with the girl. I have seen you wheedle an angry Mahdieh woman into giving you dates. This won't be a tithe as difficult. You had better not be here to-morrow afternoon, because the Nilghai and I will be in possession. It is an order. Obey.'

'Dick,' said Torpenhow next morning, 'can I do anything for you?'

'No! Leave me alone. How often must I remind you that I'm blind?'

'Nothing I could go for to fetch for to carry for to bring?'

'No. Take those infernal creaking boots of yours away.'

'Poor chap!' said Torpenhow to himself. 'I must have been sitting on his nerves lately. He wants a lighter step.' Then, aloud, 'Very well. Since you're so independent I'm going off for four or five days. Say good-bye at least. The housekeeper will look after you, and Keneu has my rooms.'

Dick's face fell. 'You won't be longer than a week at the outside? I know I'm touched in the temper, but I can't get on without you.'

'Can't you? You'll have to do without me in a little time, and you'll be glad I'm gone.'

Dick felt his way back to the big chair, and wondered what these things might mean. He did not wish to be tended by the housekeeper, and yet Torpenhow's constant tendernesses jarred on him. He did not exactly know what he wanted. The darkness would not lift, and Maisie's unopened letters felt worn and old from much handling. He could never read them for himself as long as life endured; but Maisie might have sent him some fresh ones to play with. The Nilghai entered with a gift, —a piece of red modelling-wax. He fancied that Dick might find interest in using his hands. Dick poked and patted the stuff for a few minutes, and, 'Is it like anything in the world?' he said drearily. 'Take it away. I may get the touch of the blind in fifty years. Do you know where Torpenhow has gone?'

The Nilghai knew nothing. 'We're staying in his rooms till he comes back. Can we do anything for you?'

'I'd like to be left alone, please. Don't think I'm ungrateful; but I'm best alone.'

The Nilghai chuckled, and Dick resumed his drowsy brooding and sullen rebellion against fate. He had long since ceased to think about the work he had done in the old days, and the desire to do more work had departed from him. He was exceedingly sorry for himself, and the completeness of his tender grief soothed him. But his soul and his body cried for Maisie,—Maisie who would understand. His mind pointed out that Maisie, having her own work to do, would not care. His experience had taught him that when money was exhausted women went away, and that when a man was knocked out of the race the others trampled on him. 'Then at the least,' said Dick, in reply, 'she could use me as I used Binat, —for some sort of a study. I wouldn't ask more than to be near her again, even though I knew that another man was making love to her. Ugh! what a dog I am!'

A voice on the staircase began to sing joyfully—

'When we go—go—go—away from here,
    Our creditors will weep and they will wail,
Our absence much regretting when they find that we've been getting
    Out of England by next Tuesday's Indian mail.'

Following the trampling of feet, slamming of Torpenhow's door, and the sound of voices in strenuous debate, some one squeaked, 'And see, you good fellows, I have found a new water-bottle,—firs'-class patent—eh, how you say? Open himself inside out.'

Dick sprang to his feet. He knew the voice well. 'That's Cassavetti, come back from the Continent. Now I know why Torp went away. There's a row somewhere, and—I'm out of it!'

The Nilghai commanded silence in vain. 'That's for my sake,' Dick said bitterly. 'The birds are getting ready to fly, and they wouldn't tell me. I can hear Morten-Sutherland and Mackaye. Half the War Correspondents in London are there;—and I'm out of it.'

He stumbled across the landing and plunged into Torpenhow's room. He could feel that it was full of men. 'Where's the trouble?' said he. 'In the Balkans at last? Why didn't some one tell me?'

'We thought you wouldn't be interested,' said the Nilghai shamefacedly. 'It's in the Soudan, as usual.'

'You lucky dogs! Let me sit here while you talk. I shan't be a skeleton at the feast.—Cassavetti, where are you? Your English is as bad as ever.'

Dick was led into a chair. He heard the rustle of the maps, and the talk swept forward, carrying him with it. Everybody spoke at once, discussing press censorships, railway-routes, transport, water-supply, the capacities of generals,—these in language that would have horrified a trusting public,—ranting, asserting, denouncing, and laughing at the top of their voices. There was the glorious certainty of war in the Soudan at any moment. The Nilghai said so, and it was well to be in readiness. The Keneu had telegraphed to Cairo for horses; Cassavetti had stolen a perfectly inaccurate list of troops that would be ordered forward, and was reading it out amid profane interruptions, and The Keneu introduced to Dick some man unknown who would be employed as war artist by the Central Southern Syndicate. 'It's his first outing,' said The Keneu. 'Give him some tips—about riding camels.'

'Oh, those camels?' groaned Cassavetti. 'I shall learn to ride him again, and now I am so much all soft! Listen, you good fellows. I know your military arrangement very well. There will go the Royal Argalshire Sutherlanders. So it was read to me upon best authority.'

A roar of laughter interrupted him.

'Sit down,' said the Nilghai. 'The lists aren't even made out in the War Office.'

'Will there be any force at Suakin?' said a voice.

Then the outcries redoubled, and grew mixed, thus: 'How many Egyptian troops will they use?—God help the Fellaheen!—There's a railway in Plumstead marshes doing duty as a fives-court.—We shall have the Suakin-Berber line built at last.—Canadian voyageurs are too careful. Give me a half-drunk Krooman in a whale-boat.—Who commands the Desert column?—No, they never blew up the big rock at the Ghizeh bend. We shall have to be hauled up, as usual.—Somebody tell me if there's an Indian contingent, or I'll break everybody's head.—Don't tear the map in two.—It's a war of occupation, I tell you, to connect with the African Companies in the South.—There's guinea-worm in most of the wells on that route.' Then the Nilghai, despairing of peace, bellowed like a fog-horn and beat upon the table with both hands.

'But what becomes of Torpenhow?' said Dick, in the silence that followed.

'Torp's in abeyance just now. He's off lovemaking somewhere, I suppose,' said the Nilghai.

'He said he was going to stay at home,' said The Keneu.

'Is he?' said Dick with an oath. 'He won't. I'm not much good now, but if you and the Nilghai hold him down I'll engage to trample on him till he sees reason. He stay behind, indeed! He's the best of you all. There'll be some tough work by Omdurman. We shall come there to stay, this time. But I forgot. I wish I were going with you.'

'So do we all, Dickie,' said The Keneu.

'And I most of all,' said the new artist of the Central Southern Syndicate. 'Could you tell me—'

'I'll give you one piece of advice,' Dick answered, moving towards the door. 'If you happen to be cut over the head in a scrimmage, don't guard. Tell the man to go on cutting. You'll find it cheapest in the end. Thanks for letting me look in.'

'There's grit in Dick,' said the Nilghai, an hour later, when the room was emptied of all save The Keneu.

'It was the sacred call of the war-trumpet. Did you notice how he answered to it? Poor fellow! Let's look at him,' said The Keneu.

The excitement of the talk had died away. Dick was sitting by the studio table with his head on his arms, when the men came in. He did not change his position.

'It hurts,' he moaned. 'God forgive me, but it hurts cruelly; and yet, y'know, the world has a knack of spinning round all by itself. Shall I see Torp before he goes?'

'Oh yes. You'll see him,' said the Nilghai.

Chapter 13

The sun went down an hour ago,
I wonder if I face towards home,
If I lost my way in the light of day
How shall I find it now night is come?

Old Song.

'MAISIE, come to bed.'

'It's so hot I can't sleep. Don't worry.'

Maisie put her elbows on the window-sill and looked at the moonlight on the straight, poplar-flanked road. Summer had come upon Vitry-sur-Marne and parched it to the bone. The grass was dry-burnt in the meadows, the clay by the bank of the river was caked to brick, the roadside flowers were long since dead, and the roses in the garden hung withered on their stalks. The heat in the little low bedroom under the eaves was almost intolerable. The very moonlight on the wall of Kami's studio across the road seemed to make the night hotter, and the shadow of the big bell-handle by the closed gate cast a bar of inky black that caught Maisie's eye and annoyed her.

'Horrid thing! It should be all white,' she murmured. 'And the gate isn't in the middle of the wall, either. I never noticed that before.'

Maisie was hard to please at that hour. First, the heat of the past few weeks had worn her down; secondly, her work, and particularly the study of a female head, intended to represent the Melancolia and not finished in time for the Salon, was unsatisfactory; thirdly, Kami had said as much two days before; fourthly,—but so completely fourthly that it was hardly worth thinking about,—Dick, her property, had not written to her for more than six weeks. She was angry with the heat, with Kami, and with her work, but she was exceedingly angry with Dick.

She had written to him three times,—each time proposing a fresh treatment of her Melancolia. Dick had taken no notice of these communications. She had resolved to write no more. When she returned to England in the autumn—for her pride's sake she could not return earlier—she would speak to him. She missed the Sunday afternoon conferences more than she cared to admit. All that Kami said was, 'Continuez, mademoiselle, continuez toujours,' and he had been repeating his wearisome counsel through the hot summer, exactly like a cicala,—an old gray cicala in a black alpaca coat, white trousers, and a huge felt hat. But Dick had tramped masterfully up and down her little studio north of the cool green London park, and had said things ten times worse than 'Continuez,' before he snatched the brush out of her hand and showed her where her error lay. His last letter, Maisie remembered, contained some trivial advice about not sketching in the sun or drinking water at wayside farm-houses; and he had said that not once, but three times,—as if he did not know that Maisie could take care of herself!

But what was he doing, that he could not trouble to write? A murmur of voices in the road made her lean from the window. A cavalryman of the little garrison in the town was talking to Kami's cook. The moonlight glittered on the scabbard of his sabre, which he was holding in his hand lest it should clank inopportunely. The cook's cap cast deep shadows on her face, which was close to the conscript's. He slid his arm round her waist and there followed the sound of a kiss.

'Faugh!' said Maisie, stepping back.

'What's that!' said the red-haired girl, who was tossing uneasily outside her bed.

'Only a conscript kissing the cook,' said Maisie. 'They've gone away now.' She leaned out of the window again, and put a shawl over her nightgown to guard against chills. There was a very small night-breeze abroad, and a sun-baked rose below nodded its head as one who knew unutterable secrets. Was it possible that Dick should turn his thoughts from her work and his own and descend to the degradation of Suzanne and the conscript? He could not! The rose nodded its head and one leaf therewith. It looked like a naughty little devil scratching its ear. Dick could not, 'Because,' thought Maisie, 'he is mine,—mine,—mine. He said he was. I'm sure I don't care what he does. It will only spoil his work if he does; and it will spoil mine too.'

The rose continued to nod in the futile way peculiar to flowers. There was no earthly reason why Dick should not disport himself as he chose, except that he was called by Providence, which was Maisie, to assist Maisie in her work. And her work was the preparation of pictures that went sometimes to English provincial exhibitions, as the notices in the scrap-book proved, and that were invariably rejected by the Salon when Kami was plagued into allowing her to send them up. Her work in the future, it seemed, would be the preparation of pictures on exactly similar lines which would be rejected in exactly the same way—

[The red-haired girl threshed distressfully across the sheets. 'It's too hot to sleep,' she moaned; and the interruption jarred.]

Exactly the same way. Then she would divide her years between the little studio in England and Kami's big studio at Vitry-sur-Marne. No, she would go to another master, who should force her into the success that was her right, if patient toil and desperate endeavour gave one a right to anything. Dick had told her that he had worked ten years to understand his craft. She had worked ten years, and ten years were nothing. Dick had said that ten years were nothing,—but that was in regard to herself only. He had said—this very man who could not find time to write—that he would wait ten years for her, and that she was bound to come back to him sooner or later. He had said this in the absurd letter about sunstroke and diphtheria; and then he had stopped writing. He was wandering up and down moonlit streets, kissing cooks. She would like to lecture him now,—not in her nightgown, of course, but properly dressed, severely and from a height. Yet if he was kissing other girls he certainly would not care whether she lectured him or not. He would laugh at her. Very good. She would go back to her studio and prepare pictures that went, etc., etc. The mill-wheel of thought swung round slowly, that no section of it might be slurred over, and the red-haired girl tossed and turned behind her.

Maisie put her chin in her hands and decided that there could be no doubt whatever of the villainy of Dick. To justify herself, she began, unwomanly, to weigh the evidence. There was a boy, and he had said he loved her. And he kissed her,—kissed her on the cheek,—by a yellow sea-poppy that nodded its head exactly like the maddening dry rose in the garden. Then there was an interval, and men had told her that they loved her—just when she was busiest with her work. Then the boy came back, and at their very second meeting had told her that he loved her. Then he had—But there was no end to the things he had done. He had given her his time and his powers. He had spoken to her of Art, housekeeping, technique, teacups, the abuse of pickles as a stimulant,—that was rude,—sable-hair brushes,—he had given her the best in her stock, —she used them daily; he had given her advice that she profited by, and now and again—a look. Such a look! The look of a beaten hound waiting for the word to crawl to his mistress's feet. In return she had given him nothing whatever, except—here she brushed her mouth against the open-work sleeve of her nightgown—the privilege of kissing her once. And on the mouth, too. Disgraceful! Was that not enough, and more than enough? and if it was not, had he not cancelled the debt by not writing and—probably kissing other girls?

'Maisie, you'll catch a chill. Do go and lie down,' said the wearied voice of her companion. 'I can't sleep a wink with you at the window.'

Maisie shrugged her shoulders and did not answer. She was reflecting on the meannesses of Dick, and on other meannesses with which he had nothing to do. The remorseless moonlight would not let her sleep. It lay on the skylight of the studio across the road in cold silver; she stared at it intently, and her thoughts began to slide one into the other. The shadow of the big bell-handle in the wall grew short, lengthened again, and faded out as the moon went down behind the pasture and a hare came limping home across the road. Then the dawn-wind washed through the upland grasses, and brought coolness with it, and the cattle lowed by the drought-shrunk river. Maisie's head fell forward on the window-sill, and the tangle of black hair covered her arms.

'Maisie, wake up. You'll catch a chill.'

'Yes, dear; yes, dear.' She staggered to her bed like a wearied child, and as she buried her face in the pillows she muttered, 'I think—I think. . . . But he ought to have written.'

Day brought the routine of the studio, the smell of paint and turpentine, and the monotonous wisdom of Kami, who was a leaden artist, but a golden teacher if the pupil were only in sympathy with him. Maisie was not in sympathy that day, and she waited impatiently for the end of the work. She knew when it was coming; for Kami would gather his black alpaca coat into a bunch behind him, and, with faded blue eyes that saw neither pupils nor canvas, look back into the past to recall the history of one Binat. 'You have all done not so badly,' he would say. 'But you shall remember that it is not enough to have the method and the art, and the power, nor even that which is touch, but you shall have also the conviction that nails the work to the wall. Of the so many I have taught,'—here the students would begin to unfix drawing-pins or get their tubes together,—'the very so many that I have taught, the best was Binat. All that comes of the study and the work and the knowledge was to him even when he came. After he left me he should have done all that could be done with the colour, the form, and the knowledge. Only, he had not the conviction. So to-day I hear no more of Binat,—the best of my pupils,— and that is long ago. So to-day, too, you will be glad to hear no more of me. Continuez, mesdemoiselles, and, above all, with conviction.'

He went into the garden to smoke and mourn over the lost Binat as the pupils dispersed to their several cottages or loitered in the studio to make plans for the cool of the afternoon.

Maisie looked at her very unhappy Melancolia, restrained a desire to grimace before it, and was hurrying across the road to write a letter to

Dick, when she was aware of a large man on a white troop-horse. How Torpenhow had managed in the course of twenty hours to find his way to the hearts of the cavalry officers in quarters at Vitry-sur-Marne to discuss with them the certainty of a glorious revenge for France, to reduce the colonel to tears of pure affability, and to borrow the best horse in the squadron for the journey to Kami's studio, is a mystery that only special correspondents can unravel.

'I beg your pardon,' said he. 'It seems an absurd question to ask, but the fact is that I don't know her by any other name: Is there any young lady here that is called Maisie?'

'I am Maisie,' was the answer from the depths of a great sun-hat.

'I ought to introduce myself,' he said, as the horse capered in the blinding white dust. 'My name is Torpenhow. Dick Heldar is my best friend, and—and—the fact is that he has gone blind.'

'Blind?' said Maisie stupidly. 'He can't be blind.'

'He has been stone-blind for nearly two months.'

Maisie lifted up her face, and it was pearly white. 'No! No! Not blind! I won't have him blind!'

'Would you care to see for yourself?' said Torpenhow.

'Now,—at once?'

'Oh no! The Paris train doesn't go through this place till eight to-night. There will be ample time.'

'Did Mr. Heldar send you to me?'

'Certainly not. Dick wouldn't do that sort of thing. He's sitting in his studio, turning over some letters that he can't read because he's blind.'

There was a sound of choking from the sun-hat. Maisie bowed her head and went into the cottage, where the red-haired girl was on a sofa, complaining of a headache.

'Dick's blind!' said Maisie, taking her breath quickly as she steadied herself against a chair-back. 'My Dick's blind!'

'What?' The girl was on the sofa no longer.

'A man has come from England to tell me. He hasn't written to me for six weeks.'

'Are you going to him?'

'I must think.'

'Think! I should go back to London and see him, and I should kiss his eyes, and kiss them and kiss them until they got well again! If you don't go I shall. Oh, what am I talking about? You wicked little idiot! Go to him at once. Go!'

Torpenhow's neck was blistering, but he preserved a smile of infinite patience as Maisie appeared bareheaded in the sunshine.

'I am coming,' said she, her eyes on the ground.

'You will be at Vitry Station, then, at seven this evening.' This was an order delivered by one who was used to being obeyed. Maisie said nothing, but she felt grateful that there was no chance of disputing with this big man who took everything for granted and managed a squealing horse with one hand. She returned to the red-haired girl, who was weeping bitterly, and between tears, kisses,—very few of those,—menthol, packing, and an interview with Kami, the sultry afternoon wore away. Thought might come afterwards. Her present duty was to go to Dick, —Dick who owned the wondrous friend and sat in the dark playing with her unopened letters.

'But what will you do?' she said to her companion.

'I? Oh, I shall stay here and—finish your Melancolia,' she said, smiling pitifully. 'Write to me afterwards.'

That night there ran a legend through Vitry-sur-Marne of a mad Englishman, doubtless suffering from sunstroke, who had drunk all the officers of the garrison under the table, had borrowed a horse from the lines, and had then and there eloped, after the English custom, with one of those more than mad English girls who drew pictures down there under the care of that good Monsieur Kami.

'They are very droll,' said Suzanne to the conscript in the moonlight by the studio wall. 'She walked always with those big eyes that saw nothing, and yet she kisses me on both cheeks as though she were my sister, and gives me—see—ten francs!'

The conscript levied a contribution on both gifts; for he prided himself on being a good soldier.

Torpenhow spoke very little to Maisie during the journey to Calais; but he was careful to attend to all her wants, to get her a compartment entirely to herself, and to leave her alone. He was amazed at the ease with which the matter had been accomplished.

'The safest thing would be to let her think things out. By Dick's showing,—when he was off his head,—she must have ordered him about very thoroughly. Wonder how she likes being under orders.'

Maisie never told. She sat in the empty compartment often with her eyes shut, that she might realise the sensation of blindness. It was an order that she should return to London swiftly, and she found herself at last almost beginning to enjoy the situation. This was better than looking after luggage and a red-haired friend who never took any interest in her surroundings. But there appeared to be a feeling in the air that she, Maisie,—of all people,—was in disgrace. Therefore she justified her conduct to herself with great success, till Torpenhow came up to her on the steamer, and without preface began to tell the story of Dick's blindness, suppressing a few details, but dwelling at length on the miseries of delirium. He stopped before he reached the end, as though he had lost interest in the subject, and went forward to smoke. Maisie was furious with him and with herself.

She was hurried on from Dover to London almost before she could ask for breakfast, and—she was past any feeling of indignation now—was bidden curtly to wait in a hall at the foot of some lead-covered stairs while Torpenhow went up to make inquiries. Again the knowledge that she was being treated like a naughty little girl made her pale cheeks flame. It was all Dick's fault for being so stupid as to go blind.

Torpenhow led her up to a shut door, which he opened very softly. Dick was sitting by the window, with his chin on his chest. There were three envelopes in his hand, and he turned them over and over. The big man who gave orders was no longer by her side, and the studio door snapped behind her.

Dick thrust the letters into his pocket as he heard the sound. 'Hullo, Torp! Is that you? I've been so lonely.'

His voice had taken the peculiar flatness of the blind. Maisie pressed herself up into a corner of the room. Her heart was beating furiously, and she put one hand on her breast to keep it quiet. Dick was staring directly at her, and she realised for the first time that he was blind. Shutting her eyes in a railway-carriage to open them when she pleased was child's play. This man was blind though his eyes were wide open.

'Torp, is that you? They said you were coming.' Dick looked puzzled and a little irritated at the silence.

'No: it's only me,' was the answer, in a strained little whisper. Maisie could hardly move her lips.

'H'm!' said Dick composedly, without moving. 'This is a new phenomenon. Darkness I'm getting used to; but I object to hearing voices.'

Was he mad, then, as well as blind, that he talked to himself? Maisie's heart beat more wildly, and she breathed in gasps. Dick rose and began to feel his way across the room, touching each table and chair as he passed. Once he caught his foot on a rug, and swore, dropping on his knees to feel what the obstruction might be. Maisie remembered him walking in the Park as though all the earth belonged to him, tramping up and down her studio two months ago, and flying up the gangway of the Channel steamer. The beating of her heart was making her sick, and Dick was coming nearer, guided by the sound of her breathing. She put out a hand mechanically to ward him off or to draw him to herself, she did not know which. It touched his chest, and he stepped back as though he had been shot.

'It's Maisie!' said he, with a dry sob. 'What are you doing here?'

'I came—I came—to see you, please.'

Dick's lips closed firmly.

'Won't you sit down, then? You see, I've had some bother with my eyes, and—'

'I know. I know. Why didn't you tell me?'

'I couldn't write.'

'You might have told Mr. Torpenhow.'

'What has he to do with my affairs?'

'He—he brought me from Vitry-sur-Marne. He thought I ought to see you.'

'Why, what has happened? Can I do anything for you? No, I can't. I forgot.'

'Oh, Dick, I'm so sorry! I've come to tell you, and—Let me take you back to your chair.'

'Don't! I'm not a child. You only do that out of pity. I never meant to tell you anything about it. I'm no good now. I'm down and done for. Let me alone!'

He groped back to his chair, his chest labouring as he sat down.

Maisie watched him, and the fear went out of her heart, to be followed by a very bitter shame. He had spoken a truth that had been hidden from the girl through every step of the impetuous flight to London; for he was, indeed, down and done for—masterful no longer, but rather a little abject; neither an artist stronger than she, nor a man to be looked up to—only some blind one that sat in a chair and seemed on the point of crying. She was immensely and unfeignedly sorry for him—more sorry than she had ever been for any one in her life, but not sorry enough to deny his words. So she stood still and felt ashamed and a little hurt, because she had honestly intended that her journey should end triumphantly; and now she was only filled with pity most startlingly distinct from love.

'Well?' said Dick, his face steadily turned away. 'I never meant to worry you any more. What's the matter?'

He was conscious that Maisie was catching her breath, but was as unprepared as herself for the torrent of emotion that followed. People who cannot cry easily weep unrestrainedly when the fountains of the great deep are broken up. She had dropped into a chair and was sobbing with her face hidden in her hands.

'I can't—I can't!' she cried desperately. 'Indeed, I can't. It isn't my fault. I'm so sorry. Oh, Dickie, I'm so sorry.'

Dick's shoulders straightened again, for the words lashed like a whip. Still the sobbing continued. It is not good to realise that you have failed in the hour of trial or flinched before the mere possibility of making sacrifices.

'I do despise myself—indeed I do. But I can't. Oh, Dickie, you wouldn't ask me—would you?' wailed Maisie.

She looked up for a minute, and by chance it happened that Dick's eyes fell on hers. The unshaven face was very white and set, and the lips were trying to force themselves into a smile. But it was the worn-out eyes that Maisie feared. Her Dick had gone blind and left in his place some one that she could hardly recognise till he spoke.

'Who is asking you to do anything, Maisie? I told you how it would be. What's the use of worrying? For pity's sake don't cry like that; it isn't worth it.'

'You don't know how I hate myself. Oh, Dick, help me—help me!' The passion of tears had grown beyond her control and was beginning to alarm the man. He stumbled forward and put his arm round her, and her head fell on his shoulder.

'Hush, dear, hush! Don't cry. You're quite right, and you've nothing to reproach yourself with—you never had. You're only a little upset by the journey, and I don't suppose you've had any breakfast. What a brute Torp was to bring you over.'

'I wanted to come. I did indeed,' she protested.

'Very well. And now you've come and seen, and I'm—immensely grateful. When you're better you shall go away and get something to eat. What sort of a passage did you have coming over?'

Maisie was crying more subduedly, for the first time in her life glad that she had something to lean against. Dick patted her on the shoulder tenderly but clumsily, for he was not quite sure where her shoulder might be.

She drew herself out of his arms at last and waited, trembling and most unhappy. He had felt his way to the window to put the width of the room between them, and to quiet a little the tumult in his heart.

'Are you better now?' he said.

'Yes, but—don't you hate me?'

'I hate you? My God! I?'

'Isn't—isn't there anything I could do for you, then? I'll stay here in England to do it, if you like. Perhaps I could come and see you sometimes.'

'I think not, dear. It would be kindest not to see me any more, please. I don't want to seem rude, but—don't you think—perhaps you had almost better go now.'

He was conscious that he could not bear himself as a man if the strain continued much longer.

'I don't deserve anything else. I'll go, Dick. Oh, I'm so miserable.'

'Nonsense. You've nothing to worry about; I'd tell you if you had. Wait a moment, dear. I've got something to give you first. I meant it for you ever since this little trouble began. It's my Melancolia; she was a beauty when I last saw her. You can keep her for me, and if ever you're poor you can sell her. She's worth a few hundreds at any state of the market.' He groped among his canvases. 'She's framed in black. Is this a black frame that I have my hand on? There she is. What do you think of her?'

He turned a scarred, formless muddle of paint towards Maisie, and the eyes strained as though they would catch her wonder and surprise. One thing and one thing only could she do for him.

'Well?'

The voice was fuller and more rounded, because the man knew he was speaking of his best work. Maisie looked at the blur, and a lunatic desire to laugh caught her by the throat. But for Dick's sake—whatever this mad blankness might mean—she must make no sign. Her voice choked with hard-held tears as she answered, still gazing on the wreck—

'Oh, Dick, it is good!'

He heard the little hysterical gulp and took it for tribute. 'Won't you have it, then? I'll send it over to your house if you will.'

'I? Oh, yes—thank you. Ha! ha!' If she did not fly at once the laughter that was worse than tears would kill her. She turned and ran, choking and blinded, down the staircases that were empty of life, to take refuge in a cab and go to her house across the Park. There she sat down in the almost dismantled drawing-room and thought of Dick in his blindness, useless till the end of life, and of herself in her own eyes. Behind the sorrow, the shame, and the humiliation, lay fear of the cold wrath of the red-haired girl when Maisie should return. Maisie had never feared her companion before. Not until she found herself saying, 'Well, he never asked me,' did she realise her scorn of herself.

And that is the end of Maisie.

For Dick was reserved more searching torment. He could not realise at first that Maisie, whom he had ordered to go, had left him without a word of farewell. He was savagely angry against Torpenhow, who had brought upon him this humiliation and troubled his miserable peace. Then his dark hour came, and he was alone with himself and his desires to get what help he could from the darkness. The queen could do no wrong, but in following the right, so far as it served her work, she had wounded her one subject more than his own brain would let him know.

'It's all I had and I've lost it,' he said, as soon as the misery permitted clear thinking. 'And Torp will think that he has been so infernally clever that I shan't have the heart to tell him. I must think this out quietly.'

'Hullo!' said Torpenhow, entering the studio after Dick had enjoyed two hours of thought. 'I'm back. Are you feeling any better?'

'Torp, I don't know what to say. Come here.' Dick coughed huskily, wondering, indeed, what he should say and how to say it temperately.

'What's the need for saying anything? Get up and tramp.' Torpenhow was perfectly satisfied.

They walked up and down as of custom, Torpenhow's hand on Dick's shoulder, and Dick buried in his own thoughts.

'How in the world did you find it all out?' said Dick at last.

'You shouldn't go off your head if you want to keep secrets, Dickie. It was absolutely impertinent on my part; but if you'd seen me rocketing about on a half-trained French troop-horse under a blazing sun you'd have laughed. There will be a charivari in my rooms to-night. Seven other devils—'

'I know—the row in the Southern Soudan. I surprised their councils the other day, and it made me unhappy. Have you fixed your flint to go? Who d'you work for?'

''Haven't signed any contracts yet. I wanted to see how your business would turn out.'

'Would you have stayed with me, then, if—things had gone wrong?' He put his question cautiously.

'Don't ask me too much. I'm only a man.'

'You've tried to be an angel very successfully.'

'Oh ye—es! . . . Well, do you attend the function to-night? We shall be half screwed before the morning. All the men believe the war's a certainty.'

'I don't think I will, old man, if it's all the same to you. I'll stay quiet here.'

'And meditate? I don't blame you. You deserve a good time if ever a man did.'

That night there was tumult on the stairs. The correspondents poured in from theatre, dinner and music-hall to Torpenhow's room that they might discuss their plan of campaign in the event of military operations being a certainty. Torpenhow, The Keneu, and the Nilghai had bidden all the men they had worked with to the orgy; and Mr. Beeton, the housekeeper, declared that never before in his checkered experience had he seen quite such a fancy lot of gentlemen. They waked the chambers with shoutings and song; and the elder men were quite as bad as the younger. For the chances of war were in front of them, and all knew what those meant.

Sitting in his own room a little perplexed by the noise across the landing, Dick suddenly began to laugh to himself.

'When one comes to think of it the situation is intensely comic. Maisie's quite right—poor little thing. I didn't know she could cry like that before; but now I know what Torp thinks, I'm sure he'd be quite fool enough to stay at home and try to console me—if he knew. Besides, it isn't nice to own that you've been thrown over like a broken chair. I must carry this business through alone—as usual. If there isn't a war, and Torp finds out, I shall look foolish, that's all. If there is a war I mustn't interfere with another man's chances. Business is business, and I want to be alone —I want to be alone. What a row they're making!'

Somebody hammered at the studio door.

'Come out and frolic, Dickie,' said the Nilghai.

'I should like to, but I can't. I'm not feeling frolicsome.'

'Then I'll tell the boys and they'll draw you like a badger.'

'Please not, old man. On my word, I'd sooner be left alone just now.'

'Very good. Can we send anything in to you? Fizz, for instance. Cassavetti is beginning to sing songs of the Sunny South already.'

For one minute Dick considered the proposition seriously.

'No, thanks. I've a headache already.'

'Virtuous child. That's the effect of emotion on the young. All my congratulations, Dick. I also was concerned in the conspiracy for your welfare.'

'Go to the devil and—oh, send Binkie in here.'

The little dog entered on elastic feet, riotous from having been made much of all the evening. He had helped to sing the choruses; but scarcely inside the studio he realised that this was no place for tail-wagging, and settled himself on Dick's lap till it was bedtime. Then he went to bed with Dick, who counted every hour as it struck, and rose in the morning with a painfully clear head to receive Torpenhow's more formal congratulations and a particular account of the last night's revels.

'You aren't looking very happy for a newly-accepted man,' said Torpenhow.

'Never mind that—it's my own affair, and I'm all right. Do you really go?'

'Yes. With the old Central Southern as usual. They wired and I accepted on better terms than before.'

'When do you start?'

'The day after to-morrow—for Brindisi.'

'Thank God.' Dick spoke from the bottom of his heart.

'Well, that's not a pretty way of saying you're glad to get rid of me. But men in your condition are allowed to be selfish.'

'I didn't mean that. Will you get a hundred pounds cashed for me before you leave?'

'That's a slender amount for housekeeping, isn't it?'

'Oh, it's only for—marriage expenses.'

Torpenhow brought him the money, counted it out in fives and tens, and carefully put it away in the writing-table.

'Now I suppose I shall have to listen to his ravings about his girl until I go. Heaven send us patience with a man in love!' said he to himself.

But never a word did Dick say of Maisie or marriage. He hung in the doorway of Torpenhow's room when the latter was packing, and asked innumerable questions about the coming campaign, till Torpenhow began to feel annoyed.

'You're a secretive animal, Dickie, and you consume your own smoke, don't you?' he said on the last evening.

'I—I suppose so. By the way, how long do you think this war will last?'

'Days, weeks, or months. One can never tell. It may go on for years.'

'I wish I were going.'

'Good heavens! You're the most unaccountable creature! Hasn't it occurred to you that you're going to be married—thanks to me?'

'Of course, yes. I'm going to be married—so I am. Going to be married. I'm awfully grateful to you. Haven't I told you that?'

'You might be going to be hanged by the look of you,' said Torpenhow.

And the next day Torpenhow bade him good-bye and left him to the loneliness he had so much desired.

Chapter 14

Yet at the last, ere our spearmen had found him,
  Yet at the last, ere a sword-thrust could save,
Yet at the last, with his masters around him,
  He of the Faith spoke as master to slave;
Yet at the last, tho' the Kafirs had maimed him,
  Broken by bondage and wrecked by the reiver,—
Yet at the last, tho' the darkness had claimed him,
  He called upon Allah and died a believer.

                                                                   'Kizilbashi.'

'Beg your pardon, Mr. Heldar, but—but isn't nothin' going to happen?' said Mr. Beeton.

'No!' Dick had just waked to another morning of blank despair and his temper was of the shortest.

''Taint my regular business o' course, sir; and what I say is, "Mind your own business and let other people mind theirs"; but just before Mr. Torpenhow went away he give me to understand, like, that you might be moving into a house of your own, so to speak—a sort of house with rooms upstairs and downstairs where you'd be better attended to, though I try to act just by all our tenants. Don't I?'

'Ah! That must have been a madhouse. I shan't trouble you to take me there yet. Get me my breakfast, please, and leave me alone.'

'I hope I haven't done anything wrong, sir, but you know, I hope, that as far as a man can I tries to do the proper thing by all the gentlemen in chambers—and more particular those whose lot is hard—such as you, for instance, Mr. Heldar. You likes soft-roe bloater, don't you? Soft-roe bloaters is scarcer than hard-roe, but what I say is, "Never mind a little extra trouble so long as you gives satisfaction to the tenants."'

Mr. Beeton withdrew and left Dick to himself. Torpenhow had been long away; there was no more rioting in the chambers, and Dick had settled down to his new life, which he was weak enough to consider nothing better than death.

It is hard to live alone in the dark, confusing the day and night; dropping to sleep through sheer weariness at mid-day, and rising restless in the chill of the dawn. At first Dick, on his awakenings, would grope along the corridors of the chambers till he heard some one snore. Then he would know that the day had not yet come and return wearily to his bedroom. Later he learned not to stir till there was a noise and movement in the house and Mr. Beeton advised him to get up. Once dressed—and dressing, now that Torpenhow was away, was a lengthy business, because collars, ties, and the like, hid themselves in far corners of the room, and search meant head-beating against chairs and trunks— once dressed, there was nothing whatever to do except to sit still and brood till the three daily meals came. Centuries separated breakfast from lunch, and lunch from dinner, and though a man prayed for hundreds of years that his mind might be taken from him, God would never hear. Rather the mind was quickened and the revolving thoughts ground against each other as millstones grind when there is no corn between; and yet the brain would not wear out and give him rest. It continued to think, at length, with imagery and all manner of reminiscences. It recalled Maisie and past success, reckless travels by land and sea, the glory of doing work and feeling that it was good, and suggested all that might have happened had the eyes only been faithful to their duty. When thinking ceased through sheer weariness, there poured into Dick's soul tide on tide of overwhelming, purposeless fear—dread of starvation always, terror lest the unseen ceiling should crush down upon him, fear of fire in the chambers and a louse's death in red flame, and agonies of fiercer horror that had nothing to do with any fear of death. Then Dick bowed his head, and clutching the arms of his chair fought with his sweating self till the tinkle of plates told him that something to eat was being set before him.

Mr. Beeton would bring the meal when he had time to spare, and Dick learned to hang upon his speech which dealt with badly-fitted gas-plugs, waste-pipes out of repair, little tricks for driving picture-nails into walls, and the sins of the charwoman or the housemaids. In the lack of better things the small gossip of a servants' hall becomes immensely interesting, and the screwing of a washer on a tap an event to be talked over for days.

Once or twice a week, too, Mr. Beeton would take Dick out with him when he went marketing in the morning to haggle with tradesmen over fish, lamp-wicks, mustard, tapioca, and so forth, while Dick rested his weight first on one foot and then on the other, and played aimlessly with the tins and string-ball on the counter. Then they would, perhaps, meet one of Mr. Beeton's friends, and Dick, standing aside a little, would hold his peace till Mr. Beeton was willing to go on again.

The life did not increase his self-respect. He abandoned shaving as a dangerous exercise, and being shaved in a barber's shop meant exposure of his infirmity. He could not see that his clothes were properly brushed, and since he had never taken any care of his personal appearance he became every known variety of sloven. A blind man cannot eat with cleanliness till he has been some months used to the darkness. If he demand attendance and grow angry at the want of it, he must assert himself and stand upright. Then the meanest menial can see that he is blind and, therefore, of no consequence. A wise man will keep his eyes on the floor and sit still. For amusement he may pick coal lump by lump out of the scuttle with the tongs, and pile it in a little heap in the fender, keeping count of the lumps, which must all be put back again, one by one and very carefully. He may set himself sums if he cares to work them out; he may talk to himself or to the cat if she chooses to visit him; and if his trade has been that of an artist, he may sketch in the air with his forefinger; but that is too much like drawing a pig with the eyes shut. He may go to his bookshelves and count his books, ranging them in order of their size, or to his wardrobe and count his shirts, laying them in piles of two or three on the bed, as they suffer from frayed cuffs or lost buttons. Even this entertainment wearies after a time; and all the times are very, very long.

Dick was allowed to sort a tool-chest where Mr. Beeton kept hammers, taps and nuts, lengths of gas-pipes, oil-bottles and string.

'If I don't have everything just where I know where to look for it, why, then, I can't find anything when I do want it. You've no idea, sir, the amount of little things that these Chambers uses up,' said Mr. Beeton. Fumbling at the handle of the door as he went out: 'It's hard on you, sir, I do think it's hard on you. Ain't you going to do anything, sir?'

'I'll pay my rent and messing. Isn't that enough?'

'I wasn't doubting for a moment that you couldn't pay your way, sir; but I 'ave often said to my wife, "It's 'ard on 'im because it isn't as if he was an old man, nor yet a middle-aged one, but quite a young gentleman. That's where it comes so 'ard."'

'I suppose so,' said Dick absently. This particular nerve through long battering had ceased to feel—much.

'I was thinking,' continued Mr. Beeton, still making as if to go, 'that you might like to hear my boy Alf read you the papers sometimes of an evening. He do read beautiful, seeing he's only nine.'

'I should be very grateful,' said Dick. 'Only let me make it worth his while.'

'We wasn't thinking of that, sir, but of course it's in your own 'ands; but only to 'ear Alf sing "A Boy's best Friend is 'is Mother"! Ah!'

'I'll hear him sing that too. Let him come in this evening with the newspapers.'

Alf was not a nice child, being puffed up with many school-board certificates for good conduct, and inordinately proud of his singing. Mr. Beeton remained, beaming, while the child wailed his way through a song of some eight eight-line verses in the usual whine of the young Cockney, and, after compliments, left him to read Dick the foreign telegrams. Ten minutes later Alf returned to his parents rather pale and scared.

''E said 'e couldn't stand it no more,' he explained.

'He never said you read badly, Alf?' Mrs. Beeton spoke.

'No. 'E said I read beautiful. Said 'e never 'eard any one read like that, but 'e said 'e couldn't abide the stuff in the papers.'

'P'raps he's lost some money in the Stocks. Were you readin' him about Stocks, Alf?'

'No; it was all about fightin' out there where the soldiers is gone—a great long piece with all the lines close together and very hard words in it. 'E give me 'arf a crown because I read so well. And 'e says the next time there's anything 'e wants read 'e'll send for me.'

'That's good hearing, but I do think for all the half-crown—put it into the kicking-donkey money-box, Alf, and let me see you do it—he might have kept you longer. Why, he couldn't have begun to understand how beautiful you read.'

'He's best left to hisself—gentlemen always are when they're downhearted,' said Mr. Beeton.

Alf's rigorously limited powers of comprehending Torpenhow's special correspondence had waked the devil of unrest in Dick. He could hear, through the boy's nasal chant, the camels grunting in the squares behind the soldiers outside Suakin; could hear the men swearing and chaffing across the cooking-pots, and could smell the acrid wood-smoke as it drifted over the camp before the wind of the desert.

That night he prayed to God that his mind might be taken from him, offering for proof that he was worthy of this favour the fact that he had not shot himself long ago. That prayer was not answered, and indeed Dick knew in his heart of hearts that only a lingering sense of humour and no special virtue had kept him alive. Suicide, he had persuaded himself, would be a ludicrous insult to the gravity of the situation as well as a weak-kneed confession of fear.

'Just for the fun of the thing,' he said to the cat, who had taken Binkie's place in his establishment, 'I should like to know how long this is going to last. I can live for a year on the hundred pounds Torp cashed for me. I must have two or three thousand at least at the Bank—twenty or thirty years more provided for, that is to say. Then I fall back on my hundred and twenty a year which will be more by that time. Let's consider. Twenty-five—thirty-five—a man's in his prime then, they say—forty-five—a middle-aged man just entering politics—fifty-five—"died at the comparatively early age of fifty-five," according to the newspapers. Bah! How these Christians funk death! Sixty-five—we're only getting on in years. Seventy-five is just possible though. Great Hell, cat O! fifty years more of solitary confinement in the dark! You'll die, and Beeton will die, and Torp will die, and Mai—everybody else will die, but I shall be alive and kicking with nothing to do. I'm very sorry for myself. I should like some one else to be sorry for me. Evidently I'm not going mad before I die, but the pain's just as bad as ever. Some day when you're vivisected cat O! they'll tie you down on a little table and cut you open—but don't be afraid; they'll take precious good care that you don't die. You'll live, and you'll be very sorry then that you weren't sorry for me. Perhaps Torp will come back or . . . I wish I could go to Torp and the Nilghai, even though I were in their way.'

Pussy left the room before the speech was ended, and Alf, as he entered, found Dick addressing the empty hearth-rug.

'There's a letter for you, sir,' he said. 'Perhaps you'd like me to read it.'

'Lend it to me for a minute and I'll tell you.'

The outstretched hand shook just a little and the voice was not over-steady. It was within the limits of human possibility that—that was no letter from Maisie. He knew the heft of three closed envelopes only too well. It was a foolish hope that the girl should write to him, for he did not realise that there is a wrong which admits of no reparation though the evildoer may with tears and the heart's best love strive to mend all. It is best to forget that wrong whether it be caused or endured, since it is as remediless as bad work once put forward.

'Read it, then,' said Dick, and Alf began intoning according to the rules of the Board School—

' "I could have given you love, I could have given you loyalty, such as you never dreamed of. Do you suppose I cared what you were? But you chose to whistle everything down the wind for nothing. My only excuse for you is that you are so young." '

'That's all,' he said, returning the paper to be dropped into the fire.

'What was in the letter?' asked Mrs. Beeton when Alf returned.

'I don't know. I think it was a circular or a tract about not whistlin' at everything when you're young.'

'I must have stepped on something when I was alive and walking about, and it has bounced up and hit me. God help it, whatever it is—unless it was all a joke. But I don't know any one who'd take the trouble to play a joke on me. . . . Love and loyalty for nothing. It sounds tempting enough. I wonder whether I have lost anything really?'

Dick considered for a long time, but could not remember when or how he had put himself in the way of winning these trifles at a woman's hands.

Still, the letter as touching on matters that he preferred not to think about stung him into a fit of frenzy that lasted for a day and night. When his heart was so full of despair that it would hold no more, body and soul together seemed to be dropping without check through the darkness. Then came fear of darkness and desperate attempts to reach the light again. But there was no light to be reached. When that agony had left him sweating and breathless, the downward flight would recommence till the gathering torture of it spurred him into another fight as hopeless as the first. Followed some few minutes of sleep in which he dreamed that he saw. Then the procession of events would repeat itself till he was utterly worn out, and the brain took up its everlasting consideration of Maisie and might-have-beens.

At the end of everything Mr. Beeton came to his room and volunteered to take him out. 'Not marketing this time, but we'll go into the Parks if you like.'

'Be damned if I do,' quoth Dick. 'Keep to the streets and walk up and down. I like to hear the people round me.'

This was not altogether true. The blind in the first stages of their infirmity dislike those who can move with a free stride and unlifted arms —but Dick had no earthly desire to go to the Parks. Once and only once since Maisie had shut the door he had gone there under Alf's charge. Alf forgot him and fished for minnows in the Serpentine with some companions. After half an hour's waiting Dick, almost weeping with rage and wrath, caught a passer-by who introduced him to a friendly policeman, who led him to a four-wheeler opposite the Albert Hall. He never told Mr. Beeton of Alf's forgetfulness, but . . . this was not the manner in which he was used to walk the Parks aforetime.

'What streets would you like to walk down, then?' said Mr. Beeton sympathetically. His own ideas of a riotous holiday meant picnicking on the grass of the Green Park with his family, and half a dozen paper bags full of food.

'Keep to the river,' said Dick, and they kept to the river, and the rush of it was in his ears till they came to Blackfriars Bridge and struck thence on to the Waterloo Road, Mr. Beeton explaining the beauties of the scenery as he went on.

'And walking on the other side of the pavement,' said he, 'unless I'm much mistaken, is the young woman that used to come to your rooms to be drawed. I never forgets a face and I never remembers a name, except paying tenants o' course!'

'Stop her,' said Dick. 'It's Bessie Broke. Tell her I'd like to speak to her again. Quick, man!'

Mr. Beeton crossed the road under the noses of the omnibuses and arrested Bessie then on her way northward. She recognised him as the man in authority who used to glare at her when she passed up Dick's staircase, and her first impulse was to run.

'Wasn't you Mr. Heldar's model?' said Mr. Beeton, planting himself in front of her. 'You was. He's on the other side of the road and he'd like to see you.'

'Why?' said Bessie faintly. She remembered—indeed had never for long forgotten—an affair connected with a newly-finished picture.

'Because he has asked me to do so, and because he's most particular blind.'

'Drunk?'

'No. 'Orspital blind. He can't see. That's him over there.'

Dick was leaning against the parapet of the bridge as Mr. Beeton pointed him out—a stub-bearded, bowed creature wearing a dirty magenta-coloured neckcloth outside an unbrushed coat. There was nothing to fear from such an one. Even if he chased her, Bessie thought he could not follow far. She crossed over and Dick's face lighted up. It was long since a woman of any kind had taken the trouble to speak to him.

'I hope you're well, Mr. Heldar?' said Bessie, a little puzzled. Mr. Beeton stood by with the air of an ambassador and breathed responsibly.

'I'm very well indeed, and, by Jove! I'm glad to see—hear you, I mean, Bess. You never thought it worth while to turn up and see us again after you got your money. I don't know why you should. Are you going anywhere in particular just now?'

'I was going for a walk,' said Bessie.

'Not the old business?' Dick spoke under his breath.

'Lor', no! I paid my premium'—Bessie was very proud of that word—'for a barmaid, sleeping in, and I'm at the bar now quite respectable. Indeed I am.'

Mr. Beeton had no special reason to believe in the loftiness of human nature. Therefore he dissolved himself like a mist and returned to his gas-plugs without a word of apology. Bessie watched the flight with a certain uneasiness; but so long as Dick appeared to be ignorant of the harm that had been done to him . . .

'It's hard work pulling the beer-handles,' she went on, 'and they've got one of them penny-in-the-slot cash-machines, so if you get wrong by a penny at the end of the day—but then I don't believe the machinery is right. Do you?'

'I've only seen it work. Mr. Beeton?'

'He's gone.'

'I'm afraid I must ask you to help me home, then. I'll make it worth your while. You see?' The sightless eyes turned towards her and Bessie saw.

'It isn't taking you out of your way?' he said hesitatingly. 'I can ask a policeman if it is.'

'Not at all. I come on at seven and I'm off at four. That's easy hours.'

'Good God!—but I'm on all the time. I wish I had some work to do too. Let's go home, Bess.'

He turned and cannoned into a man on the sidewalk, recoiling with an oath. Bessie took his arm and said nothing—as she had said nothing when he had ordered her to turn her face a little more to the light. They walked for some time in silence, the girl steering him deftly through the crowd.

'And where's—where's Mr. Torpenhow?' she inquired at last.

'He has gone away to the desert.'

'Where's that?'

Dick pointed to the right. 'East—out of the mouth of the river,' said he. 'Then west, then south, and then east again, all along the underside of Europe. Then south again. God knows how far.' The explanation did not enlighten Bessie in the least, but she held her tongue and looked to Dick's path till they came to the chambers.

'We'll have tea and muffins,' he said joyously. 'I can't tell you, Bessie, how glad I am to find you again. What made you go away so suddenly?'

'I didn't think you'd want me any more,' she said, emboldened by his ignorance.

'I didn't as a matter of fact—but afterwards—At any rate I'm glad you've come. You know the stairs.'

So Bessie led him home to his own place—there was no one to hinder—and shut the door of the studio.

'What a mess!' was her first word. 'All these things haven't been looked after for months and months.'

'No, only weeks, Bess. You can't expect them to care.'

'I don't know what you expect them to do. They ought to know what you've paid them for. The dust's just awful. It's all over the easel.'

'I don't use it much now.'

'All over the pictures and the floor, and all over your coat. I'd like to speak to them housemaids.'

'Ring for tea, then.' Dick felt his way to the one chair he used by custom.

Bessie saw the action and, as far as in her lay, was touched. But there remained always a keen sense of new-found superiority, and it was in her voice when she spoke.

'How long have you been like this?' she said wrathfully, as though the blindness were some fault of the housemaids.

'How?'

'As you are.'

'The day after you went away with the cheque, almost as soon as my picture was finished; I hardly saw her alive.'

'Then they've been cheating you ever since, that's all. I know their nice little ways.'

A woman may love one man and despise another, but on general feminine principles she will do her best to save the man she despises from being defrauded. Her loved one can look to himself, but the other man, being obviously an idiot, needs protection.

'I don't think Mr. Beeton cheats much,' said Dick. Bessie was flouncing up and down the room, and he was conscious of a keen sense of enjoyment as he heard the swish of her skirts and the light step between.

'Tea and muffins,' she said shortly, when the ring at the bell was answered; 'two teaspoonfuls and one over for the pot. I don't want the old teapot that was here when I used to come. It don't draw. Get another.'

The housemaid went away scandalised, and Dick chuckled. Then he began to cough as Bessie banged up and down the studio disturbing the dust.

'What are you trying to do?'

'Put things straight. This is like unfurnished lodgings. How could you let it go so?'

'How could I help it? Dust away.'

She dusted furiously, and in the midst of all the pother entered Mrs. Beeton. Her husband on his return had explained the situation, winding up with the peculiarly felicitous proverb, 'Do unto others as you would be done by.' She had descended to put into her place the person who demanded muffins and an uncracked teapot as though she had a right to both.

'Muffins ready yet?' said Bess, still dusting. She was no longer a drab of the streets, but a young lady who, thanks to Dick's cheque, had paid her premium and was entitled to pull beer-handles with the best. Being neatly dressed in black she did not hesitate to face Mrs. Beeton, and there passed between the two women certain regards that Dick would have appreciated. The situation adjusted itself by eye. Bessie had won, and Mrs. Beeton returned to cook muffins and make scathing remarks about models, hussies, trollops, and the like, to her husband.

'There's nothing to be got of interfering with him, Liza,' he said. 'Alf, you go along into the street to play. When he isn't crossed he's as kindly as kind, but when he's crossed he's the devil and all. We took too many little things out of his rooms since he was blind to be that particular about what he does. They ain't no objects to a blind man, of course, but if it was to come into court we'd get the sack. Yes, I did introduce him to that girl because I'm a feelin' man myself.'

'Much too feelin'!' Mrs. Beeton slapped the muffins into the dish, and thought of comely housemaids long since dismissed on suspicion.

'I ain't ashamed of it, and it isn't for us to judge him hard so long as he pays quiet and regular as he do. I know how to manage young gentlemen, you know how to cook for them, and what I says is, let each stick to his own business and then there won't be any trouble. Take them muffins down, Liza, and be sure you havd no words with that young woman. His lot is cruel hard, and if he's crossed he do swear worse than any one I've ever served.'

'That's a little better,' said Bessie, sitting down to the tea. 'You needn't wait, thank you, Mrs. Beeton.'

'I had no intention of doing such, I do assure you.'

Bessie made no answer whatever. This, she knew, was the way in which real ladies routed their foes, and when one is a barmaid at a first-class public-house one may become a real lady at ten minutes' notice.

Her eyes fell on Dick opposite her and she was both shocked and displeased. There were droppings of food all down the front of his coat; the mouth, under the ragged ill-grown beard, drooped sullenly; the forehead was lined and contracted; and on the lean temples the hair was a dusty, indeterminate colour that might or might not have been called gray. The utter misery and self-abandonment of the man appealed to her, and at the bottom of her heart lay the wicked feeling that he was humbled and brought low who had once humbled her.

'Oh! it is good to hear you moving about,' said Dick, rubbing his hands. 'Tell us all about your bar successes, Bessie, and the way you live now.'

'Never mind that. I'm quite respectable, as you'd see by looking at me. You don't seem to live too well. What made you go blind that sudden? Why isn't there any one to look after you?'

Dick was too thankful for the sound of her voice to resent the tone of it.

'I was cut across the head a long time ago, and that ruined my eyes. I don't suppose anybody thinks it worth while to look after me any more. Why should they?—and Mr. Beeton really does everything I want.'

'Don't you know any gentlemen and ladies, then, while you was—well?'

'A few, but I don't care to have them looking at me.'

'I suppose that's why you've growed a beard. Take it off, it don't become you.'

'Good gracious, child, do you imagine that I think of what becomes me these days?'

'You ought. Get that taken off before I come here again. I suppose I can come, can't I?'

'I'd be only too grateful if you did. I don't think I treated you very well in the old days. I used to make you angry.'

'Very angry, you did.'

'I'm sorry for it, then. Come and see me when you can and as often as you can. God knows, there isn't a soul in the world to take that trouble except you and Mr. Beeton.'

'A lot of trouble he's taking and she too.' This with a toss of the head. 'They've let you do anyhow, and they haven't done anything for you. I've only to look to see that much. I'll come, and I'll be glad to come, but you must go and be shaved, and you must get some other clothes— those ones aren't fit to be seen.'

'I have heaps somewhere,' he said helplessly.

'I know you have. Tell Mr. Beeton to give you a new suit and I'll brush it and keep it clean. You may be as blind as a barn-door, Mr. Heldar, but it doesn't excuse you looking like a sweep.'

'Do I look like a sweep then?'

'Oh, I'm sorry for you. I'm that sorry for you!' she cried impulsively, and took Dick's hands. Mechanically, he lowered his head as if to kiss— she was the only woman who had taken pity on him, and he was not too proud for a little pity now. She stood up to go.

'Nothing o' that kind till you look more like a gentleman. It's quite easy when you get shaved, and some clothes.'

He could hear her drawing on her gloves and rose to say good-bye. She passed behind him, kissed him audaciously on the back of the neck, and ran away as swiftly as on the day when she had destroyed the Melancolia.

'To think of me kissing Mr. Heldar,' she said to herself, 'after all he's done to me and all! Well, I'm sorry for him, and if he was shaved he wouldn't be so bad to look at, but . . . Oh them Beetons, how shameful they've treated him! I know Beeton's wearing his shirts on his back today just as well as if I'd aired it. To-morrow, I'll see . . . I wonder if he has much of his own. It might be worth more than the bar—I wouldn't have to do any work—and just as respectable if no one knew.'

Dick was not grateful to Bessie for her parting gift. He was acutely conscious of it in the nape of his neck throughout the night, but it seemed, among very many other things, to enforce the wisdom of getting shaved. He was shaved accordingly in the morning, and felt the better for it. A fresh suit of clothes, white linen, and the knowledge that some one in the world said that she took an interest in his personal appearance, made him carry himself almost upright; for the brain was relieved for a while from thinking of Maisie, who, under other circumstances, might have given that kiss and a million others.

'Let us consider,' said he after lunch. 'The girl can't care, and it's a toss-up whether she comes again or not, but if money can buy her to look after me she shall be bought. Nobody else in the world would take the trouble, and I can make it worth her while. She's a child of the gutter holding brevet rank as a barmaid; so she shall have everything she wants if she'll only come and talk and look after me.' He rubbed his newly-shorn chin and began to perplex himself with the thought of her not coming. 'I suppose I did look rather a sweep,' he went on. 'I had no reason to look otherwise. I knew things dropped on my clothes, but it didn't matter. It would be cruel if she didn't come. She must. Maisie came once, and that was enough for her. She was quite right. She had something to work for. This creature has only beer-handles to pull, unless she has deluded some young man into keeping company with her. Fancy being cheated for the sake of a counter-jumper! We're falling pretty low.'

Something cried aloud within him:—This will hurt more than anything that has gone before. It will recall and remind and suggest and tantalise, and in the end drive you mad.

'I know it, I know it!' Dick cried, clenching his hands despairingly; 'but good heavens! is a poor blind beggar never to get anything out of his life except three meals a day and a greasy waistcoat? I wish she'd come.'

Early in the afternoon time she came, because there was no young man in her life just then, and she thought of material advantages which would allow her to be idle for the rest of her days.

'I shouldn't have known you,' she said approvingly. 'You look as you used to look—a gentleman that was proud of himself.'

'Don't you think I deserve another kiss then?' said Dick, flushing a little.

'Maybe—but you won't get it yet. Sit down and let's see what I can do for you. I'm certain sure Mr. Beeton cheats you, now that you can't go through the housekeeping books every month. Isn't that true?'

'You'd better come and housekeep for me then, Bessie.'

''Couldn't do it in these chambers—you know that as well as I do.'

'I know, but we might go somewhere else, if you thought it worth your while.'

'I'd try to look after you, anyhow; but I shouldn't care to have to work for both of us.' This was tentative.

Dick laughed.

'Do you remember where I used to keep my bankbook?' said he. 'Torp took it to be balanced just before he went away. Look and see.'

'It was generally under the tobacco-jar. Ah!'

'Well?'

'Oh! Four thousand two hundred and ten pounds nine shillings and a penny! Oh my!'

'You can have the penny. That's not bad for one year's work. Is that and a hundred and twenty pounds a year good enough?'

The idleness and the pretty clothes were almost within her reach now, but she must, by being housewifely, show that she deserved them.

'Yes; but you'd have to move, and if we took an inventory, I think we'd find that Mr. Beeton has been prigging little things out of the rooms here and there. They don't look as full as they used.'

'Never mind, we'll let him have them. The only thing I'm particularly anxious to take away is that picture I used you for—when you used to swear at me. We'll pull out of this place, Bess, and get away as far as ever we can.'

'Oh yes,' she said uneasily.

'I don't know where I can go to get away from myself, but I'll try, and you shall have all the pretty frocks that you care for. You'll like that. Give me that kiss now, Bess. Ye gods! it's good to put one's arm round a woman's waist again.'

Then came the fulfilment of the prophecy within the brain. If his arm were thus round Maisie's waist and a kiss had just been given and taken between them,—why then. . . . He pressed the girl more closely to himself because the pain whipped him. She was wondering how to explain a little accident to the Melancolia. At any rate, if this man really desired the solace of her company—and certainly he would relapse into his original slough if she withdrew it—he would not be more than just a little vexed. It would be delightful at least to see what would happen, and by her teachings it was good for a man to stand in certain awe of his companion.

She laughed nervously, and slipped out of his reach.

'I shouldn't worrit about that picture if I was you,' she began, in the hope of turning his attention.

'It's at the back of all my canvases somewhere. Find it, Bess; you know it as well as I do.'

'I know—but—'

'But what? You've wit enough to manage the sale of it to a dealer. Women haggle much better than men. It might be a matter of eight or nine hundred pounds to—to us. I simply didn't like to think about it for a long time. It was mixed up with my life so.—But we'll cover up our tracks and get rid of everything, eh? Make a fresh start from the beginning, Bess.'

Then she began to repent very much indeed, because she knew the value of money. Still, it was probable that the blind man was overestimating the value of his work. Gentlemen, she knew, were absurdly particular about their things. She giggled as a nervous housemaid giggles when she tries to explain the breakage of a pipe.

'I'm very sorry, but you remember I was—I was angry with you before Mr. Torpenhow went away?'

'You were very angry, child; and on my word I think you had some right to be.'

'Then I—but aren't you sure Mr. Torpenhow didn't tell you?'

'Tell me what? Good gracious, what are you making such a fuss about when you might just as well be giving me another kiss.'

He was beginning to learn, not for the first time in his experience, that kissing is a cumulative poison. The more you get of it, the more you want. Bessie gave the kiss promptly, whispering, as she did so, 'I was so angry I rubbed out that picture with the turpentine. You aren't angry, are you?'

'What? Say that again.' The man's hand had closed on her wrist.

'I rubbed it out with turps and the knife,' faltered Bessie. 'I thought you'd only have to do it over again. You did do it over again, didn't you? Oh, let go of my wrist; you're hurting me.'

'Isn't there anything left of the thing?'

'N'nothing that looks like anything. I'm sorry—I didn't know you'd take on about it; I only meant to do it in fun. You aren't going to hit me?'

'Hit you! No! Let's think.'

He did not relax his hold upon her wrist, but stood staring at the carpet. Then he shook his head as a young steer shakes it when the lash of the stock-whip across his nose warns him back to the path to the shambles that he would escape. For weeks he had forced himself not to think of the Melancolia, because she was a part of his dead life. With Bessie's return and certain new prospects that had developed themselves the Melancolia—lovelier in his imagination than she had ever been on canvas—reappeared. By her aid he might have procured more money wherewith to amuse Bess and to forget Maisie, as well as another taste of an almost forgotten success. Now, thanks to a vicious little housemaid's folly, there was nothing to look for—not even the hope that he might some day take an abiding interest in the housemaid. Worst of all, he had been made to appear ridiculous in Maisie's eyes. A woman will forgive the man who has ruined her life so long as he gives her love: a man may forgive those who ruin the love of his life, but he will never forgive the destruction of his work.

'Tck—tck—tck,' said Dick between his teeth, and then laughed softly. 'It's an omen, Bessie, and—a good many things considered, it serves me right for doing what I have done. By Jove! that accounts for Maisie's running away. She must have thought me perfectly mad—small blame to her! The whole picture ruined, isn't it so? What made you do it?'

'Because I was that angry. I'm not angry now—I'm awful sorry.'

'I wonder.—It doesn't matter, anyhow. I'm to blame for making the mistake.'

'What mistake?'

'Something you wouldn't understand, dear. Great heavens! to think that a little piece of dirt like you could throw me out of my stride!' Dick was talking to himself as Bessie tried to shake off his grip on her wrist.

'I ain't a piece of dirt, and you shouldn't call me so! I did it 'cause I hated you, and I'm only sorry now 'cause you're—'cause you're—'

'Exactly—because I'm blind. There's nothing like tact in little things.'

Bessie began to sob. She did not like being shackled against her will; she was afraid of the blind face and the look upon it, and was sorry too that her great revenge had only made Dick laugh.

'Don't cry,' he said, and took her into his arms. 'You only did what you thought right.'

'I—I ain't a little piece of dirt, and if you say that I'll never come to see you again.'

'You don't know what you've done to me. I'm not angry—indeed, I'm not. Be quiet for a minute.'

Bessie remained in his arms shrinking. Dick's first thought was connected with Maisie, and it hurt him as white-hot iron hurts an open sore.

Not for nothing is a man permitted to ally himself to the wrong woman. The first pang—the first sense of things lost is but the prelude to the play, for the very just Providence who delights in causing pain has decreed that the agony shall return, and that in the midst of keenest pleasure. They know this pain equally who have forsaken or been forsaken by the love of their life, and in their new wives' arms are compelled to realise it. It is better to remain alone and suffer only the misery of being alone, so long as it is possible to find distraction in daily work. When that resource goes the man is to be pitied and left alone.

These things and some others Dick considered while he was holding Bessie to his heart.

'Though you mayn't know it,' he said, raising his head, 'the Lord is a just and a terrible God, Bess; with a very strong sense of humour. It serves me right—how it serves me right! Torp could understand it if he were here; he must have suffered something at your hands, child, but only for a minute or so. I saved him. Set that to my credit, some one.'

'Let me go,' said Bess, her face darkening. 'Let me go.'

'All in good time. Did you ever attend Sunday school?'

'Never. Let me go, I tell you; you're making fun of me.'

'Indeed, I'm not. I'm making fun of myself. . . . Thus. "He saved others, himself he cannot save." It isn't exactly a school-board text.' He released her wrist, but since he was between her and the door she could not escape. 'What an enormous amount of mischief one little woman can do!'

'I'm sorry; I'm awful sorry about the picture.'

'I'm not. I'm grateful to you for spoiling it. . . . What were we talking about before you mentioned the thing?'

'About getting away—and money. Me and you going away.'

'Of course. We will get away—that is to say, I will.'

'And me?'

'You shall have fifty whole pounds for spoiling a picture.'

'Then you won't—?'

'I'm afraid not, dear. Think of fifty pounds for pretty things all to yourself.'

'You said you couldn't do anything without me.'

'That was true a little while ago. I'm better now, thank you. Get me my hat.'

'S'pose I don't?'

'Beeton will, and you'll lose fifty pounds. That's all. Get it.'

Bessie cursed under her breath. She had pitied the man sincerely, had kissed him with almost equal sincerity, for he was not unhandsome; it pleased her to be in a way and for a time his protector, and above all there were four thousand pounds to be handled by some one. Now through a slip of the tongue and a little feminine desire to give a little, not too much, pain she had lost the money, the blessed idleness and the pretty things, the companionship, and the chance of looking outwardly as respectable as a real lady.

'Now fill me a pipe. Tobacco doesn't taste, but it doesn't matter, and I'll think things out. What's the day of the week, Bess?'

'Tuesday.'

'Then Thursday's mail-day. What a fool—what a blind fool I have been! Twenty-two pounds covers my passage home again. Allow ten for additional expenses. We must put up at Madame Binat's for old sake's sake.

Thirty-two pounds altogether. Add a hundred for the cost of the last trip—Gad, won't Torp stare to see me!—a hundred and thirty-two leaves seventy-eight for baksheesh—I shall need it—and to play with. What are you crying for, Bess? It wasn't your fault, child; it was mine altogether. Oh, you funny little opossum, mop your eyes, and take me out! I want the pass-book and the cheque-book. Stop a minute. Four thousand pounds at four per cent—that's safe interest—means a hundred and sixty pounds a year; one hundred and twenty pounds a year—also safe—is two eighty, and two hundred and eighty pounds added to three hundred a year means gilded luxury for a single woman. Bess, we'll go to the bank.'

Richer by two hundred and ten pounds stored in his money-belt, Dick caused Bessie, now thoroughly bewildered, to hurry from the bank to the P. and O. offices, where he explained things tersely.

'Port Said, single first; cabin as close to the baggage-hatch as possible. What ship's going?'

'The "Colgong," ' said the clerk.

'She's a wet little hooker. Is it Tilbury and a tender, or Galleons and the docks?'

'Galleons. Twelve-forty, Thursday.'

'Thanks. Change, please. I can't see very well—will you count it into my hand?'

'If they all took their passages like that instead of talking about their trunks, life would be worth something,' said the clerk to his neighbour, who was trying to explain to a harassed mother of many that condensed milk is just as good for babes at sea as daily dairy. Being nineteen and unmarried, he spoke with conviction.

'We are now,' quoth Dick, as they returned to the studio, patting the place where his money-belt covered ticket and money, 'beyond the reach of man, or devil, or woman—which is much more important. I've three little affairs to carry through before Thursday, but I needn't ask you to help, Bess. Come here on Thursday morning at nine. We'll breakfast, and you shall take me down to Galleons Station.'

'What are you going to do?'

'Going away of course. What should I stay for?'

'But you can't look after yourself?'

'I can do anything. I didn't realise it before, but I can. I've done a great deal already. Resolution shall be treated to one kiss if Bessie doesn't object.' Strangely enough, Bessie objected and Dick laughed. 'I suppose you're right. Well, come at nine the day after to-morrow and you'll get your money.'

'Shall I sure?'

'I don't bilk, and you won't know whether I do or not unless you come.

Oh, but it's long and long to wait! Good-bye, Bessie,—send Beeton here as you go out.'

The housekeeper came.

'What are all the fittings of my rooms worth?' said Dick imperiously.

''Tisn't for me to say, sir. Some things is very pretty and some is wore out dreadful.'

'I'm insured for two hundred and seventy.'

'Insurance policies is no criterion, though I don't say—'

'Oh, damn your longwindedness! You've made your pickings out of me and the other tenants. Why, you talked of retiring and buying a public-house the other day. Give a straight answer to a straight question.'

'Fifty,' said Mr. Beeton, without a moment's hesitation.

'Double it; or I'll break up half my sticks and burn the rest.'

He felt his way to a bookstand that supported a pile of sketch-books, and wrenched out one of the mahogany pillars.

'That's sinful, sir,' said the housekeeper, alarmed.

'It's my own. One hundred or—'

'One hundred it is. It'll cost me three and six to get that there pilaster mended.'

'I thought so. What an out-and-out swindler you must have been to spring that price at once!'

'I hope I've done nothing to dissatisfy any of the tenants, least of all you, sir.'

'Never mind that. Get me the money to-morrow, and see that all my clothes are packed in the little brown bullock-trunk. I'm going.'

'But the quarter's notice?'

'I'll pay forfeit. Look after the packing and leave me alone.'

Mr. Beeton discussed this new departure with his wife, who decided that Bessie was at the bottom of it all. Her husband took a more charitable view.

'It's very sudden—but then he was always sudden in his ways. Listen to him now!'

There was a sound of chanting from Dick's room.

> 'We'll never come back any more, boys,
> We'll never come back no more;
> We'll go to the deuce on any excuse,
> And never come back no more!
> Oh say we're afloat or ashore, boys,
> Oh say we're afloat or ashore;
> But we'll never come back any more, boys,
> We'll never come back no more!'

'Mr. Beeton! Mr. Beeton! Where the deuce is my pistol?'

'Quick, he's going to shoot himself—'avin' gone mad!' said Mrs. Beeton.

Mr. Beeton addressed Dick soothingly, but it was some time before the latter, threshing up and down his bedroom, could realise the intention of the promises to 'find everything to-morrow, sir.'

'Oh, you copper-nosed old fool—you impotent Academician!' he shouted at last. 'Do you suppose I want to shoot myself? Take the pistol in your silly shaking hand then. If you touch it, it will go off, because it's loaded. It's among my campaign-kit somewhere—in the parcel at the bottom of the trunk.'

Long ago Dick had carefully possessed himself of a forty-pound weight field-equipment constructed by the knowledge of his own experience. It was this put-away treasure that he was trying to find and rehandle. Mr. Beeton whipped the revolver out of its place on the top of the package, and Dick drove his hand among the khaki coat and breeches, the blue cloth leg-bands, and the heavy flannel shirts doubled over a pair of swan-neck spurs. Under these and the water-bottle lay a sketch-book and a pigskin case of stationery.

'These we don't want; you can have them, Mr. Beeton. Everything else I'll keep. Pack 'em on the top right-hand side of my trunk. When you've done that come into the studio with your wife. I want you both. Wait a minute; get me a pen and a sheet of notepaper.'

It is not an easy thing to write when you cannot see, and Dick had particular reasons for wishing that his work should be clear. So he began, following his right hand with his left: '"The badness of this writing is because I am blind and cannot see my pen." H'mph!—Even a lawyer can't mistake that. It must be signed, I suppose, but it needn't be witnessed. Now an inch lower—why did I never learn to use a type-writer?—"This is the last will and testament of me, Richard Heldar. I am in sound bodily and mental health, and there is no previous will to revoke."—That's all right. Damn the pen! Whereabouts on the paper was I?—"I leave everything that I possess in the world, including four thousand pounds, and two thousand seven hundred and twenty-eight pounds held for me"—Oh, I can't get this straight.' He tore off half the sheet and began again with the caution about the handwriting. Then: 'I leave all the money I possess in the world to'—here followed Maisie's name, and the names of the two banks that held his money.

'It mayn't be quite regular, but no one has a shadow of a right to dispute it, and I've given Maisie's address. Come in, Mr. Beeton. This is my signature; you've seen it often enough to know it; I want you and your wife to witness it. Thanks. To-morrow you must take me to the landlord and I'll pay forfeit for leaving without notice, and I'll lodge this paper with him in case anything happens when I'm away. Now we're going to light up the studio stove. Stay with me, and give me my papers as I want 'em.'

No one knows until he has tried how fine a blaze a year's accumulation of bills, letters, and dockets can make. Dick stuffed into the stove every document in the studio—saving only three unopened letters: destroyed sketch-books, rough note-books, new and half-finished canvases alike.

'What a lot of rubbish a tenant gets about him if he stays long enough in one place, to be sure,' said Mr. Beeton at last.

'He does. Is there anything more left?' Dick felt round the walls.

'Not a thing, and the stove's nigh red-hot.'

'Excellent, and you've lost about a thousand pounds' worth of sketches. Ho! ho! Quite a thousand pounds' worth, if I can remember what I used to be.'

'Yes sir,' politely. Mr. Beeton was quite sure that Dick had gone mad, otherwise he would have never parted with his excellent furniture for a song. The canvas things took up storage room and were much better out of the way.

There remained only to leave the little will in safe hands: that could not be accomplished till to-morrow. Dick groped about the floor picking up the last pieces of paper, assured himself again and again that there remained no written word or sign of his past life in drawer or desk, and sat down before the stove till the fire died out and the contracting iron cracked in the silence of the night.

Chapter 15

With a heart of furious fancies,
  Whereof I am commander;
With a burning spear and a horse of air,
  To the wilderness I wander.
With a knight of ghosts and shadows
  I summoned am to tourney—
Ten leagues beyond the wide world's end,
  Methinks it is no journey.

  'Tom a' Bedlam's Song.'

'GOOD-BYE, BESS; I promised you fifty. Here's a hundred—all that I got for my furniture from Beeton. That will keep you in pretty frocks for some time. You've been a good little girl, all things considered, but you've given me and Torpenhow a fair amount of trouble.'

'Give Mr. Torpenhow my love if you see him, won't you?'

'Of course I will, dear. Now take me up the gangplank and into the cabin. Once aboard the lugger and the maid is—and I am free, I mean.'

'Who'll look after you on the ship?'

'The head-steward, if there's any use in money. The doctor when we come to Port Said, if I know anything of P. and O. doctors. After that, the Lord will provide, as He used to do.'

Bess found Dick his cabin in the wild turmoil of a ship full of leave-takers and weeping relatives. Then he kissed her, and laid himself down in his bunk until the decks should be clear. He who had taken so long to move about his own darkened rooms well understood the geography of a ship, and the necessity of seeing to his own comforts was as wine to him. Before the screw began to thrash the ship along the Docks he had been introduced to the head-steward, had royally tipped him, secured a good place at table, opened out his baggage, and settled himself down with joy in the cabin. It was scarcely necessary to feel his way as he moved about, for he knew everything so well. Then God was very kind: a deep sleep of weariness came upon him just as he would have thought of Maisie, and he slept till the steamer had cleared the mouth of the Thames and was lifting to the pulse of the Channel.

The rattle of the engines, the reek of oil and paint, and a very familiar sound in the next cabin roused him to his new inheritance.

'Oh, it's good to be alive again!' He yawned, stretched himself vigorously, and went on deck to be told that they were almost abreast of the lights of Brighton. This is no more open water than Trafalgar Square is a common; the free levels begin at Ushant; but none the less Dick could feel the healing of the sea at work upon him already. A boisterous little cross-swell swung the steamer disrespectfully by the nose; and one wave breaking far aft spattered the quarter-deck and the pile of new deck chairs. He heard the foam fall with the clash of broken glass, was stung in the face by a cupful, and sniffing luxuriously, felt his way to the smoking-room by the wheel. There a strong breeze found him, blew his cap off and left him bareheaded in the doorway, and the smoking-room steward, understanding that he was a voyager of experience, said that the weather would be stiff in the chops off the Channel and more than half a gale in the Bay. These things fell as they were foretold, and Dick enjoyed himself to the utmost. It is allowable and even necessary at sea to lay firm hold upon tables, stanchions, and ropes in moving from place to place. On land the man who feels with his hands is patently blind. At sea even a blind man who is not sea-sick can jest with the doctor over the weakness of his fellows. Dick told the doctor many tales—and these are coin of more value than silver if properly handled—smoked with him till unholy hours of the night, and so won his short-lived regard that he promised Dick a few hours of his time when they came to Port Said.

And the sea roared or was still as the winds blew, and the engines sang their song day and night, and the sun grew stronger day by day, and Tom the Lascar barber shaved Dick of a morning under the open hatch-grating where the cool winds blew, and the awnings were spread and the passengers made merry, and at last they came to Port Said.

'Take me,' said Dick to the doctor, 'to Madame Binat's—if you know where that is.'

'Whew!' said the doctor, 'I do. There's not much to choose between 'em; but I suppose you're aware that that's one of the worst houses in the place. They'll rob you to begin with, and knife you later.'

'Not they. Take me there, and I can look after myself.'

So he was brought to Madame Binat's and filled his nostrils with the well-remembered smell of the East, that runs without a change from the Canal head to Hong-Kong, and his mouth with the villainous Lingua Franca of the Levant. The heat smote him between the shoulder-blades with the buffet of an old friend, his feet slipped on the sand, and his coat-sleeve was warm as new-baked bread when he lifted it to his nose.

Madame Binat smiled with the smile that knows no astonishment when Dick entered the drinking-shop which was one source of her gains. But for a little accident of complete darkness he could hardly realise that he had ever quitted the old life that hummed in his ears. Somebody opened a bottle of peculiarly strong Schiedam. The smell reminded Dick of Monsieur Binat, who, by the way, had spoken of art and degradation. Binat was dead; Madame said as much when the doctor departed, scandalised, so far as a ship's doctor can be at the warmth of Dick's reception. Dick was delighted at it. 'They remember me here after a year. They have forgotten me across the water by this time. Madame, I want a long talk with you when you're at liberty. It is good to be back again.'

In the evening she set an iron-topped cafe-table out on the sands, and Dick and she sat by it, while the house behind them filled with riot, merriment, oaths, and threats. The stars came out and the lights of the shipping in the harbour twinkled by the head of the Canal.

'Yes. The war is good for trade, my friend; but what dost thou do here? We have not forgotten thee.'

'I was over there in England and I went blind.'

'But there was the glory first. We heard of it here, even here—I and Binat; and thou hast used the head of Yellow 'Tina—she is still alive—so often and so well that 'Tina laughed when the papers arrived by the mail-boats. It was always something that we here could recognise in the paintings. And then there was always the glory and the money for thee.'

'I am not poor—I shall pay you well.'

'Not to me. Thou hast paid for everything.' Under her breath, 'Mon Dieu, to be blind and so young! What horror!'

Dick could not see her face with the pity on it, or his own with the discoloured hair at the temples. He did not feel the need of pity; he was too anxious to get to the front once more, and explained his desire.

'And where? The Canal is full of the English ships. Sometimes they fire as they used to do when the war was here—ten years ago. Beyond Cairo there is fighting, but how canst thou go there without a correspondent's passport? And in the desert there is always fighting, but that is impossible also,' said she.

'I must go to Suakin.' He knew, thanks to Alf's readings, that Torpenhow was at work with the column that was protecting the construction of the Suakin-Berber line. P. and O. steamers do not touch at that port, and, besides, Madame Binat knew everybody whose help or advice was worth anything. They were not respectable folk, but they could cause things to be accomplished, which is much more important when there is work toward.

'But at Suakin they are always fighting. That desert breeds men always —and always more men. And they are so bold! Why to Suakin?'

'My friend is there.'

'Thy friend! Chtt! Thy friend is death, then.'

Madame Binat dropped a fat arm on the table-top, filled Dick's glass anew, and looked at him closely under the stars. There was no need that he should bow his head in assent and say—

'No. He is a man, but—if it should arrive . . . blamest thou?'

'I blame?' she laughed shrilly. 'Who am I that I should blame any one— except those who try to cheat me over their consommations. But it is very terrible.'

'I must go to Suakin. Think for me. A great deal has changed within the year, and the men I knew are not here. The Egyptian lighthouse steamer goes down the Canal to Suakin—and the post-boats—But even then—'

'Do not think any longer. I know, and it is for me to think. Thou shalt go—thou shalt go and see thy friend. Be wise. Sit here until the house is a little quiet—I must attend to my guests—and afterwards go to bed. Thou shalt go, in truth, thou shalt go.'

'To-morrow?'

'As soon as may be.' She was talking as though he were a child.

He sat at the table listening to the voices in the harbour and the streets, and wondering how soon the end would come, till Madame Binat carried him off to bed and ordered him to sleep. The house shouted and sang and danced and revelled, Madame Binat moving through it with one eye on the liquor payments and the girls and the other on Dick's interests. To this latter end she smiled upon scowling and furtive Turkish officers of Fellaheen regiments, was gracious to Cypriote commissariat underlings, and more than kind to camel agents of no nationality whatever.

In the early morning, being then appropriately dressed in a flaming red silk ball-dress, with a front of tarnished gold embroidery and a necklace of plate-glass diamonds, she made chocolate and carried it in to Dick.

'It is only I, and I am of discreet age, eh? Drink and eat the roll too. Thus in France mothers bring their sons, when those behave wisely, the morning chocolate.' She sat down on the side of the bed whispering:—

'It is all arranged. Thou wilt go by the lighthouse boat. That is a bribe of ten pounds English. The captain is never paid by the Government. The boat comes to Suakin in four days. There will go with thee George, a Greek muleteer. Another bribe of ten pounds. I will pay; they must not know of thy money. George will go with thee as far as he goes with his mules. Then he comes back to me, for his well-beloved is here, and if I do not receive a telegram from Suakin saying that thou art well, the girl answers for George.'

'Thank you.' He reached out sleepily for the cup. 'You are much too kind, Madame.'

'If there were anything that I might do I would say, stay here and be wise; but I do not think that would be best for thee.' She looked at her liquor-stained dress with a sad smile. 'Nay, thou shalt go, in truth, thou shalt go. It is best so. My boy, it is best so.'

She stooped and kissed Dick between the eyes. 'That is for good-morning,' she said, going away. 'When thou art dressed we will speak to George and make everything ready. But first we must open the little trunk. Give me the keys.'

'The amount of kissing lately has been simply scandalous. I shall expect Torp to kiss me next. He is more likely to swear at me for getting in his way, though. Well, it won't last long—Ohe, Madame, help me to my toilette of the guillotine! There will be no chance of dressing properly out yonder.'

He was rummaging among his new campaign-kit, and rowelling his hands with the spurs. There are two ways of wearing well-oiled ankle-jacks, spotless blue leg-bands, khaki coat and breeches, and a perfectly pipeclayed helmet. The right way is the way of the untired man, master of himself, setting out upon an expedition, well pleased.

'Everything must be very correct,' Dick explained. 'It will become dirty afterwards, but now it is good to feel well dressed. Is everything as it should be?'

He patted the revolver neatly hidden under the fullness of the blouse on the right hip and fingered his collar.

'I can do no more,' Madame said, between laughing and crying. 'Look at thyself—but I forgot.'

'I am very content.' He stroked the creaseless spirals of his leggings. 'Now let us go and see the captain and George and the lighthouse boat. Be quick, Madame.'

'But thou canst not be seen by the harbour walking with me in the daylight. Figure to yourself if some English ladies—'

'There are no English ladies; and if there are, I have forgotten them. Take me there.'

In spite of his burning impatience it was nearly evening ere the light-house boat began to move. Madame had said a great deal both to George and the captain touching the arrangements that were to be made for Dick's benefit. Very few men who had the honour of her acquaintance cared to disregard Madame's advice. That sort of contempt might end in being knifed by a stranger in a gambling-hell upon surprisingly short provocation.

For six days—two of them were wasted in the crowded Canal—the little steamer worked her way to Suakin, where she was to pick up the superintendent of lighthouses; and Dick made it his business to propitiate George, who was distracted with fears for the safety of his light-of-love and half inclined to make Dick responsible for his own discomfort. When they arrived George took him under his wing, and together they entered the red-hot seaport, encumbered with the material and wastage of the Suakin-Berber line, from locomotives in disconsolate fragments to mounds of chairs and pot-sleepers.

'If you keep with me,' said George, 'nobody will ask for passports or what you do. They are all very busy.'

'Yes; but I should like to hear some of the Englishmen talk. They might remember me. I was known here a long time ago—when I was some one indeed.'

'A long time ago is a very long time ago here. The graveyards are full. Now listen. This new railway runs out so far as Tanai-el-Hassan—that is seven miles. Then there is a camp. They say that beyond Tanai-el-Hassan the English troops go forward, and everything that they require will be brought to them by this line.'

'Ah! Base camp. I see. That's a better business than fighting Fuzzies in the open.'

'For this reason even the mules go up in the iron-train.'

'Iron what?'

'It is all covered with iron, because it is still being shot at.'

'An armoured train. Better and better! Go on, faithful George.'

'And I go up with my mules to-night. Only those who particularly require to go to the camp go out with the train. They begin to shoot not far from the city.'

'The dears—they always used to!' Dick snuffed the smell of parched dust, heated iron, and flaking paint with delight. Certainly the old life was welcoming him back most generously.

'When I have got my mules together I go up to-night, but you must first send a telegram to Port Said, declaring that I have done you no harm.'

'Madame has you well in hand. Would you stick a knife into me if you had the chance?'

'I have no chance,' said the Greek. 'She is there with that woman.'

'I see. It's a bad thing to be divided between love of woman and the chance of loot. I sympathise with you, George.'

They went to the telegraph-office unquestioned, for all the world was desperately busy and had scarcely time to turn its head, and Suakin was the last place under sky that would be chosen for holiday-ground. On their return the voice of an English subaltern asked Dick what he was doing. The blue goggles were over his eyes and he walked with his hand on George's elbow as he replied—

'Egyptian Government—mules. My orders are to give them over to the A. C. G. at Tanai-el-Hassan. Any occasion to show my papers?'

'Oh, certainly not. I beg your pardon. I'd no right to ask, but not seeing your face before I—'

'I go out in the train to-night, I suppose,' said Dick boldly. 'There will be no difficulty in loading up the mules, will there?'

'You can see the horse-platforms from here. You must have them loaded up early.' The young man went away wondering what sort of broken-down waif this might be who talked like a gentleman and consorted with Greek muleteers. Dick felt unhappy. To outface an English officer is no small thing, but the bluff loses relish when one plays it from the utter dark, and stumbles up and down rough ways, thinking and eternally thinking of what might have been if things had fallen out otherwise, and all had been as it was not.

George shared his meal with Dick and went off to the mule-lines. His charge sat alone in a shed with his face in his hands. Before his tight-shut eyes danced the face of Maisie, laughing, with parted lips. There was a great bustle and clamour about him. He grew afraid and almost called for George.

'I say, have you got your mules ready?' It was the voice of the subaltern over his shoulder.

'My man's looking after them. The—the fact is I've a touch of ophthalmia and I can't see very well.'

'By Jove! that's bad. You ought to lie up in hospital for a while. I've had a turn of it myself. It's as bad as being blind.'

'So I find it. When does this armoured train go?'

'At six o'clock. It takes an hour to cover the seven miles.'

'Are the Fuzzies on the rampage—eh?'

'About three nights a week. 'Fact is I'm in acting command of the night-train. It generally runs back empty to Tanai for the night.'

'Big camp at Tanai, I suppose?'

'Pretty big. It has to feed our desert-column somehow.'

'Is that far off?'

'Between thirty and forty miles—in an infernal thirsty country.'

'Is the country quiet between Tanai and our men?'

'More or less. I shouldn't care to cross it alone, or with a subaltern's command for the matter of that, but the scouts get through in some extraordinary fashion.'

'They always did.'

'Have you been here before, then?'

'I was through most of the trouble when it first broke out.'

'In the service and cashiered,' was the subaltern's first thought, so he refrained from putting any questions.

'There's your man coming up with the mules. It seems rather queer—'

'That I should be mule-leading?' said Dick.

'I didn't mean to say so, but it is. Forgive me—it's beastly impertinence I know, but you speak like a man who has been at a public school. There's no mistaking the tone.'

'I am a public school man.'

'I thought so. I say, I don't want to hurt your feelings, but you're a little down on your luck, aren't you? I saw you sitting with your head in your hands, and that's why I spoke.'

'Thanks. I am about as thoroughly and completely broke as a man need be.'

'Suppose—I mean I'm a public school man myself. Couldn't I perhaps—take it as a loan y'know and—'

'You're much too good, but on my honour I've as much money as I want. . . . I tell you what you could do for me, though, and put me under an everlasting obligation. Let me come into the bogie truck of the train. There is a fore-truck, isn't there?'

'Yes. How d'you know?'

'I've been in an armoured train before. Only let me see—hear some of the fun I mean, and I'll be grateful. I go at my own risk as a non-combatant.'

The young man thought for a minute. 'All right,' he said. 'We're supposed to be an empty train, and there's no one to blow me up at the other end.'

George and a horde of yelling amateur assistants had loaded up the mules, and the narrow-gauge armoured train, plated with three-eighths-inch boiler-plate till it looked like one long coffin, stood ready to start.

Two bogie trucks running before the locomotive were completely covered in with plating, except that the leading one was pierced in front for the nozzle of a machine-gun, and the second at either side for lateral fire. The trucks together made one long iron-vaulted chamber in which a score of artillerymen were rioting.

'Whitechapel—last train! Ah, I see yer kissin' in the first class there!' somebody shouted, just as Dick was clambering into the forward truck.

'Lordy! 'Ere's a real live passenger for the Kew, Tanai, Acton, and Ealin' train. "Echo," sir. Speshul edition! "Star," sir.'—'Shall I get you a foot-warmer?' said another.

'Thanks. I'll pay my footing,' said Dick, and relations of the most amicable were established ere silence came with the arrival of the subaltern, and the train jolted out over the rough track.

'This is an immense improvement on shooting the unimpressionable Fuzzy in the open,' said Dick from his place in the corner.

'Oh, but he's still unimpressed. There he goes!' said the subaltern, as a bullet struck the outside of the truck. 'We always have at least one demonstration against the night-train. Generally they attack the rear-truck where my junior commands. He gets all the fun of the fair.'

'Not to-night, though! Listen!' said Dick. A flight of heavy-handed bullets was succeeded by yelling and shouts. The children of the desert valued their nightly amusement, and the train was an excellent mark.

'Is it worth while giving them half a hopper full?' the subaltern asked of the engine which was driven by a Lieutenant of Sappers.

'I should just think so! This is my section of the line. They'll be playing old Harry with my permanent way if we don't stop 'em.'

'Right O!'

'Hrrmph!' said the machine-gun through all its five noses as the subaltern drew the lever home. The empty cartridges clashed on the floor and the smoke blew back through the truck. There was indiscriminate firing at the rear of the train, a return fire from the darkness without and unlimited howling. Dick stretched himself on the floor, wild with delight at the sounds and the smells.

'God is very good—I never thought I'd hear this again. Give 'em hell, men. Oh, give 'em hell!' he cried.

The train stopped for some obstruction on the line ahead and a party went out to reconnoitre, but came back cursing, for spades. The children of the desert had piled sand and gravel on the rails, and twenty minutes were lost in clearing it away. Then the slow progress recommenced, to be varied with more shots, more shoutings, the steady clack and kick of the machine-guns, and a final difficulty with a half-lifted rail ere the train came under the protection of the roaring camp at Tanai-el-Hassan.

'Now, you see why it takes an hour and a half to fetch her through,' said the subaltern, unshipping the cartridge-hopper above his pet gun.

'It was a lark, though. I only wish it had lasted twice as long. How superb it must have looked from outside!' said Dick, sighing regretfully.

'It palls after the first few nights. By the way, when you've settled about your mules, come and see what we can find to eat in my tent. I'm

Bennil of the Gunners—in the Artillery lines—and mind you don't fall over my tent-ropes in the dark.'

But it was all dark to Dick. He could only smell the camels, the hay-bales, the cooking, the smoky fires, and the tanned canvas of the tents as he stood, where he had dropped from the train, shouting for George. There was a sound of light-hearted kicking on the iron skin of the rear trucks, with squealing and grunting. George was unloading the mules.

The engine was blowing off steam nearly in Dick's ear; a cold wind of the desert danced between his legs; he was hungry, and felt tired and dirty—so dirty that he tried to brush his coat with his hands. That was a hopeless job; he thrust his hands into his pockets and began to count over the many times that he had waited in strange or remote places for trains or camels, mules or horses, to carry him to his business. In those days he could see—few men more clearly—and the spectacle of an armed camp at dinner under the stars was an ever fresh pleasure to the eye. There was colour, light, and motion, without which no man has much pleasure in living. This night there remained for him only one more journey through the darkness that never lifts to tell a man how far he has travelled. Then he would grip Torpenhow's hand again—Torpenhow, who was alive and strong, and lived in the midst of the action that had once made the rep-utation of a man called Dick Heldar: not in the least to be confused with the blind, bewildered vagabond who seemed to answer to the same name. Yes, he would find Torpenhow, and come as near to the old life as might be. Afterwards he would forget everything: Bessie, who had wrecked the Melancolia and so nearly wrecked his life; Beeton, who lived in a strange unreal city full of tin-tacks and gas-plugs, and matters that no men needed; that irrational being who had offered him love and loyalty for nothing, but had not signed her name; and most of all Maisie, who, from her own point of view, was undeniably right in all she did, but oh, at this distance, so tantalisingly fair.

George's hand on his arm pulled him back to the situation.

'And what now?' said George.

'Oh yes, of course. What now? Take me to the camel-men. Take me to where the scouts sit when they come in from the desert. They sit by their camels, and the camels eat grain out of a black blanket held up at the corners, and the men eat by their side just like camels. Take me there!'

The camp was rough and rutty, and Dick stumbled many times over the stumps of scrub. The scouts were sitting by their beasts, as Dick knew they would. The light of the dung-fires flickered on their bearded faces, and the camels bubbled and mumbled beside them at rest. It was no part of Dick's policy to go into the desert with a convoy of supplies. That would lead to impertinent questions, and since a blind non-combatant is not needed at the front, he would probably be forced to return to Suakin. He must go up alone, and go immediately.

'Now for one last bluff—the biggest of all,' he said. 'Peace be with you, brethren!' The watchful George steered him to the circle of the nearest fire. The heads of the camel-sheiks bowed gravely, and the camels, scenting a European, looked sideways curiously like brooding hens, half ready to get to their feet.

'A beast and a driver to go to the fighting line to-night,' said Dick.

'A Mulaid?' said a voice, scornfully naming the best baggage-breed that he knew.

'A Bisharin,' returned Dick with perfect gravity. 'A Bisharin without saddle-galls. Therefore no charge of thine, shock-head.'

Two or three minutes passed. Then—

'We be knee-haltered for the night. There is no going out from the camp.'

'Not for money?'

'H'm! Ah! English money?'

Another depressing interval of silence.

'How much?'

'Twenty-five pounds English paid into the hand of the driver at my journey's end, and as much more into the hand of the camel-sheik here, to be paid when the driver returns.'

This was royal payment, and the sheik, who knew that he would get his commission on the deposit, stirred in Dick's behalf.

'For scarcely one night's journey—fifty pounds. Land and wells and good trees and wives to make a man content for the rest of his days. Who speaks?' said Dick.

'I,' said a voice. 'I will go—but there is no going from the camp.'

'Fool! I know that a camel can break his knee-halter, and the sentries do not fire if one goes in chase. Twenty-five pounds and another twenty-five pounds. But the beast must be a good Bisharin; I will take no baggage-camel.'

Then the bargaining began, and at the end of half an hour the first deposit was paid over to the sheik, who talked in low tones to the driver. Dick heard the latter say: 'A little way out only. Any baggage-beast will serve. Am I a fool to waste my cattle for a blind man?'

'And though I cannot see'—Dick lifted his voice a little—'yet I carry that which has six eyes, and the driver will sit before me. If we do not reach the English troops in the dawn he will be dead.'

'But where, in God's name, are the troops?'

'Unless thou knowest let another man ride. Dost thou know? Remember it will be life or death to thee.'

'I know,' said the driver sullenly. 'Stand back from my beast. I am going to slip him.'

'Not so swiftly. George, hold the camel's head a moment. I want to feel his cheek.' The hands wandered over the hide till they found the branded half-circle that is the mark of the Bisharin, the light-built riding camel. 'That is well. Cut this one loose. Remember no blessing of God comes on those who try to cheat the blind.'

The men chuckled by the fires at the camel-driver's discomfiture. He had intended to substitute a slow, saddle-galled baggage-colt.

'Stand back!' one shouted, lashing the Bisharin under the belly with a quirt. Dick obeyed as soon as he felt the nose-string tighten in his hand, —and a cry went up, 'Illaha! Aho! He is loose.'

With a roar and a grunt the Bisharin rose to his feet and plunged forward towards the desert, his driver following with shouts and lamentation. George caught Dick's arm and hurried him stumbling and tripping past a disgusted sentry who was used to stampeding camels.

'What's the row now?' he cried.

'Every stitch of my kit on that blasted dromedary,' Dick answered, after the manner of a common soldier.

'Go on, and take care your throat's not cut outside—you and your dromedary's.'

The outcries ceased when the camel had disappeared behind a hillock, and his driver had called him back and made him kneel down.

'Mount first,' said Dick. Then climbing into the second seat and gently screwing the pistol muzzle into the small of his companion's back, 'Go on, in God's name, and swiftly. Good-bye, George. Remember me to Madame, and have a good time with your girl. Get forward, child of the Pit!'

A few minutes later he was shut up in a great silence, hardly broken by the creaking of the saddle and the soft pad of the tireless feet. Dick adjusted himself comfortably to the rock and pitch of the pace, girthed his belt tighter, and felt the darkness slide past. For an hour he was conscious only of the sense of rapid progress.

'A good camel,' he said at last.

'He has never been underfed. He is my own and clean bred,' the driver replied.

'Go on.'

His head dropped on his chest and he tried to think, but the tenor of his thoughts was broken because he was very sleepy. In the half doze it seemed that he was learning a punishment hymn at Mrs. Jennett's. He

had committed some crime as bad as Sabbath-breaking, and she had locked
him up in his bedroom. But he could never repeat more than the first two
lines of the hymn—

'When Israel of the Lord beloved
Out of the land of bondage came.'

He said them over and over thousands of times. The driver turned in the
saddle to see if there were any chance of capturing the revolver and ending the ride. Dick roused, struck him over the head with the butt, and
stormed himself wide awake. Somebody hidden in a clump of camel-thorn
shouted as the camel toiled up rising ground. A shot was fired, and the
silence shut down again, bringing the desire to sleep. Dick could think
no longer. He was too tired and stiff and cramped to do more than nod
uneasily from time to time, waking with a start and punching the driver
with the pistol.

'Is there a moon?' he asked drowsily.

'She is near her setting.'

'I wish that I could see her. Halt the camel. At least let me hear the
desert talk.'

The man obeyed. Out of the utter stillness came one breath of wind. It
rattled the dead leaves of a shrub some distance away and ceased. A handful of dry earth detached itself from the edge of a rain trench and crumbled softly to the bottom.

'Go on. The night is very cold.'

Those who have watched till the morning know how the last hour before the light lengthens itself into many eternities. It seemed to Dick that
he had never since the beginning of original darkness done anything at all
save jolt through the air. Once in a thousand years he would finger the
nail-heads on the saddle-front and count them all carefully. Centuries
later he would shift his revolver from his right hand to his left, and allow
the eased arm to drop down at his side. From the safe distance of London
he was watching himself thus employed,—watching critically. Yet whenever he put out his hand to the canvas that he might paint the tawny
yellow desert under the glare of the sinking moon, the black shadow of
the camel and the two bowed figures atop, that hand held a revolver and
the arm was numbed from wrist to collar-bone. Moreover, he was in the
dark, and could see no canvas of any kind whatever.

The driver grunted, and Dick was conscious of a change in the air.

'I smell the dawn,' he whispered.

'It is here, and yonder are the troops. Have I done well?'

K

The camel stretched out its neck and roared as there came down wind the pungent reek of camels in square.

'Go on. We must get there swiftly. Go on.'

'They are moving in their camp. There is so much dust that I cannot see what they do.'

'Am I in better case? Go forward.'

They could hear the hum of voices ahead, the howling and the bubbling of the beasts and the hoarse cries of the soldiers girthing up for the day. Two or three shots were fired.

'Is that at us? Surely they can see that I am English,' Dick spoke angrily.

'Nay, it is from the desert,' the driver answered, cowering in his saddle. 'Go forward, my child! Well it is that the dawn did not uncover us an hour ago.'

The camel headed straight for the column and the shots behind multiplied. The children of the desert had arranged that most uncomfortable of surprises, a dawn attack for the English troops, and were getting their distance by snap-shots at the only moving object without the square.

'What luck! What stupendous and imperial luck!' said Dick. 'It's "just before the battle, mother." Oh, God has been most good to me! Only'—the agony of the thought made him screw up his eyes for an instant— 'Maisie . . .'

'Allahu! We are in,' said the man, as he drove into the rearguard and the camel knelt.

'Who the deuce are you? Despatches or what? What's the strength of the enemy behind that ridge? How did you get through?' asked a dozen voices. For all answer Dick took a long breath, unbuckled his belt, and shouted from the saddle at the top of a wearied and dusty voice, 'Torpenhow! Ohe, Torp! Coo-ee, Tor-pen-how.'

A bearded man raking in the ashes of a fire for a light to his pipe moved very swiftly towards that cry, as the rearguard, facing about, began to fire at the puffs of smoke from the hillocks around. Gradually the scattered white cloudlets drew out into long lines of banked white that hung heavily in the stillness of the dawn before they turned over wave-like and glided into the valleys. The soldiers in the square were coughing and swearing as their own smoke obstructed their view, and they edged forward to get beyond it. A wounded camel leaped to its feet and roared aloud, the cry ending in a bubbling grunt. Some one had cut its throat to prevent confusion. Then came the thick sob of a man receiving his death-wound from a bullet; then a yell of agony and redoubled firing.

There was no time to ask any questions.

'Get down, man! Get down behind the camel!'

'No. Put me, I pray, in the forefront of the battle.' Dick turned his face to Torpenhow and raised his hand to set his helmet straight, but, miscalculating the distance, knocked it off. Torpenhow saw that his hair was gray on the temples, and that his face was the face of an old man.

'Come down, you damned fool! Dickie, come off!'

And Dick came obediently, but as a tree falls, pitching sideways from the Bisharin's saddle at Torpenhow's feet. His luck had held to the last, even to the crowning mercy of a kindly bullet through his head.

Torpenhow knelt under the lee of the camel, with Dick's body in his arms.

DATE DUE

DEMCO, INC. 38-3011